THE INQUISITION WAR

DRACO • HARLEQUIN • CHAOS CHILD

'In an Imperium of a million worlds, what does the death of one world matter in the cause of purity?'

IN THE GRIM darkness of the 41st millennium, the Inquisition protects mankind from its many enemies, whether foul daemons or savage alien races. But who will protect humanity if the Inquisition becomes corrupted? Renegade Inquisitor Jaq Draco and his group of motley companions find themselves caught in a war that no one can win... unless he can somehow access the ancient secrets hidden in the legendary Black Library.

DAZZLING AND FRENETIC, Ian Watson's Inquisition War trilogy presents a unique vision of the Warhammer 40,000 universe and explores areas that few other authors have dared to tackle. His prestigious career has included winning a slew of awards and several of his stories have been finalists in the Hugo awards. Ian Watson's other work has included credit for the Screen Story of Steven Spielberg's movie *A.I.*, on which he worked with Stanley Kubrick.

More Warhammer 40,000 Omnibuses from the Black Library

EISENHORN
By Dan Abnett
(Includes the novels *Xenos, Malleus* and *Hereticus*)

GAUNT'S GHOSTS: THE FOUNDING
By Dan Abnett
(Includes books 1-3 in the series: *First and Only, Ghostmaker*
and *Necropolis*)

GAUNT'S GHOSTS: THE SAINT
By Dan Abnett
(Includes books 4-7 in the series: *Honour Guard, The Guns of Tanith,
Straight Silver* and *Sabbat Martyr*)

THE ULTRAMARINES OMNIBUS
By Graham McNeill
(Includes the novels *Nightbringer, Warriors of Ultramar*
and *Dead Sky, Black Sun*)

THE BLOOD ANGELS OMNIBUS
By James Swallow
(Includes the novels *Deus Encarmine* and *Deus Sanguinius*)

IMPERIAL GUARD: OMNIBUS ONE
By Mitchel Scanlon, Steve Lyons and Steve Parker
(Includes the novels *Fifteen Hours, Death World* and *Rebel Winter*)

CIAPHAS CAIN: HERO OF THE IMPERIUM
By Sandy Mitchel
(Includes the novels *For the Emperor, Caves of Ice*
and *The Traitor's Hand*)

THE SPACE WOLF OMNIBUS
By William King
(Includes the novels *Space Wolf, Ragnar's Claw* and *Grey Hunter*)

THE INQUISITION WAR

Ian Watson

For Mike Allen

A Black Library Publication

Draco, Warped Stars and The Alien Beast Within
copyright © 1990, Games Workshop Ltd.
Harlequin copyright © 1994, Games Wokshop Ltd.
Chaos Child copyright © 1995, Games Workshop Ltd.

Omnibus edition first published in Great Britain in 2004.
This edition published 2009 in Great Britain by
BL Publishing,
Games Workshop Ltd.,
Willow Road, Nottingham,
NG7 2WS, UK.

10 9 8 7 6 5 4 3 2 1

Cover illustration by Clint Langley.

A CIP record for this book is available from the British Library.

ISBN 13: 978 1 84416 767 8
ISBN 10: 1 84416 767 4

See the Black Library on the Internet at
www.blacklibrary.com

Find out more about Games Workshop
and the world of Warhammer 40,000 at
www.games-workshop.com

Printed and bound in the UK.

IT IS THE 41st millennium. For more than a hundred centuries
the Emperor has sat immobile on the Golden Throne of
Earth. He is the master of mankind by the will of the gods,
and master of a million worlds by the might of his
inexhaustible armies. He is a rotting carcass writhing invisibly
with power from the Dark Age of Technology. He is the
Carrion Lord of the Imperium for whom a thousand souls are
sacrificed every day, so that he may never truly die.

YET EVEN IN his deathless state, the Emperor continues his
eternal vigilance. Mighty battlefleets cross the daemon-infested
miasma of the warp, the only route between distant stars, their
way lit by the Astronomican, the psychic manifestation of the
Emperor's will. Vast armies give battle in his name on
uncounted worlds. Greatest amongst his soldiers are the
Adeptus Astartes, the Space Marines, bio-engineered super-
warriors. Their comrades in arms are legion: the Imperial
Guard and countless planetary defence forces, the ever-vigilant
Inquisition and the tech-priests of the Adeptus Mechanicus to
name only a few. But for all their multitudes, they are barely
enough to hold off the ever-present threat from aliens,
heretics, mutants – and worse.

TO BE A man in such times is to be one amongst untold
billions. It is to live in the cruellest and most bloody
regime imaginable. These are the tales of those times.
Forget the power of technology and science, for so much has
been forgotten, never to be re-learned. Forget the promise of
progress and understanding, for in the grim dark future
there is only war. There is no peace amongst the stars,
only an eternity of carnage and slaughter, and the
laughter of thirsting gods.

CONTENTS

INTRODUCTION

I WROTE THE trilogy of novels and the two short stories in this omnibus volume in the early 1990s, when Warhammer and Warhammer 40,000 fiction were just beginning. I believe I was the first writer to tackle Warhammer 40,000 fiction. Other early scribes fled in consternation from the *Encyclopaedia Psychotica* of 40K rulebooks into the more familiarly medieval Old World or into the post-apocalypse America of Dark Future.

The then-owner of Games Workshop yearned for real novels by real novelists set in his beloved games domains – yet how could one possibly imagine that those little Citadel Miniatures of Space Marines were real human characters? Or even real superhuman characters? Never mind the array of abhumans, inquisitors, assassins and aliens as sketched in the rulebooks of those bygone days? (The aliens, of course, being unhuman characters!) How could these possibly come alive? Some voices muttered darkly that the task was impossible.

Here was a challenge. So I attacked the mountain of information, and I climbed it. Or ate it. And then I hallucinated myself into a strange state of mind whereby I could believe in such an insane future 40,000 years ahead. I only needed to remind myself that during the course of human history to date huge numbers of people have entertained delusionary belief systems which often lead to ultra violence. Need I mention the Crusades, the massacre of the Albigensians, the activities of the Spanish Inquisition, the horrors inflicted on suspected witches? Barbara Tuchman's *A Distant Mirror: The Calamitous 14th Century* provided a bit of a model for the Warhammer 40,000 universe. However, the daemonic presence in the universe of 40K is real and actual – so to survive in such a future era you need to be psychotic, from our point of view.

For me the secret of writing Warhammer 40,000 fiction, and making it believable, was to go completely over the top in style and also in content – to be lurid and brooding and hyperbolic and generally crazy, although in an elegant, ornate way where a dark beauty pervades the atmosphere as in a painting by Gustave Moreau. (Some years earlier I wrote a story about Moreau's painting of the disembodied floating head of John the Baptist.)

Just to be educational, I put in passages in Latin. For some comic relief, as Shakespeare has a fool in the tragedy of King Lear, so I created Grimm the squat. (Subsequently, I understand that tyranids ate all the squats, which is a shame.) And I enjoyed myself enormously, and I grew fond of my brave, mad characters. I became deeply involved in their destinies, and to this day I still think of them – particularly since by the end one is very insane, another is dead, and one is hopelessly lost; which suggests that perhaps I ought to write a fourth volume some time to rescue them from lunacy, death and solitude. For a while, anyway. In the 41st millennium, where all is whelmed in darkness, any moderately happy ending seems unrealistic.

Fortunately I was able to switch on my own psychosis in the morning at the same time as I switched on my computer, then switch it off again later in the day – or else I might have been possessed by Chaos! Something similar happened to me when I was writing my novel about the UFO experience, *Miracle Visitors*. Reports began to appear in the local newspaper of UFO sightings closer and closer to where I was writing. If I didn't finish the book soon, who knows what might happen to me?

I was so happy with the resulting 40,000 books that I used my own name on them. Other tech-scribes used pseudonyms. They preferred to distance their Games Workshop fiction from their 'real' artistic endeavours, but I didn't feel this way – and as it turns out, my 40K novels appear to be the most popular things I've written in terms of sales and fan mail.

A kindly reviewer once wrote that I resemble HG Wells 'in invention, and impatience.' I also quite resemble him physically too, consequently I have appeared as HG Wells at various events in England, Romania and Italy. But I do not mention a similarity to Wells out of egotism – perish the thought! I mention it because HG Wells is actually the chief inventor of modern-day wargaming. In 1913 Wells published a book entitled *Little Wars, a game for boys from twelve years of age to one hundred and fifty and to that more intelligent sort of girl who likes boys' games and books; with an Appendix on Kriegspiel.* In that book is a photograph of a layout which Wells built for what he called 'The Battle of Hook's Farm.' In an early Games Workshop manual, *Rogue Trader*, lo and behold, there's a very similar photo of a layout for a fight between orks and Space Marines. Gosh. So my resemblance to Wells in various respects holds true in the realm of Warhammer 40,000 too!

Wells's reason for pioneering wargaming to be played on a carpet or table or lawn was, in his words, 'to show that Great War, real war, is the most expensive game in the universe and is a game out of all proportion.' He goes on to say that to the blundering insanity of war he opposes the striving for utopia, and that excitable self-proclaimed patriots and adventurers should be locked up in a room to play wargames to satisfy themselves.

Well, almost immediately the First World War happened. The trenches, the slaughter. To be followed by Hiroshima and Dresden, Vietnam, the Congo, the Twin Towers… Is the universe of the year 40,000 actually madder than ours?

Fortunately, yes, it is. So far. But just as the daemonic visions of Hieronymus Bosch compare to horrors in the Netherlands a few hundred years ago, so perhaps Warhammer 40,000 compares to our own recent history. At the moment we are semi-enlightened and fairly civilised, on the whole. In a few hundred more years, who knows? If the climate changes radically, if resources run out and are not replenished, if jihads succeed, if x, y, and z, might there be a new Dark Age? Might our own daemons stalk a ravaged world?

To write stories set in the deranged future of 40K is to adopt, for a while, the medieval mind of Bosch – if Bosch could have written space opera.

Ian Watson, 18th March 42,004

THE ALIEN
BEAST WITHIN

THE GIANT EXERCISE wheel accelerated yet again while Meh'Lindi raced, caged within it. The machine towered two hundred metres high, under a fan-vaulted roof. Shafts of light, of blood-red and cyanotic blue and bilious green, beamed through tracery windows which themselves revolved kaleidoscopically. Chains of brass amulets dangling from the rotating spokes of the wheel clashed and clanged deafeningly like berserk bells as they whirled around.

Elsewhere in the gymnasium of the Callidus shrine, high-kicking initiate assassins broke plasteel bars, or else their own tarsal or heel bones. Injury was no excuse to discontinue the exercise – now they must master pain instead. Others dislocated their limbs by muscle tension so as to escape from bonds before crawling through constricted, kinking pipes. A pump sucked blood dazingly from two youths prior to their practising unarmed combat, and from another before he would attempt to run the gauntlet along a corridor of spinning knives. Scarred veteran instructors patrolled, ever willing to demonstrate to the unbelieving.

Callisthenics machines shrieked and roared and spun so as to disorient their users.

Meh'Lindi had been running for half an hour, trying to catch a fellow assassin who ran vertically above her, upside-down, wearing an experimental gravity-reverser belt. She ran in a self-induced trance, imagining that she might presently reach such an enlightened state of mind that she could speed up inhumanly and loop the loop, stunning her quarry as she passed by. Whenever she was about to put on such a spurt, the wheel speeded up to frustrate her.

Suddenly, with a thunderous crash of engaging sprockets and a screaming of its gears, the wheel halted.

Meh'Lindi was hurled forward violently. Though the event was entirely unexpected, she was already fully alert, and arching herself into a hoop so as to roll. Uncoiling, she somersaulted backwards. She leapt about-face. The wheel was already beginning to turn in the opposite direction. It was picking up speed. High overhead, her quarry was tumbling. She sprinted, up, up, willing the friction of her bare feet and her sheer renewed momentum to stop her from toppling back down the giant curved track.

Presently a siren wailed, signalling the end of her session – just when she fancied she had a slight chance of succeeding in what was virtually an impossible task.

Dismissing any temptation to feel annoyed, she skipped about, and ran back down the wheel. A filigree gate opened; she stepped out.

'Director secundus invites your presence in an hour,' the wheelmeister told her. The bald old man, one of whose eyes was a ruby lens, forbore to comment on her performance. As a seasoned graduate of the Collegia Assassinorum, Meh'Lindi should be able to assess that for herself. If not, she was less than devout.

'Invites?' she queried. The director secundus was none other than deputy to the supreme director of the Callidus shrine of assassins. Did such a high official *invite*?

'That was the phrasing.'

In a domed cubicle in the baptisterium, Meh'Lindi peeled off her clingtight black tunic. As hypersound vibrated sweat and grime loose from her, she gazed at her body in a tall speculum framed with brass bones interwoven and knotted. She permitted herself a certain degree of admiration over and above mere physical assessment. For she was trained as a pedigree courtesan as well as a sleek and cunning killer. A courtesan – even one who largely pretended to fulfil the role of a pleasure-bringer – must be conscious of sensuality.

Meh'Lindi was tall, long-limbed, with puissant biceps and calf-muscles, though her sheer height diluted the impression of power. Enticing black tattoos concealed her scars. A giant hirsute spider wrapped around her midriff. A snake, baring fangs, climbed her right leg. Scarablike beetles trod the modest swell of her bosom. Her breasts, which no exercise could mould into weapons, were small and unimpeding, though agreeably firm – dainty little beetle-tipped cones. Her coaly hair was cropped short so that no one could seize it. In her courtesan role she might, or might not, opt to wear a lustrous wig. Her eyes were golden, her ivory face oddly anonymous and unmemorable in repose. But then, she could alter her features to those of an enchantress – or equally, of a hag.

The director secundus did not summon her. He *invited* her…

She probed at the word just as the tip of one's tongue might tease at a hollow tooth loaded with catalepsin for spitting into a victim's eye to paralyse him.

It was unthinkable that the secundus dreamed of exploiting this wonderful instrument – herself – which his Collegia had crafted from feralworld flesh, for any private aphrodisiac satisfaction of his own. That would be blasphemous. Had Meh'Lindi not been a sham-courtesan as well as an assassin, this thought would hardly have occurred to her at all.

Invite. The word hinted at the protocol of the Mors Voluntaria, the permission to commit exemplary suicide which was granted to an assassin who had failed calamitously, though honourably, in some enterprise. Or whose suicide might be required, so as to erase the principal witness of an error on the part of the Officio Assassinorum…

Meh'Lindi knew that she had in no way failed in her vocation.

Puzzled, she anointed the soles of her feet with consecrated camphor oil, her loins with oil of frankincense, and the crown of her head with rosemary, then performed a devotion to the Emperor before resuming her tunic.

AT THE INVITATION of Tarik Ziz, the secundus, Meh'Lindi seated herself in a double lotus position, facing him.

She bowed her head. The lotus that locked her legs together and the aversion of her gaze were both modes of obeisance towards a superior in his private studium. Thus she signified that she was hampering herself from any assassination bid. True, she could uncoil in an instant and launch herself – nor did a skilled assassin need to be staring at her target. The faint sigh of the man's lungs, his odour, the mere pressure of air in the room located Ziz for her.

But nor would any such traitorous, motiveless attack succeed. Tarik Ziz was reputedly omega-dan.

The black-robed secundus knelt on a brocaded dais, which was also his spartan bed, facing an ancient baroque data-console. His long beringed fingers occasionally tapped a sequence of keys, one side of his mind seemingly involved in other concerns. Tomes bound in skin and data-cubes crowded one wall up to the groin-vaulted ceiling.

A collection of thousands of tiny, burnished archaic knives, many no larger than fingernails, ornamented another wall, resembling a myriad wings torn from metallic moths, shattering the light from an electro-flambeau into quicksilver fragments.

'You may look at me, Meh'Lindi.'

Ziz was swarthy, short, and compact – almost a dwarf, save for his sinuous fingers. The many rune-wrought rings he wore undoubtedly concealed a pharmacy of exotic hallucinogens and paralytic agents, even though the secundus no longer operated in the field. His artificial teeth, alternately of jet and vermilion, were all canines.

'You are one of our finest chameleons,' Ziz said to her softly.

Meh'Lindi nodded, for this was the simple truth. An injection of the shape-changing drug polymorphine would allow any trained assassin of her shrine to alter their appearance by effort of will. This was one of the specialities of the Callidus shrine, the keynote of which was cunning – just as the Vindicare shrine specialized in vengeance, and the Eversor shrine in unstoppable attack.

Under the stimulus of polymorphine, flesh would flow like heated plastic. Bones would soften, reshape themselves, and harden again. Altering her height, her frame, her features, Meh'Lindi had frequently masqueraded as other women – gorgeous and ugly, noble and common. She had mimicked men. On one occasion she had imitated a tall, hauntingly beautiful alien of the eldar race.

Always, with the purpose of eradicating someone whose activities imperilled the Imperium; with the aim of destroying a foe physically or – more rarely – psychologically...

Yet the drug polymorphine on its own was no miracle elixir. The business of shape-shifting demanded a deep and almost poignant sympathy with the person who was to be copied, killed, and replaced. The trick required empathy – deep identification with the target – and inner discipline.

Inject a non-initiate with polymorphine, and the result would be a protoplasmic chaos of the body, an agonising anarchy of the flesh and bones and organs, an on-going muddled upheaval and meltdown resulting finally in blessed death.

Meh'Lindi was an excellent, disciplined chameleon, exactly as the secundus said. Though she was no psyker, yet inscribed in the cells of her flesh and in the chambers of her brain was assuredly a wild gene-rune for apeing the appearance and traits of strangers – for metamorphosing herself – which the drug allowed her to express to the utmost.

If she had been born on a cultured world she might have been an actress. On her own feral home world she might have become a priestess of some cult of mutability. Recruited willy-nilly when a child from her barbarian tribe, she could now – as a Callidus assassin – become virtually any stranger, which was a fine fulfilment for her.

Ziz leaned forward. 'Because of your talent, our shrine invites you to participate in an epochal experiment.'

'I am but an instrument,' she replied, 'in the service of our shrine.' Her answer was obedient and dutiful, with the merest hint of caution, as one might expect from a Callidus initiate.

'You are a thinking instrument, my daughter. A wise one. One whose mind must be in perfect tune with the changes you will undergo, or else the result could prove fatal.'

'What changes, secundus?'

When Ziz told her, Meh'Lindi gasped once, as if her dwarfish omega-dan superior had punched her in her muscle-stiffened stomach.

WHEN SHE LEFT his studium, she trotted through the labyrinth of shadowy corridors where any but an initiate would soon be hopelessly lost. Reaching the gymnasium, she begged the wheelmeister to evict a novice from the apparatus, and re-admit her. Scrutinising her, the bald old man seemed to appreciate her need.

Soon Meh'Lindi was running, running, as if to race right away from the shrine, away to the very stars, to anywhere else where she might lose herself entirely and never be found again.

As if the worst nightmare in the world was pursuing her, she sprinted. Thus she vented her feelings of appalled anguish without absconding disobediently to anywhere else whatever. Finally, hours later so it seemed, at a point of exhaustion such as Meh'Lindi had never verged on before, she achieved a kind of acceptance of her fate.

Just as the exercise wheel had changed direction of a sudden previously, so had the wheel of her own fortune reversed shockingly.

Out of binding allegiance to her shrine, on account of the solemn and sinister oaths she had sworn, because the Collegia Assassinorum had made her everything that she was, she must comply.

She was invited to do so, but refusal was unthinkable.

The only alternative was exemplary suicide – to volunteer for a mission that was guaranteed to destroy her, after destroying many other foes.

Meh'Lindi was Callidus, not Eversor. Until now, she had never felt suicidal. Till now. Nor, after her passion-purging run in the wheel, did that alternative tempt her. Even if her shrine, in the unrefusable person of Tarik Ziz, seemed bent on amputating her talent. Aye, mutilating it! By way of an epochal experiment.

* * *

As THE LASER-SCALPELS hovered over her naked, paralysed body, Meh'Lindi gazed askew at the senior chirurgeon whose robe was embroidered with purity symbols and prophylactic hexes.

She could move her eyeballs fractionally. Her field of view additionally took in the robed, tattooed radiographer-adept mounted and wired into the brass-banded examinator machine. This towered alongside the operating table like a predatory armadillo, scanning the inner strata of her body with multiple snouts. Its lens-eyes projected four infant-sized holograms of herself into mid-air, side by side.

One hologram was of her body flayed so that all her muscles were exposed. Another revealed only the rivers, tributaries, and streams of her circulatory system. A third dissected out her nerve network. A fourth stripped her skeleton bare. These homunculi of herself rotated slowly as if afloat in invisible bottles, displaying themselves to her and to the chirurgeon.

The lanky soporifer-adept, who monitored the drips of metacurare that numbed and froze her, sat in a framework resembling a giant spider. Its antennae reached out to sting her insensible, though not unconscious – for her mind must understand the procedure she was about to undergo. An elderly, warty, gnome-like medicus knelt on a rubber cushion to whisper in her ear. Meh'Lindi could hear him but not see him; nor could she see other adepts in the surgical laboratory who superintended the body implants and extra glands awaiting in stasis tureens.

Meh'Lindi felt nothing. Not the clamp that held her mouth, nor the silver nozzle that gargled saliva from it. Nor the grooved operating table underneath her, with its runnels for any spilled blood or other fluids. Unable to shift her head, yet capable of rolling her eyeballs a fraction, she merely saw somewhat. And heard, the murmurings of the warty gnome.

'First we transect your shoulders and your arms. Later, we will of course be heedful of the topography of your tattoos...'

She heard a laser-scalpel descending, buzzing like a busy fly. The process was beginning.

An assassin could block off agony, could largely disconnect her consciousness from the screaming switchboard of pain in the brain. Thus was an assassin trained. Thus was the web of her brain restrung. How, otherwise, could she fulfil her missions if injured? How else could she focus her empathy without distraction during the polymorphine change? However, during a total dissection such as this some muscles might well spasm instinctively, thwarting the chirurgeon's delicate manoeuvres. Consequently she was anaesthetised, awake.

The gnome's words registered. Yet in her heart – in her wounded heart – Meh'Lindi was still hearing Tarik Ziz announce how she would be desecrated.

'INITIATES OF CALLIDUS can imitate all sorts and conditions of people. Who can do so better than you, Meh'Lindi? You have even mimicked a humanoid eldar, sufficiently well to convince human beings.'

'And well enough to persuade another eldar for a while, secundus,' she reminded him discreetly.

Ziz nodded. 'Yet we cannot adopt the form of other alien creatures whom we might wish to copy. We are constrained by our limbs, by our bones, by the flesh that is available... What do you know about *genestealers*, Meh'Lindi?'

At that point Meh'Lindi had experienced a chilling, weakening, cavernous pang, as though her entrails had emptied out of her. It took her moments to identify the unfamiliar sensation.

The sensation was terror.

Terror such as she believed had been expunged from her long since, torn out of her by the root during training.

'What do you know?' he repeated.

'Genestealers have four arms,' she recited robotically. 'Two arms equipped with hands, and two with claws that can tear through plasteel armour as if it is tissue. Their heads are long and bulbous, with fangs. Their horny spine bends them into a permanent crouch. They have an armoured carapace and a powerful tail...'

Yet it was not the creatures themselves that appalled her. Oh no. It was the implication behind Ziz's question.

'Polymorphine could never turn us into one of those, secundus.'

'Not polymorphine alone, Meh'Lindi.'

As THE MEDICUS murmured his commentary, interspersed with pious invocations to the Emperor – echoing those of the presiding chirurgeon – she squinted askew at the homunculi of herself being dissected open and knew that the very same was happening to herself. Tiny stasis generators were clipped inside her to stop her blood from spurting and draining away.

She was a snared hare stretched out on a butcher's block.

'WE SHALL USE body implants,' Ziz had continued. 'We will insert extrudable plastiflesh reinforced with carbon fibres into your anatomy. We will introduce flexicartilage which can toughen hard as horn. In repose – in their collapsed state – these implants will lurk within your body imperceptibly. Yet they will remember the monstrous shape and strength programmed into their fabric. When triggered, while polymorphine softens your flesh and bone, those implants will swell into full, active mode.'

The mosaic of tiny, glittering knives on the wall had seemed to take wing, to leap at Meh'Lindi to flay her.

'We will graft extra glands into you to store, and synthesise at speed, growth hormone – somatotrophin – and glands to reverse the process…'

'But,' she had murmured despairingly, 'I still could not become a perfect genestealer, could I?'

'At this stage that is not necessary. You will be able to transform into a convincing genestealer hybrid form. A hybrid with only one pair of arms, and lacking a tail… One closer to the semblance of humanity – yet sufficiently polluted, sufficiently grotesque to persuade those whom you must infiltrate. If this experiment succeeds as we hope, subsequently we shall attempt to implant secondary limbs.'

'Into me?' Did her voice quiver?

Ziz shook his head. 'Into another volunteer. You will be committed to the hybrid form, only able to alternate between that and your own human anatomy.'

Meh'Lindi's horror grew. What Ziz proposed couldn't simply be a gratuitous experiment, could it? One conducted merely out of curiosity?

Meh'Lindi licked her lips. 'I take it, secundus, that there's some specific mission in view?'

Ziz smiled thinly and told her.

To Meh'Lindi, that mission almost seemed to be a pretext, a trial to test whether she would perform to specification and survive.

Yet of course, she was no arbiter of the importance of a mission. The art of the assassin was to apply lethal pressure at one crucial, vulnerable point in society, a point which might not always even seem central, yet which her superiors calculated was so. Often a target was prominent – a corrupt planetary governor, a disloyal high official. Yet dislodging a seemingly humble pebble could in some circumstances start an avalanche. A Callidus assassin wasn't a slaughterer but a cunning surgeon.

Surgery…

'You are one of our most flexible chameleons, Meh'Lindi. Surely our experiment will succeed best with you. This can lead to wondrous things. To the imitating of tyranids, of tau, of lacrymoles, of kroot. How else could we ever infiltrate such alien species, if the need arose?'

'You honour your servant,' she mumbled. 'You say that I will be... committed...'

'Hereafter, when using polymorphine, you will unfortunately only be able to adopt the genestealer hybrid form; none other.'

It was as she had deeply feared. She would lose all other options of metamorphosis. She would be flayed of her proud talent, of what – in her heart – made her Meh'Lindi.

Was it so strange that an outstanding ability to mimic other people could reinforce her sense of her own self? Ah no, not so odd... For Meh'Lindi had been snatched away as a child from home and tribe, from language and customs. After initial stubbornness – insisting on her own sovereign identity – she had yielded and thereafter had found her own firm foundation, in flexibility.

'I'm also trained as a courtesan, secundus,' she reminded Ziz humbly.

A momentary bitter grimace twisted the lips of the swarthy, stunted omega-dan.

'You are... splendid enough to be one exactly as you are. We must be willing to prune our ambitions according to the needs of our shrine, and of the Imperium. Ambition is vanity, in this world of death.'

Had Tarik Ziz sacrificed his own ambitions in the process of rising to the rank of director secundus? Ziz was in line to become supreme director of the Callidus shrine, and thus perhaps grand master of the assassins, a High Lord of Terra.

This experiment, if successful, might play a significant role in his personal advancement...

'I am but an instrument,' Meh'Lindi echoed, hollowly.

And that was why she had fled to the exercise wheel, to run until she felt utterly empty, empty enough to accept.

THE SURGICAL PROCEDURE had already lasted for three painstaking, pious hours. The whispery voice of the warty gnome was growing hoarse.

A sub-skin of compacted, reinforced, 'clever' plastiflesh was now layered subcutaneously within Meh'Lindi's arms and legs and torso. This pseudoflesh was 'clever' in two regards. It was sending invasive neural fibres deeper into her anatomy, fusing physiologically. In this, it was cousin to the black carapace which was grafted into every Space Marine as the crowning act of his transformation into a superhuman. Furthermore, the false flesh could remember the evil contours it was programmed to assume, and would forever override any rebellious impulse of Meh'Lindi to counterfeit a different form.

It was like a map embroidered on supple fabric, which, upon stimulus, would expand, springing into shape stiffly, extruding from its contour lines the mountains of monstrosity.

The anatomical experimentum adepts of Callidus had been ingenious.

Likewise, blades of flexicartilage were inset under her finger and toe nails and sheathed her phalanges, her metatarsal and metacarpal bones. Stubs of the same had been grafted to her vertebrae, to her splint bones and femurs... And elsewhere.

In the phantom holo-dolls hanging above the operating table her new glands glowed as nuggets high inside her chest, not unlike a second set of nipples pointing inward.

Oh, she had been thoroughly, devoutly operated on.

And now the climax was coming, as the laser-scalpels swung down towards her staring face. Instruments came into play around her eyes, her nose, her clamped-open mouth, her cranium.

The medicus murmured huskily, 'By submucous resection we now incise inside the nostrils, to elevate the lining membrane from the septum and insert spurs of flexicartilage; thus to develop the genestealer snout...'

And this was happening to her.

'We drill all the frontal teeth to replace the roots with fangplasm...'

And this was happening to her, too.

'We sever the frenulum-fold under the tongue, for greater flexibility of that organ. We perform a partial glossectomy – akin to a coring of your tongue, were it a rose-red apple – to insert a similitude of genestealer tongue...'

And this was also happening to her, as she squinted askance at the spinning stems of silver precision tools, while the gurgling pipe sucked away minced and vaporized flesh.

Presently: 'We lift your scalp, so as to trepan the skull. We perform a frontal craniotomy so that islets of skull will spread more easily, to assume the genestealer profile...'

Aye, that profile – and none other!

No eerily elegant alien eldar's silhouette.

No glory-girl's, nor hag's.

No one else's, ever, other than that single bestial shape.

And this was happening to her.

As laser-scalpels sliced her face and skull she screamed within.

Boiling outrage welled in her heart. Grievance, gall, and bitterness mixed their corrosive, acid cocktail in her belly. Her spirit shrieked.

Yet, necessarily, she lay silent as a stone.

She lay silent as a marble woman whom ruthless sculptors were carving into an evil idol.

Aye, silent as the very void that now opened in her tormented soul, swallowing her scream, sucking it away as surely as the silver tube sucked away parts of herself.

And in that terrible silence part of Meh'Lindi still listened to the medicus explaining; for she must understand.

ALONE, ALONE, AND now ever more alone, Meh'Lindi walked towards a huge eroded sandstone temple under a coppery sky inflamed by a giant red sun. That awesome sun filled a quarter of the heavens. Nevertheless, the air was chilly, for such suns yielded only meagre heat.

The temple complex dominated the end of a dusty boulevard lined by arcaded buildings of glazed terracotta with interior courtyards sheltered by domes. The arcades were crowded with vendors of barbecued birds' legs, stuffed mice and hot spiced wine, of holograms of this holy city of Shandabar, of supposed fragments of relics embedded in crystal, and models of relics. Those loggia were thronged with beggars and cripples and conjurors, with fortune tellers and robed pilgrims and gaudy tourists.

Temple concessionaires, some of them retired priests, were selling icons guaranteed as Imperially blessed and, to those who underwent the trivial test of sticking their hand inside a humming hex-box, lurid silken purity tassels, so called. These promised protection from evil in proportion to the size and number and floridity of tassels purchased.

The Oriens temple of Shandabar, built at what had once been the eastern gateway, was in fact the least of the holy city's three major temples. However, it boasted a giant, guarded jar of long, curving, talon-like fingernails. These were undoubtedly clippings from the Emperor's own hands, dating from the mythic days before He had been encased in the golden throne. Due to His immortal power and reach throughout the galaxy, these disembodied nails were understood to continue growing slowly as if still connected to His person. Thus priests could trim and shave off authentic parings for sale to the faithful, who might wear them or grind them to dust so as to drink in potions.

The temple also housed, in a huge silver reliquary, the thigh bones of a Space Marine commander from long ago – and, in a baroque copper cage, what was reputed to be the partial skeleton of a 'daemon.'

Carts, drawn by cameleopards with humps suggestive of huge inflamed boils, with snaking necks and lugubrious, whiskery, stupid faces, creaked to and fro along the boulevard, carrying sightseers and vegetables. Balloon-tyred cars and the occasional armoured police or security vehicle growled by. Even the Oriens temple was notably wealthy.

Meh'Lindi wore the capacious brown robe of a pilgrim, with a cowl that hid her features in shadow. Cinching the waist was her scarlet assassin's sash which concealed garrottes, blades, phials of chemicals, and a digital needle gun. Within her robe were other articles of her primary trade.

And what was hidden within her?

Why, the most evil shape. A vile shape that forever constrained her now; that denied her the option of masquerading as anyone she pleased. That shape, which was indelibly inscribed within her healed anatomy – physically implanted in collapsed form – denied her access to any of the sham physiques and physiognomies that she had thought of as... well, sisters, mothers, cousins to herself.

Thus she was utterly alone. Her only doppelganger was a monster: the alien beast within.

Meh'Lindi grieved as she entered a caravanserai near the temple. Camelopards were tethered to steel rings set in the flagstones of the vast courtyard. Ropes hobbled their lanky legs, fore and aft, lest they lash out. Flies buzzed around their orange droppings. Guyed to other rings, tents were pitched under the dome. Galleries, reached by curving iron stairways, housed three upper tiers of semi-private rooms with linked balconies. Smoke from several bonfires of dried dung drifted out through the open eye at the zenith of the dome. These fires notwithstanding, the chill of the night would creep in from outside. The more traditional breed of traveller who shunned the shivers of the early hours, and who sought privacy, would rent a tent. Poorer cousins would wrap themselves in bedrolls on the hard flags.

The hunchbacked, sallow-complexioned proprietor asked, in the common language of Sabulorb, 'Seeking lodgings?'

Any assassin was already fluent in major dialects of Imperial Gothic as well as a number of human languages which had drifted far enough from their origins as to bear no resemblance to their roots. An assassin constantly added new languages to her repertoire. Meh'Lindi had done likewise, using a hypno-casque – a knowledge-inducer – on the cargo ship en route to the sandy world of the giant red sun. The electronic tattoo on her palm currently declared her to be the daughter of a planetary governor intent on a pilgrimage.

'Preferring lowest room,' she replied. 'Being from cavern world, surface uninhabitable. Suffering from vertigo and sky-fear.' She pulled the capacious hood even further forward, implying that this headgear was her private cave. She paid the proprietor a week in advance in Sabulorb shekels, exchanged at the spaceport against Imperial credit programmed into her tattoo, and added a shekel as a modest sweetener.

'Being cellar rooms under your caravanserai?' she asked. A reasonable question, given her explanation. She allowed a hint of vulnerability and pleading to colour her voice, though a harder overtone – of someone accustomed to be indulged and obeyed – warned that she was not to be taken advantage of.

'Being, indeed... though not habitable.' The hunchback's palm seemed to itch. 'Being even an old tunnel, perhaps, if this guest is preferring to visit the Oriens by risking sticky cobwebs, but avoiding open sky.'

'Oh no,' she demurred. 'Being pilgrim, same as others. But thanking you for offering favour.' She slipped him an extra half-shekel.

NEXT MORNING MEH'LINDI took the full-scale guided tour of the Oriens temple, alert for signs of covert genestealer infestation, such as any four-armed idol, however small, tucked away in however inconspicuous a niche.

A scrawny, long-nosed priest guided her party. In the Hall of the Holy Fingernails, robed guardian deacons sat hunched on tripod stools around a tall crystal jar of parings, nursing what seemed to be some kind of stun gun of local manufacture. While the guide enthused about the miracle of how the Emperor's nails continued to grow, Meh'Lindi pretended that she was about to make an offering. She contrived to spill some half-shekels far and wide from her purse. Recovering her coins, she stooped to squint inside the hoods of the guards.

Two of those deacons certainly possessed the sharp teeth and glaring mesmeric eyes of hybrids who could hope to pass for true human, at least in shadow.

Massive candles burned, rendering the rune-mosaics of the walls waxy as the inside of a beehive. Bowls of smouldering incense flavoured the honey of the air. She thought of cellars under the caravanserai, and of the tunnel. Under this elderly temple there must be crypts and catacombs, and tunnels extending who knew how far beneath the ancient city...

'Now conducting you to the Hall of Femurs,' announced their guide.

Her journey through the warp to Sabulorb had been brief enough, but some years of local time would have passed since whichever spy of the Imperium had left to report his or her suspicions. The infestation by genestealers had plainly been under way for a number of generations. Genestealers would hide, seeking to maintain a facade of normality for as long as possible. Ultimately the evil brood would hope to control the city through their more presentable offspring, and even the planet, while still maintaining the pretence that life was normal. Long before that stage was reached, the Imperium ought to take utmost measures.

Meanwhile Tarik Ziz judged – cunningly, or rashly? – that there existed leeway for an experiment... Had he consulted with the supreme director of Callidus? Had the supreme director consulted with the grand master? And had the grand master consulted with... whom? The lord commander militant?

An instrument of Callidus should not dream of asking such questions. Nor did Meh'Lindi understand the hierarchy of the Imperium in its complex entirety. She was but an instrument.

Yet she was aware that the rapid and total destruction of genestealers, wherever found, was a military priority.

'Please coming this way, pious pilgrims–'

In a crypt beneath the temple, the genestealer patriarch – the first of the evil aliens to pollute a victim – would roost on its throne, attended by its offspring in hybrid or quasi-human form. By the fourth generation, these would each be able to sire or bear new purestrain stealers. Had that stage yet been reached? The nominal leader of the brood, the charismatic, human-seeming magus, would undoubtedly have become high priest of the Oriens temple, which would seem to continue to worship the Emperor of all Mankind.

Humans who had been polluted by stealers were mesmerized. The human-seeming offspring heeded a brood-bond so that they loved their bestial cousins and uncles intensely. Would Meh'Lindi, in her altered body, possess enough chameleon empathy to fool that brood-bond?

She almost ignored the sacred, pitted thigh bones of the Marine poised in their reliquary. At that moment, beneath her feet perhaps lurked the fierce, bloated, armoured, cloven-footed patriarch...

Just as inside herself there lurked an example of its bastard progeny, as if it had kissed her deep with its spatulate, seed-planting tongue...

When presently she saw the partial skeleton of the supposed 'daemon' in that copper cage, filigreed with hexes and a-crackle with blue sparks – energized so that no daemonic claimant could return – she wondered whether the hunched alien bones were actually those of a purestrain stealer, set up sardonically in that place of honour by the patriarch while the real relic languished elsewhere... The tour lasted for two hours, comprising lavishly decaying halls, sacrariums, and lesser shrines. She saw some evidence of on-going embellishment and repair, yet evidently wealth was not being squandered on the Imperial cult.

The donated shekels, and those gleaned from sale of relics, would be sustaining an ever-extending family of unhumans underground.

When Meh'Lindi and her party at last returned to the great courtyard, a liturgical pageant was about to begin.

'Seeing the blessed Emperor defeating the daemon you were witnessing within!' cried a herald.

Daemons and aliens were creatures of a very different stripe; and genestealers certainly fell into the latter category, of natural beings. The less known about the daemons of Chaos, the better! Ironically the herald – knowing no better – blared out something forbidden so as to advertise whatever flummery would be staged…

'A shekel apiece, good pilgrims, so that we may be proceeding!'

A scrofulous dwarf scurried to and fro, collecting coins in a sawn-open skull fitted with silver handles, till he was satisfied with the height of the pile. The herald clapped his hands.

The illusion of a huge and ornate, though melancholy, throne room sprang into being all around, cast by hidden holographic projectors. The sandy ground of the courtyard now seemed to be tessellated marble. A horde of gorgeous, abject lords and ladies grovelled before a leering, green-hued, sag-bellied monster sprawling in a great, spike-backed throne. Mutant guards wearing obscene and blasphemous armour kept vigil, cradling bolt pistols and power axes. The 'daemon' glowed luridly. Jagged threads of lightning flickered between its froggy hands. Meh'Lindi was wryly amused.

At that moment a parody of Space Marines with brutish, bulbous heads burst into the throne room. They fired explosive bolts at the guards, who fired back in turn. Caught up in the illusion, the audience of pilgrims screamed. Rapidly, as if matter met anti-matter, all of the guards and all of the mock Space Marines died and vanished. So did the lords and ladies, leaving the stage clear…

A tall, aura-cloaked figure entered, wearing a flashing golden crown. A mask of wires and tubes hid the 'Emperor's' face. From his outstretched hands sprouted nails which were as long again as his fingers. He gestured challengingly at the daemon – or alien – lord. As Meh'Lindi stared, transfixed, these nails swelled into claws, and an extra set of hands, and arms, burst forth from the sides of the 'Emperor's' rib-cage.

Plainly this pageant was designed to confuse the beliefs of onlookers – already confused – so that they would identify the holy Emperor with the image of a genestealer... who would soon tear the fat green dae-mon-alien apart and claim that throne...

'Fool!' cried a voice. 'This being the climax, not the prelude!'

Behind the goggling, gasping pilgrims a tall purple-cloaked man was rebuking the herald, whom he was hauling along by the scruff of the neck. Like a ventilator cowl or a radar dish, the newcomer's high stiff-ened hood cupped a long, menacing, yet enchanting face. His cranium was shaved bald. Knobbly bumps above his brows were tattooed with butterflies unfurling their wings, as if beauteous thoughts were bursting forth from chrysalises there.

It was indeed a magus.

Meh'Lindi slipped closer to him.

'Not noticing our error, exalted one,' babbled the herald. 'Being out-side of the holorama. Apologizing. Soon rectifying. Recommencing the performance–'

As Meh'Lindi concentrated all her attention on the magus, the man seemed to sense her scrutiny and gazed towards her piercingly. His nos-trils flared like a horse scenting fire on the wind.

His gaze was compelling... but did not compel her.

Shucking her hood further forward, the more to gloom her shadowed face, she withdrew, and walked through the illusory walls of the throne room. She strolled away across the gritty courtyard back towards the boulevard and the caravanserai. The bloated sun of dull blood was sink-ing.

Let her not be distracted by grief at what she must now do! Let her not betray her shrine – even if her shrine had, in a sense, betrayed her.

She was an instrument.

And now the shape of the tool must change.

THAT EVENING MEH'LINDI crept through a twisting, turning, cobwebbed tunnel, exerting her chameleon instinct. Best that she should be quite close to those whom she copied. The metamorphosis would proceed more speedily; and she by no means wished to linger over it.

The electrolumen in her hand feebly lit ancient, rune-carved stones matted with dusty spider-silk in which the bones of little lizards hung.

Presently she reached an appendix to a deserted crypt, in which a soli-tary nub of candle burned low. Ahead were branching catacombs lit by the occasional oil lamp, leading towards a brighter glow and the moan of a distant choir.

Her robe was loose, and would accommodate the changes, but she dropped it nonetheless. She did not wish to disguise her new form.

She injected polymorphine, and swiftly hid the tiny empty syringe in a crevice where no one should ever find it. She had left her assassin's sash in the caravanserai. With her hands transformed into claws, she could hardly have manipulated garrottes or knives, let alone a miniature jokaero gun that was meant to slip on to a fingertip. She hoped the device she had rigged up in her room to re-inject her and restore her, would penetrate her toughened body. Maybe she would be obliged to inject through her eye.

A wave of agony coursed through her, and she blocked it.

She hunched over. Her body was molten. As she focused her attention, the implants began to express themselves. Bumps thrust up along her bending spine. Her jaw tore open, elongating into a toothy snout. Her eyes bulged. Her arms swelled, and the phalanges of her fingers became long thick claws. Her hips distorted. Now her very skin was hardening into a tough carapace, which she knew would be a livid blue, just as her cordy ligaments were a purple-red in hue.

Fairly soon, she was an extreme specimen of genestealer hybrid, whom no one could surely suspect to be anything else underneath the skin, underneath the carapace.

SHE EXERTED ALL of her empathy as she loped onward through the catacomb… and into a great subterranean chamber, pillared and vaulted, awash with torchlight, alive with brood kin, many of whom were brutish, others of whom might pass muster as human.

The hiss of many throats silenced the unhuman choir that was serenading, or communing with, the patriarch on its horned throne.

Human-seeming guards directed weapons at her. Broodkin rushed towards her, snarling.

Oh, the hunchbacked steward of the caravanserai had dreamed of a pretty prank to play on this high-born pilgrim daughter from another world. He must have been well aware of what he would guide her into.

Hybrids, more human than herself, formed a menacing circle around Meh'Lindi.

On his throne, nostrils flaring, the patriarch bared his fangs.

Through the midst of the deadly cordon, strode the magus, cloak swirling.

'I…,' Meh'Lindi hissed, 'seeeeking sanc-tuary… with my kiiind.'

Issuing from a distorted larynx, over a twisted tongue, her voice was far from human. Yet the magus must be well accustomed to such voices.

'Where coming from?' he demanded, fixing Meh'Lindi with his mesmeric gaze.

'Hiiiding on starship,' she replied. 'Imperials des-troying my brood, all of my clan but meeee. Craving sanc-tuareee–'

'How finding us here?'

'Wrapping myself in robe… skulking by night… checking temples. Temples being where maybe finding my distant kin.'

The magus scrutinized Meh'Lindi searchingly. 'You being first genera-tion hybrid… Excellent stealer body, mostly…' He locked his gaze with hers, and she felt… swayed; but was trained to resist ordinary mesmeric enchantments.

The magus chuckled. 'Of course we are not compelling one another… We are only compelling the human cattle. Our own bond being one of mutual devotion. Of heeding the calls, which you cannot heed, being not of our brood.' He turned. 'As I am now heeding… our Master. Be coming with me.'

The patriarch was gesturing with a claw.

'Escort her carefully, brothers and sisters,' the magus told the guards with a radiant yet twisted smile.

And so Meh'Lindi approached the monster on the throne: a leering, fang-toothed, armoured hog of a grandsire alien. Its eyes glared at her from under ridged bony brows. One of its lower, humanoid hands, adorned with topaz and sapphire rings, contemplatively stroked a fierce claw-hand that rested on its knee. One of its hooves tapped the floor. Loaves of armour-bone jutted from its curved spine, and it rubbed these against the carved back of its throne grindingly, as if to dispel an itch. Its spatulate tongue stuck out, tasting.

Meh'Lindi bowed lower than her stoop dictated, thrusting from her mind any hint of assassin thoughts, soaking up and re-radiating as best she could the ambience of grotesque, evil worship.

'Craving sanc-tuary, greatest father,' she hissed.

This was the crucial moment.

The patriarch's nostrils flared, sniffing the faintly oily odours of her spu-rious body. Its violet, vein-webbed eyes, at once odious and alluring, scrutinized her intently. Its gaze caressed her and pried intimately like some dulcet scalpel blade smeared with intoxicating, aphrodisiacal mucus. The grandaddy of evil clicked its claws together contemplatively. One of its hooves drummed the flagstone which was worn, at that spot, into a rut.

No, not evil… That was no way to be thinking of this fine patriarch! Empathy was the key to impersonation.

Identification.

How Meh'Lindi's yearned to flee from this den of monsters and demi-monsters! – though of course it was far too late to flee.

Flee? Ha! While the very same monstrosity resided within herself?

In such circumstances, fleeing made no sense whatever. For she was monstrous too.

So therefore she must perceive the patriarch as the incarnation of...

Benevolence. Fatherliness. Wisdom. Maturity.

The armoured monster that confronted her personified love. A profound depth of love. Love which quite transcended the passions and affections of mundane men and women – whatever such sentiments might feel like to the possessors.

Meh'Lindi had certainly mimed such emotions in the past. With an assassin's eye she had studied the victims of amorousness, lust, infatuation, and fondness, even if she herself had not been vulnerable...

This genestealer patriarch radiated such a powerful, protective, brooding love – of its true kin, and of itself, of the monster that it could not help but be: the perfect, passionately dedicated, self-sanctified monstrosity.

Yes, love, fierce, twisted love.

And utter, biological loyalty.

And a dream that possessed it, almost like some daemon: an inner vision of its mission.

The mission was to perpetuate its kind. Human beings seemed to manage this same feat almost incidentally and accidentally – all be it that the result was a thousand times a thousand human worlds, many pulsing to bursting point with the festering pus of the human species.

Genestealers were compelled to try harder. They couldn't simply writhe in copulation with their own species and produce a litter of brats.

Genestealers would willingly – nay, compulsively – infiltrate any species. Human. Ork. It didn't matter which. Eldar. To bring about, incidentally, the corruption and downfall of those species.

In a sense, a genestealer almost represented cosmic love. A love that knew no boundary of species. That heeded no distinction between male and female. Between human and abhuman, human and alien.

So this patriarch was love incarnate! Hideous, enslaving love. Almost...

Its mission also demanded hair-trigger, homicidal fury in defence of its own destiny.

And, at the same time, cunning restraint – intelligence.

Its intelligence knew naught of machines, of starships or bolt pistols, of dynamos or windmills. Tools? Our broodkin can use those things for us! Yet its mind kenned much of glands and feelings, of hormonal motives, of genetic and hypnotic dictates.

The patriarch's rheumy, violet, magnetic eyes, set in that hideous magenta countenance, considered Meh'Lindi in her hybrid guise...

Seeing... true kindred?

Or seeing through her? About to turn down its claw?

Loving you, she thought. *Revering you. Admiring you utmostly.*

In the same fashion as she revered Callidus. As she honoured her omega-dan director...

(No! Not that one. Not Tarik Ziz!)

In the same way as she reverenced... the Emperor on Terra.

This clever, loving patriarch was her Emperor here. Her great father-of-all.

Did it possess a personal name? Did any genestealer?

The patriarch grunted wordlessly.

Beside her, the magus rocked to and fro, heeding the alien monster's mental sendings. A hybrid from another star system need not be similarly attuned to those.

'Granting refuge,' murmured the magus at last. 'Embracing you in our tabernacle, and in our crusade.'

The patriarch closed its eyes, as if to dismiss Meh'Lindi. It folded its humanoid hands across its jutting, carapace-banded belly, and seemed to drift into a reverie. Its claws twitched rhythmically. Perhaps it was numbering its children, grandchildren, and great-grandchildren. Of whom, Meh'Lindi of course was not one. So though it accepted her into the fold, or at least into the fringe of the fold, she was hardly a total communicant, as were all others in this subterranean stronghold.

And how many there were! Brutishly deformed broodkin rubbed shoulders and preened and sang praise. They hissed intimacies to one another. They went about their cult duties. They kept watch and ward. They nurtured the juveniles of the clan, some of whom were marked with the taint, others of whom almost appeared to be sweet, comely children, save perhaps for bumpy brows and the eerie light in their eyes.

As Meh'Lindi gazed at a nursery area, she wondered how many of the deadly, infected children she might need to kill before she could leave this place.

If the patriarch – in the wisdom of its alien glands – had chosen to tolerate her presence, the quasihuman magus retained an edge of scepticism.

'Most welcome refugee from far planet,' he said, 'how being speaking Sabulorbish so readily?' He stroked one of the butterflies – of saffron and turquoise hue – upon his knobbly forehead, as if deep in thought.

'After hiding on ship? After skulking in city? What opportunity of

learning? Seeming remarkable to me! Knowing of the plurality of languages in the galaxy. Many worlds; many lingos and dialects, hmm?'

The magus was sufficiently persuaded by her body; that passed muster.
How could he disbelieve the evidence of the hybrid body that he saw
before him? He could not. Yet he had come up with a question which
she had hardly expected from a fanatic posing as high priest of a somewhat dodgy provincial cult devoted to miraculous Imperial fingernails.

His question was cool and logical.

Ought she to have burst in upon the genestealer clan inarticulately,
unable to express herself at all? Incoherently? Babbling in some off-
world tongue, without explanation?

In that event, she might now be caged behind bars strong enough to
hold even a genestealer, while her hosts investigated her at their leisure.

Meh'Lindi's mind raced.

She was Callidus, wasn't she?

'My human mother beeeeing a Psittican,' Meh'Lindi hissed. 'You hearing of planet Psitticusss? Itsss lingo-mimes?'

No such planet as Psitticus, the parrot-world, existed. In an Imperium
of a million worlds, no one individual, however well informed, could
know much about more than a tiny fraction of planets. Better, by far, to
name a world which didn't exist, than one which did, concerning which
she might conceivably be faulted…

'Ah,' said the magus. 'You enriching my knowledge. Being a fertile
world for our kind, that Psitticus?'

'Inishhhially. Then the killersss coming, in the cursed name of their
Emperor… The ruthlessss Space Marinesss… blasting my famileeee,
missssing only meee.'

'Condolences. Have you been seeing inside our temple up above?'

'Only from a dissstance,' lied Meh'Lindi.

'We are using theatrical skills to ensorcel the superstitious pilgrims.
We are confusing their image of the God-Emperor with that of… Old
Four Arms.' The magus nodded towards the throne, his tone humor-
ously affectionate in that moment. Oh how the magus basked in an
embracing, patriarchal love… of the foulest breed. How he relished the
monster's wisdom. What a twisted parody of fondness the man exhibited. A fondness that did not make him exactly a fool, however…

The patriarch had nodded off. Its claws and fingers spasmed fitfully as,
bathing in adoration, it dreamt… of what? Of mating with human
beings gulled here or dragged here by its broodkin? Of the glory and
ecstasy of disseminating its genes, carving its own image into the tormented flesh of the galaxy?

'After we are expanding here enough and consolidating our hold enough,' the magus declared, 'we shall be smuggling missionaries out to other worlds to stage religious pageants – to spread the cult of the true, four-armed ruler of existence. We shall be subverting other temples, other pilgrims, other worshippers of that moribund god on Terra – of that brittle stick, that rag-doll locked in his golden commode.'

His eyes glowed. 'How vivid, how *alive* a four-arm being! How truly superhuman. What other species truly uniting all the strife-torn stars? What other breed of being physically making men and aliens into cousins? And nurturing and preserving the myriad worlds for its breeding ground forevermore? Nor ever casting aside the heritage of men or aliens – those being like nourishing milk to the four-armed ones!'

'You being wisssse,' hissed Meh'Lindi.

'Oh yes, myself studying reports and rumours of other worlds that we might be making our own. But, dear refugee, you being tired and famished. Was I speaking of mere milk? Ha! You be coming this way…'

Meh'Lindi was indeed ravenous. Soon she was feasting on imported grox steaks and offworld truffles and sweetmeats bought with donated shekels. She and the brood tore into the dainties with their fangs. She fed, but took no gourmet satisfaction in the costly foods.

What of the hunchbacked proprietor of the caravanserai? He had to be in league with the stealer clan. Or at the very least he had to be aware of their existence, in relatively friendly fashion. Would he otherwise have mischievously told the lone lady traveller of the tunnel?

If Meh'Lindi remained long amongst the broodkin, and the hunchback noted her absence – then decided to pry into her room, and into her belongings – might he report his puzzlement to the temple guards?

If Meh'Lindi died here, would she care? If she was torn apart by the enraged kin of that vile form which possessed her, would that matter? Would the genestealers, in the act of destroying their own semblance, symbolically annul what desecrated her, as no other death could, thus bringing her a moment's blessed balm before the long dreamless sleep of nullity?

Yes, by Callidus it mattered!

And by Him on Terra it mattered.

Yet had not Callidus… betrayed her?

How long dared she remain here? Alternatively, did she dare to try to leave?

Brooding, Meh'Lindi picked her fangs clean with a claw.

She lay that night in the torch-lit vault among monsters and demi-monsters, a monster herself.

* * *

SHE WOKE EARLY.

She woke into a nightmare – and almost cried out in horror. A convulsive spasm racked her. She flinched from…

…*from herself.*

For she was the nightmare. She herself. None other.

Oh there were times in the past when she had woken in metamorphosed bodies. In comely bodies. In ugly bodies. Even in an alien, eldar body – ethereally beautiful, that one had been, radiantly lovely…

But she had never woken as a monster.

An assassin was trained to respond instantly, to come wide awake at once and attack instantly, if need be. Yet in that brief instant of awakening Meh'Lindi was almost impelled by the nightmare of reality to attack her own altered person.

She rolled over, rose to a crouch, and stretched… casually, attempting now in alien body language – should any eyes be scrutinizing her – to express relief at finding herself amongst monster kin. Her spasm had merely been the instinctive reflex of the fugitive, the supposed former stowaway amidst hostile human beings. Had it not? Had it not?

A snouty hybrid guard had indeed been eyeing her, she noted. A couple of young whelps of the brood, as well. Another hybrid raised its head, darting a look in her direction. Here was family, hypersensitive to an occult, sticky web of relationships, to hormonal bonds of gossamer that were nevertheless as strong as the steel of a coiled spring.

She was now a fly in that web, permitted to conduct herself as a guest spider. It was a web that would spin outward from here, and from other genestealer lairs – so the magus dreamed – to entrap all sentient creatures of the galaxy in its domineering, adhesive embrace.

As any sensible being – honed to survival – would, in a new environment, she roamed.

The brats and the guard ambled after her as she sauntered, stooped, hooves clicking flagstones, through crypt and vault lit with aromatic oil burning in golden lamps, hung with tapestries depicting abstractly the deserts of Sabulorb, its seas of sand. Here was a librarium full of tomes about worlds, worlds, worlds.

What a hunger for worlds a genestealer must feel. What a blind, frustrated hunger – until a captured species of breeders gave it the means to sate its greed. How appropriate that next to the librarium was a great kitchen and larders piled with extraterrestrial imports.

Here, behind a gaol-like barred door was a treasury, banded chests abrim with shekels. Behind other bars, an armoury storing different treasure: stun guns, stub guns, bolt pistols, lasrifles.

In a birthing chamber, adjacent to a well-equipped surgery, several hugely pregnant females lay in silk upon the softest feather beds – human-seeming females, bestial females side by side.

Meh'Lindi noted stone stairways leading upward; vaulted tunnels that vanished away darkly. She memorized the subterranean layout, matching it against her recollection of the temple above.

Here, a long stone ramp led up to a great trapdoor that would rise on chains. Garaged below: a long purple limousine with toughened, reflective, curtained windows, its radiator grille a great grin of brass teeth, its armoured panels studded elegantly with chromium-plated rivets. The magus's personal transport, no doubt. Could it be that the patriarch itself ever rode unseen through the dusty streets of Shandabar, leering out at its... pasture of people, its great paddock of prey?

She trotted lithely back from her tour, to the main family chamber. All these tunnels and chambers below the temple were a sewer of alien evil – of an evil compelled by a foul, cunning, imperative joke of nature to be none other than just that; evil that even wore a mask of ultimate community. However, Shandabar City was also plumbed in the sanitary sense. In a privy, Meh'Lindi defecated her transformed supper of the previous night and before flushing that away with a push of her claw wondered whether her excrement had been doubly metamorphosed, the food transformed not only into dung, but into identifiably genestealer dung.

Perhaps her bowels remained her own. Perhaps her dirt was the talisman of her identity.

If so – considering the keen senses of genestealers – thanks be for plumbing. In the Callidus part of her she made a mental note to mention this aspect of her mission. Could an assassin, transformed into an alien, be tripped up... by an all too human stool?

THE BROOD HAD stirred. The brood fed – she too – and dispersed about their duties, though the throne room was always well visited, as if kin loved to bask regularly in the presence of their patriarch.

That vile eminence, which had snoozed nightlong in its horned throne, stirred at last.

Immediately its violet eyes, rheumy from slumber, sought out Meh'Lindi. It beckoned with a claw.

Its hybrid guards were alert now. The magus hastened to its side as Meh'Lindi approached, sidling deferentially. Not bowing, no. Straightening herself somewhat, indeed. She had decided by now that a frontal stoop might be misconstrued as the attack-crouch.

The magus rocked gently to and fro, heeding.

'We being the dreamers of bodies,' he said to Meh'Lindi. 'We kissing the dream of ourselves into the bodies of human beings, a dream that is enrapturing them. Our grandsire was dreaming of your body, New One.'

Meh'Lindi experienced a brief squirm of courtesanly disgust, of the apprehension felt by a paramour when first confronting a singularly bloated and repulsive debauchee – that virgin instant before professionalism and pretence triumph. But of course, a genestealer was quite without sexual lust as such. A genestealer's loins were blank save for an anal vent protected by a tough flap.

She projected her semblance of love.

'Grandsire's dream was highlighting patterns on your body, which indeed he is perceiving faintly, now that his dream has been showing him those... Dim, distorted images of spider, snake, strange beetles...'

The patriarch could see the trace of her tattoos! Those should have been engulfed, submerged, by the purple-red pigment of her swollen new muscles, by the deep blue of her horny carapace. Certainly they had seemed to vanish utterly when she had first transformed herself, with Tarik Ziz and chirurgeon adepts as audience. No human eyes had spied her eerie – her provocatively sinister – tattoos, which so much spelled out herself, as to be her own private heraldry.

No human eyes.

The mesmeric, veinwebbed orbs of the granddaddy of evil saw somewhat differently.

'Aaah,' she sighed. 'On Psitticusss, being many large poisonousss arachnids and serpentsss. Mottled skins of the human lingo-mimes mimicking those... My human mother passing such blemishes on to me. Slight birthmarksss...'

The patriarch grunted several times, ingesting her story like a hog its swill. The magus glared sceptically.

'A variant upon genetic inheritance of acquired characteristics,' he said primly, 'being the genestealer glory. That, and the later expression of our own lurking somatotype. Yeah, the pirating of genes – the boarding of the vessel of an alien breed's body – being what is giving us our holy name. But for a human being to be transmitting her personal acquired marks as opposed to a capacity for acquiring such–' Damn his clever mind and his grubbing in that librarium!

'Not undersssstanding,' hissed Meh'Lindi; and truly she didn't.

It was all irrelevant.

All utterly irrelevant.

From the direction of the tunnel by which she had first entered the lair of the brood, bustled the hunchbacked, yellow-faced landlord of the caravanserai.

He held Meh'Lindi's discarded robe and the device she had rigged up in her room that held the syringe of polymorphine. Around his neck he had draped her red sash.

'Being treachery! Bewaring!' he cried.

Guards raised their bolt pistols, staring around for an enemy.

'Seizing that New One!' spat the magus, saliva spraying at Meh'Lindi. Four strong hybrids leapt to pinion her by the arms.

For a moment she stiffened, as if in surprise, both testing their vigour and about to fight, yet then – before they would even have sensed resistance – she relaxed.

She could probably throw them off.

What then?

Could she trigger a salvo of explosive bolts, some of which might strike the patriarch? If she leapt at it? Bolts that would destroy her in the process, too…

No, the brood wouldn't recklessly put their patriarch in such peril. They would surely hold their fire at close quarters.

With her claws and fangs alone she, a hybrid, would never be able to kill a full-blown, mature patriarch. Who might loll. Who might snooze. Yet who was probably the most lethal fighting creature in all the galaxy. Whose claws could rip through a Space Marine's powered combat armour as if that was a mere sheath of thin tin.

She couldn't hope to snatch a boltgun. Her claws were too crude to operate the trigger.

The sash left behind in her lodging… the improvised frame for the little hypodermic… where else could she have left those? And her robe in the tunnel… where else?

Nevertheless, she felt that she had walked into a trap of her own making – marched into it through self-hatred. Or at least through hatred of what Tarik Ziz had done to her.

The patriarch crunched its claws together malevolently. The magus almost jigged with the power of its sendings. That mesmeric, clever leader of the brood was a puppet now, his true role blatantly apparent – that of a lordly, willing slave to the gross granddaddy. For that magus, who boasted of the glory of the genestealers, was not a full genestealer himself. He wasn't a purestrain. He was a sublimely talented, puissant tool of the patriarch and of the genestealer mission. A tool.

Just as Meh'Lindi herself was an instrument.

And thus it would be under the perverted, loving tyranny of gene-stealers triumphant: a cousinhood of captivated, obedient, cattle-like species, lowing their praise of their predator.

It seemed almost as though genestealers had been, well, consciously devised... to enslave the different races of the galaxy, to prepare the ground, to sow the seed which something else unimaginable might reap...

Meh'Lindi thrust this speculation from her mind, as the hunchback proclaimed slyly: 'A pilgrim woman coming to my caravanserai, from a cavern world saying, seeming an imperious princess in disguise. Then finding her gone, and this sash of many deadly marvels in her room – some enigmatic, some plain in purpose such as a garrotte – and this device for injecting some substance. Discovering her robe in the tunnel I was telling her of, prankfully, so as to be presenting a fine fertile vessel to our lord, His tongue to be kissing deep... A New One being here! And where is that covert princess of the caverns, eh?'

'Cousin,' said the magus, 'we too are having our suspicions of the New One.'

'Oh, are we?' retorted the hunchback.

'Yet that a pilgrim woman should be becoming a mighty hybrid... being contrary to anatomy.'

'Big galaxy, cousin! Full of strange marvels, no doubt!'

'Being well aware.'

'Pedantically aware, at times! Despite charisma of glowing eyes, despite charm of handsome countenance, and splendid limbs!'

'So there we are having it,' said the patriarch's supreme puppet. 'You yourself might be being magus, but for your exaggerated deformity, and because of your lacking sufficient... grace. So our grandsire was not countenancing you, my jealous, loving cousin. Thus you are seeking undermining me, maybe, with this story of a woman.'

Was it possible, thought Meh'Lindi, that the hunchback and the magus might quarrel bitterly enough to allow her some grace, some lee-way?

No. For the patriarch arose, exerted its control of kindred.

'Bringing that needle against the New One,' ordered the magus. 'Piercing a part. Testing...' He mused. 'Though which part? Where...? New One, will you be sticking out your tongue?'

'That ssstooped man planning poisssoning this refugee?' Meh'Lindi asked, as if in ignorance. 'This being asssylum in your tabernacle? Yet... willingly, trussstingly, I am obeying my newly adopted lord.'

As she had hoped, at the hunchback's approach, two of the hybrids who had held her moved aside out of the way. The patriarch was watching her fixedly, unblinkingly. She let herself be limp in the grip of her two remaining captors.

Two. Only two.

Yes, she relaxed. However, in her spirit she was back inside the exercise wheel, racing, accelerating. Within her a fly-wheel was accumulating momentum, ready to release it in one great burst, in one transcendental surge of power that would carry her right over the top. A spring was winding up, coiling tight.

She must be utterly lucky too…

Yet luck was often a gift of grace; and who was more graceful than a Callidus assassin? She prayed fervently to the God-Emperor on Terra. Never had she needed his grace more.

The wheel spun wildly. The spring tightened towards that point where it must either snap or be released.

Utterly lucky… if she was to succeed before she died.

For surely she would die.

A suicide song keened through her soul, the harmony of exemplary suicide.

And of course at such a moment an assassin – by bidding farewell to self – could survive and survive, weaving through a host of foes and weapons, killing, killing; as did her cousins of the Eversor shrine.

But she was Callidus.

And Callidus had betrayed her…

So something was missing from her song.

Rage arose in her once more. Utmost fury at her violation. She saw the patriarch before her as a monstrous Tarik Ziz who could blithely implant this vile form within a violated human being.

Alas, she could never vent her scalding vengeance upon the director secundus, on account of her oaths, her loyalties…

But she could aim all of that venom at the patriarch.

Now the wheel was white-hot. Now the spring was razor-edged.

The hunchback held the hypodermic in its framework towards her snout. By a sudden slump, with a twisting spin, with a violent upthrust of her arms, she shucked off her captors. In her claws she seized the framework. She rotated it in a trice. Brushing the hunchback aside, she threw herself at the patriarch, that jutting little needle aimed at its left eye.

The patriarch uttered a squeal – more of surprise than of a pig being impaled. What, impaled by a pinprick, even in the corner of one eye?

Snarling, the patriarch was already batting Meh'Lindi aside. She rolled. She rose, to grip the magus as a shield. Some lurid magenta blood flecked the patriarch's eye. Some violet liquid seemed to leak. It reared its mighty head and roared. This stupid, insignificant injury was as nothing to it. Nothing. A flea-bite. Pure, raw, ravening genestealer now, the patriarch reached out its claw-arms.

Yet it did not attack at once. Perhaps perplexity at the feebleness of her assault caused it to pause. Perhaps, detecting no further threat, it was turning its senses inwards, attempting to diagnose what substance had entered it. A poison? Hardly!

How soon, dear Emperor, how soon?

Abruptly the polymorphine began to work – on an untrained anatomy, on a creature which had no idea of what was happening to it, and hardly enough time to guess by introspection.

The patriarch's body rippled as its carapace softened, as though a coating of worms crawled underneath its previously horny hide. Its head distorted sidelong. Its injured eye solidified into a marble ball. Its teeth fused together – then, as it howled, the joined teeth softened, to stretch like rubber. Its claws began to bud teeth. Its lower, simian hands became floppy pincers.

It was in flux. Nothing could teach it how to hold its form intact. It vented excrement. Its tongue pressed out between the elastic teeth, longer, longer, thinner, thinner. The monster – even more monstrous now – collapsed back across its throne. And now, in its one true eye, Meh'Lindi could see how fiercely, how desperately it was willing itself to keep its shape amidst the anarchy that engulfed it.

Willing itself. Yet failing, since it couldn't perceive the proper shape of its own internal organs... while those swelled or pinched or stretched. And since it was in flux, its broodkin were in confusion. Appalled at its continuing transformation, they were rocked by its now incoherent sendings.

The patriarch's organs and appendages were dissolving and reforming while its tormented will still endured. Suddenly its softened thorax split open. Pulsing mauve and silver coils spilled out, liquefying. The exposed innards of the true master of the Oriens temple melted into protoplasmic jelly.

With her own claws Meh'Lindi crushed the arms of the magus. She drew up her stealer knee to break his spine. Throwing him at the nearest guards, she darted to the hunchback. Seizing him under one arm, she bore him away, the sash still hanging round his neck.

As she raced into a tunnel that would lead to a certain stairway, explosive bolts whined past her inaccurately, detonating against the stonework, spraying splinters. Behind her, broodkin screeched as the patriarch's death agony communicated itself. Confusion, chaos – then an onrush of broodkin in her wake intent on vengeance.

SHE EMERGED IN the Hall of the Holy Fingernails, and sprinted for the great doorway through the reek of candle smoke and incense. Pilgrims scattered. She tossed a hybrid deacon aside, eviscerating him with her free claw, as brutish broodkin boiled up into the hall behind her.

Outside, a morning pageant was in progress. She rushed through the illusory walls of the phantom throne room just as the parody Space Marines were opening fire at the green daemon's guards.

As guards and Marines died and vanished, along with the grovelling lords and ladies, for a moment the gawping audience of pilgrims and tourists must have imagined that the monster Meh'Lindi and her struggling burden were a part of the spectacle.

Then the caricature Emperor entered behind her, gesturing with those extraordinary fingernails. Rushing around him, bursting right through his holographic image, snarling parodies of humanity invaded the throne room.

The brood had temporarily lost all leadership. A salvo of bolts winged into the crowd, blasting bloody craters in flesh. For the spectators were in the way. Their toppling corpses nevertheless served to shield Meh'Lindi. She leapt through the phantom wall into the actual sandy courtyard – and raced. Behind, she heard no more firing; only hideous screams. Nor were the broodkin following her out into the open, under the ballooning red sun.

Perhaps a collective caution prevailed. Perhaps the broodkin were busy slaughtering all witnesses of their wanton exposure prior to withdrawing. Or, insensate, the brood may have decided to wreak their wrath, bare-handed, sharp-clawed, upon any available human victims. Certainly none escaped through the illusory walls – which, in their panic, may have seemed all too real.

Voices cried out around Meh'lindi in disbelief or pious terror about a 'daemon' on the loose.

Sirens of armoured militia vehicles were beginning to shriek, but Meh'lindi was an expert at evasion. Darting down one side alley, then another, she found a sewer hatch and tore it open. She thrust the hunchback down inside the tiled hole to drop to the bottom with a splash, then inserted herself with legs and bony back braced, so as to slide the lid back into place above her. Difficult, with claws instead of fingers!

In part-flooded, stinking darkness, she regained hold of the hunchback. She squeezed him.

'Ssso, would-be magusss,' she wheezed, 'I being helping you, eh? You mussst be waiting for a new puressstrain being born, to whom you shall becoming uncle... then high ssservant and oracle. Who better?'

'What being you?' the hunchback managed to ask, terror and cunning warring in his voice.

'An ally... Would you seeeeing a miracle?'

'Yes. Yes.'

'Tiny electrolumen being in my sssash. You lighting it.'

The hunchback groped for a long while before the tiny light brightened the cramped cloacal tunnel they were crouched in.

'Being needle in my sssash. Hold it out at meee. And I am becoming harmless to you then, as a pilgrim woman, hmm?'

The hunchback nodded. He held the needle firmly. Meh'Lindi bit the tip of her tongue between her fangs. Impaling the injured, softer inner tissue upon the sharp needle point, she pressed her tongue forward to discharge the drug into herself.

Soon her body was molten. Soon her implants were slackening, shrinking. The hunchback stared, goggle-eyed.

SHE SPAT SOME blood from her mouth. Despite the stenchful surroundings, the hunchback now gazed hungrily at the nude tattooed body amazingly revealed to him.

'Safer as a woman,' he agreed, licking his lips. 'Softer to be questioning – about this wondrous liquid that is altering bodies. With such guile we could be disguising our hybrids perfectly.'

He shifted his left hand from behind his back. On one finger he wore the jokaero needle gun. While the convulsive changes had distracted her, while her vision had glazed, the hunchback had filched that miniature weapon from her sash and slipped it on. Or maybe he had already transferred the tiny gun to the pocket of his robe much earlier, recognizing it for what it was, and determined to reserve it for himself.

'Not being fooled into thinking this a ring, princess. My cousin being duped, perhaps. Not I. Ah, how poetically you were bending his spine, making him just like me in death.' He pointed his armed finger at her.

'When I am bending my finger sharply, this gun is discharging, I am supposing?'

Yes. By and large. Yes. The hunchback might well succeed in firing the gun.

'Staying here a while till excitement is dying... Then sneaking to my fine establishment, and into a certain cellar. You ravaged my clan, witch. Softer to question, ah yes.'

He was wrong. Meh'Lindi was herself again, no longer encumbered by clumsy claws and a stoop. Once again, she was a Callidus assassin. If the environs were cramped, what of that? She shuffled ever so slightly.

FIVE MINUTES LATER, during a moment of mild inattention when boots rang on the sewer lid overhead, the hunchback died quickly and silently – throat-punched, nerve-blocked, broken-necked – without even crooking his finger once.

Meh'Lindi was ravenous after the change. She had to feed. She only knew one immediate source of protein. The proprietor of the caravanserai had stared at her hungrily.

Now she repaid the compliment, somewhat reluctantly.

In her famished state, his corpse tasted sweet.

SHE BALLED UP his robe to haul behind her, tied to one ankle. She reasoned that she should crawl for a mile or so to escape from the immediate neighbourhood.

Some pipes were to prove tight and deep in effluent. She needed to dislocate her joints and hold her breath. She did so. She was an instrument. She was Callidus.

WRAPPED IN THE hunchback's sodden robe, cinched with her scarlet sash, she trotted through the city under the cold constellations, heading back towards the spaceport.

Patriarch and magus were both dead. Yet the evil clan remained. Maybe the city militia would react and call in heavy assistance. Or maybe the local forces were themselves infiltrated by hybrids. Meh'Lindi had no intention of discussing matters with any militiamen in Shandabar.

She had infiltrated a genestealer stronghold – for a night and a morning – and had survived. By luck. Through rage. And courtesy of polymorphine, misused as no assassin had misused the drug before. Perhaps that would be a bright enough feather in Tarik Ziz's cap...

The alien beast lurked within her, as it always would: tamed, yet holding her captive too.

How her heart grieved.

DRACO

My lord high inquisitor,

I have now examined this particular archive, as you requested of me. I can state that the text does truly date from a time around twelve hundred years before the present day. However, in the absence of a true physical copy of the work, dating a record that exists only as a data file upon our cogitator with any real precision is beyond the abilities of even my most skilled tech-priests.

As to its content, there is little to tell. I have been unable to acquire any evidence of the existence of an inquisitor of our Ordo by the name of Jaq Draco. Indeed, my researches have led me to believe that none of the Ordos have any record of such a personage. However, I have not been permitted access to their most hidden archives, and I cannot therefore offer a definitive answer as to his non-existence.

Of his outlandish companions, I have more mixed feelings. The work itself states that the Callidus temple acknowledges the presence upon its roll of infamy a such-named assassin. Yet in all my years I have never heard of such a request for information producing such an unequivocable result – that the secretive leaders of the assassins' shrines openly would even acknowledge any such query from those outside their order is frankly unbelievable. The Navigator… well, well we know of old the scorn with which our 'brothers' in the Navis Nobilite regard outside enquiries. As to the abhuman, the thread is cut. The accursed hive fleet of the tyranid put paid to that line too long ago. I cannot believe, however, that even a renegade inquisitor, if that is what this Draco really was, would tolerate the presence of such a disgusting mutation.

Lord, I understand full well that my role is to examine the facts as they are presented, to report upon the technical aspects of this archive alone. But I must confess to you now: I am sorely troubled. I have been serving you in my capacity as master librarian for two centuries now, but never have you asked me to report upon such a tangled morass of bare half-truths and inferences. If even a fragment of what this memoir purports to reveal is truthful, it implies a conspiracy of the most mind-warping complexity.

Yet where is the evidence? Without it, this work can be nothing but a blasphemous heresy, a traitorous farrago of the most evil kind. This work would be better destroyed than be recorded in any form, lest it one day be revealed, to cause who knows what damage to the minds of scholars less sceptical than ourselves. I implore you, lord, let me erase this heresy.

May the Golden Throne watch over you,

R.

Ordo Malleus Archive Decimus-Alpha
Record 77561022/a/jj/fwr/1182/i
Added 3721022.M39
Reclassified 1441022.M40
Clearance level: Vermilion.

WARNING!

What follows is the so-called Liber Secretorum, or Book of Secrets of Jaq Draco, the renegade inquisitor.

This is a book which may have been deliberately designed as a weapon to sabotage faith and duty. The primary purpose of the Liber may be to sow distrust and discord among the Hidden Masters of our order so as to undermine the Ordo Malleus from within. The intention might also be to cast doubt upon the motives of our immortal God-Emperor himself, praise His name. We do not know.

Anyone authorised to scan this Liber Secretorum is privy to the darkest of conspiracies. Anyone not thus authorised faces the penalty of mindscrubbing or death. In either event, you are warned.

PROLOGUE

Believe me. I intend to tell the truth as I experienced it.

What does the name of *inquisitor* mean? Many people would answer: destroyer of mutants, hammer of heretics, scourge of aliens, witch-hunter, torturer. Yet really the answer is: a seeker after truth, however terrible the truth may be.

As a member of the Ordo Malleus I am already a secret inquisitor. Yet the truth I must disclose involves the revelation of even deeper, more sinister secrets than those known to members of our covert order.

My story includes a journey to the Eye of Terror itself. Not to mention an incursion into the Emperor's own throne room in the heart of his heavily guarded palace on Earth, something that you may consider almost impossible; yet I have achieved it.

Ah yes, I won through – only to find that the Emperor may keep secrets even from himself, in his fragmented mind; which you may not believe, either. But such is the case. So I swear.

My story involves a sleeping menace which you yourself may harbour. And you, and you, unknowing!

In a galaxy where more than a million worlds harbour human beings – or variations upon human beings – and where this multitude is but the tip of the iceberg of worlds, and where that vast iceberg itself floats in a deeper sea of Chaos, there must be many secrets. Likewise: guardians of secrets, betrayers of secrets, discoverers of secrets. The whole universe is a skein of secrets, many of which are dire and hideous. Possession of a secret is no blessing, no hidden jewel. Rather, it is akin to a poison toad lurking inside a gem-encrusted box.

Yet now I must open that box for your inspection. I must betray my secret, or as much as I know of it.

Believe me.

I! Me! It sounds odd for a hidden inquisitor to reveal his identity in this fashion. Aside from the obvious considerations of security, who can doubt what a powerful instrument a name can be? Why else will a daemon use almost any trick to avoid vomiting its true name forth from its own treacherous lips? For instance, whosoever knows the name of Thlyy'gzul'zhaell can bind and summon that vile entity... until such time as Thlyy'gzul'zhaell gains the upper claw; whereupon woe betide the foolish summoner. Naturally, a malicious daemon will readily reveal a rival daemon's name...

Though no daemon I, I feel in my bones that it might prove inauspicious to utter my own name overmuch *in my own voice*, lest somehow I may be summoned and bound – by hostile human forces. Therefore, I shall become he. I, Jaq Draco, will tell the story of Jaq Draco as witnessed by a fly upon the wall, committing Jaq Draco's experiences to this data-cube in the hope that the Masters of the Malleus or of the Inquisition itself may authenticate the truth of what I report and determine to take action.

In that event, you (whoever you are, wherever, whenever) may be scanning these words as part of a briefing, poised on the brink of a deadly mission.

I hail you – fellow inquisitor, Space Marine commander, whomever.

Firstly I should briefly introduce Jaq Draco's travelling companions, without whom he would surely have failed. They were three: Meh'Lindi the assassin, Vitali Googol the Navigator, and Grimm. (Little Grimm the squat; do not despise this plucky, ingenious abhuman. Do not mock his youthful foibles.) When Draco landed on the planet Stalinvast accompanied by these three, the inquisitor was in the guise of a rogue trader, an incognito that he often used. Googol was his pilot; Grimm, his engineer. Seemingly, Meh'Lindi was the trader's mistress, though in truth... a secret inquisitor needs a secret assassin, does he not?

One of the nastier poison toads of the universe was about to launch itself out of its box, under the energetic prodding of a much more public inquisitor by the name of Harq Obispal. Draco would keep vigilant watch in case any toadspawn remained behind uncleansed. He was likewise keeping watch on Obispal, a surveillance of which Obispal should ideally have remained unaware, though doubtless he might have relished the scrutiny, since Obispal was a performer...

ONE

SOME HIVE WORLDS consist of shell upon shell of plasteel braced by great pillars, as if the planet has grown a metal skin and then another skin and yet another, each successive skin being home to billions of busy human maggots, fleas, lice.

Other hive worlds are poisoned wildernesses punctuated by rearing plasteel termite mounds, vertical cities that punch through the clouds.

The cities of Stalinvast were more like coral reefs looming above a sea of hostile jungle. Kefalov bulged like some fossil brain adorned with innumerable ridges. Dendrov branched every which way, a forest of tangled stags' horns. Mysov was a mass of organ pipes, from which sprouted the fungi that were suburbs. Other cities were stacks of fans or dinner plates.

A thousand such cities, soaring, bulging, branching from the surface of Stalinvast and almost all involved in the manufacture of weapons for the Imperium. Stalinvast was a rich, important world. Its thronged reefs were proudly stained rose-red, scarlet, purple, pink. Between the cities the blue-green jungle was riven with great scars where plasma cannon and barrage bombs had been tested. Warrior robots, juggernauts, and great armoured vehicles used the jungles as a proving ground.

The capital, Vasilariov, partook of most of the styles of coral architecture. Fifty kilometres long by forty wide by five high, currently Vasilariov was being scarred by some of its own weapons as Harq Obispal raged through the hive like an angry bear. Doing good work, oh yes.

* * *

In the Emerald Suite of the Empire Hotel, a plate jutting high above raw jungle at the southern edge of Vasilariov, Meh'Lindi said, 'I think I shall go into town to practise.'

'Against the rebel hybrids?' asked Grimm. 'Huh! Count me out.'

Which meant, as they all knew, that Grimm didn't intend to miss any of the action.

'Dressed like that, Meh'Lindi?' Googol drawled archly.

The Navigator's large eyes assessed her gown of iridescent Sirian silk tied at the waist with a casual scarlet sash, her silverfur stole, her curly-toed slippers.

True, even costumed thus as a trader's mistress she would be armed – with a garrotte or two, some tiny digital weapons for slipping on to her fingers, phials of the chemicals she used.

Reclining on a couch, Googol appraised Meh'Lindi's figure as she began to twitch subtly. The assassin was running through some muscle exercises, using her enhanced body sense to tense and untense. She was artful steel expanding and contracting, tempering itself. Googol's own pose suggested languor. The spindly Navigator yawned.

Yet he was watching Meh'Lindi. As was Grimm; as was Jaq himself.

Meh'Lindi was taller than most men, long-limbed and sleek. Her height served to distract attention from the power in her calves and biceps. Her face, framed by curly, cropped raven hair, was curiously flat and anonymous – almost forgettable. Its smooth ivory planes suggested beauty without exactly expressing it, as if awaiting a stimulus to burst into life. Her eyes were golden.

Meh'Lindi. She had been taken as a child from a wild jungle world of carnivores, flesh-sucking plants and hunter-warriors who had lost most of the arts of civilisation save for those of cunning, combat and survival. Borne away to commence a decade of training in the temple on Callidus, she had stubbornly insisted longer than most recruits on maintaining her identity. In her outlandish, simple dialect she had declared, 'Me, Lindi! Me, Lindi!' Soon enough the seven-year-old girl had killed an older pupil who mocked her. She became known as 'Meh'Lindi' thereafter among her instructors. They let her keep that part of herself, though much else changed. Now she smiled down faintly at the jungle below the crystal windows of the suite as if remembering home – though this day the really deadly jungle was within the city, not without.

Googol and Grimm both fed on her smile. As did Jaq. As did Jaq himself.

The inquisitor knew that he should only think of Meh'Lindi as a wonderful, living weapon. He sincerely hoped that the Navigator would never be foolish enough to try to charm Meh'Lindi into his bed. Meh'Lindi could crush him to straw like a constrictor. She could crack his hairless head like an egg. Googol's ever-hidden warp-eye would pop out from beneath the black bandana tied around his brow.

As for the red-bearded squat who only stood waist-high to Meh'Lindi... dapper in his quilted red flak jacket, green coveralls and forage cap, his was obviously a comically hopeless passion.

'Meh'Lindi...'

'Yes, inquisitor?' She inclined her head. Was she conceivably teasing him?

'Don't use that title while we're on a mission!' He hoped that his tone sounded severe. 'You must address me as Jaq.'

Ha, the power to order this remarkable and disturbing woman to address him intimately.

'Well, Jaq?'

'Yes is the answer. By all means go and practise within reason. Don't pull any stunts that draw lurid attention to yourself.'

'Vasilariov's in chaos. No one will notice me. I'll be helping the Imperium a little, won't I?'

'That isn't my purpose at present.'

Googol flapped a hand languidly. 'The whole of Stalinvast may be in chaos in the ordinary sense, but Chaos as such has nothing to do with it. Genestealers aren't creatures of Chaos even if they do hang out in hulks in the warp until they can find a world to prey on.'

Jaq frowned at the Navigator. To be sure, his companions needed to know enough about him and his goals to perform effectively, but Malleus policy on the subject of Chaos and its minions was one of censorship. Chaos – the flipside of the universe, domain of the warp – spawned many vilenesses of the ilk of Thlyy'gzul'zhaell which sought to twist reality askew. Innumerable such specimens? The Ordo Malleus attempted to numerate them! Yet *not* to broadcast knowledge of those. Oh no, quite the contrary. Even the natural menace of genestealers was daunting enough to require utmost circumspection.

'Huh,' said Grimm, 'nobody knows the stealers' true origin, so far as I'm aware. Unless you do, Jaq.'

Before Jaq could respond, Meh'Lindi kicked off her slippers. She discarded her stole. She loosed her sash, sending it snaking with a flick of her wrist so that Grimm jumped back a pace. Without ceremony she dropped her silk gown, standing naked but for her briefs and her tattoos, which were all black. A hairy spider embraced her waist. A fanged serpent writhed up her right leg as if to attack the spider. Beetles walked across her breasts. Most of her tattoos concealed long-healed scars, embellishing those cicatrices eerily.

Her hand now cradled a tiny canister; what a conjuror she could be. That would have been clipped somewhere inside the scarlet sash.

Poising acrobatically upon one leg then the other, Meh'Lindi proceeded to spray her body from toe to neck with black synthetic skin. Contorting herself elegantly, yet always remaining perfectly balanced, she missed no cleft or crease or dimple. At what stage did her briefs tear loose? Jaq hardly saw. He sensed her excitement and his own excitement; knew that those were two different species of excitement.

Hastily he redirected his attention towards the circular screen that he had hung on the wall in place of an oil painting of some horned, scaly jungle monster.

His psychic sense of presence buzzed as he recontacted his spy-flies. The screen lit with a hundred crowded little images, a mosaic of miniature scenes. Now that screen was the faceted eye of a fly, though the view from each facet was unique.

The mosaic occupied much of his consciousness so that he was only dimly aware – out of the corner of his eye, and mind's eye – of Meh'Lindi, a flexible ebon statue of herself, yet still with an ivory face. Now she was inserting the throat and ear plugs with which she would hear and communicate and breathe.

Jaq summoned a facet into full prominence. It swelled. Around it, like a thronged ring of moonlets each with its own scenery, all the other facets squeezed.

A skirmish in a hovertank plant...

Arrows of light cross-hatched a grey cavern housing half-completed vehicles. Hybrids armed with lasguns were pressing hard against a picket line of planetary guardsmen. Those guards were a loyal, uninfiltrated unit and they were losing. What brutish caricatures of human beings the hybrids were, with their jutting, swollen, bone-ridged heads, their glaring eyes, their jagged bared teeth. In place of a human hand, several hybrids sported the terrible, strong claw of the purestrain genestealer. When those hybrids overran the guards they might simply tear the last survivors apart.

Yet this wasn't the whole picture, oh no, not by any means. Jaq shrank that grim facet and expanded another...

Many hundreds of rebels swarmed across the roof of a rose-red plate-district, heading for a tree of administrative towers.

Mingling with hybrids, indeed outnumbering them, were rebels who looked truly human. Some of these would be the firstborn spawn of hybrids, human in looks yet able to procreate a purestrain genestealer. Others would be subsequent offspring, genuine human beings who still heeded the hypnotic brood-bond.

A series of explosions tore at the stem of the plate district where it was attached to the rest of the city. The entire plate sagged and snapped free. Briefly, the whole huge structure sailed on the air, then fell. Rebels slid and scrabbled for hand holds, claw holds, as the district plummeted towards the fringe of the jungle two kilometres below.

On impact – a tree-flattening impact – dust arose. The dust was rebel bodies. Even the plasteel of the plate cracked open. A well-aimed plasma beam from above ignited fuel storage tanks. Within and without, flame engulfed the fallen plate-district. The dust burned; as did any populace who lived in that plate, supposing they had survived the plunge of their factory-homes.

Many hundreds more rebels were dead now. Really the rebellion was entering its final, frantic, suicidal phase.

'Some people believe the genestealers were designed – as a living weapon,' Googol was informing Grimm. 'A fine joke, dreamed up by some vicious alien!'

'Huh.'

'Well, why not? Do you think they evolved that way? Genestealers can't breed on their own. How could they have come into existence in the first place without malicious midwives? They're compelled to infest other races and multiply like a cancer within.'

In his travels throughout the galaxy, doubtless Googol would have heard many rumours, despite best official efforts to suppress scaremongering talk.

'Perhaps,' suggested Grimm, 'a Chaos storm warped them from whatever they were before? Seems the purestrains can't pilot a ship, can't fire a gun, can't fix a fuse. Otherwise, they'd be all over the place under their own steam. What a clumsy weapon! Huh!'

'Yet what an excellent dark joke against life and family and love.'

The stout abhuman muttered some oath in his own outlandish dialect.

'Now, now, Grimbo,' reproved the Navigator, 'we all speak Imperial Gothic here–'

Another, darker oath in the same patois.

'–like civilised beings.'

'Well, kindly don't call me Grimbo, then. Me name's Grimm.'

'Grimm in name though not grim in nature necessarily. You're but a sprout of a squat.'

'Huh. You're hardly antique yourself, despite appearances.'

Those wrinkles on the Navigator's face; and his mournful tunic...

Meh'Lindi's hair was slicked down tight. When she sprayed her face, her visage became more of a blank than ever, a black mask with the merest hint of features. The syn-skin would protect her against poison gas or flame or the flash of explosions; it would boost her already-honed nervous system and her already-notable vigour.

By the time she wound the scarlet sash around her waist once more, miniaturised digital weapons hooded her fingers like so many baroque thimbles. The needler, laser and flamer were precious, alien, jokaero devices.

Jaq summoned another facet...

In a transit-tube station two different units of planetary defence troopers were fighting each other furiously at close quarters. Rainbow light sprayed and arced as the vibrating edges of power axes met the energy fields of power swords. One of these units must have been entirely genestealer brood in human guise. But which was which? Those who wore the black basilisk insignia, or the blue deathbats?

Reinforcements were arriving on foot through the tunnel. Flamers sprayed at the fracas, and at last rebels could be distinguished from loyalists, just as it became obvious that the new arrivals on the scene – pink salamanders – were also loyalists. For the black basilisks screamed and writhed and quit fighting as soon as superheated chemicals clung burning to them. Deathbats – those of the brood – rushed frenziedly, even as they blazed, to attack the wielders of the flame guns. Precision laser fire sliced through the berserkers, killing human torch after human torch until the last had fallen.

Presently, perhaps tardily, foam engulfed the platforms to douse the clingfire – blinding this particular spy-fly, though by now Jaq had registered the loyalists' hard-won gain...

Another facet: a ribbed hall of towering, icon-stencilled machine tools, littered with corpses, many of them as grotesque in death as they had been in life...

Jaq's hundred roving spy-flies and the screen-eye were another jokaero invention, perhaps unique, which the Ordo Malleus had captured. Those simian, orange-furred jokaero were forever improvising ingenious equipment, not necessarily in the same way twice, though with an accent on miniaturisation.

Debate still waxed hot as to whether the orange ape aliens were genuinely intelligent or merely made weapons as instinctively as spiders make web. Grimm, a born technologist himself – as were all of his kind, it seemed – had pointed out that this eye-screen required psychic input from the operator. So some Jokaero must have psyches. At least.

Most planets seemed to harbour biological flies. Swamp-flies, dung-flies, offal-flies, sand-flies, flies that liked to sip from the eyeballs of crocodiles, corpse-flies, rotting-vegetation-flies, pseudo-flies that fed on magnetic fields. Who would notice a little fly buzzing around nimbly? Who would mark that fly watching you, transmitting what it saw and heard back to the eye-screen from anywhere within a compass of twenty kilometres? Who would expect that the fly and its fellows were tiny vibrating crystalline machines?

'I go!' announced Meh'Lindi.

If she chose, she could speak as gracefully as a courtier, as deviously as a diplomat. In the face of imminent deadly action, she sometimes reverted to a more basic style of utterance, recalling her original primitive tribal society. Lithely and silently, swift as a razorwing, she departed the Emerald Suite.

With a piercing thought and a twist of will, Jaq detached one of several spy-flies hovering in the otherwise deserted corridor outside, detailed it to follow her.

He magnified that viewpoint, allowing it a quarter of the eye-screen. Meh'Lindi paused momentarily, glanced back in the direction of the spy-fly, and winked. Then she padded quickly away, pursued.

'Huh, so I'll be off too.' Grimm jammed his cap down hard, patted his holstered laspistol, checked his 'bunch of grapes' – his grenades – and scampered after her. Unlike when Meh'Lindi exited, this time the suite door banged shut.

'Noisy tyke,' commented Googol, uncoiling from the couch. 'Surprised he doesn't favour a boltgun. *Clatter-clatter-clatter.*'

'You know very well,' said Jaq, 'that he slammed the door to signal he was following her.'

Googol laughed giddily. 'He needs to run around to keep his legs short. And Meh'Lindi, to keep hers long.'

'She'll be back, Vitali, never fear. As will Grimm.'

'Grimm racing off to protect her... as soon set a mouse to escort a cat! It's really pathetic the way he dotes on her then pretends to bluff it all off with a *huh*. I suppose in the absence of any dumpy squat females Meh'Lindi must seem like a goddess to the little chap.'

And, thought Jaq, likewise to you? And even – somewhat – to me? 'A deadly goddess,' he said, 'who always has other things on her mind. As I have. So hush.'

The Navigator prowled to and fro. He picked up a crystal decanter of amber liqueur, set it down. He pricked his thumb against the corkscrew horn of a baby teratosaur skull mounted on one wall, its brow inset with a green jewel. He stirred a courtesy bowl of dream-dust, untouched within its force-membrane by any of them hitherto, then went and cleaned his hands under the vibrostat.

Nervous for Meh'Lindi's safety? What was Meh'Lindi's whole purpose, what was her very life, but to go into perilous places, always to emerge alive? What was her daily rationale but to keep herself tuned to a pitch, taut as a bowstring? Yet in those golden eyes of hers was a lively intelligence and even wit. Of course, her sense of wit could be alarming.

Jaq riffled through facets, summoning scene after scene into prominence in swift succession until he came to the spy-fly that was tracking...

Harq Obispal.

TWO

BRANDISHING A BOLTGUN in one hand and a power sword in the other, the burly inquisitor strode along a broad boulevard, glaring to right and left.

Obispal's ginger beard forked three ways as if hairy tentacles sprouted from his chin. His eyebrows were bushes of rusty wire. His belted black robe was appliquéd with glaring white death's heads. His swamp-hunter boots could have been a pachyderm's great feet lopped off and hollowed out. Weapons and other devices hung within his blood-red, high-collared cloak; and a communicator dangled from one earlobe.

The inquisitor was advancing in the vanguard of a squad of armoured Imperial Guardsmen. Guardsmen from the local garrison, rather than Space Marines from off-world. Obispal believed in the force of will, in his own ruthless aura; and indeed, except for the evidence of lurid, puckered scar tissue across one cheek, he might have seemed invulnerable.

Presumably he didn't rate the Stalinvast operation as requiring really major surgery – even though thirty hive cities had been devastated to date and several totally destroyed. Casualties? Twenty million civilians and combatants? Out of a thousand cities, housing billions...

Wistfully, Jaq quoted to himself the words of an ancient leader of the middle kingdom on bygone Terra: 'In the land of a thousand million people, what does the death of one million of these count in the cause of purity?'

Still, suppressing such a plague wasn't the same as purging it totally. Only one fertile genestealer needed to remain alive in hiding to undo all the good work within a few decades. Highly trained Space Marines would have been utterly thorough, and would never yield to the malaise of combat, that battle-weary yearning to be done with a ghastly campaign, to rate it a *probably* total triumph, a *practically* unqualified success.

Wrecked ground cars and tanks smouldered along the boulevard under a leaden ceiling so high that utility tubes and power cables seemed to be but a delicate tracery.

Many glow-globes had been shot out or had failed, so shadows lurked like intangible behemoths. Baleful fumes drifted from slumped ducts; corrosives dripped. Gloomy tunnels led aside into blitzed factories.

Jaq allowed sound to invade his awareness.

Obispal was howling execrations that echoed, multiplying as if his voice was that of many men.

'Death to the alien scum that steal our humanity! Death to polluters! Death to the polluted! With joy may we burn and cleanse!'

The inquisitor's voice, as picked up by the spy-fly, almost drowned the crackle of gunfire. Obispal whirled his sword around so that his right arm resembled a circular saw. He threw the deadly, humming weapon into the air and caught it deftly by the shaft. He could have been leading a parade, twirling the baton.

Yes: a parade... of extermination.

Obispal had certainly taken his time over the cleansing, even protracting the process. Backed by his men and by the many planetary defence troopers who were unpolluted and loyal to the governor, he had commenced his activities around a ring of other cities than the capital, moving from one to the next, destroying. His actions had triggered full-scale rebellion by the hybrids and by the vaster genestealer brood of true-seeming humans. For decades these latter had been infiltrating the administration and even the troopers.

If Obispal had started by cleansing the capital the genestealer broods might have dispersed, escaping through transit tunnels or even overland through the jungle to more distant cities. So his strategy made sense at the same time as it seemed wantonly ruinous.

It was as if game birds had been flushed by beaters and driven towards a central point, forced to attack the heart of power and authority in a desperate bid to secure this for themselves and seal the planet.

Bees flying into a bonfire.

Troopers fought troopers. Administrators murdered their superiors and released stocks of weapons to the rebels. For the first time the ordinary workers and managers glimpsed the true faces of the hybrids who had lurked in their midst, cloaked and hooded, or masked.

Jaq scanned another swarm of these hybrids, on the rampage with guns and blades. Their stooping posture was of a person melting down, slumping into the stance of a vicious carnivore. Amidst the swarm, handsome if eerie human beings orchestrated the pandemonium.

'One has always heard whispers,' remarked Googol, 'yet to behold with one's own eyes is quite an experience.'

It was on the tip of Jaq's tongue to point out that the Navigator was only beholding courtesy of the eye-screen. He refrained, not wishing to goad Googol into some display of bravado which might rob Jaq of such an excellent warp pilot.

'Whispers?' Jaq enquired instead. '*Loud* whispers? You were giving Grimm the benefit of your theories about genestealers. Do Navigators gossip much? Might *you* gossip?'

'Navigators travel to many places, hear many things. Some true, some half-true, some concoctions. Stories alter in the telling, Jaq.' A half-pleading, half-impertinent tone had entered Googol's voice.

The Navigator was remembering that Jaq might be attired right now as one kind of person, whereas actually he was someone else entirely... and Googol needed to be reminded of this.

Masquerading as a rogue trader of reasonable success, Jaq wore a pleated frock coat with silver epaulettes and baggy crimson breeches tucked into short white calf boots. The coat was capacious, a home to guns, and the boots were home to knives. Quite in line with any ordinary trader.

Googol licked his upper lip nervously. 'A true story that crosses the galaxy becomes a lie, Jaq.'

'So, can a lie similarly become the truth?'

'That's too sophisticated for me, Jaq.'

It wasn't, of course. No one who had stared into the insanity of the warp, no one whose living was to do so, could be unsophisticated and survive. In a sense the warp was the ultimate lie, since it continually strove to betray those who traversed it. Yet at the same time the warp was the ultimate background to existence.

Vitali Googol actively cultivated an air of sophistication, aided in this by the premature age lines wrought in his visage due to long immersion in deep space and in the warp. These lent a world-weary cast to a face that might otherwise have been babyish.

Within, the Navigator was still young and vulnerable – liable to foolish enthusiasms such as his attraction to Meh'Lindi. Knowing this, Googol tried to be wry about his own feelings and eschewed any dandified garb such as Jaq now sported. Vitali wore a black tunic stitched with purple runes which were hardly visible. Black was the void. Black was sophisticated. (Black was the colour of Meh'Lindi in her war paint.)

Jaq tried to imagine how Googol viewed him. The trader costume suggested a certain piratical business acumen, though not without honour, and in the service of a deeper sensuality. Which was all a pretence. Jaq's sensual lips were definitely at odds with his sceptical ice-blue eyes. On the one hand, Jaq must seem capable of irony and flexible tolerance – perhaps only so as to spring a trap. On the other hand, he had to be as hard as granite inside, harder even than a brutally flamboyant exhibitionist such as Obispal – since Jaq was a guardian of those who guarded humanity, an investigator of the investigators.

Am I really hard enough, Jaq wondered? Or am I vulnerable too?

'Let Navigators gossip among themselves like fishwives,' he said sharply. 'The genestealers must remain a secret from our multitude of worlds, save for leaders who need to know, lest confusion spreads.'

'If people in general knew–'

'That, Vitali, is what inquisitors are for. To find out, and to root out. Confusion is the cousin to Chaos. Knowledge causes confusion. Ignorance can be the strongest shield of the innocent.' The ghost of a smile twitched Jaq's lips. Did Jaq Draco really believe these maxims?

Quarter-facet... Meh'Lindi had quit a transit capsule, had ridden an elevator down and was sprinting effortlessly along empty north-bound mobile pavements.

The south-bound pavements were crowded with refugees fleeing from the fighting. A river of people surged, fighting to gain the central express strip where that panic-stricken river raced fastest. Some citizens were injured, bleeding; others bore bundles of possessions. Often a would-be escapee, whose one foot was on the express path and whose other was still on the slower acceleration strip, was whirled aside in an eddy and sucked underfoot.

Drizzle fell from malfunctioning fire-control nozzles. Lightning crackled overhead as cables shorted.

Quarter-facet... Mounted on a stolen power-trike, Grimm roared up the north-bound speedstrip.

Meh'Lindi glanced once over her shoulder then ran on, taking huge strides.

The abhuman stood up on the foot rests, throttling back.

'You want a lift somewhere?' he bellowed.

Meh'Lindi merely increased her pace. Impulsively, the squat swung the trike to pull alongside, so that one wheel dragged on the slower strip. The manoeuvre failed. The trike skidded and tumbled, throwing

Grimm over the handlebars. Tucking himself into a ball of boots and flak jacket, the squat bounced and rolled half a dozen times. Briefly, Meh'Lindi broke step.

However, Grimm was already picking himself up, swearing, dusting himself off, retrieving his cap.

Meh'Lindi jerked one hand – in salute, or as a warning to stay away from her? – then she surged ahead.

Casting a disgusted glance at the buckled trike and at the throng pouring past him, south-bound, Grimm trotted northwards after the assassin.

Jaq surprised Googol – and himself – by chuckling, sympathetically, almost affectionately.

Meh'Lindi was soon way out of sight of the squat around a wide bend. There she quit the throughway, to race along feeder lanes, dodging through refugees who shrank from the fleeting, faceless, coaly-skinned woman. The spy-fly zipped along in her wake, down narrower, abandoned, grim alleys. Noise of battle grew audible. Shocks jerked at the fabric of the city, rupturing ancient sewage pipes.

Quarter-facet... and Jaq uttered a malediction. 'There's one of the fathers of evil.'

A middle-aged man and woman were escorting a purestrain genestealer through aisles lined with crates in some ill-lit and claustrophobic warehouse.

How commonplace the human couple looked in their workers' overalls. Apart from the laspistols both held, awkwardly if purposefully. And apart from the glazed, doting madness in their eyes.

For these two were emotionally fixated on that monster, bonded to it by sentiments which were the cruellest parody of love and of family attachment.

The puissant alien walked crouched over in a permanent posture of attack so that the horns along its spine projected highest. Its long cranium jutting forward, fangs dripping gluey saliva. Its upper set of arms ended in claws which could tear armour open; and its carapace was as tough as armour. Fibrous ligaments corded its limbs. A horny tube of a tongue flicked out: that tongue which could kiss its own gene material into a host.

Momentarily, Jaq flinched at the creature's hypnotic gaze, even seen through the medium of the screen, and although he was psychically immune.

'Father of evil,' he intoned as if in a travesty of prayer, 'and grandfather too...'

Yes indeed. The human mother who gave birth to a deformed, bestial hybrid would dote on it blindly, as protective as a tiger of her cub, and as cunning. Offspring of hybrids would seem less alien in appearance. By the fourth generation, save for the charismatic light in their eyes, the spawn would appear human.

Yet the firstborn of such a semblance would be purestrain stealer again. With appalling, instinctive inevitability the cycle would recommence.

By then a whole family coven numbering thousands of warped persons would be infesting society secretly, a brood keenly alert to each other's alien needs. Somewhere, in deepest luxurious hiding, the overgrown patriarch which first began the pollution of a world would relish empathetically all the doings of its kin...

Quarter-facet... A genestealer tore a planetary defence trooper's chest open before darting back into concealment...

FOR A WHILE, Jaq let all hundred spy-fly images be present at once in mosaic on the eye-screen. Extending his psychic sense of presence, he felt how the battle inside Vasilariov was congealing, slowing and centring desperately about fifteen kilometres north of the hotel. That was where the surviving purestrains and minions were concentrating. Maybe the patriarch was already dead. That was where Obispal was heading from one direction. And Meh'Lindi from another.

Quarter-facet once more... A darkened, elevated observation booth overlooked what seemed to be a laboratory. Under flickering emergency lighting, arcane apparatus fumed and sparked, abandoned by its operators. The strobing of the light froze monsters in mid-motion, gathering for some assault.

Jaq willed the spy-fly to see in infra-red.

Inside the booth above that scene, black in syn-skin, Meh'Lindi crouched. She had dogged the plasteel door shut. The observation window was doubtless of armoured glass. And she was crouching over. Hiding? Had she locked herself in a place of comparative safety?

The assassin was stowing her jokaero weapons away inside her sash. She sprayed solvent onto a tiny patch of her arm then stuck a needle through the little gap in her syn-skin, injecting herself. She hunched even lower, rabbit-legged as if about to hop.

Presently, bumps arose from her spine. Her head began to elongate. Her fingers were fusing into claws.

'What's happening to her?' cried Googol. 'Has she been infected?'

Jaq shuddered. 'I must say she does believe in challenging herself!'

'What's happening to her, man?' Googol clutched Jaq's arm, appalled, for Meh'Lindi was becoming a monster.

'She injected polymorphine.'

'Polymorphine... Sounds like a painkiller, doesn't it?'

'It isn't.'

Assassins were proofed against pain, but surely Meh'Lindi must be aware of some agonies as her body strained to adopt a new shape in obedience to her will.

Googol cackled hysterically. 'Assassins' drug, right? They use it to assume a new appearance. To disguise themselves. Masquerade as someone else. Someone *human*, Jaq! I've heard of polymorphine. It can't possibly change someone's body as much as that!' His finger jerked towards the screen. 'Nor as quickly, neither!'

'She's in propinquity to other stealers,' muttered Jaq. 'She's concentrating on their body forms, feeling them with her senses...'

'That can't account for it!'

'Well, the syn-skin helps speed the reaction. It's galvanising her whole metabolism, accelerating her vitality. It's designed to do that as well as protect her.'

'You're lying, Jaq!'

'Control yourself. There is another reason... But you have no right to know, do you understand?'

Googol flinched, and gnawed at the ball of his thumb as if to stifle anguish or panic. But still he persisted, anxiously. 'I've heard how assassins are trained to dislocate their own limbs and even break their own bones so that they can writhe like snakes through narrow tubes–'

'You have no right to ask whatever! *Quieta esto, nefanda curiositas, esto quieta!*' The resonant hieratic words acted as a slap in the face.

True enough, Jaq had known the secret essence of the matter ever since his application to the Officio Assassinorum was fulfilled – his request for an assassin with previous experience of a genestealer-infested world, and one who could pose as a sophisticated mistress.

Meh'Lindi had formerly undergone experimental surgery to implant extrudable, shape-remembering plastiflesh reinforced with carbon fibre and flexicartilage which could toughen hard as horn. Thus she could pose as a stealer hybrid, could behave as one; and afterwards could suck those implants back into herself, softening, shrinking, reabsorbing them.

Extra glands had been grafted into her to store and synthesise at speed the somatotrophin growth hormone that ordinarily promoted growth of long bones and protein synthesis in a child... and glands to reverse the process. Her artificial implants were a living organic part of her. By the same token her body of flesh and blood and bone was partly artifice and artefact.

This, coupled with the polymorphine and her own apparently chameleonic talent – perhaps potentiated by the syn-skin, though of this aspect Jaq was truly unsure – enabled her to undergo a wilder, faster transformation than fellow assassins: a radical transmutation of her body into, at least, stealer semblance.

Jaq knew that she was an initiate of the Callidus Shrine of the Assassins – speciality: cunning – and the experiment in the Callidus medical laboratory perhaps marked a perilous, agonising zenith of dissimulation. This much had been confided to him; and he had deemed it discreet to pry no further, had been persuaded of the wisdom of discretion.

Presumably Meh'Lindi's previous mission had succeeded and the Director of the Callidus Temple was inclined to field-test her again... Or maybe the mission had failed but she had survived. Maybe the extreme and somewhat specialised experiment had been abandoned? Maybe Meh'Lindi was the lone surviving product of it. Jaq knew not to enquire too deeply into the secrets of the Officio Assassinorum when such particulars were not within his brief.

Jaq had known... intellectually. Yet even so, the rapidity and utterness of her transformation shocked him.

'She's becoming a genestealer!' babbled Googol. 'Well, isn't she? Isn't she? She can't possibly be attempting a perfect copy...'

Indeed she wasn't. Meh'Lindi did not develop the lower set of arms nor the bony, sinuous tail. Too much to expect a new pair of arms to grow out of her ribs, or her coccyx to elongate so enormously. Nor could Jaq imagine that she could attain the full strength of a purestrain stealer – though her own strength was formidable, even when unenhanced.

Yet in dark silhouette she seemed almost a genestealer. She was at least the image of an injured stealer, blackened and fused by fire, one which had lost some appendages, perhaps lasered off, perhaps in an explosion; a stealer which still remained very much alive and able to use its deadly main claws. Syn-skin still wrapped her, having stretched to accommodate her new shape. The syn-skin sealed her toothy snout shut. Her face, her jaw had been implanted too in the Callidus laboratory...

Injured stealer... or hybrid shape. One or the other... Hybrids comprised a whole gamut of deformities. If taken for a hybrid, could she really fool a stealer brood, or their patriarch, over a period of time?

Maybe, thought Jaq, that was where the Callidus experiment had come unstuck... if indeed it had come unstuck.

'That's... the woman we share quarters with?' Googol's voice was filled with black wonder, with a fearful admiration, a certain desolation of the heart, and yes, a horror that nevertheless coursed thrillingly through his nerves. Jaq too felt deeply perturbed.

Already, Meh'Lindi's own skin seemed to be stiffening under that black second skin. It was forming a tough bony carapace as stimulated cells altered their nature, hardening to horn.

'Can any assassin ever have tried this trick before?' exclaimed the Navigator. 'Wrenching her organs, distorting herself so utterly? And tried it in the midst of a combat zone?'

'*Curiositas, esto quieta!*'

'She did say she needed exercise.' If Googol hoped to sound supercilious, he failed.

The black creature which had been Meh'Lindi unlatched the door and darted into a wide corridor, misty with smoke. Several armed hybrids roamed, seeming lost. Was Meh'Lindi thinking any of the alien thoughts of a genestealer? Understanding how it would react? Perhaps even radiating some protective aroma of brood empathy around herself? She bore down on the hybrids and, with her claws, she killed them almost before they realised.

A cloaked man who accompanied them gaped. His mouth opened in mute protest at this perversion of the proper order of affairs. Meh'Lindi ripped his head off.

No one seeing her on the move, rushing headlong through drear fuming tunnels, would really note the missing arms and absent tail, the sealed face, the scarlet sash. Or at least not note those betraying absences until far too late. She was keeping to the more furtive by-ways of the city and away from loyal troops.

Quarter-facet... Grimm arrived, puffing, at a narrow archway leading into a domed plaza. Three great avenues radiated away, choked with fighting, reeking with smoke. Explosions flared like novas inside a dust nebula. Shockwaves rippled downward from some higher level of the city which boomed with devastation. Walls and braced ceiling groaned. Drums of architecture were being beaten until they burst.

A smoky miasma masked glow-globes, reddening the scene as if here was the lurid sunset of the heart of this city before final night consumed and extinguished it. A massive detonation shook the plasteel heights. Had a munitions factory exploded? The roofs of the avenues sagged, pillars buckling. Abruptly the dome collapsed, shattering like an eggshell.

Whole buildings, vehicles, and machinery came tumbling from above, wearing necklaces of fire.

Grimm scuttled away up a ramp, pursued by debris and clouds of dust.

Half-facet... Obispal spotted a lone purestrain genestealer lurking some way down a dismal arcade lined by shuttered clothing stores. The stealer loped slowly away as though injured, dodging from one steel column to the next.

Swinging his power sword and shouting to guardsmen, the inquisitor pounded after the fugitive alien. Was it sheer bravado on Obispal's part that he disdained to fire explosive bolts at that creature which itself could not manipulate a gun? Or was it blood lust? He intended to cut it apart personally with his power sword – sword against claw – and be seen to do so.

The arcade proved to be a cul-de-sac. Twisted steel blocked the far end. As the inquisitor realised this, he grinned hugely. Though only briefly.

Activated by some unseen hand, a disaster-shutter of woven steel crashed down behind him, cutting him off from his guardsmen.

Obispal whirled.

'Carve through with a power axe, and quickly!' he bellowed.

The genestealer was no longer fleeing but racing towards the inquisitor, claws outstretched. Swiftly, Obispal confronted it; and now bolts from his hand-tooled, burnished-steel gun hammered at the alien. Many of the explosive-tipped shells missed entirely. Some caromed off its carapace. One, however, detonated successfully, making instant *purée* within the creature's armoured head.

Yet already hatches in the ceiling were springing free. A dozen hybrids and another purestrain dropped down into the arcade. Still more hybrids followed. A whole rabid pack was rushing at Obispal, firing a medley of weapons inaccurately, hatred written on all their twisted faces.

Las-fire, gouts of flame, and ordinary bullets ripped and charred his clothes but were deflected by the ornate armour he wore beneath. His head was unprotected. With a juggler's dexterity he switched the boltgun swishingly to full automatic. Ejected cartridges sprayed like grain at harvest time on some granary world. Firing the bolter with one hand he waved the sizzling power sword frantically in front of his face as if fanning wasps away. The explosive clatter in the arcade was ear-splitting. Obispal's cloak caught fire.

As Obispal backed against the front of a store the grille that sheathed it tore open from within. A genestealer claw reached and plucked the inquisitor through the gap.

THREE

BACK THROUGH THE gap flew his blazing cloak, still weighted with a few grenades. These exploded in the face of the mob. Obispal's power sword sailed out in an arc and danced across the floor, severing several feet. All of a sudden, the point of view shifted into the darkness beyond the torn grille, just as the purestrain leapt over the bodies of its kin to force entry.

Claws as mighty as its own batted the purestrain's claws aside and ravaged its head so that the purestrain shrieked and hung incapacitated, blocking the gap. In infra-red the scene was clear. It was the monster-Meh'Lindi who had jerked the inquisitor to safety. She had disabled the stealer which tried to follow. Now she was simply restraining Obispal, holding the disarmed man firmly at claw's length.

That high-pitched whine must be the sound of a power axe or two butter-slicing through the disaster shutter outside.

Obispal writhed. 'What?' he cried. 'Who? You aren't a genestealer. You aren't a hybrid. What are you?'

How clearly could Obispal see? Meh'Lindi didn't reply. How could she through that snout of teeth sealed with syn-skin, even if she wished to?

Outside, now: gunfire, screams, sizzling. The guards must be through the barrier.

'Aaaah—' Obispal sounded to be on the verge of deducing the truth.

'Watch out within!' came a call. Laser fire began to slice through the crippled purestrain. The claw released Obispal, thrusting him away. Meh'Lindi turned and raced off up a steel stairway. Obispal stamped his elephantine boots in furious pique before composing himself, locating his discarded boltgun and preparing to welcome his rescuers.

'Shade ungrateful, ain't he?' drawled Googol.

'He walked into a trap,' said Jaq. 'The whole universe is full of traps for the unwary. For a moment Obispal was unwary and he knows it. He knows that someone else knows, which is humiliating. At the eleventh hour, he underestimated the genestealers – as if they had only been his playthings. His campaign went so well up until now.'

'Ah yes, he did so well,' echoed Googol sardonically. He scrutinized the tiny facets of devastation aswirl around the eye-screen. 'Whole cities destroyed, millions slaughtered. So splendidly.'

'Stalinvast will very soon be cleansed, Vitali. There can be worse fates for a world.'

'Can there be?'

'*Exterminatus*,' Jaq whispered to himself.

'What?'

'Never mind. Vasilariov won't be totally ruined. The tide of battle won't even reach us here in the hotel.'

'That's consoling to know.'

'No more does the tide of Chaos threaten our Emperor.'

Meh'Lindi in stealer guise was racing at a crouch through dark ducts and service tunnels. She mounted ancient stairways that spiralled so high around shafts dribbling with condensation as to shrink into their own vanishing points. She crossed gantries bridging delving chasms. She descended other stairways. She popped through hatchways into alleys and back into ducts again. Always she chose the most deserted routes. Only occasionally did she encounter fugitives from the slaughter who had wisely dodged into such hidey holes. These she brushed aside and raced by, to their evident great relief. Still, from the major avenues the rumble and squall of flight reached her constantly, a doleful drum-backing to her own claw-clicking progress.

At one intersection, she paused, senses alert.

Quarter-facet... Grimm trotted along a precarious overhead catwalk above a river of humanity, puffing, 'Huh, huh, huh.'

Below, the surge was growing ever denser as if that river had met a dam ahead. Moving pavements must have failed under the weight they bore, otherwise one side of the crowd would surely be pulled to the rear.

Bodies were conglomerating together, asphyxiating. Corpses were carried along, standing upright. The nimblest escapees hopped across the heads of the living and the dead, until a twisted ankle or a gasping angry hand brought them down. Then they sprawled afloat upon the waves of craniums, arms thrashing.

The very walls of the avenue seemed likely to burst. Upthrusts of men and women forced cones of tangled, crushed bodies higher than the rest of the mass. The flood of tormented flesh appeared to be one single myriad-headed entity which was now compressing itself insanely until eyes started, skin split, until blood vessels sprayed. If Grimm fell into that...

Already human trees were growing towards his catwalk as survivors clawed and clutched upward. Glow-strips flickered, as if to this stifling hell of pain and terror was soon to be added darkness.

'Why no knock-out gas?' Grimm shouted over the groans and shrieks, as though some responsible official might heed him. 'Does your governor want even more of his population culled?'

A hatch popped. A black claw seized Grimm. Lifting him clear off his feet, a horny black arm hugged him. The little man's head was pressed against a jutting jaw.

Grimm gibbered in his own tongue, obviously regretting his impetuous excursion to visit the war front.

Then Jaq and Googol heard him pray squeakingly in proper Imperial Gothic, as if thus he might be heard across the galaxy. 'Oh my ancestors! Oh let me not betray my race!' That prayer might as well have been couched in his own patois. In Imperial Gothic he should have been praying to the God-Emperor for help.

Googol guffawed. 'The poor tyke must think she's going to give him the genestealer kiss. Oh, *la belle dame sans merci*.'

'Don't utter sorcerous spells,' Jaq said sternly.

'I wasn't. That's a phrase from some antique poem. It suggests, well... a fatal woman. Meh'Lindi.'

'Very fatal,' agreed Jaq.

'Not towards our friend Grimm; though he doesn't realize.'

Meh'Lindi had darted back into a service tunnel and was decamping as fast as could be, cradling Grimm, who was wailing like a baby.

'She's taking him somewhere special and secret to deliver the fatal kiss,' decided Googol. 'That's what he'll be thinking. Forever after he'll have to stay celibate to avoid polluting his people.'

'Celibate? You're joking. The victims of stealers forget that they've been infected. The stealer that kisses mesmerizes too. So the victim simply yearns to mate?'

'With ordinary mortals, ha! And enthral those in the same enchantment.'

The hybrid babies that were born would likewise hypnotize their parents to perceive beauty where there was twisted ugliness.

'Alas,' sighed Googol, 'our flustered friend hasn't noticed certain discrepancies yet. He must really be wetting his britches.'

Hugging Grimm to her, Meh'Lindi scaled gloomy networks of girders bracing shafts, dived along murky tunnels.

'Even so,' murmured the Navigator, 'to languish in her arms...'

'Are you a *poet*, Vitali?' Jaq asked. 'I do believe you're blushing.'

'I compose a few things during slack times on journeys,' Googol admitted. 'A few verses about the void. Love. Death. I might scribble them down if I like them well enough.'

And you probably *do* like them well enough, thought Jaq.

'Beware,' he said, 'of romanticism.'

Meh'Lindi had reached a small neglected storeroom cluttered with dusty, cobwebbed tools. A glow-globe on stand-by provided a dim orange light.

Shouldering the door shut, Meh'Lindi set the squat down somewhat abruptly, though not ungently. Grimm stumbled away a few paces. Since there was nowhere else that he could go, he faced the seeming monster almost defiantly.

'Huh! You shan't. Huh, I'll kill myself.'

'How very bashful.'

Googol's tone suggested not only mockery but yearning, impossible desire.

The mock-stealer gestured at her snout, clad in syn-skin. With her claws, which were hardly designed for delicate manipulations, she displayed her sash, tapped the various items of equipment clipped inside the fabric.

At last the light of understanding dawned in the little man's eyes. Hesitantly he approached her, reached for a little canister. Meh'Lindi nodded her horse-like head. The solvent, yes.

Grimm sprayed her, and first her jaws snapped open, revealing dagger-fangs. She hissed at him. Was she trying to force that alien throat and ovipositor of a tongue to master human words? Still he sprayed, now almost without flinching – her chest, her arms, her back – until all the syn-skin had dissolved away. If anything, revealed, she looked even more evil.

'She needed his hands,' sneered Googol. 'That's the reason she snatched him. Soon as he injects her with the antidote to polywhatnot, she'll leave him to find his own way home.'

But Meh'Lindi neither gestured for the hypodermic nor did she abandon Grimm. Picking the squat up again, she tore the door open and resumed her journey through the obscure, sombre entrails of Vasilariov. She could scale the heights and shin down depths that the squat could never have tackled on his own, or at least not so swiftly.

'Damn it, Grimm looks positively snug now. He's enjoying his ride in her arms, don't you think, Jaq? I suppose he's just her voice in case she needs to identify herself!'

'Jealousy, Vitali, is a consequence of romanticism...'

THE DOOR TO the Emerald Suite flew open and in darted the monster-Meh'Lindi. She set Grimm down. The squat tugged his flak-jacket straight, brushed dirt off it, combed his gingery beard with his fingers, flicked at his knotted ponytail as if a fly had landed on it. For a moment he smiled lavishly at Meh'Lindi, then thought better of it.

'Huh, huh, quite a caper.'

'We've been watching,' said Googol. 'A virtuoso exhibition, my dear!' He sketched a graceful bow in the direction of the assassin.

'I did tell you not to pull any stunts,' Jaq reminded her. 'Now Obispal knows that there are other Imperial agents on this world unbeknown to him. On the other hand, he's still alive, which might salve his ego.'

Meh'Lindi advanced and knelt before Jaq. Was she begging his pardon? No, she was presenting her genestealer semblance for his inspection.

He reached out his hand and stroked her horny, savage face. Googol whistled agitatedly. Despite himself, Jaq felt fascinated. He could touch – he could caress – Meh'Lindi in this murderous alien guise like someone stroking a kitten, as though he was absolved from the normal punctilios of duty and common sense. In this form she was perhaps more deadly than ever; yet for that very reason she refrained from causing harm, suppressing her reflexes.

He examined her carapace, her tough coiled-spring legs; and knew that he was examining Meh'Lindi intimately, yet at the same time he wasn't. He was hardly aware of his audience. Meh'Lindi hissed cacophonously.

'She needs to eat, boss,' said Grimm. 'For energy, before changing back.'

'Can you understand her?' Googol asked incredulously.

'Understand her? Understand? Huh! Who can plumb and penetrate such a person? Her mouth makes noises and I interpret. I have, after all,' and Grimm grinned raffishly, 'enjoyed rather longer in her company than either of you two. Just recently.'

'Shall I call room service for something special?' Googol enquired coolly. 'Such as a whole genuine roast sheep? Supposing that chefs and scullery lads are still alive, haven't fled, or aren't all pressed into service to boil up synthdiet for all those refugees. Our lady needs a banquet. Or would that be too flamboyant? Would we draw attention to ourselves?'

'As you know full well,' said Jaq, 'she can make free with our own food stocks.'

Which, presently, Meh'Lindi did, ravenously consuming fish, flesh and fowl from out of the stasis-boxes which they had brought to the suite from Jaq's ship, the *Tormentum Malorum*, which went by the alias of *Sapphire Eagle* while they were visiting Stalinvast. Rich planet though Stalinvast was, real food couldn't necessarily be guaranteed in a hive city, even in a wealthy hotel, not least in a time of strife.

Jaq noted how wistfully Grimm regarded what he rated as gourmet ambrosia disappearing into the monster's maw remorselessly.

Did Meh'Lindi relish exotic veals, smoked fillets of sunfish, sirloins of succulent grox? Or was she trained, and her body geared, to subsist on any available fodder whatever, algae, cockroaches, rats, who cares? Could she taste the difference?

Grimm could.

Which wasn't wholly surprising. The race of squats had evolved away from the human norm inside the caves and cramped, carved-out seams of bleak mining worlds which were barren save for minerals. Squats had become stocky, tough and self-reliant. During the millennia of genetic divergence, while warp storms cut their worlds off from the rest of the galaxy, they were forced to manufacture their own food and air. They knew famine – and still commemorated those hard times. Squats thrived in adversity. Often they preferred a harsh world to a sweeter one.

Yet they did like to eat, and handsomely, if they could.

Their artificial hydroponics gardens were famous for nutritious output; and after recontact by the Imperium they spent a fair tithe of their mineral wealth on importing exotic foods. If their staple diet still consisted of hydroponically grown vegetables, these were deliciously spiced and sauced – a far more piquant diet than the recycled synthfood that was the lot of the majority of most populations on crowded worlds. Given the slightest encouragement, a squat's appetite was – to judge by Grimm – that of a keen connoisseur.

Oh yes, Jaq noted the hungry glint in the squat's eyes. It wasn't greed. In his bluff, homespun way Grimm was courteous, even chivalric. It was plain to the little man that the assassin, who had exerted herself hugely, must eat first. Yet he too was also at least a little famished; and he did appreciate cuisine.

'Eat something yourself, Grimm,' invited Jaq. 'Go ahead: that's virtually an order.'

Gratefully, the little man chose from stasis the smoked drumstick of some bulky flightless avian.

He nodded appreciatively.

Plenty more such finger-licking, lip-licking food on board *Tormentum Malorum*. An inquisitor could commandeer whatsoever he wished and Jaq had provisioned his own ship exquisitely. For Jaq by no means equated iron duty with iron rations. That was a false and sanctimonious puritanism, such as had dogged the inquisitor's own youth.

To be sure, one could sympathise with the sentiments of some of those penitents who refused themselves pleasures because the Emperor, undying saviour of mankind, could experience no pleasure whatever, locked as he had been for millennia in his prosthetic throne...

Though Jaq, in his role as a rogue trader, pretended to patronise a mistress, the reality was that during his thirty-five years of life he had only bedded one woman – almost on an experimental basis so that he should at least be acquainted with the spasm of sex.

Those who yielded to passion forsook their self-control.

Jaq similarly drew the line at wine, which could fuddle the senses and put a person in needless peril.

Thus his stocking of the ship's larder with delicacies was, to his mind, a far cry from self-indulgence. Rather, it was a way of rejecting unctuous, masochistic denial – which might narrow his perspectives.

Unlike Grimm, Googol hardly seemed ever to notice what he ate. How could a self-styled poet be so oblivious to taste? Ah, perhaps he who gazed so much into the warp existed on a more ethereal plane... except when a Meh'Lindi was around.

Grimm, however, had set the drumstick aside after a single bite.

'Something amiss?' asked the Navigator.

'I'm thinking about those trampled mobs, those shattered streets. Millions dead, and here I munch. Why didn't anyone use knockout gas on all those panicking refugees?'

'They were a sacrifice to purity,' murmured Jaq.

'More like a sacrifice plain and simple, an offering on a bloody altar, if you'll pardon me. Huh!'

'Do you really think so?' Jaq brooded. So many corpses; and then some more, to sugar the porridge of death.

Ruefully, Grimm took up the drumstick again and gnawed. Meh'Lindi seemed sated at last.

Emerging from his reverie, Jaq wondered whether he would be able to watch her changing back, whether he might witness the melting of the monster and the re-emergence of a perfect female human body. But Grimm nodded towards Meh'Lindi's bedroom enquiringly and she too nodded her horse-head. Discarding the bird bone, Grimm gathered up Meh'Lindi's silk gown, stole and slippers from where they still lay and headed for the bedroom door, followed by Meh'Lindi.

'I say,' protested Googol.

Grimm rounded on him. 'And *what* do you say, eh?'

The Navigator glanced appealingly at Jaq.

Jaq wondered at his own motives for wishing to view the mock-stealer changing back into a woman – teasing, ambivalent motives. An inquisitor must not be ambiguous. Alert to subtleties and paradoxes, oh yes. But not fickle. It was wiser not to tantalise oneself. He gestured for Grimm to proceed.

As the bedroom door closed, Googol adopted a peeved expression and pretended great interest in a fingernail.

Jaq concentrated on his spy-flies.

The havoc was all but over. Obispal was triumphantly mopping up. Soon only ruin, death and injury remained.

Presently, Jaq blanked the eye-screen and relaxed, though with a puzzled air.

When Meh'Lindi emerged from the bedroom, begowned and jewelled as Jaq's mistress once more, her face was a study in expressionless hauteur; though when Grimm trotted out after her, looking dazzled, fleetingly a hint of mischief twinkled in her eyes.

'Let us pray,' said Jaq. 'Let us thank our God-Emperor who watches over us – for the purification of this planet, for its redemption from alien evil...'

As he recited familiar words, Jaq puzzled why he had really been detailed to be present on Stalinvast during its purge. The proctor minor of his chamber, Baal Firenze, had assigned him this mission, presumably acting on the instructions of a Hidden Master.

'Watch whether anything remains uncleansed,' Baal Firenze had said.

What puzzled Jaq was that the genestealer rebellion, now so bloodily suppressed, was a *natural* threat. Stealers weren't Chaos spawn. Their imperatives were comparatively simple: to procreate and protect themselves and perpetuate the social order – preferably under their own control – so as to ensure a supply of human hosts.

Whereas Jaq was of the Malleus and a daemonhunter. His Ordo was primarily concerned with the forces of Chaos from the warp which could possess vulnerable individuals of psychic talent, twisting them into tools of insanity.

That was hardly the situation on Stalinvast. So why was he trouble-shooting a non-psychic threat?

Protect us from the foul ministrations of Khorne and Slaanesh, Nurgle and Tzeentch...

He spoke those words silently, only to himself. A common squat, a Navigator, even an assassin – should not even hear those arcane names of the Chaos powers.

His companions' heads remained bowed. The names would only have sounded to them like unfamiliar ritual incantations.

Or, he thought grimly, like eldritch poetry.

'Protect us from those who would twist our human heritage,' he recommenced.

Why Stalinvast, why?

True, his own Ordo also served as a secret watchdog over the Inquisition at large. Could Harq Obispal's furious, if successful, excesses be regarded as a symptom of potential possession by daemonic forces from the warp? Hardly, thought Jaq. Nor could Obispal exactly be viewed as incompetent, despite his last-moment slackening of judgement when he charged into that trap in the arcade.

A cynic might say that Obispal's activities were directly responsible for triggering the rebellion, and thus for all the deaths, including those of millions of bystanders. Yet could such a nest of vipers have been left to writhe and breed unstirred? Of course not. Though Obispal might have adopted a more subtle surgical strategy than hacking the body to pieces to extract the festering organ.

The squat's remark about a sacrifice upon the altar worried Jaq. The death-scream of millions could serve as a call to Chaos; could be part of a conjuration.

'And protect us from ourselves,' Jaq added, drawing a curious glance at last, from Grimm.

By now Jaq too felt starved.

He dined discriminatingly, from out of a stasis-box, on spiced foetal lambkin stuffed with truffles; and he sipped gloryberry juice.

FOUR

'Do you suppose any wild natives live in those jungles?' Meh'Lindi asked Jaq, exhibiting a hint of nostalgia.

Half-facet... an aerial view of the sprawling spaceport, an island of ferroconcrete within a sea of rampant vegetation...

'Human natives?' he asked incredulously.

'Descendants of runaways? Criminals? Disaffected workers who have formed their own tribes?'

'I suppose it's possible. Human beings will adapt to almost any vile conditions. And now, the ranks of these hypothetical runaways might be swelled?'

Most of the jokaero spy-flies were transmitting tiny facets of war's aftermath within the city, a grim mosaic. Vehicles smouldered amidst wreckage. Foetid flooded sumps bobbed with bodies. Corpse collectors were sorting fresh human meat for recycling. Rotten meat and all cadavers of genestealer kin were destined for furnaces. Troopers and vigilantes patrolled. Gangs looted; looters were executed. Tech-priests and servitors were bracing and splinting Vasilariov's terrible urban wounds, the city's ripped skin, its splintered bones, injured organs, torn arteries. Acrid miasmas coiled from ventilation ducts and sewage flooded avenues.

On Vasilariov's many levels – some of which had slumped into chasms – surviving refugees trudged through debris or foul floodwater back to their shattered factory-homes. They crowded whatever elevators still worked or wearily scaled buckled stairways or girders. These refugees fell prey to marauding gangs, even to troopers, or to one another. It seemed as though rival nests of ants had been poured together willy-nilly.

Nevertheless, the stringent regimen that was normality for many – even in a lavish burg – was staggering back towards normal. The ants were trying to return to their separate nests, or what was left of them, if anything. Jaq had spied no absconders from the devastated city, the alternative to which was hardly inviting...

A plasteel wall circled that spaceport, which lay some fifteen kilometres from the southern edge of Vasilariov. Heavy defence lasers and plasma cannons studded the rim. Jaq presumed that periodically these would be switched on to prune the jungle back.

Armoured train-tubes on pylons linked the port with Vasilariov, from where other elevated tubes radiated towards other cities, high above the tangled savage vegetation.

The flora of this world was forever bubbling and festering, like a green soup on the boil. Vines in tree-tops strangled each other. Lianas writhed towards the light from bilious decaying depths. Lurid parasites swelled and bloomed and rotted.

'You aren't thinking of going out into the jungle to exercise for old times' sake?' Jaq enquired of Meh'Lindi. 'By any chance?'

'No, now is the real job. Right?'

'Hostile environment,' Grimm hastened to remind the assassin, to be on the safe side. 'Don't suppose anything intelligent lives out there. If the saurians don't get you, barrage bombs or juggernauts will.'

'I lived in such a jungle once,' said Meh'Lindi. 'Somewhere very like out there. Am I not intelligent?'

'Oh yes! But–'

'But what?'

'You have matured.'

At which, Googol tittered.

Some thirty great cargo shuttles sat in blast-bays, and other vessels too, including the *Tormentum Malorum*. Jaq summoned a different half-facet, the scene close to the customs house, which quite belied the spectacle of ruin within much of Vasilariov.

The planetary governor, Lord Voronov-Vaux, and his entourage were seeing the victorious Harq Obispal off with a fanfare.

Several hundred loyal planetary defence troopers stood to attention. A band in gold-braided uniforms blew long brass trumpets. Lesser lords and bodyguards thronged two reviewing stands. Servants circulated with wines and sweetmeats. Banners fluttered. Preachers chanted prayers to the Emperor. Privileged merchants patted their paunches. Near-naked performers danced and juggled. Chained jungle-beasts, doubly confined within force fields, fought each other with horns, fangs and claws, sliding in pools of vermilion blood. Ladies eyed one another's gowns and intricate, suspensor-lifted, rainbow-hued hairstyles. Beefy Obispal would have enjoyed a number of those ladies' favours since the fighting died away. He had, Jaq noted, obtained a new cloak trimmed with dazzling white ermine death's heads. A gift of gratitude. Voronov-Vaux himself wore a casque that covered his whole head, making him seem to be a human lizard with great red eyes.

Tiring of the distant ceremonies and speeches and festivities, so at odds with the gangrenous suffering inside the city – climax to so much other death on Stalinvast – Jaq opened a case keyed to the electronic tattoo on his palm and removed a small package of flayed, cured mutant skin.

Inside, his Tarot deck.

The Emperor's Tarot was supposed to partake of the very spirit of the Master of Mankind, forever on overwatch throughout the warp. Immobile in his throne on Earth, that godly paragon who was so old that his personal name had long been forgotten both beamed out a beacon and sensed the flow of Chaos, through which his starships must swim and out of which could congeal... abominations.

The Emperor trawled, the Emperor sifted unsleepingly.

These cards, rumoured to be of his design, and said to be blessed by virtue of that design – psychically imbued with his influence – also sieved.

They sieved the tides of fate. Of probability and improbability. Of strengthening influences and weakening influences. They were an X-ray of embryo events in the womb of the universe.

The seventy-eight wafers of liquid crystal formed a chart of the human Imperium, its champions and its foes. Each image pulsed animatedly, responsive to the currents of fortune, to the ebb and flow of events, to the forces of cleansing light and of dark malevolent corrupt insanity.

Jaq rifled through the pack to find the card he used to signify himself: the black-robed High Priest, enthroned, gesturing with a hammer.

His very own face frowned back at him doubtfully as if a homunculus was imprisoned in the card, a mute model of himself. This homunculus could not speak to him. It could not foretell the future. It could only show, in conjunction with other cards.

Placing the High Priest on a table, Jaq slipped into a routine of slow rhythmic breathing to attune his psychic sense. Almost of their own accord his hands shuffled the rest of the pack. He felt the cards vibrate.

'Thee I invoke, oh our Emperor,' he prayed, the formula glowing neon in his mind's eye, 'that thou wilt infuse these cards this hour; that thereby I may obtain true insight of things hidden, to thy glory and to the salvation of humanity–'

Shutting his eyes, he dealt a star of five cards.

Then he looked at what he had dealt.

The Emperor card was present, the Emperor card itself! In its position, it marked the outcome of the matter. Consequently, this was a divination of deep significance.

Yet that card lay reversed. The grim blind face, locked into the prosthetic throne, confronted Jaq upside-down.

This orientation could signify confusion amongst the Emperor's enemies. Equally it could signal obstructions and contradictions of a more frustrating sort.

And, of course, it might signify compassion as opposed to stern authority. Though how could *that* be the case?

The other cards were Harlequin, Inquisitor, Daemon and Hulk – one each from the suits of Discordia and Mandatio, and two major arcana trumps, both menacing.

The Hulk was a towering, ruined spacecraft adrift in black void, wreathed with... spewed-out gases?

The Daemon was curiously amorphous. Usually the Daemon in that card snarled with bared fangs and reached out with wicked claws. Now it showed no face at all. Its arms were many, a writhing knot of arms more like tentacles. Sniffing, Jaq detected a cloacal effluvium of sewers.

The Mandatio suite concerned wealth, stability, the burdens of government. The Knight of Mandatio was a cloaked inquisitor brandishing a power sword and his face was that of... Harq Obispal.

Jaq heard the crackling hum of the sword, smelled ozone. Right now the real Obispal was on the verge of departing from Stalinvast with a flourish of trumpets and hallelujahs. He would fly through the warp to any one of a million worlds. Why should Jaq encounter Obispal again in the near future? In all likelihood Jaq would presently run across some other inquisitor entirely. Obispal was simply uppermost in his mind because of that particular inquisitor being on the eye-screen. Thus the card conformed.

The truth might be that Obispal had left unfinished business behind on Stalinvast. Which would be unfortunate. It was exactly what Jaq was here to watch out for.

The Discordia suit comprised enemies and aliens and fiends. In this particular Discordia card pranced a tall, lithe, deadly Harlequin of the eldar race. A clownish mosaic of shifting hues attired the Harlequin. A rainbow coxcomb crested its head. Faintly Jaq heard a skirling of wild, unearthly music. However, this Harlequin didn't wear the customary mask. Nor was its bare face the ethereally lovely, angular visage of that alien species. This particular Harlequin's face was purely human.

A man's face. The chin was slightly hooked, the nose long and jutting, the eyes of piercing green. The Harlequin man pursed his lips and sucked in his cheeks not in a cadaverous but in a speculative, mischievous style which nevertheless bespoke some fatal intent.

As Jaq leaned over this Discordia card, deep in concentration, the image smirked.

Its lips moved.

'The hydra is kindled,' Jaq heard the false Harlequin whisper inside his head.

Jaq recoiled, gesturing a hex.

Cards could not speak, only show!

Cards could not talk to the divinator. Yet this one had whispered to Jaq. Could the Tarot cards become a channel for daemonic possession? Could a divinator be invaded? Surely not while the Emperor's spirit imbued his Tarot!

Yet the image had addressed Jaq as if some outside force had been able to intervene in his holy trance through the agency of that Discordia card, hacking into the pack.

To what purpose? To alert him? To mock him?

A 'hydra' was no known daemon of the warp. It was... yes, some legendary creature from the distant prehistory of Earth. A many-headed monster: yes, that was it. If you cut off one head of a hydra, two others promptly sprouted in its place. A hydra might be a deal more plaguesome to purge than even genestealers... Surely one or two stealers must remain even after Obispal's campaign? Didn't the man care about that possibility? Off he was going, in triumph, almost as soon as could be.

Jaq refused to be distracted. He peered at the tangled convulsions in the Daemon card. He could see no definable head, nothing which could be stricken off even with doleful consequences.

The card squirmed, flickering within itself as if aflame, although all the tongues of fire were cold. The longer he looked, the more the tentacles seemed to stretch out thinly into obscure distance as if there was no limit to their elasticity. New tentacles writhed and grew, variously greasy and glassy and jelly-like.

If this was the hydra of which the false Harlequin spoke, then *what was it?* Where was it? And why?

Jaq considered the disposition of the star of cards. Ought he to deal out a full corona pattern? A full corona might tell him far more than he needed to know – so much that he would end up by knowing nothing precise at all.

Meh'Lindi peered past him. Her fingernail stabbed swiftly at the Harlequin.

'Who's he? He looks rather... delicious.'

Wearing that eldar body, the mysterious figure was indeed configured like Meh'Lindi herself.

'Or is that just an eldar wearing a human mask?' she asked.

'No, it's a human all right – I'm sure of it. I believe he has just left me his calling card.'

Meh'Lindi knew all about calling cards. Many assassins would plant their own special card from the Adeptio suit in an intended victim's vicinity, to announce to that target his impending and unavoidable doom. The condemned person might be well advised to commit suicide rather than await whatever fate the assassin was designing.

'Mark his face well, Meh'Lindi.'

'I already have, Jaq.'

Such was her instinct, such was her duty. But above and beyond... did that enemy face perversely *appeal* to her?

What did the word 'delicious' mean to someone who cared not a fig about cuisine? Something to rend, to consume, to digest in her stomach acids? Meh'Lindi had once mentioned a legendary assassin who swallowed a rebel governor's young son whole so that the child should seem to vanish into thin air. That heroine of assassins had distended her jaws and throat and belly by means of polymorphine, like a python. Disguised and obese, she had waddled away.

'Huh! You're missing out on the carnival.'

Harq Obispal and entourage were stomping towards their many-buttressed ship. Trumpets wailed, acrobats somersaulted, torn beasts died; some bejewelled ladies blew kisses, perhaps only so as to kindle the jealousy of rival ladies or of their own lords.

'I don't suppose you've seen many such splendid sights,' Googol teased. 'You, from your pokey little caverns.'

'Splendid?' queried the squat. 'Do you rate such a farrago as splendour? You with your eyes forever trained on the gloomy sludge of the warp?'

'Touché!' the Navigator applauded.

Troubled, Jaq gathered the star of cards back into the deck, feeling them grow inert and passive as he did so. He picked up the wafer of liquid crystal which represented himself and stared at the High Priest's face, his own, wishing that his own image could confide in him in the same way that the Harlequin had.

And in a sense it could. For as Jaq gazed he sank deeply into himself and he dreamed back to his youth...

A time of hope, a time of horror. Jaq was born on Xerxes Quintus, fifth planet of a harsh white sun. Xerxes Quintus was a world of farmers, fisherfolk – and of mutants and wild psykers.

The planet had only been recontacted a century earlier. For thousands of years, Xerxes Quintus had gone its own course, ignorant of the Imperium. Memories of star-travel had mutated into bizarre myths. Human beings had begun to mutate too, in body and in mind.

Eyeless men could see through psychic eyes. The dumb could talk without tongues. The mouthless could feed through their skins. More sinister changelings became channels for daemons which walked the land in those host bodies, twisting and melting their anatomy into devilish monstrosities with scales and horns, claws and feelers – until the possessed bodies finally fell apart, until the vestiges of corrupted mind were sucked away as spirit-meat for those parasites from outside of normality.

Quintus was paradise and hell at once. Paradise was the lush coastal farms and the fishing islands where normal human beings preserved their traditions and their shapes by expelling all those who were born changed or who changed subsequently. Or by killing them.

Always, as worms out of an apple, as maggots out of meat, mutants emerged and fled – if they could – into the hinterland. There, if fertile, those mutants mated to make more and even stranger mutants.

The coastal inhabitants did not worship a god who might safeguard them in their own true image. Instead, they reviled the Lord of Change. Every tenth day, in special temples of execration, they cursed ritually and shouted abuse, before turning their attentions back to their beloved bountiful sea and soil.

Theirs was a religion of damning exorcisms. Their language, hardly even a bastard grandchild of Imperial Gothic, was salted with oaths, the whole intention being to drive their meddling malicious deity and its minions as far away as possible. They even expressed affection obscenely, as if to purge their relationships of any possible betraying taint. Neighbours always raised a child so as to exonerate parents from the need to reject their own offspring.

Recontact brought an Imperial expedition which admired the farming and fisheries potential of Quintus. One day, this planet could become an agricultural export world. If so, the Imperium could convert the barren fourth world, Quartus, into a valuable mining planet, its population fed from Quintus.

The expedition also found the coastal population to be a potentially fertile field where the Imperial cult could take root. Was not the God-Emperor the great guardian against change? Missionaries and preachers strove to switch the focus of hatred from the Lord of Change to the products of change dwelling in the interior. Ideally, the Imperium ought to seek to supplant the blasphemous Quintan language with Imperial Gothic; though this was no doubt too major a task.

Both of Jaq's parents were adepts of genetics. The Imperium had assigned them for life to Quintus, to assist in its uplift. Even in rapport with his significator card, Jaq only dimly remembered his mother and father. He recalled smiles and fondling and sensed that his parents were happy to conceive him and care for him. Imperials both, they did not follow the local custom of farming him out to a neighbour. Indeed, they seemed to cherish him. Certainly – from what little he was later told – both parents were fervent in their work and their loyalty to the Imperium. How proud they might have been to see him now, risen so high above their status; how fulfilled. But they hadn't conceived him as a duty, merely to increase the number of Imperials on the planet. Nor with a curse, as was the local habit. Rather, in happiness.

Vain happiness.

Jaq was barely two years old when daemon-possessed psykers slaughtered both his parents during a scientific probe into the wilderness. Jaq was raised thereafter as an orphan in a mission school.

Ultimately the scrupulous, strait-laced upbringing had left him distrusting the strictures of rigid minds. Oh, he remembered honeyed, frail evenings walking in the walled grounds of the orphanage. The tulip trees, the bowers. He remembered games and infrequent feasts. He likewise remembered punishments, usually caused by asking awkward questions.

'Magister, if the Quintans curse their god, won't they also curse the God-Emperor?'

'Beware, boy!'

'The Quintans don't have the voc-voc-vocabulary to adore our Emperor, do they?'

'Draco, you will write out the *Codex Fidelitatis* forty times, then you at least will possess the correct vocabulary!'

In his heart, the boy Jaq vowed vengeance against daemons and against psykers who were conduits for daemons for stealing his parents from him and bestowing upon him the honour of being raised by missionaries.

He learned piety, dedication. He learned restraint. Some of that restraint was protective camouflage for passions which he both felt welling within himself and denied.

When he was twelve, his psychic sense blossomed and he realised that he himself was one of those whom he had learned to loathe, taught both by his personal tragedy and by the missionaries.

He would lie abed in the darkened dormitory, sensing a sloshing sea of human and mutant existence surrounding him. In that sea twists and clumps of phosphorescence marked the minds of other psykers. Many displayed the malign green of corruption, the verdigris of spiritual gangrene. Some swelled bloatedly, streaked with red, as power from the deeps infused them. From such, tendrils descended into the abyss.

Indeed, threads dangled down from all life, psychic and non-psychic alike. Filaments linked living beings with the seeds of themselves in the deep-down ooze. Up some of these tendrils the substance and energy of the ooze could travel parasitically. This material was hostile to life yet also greedy for life and jealous of life. This energy was hungry and destructive, bestowing power upon a person but invariably injuring that person by virtue of the power it bestowed.

The abyssal ooze wasn't exactly like mud at the bottom of an ocean. As he peered through his mind's eye it seemed rather that the deepest water changed into a different type of material which sank down and down forever, tossed by its own fierce storms, swayed by its own currents that were swifter than any ocean's – until far off elsewhere there surfaced from this *immaterium* yet other seas of life, which were other worlds.

Potent creatures swam in the dark sub-ocean in between worlds. These creatures should be distrusted, not desired. Yet oh so many sparks of phosphorescence yearned for the potency of the denizens of that other realm, or else signalled obliviously to those creatures, blinking their little lamps – to summon the equivalent of sharks, or krakens of twisted intelligence.

One evening Jaq perceived a material vessel emerging from the ultimate deep. The vessel was diving upward towards his world. Jaq understood that this must be a warp-ship, protected against the forces in that ocean.

By straining his vision he glimpsed far off a beacon of white radiance by which that warp-ship strove to navigate. His heart swelled with joy and gratitude to the Emperor on Terra, whose mind was that lamp.

Already, like flowers turning towards the sun or like bees seeking pollen, in the wastelands of his world and in the ooze below – in that deep dark underocean of power and Chaos – Jaq sensed attentions focusing upon him tentatively; and he blanked his own white spark. He hid it.

A white spark, yes. Not curdled, nor stained by influences from below.

Few other sparks seemed white. Was that because those couldn't blank themselves, as he had just done? They attracted pollutants as a light attracts filthy bugs.

'Surely, magister, the rogue psykers could shine whitely if they could learn how to shade themselves?'

'What heretical paradox is this, Draco? You will commit to memory the Codex Impuritatis!'

And so, resentfully, he learned concepts that could stand him in good stead. In a sense, unknowingly, he had already entered the kindergarten of the Inquisition.

Imperial preachers were haranguing the coastal populace to destroy... people like Jaq himself, people who would become polluted through no real fault of their own, in many cases. Or so it seemed to Jaq. His missionary teachers sternly announced the message that deviation from normality was a sin against the Emperor.

Surely the real enemy must be those warped, fierce, cunning entities which feasted on vulnerable human beings who shone their lights unshaded.

If he, Jaq – being a child of genetically wholesome parents – had begun to shine this light too, might not something in the nature of the world of Xerxes Quintus itself be to blame?

'Perhaps, magister, the water or the white sunlight poisons people so that mutants are born?'

'Perhaps! Expand your thesis, Draco.'

'But the really grotesque and venomous distortions of the human form only occur after daemons–'

'Daemons, daemons? Do not dote on daemons! Do not even think of daemons. Daemons are forbidden effluvia of the human phantasy, turned sick and evil. This must be stamped out.'

'After daemons possess those souls who, as it were, shine a light.'

'A light? What light?'

'The psyker light... as it were. Maybe this arises naturally within a person, naturally and purely? Are there not astropaths and other psykers in the service of the Imperium? Could not all psykers shelter within its fold?'

'Faugh! Purify yourself, Draco.'

He was whipped. So as to purge him of wicked curiosity? Or so as to test him?

He brooded for weeks. Finally he nerved himself and confessed about his visions.

After the senior missionary had interrogated him, the man folded pleased hands across his belly. The gleam in the missionary's eye suggested that Jaq's account of how much he could perceive– 'Even to a glimpse of the Emperor's beacon?' – and of how he could hide his own spark of phosphorescence, meant that this lad was singularly blessed.

This in turn would bless the mission and its master. Smug devious bastard, thought Jaq, of that missionary.

A few months later a shuttle carried Jaq up to a great black ship circling in orbit. He left the sun Xerxes behind forever.

A DIFFERENT SHIP was departing from a different world. Lifting from the spaceport of Vasilariov, Harq Obispal's shark-shaped ship rapidly diminished to the size of a bug, of a sparkle of dust in the sky. Then it was gone, on its journey of several weeks through normal planetary space to that zone on the rim of the system far from the worlds and moons where it could dive into the warp.

On impulse, Jaq slipped the High Priest card into a pocket then slid the other Tarot cards back into their box and wrapped the box again in its sheath of skin.

The skin was a souvenir of an exorcism which had, in common with most trouncings of daemons, both succeeded – and failed. The daemon was defeated, but the daemon's living vessel had been destroyed, not redeemed.

How could the outcome be otherwise?

Yet Jaq feared that for all its power the Imperium was slowly succumbing to the attentions of aliens, of renegades, of daemons. Each Imperial victory seemed to involve the crushing of some part of the vital substance of the Imperium itself, of humanity itself.

How could it be otherwise? Fire must fight fire, must it not?

Thus that dappled skin, peeled from a mutant, both reminded him of how he had been orphaned and reproached him too.

'There, but for the grace of the Emperor,' he muttered, 'go I.'

'Where?' asked Grimm brightly.

Jaq was pleased that his companion had been perturbed by the trashing of Vasilariov and the evisceration of other cities, destroyed in order to save them. He valued the squat's presence and his occasional sallies

Ian Watson

of sarcasm – just as, in a way, he valued Googol's pose of disdain. Fanatics such as Obispal were invaluable; yet they were akin to bulls set loose in china shops. Certainly the Imperium embraced a million china shops and more; much crockery could be wasted. However, a sceptic could often see what rigid enthusiasts overlooked.

'Why, here,' Jaq told Grimm. 'Right here, wrapping up this little box. In different circumstances this might have been my skin.'

The little man stared at Jaq, bemused, then simply retorted, 'Huh.'

Perhaps the concept was indeed too complex.

FIVE

'THERE SHE IS!' cried Grimm.

Meh'Lindi was waiting inside an odour bar in the grotesque, extravagant concourse of the station where elevated trains left for Kefalov and hives beyond. The walls were a collage of tens of thousands of reptile skulls carved in gloomy green jade and malachite, as if this place was a saurian necropolis. Pillars were massive columns of vertebrae.

Of the nearby cities, Kefalov alone had remained unpolluted and unwrecked. Now, a week after Obispal's departure, traffic between the partly ravaged capital and Kefalov seemed to have returned almost to normal. Planetary defence troopers patrolled, scanning arrivals. Licensed hawkers were circulating, braying the merits of spiced sausages containing only real animal protein – so they claimed.

Perhaps truly. Bearing in mind the recent huge casualty statistics, their sausages probably contained minced human flesh. Suchlike suspicions did not deter prospective travellers from paying the high prices asked for such authentic delicacies; maybe even encouraged brisker sales. Such train travellers, of course, would have funds; most Vasilariovites never left their reef-hive during a lifetime...

Two burly bodyguards stood by Meh'Lindi, eyeing anyone who so much as glanced in her direction. The sleek, expressionless woman wore a silvery skintight jumpsuit which almost appeared to have been sprayed onto her limbs, not donned. A score of fleshy-hued silk scarves fluttered from strategic points, acting as veils. The guards were clad in tough green leather from some jungle beast and draped in weapons.

They had no idea that the woman they escorted was far more lethal than ever they could hope to be. Jaq had hired these bodyguards to lend credence to Meh'Lindi's role as a mistress, of perverse tastes, a tourist of disaster through the savaged and demolished sectors where a degree of anarchy still ruled. She had been on the prowl for days, though it seemed highly unlikely, to say the least, that she would come across the Harlequin man by chance... As soon hope to catch a particular fish by jumping at random into an ocean. But that individual had chosen to draw himself to Jaq's attention once already, had he not?

AN HOUR EARLIER in the Emerald Suite, Jaq's comm-unit had bleeped.

In jumblespeech Meh'Lindi had reported, 'I've just seen the Harlequin man. I'm following.'

Jaq promptly consulted the eye-screen. Several spy-flies were tailing Meh'Lindi.

She was on a balcony level of an arcade which must specialise in manufacturing small components, and was still doing so. Baggy women and runty, raggy children slaved alongside their menfolk in a veritable honeycomb of family workshops, tier upon tier of plasteel caves linked by ladders and gantries. Swarf from lathes lay thick on the floor below. Wading through this, apace: a man taller than any of the artisans.

He wore a pastel-hued cloak and cockaded purple hat quite out of keeping with his surroundings. He attracted whistles and jeers and minor missiles, such as nuts and bolts.

Meh'Lindi's rented, streetwise duo guaranteed her much more anonymity; as to her motives, they exhibited no interest whatever.

Jaq had willed a spy-fly to home on the man, whose face he recognized from the Tarot card. Thus, while Meh'Lindi padded in pursuit with her mute chaperones, Jaq was also tracking the Harlequin man. At the Kefalov station the dandified fellow had boarded the transjungle transport, while Meh'Lindi stayed. The accompanying spy-fly clung to the ceiling of the carriage, surveying the Harlequin man until the train carried the spy-fly beyond its transmitting range. Until then, its quarry sat twiddling his thumbs and not quite smirking.

Jaq knew that he must give chase; he was virtually being challenged to do so. The Harlequin man had invaded Jaq's Imperial Tarot with the slickness of a lashworm snatching some flesh from a passer-by, and now that damned individual was contemptuously trailing his cloak for Jaq to follow. This, Jaq did not care for one little bit. Yet to ignore such provocation would surely be a greater folly than heeding it. Leaving Googol to safeguard their equipment, he had hurried with Grimm to the station to meet up with Meh'Lindi.

THE BAR WAS heady with attar of jungle parasite-blooms and other alien aromas that tweaked at Jaq's senses, causing mild wobblings of perception and confusions of taste and smell. Some of the odours were hallucinogenic and patrons wore a glazed look.

Perhaps those individuals were still shell-shocked by the ravaging of their city – of which Jaq and the squat had seen, and smelled, evidence aplenty en route to this rendezvous. Equally, the customers of the odour bar might be adopting a glassy-eyed demeanour so as to avoid seeming to scrutinise Meh'Lindi in what might be construed as an impertinent fashion.

'Sir Draco!' one of the guards greeted Jaq.

The bodyguard eyed Grimm as though the squat was some pet monkey of this merchant and ought to be on a lead. The mood-shifting scents were allowing sentiments to slip out.

'Huh! You can scoot off now,' cried the little man. 'Scram and skedaddle.'

Darting Grimm a cautioning glance, Jaq paid off the hired guards in local voronovs, plus a retainer so that they would continue on call if need be.

As soon as the two men had departed, in the direction of a food vendor, Jaq said to Meh'Lindi: 'Of course, he let you see him. He put himself in your way deliberately.'

She nodded. 'Question is, Jaq, dare you ignore this bait?'

'Probably not. I hardly think the aim can be to lure us somewhere to murder us.'

'Still,' Meh'Lindi said wistfully, 'the Harlequin man has the look of an assassin. Maybe even... a renegade assassin? Surely there can be no such animal!'

'Who employs him, eh?' asked Grimm. 'Or does he employ himself?'

She shrugged.

'And don't you fancy him just a jot?'

To which mischievous gambit, Meh'Lindi glared. 'Perhaps Obispal left him behind,' she suggested. 'Maybe the intention is to humiliate you somehow, Jaq? I did betray our presence to Obispal.'

'And splendidly so indeed!' agreed the squat.

'Be quiet,' said Jaq. 'If Obispal decided that a secret inquisitor was watching him, surely he'd be a fool to seek vengeance – especially when he hardly put a foot wrong. I think the idea has to be to show me something, in case I miss it.'

'Yeah, what is the hydra?' said Grimm.

'I find this somewhat galling, don't you?' Jaq asked his pretend-mistress. 'To be manipulated!'

Really, they had no other option but to board the next train bound for Kefalov.

As THE PASSENGER capsule whisked through the crystalline tube above the blurred green hell of jungle, Jaq scrutinised his personal Tarot card and recalled his trip to Terra as a boy aboard the Black Ship.

Only en route had he understood the true implications.

To his keen senses, that cavernous crowded ship had been awash with psychic turmoil – despite the dampening field projected by a suppressor adept linked in to arcane machinery. This deadening field was subtly nauseating, a psychic equivalent of the stale, rebreathed air. In spite of it, Jaq easily read raw talent, hope, muted dread; and on the part of some of the officers boredom mixed with disgust, on the part of others fierce dedication, occasionally mixed with regret.

The suppressor field seemed to work perversely on Jaq, who already knew how to hide his own light. He hadn't read moods before, but now almost everyone on board appeared to broadcast sludgy feelings.

Stray whispers in a hundred distant-cousin tongues twittered through the ship, as if voices were trying to inform him of his fate, the ghost echoes from a million previous passengers, ten million down the centuries that this ship had been in service.

Of course, the ship was rife with ordinary gossip too, in various versions of Imperial Gothic, some halting, some fluent, in a waveband of accents from mellow to harsh, sibilant to guttural.

'A great fleet of ships like this tours the galaxy–'

'They trawl for promising psykers–'

'Wayward, twisted psykers are hunted down ruthlessly on a host of worlds. They're preached against and purged. The Inquisition scourges them. Planetary governors destroy them–'

'At the very same time fresh, uncorrupted psykers are being harvested. They're sent to Earth in Black Ships such as this–'

Psychic talent was the floodgate by which the malevolent lunacy of powers in the warp could invade and ravage worlds, could corrupt the human race into polluted slaves of evil.

Yet psychic talent was also the hope of the future, of a galaxy in which the human race, free and strong, could defend itself mentally.

Meanwhile, the God-Emperor must defend all his scattered multi-billions of subjects by ruthless sacrificial force. For a terrible equation prevailed: that which would ultimately save the human race – the evolution of a higher consciousness – was, in its long and vulnerable gestation, exactly what could so easily destroy humanity by letting it be corrupted, polluted, warped and ruined. Only the utter ruthlessness of one ravaged, machine-sustained tyrant and the overstretched forces of his fierce yet fragile Imperium kept the human race tottering along its fraying tightrope.

'Sacrifice–'

Sacrifice on his own part, yes indeed. Was not the Emperor tormented and exhausted by his own ceaseless vigilance?

'Sacrifice–'

But also by the sacrificing of his own subjects...

Of the gathered talents on board the Black Ship, a fraction – the brightest and the best – were destined to be recruited as psykers in the service of the Imperium. Most of this fraction would be soul-bound to the Emperor for their own protection.

'Soul-binding is agony–'

The ghastly mental ritual would burn out optic nerves and leave those chosen psykers blind forever.

'Sacrifice–'

Many of those on board who were of merely ordinary calibre would serve by yielding up their vital force to feed the Emperor's insatiable soul, so that he could continue to be a watchful beacon and protector. After suitable lengthy training for the sacrifice, these psykers would be consumed within a few scant weeks or months, drained of their spirits until they died.

'SACRIFICE!'

Which did not pleasure the Emperor. Oh no. Each soul he devoured lanced him with anguish, torment, it was rumoured. Such was the cruel equation by which humanity survived in a hostile universe.

'SACRIFICE!'

No passenger on board the Black Ship was older than twenty standard years. Many were as junior as Jaq. One girl in particular... he refused to think of her right now. As the ship's officers administered tests and counselled their human cargo, it became evident that almost all were going to their deaths.

Worthy deaths, necessary deaths; but still, deaths.

In what manner – other than its worthiness – was this fate different than being slaughtered on one's home world?

The difference was...

'SACRIFICE! TO THE GOD AND TO HUMANITY!'

Some young psykers wept. Some prayed. Some raged. Those who raged were restrained. In later life, Jaq understood that this particular Black Ship had been carrying a higher percentage of individualists hailing from less longstandingly pious worlds, than most such shipments. Yet many of the young passengers adopted an air of cool nobility, even of passionate complicity in their own fate; these were praised. Devout dedication was the desideratum for soul-sacrifice.

Death laid a numbing hand on Jaq's heart. He bargained in his soul with fate, promising to dedicate his life to Imperial service without scruple – if only a life was left to him to dedicate.

Jaq still clearly remembered his reprieve and how annoyed he had been not to have foreseen it.

'You can blank out your light, boy,' the goitrous officer had told him, almost respectfully. 'Without training, that's rare. You'll certainly be recruited. I suspect you won't need soul-binding. I may well be addressing a future inquisitor–'

To hunt down those who resembled him, yet who had gone astray? To purge his – cousins – who had been twisted askew? To destroy his diseased psychic kin without a qualm?

Yes.

Jaq had spent the remainder of the voyage feeling exalted, yet pitiful. Sad for the bulk of his travelling companions; glad that his own destiny was different. His fellow travellers saw him praying to the Emperor, as he had been schooled to. They presumed that Jaq was honing his soul serenely in expectation of sacrifice. His example had a calming effect on others. Already he was mentally a secret agent, privy to hidden knowledge.

'Yet seemingly the Harlequin man can pierce my cover,' Jaq murmured under his breath. 'What manner of man must he be?' He tucked his Tarot card away.

Presently the city of Kefalov loomed ahead. From a distance Kefalov was a grey brain bereft of a skull, ten kilometres high at least. Its tiers of convoluted ridges would be harder than any bone. As the train neared, great windows, air-vents and portals became visible. Seeming to be merely speckles and punctures at first, actually they were as tall as the highest trees.

A stream of military ram-jets flew from one such vent, into a sky the hue of bruised blood in a badly beaten body. Dirty clouds glowered and snake-tongues of lightning flickered. Soon bombs would rip the surging vegetation somewhere, punching holes which would rot and quicken with parasitic blooms.

The petrified brain smoked and steamed lazily, venting effluvia. Kefalov leaked effluent into the jungle, poisoning the vicinity, forming a deep sickly vaporous swamp over which the train raced, insulated in its tube.

SCARCELY HAD THEY left the station concourse than 'Rogue Trader Draco' was voxed to a public comm-screen.

From the viewplate in the open booth *that face* looked out at Jaq, eyes twinkling like ice in chartreuse, a playful and predatory smile puckering the lips.

'Zephro Carnelian at your service!' announced the Harlequin man.

This call just had to be an act of purest derision, a flaunting of how well this enemy had foretold Jaq's actions – or even was psychically alert to Jaq's whereabouts.

Enemy?

Most likely. Stalinvast couldn't very well be hosting a second secret inquisitor, could it? Surely Proctor Firenze would have advised Jaq of the presence of another Malleus man? If Baal Firenze *knew*; if he knew!

This mysterious man had penetrated Jaq's Tarot. He was dangerous, dangerous. He was playing with Jaq, as though Jaq was a card in his own paw.

'Do you imagine you have some business with me?' Jaq asked the image non-committally. Meanwhile, his mind raced.

With a giggle, Carnelian tipped his foolish foppish cockaded hat to Jaq.

'Business? Oh yes: *hydra* business. A terrible menace, hmm? Thought I'd draw your attention to it. Good specimen here in the undercity. Fancy a spot of big game hunting with me?' The man spoke Imperial Gothic with no trace of the local husky accent, but rather with a kind of spooky affectation – almost, thought Jaq, an alien affectation.

At Jaq's back, Meh'Lindi and Grimm warily eyed loitering beggars, pedlars, riff-raff. Naturally, passers-by eyed Meh'Lindi. In particular two small groups of vigilantes wearing diversely blazoned combat fatigues seemed to be sizing up Jaq's trio, either with a view to offering their services or with less savoury intent. One group, decorated with motifs of gaping, dagger-toothed mouths, had tattooed their shaved skulls with leering lips and a view of the brain tissue below. The other, adorned with green toad-badges, wore steel skullcaps piled with simulated excrement. Or perhaps their own hair, waxed solid and stained, coiled through a hole in the cap.

Tension brooded in the air. Décor was at once oppressive and lurid. Brown entrails seemed to bulge from the walls, sprayed with pious mottos.

Dingy pillars were subtly phallic. It wasn't so much that Kefalov appeared already to be a more sordid city than the capital, as that this particular city hadn't been devastated at all. Thus aggressions and desires bubbled and brooded, as yet unpurged.

If the brain was letting off steam and smoke into the sky while filth flowed down its flanks, it remained a pressure vessel of packed humanity, a vat of frustrations, oppressions and twisted longings.

'Do you fancy potting a fine trophy, sir inquisitor? Oops! My apologies, honourable *trader*.' Carnelian chortled hectically.

Jaq peered at the face in the screen – especially at the eyes – for signs of a daemon rooted within the man's psyche. Those eyes seemed rational and unhaunted. Was this clownish farrago all a pretence?

'Whereabouts in the undercity?' asked Jaq.

'Why, everywhereabouts. That's the nature of the beast.'

Jaq made a guess. 'And I suppose the death of so many millions – the psychic shockwave – conjured up this new abomination, whatever it is?'

'You're catching on, Sir Jaq.'

'Why should you tell me? And what do you have to do with this hydra? Well?'

'Ah, tetchy, tetchy... *You're* the adept investigator! Must I dot every eye and cross every tee?'

'Damn you, Carnelian, what's your game?'

'Do call me Zephro! Please! Shall I show you some of the pieces and let you try to guess the rules? Pray to visit sub-level five in the Kropotnik district of this fair burg.'

Meh'Lindi hissed. The hesitancy of the vigilantes seemed only due now to mutual dislike, which would soon resolve itself one way or another. Jaq quickly cut the connection.

POXED, DISFIGURED SCAVENGERS scuttled across hillocks of debris which rained into this underworld from a low steel sky by way of chutes and grilles.

Once upon a time this plasteel cavern with its ranks of mighty support pillars must have seemed spacious, voluminous, gargantuan. Now it was merely extensive horizontally, connecting to other such caverns through vast arches in its barrier walls a couple of kilometres distant. In places the dross almost brushed the roof. Feeble illumination came from phosphorescent lichens mottling the ceiling and from the furnaces of the many tribes of recyclers whose smelting activities and whose upward export-trade in reusable elements to higher zones of the city alone prevented their home-space from filling as full as a constipated bowel.

Perhaps these inhabitants of the underworld were slowly losing the struggle. On the other hand, nourished on the synthdiet they must exchange for their impure ingots, maybe the tribes were breeding fast enough to fend off being buried alive in swarf and shavings and other detritus.

Just as a queen bee unwittingly hosts tiny mites that have specialised to graze on her mouth parts, so at the bottommost end of the city did Kefalov house its recycler and scavenger tribes. Nay, they were useful – some might say vital – to the economy of the city.

They weren't such people as would, or could, send reports to the administration high above, not even of anything monstrously peculiar. Given their foreshortened horizons, and their own abnormality, how could they really think in terms of something as being significantly abnormal?

They scuttled like crabs. They burrowed like worms. They rolled balls of wire about like dung-beetles. Jaq suspected that their recycling and export trade had practically become instinctive. What did these know of the rest of the city, let alone of planet or galaxy? As much as the mite on the bee's mouth parts knew about the rest of her body, or about the throbbing hive.

'How must it seem,' Jaq asked, 'to live one's whole life down here?'

He already knew the answer. Blessed are the ignorant; cursed are those who know too much.

'At least it's warm enough down here,' remarked Grimm.

From the catwalk they surveyed this choked cavern which lay beneath even the underbelly of the city. Furnaces winked like fireflies. Holding a lens to one eye, Jaq scanned tunnel mouths that were almost buried.

Sprawling out from one tunnel, glassy branching tentacles pulsed as if they were huge muscles dissected out of the body of a leviathan.

As soon as Jaq noticed those translucent, almost immaterial shapes, their extent appalled him. They wove across the metallic dunes, submerging themselves like roots, surfacing again, twitching, throbbing sluggishly. Tendrils coiled and uncoiled, seeming to exist one moment yet not the next.

What did the scavengers think of this intrusion into their domain by a rubbery multi-octopus? The human crabs scuttled clear of its feelers.

Or should that be: *their* feelers? Jaq couldn't tell whether the hydra was single or plural, connected or disconnected. Or how much more of it existed out of sight, packed within the tunnel complexes.

Those tentacles did not appear interested in trapping the denizens of this underzone. Rather, the hydra seemed to be waiting. Meanwhile, it signalled a menace that alarmed Jaq's psychic sense.

'Yuck,' said Grimm, as he too became aware of it. 'It's like those pesky jelly strings in eggs that stick between your teeth – really monstrous ones from an egg the size of a mountain! It's like umbilical cords and nothing but. Yuck, yuck.'

'Shall we see how it reacts to laser and plasma?' suggested Jaq.

'Oh yes, let's slice it and fry it.'

Meh'Lindi sniffed the stale, hot, ferrous air like a fretful horse.

The three headed along the catwalk, descended a rusty ladder on to the dunes of debris. They waded across until they reached a vantage point fifty metres short of the closest tentacle.

Jaq aimed his ormolu-inlaid laspistol and squeezed. Hot light leapt out from the damascened chromium steel nozzle in a dazzling silver thread. He drew the sliver of light across that limb of the hydra as if slicing cheese. He sliced and resliced. Severed portions writhed. Gobbets seemed to wink in and out of existence. Though chopped every which way, the whole tentacle squirmed towards where they stood as if still joined together, glued by some adhesive force from outside the normal universe.

'Plasma,' Jaq said to himself and switched weapons. The frontal hood of the plasma gun was gilded with safety runes. Ventilator holes in that hood doubled as the hollow pupils of slanting crimson eyes that focused faithfully on the chosen target, since a single discharge of super-heated plasma would completely exhaust the capacitor. A couple of minutes must pass before the accumulator vanes behind the hood re-energised the conductors and insulators. This target, though, was large and various.

The gun bounced in his grasp as incandescent energy leapt to evaporate a stretch of that many-times-severed, yet still tenacious limb. Its boiling substance sprayed across the dune beyond, lacquering the metallic hillock. A backwash of heated air caressed Jaq's face. He smelled the bitter fragrance of ablated chromium steel. And he sensed... eagerness.

Of a sudden, the Harlequin man sprang up from behind the dune beyond.

'Yes, yes!' he shrieked, capering and applauding. 'Shoot it to smithereens!'

Jaq jammed the discharged plasma gun away and was about to aim his laser.

Blessed are the ignorant.

But not if they are inquisitors!

'Meh'Lindi...'

'Yes, Jaq, I'll take him for you.'

'Unharmed,' he called after her.

She had already started down the scree of debris in pursuit.

'Or reasonably unharmed!'

He need not have bothered.

SIX

Once more the turbulent bilious jungle rushed by beneath the plascrystal train-tube.

Jaq said patiently, 'Let's recap what happened just once more.'

In truth he felt far from patient. Vitali Googol had failed to answer vox messages sent from Kefalov; again and again, no reply from the Navigator. This enigma demanded their return as soon as possible. Jaq felt extremely irked to be manoeuvred thus – in addition to the fury he felt on Meh'Lindi's behalf because of the way she had been used.

Her emotions, her nervous system, tampered with! She who could transform herself by force of will into a passable semblance of a genestealer. She who could kill with a single fingertip. For her to be subjected to the whimsical will of a clown! To be twisted, as it were, around Carnelian's little finger: that was abominable.

The assassin said softly, 'I request permission to commit exemplary suicide. I'm dishonoured.'

Jaq sensed the distress behind the expressionless face and the profundity of her request.

Not so Grimm, apparently. He thumped his fists on his knees. 'Huh,' he jeered. 'Exemplary suicide, indeed? What's that? Suicide that sets us an example of useful behaviour? Such as a solo death-charge against a whole renegade army? A wrestle to the death with Titans? An unarmed hike across a deathworld? Huh.'

Meh'Lindi growled deep in her throat.

'Huh. Growl away. You'd be snapping, "Don't scorn me!" – if you weren't so busy scorning yourself.' Maybe the little man did understand, after all, and this was his rough form of therapy. 'I don't scorn you, you know,' he added. 'I could never scorn you, whatever happened.' Did the abhuman blush at this avowal?

'I request permission, nevertheless,' repeated Meh'Lindi, still poker-faced.

Jaq sincerely hoped that she felt obliged to make such a demand by her own code of honour rather than that the demand was due to an abrupt, intrinsic sense of genuine worthlessness. If the latter, then the Harlequin man would really have hamstrung her, sowing self-sabotage within her heart.

'Refused,' he told her firmly. 'I was to blame for ordering you not to harm him. I tied your hands.'

Her eyes widened ever so slightly and Jaq regretted his phrasing. Grimm smirked. Did he suppose that Jaq had made a joke? Perhaps Grimm devoutly wished that joking was possible in the circumstances; and would do his best to make it so.

'Just tell me the facts again, Meh'Lindi. We may be overlooking some vital detail.'

Did not everyone, of necessity, overlook a large part of what might be termed, for want of a better word, the truth? Those scavengers living their entire lives in those caverns underneath Kefalov were merely an extreme example of segmented vision – their whole cosmos reduced to a few cubic kilometres of debris. Even the rulers of this planet of Stalin-vast, luxuriating high up in their hives, must take a very partial view. Even an inquisitor such as Obispal suffered from – well, tunnel-vision.

Jaq struggled to see like the Emperor. He strove to think on a different plane of reason and insight. Only thus could he step outside of the present situation and hope to puzzle out the riddle of Zephro Carnelian – even while being forced to react predictably...

'I RUN TOWARDS Carnelian,' Meh'Lindi related. 'I run through the gap you blasted in the tentacle. Already the wounds sprout new growth. Each severed section seems alive independently. A few loose slices quiver with intent. As for the atomised material – well, I don't know. That is not ordinary matter.'

'I realise,' said Jaq.

The substance of the hydra must be partly normal matter and partly immaterium – partly the stuff of the warp, which was raw Chaotic fluid energy.

Where warp substance flowed into the world, daemons could follow presently.

'He darts away across the wasteland, cloak flapping. I chase. Bold Grimm tries to keep up but flounders.'

How Grimm basked in that word 'bold' – not from pride, Jaq sensed, but because to utter such a compliment Meh'Lindi could not be wholly filled with self-loathing.

'Carnelian is swift. "Follow and find!" he hoots. "Follow and find!" I follow. Far. Exactly in his footsteps, in case of some pitfall.

'Then a nest of tentacles writhes from the swarf, trapping my feet in a grip so strong. Even as I snatch for weapons, whip-tendrils seize my wrists and my neck. I am pulled down, spread out.

'Carnelian doubles back. I could crunch a tooth and spit death–'

'I forbade that, Meh'Lindi.'

'Yes. Now a tendril gags my mouth. He kneels by my head, grinning. I flex, but can't break free.

'He whispers in my ear: "This'll soon be everywhere on Stalinvast and when it's everywhere, ah then..."

'I don't know whether he uses a slim feeler of the hydra – I can't see if he does – but I suppose he does. An immaterium feeler, used as a probe.

'He reaches into my head, into my brain. He finds the pleasure centre there. He stims it again and again. I am hating him, but I writhe in a betraying ecstasy, an agony of pleasure. Hating him still, I burn with utter delight.

'He says, "Sir Jaq's correct in his supposition that all the slaughter brought it to life – exactly like a conjuration."

'I am hardly able to think, only feel. But I gasp, "What is a hydra? What's its purpose?"

'"Dissect it and see," he says. "Cut it into little bits." I cannot block the stimming. If he stims me much more, I know that I may seek such stimming again, however unwillingly. I imagine killing him. I link that image to the hot ecstasy.

'We are taught to resist pain. We are taught to block pain. But to resist ecstasy: who would have thought of such a thing?

'He laughs and stops his probing of my pleasure centre. "Enough!" he cries. "Your little friend is coming clumpingly along. He can never – and Jaq can never – make you feel the way I have made you feel today. Should you ever wish them to! So remember the *ideal*. Remember Zephro Carnelian, master of the hydra!" And off he flees, out of sight.

'I am still moaning. Kindly Grimm cradles my head, as I cradled him. I snarl at him. He blasts me free. I roll away. The cut tentacles and whip-tendrils sprout anew, budding and stretching elastically. Grimm has collected Carnelian's hat, which fell off as I chased him. We return. I am disgraced. I lust. I beg permission.'

'No, Meh'Lindi. Carnelian is guilty of psychic rape. You aren't guilty, believe me.'

'Huh,' said Grimm, 'a different case from physical rape, which principally *hurts*, so I hear. Why should an enemy inflict *pleasure* on you?'

'To insult,' she replied distantly.

'To undermine you,' the squat said briskly. 'To make you doubt yourself – just as you are doubting now. I don't doubt you.'

Jaq frowned. Could that have been Carnelian's prime motive? Perhaps it was. Jaq felt that he was missing something. He strove to analyse events...

Carnelian's scheme couldn't have been to expose Jaq to whatever type of recycling of human bodies occurred in that underworld. True, the crab-men had begun to take an unhealthy interest in him once his companions had rushed off after the Harlequin man. He had needed to shoot two or three. By the time Grimm and Meh'Lindi returned, a tribal attack seemed imminent. However, they evaded this easily enough.

No, Carnelian definitely seemed uninterested in killing or injuring Jaq and companions; aside from the injury to Meh'Lindi's esteem, and Jaq's own, which might have been purely incidental...

Assuming that agents of Carnelian had interfered with the Navigator back in Stalinvast, therefore Vitali was probably still alive.

The Harlequin man had entered Meh'Lindi's head. After a fashion he had controlled her – not exactly in the way that a slavering daemon from the warp might control a victim.

Was his psychic ravishing of Jaq's assassin and his blithe withdrawal some kind of message that the true purpose of the hydra was a similar ravishment?

If so, why should he show Jaq this?

'Let me see his hat,' said Jaq.

Grimm tugged a crumpled purple handful from his pocket and restored some shape to the hat.

Jaq examined the cockade. It showed a naked infant seated upon a stylized cloud against a starry background, each star being a tiny red carnelian stone. The infant was either blowing or hallooing through chubby cupped hands.

The child was a zephyr, a wind-spirit. Hence this was Zephro's personalised hat. Apart from those blood-hued stars, the image seemed curiously benign and harmless.

'Well?' asked Grimm eagerly.

Jaq tore the cockade loose and pocketed it, for the minor satisfaction of having at least a scrap of the Harlequin man in his grasp.

'He dropped his hat, that's all. Not so that you could find it as a clue. It simply fell off.'

'Huh. At least he isn't perfect. Eh, Meh'Lindi?'

'Is that,' she asked icily, 'meant to console me?'

The squat withered somewhat. When it fell to his lot to cut her free from the coils of the hydra, had his poignant fixation received a body-blow – or a boost? For a while, did she seem almost within his reach? And was she now an absolute stranger again?

Jaq wondered how much effort of will it had cost her to resist ultimate, engulfing pleasure so as to gasp out a question or two to her tormenter and enchanter. How much might that experience have twisted her within?

On that doleful Black Ship on the way to Earth years ago, Jaq had kissed a girl psyker. Olvia had been her name. Her unformed talent was for curing injuries; and she was destined to die.

Olvia thought that Jaq would die too, and he had not disabused her. They had embraced for mutual comfort. They had kissed, though that was all.

Afterwards Jaq had felt that he had betrayed Olvia. Maybe his self-denial in the matters of the flesh had begun then and there. What of the woman to whom he had recourse subsequently, on an icy world, as a fledgling inquisitor? The woman whom he paid for her favours so as to learn of that enchantment that could fuddle men and women? He never asked her name. The experience had cheated him.

He would only ever, he sensed, be able to pair with a woman who was his own match – professionally, as it were. How few human beings in the entire galaxy could fulfil that criterion! If they did fulfil it, surely they must be potential rivals, competitors even in the guise of colleagues.

So therefore: loneliness and duty.

He had begun to think of Meh'Lindi as someone who might... As someone who was strong enough, strange enough...

Jaq staunched the thought, like an open wound. Carnelian had dealt that wound with devastating accuracy. Not because the Harlequin man had sullied Meh'Lindi in Jaq's eyes, oh no, no question of such a despicable thought – but because Carnelian had used pleasure as a weapon, therefore Meh'Lindi must reject dalliance with any such delights; even if she had felt the faintest inclination to dally in the first place, and that was a dubious proposition.

Folly, thought Jaq! I'm reacting to her as dotingly as infatuated Grimm or mooning Vitali. Double folly, now. Carnelian's attack on Meh'Lindi has fuddled me.

And her too...

'We must both think very clearly,' he said to her. 'We mustn't indulge our feelings at all.'

There in the train, Jaq prayed for clarity.

THEY FOUND GOOGOL tied up securely in the Emerald Suite with a leather hood over his head. The Navigator ached almightily with cramps and had soiled himself. The eye-screen was missing.

Grimm released Googol, cleaned him, massaged him. Then Googol sprawled wretchedly on a couch, whispering of how a power axe had sliced a hole through the door and how stun-gas had billowed into the suite, all within seconds. Googol glanced perplexedly at the door, which was perfectly intact. The assailants had replaced it. Was that so as to cast doubt on Googol's word? Or only to prevent prior discovery?

'Three of them, I'd say. Never saw their faces. Only heard their voices when I woke, all trussed up. I pretended to be still unconscious.'

'Let's assume they realised you were awake,' said Jaq. 'They probably saw you twitch. Let's assume they waited around so that you could overhear them talking.'

'That didn't occur to me.'

'No? Well, I'm cultivating suspicion, Vitali.'

'Surely not of me, Jaq? You don't think that... They did cut through the door, I swear it!'

'Yes, yes, I'm sure they did. As well as blinding me by stealing the screen, what did they want me to know?'

'Ah, let's see... It's coming. "Now Draco won't be able to see how Vasilariov is infested." Something along those lines. They mentioned names of lots of other cities too, but I couldn't hear what they were saying about them clearly with that leather over my lugs.'

'Meh'Lindi.' Jaq spoke with a casualness which, in the circumstances, brought her to full alert. His gaze flicked.

It only took her moments to locate the spy-fly roosting in a shadow, to aim her digital laser and evaporate the tiny surveillance device. Her accuracy was unimpaired.

'Spider time,' said Jaq. He fetched a detector from his luggage. This chittered in his hand as he swept the suite, uncovering four further spy-flies, which Meh'Lindi despatched.

'Now that Carnelian can't overhear us,' he said, 'I can perhaps plan something unexpected.'

'Outside of here: more flies? Wherever we go?'

'Undoubtedly,' he told her.

'Use jumblespeech?'

'Carnelian may understand it.'

'He reached you through your Tarot before. Can he eavesdrop through a card, Jaq? Sense what you're thinking?'

'When I activate them. Maybe! Otherwise, I strongly doubt it. I shall leave them inert, even if that closes off the currents of the future. Any more gossip, Vitali?'

'Not that I recall.'

'By the way, trusty watchman,' said Grimm, 'how fruitfully did you occupy yourself while you were lying there with nothing to do and a hood over your bean?'

'I contemplated ways of killing my attackers.'

'Huh, that isn't very grateful, seeing as how they left you alive. Don't you mean that you replayed the episode with yourself as hero? Didn't you fantasise about what might have occurred if only you'd been holding your breath at the time and a gun as well? Ah, I bet by the end of it you were quite amazed to find yourself still inexplicably tied up.'

Googol sighed. 'I *would* have killed them, hot-shot. No coward navigates the warp. As to my... period of meditation, there are mental disciplines in which I fear you're sorely lacking, Grimbo, though I thank you for rubbing life back into my limbs.'

'And changing your dirty underwear.' Grimm sniffed at his blunt, though nimble, fingers. He disregarded the Navigator's diminution of his name, perhaps sensing the undertone, this time, of almost fond indebtedness. Almost.

'Actually,' confessed the Navigator, perking up, 'I composed a poem and quite a good one.'

'What?' said Grimm.

'Did you really do that, Vitali?' Meh'Lindi asked, with more than a note of admiration in her voice. 'I salute you.'

'What for?' asked the squat, perplexed. Meh'Lindi's reaction was her first really affirmative one since her humiliation at Carnelian's hands. 'I like poems, too,' he ploughed on hopefully. 'We sing many epic ballads – about our wars with the foul orks and the deceitfulness of the eldar. Our ballads are all quite long. Take a day or so to recite.'

'Mine are generally quite short,' said Vitali. 'Verses should aim to be gems, not gasbags.'

'Huh! Let me tell *you*–'

Were the squat and the Navigator on the brink of a poetical competition with which to court Meh'Lindi? But then she interrupted.

'One's whole previous life becomes a poem by means of the suicide-ode.'

Jaq didn't wish to hear any more. 'Grimm,' he said, 'I want you to go deep into the ruptured entrails of Vasilariov to search for another hydra. I'm sure you'll find one down where the dross and scum gather.'

'If I find it, should I slice it up a little?'

'Absolutely not! Just report back here.'

'I should go,' Meh'Lindi said disconsolately. 'I could atone.'

'The role of an assassin,' Jaq reminded her, 'is not to feel remorse in any respect. I'd prefer that you stay here. I need to think.'

'Her presence assists you to *think*?' enquired Googol. Irony was returning to his voice. Consequently he was recovering from his minor ordeal.

THINK.

'Search for another hydra.' That's what he had told Grimm.

As Jaq questioned Meh'Lindi yet again so as to compare her impressions with his, a sickening realisation about the probable nature of the hydra dawned on him.

'Dissect it. Pot a trophy.' Thus Carnelian had goaded Jaq, wishing him to do exactly that, wanting him to attack the hydra in the axe-swinging style of an Obispal.

Not only would the creature regenerate severed scraps of its body into new limbs, not only would gobbets of its substance give rise to more of it, but in some fashion – through the medium of the warp – its substance could remain connected together, could still function as a unit even when slashed apart.

And therefore, *therefore*, the hydra that lurked under the city of Kefalov and any hydras roosting in the underbelly of Vasilariov and other cities on this planet were all *one and the same*.

Had even Jaq's plasma blast truly damaged the beast – or simply stimulated it, spraying elements of it hither and yon?

All the millions of deaths resulting from the genestealer rebellion – a great psychic bellow of rage, pain and extinction – had served to trigger the growth of this creature.

The rebellion had been sparked deliberately, primarily to feed the creation of this creature. To forge that strange blend of protoplasm and the fluidium of the warp – or more exactly, to quicken it, since its ultimate origin must surely lie elsewhere, in some dire biological crucible.

Why here, why Stalinvast, and not some other world? Jaq imagined arcane astromantic calculations and perversions of Tarot divination – conducted by Carnelian, the Tarot-sneak? – before this planet was chosen for the first emergence of the entity.

The first. There had to be a first emergence somewhere. And this world harboured enough infesting furtive stealers to cause a huge conflagration of lives – the calculated level of obscene sacrifice – without leading to really major devastation.

All to what end? If guided by an adept, the hydra could enter people's minds on a deep-down level where the ultimate biological controls of behaviour existed, the pleasure centre and the pain centre...

Daemons did not seem to be involved at all. *Someone* – human or alien – had engineered a mighty and sinister living tool for an unknown purpose.

Jaq had been chosen as a dupe.

On discovering a macabre entity such as the hydra, any inquisitor worth his salt would call in the nearest available force of Space Marines – Blood Angels, Space Wolves, whichever – to root out the malevolent lifeform.

The result of this obvious strategy would be to spread the hydra around still further, so that more and more of it grew from the savaged fragments left behind. As soon attempt to slice water with a sword, or chop up the sea.

Jaq had been blinded – had his eye-screen stolen by agents of Carnelian – so that he would see even less of the picture than before and would be the more likely to call in such a vigorous and essentially useless assault. Carnelian even teased him with the truth, assuming that Jaq would fail to perceive it.

Therefore, Jaq would not call in a Space Marine unit to assist him. Would not, must not.

That only perhaps left him one alternative – an ultimate alternative which no one, not even Carnelian, could reasonably expect him to invoke, let alone soon...

The name of that alternative was *exterminatus*.

'In an Imperium of a million worlds,' he repeated to himself, 'what does the death of one world matter in the cause of purity?'

For such was *exterminatus*: the total destruction of all life on the surface of a planet by means of virus bombs delivered from orbit.

The life-eater virus, spreading at amazing speed, would attack anything whatever that breathed or grew or crawled or flew as well as anything of biological origin: food, clothes, wood, feathers, bone. The life-eater was voracious. The jungles of Stalinvast would swiftly rot into sludge that would form shallow festering inland seas and lakes, where rot continued to feed so that the very air burned planet-wide, searing the whole surface to ashes and bare rock.

In the cities all protein would eat itself and ooze in a tide into the underbelly, rot eating rot, until the firegas detonated, leaving the cities like mounds of dead, blasted coral.

What if the hydra was not... life exactly? No matter. What would it have left to prey upon, if such was its design and its destiny?

Exterminatus.

The word tolled like a woeful bell.

'What does the death of one world matter...?'

When one person dies, that person's entire world – their whole universe – vanishes for them. A cosmos is snuffed out and quenched. Any individual's death essentially involves the death of an entire universe, does it not? The death of a planetful of people could hardly involve any more than that.

Yet it did.

By now Jaq was on his knees, praying. He yearned to consult his Tarot so as to connect himself however tenuously with the spirit of the Emperor. He dared not, lest his inner thoughts might be snooped upon by an interloper.

Exterminatus.

It did matter. He would be sacrificing a rich industrial world, a bastion of the human Imperium. He would also be slaying a part of himself, burning out certain aspects of... sensitivity, of scepticism. Aspects which made him remember an Olvia and mourn the death of that comparative stranger. Yet was not everyone essentially a stranger? Maybe he should have cauterised those aspects of himself long since.

To contemplate causing the death of a world was, he realized, akin to contemplating one's own suicide. A harsh, chilling light shone through the soul, and where it shone, in its wake the ultimate darkness began to gather.

His knees ached as he had knelt there for hours. Googol had gone to sleep and was snoring gently. Meh'Lindi sat cross-legged regarding Jaq expressionlessly all this time. She had become a statue; he hardly heeded her. An inner light shone upon his wounded, confused, hopeless feelings for her; and soon in its wake a healing shadow swept across those feelings, obscuring them.

Exterminatus.

SEVEN

FAR BELOW THE windows of the suite, the jungle exhaled mists of early morning to dazzle the eye as the sun brightened. Along the horizon dirty clouds were already bunching up, to suffocate the radiance falsely promised by the dawn.

Jaq had prayed all through the night and felt giddy but purified.

At long last Grimm returned. 'There's a hydra down below all right,' he reported. 'All over the place! Appears to be influencing the human rats and roaches down there not to notice it. No, not to be properly *aware* of it; that's how it seemed to me. Now you spy it, now you don't, like some mirage. Its jelly shifts in and out of reality.'

'I dreamed about it,' said Meh'Lindi. 'Attacking it increases its vigour. Is some of it still in my head?'

Jaq arose at last, staggering slightly. Crossing to her, he placed a palm against her brow. She flinched momentarily. Extending his psychic sense, he spoke words of power in the hieratic ritual language.

'*In nomine imperatoris hominorum magistris ego te purgo et exorcizo. Apage, Chaos, apage!*' He coughed as though to banish a clot of phlegm, the taste of Chaos. 'I exorcize you,' he told her. 'You're free of it. *I'm a daemon-hunter*; I should know.' Though truly the hydra was no daemon.

Meh'Lindi relaxed. How perceptive of her to realize that the entity might thrive on violent opposition.

Nothing could thrive after the wholesale scouring of the planet.

Googol had risen earlier to consult the comm-screen. 'I've checked with spaceport registry, Jaq. Zephro Carnelian has his own interstellar craft in a berth. It's registered as belonging to something called the Zero Corporation.'

'Meaning that no such corporation exists.'

'Ship exists. She's called *Veils of Light.*'

'How did you confirm it belongs to Carnelian?'

'Ah... we Navigators have some influence where matters of space are involved.'

'The famous Navis Nobilitate spider's web?'

'Depending on our particular family allegiances...' Googol seemed pleased with himself.

Grimm yawned, and yawned again.

Jaq wished that he himself could slumber. He musn't. He must act in the purity of the moment. He located a powerful stimulant.

'I shall pay a call on Governor Voronov-Vaux,' he announced. 'Dawn is a good time to do so. I shall reveal myself. He will be less alert, more pliable. I need his astropath to send an interstellar message.'

'If I was a lord,' observed Grimm, 'I'd be tetchy first thing in the morning.'

'Be glad you aren't a lord, then, my buoyant mankin,' said Googol. 'May I come along too, Jaq? Leaving me seems to lead to embarrassments. I'm restless. I've been cooped up. A Navigator needs... to explore space.'

Jaq nodded. If they needed to leave Stalinvast rapidly, the pilot musn't be languid. A false, drug-induced vitality coursed through Jaq's blood and muscles and illuminated his mind harshly, sweeping away fatigue and any remaining perplexity. In such a state, he knew, he could make judgments which were almost too pure, too unrelenting. Perhaps he needed an ironist to accompany him – at his left hand; and at his right hand, his assassin.

'We eat first,' he said, 'and we eat *well.*'

THE VESTIBULE LEADING to the governor's quarters was the mouth of a toothed monstrosity. Sculpted from marble blocks, the vestibule was capacious enough to gulp all but the bulkiest of actual jungle monsters whole. Jaq wondered whether this menacing foyer was designed to close up exactly like a mouth, using hidden plasteel muscles to move the marble blocks.

Certain ancient stains along the approach corridor – which resembled the rib cage of a very long whale – had suggested that those ribs could clash shut at any sign of unwelcome visitors, imprisoning or crushing intruders.

Within the vestibule, red lighting ached drearily on the eye. It stole away all other colours or rendered them purple, black. Air puffing from the ventilator gargoyles, styled after lizards of the jungle, smelled musky rather than fresh. Despite his drug-boosted clarity, Jaq felt half-blinded and stifled.

'How strange,' the majordomo was saying, 'another honourable inquisitor presenting his credentials so soon after we have seen the last one off!'

The fat man fluttered chubby, ringed fingers. He wore corrective goggles which must translate the rubicund gloom of this vestibule into the true spectrum. A seemingly black Voronov-Vaux monogram emblazoned his silk robes.

'Our world has just been cleansed, sir, at enormous cost – and with the whole-hearted co-operation of his lordship. Our population is culled. The economy will boom.'

'Ah yes, the economic stimulus of slaughter!'

Jaq held up his palm once more, activating the electronic daemon-head tattoo of the outer Inquisition. The guards in saurian leather and goggles, who manned this last of many checkpoints, stiffened. An Obispal had recently reinforced the Inquisition's authority.

'I simply require the use of your master's astropath,' said Jaq.

'Ah, you need to send an interstellar message? His lordship will be curious. You'll be reconfirming that our whole world is cleansed, I take it?'

'The message is *my* business.'

'Our astropath might mention the content to his lordship later on, so why not divulge it now?'

Unlikely, thought Jaq, that the astropath would mention anything at all ever again... He doubted that the astropath would wholly understand the message that Jaq intended to send. If at all, if at all. The message would be couched in Inquisition code; the astropath would parrot the words out telepathically.

Still, the astropath would remember, and some scholar on the governor's staff might construe the meaning.

On this occasion the astropath must seem to succumb to the pressure of his work. Meh'Lindi would see to this subtly. The astropath must suddenly appear to be possessed – with lethal consequences.

The astral telepath would die in any case when *exterminatus* arrived. So this would almost be a mercy killing. A grain of dust to set beside the mountain of several billion other deaths...

'Ah,' said the majordomo, 'I'm well aware that the college of the priesthood here in the capital was destroyed during the rebellion. You can't use their astropath. What of commercial ones?

'Less reliable.'

'Reasonably reliable.'

'Reasonably is not enough. Your master's astropath will be the very best on this world.'

'Oh yes. Granted. Utterly true. Only the best for an inquisitor. Still, the priestly colleges in other cities boast of some fairly excellent specimens...'

Such would die too, along with many good priests. Was the *cause* sound enough, when the true nature of the hydra remained so opaque and ambiguous?

The *hydra* had to be sinister. The obvious response – of summoning in an exterminator team – just had to be wrong. Briefly Jaq entertained the notion that he was being tested by some Hidden Master of his secret order who had instructed Baal Firenze to send him to Stalinvast to assess whether Jaq possessed supreme courage and insight – enough for him to become a Hidden Master himself.

If so, that master must already have known about the hydra. Would even such a power squander a whole planet simply to test one individual? Maybe Jaq would send the signal for *exterminatus* – and that command would already have been countermanded, light years away. The red light grated on Jaq's eyes as if his own eyes were bloodshot, dazed with the blood of billions.

He tried to spot any spy-flies lurking in this foyer, little spies which so recently had been his own to command, until they were stolen. The dire light and dark shadows foxed him. A spy-fly might be hiding in the open mouth of any gargoyle. It could be peeping from the eye-socket of any of the saurian skulls with jewels atip their horns mounted on the walls.

Jaq hadn't told either of his companions exactly what he intended to do, and just then it occurred to him how Googol might resent the deaths of fellow Navigators caught on this world when the flesh-eater came.

'Thus,' said the fat man, 'your message must be distinctly *urgent*...'

Aside from the pre-eminence of a governor's own astropath, Jaq had one further reason for visiting Lord Voronov-Vaux's domain. He would have felt it demeaning to condemn this world utterly without first paying a visit to the vicinity of its ruler.

Just so, did an assassin care to leave a calling card...

Nor had he wished to leave the capital a second time. Nor had he wanted to... The thought tried to elude him. He brought it into sharp, cruel focus.

Nor had he wanted to have recourse to the services of an astropath belonging to a pious and loyal fraternal organisation. Whom, and which, he must sacrifice to the flesh-eater.

Had he come here to the governor's court out of cowardice? Out of craven abdication of his moral duty masquerading as brazen confrontation?

'Don't hinder me,' said Jaq. 'I demand access in the Emperor's name.'

What name, Jaq wondered fleetingly, was *that*?

Meh'Lindi moved closer to the majordomo, her fingers flexing. Googol fiddled ostentatiously with the bandana round his brow as if toying with the idea of removing what masked his third eye, the warp-eye, a hostile glare from which could kill, as was widely known though seldom tested.

'Of course you must be admitted to His Lordship,' burbled the majordomo. 'An inquisitor, oh yes! Though it's inconvenient.'

'If so, I don't need to see the governor – only his astropath.'

'Ah... His lordship must needs give consent. Do you see? Do you see?'

Not very well, thought Jaq. Not in this ruddy obscurity.

THE GOVERNOR'S SANCTUM was a leviathan suffused with the same dreary red light. Above the tenebrous vault of the ceiling, sunshine must reign. Jaq doubted that even the most towering of storms could engulf the uppermost reaches of Vasilariov. Of that outside brightness, no hint existed.

Now Jaq understood the function of that helmet he had seen the governor wearing out at the spaceport under the open sky. Voronov-Vaux must see best at red wavelengths. Probably in infrared too. The governor must see the heat of bodies as much as the physical flesh.

That was a mutation, a deviation. Since this affected the ruling family, no one might dare oppose it. Conceivably it contributed to the family's mystique.

Censers burned, further hazing the air. Goggled officials hunched over consoles around tiers of cantilevered wrought-iron galleries, listening to data, whispering orders. A string orchestra wailed as if in torment. Caged mutants with abnormally large eyes played complicated games on three-dimensional boards. Were those bastards of the Voronov-Vaux clan? Inbred freaks? Talented advisers, held in permanent captivity?

Jaq smelled the whiff of genetic pollution.

The busy galleries were attached to the ribs of the leviathan. Between those ribs, at floor level, sub-chambers formed deep caves. At the heart of the enormous room an ornate marble building shaped like a pineapple squatted on a disc of steel. That disc must be a lifting platform which could raise and lower the governor's sanctum sanctorum, his travelling tabernacle. Up into his government's headquarters; down into his family apartments and bunker.

Give thanks that the sanctum sanctorum was present, not sealed away below.

Liveried guards admitted the majordomo and those he escorted into the marble pineapple. The fat man loudly prattled unctuous apologies. From a dim inner room Jaq heard flesh slap flesh. With a squeal, a scantily clad girl whose eyes were twice the normal human size scampered out, to be caught by one of those guards and led away.

Lord Voronov-Vaux followed bare-footed, adjusting a black robe on which dragons of seemingly purple hue writhed at the edge of visibility.

'YOU'RE THE HEREDITARY lord of a whole world,' Jaq found himself saying presently. 'Whereas I'm the emissary from the lord of the entire galaxy.'

'Lord of parts of it,' growled the governor.

'Of the human parts.' Jaq stared at those mutant, red-seeing eyes accusingly.

'True. Well, I'm hardly rebellious! I placed all my loyal guard at the previous inquisitor's service, did I not? Did I not sustain terrible losses?'

'Much to your benefit, may I remind you? Otherwise, within a few decades genestealers would have begun to infiltrate your own family, polluting and hypnotising.'

'I realise.'

'Now I only wish you to place your finest astropath at my service.'

Standing before the man, Jaq's various rationalizations evaporated. In coming here, he was actually following psychic instinct, an indefinable but insinuating impulse to visit the court of Governor Voronov-Vaux.

In the psychic economy of the universe a compensation must exist for the reverses Jaq had suffered at the hands of the Harlequin man. Something was going to balance his previous contretemps. Because he had prayed with a pure heart throughout the night, a tendril from the God-Emperor was now nudging him like a guardian spirit.

The monstrosity of the *exterminatus* he contemplated had eclipsed that thread of instinct until now, all be it that *exterminatus* was the correct course of action. Exhilaration keened through Jaq. Could the drug alone be responsible? No. He felt subtly in touch with higher forces, as though he had become the Tarot card that represented him.

'Hmm,' said the governor, 'but why? What have you discovered?'

Voronov-Vaux, a stout, balding fellow, was plainly a sensualist. To rule a planet he must be capable of severity. Yet his curiosity as to Jaq's request seemed to proceed from reasonable concern rather than from the paranoia which often afflicted rulers. Actually, the governor would have ample reason to feel paranoid if he did but know the gist of the message Jaq intended to send.

Led by the tendril of intuition, Jaq said lightly, 'Let's hope that, after all your loyal assistance, Inquisitor Obispal doesn't report adversely to the Imperium about your mutation... I certainly shan't.'

What need to? Voronov-Vaux and everyone else on this world would soon be dead.

The governor twitched. 'Harq wouldn't. He swore on his honour.'

There was the key! Obispal had virtually blackmailed Voronov-Vaux to allow him to root out the rebellion with wanton use of force, resulting in all those millions of deaths.

Voronov-Vaux's red vision was his vulnerable flaw; for the Imperium might just decide puristically that a mutant should not continue as governor. His lordship was glancing askance at Meh'Lindi. Did he detect the heat-profile of an assassin?

Did he imagine he had already been judged and condemned? Lesser lords would be only too eager to step into his shoes.

'So do I also swear on my honour,' Jaq assured the man. 'A good governor does as he pleases on his world, just so long as he pays his tithes in treasure and people. Or in your case, weapons. A minor mutation should be deemed an eccentricity and nothing more. Out of curiosity, how long has this variation been in your family?'

'Since my grandfather's time.'

'May it endure until the end of the world! I promise. Harq promised. I suppose Zephro promised too?'

'Carnelian, yes... A peculiar individual... He almost seemed to regret the necessary slaughter of my people as much as I did.'

Ha, it was proven. The Harlequin man was Obispal's associate, utterly. Could Obispal really be loyal to the Imperium? It hardly seemed so. Surely here was the evidence that Jaq's Emperor-sent impetus had been leading him toward.

'Now may I use your astropath without further ado?'

'Yes. Yes, inquisitor.'

'I'm glad you are so loyal.'

Your reward, thought Jaq grimly, will be exterminatus.

As soon as Jaq met the astropath he guessed that there was more awaiting.

EIGHT

THE PRIME ASTROPATH of Stalinvast was a small, thin, dark-skinned woman. And she was old, *antique*. Deep lines grooved her prune of a face. Her hair, which shone so brightly red, must really be purest white. Due to the long-past agony of soul-binding her blind eyes were opaque and curdled.

She leaned on a staff as tall as herself, and could not see the visitors to her fur-lined chamber, but her nearsense informed her.

'Three more come,' she sang out. 'One with the vision. One with the sense. And one who is more than she seems!'

Momentarily Jaq imagined that the majordomo had led them, in error of mischief, to a soothsayer. However, the old woman's dark purple habit would, in true lighting, be some hue of green appropriate to an astropath.

'I'm the one with the vision,' agreed Googol. 'It's warp vision – the Navigator's eye.'

And I, thought Jaq, am the one with the sense. Whereas Meh'Lindi... she's the one who will presently cause this old woman's heart to stop.

The astropath reached towards a fur-cloaked ledge; and the fur shifted. Glowing eyes opened. Sharp small claws flexed. She toyed with an animal, which must be her companion. The creature looked both voluptuous and savage. Would it defend its mistress fiercely?

'What is that?' whispered Jaq.

'It's called a cat,' Meh'Lindi told him. She also answered his deeper question. 'It will merely look on, observing what it sees. Who knows what it understands? Its actions are usually self-centred and autistic.'

'Why do you keep such a creature?' Jaq asked the old woman.

'For love,' she replied bleakly. 'I have kept at least a score of them during my life here, until each decayed in turn. They are my consolation.' She held up a wizened hand. 'Look, here are some of its recent scratches. I can *feel* those.'

'Leave us now,' Jaq told the majordomo. The fat man withdrew, drawing a baffle-curtain across the mouth of the astropath's furry womb-cave.

Meh'Lindi whisked an electrolumen from her sash to supplement the dull rubescence of the single glow-globe. In true light the old woman's skin was brown and her hair indeed was white as cotton, while her eyes were the boiled white of eggs. The fur lining the cave was a brindled orange; that of the cat creature too. The animal's pupils widened into black marbles at this sudden intrusion of a wholly novel radiance, then narrowed to slits. Its jaws widened, baring sharp little teeth.

It was, however, yawning. A yawn, in the face of a whole new world of light!

'Your name?' Jaq asked the old woman.

'People call me Moma Parsheen, perhaps because I have no children except for...' She stroked the cat creature.

'I'm Inquisitor Draco.'

'An inquisitor? Then you probably know how much was burnt out of me. I neither see nor smell nor savour any tastes. I only touch.' The cat writhed sensuously, throbbing. To kill this woman might indeed be a blessing to her...

'Moma Parsheen, I wish you to send a message to the Imperial Ravager Space Marines' headquarters, orbiting Vindict V.'

That fortress-monastery was the nearest roost of ultimate warriors capable of obliterating a world. Jaq already had his fatal signal concisely formulated: *Ego, Draco Ordinis Mallei Inquisitor, per auctoritate Digamma Decimatio Duodecies, ultimum exterminatum planetae Stalinvastae cum extrema celeritate impero.* The triple-D code phrase, sometimes vulgarised as Death-Destruction-Doom, would itself suffice to launch *exterminatus.* Thus the Inquisition mission stationed on the orbital fortress would advise. Jaq had included the phrase *Ordinis Mallei* by way of double indemnity; the mission was almost bound to include a covert member of his own Ordo. Never before had he sent such an order, never. This weighed on him like an inactive dreadnought suit of combat armour, imprisoning him; and he sought his enhanced clarity, as it were, to restore power to that suit.

'Listen to me carefully, Moma Parsheen.' He recited the words. She might not understand them, but she repeated them back faithfully.

'Now commence your trance.'

The blind woman quivered as she skryed light years outward through the warp, obeying the disciplines of the Adeptus Astra Telepathica, seeking contact with the mind of some other astropath serving the fortress-monastery at Vindict V.

Yet then she hesitated. 'Inquisitor?'

'What is it, old woman?'

'Such a resonant message... '

'Send it *now*.'

Now, before the Harlequin man could intervene. A spy-fly could be nestling in these furry walls. An agent might be poised nearby, prepared to burst in here on a suicide mission.

'Inquisitor... I'm sensing warp portals opening deep down in our city. And yes, in other cities across this world...'

'You must send my message immediately!' To sense portals in distant cities, she must possess impeccable talent... 'What is entering through these portals?'

The astropath shook her head. 'Nothing is entering. Strange... substances are departing from this world.'

'*Leaving*? Are you sure?'

'I am. A life that isn't exactly life. A creation... I can't really tell. There's so little mind. It's as if its existence is almost blank as yet. Embryonic... awaiting. I sense it all passing away through those portals. So many little portals! What is happening?'

'Don't send that message, Moma. Absolutely don't.'

'No?'

'New circumstances. Meh'Lindi, there's a spy-fly somewhere in here with us–'

'Who are you, inquisitor?' asked the astropath, relaxing from her trance state. 'What is happening?'

'Our hydra's withdrawing into the warp whence it came,' Googol murmured, half in answer to her. 'Never find it again, I don't suppose.'

'Can't you track it with warp vision, Vitali?'

'I'm a Navigator, not a magician. In case you hadn't noticed, I'm not in the warp at the moment. We're a week's travel away from the jump zone.'

'Exceptional Navigators can see into the warp from the normal universe!'

'Yes, yes, yes, Jaq. But the hydra isn't flying away *through* the warp. It's using portals to leap directly from here – to Grimm knows where.'

'Damnation...'

For a short while Jaq had believed he had achieved something admirable. The draconic decision to declare *exterminatus* had been exactly right, a model of resolute courage and pure thinking. Carnelian, spying through the eye-screen from wherever, had immediately begun withdrawing the hydra into the warp of Chaos to save it from extinction. Thus Jaq was saved from the consequences of his pronouncement. Now he had no way to track the cursed creature.

How very quickly Carnelian had acted! Surely the Harlequin man understood that *exterminatus* wouldn't arrive instantly? Time for the Space Marines to equip and load virus bombs... warp-time versus galactic time... Ten local days at the earliest. It was almost as though Carnelian hoped charitably to save this planet...

'Damnation, it's escaping...'

The old woman lapsed into a semi-trance. 'If the... existence... possessed a higher consciousness,' she mused, 'I could place a psychic homer in it for you, a little beacon. Though only I could follow such a trace.'

'Well, it doesn't,' snapped Jaq, 'and meanwhile it's sliding away like slops down a drain.'

Outcry assaulted his ears. As Meh'Lindi doused her electrolumen, Jaq whirled and tore the baffle-curtain aside.

Through the crepuscular afterglow, from behind the marble pineapple, there came skipping a true-light figure. Aglow, the intruder radiated his own natural wavelengths luminously like some alien eldar attired in a holo-suit. He pirouetted. He bowed.

'Carnelian!' Meh'Lindi hissed and tensed.

'Sir Draco,' cried the figure. 'Nice try, but not nice enough, so it seems. Follow me, find me! Follow me, find me!' Did Carnelian think he was playing some childhood game?

'No one is really there,' warned Moma Parsheen. 'The space he speaks from is empty.'

Jaq understood. The figure was holographic. Spy-flies hovering beside that astral shape must be projecting it, weaving it of light.

To reverse the mode of operation of the jokaero spying device in this manner, the Harlequin man must understand the technology better than Jaq did. Carnelian must know special runes to inscribe around the eye-screen and arcane litanies to incant, to make it serve this two-way purpose, which perhaps had been the true purpose of the device in the first place...

'I'm listening,' Jaq shouted. 'I'm all ears!'

Did Carnelian hope that Jaq or Meh'Lindi would rush, or fire, impetuously – only for their laser beams or needles to pass through the phantom without effect, until they hit some bystander or the governor's tabernacle? As soon as Jaq realised how Carnelian was accomplishing this intrusion, he knew that he hadn't lost.

'Moma Parsheen,' he whispered, 'place your tracer in the man that sends this illusion. His tiny toys are nearby, linked to the real man somewhere in the city. Feel out those links. Snare him.'

'Yes... yes...' she mumbled, en-tranced.

'What do you want with me, Carnelian?' Jaq shouted, to persuade the illusion to linger long enough.

If only the governor's guards refrained from opening fire... Obviously they had seen Carnelian before in this sanctum, though not in that eerie, invasive guise. They were leery of the figure of light who had appeared as if by magic yet who looked so solid.

'Ask not,' Carnelian taunted, 'what you can do for me, but what I can do for you.'

'And what might that be?'

Once more, Jaq surmised that he was being tested, his every action scrutinised by a cunning, manipulative intelligence.

'Follow me, find me. If you can!' The figure levitated, spinning, darting out its arms menacingly, hands crackling with light – and vanished, just as the guards opened fire in alarm. Ruby laser light stitched the interior of the sanctum like thinnest threads of stronger flame within a dully glowing oven.

In vain.

Worse than in vain.

Screams rang out from the galleries, where spectators had been gazing down instead of hiding. Some data screens exploded. The laser fire ceased too late.

'Did you succeed?' Jaq asked the astropath urgently.

'Oh yes. I marked him without him knowing. I can track him, and he won't know. You'll have to take me with you, Inquisitor Draco. Take me from this place. I have been here for decades untold in this court, never leaving it except in my mind, ranging to far stars yet never truly experiencing those elsewheres. Only terse commercial messages. Is it one and a half centuries, is it two? I was rejuvenated... was it twice, was it thrice? Because I'm so valuable. Oh I am sightless but I can sense my environs and weary utterly of them. Food is always ashes in my mouth. Incense only stifles me; it has no aroma. I can only touch. Take me far away.'

'If Carnelian leaves Stalinvast,' Jaq said bluntly, 'we may need to take you a vast distance.'

Oh yes, Jaq's intuition to visit Voronov-Vaux had been right. She, Moma Parsheen, had been the true goal of his guardian spirit, of the tiny fraction of the Emperor's potence that walked with him.

'Why should I have feared the sending of your message, inquisitor? Because I feel any tenderness towards my prison where all luxuries are insipid? Because I feel any attachment to this city or this world where I have laboured?'

She must indeed have plumbed the general sense of Jaq's message.

'Ah, but to be released by death before I could ever sense somewhere else directly! That would have been cruel comfort.'

'From an inner sanctum to the inside of a ship,' said Googol. 'You mightn't find the contrast all that stunning.'

'Even the brief journey to your ship will be a great liberating expedition for me.'

'Yes, we must go to the *Tormentum* right away,' said Jaq. 'Now that the hydra has gone into the warp, where else would Carnelian head?'

'You are old, Moma Parsheen,' Googol observed doubtfully.

'I will *stride* out with you,' she promised.

'What of your cat-animal?'

'Ming will cling to his home, not to me.'

'Yet you loved such a creature?'

The old woman ducked quickly back into her soft cave, to linger for a few seconds by the animal. She fondled its scruff, then snatched up a simple sling-bag of possessions embroidered with fidelity emblems.

'I'm ready.'

'Now's the best time,' said Meh'Lindi.

The injured were crying out up above. A console sprayed electric sparks and began to blaze. Distraught, the fat majordomo was bustling into the chamber. Guards were arguing. The Harlequin man couldn't have provided a better distraction.

EN ROUTE TO the train-tube terminal Jaq voxed Grimm to carry away as much as he could from the hotel suite, settle their account if challenged and rendezvous at the *Tormentum*.

At one point in their journey, Moma Parsheen was overcome by frailty. Limp and detached from her fast-shifting surroundings – maybe overwhelmed by those – she needed to be guided, almost carried along by Meh'Lindi for a while. Then the old woman recovered vigour and strode, favouring her staff.

EVEN BY THE standards of ships that could set down upon the surfaces of worlds, the *Tormentum Malorum* was singularly sleek and streamlined for rapid departure or arrival through atmosphere. Only warp-vanes jutted notably from the hull, and those were contoured cleverly as wings.

Within, the vessel in no wise resembled a rogue trader's treasure den or seraglio. The *Tormentum* was a sepulchral temple to the Master of Mankind, atrabilious and funereal.

In its layout the interior resembled black catacombs. Narrow corridors linked cells housing bunks or stores to crypt-rooms housing instruments or engines. Walls, ceilings and floors were clad in smooth obsidian and jet carved with runes, sacred prayers and holy texts. In niches, each lit by an electrocandle, images of the distorted enemies of humanity seemed to writhe in flames. The dark glassy surfaces reflected and re-reflected these flickering lights so that walls seemed to be the void – solidified – with stars and smeared veils of nebulae glinting within. Portholes were few and usually hatched over with leering daemon masks.

One bulkhead was a great bas-relief representing the heroic features of the Emperor stood astride the cowering form of the arch-traitor, Horus. A far cry from the shrivelled but undying form, embedded in the very centre of his throne amidst a forest tubes and wires. A virtual mummy, a living corpse that could not twitch a fingertip – though did any fingers or even fingerbones remain within that mass of medical machinery? Yet the Master's mind reached out afar.

Jaq often prayed to this bas-relief. The whole décor of the ship reinforced his faith.

As to Jaq's companions... Meh'Lindi's attitude to the *Tormentum* was impassive, inscrutable, while the corridors and crypts reminded Grimm nostalgically of mine workings and coaly caverns. The little man would trot around, mumbling contentedly, reenacting heroic skirmishes with rabid orks in cramped subterranean strongholds.

Googol talked to himself in a muffled manner or merely droned – hard to say which – whenever he was in space. At first Jaq had assumed the Navigator's idea was to sustain, sympathetically, the pitch of the ship's engines which sometimes skipped a beat, by chatting or humming to them. Jaq now surmised that Googol was reciting his own verses under his breath, polishing old ones, composing new ones. *Gloom. Tomb. Doom.*

Moma Parsheen embraced her new surroundings intently. Though more restricted, she declared them to be 'charged with potential space' – the potential to be elsewhere, anywhere else, in the galaxy.

Grimm, when he arrived, treated the old woman with a teasing reverence.

'A century or two? That's not so old! Me, I'll live at least three hundred years–'

'And still be none the wiser,' Googol said airily.

'Huh. You shorten the body, you increase the length of lifespan, I'm thinking.'

'Maybe we should breed men a span high so as to live a million years.'

'Sour grapes, Vitali! You're prematurely aged. It's all this warping you do.'

'That's my talent, sprat. Doesn't mean I'm going to die prematurely just because my face has character.'

'Wrinkles is the word. Anyway, I thought you wished to retire to some asteroid to be a bard. When will you entertain us with one of your effusions, by the by?'

Googol scuffed the abhuman lazily.

'Do you ever compose elegies?' Moma Parsheen asked unexpectedly. 'Dirges? Songs of lamentation?'

'For you, dear lady,' Googol replied gallantly, 'I might attempt such a challenge, though that isn't my usual style.'

'Huh, what about me?' protested Grimm. 'What I'm saying, Vitali – what I've been driving at in my own bluff way – is that I would very much appreciate, that's to say, well...'

The little man tore off his forage cap and twisted it in his hands. 'Ahem. The epic ballad of Grimm the squat who helped trounce the hydra. For my old age. I will teach you the modes, the verse form. If I live past three hundred or so, you see, I become a living ancestor; and an ancestor needs an epic under his belt. If I live past five hundred...' He grinned lamely. 'I reckon I'll become psychic then. Oh Moma Parsheen, in that respect you're a living ancestor already. I guess for a true human you've reached a decent age.'

'Decent?' she echoed disbelievingly. 'To be psychic is a blessing? My talent has robbed me utterly.'

'Would that robbery be the subject matter of your elegy?' Googol asked.

'Oh no. Oh no.' She didn't amplify further. 'How old are you, Grimm?'

'Oh, no more than fifty. That's standard Imperial years.'

'And bouncing along like a rubber ball.' Googol laughed. 'Maybe you do need an epic – of naivety.'

'I'm a sprat, it's true. A clever sprat; that's true too. But,' and he eyed Meh'Lindi puppyishly, 'my heart can be heavy at times.'

Meh'Lindi frowned. 'Mine too. For other reasons.'

She had quickly abandoned her sensual mistress's garb and was attired in a clingtight assassin's black tunic.

Jaq had likewise divested himself of his trader's gaudy gear and now wore the black, ornamented, hooded habit of his Ordo.

Along with Googol in his affectedly fluted black silk on-board suit, these three seemed to be a trio of tall-standing predatory bats who eclipsed the false star-void of the walls, wherever they stood, like dense hungry shadows eating the fire-flies of the night.

Moma Parsheen sank into a semi-trance.

'I warn you: the man called Carnelian is hurrying towards this spaceport.'

A WEEK LATER, in pursuit of the *Veils of Light* – not trying to catch Carnelian, only follow him – the *Tormentum Malorum* entered the ocean of Chaos which was warp-space.

Only then did Moma Parsheen say to Jaq, 'I sent the message anyway.'

'Message?'

'Your message to Vindict V. I sent it while we were still in Vasilariov.'

'Unsend it!' he cried. 'Cancel it!'

Sightless, she smiled thinly and inhumanly; she who had not seen a smile with which to compare since her girlhood, nor a mirror either.

'From here, in the very warp? Impossible.'

Was she telling the truth? *He did not know.*

'In that case,' said Jaq, 'let us drop back into true space.'

'And lose the scent of Carnelian? While we dilly-dally in the ordinary universe, his ship will forge onward through the warp out of my range.'

'Surely you can transmit from the warp.'

'I'm sure I wouldn't know how, inquisitor. That's quite outside of my experience. If I was trained in that, I've forgotten long since. Please recall how I've been penned in a sanctum on a planet for most of my days. I haven't known the pleasures of star-cruising. So, supposing I tried, the task would demand *total* concentration. I might easily lose my sense of our quarry.'

'You're lying.'

'The application of torture,' she said idly, 'would certainly distort my talent.'

Jaq wished she had not alluded to any such notion. To administer torture while within the warp – to a talented astropath of all people –

would be plain lunacy. *Tormentum* mightn't be heavily screened against evil; what would be more likely to pierce the membrane between reality and Chaos than mind-screams of pain? What more likely to attract the attention of... the hyenas of Chaos?

From his Navigator's couch, Googol looked on anxiously. He fingered some of the amulets and icons that dangled around his neck now that he was in the warp.

'Jaq?'

'We carry on,' Jaq said anguishedly.

Time passed faster in the warp than in the real universe, but was also inconstant, unpredictable. Moma Parsheen had sent the *exterminatus* signal just over a week earlier. The Ravagers might already have sailed towards their jump zone, or be on the point of sailing. Once in the warp, how quickly would they arrive in the vicinity of Stalinvast?

Jaq imagined the priests of the squadron instructing the ultimate warriors righteously and reverently, honing their spirits for a task that was awesome – and yet almost abstract. How much more eager those warriors would have been to contact a foe face to face.

If the government of Stalinvast realised the import of the death-fleet's arrival, the orbital monitors might resist for a while. A day. A few hours. Armageddon would soon enough descend – enforced almost with a sense of regret.

Out of a million worlds, what did one matter?

Yet it did. For this would be one more loss suffered by the Imperium. The granite rock of the Imperium, which rested upon shifting sands of malevolent Chaos, could not endure an infinity of such cracks in its fabric. Indeed that rock was already much riven.

It could crumble, and all human culture could collapse, just as it had collapsed once before, but this time never to rise again. It must not crumble. Or daemons, loosened from Chaos, would feast.

Yes, it did matter! For Jaq called to mind the fat, fussy majordomo and Lord Voronov-Vaux of the red vision, but not a bloodthirsty vision, and the great-eyed girl who had scampered from his bed, and all the survivors of the genestealer uprising who had dolefully expected that their lives would at least continue after the disaster.

All were to die, all.

Not even in the way that Olvia must have died years ago to serve the Emperor – but to sate one mad woman's vengeance. When the time came, would Moma Parsheen tune in to the deaths of fellow astropaths on Stalinvast?

Jaq could order Vitali to drop back into normal space and no doubt could force the old woman to comply. He himself. He wouldn't order Meh'Lindi to do the task.

Yet then a terrible, enigmatic conspiracy might succeed...

'You have murdered a world,' he accused her.

'And now that world needs an elegy,' she said. 'Our resident poet could sing of Stalinvast's lethal festering jungles which I never saw; and of viscous scabs blasted in those jungles by a host of weapons; and of all the reef-cities which I never saw either, infested with their slaving grimy weapons-makers. He could sing of lizard-clad nobles hunting for trophies, and of body-heat orgies and mutations of the eye, and of a lone white-haired woman whose senses had been scarified, locked in a sanctum forever, her mind reaching to the stars; and out among all those stars and worlds that she spoke to in her mind, no fellow spirit yearned towards her or was able to express any such feeling–'

'Enough! Later, I will – I *ought* to execute you.'

'I do not much care if you do.'

'Oh you will, Moma Parsheen, you will. When it's too late, near the end, everyone cares. They may even wish for death, but they still care.'

'Perhaps,' she said, '*yours* should be the ballad of naivety? I shall have travelled away in the flesh from that wretched court – light years away by then, light decades. With every light year I redeem a year of my lost life.'

'And how about your cat-creature?' Meh'Lindi asked the old woman softly.

At that, in Moma Parsheen's visionless eyes a few tears welled.

For several minutes a sense of utter paralysing futility overwhelmed Jaq.

NINE

Should anyone be foolish enough to don space armour and climb through the airlock, nothing whatever would be strictly *visible* – save for what had already come from the ordinary universe.

No stars shone in the realm of the warp, for no stars were present, nor any nebulosities of gleaming gas. Neither did darkness absolute prevail, as at the bottom of a well at midnight; for even blackness – the opposite of light – was absent.

On other wavelengths of perception than the visible, the warp was far from empty. It was super-saturated with virtual existence. Vitali Googol's warpscreen displayed an iridescent soup of energies riven by currents both swift and sluggish, poxed with vortices and whirlpools.

Here was the domain which glued the Imperium together since ships could slip through it to distant stars within days – or months at most – instead of taking impossible thousands of years over such voyages.

Yet here too was the realm where Jaq's special foes coagulated. Here was the infinite region where powers of Chaos achieved a twisted consciousness and a purpose anathema to all that was real and true.

Yes, the standing waves of warp storms became animate as great Powers. They drank the rage or the lust or the caprice of mortals whose souls returned to dissolve in this sea of energy.

These bloated Powers dangled lesser daemons. Avatars, made out of their own perverse essence, would hook into the spirits of vulnerable psykers, into greedy, heedlessly ambitious mortals, and would offer those dupes a little power – playing them like living puppets on intangible strings – before twisting them into tools of evil and eventually consuming them.

Thereby did the diabolical Powers seek to mutate the substance of the universe and to destroy Man's far-flung yet ultimately frail empire of sanity – a sanity that must needs defend itself with unrelenting savagery...

Jaq had learned all this during his training in the headquarters of his Ordo, that labyrinth many contorted thousands of kilometres in extent which cut through the bedrock deep beneath the massive concealing ice-cap of Terra's south polar continent.

'Astronomican strong and clear,' reported Googol. 'South declination eighty-two point one, ascension seventeen point seven. No significant warp storms evident.'

The warpscreen might have been a tank choked with bubbling prismatic frogspawn. Through that viewer they could all peer into the warp as if through one-way mirror-glass. Nothing from the warp could intrude into *Tormentum Malorum*, for the ship – this bubble of reality – was strongly shielded with force-fields and prayers.

Of course, with his warp-eye Googol saw far beyond the portion of warp space shown in the viewer – clear to the Emperor's aching beacon.

Starfarers in less well-protected vessels might hear the scrabbling of claws upon their hulls, or wailing incoherent voices, lascivious enticements, rumblings of wrath. If a vessel's force-skin was penetrated, daemons might congeal ectoplasmically within.

Let those be sirens of Slaanesh rather than harpies! Perhaps the death was sweeter. Or merely more prolonged.

The Inquisition schola was a vast, almost deliberately confusing maze of baroque halls, dormitories, sanctums, reclusia, libraria, scriptoria and apothecaria, dungeons, theological laboratories, psychic gymnasia and weapons arenas.

Fierce, sourly wise old adepts, who had retired from the field of stars, coached the intake of novices in the outer secrets of the art of the inquisitor, his ken and practice.

Jaq thrived at acquiring the necessary skills; yet already it was plain that he would never be a dogmatist, nor a flamboyant practitioner of the art of suppression.

'Why?' he would ask; and, 'Wherefore?'

He voiced such questions reverently, righteously, but voiced them nonetheless.

One day an instructor said to Jaq, 'We have our eye on you.'

Jaq feared being marked as a heretic; but that was not the reason why he was being specially scrutinised.

'CARNELIAN IS AT two-thirds of my tracking range,' commented Moma Parsheen, the murderess of a world.

Aft, Grimm was labouring in the stygian engine crypt by electrocandle and lantern light, tuning the drive that bore them through the warp. He only used spanners and gauges, scorning the runes or litanies which all other techs deemed so essential to woo the spirit of a machine.

Jaq lit incense sticks – frangipani, myrrh and Vegan virtueherb – in the obsidian control room. The air gargoyles gently sucked and puffed the aromatic smoke into strange curlicues as if sketching the features of potential daemons which might lurk outside the hull. His thoughts drifted forward in time from his novitiate. Years elapsed in his memory just as light years were elapsing in ordinary space as they fled onward.

HE HAD TAKEN all his oaths as a journeyman agent. He had served on a dozen worlds, rooting out aberrant psykers and heretics scrupulously and astringently – never succumbing to excess of zeal, though zealous none-the-less.

He was always willing to entertain a doubt – before, as was so often sadly the case, needing to crush all doubt. He never destroyed a witch simply on the say-so of vindictive enemies.

Came the day when a robed elder inquisitor activated a palm-tattoo that Jaq had never seen before, and spoke to him the words: 'Inner Order.'

A wheel within a wheel...

MEH'LINDI COMMENCED SOME isometric combat exercises as if to repel the oppression of being in the warp, which at times could generate a spiritual migraine, an ache of the soul.

She flexed. She tensed. Presently she danced – slowly. Each gesture, each step, each posture and nuance of limb or finger was part of a complex killing ritual. For a while she became the priestess of her own cult of Assassins, carrying out a deadly ceremony which appeared suave and innocuous, but was not.

Moma Parsheen took heed. Perhaps her nearsense completed for her – in her mind's eye – those abbreviated gestures so that she perceived the weaving of a skein of death. The old woman smiled distortedly, her brown, lined face a mask dropped into rippling water.

Vitali Googol began to recite:

'*Lovely lady of death*
Steals away my breath
With kisses that kill
Or ensorcel the will.
Her limbs mock my bones.
My squeezed heart moans.
The endearment: begone.
Lovely lady of death...'

The Navigator shuddered and focused himself more acutely on the immaterium without, alert for maelstroms. Presently he began to hum, somewhat tunelessly, a Navigator song, *The Sea of Lost Souls*.

Moma Parsheen stroked the air. In her mind was she comforting her cat-creature as the virus bombs began to rain down?

JAQ DAYDREAMED ABOUT a subsequent year when Baal Firenze had first made himself known. For there existed wheels within wheels within wheels. The Inquisition was by no means the be-all and end-all of the fight against corruption; nor was the secret inner order of the Inquisition the ultimate either.

The order of the hammer, Ordo Malleus, had been founded thousands of years in the past in deadliest secrecy – before the wounded Emperor had even entered his life-support throne. One of its mottos was: *Who Will Watch the Watchdogs?* The Ordo had even executed masters of the Inquisition when those mighty figures had shown signs of straying from true purity or diligence.

Yet its main task was to comprehend and destroy daemons. Jaq learned the appellations of those great entities of Chaos: Slaanesh the lustful, Khorne the blood-soaked, Tzeentch the mutator, Nurgle the plague-bearer. He would not utter those names lightly. All too often, human beings showed a literally fatal attraction towards such poisonous powers and their sub-daemons; as indeed perhaps people must, since those selfsame entities had agglutinated from out of the foul passions of once-living souls.

The training and conditioning of a Malleus man quite eclipsed the rigours of Jaq's training as a regular inquisitor. At the climax of a blood-chilling ceremony he swore even more secret oaths.

How could he forget the first daemon he had combatted in full knowledge of its nature? A lurid tattoo on his thigh commemorated his victory.

By now, underneath his garments, his frame sported a tapestry of such tattoos, though he kept his face clear, for secrecy.

* * *

ZEUS VI THE planet had been a farming world.

Peasants tilled the soil and herded sheep. They thought that the stars were holes in a blanket which the fabled Emperor draped across the sky each night. An outstretched fist could eclipse the sun that burned them by day. How fiercely they would be incinerated by a whole skyful of such light! This evidently existed, since from one horizon to the other dribs and drabs leaked through the little frays in the Emperor's blanket.

The peasants sacrificed lame children in honour of the celestial *blanket-holder*. If such propitiation did not result in the sewing-up of any chinks, at least it stopped new chinks from showing through.

A well-armed little colony had settled in this ignorant hinterland, calling themselves the 'Keepers of the Blanket's Hem'.

Spurious preachers began to declare that the peasants were going about matters in a foolish way by sacrificing crippled infants. Cripples! This was the reason why the night-blanket was tattered. From now on the peasants must offer to the Keepers a tithe of more mature, and physically intact, sons and daughters who had some pretence to comeliness. Parents who objected were torn apart as heretics. A new cult established itself over twenty years, its shrine being the domed town of the Keepers, which was built up against the entrance to caverns.

In the final confrontation Jaq and a company of Grey Knights had fought through savage ranks of cultists who all showed some mark of Chaos – a tentacle, a sting, tendrils instead of hair, suckers, claws; through to the warlock of the coven ensconced deep within the caverns where young captives whimpered piteously in cages.

That warlock was a bloated, horned hermaphrodite draped in bilious green skin. Oozing sexual orifices puckered his/her slumping belly. His/her long muscular tongue lashed and probed the air like a sense organ as if to supplement his/her tiny shrunken eyes. Plainly that tongue had other uses too.

Acrid musk saturated the air. Jewel-tipped stalactites hung from the cavern roof, aglow like many little lamps. The warlock likewise was aglow. His/her foul body shone phosphorescently as if lit from within; as if his/her flesh acted as a window to a lascivious light from elsewhere.

The warlock had once been human; now he/she mirrored the warp-form of the daemon which possessed and which had remoulded him/her.

He/she fought by projecting an obscene delirium of dizzying debauched desire. Even though psychic hoods shielded the Grey Knights, they were rocked. Despite all his own psychic training, Jaq felt twisted within. A lurid miasma dazed his vision.

Blasts from weapons went astray or were turned back to their sources so that the warlock seemed to be using his/her assailants as puppets to fight themselves.

Two Grey Knights died. But Jaq girded himself with his own tormented chastity and fired true, from psycannon and boltgun.

For a few moments more the warlock held his/her shape and Jaq almost despaired. Then the monstrous green body exploded like a balloon of filth, spattering the walls of the cavern and the cages of the cowering young prisoners – the last time he/she would set a mark upon them.

On his thigh Jaq wore that warlock's image in phosphorescent green.

Other daemons, which he confronted subsequently, had proved to be – if anything – even less appealing.

'The hydra isn't a daemon,' he murmured to himself. 'Yet how can it come from the warp, and not be steered ultimately by a Ruinous Power of the warp?'

The daemonological laboratories of the Ordo Malleus – its Chamber Theoretical – needed to know about this strange new entity. Jaq prayed that this Harlequin man might lead him to it.

GOOGOL SLOWED THE *Tormentum* to a virtual halt. The ship drifted in the sea of lost souls as the occupants of that bubble of reality stared at what the warp-scope showed.

A space hulk wallowed in the spangled spectral abyss, in thrall to the random currents of the warp; and it was there that *Veils of Light* had docked, slipping in to some gaping port.

The hulk wasn't one single derelict craft. The hulk was many, and more. It was a titanic conglomerate constructed by madmen, even by mad aliens too. The hulk might be ten thousand years old, so scoured, pockmarked and ancient did some parts appear.

Once, there must have been a single core-vessel which had lost its way or had lost the use of its warp-vanes so that it could no longer jump back into truespace.

Maybe its Navigator had died, his mind disrupted by daemonic intrusion. Maybe a warp storm had battered the ship and broken its warp-vanes when their runes failed.

The survivors must have tried to live out their lives by hook or by crook, descending into despair and lunacy, their offspring – if any – mutating into warp-monkeys.

Over the millennia, other wrecks and crippled vessels were welded to the first, in whole or in part, or were crashed into place in what became a vast assembly kilometres across and deep.

Many of these were deep-space vessels that never landed on worlds. Crenellated towers and buttressed spires jutted from the hulk as if a multiple collision had occurred between baroque flying castles.

The whole mass resembled, too, some jointed megawhale of metal which had sprouted metastasising cancers. Exotic cruciform antennae arose. Corbelled gargoyles bristled, as if spewing into the warp. Wrecked balustrades hung loose below stained-glass galleries. Heavily ornamented fins and flukes protruded. One pier intended for shuttles to dock at was studded with statues of dwarfs, another was embellished with runes. Weapons turrets were moulded in the shape of snarling wolves and savage lizards. A portal gaped: leering vermilion plasteel lips with bared ebon teeth each inscribed with golden texts. This portal was swallowing, or vomiting a fat endless worm...

Around the hulk clung the waxen coils of the hydra like some giant wreath of spilled intestines. Glassy tentacles delved through hatches and fissures. Tendrils rippled lazily in the warp current like weed in a stream. Some parts of the creature – hugely swollen parts – pulsed sluggishly, suggestive of disembowelled organs.

Other great sections of the entity hung almost loose, huge gobs of spittle on glassy strands. The hulk was vast; the hydra possibly vaster.

Jaq gave thanks to the Master of Mankind for their arrival.

Should he give thanks to Moma Parsheen too?

'Can you take us somewhat closer?' he asked Googol. 'Whilst steering clear of any dangling hydra?'

'Question is, will it steer clear of us, Jaq?'

'We'll find out. I spy a vacant cavity. Starboard top quadrant, see?'

Indeed. The hugging, questing, gelatinous limbs did not block all possible entrance into the multiple hulk.

As the Navigator nudged *Tormentum Malorum* slowly nearer to the indicated zone, using only attitude jets, for Jaq a strange intuition of security began to percolate through the dread engendered by hulk and warp alike. Tuning his psychic sense, he strove to analyse this feeling until he was virtually positive of its origin.

Once more the *Tormentum* hung almost motionless with respect to the convoluted crumpled cliffside of the hulk. A hundred metres of the emptiness-that-was-not still yawned, separating their ship from a ragged hole large enough to admit several armoured Terminator Marines abreast. Would that such were here!

Googol fretted. 'If we push closer than this, any sudden warp-eddy could impact us...'

'Here will do, then,' said Jaq. 'We can cross the remaining space in power suits.'

The Navigator's face blanched. 'You mean, leave the ship... at this point?'

The squat's teeth chattered momentarily. 'Er, boss, you aren't by any chance pro-pro-proposing warp-walking?'

'But that's an insane risk,' protested Googol. 'Things can materialise anywhere in the warp. Things I'd rather not try to name!'

'We'll be safe,' said Jaq. 'I'm picking up a powerful field of daemonic shielding from this hulk. The field spills out beyond. We're within the fringe. Daemon spawn won't be able to home in and manifest themselves. We can leave the shield of *Tormentum* in almost total confidence.'

Grimm hummed and hawed; he cleared his throat. 'That's what he tells us... You aren't, um, merely saying that to, um, jolly us on?'

'*Damnatio!*' swore Jaq. 'What sort of fool do you think I am?'

'Okay, okay, I believe you, lord. We'll be shielded.'

The fact that the hulk was protected against daemonic intrusion piqued Jaq's curiosity at the same time as it relieved his mind. For in that case how could daemons and evil have any connection with the hydra?

'Right,' said Googol. 'I withdraw my objection, which as a warp pilot I felt bound to register.' He affected a sigh. 'So I presume I'm obliged to stay with the ship.' He glanced Moma Parsheen's way. 'I've no desire to stay with her, though. My gaze can kill, but obviously not a blind woman. She's unreliable, tricky. I wouldn't even trust her under lock and key.'

Oh yes, Googol had been left safely in a locked room once; and he had been taken by surprise.

'Huh!' exclaimed Grimm. 'So you've decided to opt out of this little excursion, eh, Vitali? That's nice to know. Of course a chivalrous fellow such as yourself couldn't contemplate *shooting* that... parody of a living ancestor. If need be, if need be.'

'I do feel a profound antipathy to firing any type of gun inside a ship I'm piloting,' the Navigator said loftily.

Grimm's attitude to Moma Parsheen had altered drastically since she revealed her sabotage of Stalinvast's future.

'Do we have to be saddled with her?' demanded the little man. 'Is that it? While we fight our way through the coils? That doesn't make much sense.'

'You're to stay with *Tormentum*, Vitali, quite right,' confirmed Jaq. 'As to our astropath...'

Logic said that Jaq should execute her now – and quite justifiably too – for the murder of a world, for the sabotage of the Imperium. However, maybe Stalinvast still survived, and the *Tormentum Malorum* might yet leave the warp in time for him to compel the old woman to send a signal to save the situation. And even so, she deserved to die for attempted treason.

Meanwhile, here they stood, in effect discussing the advisability of killing Moma Parsheen. The astropath listened, wearing a faint rictus of a smile, and thinking who knew what. How could such a debate stimulate any sense of loyalty towards her travelling companions?

What sense of loyalty? Plainly she possessed none, except perhaps to her cat-creature far away, which she had condemned to death.

'I sense when warp portals open,' she remarked in Jaq's general direction. 'Your hydra is at least partly a thing of the warp, is it not?'

She wasn't pleading for her life. She was simply reminding Jaq of how she might continue to be useful.

'Besides,' she added, 'I presume you need to know *precisely* where Carnelian is within that great mass?'

If only Jaq could sense ordinary human *physical* presence at a distance, as some psykers could. The firefly of a psychic spirit gleaming in the nightscape of existence: ah, that he could pinpoint by and large. Exerting this sense, he encountered the fog of daemonic shielding which was hiding whosoever occupied the hulk.

'Are you sure you can still fix him clearly, astropath?' he demanded.

Moma Parsheen gazed blindly. 'Oh yes,' she said. 'I'm good at harking through warped spaces, very good. I'm not *looking* for him. I'm listening to the echo of my tracer.'

'Our astropath will accompany us,' Jaq said. If he could but consult his Tarot! Yet Carnelian might be alerted. Jaq dearly wished to surprise that man.

Meh'Lindi spoke up. 'We'll be wearing powered space armour all the time we're inside the hulk? That disposes of the problem of Parsheen's muscular atrophy.' Oh no, Meh'Lindi would not call the astropath Moma.

'Huh! Give a madwoman the strength of a tigress?'

'I presume, Grimm,' she said, 'you can gimmick her armour so that she can be switched off by any of us if she misbehaves?'

'No problem, lady.'

'I thought not! I could do so easily enough myself.'

'Do you suppose *thinking* of doing so requires true genius, huh? Oh damn it, I'm sorry. I bite my tongue. Give me ten minutes to insert a governor into Vitali's space gear.'

'Into *mine*?' protested the Navigator.

'Whose else do you think the hag'll wear? Did she bring her own spacesuit in that little satchel, shrunken by magic?'

'She has never worn such gear in her life.'

'You want rid of her, yet you don't want her to wear your suit.'

'No, I do not! She might taint it psychically. Interfere with the protection runes.'

Grimm chortled. 'Our inquisitor can exorcise and asperge and reconsecrate it afterwards.'

Obviously the squat didn't place much faith in any such techno-theological procedures, the efficacy of which was perfectly evident to Jaq and to most right-minded people. Still, the little man seemed somehow to get by. Unconsecrated, he certainly wouldn't survive in the warp!

'I will bless all our armour beforehand,' vowed Jaq. 'Triply so, when we are about to undertake a short swim in the sea of souls! I will seal and sanctify. You, Moma Parsheen, world-slayer, will lead us to Carnelian. We will surprise him, net him, wring the juice of confession out of him.'

Jaq thought of the collapsible excruciator that any inquisitor carried, to extort information from the unwilling. It had rarely been his style to use that instrument. Even though the device was righteous, he felt a certain repugnance towards it. Sometimes the whole galaxy seemed to reverberate with a sob of pain, a moan of anguish.

SOON JAQ AND Meh'Lindi were donning their stout suits of power armour and Grimm his smaller version of the same, while Googol disdainfully assisted Moma Parsheen into his own suit, his lips curled, as if he was packaging excrement.

Cuisses on to thighs... locking on to the hip girdle. Flared greaves on to shanks; magnetic boots locking into the greaves...

'*Benedico omnes armaturas*,' intoned Jaq. '*Benedico digitabula et brachiales, cataphractes atque pectorales.*'

Presently they were testing their sensor pick-ups, temperature regulators, air purificators...

TEN

LIKE FOUR BLACK-CARAPACED beetles decorated with protective runes, fluorescent red icons, and weapons pouches, Jaq and Meh'Lindi and little Grimm – who was tugging Moma Parsheen – jetted their way into a ruptured, cavernous hold. They hoped to maintain radio silence.

Junk of aeons hung aimlessly nearby: strange knobbly skulls of some humanoids reminiscent of irregular, cratered moonlets, an antique plasma gun half melted into slag, broken crates, and a buckled cage that was still confining a corpse dressed in a spotted leotard. A tumble of yellow silken hair suggested woman, though the long-exposed flesh was purple leather.

Their light beams played around the interior. Shadows jerked about. The corpse in the cage seemed to shift as if seeking release. In the deeps grim giant ghosts appeared to swell. This was all illusion.

Jaq carried on his suit a force rod, power axe and psycannon. The force rod, resembling some solid black flute embedded with enigmatic circuits, stored psychic energy so as to augment a psyker's mental attack. Unknown aliens had crafted all such force rods which had fallen into the hands of the Imperium, most notably the cache found in the ice-caverns of Karsh XIII. Impervious to any probing, a rod never needed or offered the possibility of any overhaul, so it was perhaps the least adorned of all weapons. By contrast, the shaft of Jaq's power axe was embossed with rococo icons, the pommel of that halberd was a brass ork skull, and complex purity seals embellished the power-pack to which a cable resembling a gem-serpent ran. The psycannon likewise was adorned with supernumerary ribs and moulded flanges painted with esoteric, exorcistic glyphs.

Jaq drew Meh'Lindi's attention to the bio-scanner in its filigreed, jade-studded frame. A blotch of green light registered the psychic throb of life deep in the interior of the hulk. However, his scanner was fogged by emanations from the aspect of the hydra that was alive, almost masking the trace.

That pocket of life was plainly still some distance away, yet it was apparent to Jaq that the instrument was attempting to distinguish more than the single sharp blip that would represent Carnelian alone.

He held up his gauntlet questioningly, opening five fingers once... then twice.

Meh'Lindi signalled another ten possible presences far ahead, in her opinion. Maybe more.

When Jaq turned up the gain on his sensor, static flooded it. Too much interference from the hydra. To his annoyance the sensitive instrument failed like a night-flower wilting in too bright a light. He muttered an invocation but the machine's soul had perished and did not revive.

Ever since entering the hulk, Jaq had been aware of daemonic shielding. While this relieved his mind in one regard – daemon spawn would be unable to home in and manifest themselves – the precaution piqued his curiosity afresh.

Jaq heartily disliked space hulks. It was well known how these sinister plasteel cadavers could house genestealer broods, adrift for centuries or millennia until a fluke of the warp vomited the derelict into truespace close to some vulnerable world.

Or they might shelter piratical degenerates who had become creatures of Chaos.

Loyal subjects of the Imperium always feared hulks. Imperial merchantmen traversing the warp would flee at the sighting of one. Space Marines were honour-bound to board a hulk, to cleanse any threat it posed, and to recover any valuable or enigmatic pieces of ancient technology from millennia earlier which might be encysted in the wreck like pearls held in a lethal clam.

Too often, the consequences of such boardings proved quite dire.

Where better, then, to hide the heart of some treacherous web of intrigue than in such a megavessel lost in the vastness of the warp, that all sane voyagers would shun?

The four intruders drifted through the hold. Half a dozen different black-mouthed corridors beckoned, angling away variously. Tentacles of the hydra protruded from two; stout soapy cables, undulating sluggishly.

Moma Parsheen pointed to a third, empty mouth. That direction corresponded with the earlier bearings for the green splotch of life signs.

HAD IT NOT been for the psychic tracer, they must surely have lost themselves in the labyrinthine entrails of what was not one vessel but many, some of these enormous in their own right.

They traversed sooty halls so crammed with long-dead machinery as to be mazes in themselves. They floated down dismal lift shafts; they mounted crazily angled corridors where friezes showed forgotten battles between impossible ships shaped like butterflies with wings of spectral energy. Other walls were gouged as if claws had ravaged them. Some walls glowed with runes.

Their lights picked out the graffiti of long-dead people – prayers, curses, obscenities, threats – and what might have been messages in alien script or in the calligraphy of madness. In one zone a drift of loose bones, kippered limbs, and dehydrated heads suggested cannibalism.

At last, a functioning airlock admitted them into a section where a breathable atmosphere survived, and warmth.

Survived? Ah no, thought Jaq. Where air and heat had been *restored*.

He raised his visor and breathed cautiously. Oxygen enough, a spike of ozone – and a hint of sensuous cloying patchouli, perhaps injected to mask the undertow of smouldering embers, as of charring insulation.

The others copied him, Grimm assisting Moma Parsheen.

'He's very close,' the astropath commented dully.

Through a plascrystal port they gazed upon a vast hazy hangar lit by the occasional glowstrip. *Veils of Light* was berthed there, tethered magnetically. So were six other starcruisers. One, shaped like a terrestrial shark; another like a rippy-fish; a third like the sting of a scorpion. Jaq looked in vain through a lens for identification marks, badges, or names. All the usual safety runes, of course. Otherwise, so far as he could see, the vessels were anonymous, identities concealed. Servitors – half-human, half-machine – rolled to and fro, stepped like spiders across the hulls on sucker pads. The haze in the hangar was exhaust gas expelled during docking.

That shark ship reminded him–

A speaker crackled to life.

'Welcome, Jaq Draco!' That was Carnelian's voice: part merry, part crazed. 'Congratulations! You're everything we hoped for.'

'Who is we?' Jaq shouted in response and promptly slammed his visor shut in case of gas attack. Meh'Lindi and Grimm followed his lead, and Meh'Lindi flipped the blind woman's visor shut too.

Jaq drew his power axe. The assassin and the abhuman both favoured laspistols at this point. In the gravityless environment of the hulk any unexploded bolts or similar projectiles could ricochet unpredictably for a long time within a confined space.

'All will be explained!' came the voice, now over their audio pickups. 'First, you must shed your armour and weapons. Especially, your assassin must divest herself of every tiny hidden trick. Except herself, of course! She's the funniest trick of all.' Carnelian giggled. 'Do it now. You're being scanned.'

Jaq switched on the magnetics in his boots to give him purchase for possible combat. Grimm and Meh'Lindi didn't need to be told to do likewise.

'Ah, you're rooted to the spot!' mocked the voice.

Moma Parsheen still floated blindly near the plascrystal port. Jaq gestured urgently ahead, and swung a boot forward.

At that very moment, from the air-gargoyles furthest away, fingers then arms of grey jelly erupted to interlace across the corridor. Behind the little party similar tentacles of hydra burst forth, blocking any retreat.

Jaq activated his power axe and strode forward. Meh'Lindi and Grimm flanked him, firing their lasers, slicing through the impeding arms.

Severed segments writhed and melted. Globules filled the air. Still more tentacles poured into the corridor – from every gargoyle now. The hydra's substance reformed and repaired itself, recoagulating and stiffening even as Jaq hewed with his power axe and as his companions lasered.

A force greater than magnetism gripped Jaq's feet. The floor was ankle-deep, knee-deep soon in viscid, melted and disjoined hydra which sought to set like glue. Jaq powered a boot free, then the boot was trapped once more.

Quite quickly the whole corridor filled to the brim with the substance of the hydra. Pressure mounted against Jaq's armour, and though the armour could withstand far greater stress before crumpling he could hardly move even under full power. Red tell-tales blinked as he exerted himself.

Rather than overload the suit's resources, he relaxed. The power axe, clenched in his mailed fist, still hewed away at the same small area in front of him, but for the life of him he couldn't push himself into the space it liquefied, nor could he shift the weapon to left or to right, so firmly was his arm held by the hydra.

All he could see was tough grey jelly plastered across his visor. He felt such a writhing impotence. He was outguessed. Paralysed. Though nothing as yet had touched his flesh, he was a titbit trapped in stiffest aspic.

So were they all.

'Cease fire, if you can,' he radioed to his invisible companions. 'We may only hurt ourselves.'

As he strove to release his grip on the control of the power axe, so the jelly appeared to co-operate. It slackened, then tightened once again as soon as the axe was inactive.

Presently, Jaq felt the fingers of his gauntlet being forced apart; and his axe was lifted away. Soon after, he realised with a chill in his groin that something was opening the clasps of his suit.

Those cold touches of steel! He realised that a servitor was stripping him of his armour and removing all detectable weapons. The robotic thing was working within the substance of the hydra and with its apparent complicity.

Recalling how Meh'Lindi had been violated on that other occasion, Jaq feared for her sanity once her psychic hood was removed. Yet he also hoped that she might retain some weapon, hidden in a hollow tooth perhaps.

When Jaq's helmet lifted clear, the hydra did not flow up against his face to suffocate him.

'Can you hear me?' he cried.

Only centimetres from his eyes and mouth, the hydra blurred and soaked up his voice so that he seemed to be shouting underwater.

Yet soon the glutinous entity was withdrawing far from his head, allowing him to see it squeezing portion by portion back into the ventilation system. He still couldn't move. Burly, fearsome servitors held all four of the intruders inflexibly.

The machines were hideous parodies of the human form, their metal casings and flanges moulded so that the robots seemed to be sculptures made of bones welded together, interspersed with flattened, grimacing skulls. Each sported two flails of sinuous steel tentacles and a crab-like claw. The sensors of their faces were indented into a snarling, tusked daemon mask.

Finally, save for inchoate puddles adhering to the floor and the walls, the hydra was all gone.

'What a deal of nuisance we could all have saved ourselves,' remarked Carnelian's voice. 'And now, dear guests, it's party time.'

These disconcerting servitors slid on magnetised feet along the corridor, carrying their prisoners suspended weightlessly. Suits and weapons remained adrift. At least Jaq and the others hadn't been stripped naked. Only Grimm bothered to wriggle and kick.

IN THE VAULTED auditorium to which they were carried, a score and a half of robed figures sat around a horseshoe of data-desks. The robes were of black or crimson velvet – over body armour – and all of those seated at the desks wore identical long masks.

Thirty mock-Emperors regarded the prisoners through tinted lenses; for those masks mimicked the shrivelled features of the Master of Mankind, including some of the tubes and wires which sustained that living corpse.

Only the capering Carnelian showed his true, mischievous face. He was wearing a domino costume of black spots on white on his left side, white spots on black on his right. His high collar was white and fluted. His black half-cloak swirled as he turned to display himself. Magnetic shoes, studded with pearls, were pointy and golden in hue. On his head, a gilded tricorne hat. What a lethal, sly fop the man was.

'In the Emperor's name,' said Jaq. 'You, who mock the Emperor–'

'Be quiet,' growled a voice. 'We *are* of the Emperor. We do His bidding.'

'Hiding here in the warp? Manipulating a creature of the warp?'

One of the pretend Emperors hauled off his mask abruptly. That triforked ginger beard! Those bristling eyebrows!

Shock coursed through Jaq. 'Harq Obispal!'

Yet of course: that shark ship…

The ruthless inquisitor roared with laughter, steel teeth showing amongst his ivories.

'Ostentation can be a mask too, Jaq Draco! A brazen display can distract attention from the true purpose. Though you cannot deny that Stalinvast needed cleansing of its parasites! Ah, those convenient genestealers…'

Obispal's gaze drifted towards Meh'Lindi, and he frowned as if adding the final piece to a puzzle which had been perplexing him, but not liking the pattern that he saw.

Did Obispal's associates realise that the rashly rampaging inquisitor was only present in this auditorium courtesy of Jaq's assassin who had plucked him to safety? Jaq smiled at the impassive Meh'Lindi, blessing her impetuous intervention in that arcade in Vasilariov.

'Hear me, inquisitor ordinary,' he said. 'Obey me. I am of the Malleus.'

Obispal grinned. 'I know full well. What else could you be, snooping on my activities?'

Jaq pressed his advantage, however slim. 'It's as well that I was, otherwise you'd be dead now, torn apart by genestealers, wouldn't you be?'

Several masked figures stirred. One asked, 'Is this true?' Even Carnelian registered surprise.

'It's accurate enough,' allowed Obispal, 'though by that stage my death wouldn't have made a whit of difference to the outcome. I was merely somewhat incautious at one point. One risks one's life for the Emperor always, blessed be His name.' The man's tone was dismissive, and Jaq had to allow him more credit for flexibility than he would have supposed.

'Still,' hissed another mask, 'it would have been a shame to lose so bold a partner in this enterprise of ours; and of His Supremacy's. Recruiting suitable candidates is a delicate business. Which brings us to yourself, Jaq Draco–'

Further around the horseshoe, a voice which struck Jaq as familiar asked him: 'Draco, what is the greatest need in this galaxy?'

Jaq replied immediately: 'The need for control.'

'So let me tell you about our Emperor's hopes for the fullest possible form of control...' The owner of that voice pulled off his mask.

Jaq felt stunned anew. For the man looking at him through one natural eye and a lens in the socket of his other eye, the silver-haired man with a scar bisecting his cheek, to which he had sewn rubies so that the long-healed wound seemed still to gleam with blood – was none other than Baal Firenze.

'Proctor!' Jaq sketched a minor adoration of respect. 'You sent me to Stalinvast–'

'And you have been more quick-witted than even I expected.' Firenze nodded towards Jaq's companions. 'Let's have some total privacy, Zephro.'

Carnelian produced null-sense hoods and proceeded to fit these over Grimm's head, and Moma Parsheen's. Dartingly as a lizard's tongue he kissed Meh'Lindi on the side of the brow before plunging her, too, into silence and blindness.

'As you know, Draco,' resumed the proctor, 'there is an outer order of the Inquisition, and there is an inner order. And then there is the Ordo Malleus – with its Hidden Masters. Within the ranks of those Hidden Masters exists a secret, innermost conclave founded in recent centuries by the Emperor himself, answerable to no one else, and now here in session. This most secret group is the Imperial Order of the Hydra. Its main tool is, of course, the hydra. Its long-term purpose is none other than the total control of all human minds throughout the galaxy.'

And Proctor Firenze proceeded to explain the plan that motivated this cabal of Hidden Masters gathered there in the hulk.

WAS IT AN hour later? Jaq still reeled at the grandeur and abomination of the enterprise.

Some twenty of the cabalists had removed their masks by now, as if in earnest of good faith. Jaq knew none by sight – unless they had been surgically altered; nevertheless he could perceive that they were true-human, no marks of Chaos blemishing their features. He would know those faces again.

Eight others retained their incognitos. Cloaked in crimson, those were the High Masters of the Hydra. Jaq detected psychic strength of the utmost degree, yet no taint of daemonic pollution. This was undoubtedly human business.

Obispal was a member of this very special Ordo. So too had Jaq now sworn to become. He had repeated his oaths dully like a sleeptalker. One of those oaths bound him never to return to Terra, never to revisit the headquarters of the Inquisition, nor the even more elusive bastion of the Ordo Malleus.

In return Jaq had received a new electro-tattoo, imprinted on to his right cheek by Carnelian. The design was of a squirming octopus clinging round a living human head. All of those present who had shed their masks activated their own identical tattoos then willed the image to vanish again.

So it transpired that the elusive Zephro Carnelian was a trusted roving agent for the Ordo Hydra. Not an enemy at all – but an ally in the greatest, most righteous, yet perhaps also the vilest of plans.

Jaq now had custody of portions of the hydra packed in an adamantium stasis-trunk fitted with coded locks. When in future he removed coils of tentacle to seed the guts of the worlds he visited, so – he was assured – the entity would replenish itself, stasis notwithstanding, since the Chaos that underlay the universe connected the hydra together subtly, no matter how scattered its parts.

'I have no further questions,' Jaq finally told the conclave.

'Unhood those useful iotas, then,' Firenze instructed Carnelian.

Meh'Lindi, Grimm, Moma Parsheen: *iotas*, mere jots, tiny ciphers in the vastness of the Imperium and in the huge insidious scheme of the cabalists. Jaq, for his part, wondered whether he too was merely an iota, or had genuinely been promoted to become a moulder of destiny.

Even with rejuvenations it seemed highly unlikely that any of those present could possibly live long enough to experience – to *enjoy* seemed totally the wrong word – the fruits of the hydra enterprise. Unless those eight masked High Masters were sufficiently confident in their associates to try to journey to the next galaxy and back – in some incredible megaship – to take advantage of time-compression! Or to place themselves in stasis for centuries on end? Unless they dared to absent themselves from the slow unfolding of the plan – would not their keen minds continue to be needed?

Therefore the scheme must indeed be altruistic and unselfish, without personal benefit to those who were currently involved. This must indeed be a scheme for salvation in the long term: salvation through utter enslavement.

Carnelian unhooded Jaq's companions, re-admitting noise and light to their senses.

Held motionless in zero gravity by the servitors with no input of information whatever, the three had been undergoing sensory deprivation for the past hour. Grimm dribbled like a happy baby. Meh'Lindi wore a mildly blissful smile which vanished as she came alert again. Moma Parsheen cried out as she sensed environment flooding back, the way that sensation needles through a frozen limb. For the first time in her life, perhaps, the astropath had been psychically blind as well as visually so; utterly isolated.

'It's great that you arrived here, Jaq,' enthused Zephro Carnelian as he folded away the hoods. 'Without wishing to expose myself to obloquy, as you exposed friend Harq before we all became colleagues–'

Obispal guffawed, though there was a sour note to his humour.

'–would you mind confirming exactly how you distinguished yourself by finding us? Purely for the record?'

Surely the Harlequin man must have guessed?

'For the record,' said Jaq, 'it was an astropath trace. A homer in your mind.'

'Ah, ah, of course. Inserted *when*?'

'Don't worry, it'll decay within a few days.'

'*When exactly*?'

Didn't the man know? Hadn't Jaq virtually been led here by Carnelian?

'Why, it was when you transmitted your goading holo into Voronov-Vaux's sanctum, through the spy-flies you stole from me.'

'Ah! The biter, bit. The spy, spied on. That would be just after you decided not to declare *exterminatus* after all... I guess your *exterminatus* decision was really what clinched my respect for your ability to think on a grand scale, Jaq. Be damned if we didn't hope you would simply call in the Space Marines and spread our hydra around some more! Yet no, you think in ultimates. And that is excellent. We need ultimate thinking in the Ordo Hydra, Jaq. So: no harm done and no hard feelings.'

'Except perhaps on the part of the whole population of Stalinvast,' Jaq commented acidly.

Carnelian froze. 'You didn't send the *exterminatus* message, Jaq. As soon as the hydra began withdrawing, you changed your mind.'

Jaq nodded towards the astropath. 'She still sent it. Of her own accord.'

For a few brief moments Carnelian's face might have been that of a polymorphine shape-shifter viewed at speed, passing through absurdly accelerated transformations. For a few instants only, until he laughed.

Carnelian rounded on Moma Parsheen, laughing. And still laughing, he plucked a laspistol from his belt and shot her through one of her blind eyes, boiling her brain.

ELEVEN

'OH NO, WE can't tolerate an astropath who puts homers into people's heads. Not when you consider the calibre of people who are collected here. Oh nil and nunquam and nullity. In a word, no.'

Thus had Carnelian swiftly explained his shooting of the old woman.

REUNITED WITH THEIR space armour and weapons, Jaq and Meh'Lindi and Grimm were escorted through the eerie maze of the hulk by the savage servitors. Grimm towed the Navigator's weightless empty suit along behind him, and Jaq manoeuvred the adamantium trunk. At the hold where all the alien skulls floated, the automatons left the trio.

Out to *Tormentum Malorum* they jetted, only to be greeted with scepticism by the Navigator ensconced inside.

'Come on, open up,' said Grimm. 'You've locked the airlock.'

'Aha,' came Googol's response over the radio, 'but you may say you are those same three people inside those suits...'

'What's this,' asked Jaq, 'a fit of warp-psychosis? It's us who untied you back in the Emerald Suite. Remember?'

'Aha, but if you are my enemies you'll know about that. Because you would have tied me up.'

'If you don't open up, Vitali,' said Meh'Lindi, 'lovely lady of death will steal away your breath and mock your bones and squeeze your heart and all the rest of it.'

Could a radio wave blush? 'Ah, right, yes,' came Vitali's voice, and the airlock cycled.

* * *

Now THAT THEY were safely back aboard, minus an astropath but plus one locked stasis-trunk, the Harlequin man's excuse for shooting Moma Parsheen failed to satisfy Jaq.

'Was it your impression,' he asked Meh'Lindi, 'that Carnelian was performing a lightning calculation as to whether we might stand any chance of still saving Stalinvast if we jumped back into normal space?'

'Huh, fat chance of saving the planet now,' interrupted Grimm. 'He shot our message service. Was that his idea?'

'It's my impression,' said Meh'Lindi slowly, 'he may have decided there was no hope whatever for Stalinvast. That we'd be too late.' Her tone said that she still loathed the Harlequin man, yet she felt compelled to be accurate.

Jaq agreed. 'I think the news filled him, just for a moment, with grief and rage. I think he cared about the murder of a world.'

'Makes sense,' said the squat, 'if he was hoping to use Stalinvast as a playground for his bally hydra.'

'No, it was a deeper caring than that. He visited... justice, true justice upon Moma Parsheen. For a moment he was a billion people seeking some slight recompense for the waste of their lives.'

So therefore the Ordo Hydra genuinely was a caring organisation. Ruthless and totalitarian, of necessity, yet also in the long run cherishing the human race, although it must needs manacle the minds of men; absolutely, as never before.

Alas for this interpretation, Baal Firenze had reacted with apparent amusement to the revelation that Stalinvast had indeed been flushed down the sink of history. With Stalinvast gone, any remaining evidence of the kindling of the hydra had been obliterated; and Jaq would need to think up an almighty lie to exonerate the command he gave, should official query ever reach him. Which it might not... for twenty years, or more. (In a galaxy of a million worlds!) Jaq would be well advised to steer well clear of Earth until the end of his days and serve the Ordo Hydra loyally. Should he do so – as he had sworn – why, his proctor would of course rubber-stamp the eradication of Stalinvast...

'What went on while we were hooded, lord?' the squat asked. 'And what's in that trunk?'

'What is in the trunk is utterly secret,' Jaq said sternly.

'Just thought it might be something tasty to eat. Pickled grox tongues, for instance. A going-away gift.'

'Maybe it's a bigger, crueller rack, little fellow!' Jaq snapped.

'Sorry, inquisitor. I'm the right size for me already.'

'Then stay that way.'

'Where do we transport it to?' asked Googol.

'Don't concern yourself about it at all, Vitali. I shall lock it away. Erase all memory of it. Where to next? Obviously some world in need of scrutiny.'

As JAQ LAY in his sleep-cell at quarter-light with the trunk sealed in the nearby oubliette, he recalled all that he had learned at the conclave.

That cabal had created the hydra after long research in covert theological laboratories located on the frozen fringe of some barren solar system unclaimed by either the Imperium or by aliens.

Guided by the Emperor's own harsh wisdom and foresight, they had experimented on the very stuff of Chaos and upon slaves permanently immobilised in nutrient vats, and upon prisoners.

The result was a multiform entity against which normal weapons were useless.

However, the hydra's material manifestation was only the tip of the iceberg. When mature, each hydra – all part of the same hydra – would sporulate psychically, infesting human minds planet-wide, while all body traces would melt away. The hydra's psychic spores would remain dormant in human brains for untold generations, passed from parent to child.

'Our aim,' Baal Firenze had explained, 'is to seed the hydra on innumerable human worlds. On the majority. On all. We hope each hydra might escape detection during the period while it grows to maturity – or only be detected by riff-raff, whom no one in power will heed. A vain hope, obviously! Yet let it be detected, let it! *Nihil obstat*, as we say. Eradication programmes by planetary governors or by ordinary inquisitors will seem to succeed yet will simply enlarge the span and final influence of the hydra. Even Malleus men who aren't privy to our secret will only scatter the hydra in their zeal, and then subsequently lack all proof or comprehension of what occurred.'

'Zeal short of *exterminatus*,' Jaq had reminded the proctor.

'Agreed. If nothing remains alive on a world, why then, nothing can be controlled. I warrant there will be few such instances of *exterminatus*. A minuscule percentage.'

Control was the watchword. The hydra would obey the thoughts of its makers. Ultimately the spores of the entity would pervade all of humanity, to which it vectored by design. Eventually the Masters of the Ordo Hydra would activate those psychic spores. These would sprout: tiny hydras in the heads of trillions of people, all linked subtly through the medium of the warp.

Whereupon those masters – the self-proclaimed servants of the Emperor – could control the entire human species galaxy-wide, almost instantaneously.

Jaq had already witnessed, and Meh'Lindi had experienced, how the hydra could be used to invade the pleasure centres of the brain. The pain centres likewise.

'In chosen instances,' Firenze had revealed, 'the total human population of the galaxy will be compelled to function as one mighty mind. Its combined psychic power will be vast enough to scour away all alien life forms and to purge the warp of malign entities. If our Emperor's Astronomican is a lighthouse shining through the warp, this new linked mind will be a flamethrower.'

A SMALL CABAL would control all the minds of men and women for ever more. Able to twist them, direct them, fill them with ecstasy, or torment them. But mainly: to *focus* them collectively, whithersoever the cabal chose.

'This,' the proctor had concluded, 'will be the Emperor's legacy and greatest achievement. No doubt you know he is failing – just as the Imperium is failing, slowly and haphazardly, but failing nonetheless. His Supremacy will leave behind him a cosmic creature which a group of utterly dedicated masters can operate.

'Farewell, then, to daemons when we tap all human psychic potential simultaneously. Farewell to the Powers of the warp.

'Farewell to vicious genestealers and to sly eldar and to vicious pillaging orks. Farewell to the hordes of tyranids like locusts, to all aliens and their mocking, inhuman heresy.

'But most of all, farewell to all the excesses of Chaos – flayed and tamed by the human multi-mind at last!'

A grand and dire vision indeed. And Jaq would spread the hydra far and wide. As he lay musing in his sleep-cell, doubts assailed him.

If he tried to return to Terra in defiance of his oath he strongly suspected that he might never be allowed to reach the homeworld. Surely he would be watched for several years, to ensure his fidelity.

Yet, what *guarantee* did he have that the Emperor was actually the begetter of the hydra project? A project so covert that most Hidden Masters of the Ordo Malleus itself remained ignorant of it! How could the God-Emperor have sanctioned such a plan, if the human race were ever to achieve the destiny he had dreamed of for it? One of eventual freedom and fulfilment? Would the hydra eventually wither away spontaneously? Or had the Emperor... despaired of his dream?

In which case, the core of everything was rotten.

The Emperor, popularly supposed to be immortal, only endured by virtue of adamantine, anguished courage and willpower. The seemingly potent forces of his Imperium were stretched as thin as strands of spider-silk in a giant galactic web which was mostly vacant space. Strands of a cobweb are surprisingly strong but they can snap. When too many snap, the whole web collapses into a sticky mess.

Might the object of ultimate attack by the controlled mass-brain of humanity be the Emperor himself? The sick spider at the heart of the web? Thus leaving the descendants of the cabal in charge of the Imperium?

How could Jaq know for sure?

Those gruesome servitors which had restrained the trio – and the astropath – reminded Jaq so strongly of images he had viewed of traitor legionnaires, the polluted renegades spawned by the would-be Emperor-slayers of long ago who now lurked in a certain terrible, twisted zone of the galaxy...

His door slid aside.

Meh'Lindi slipped silently into his cell and shut the door. Outlined in the dim light, she was such a menacingly poised silhouette that Jaq's hand closed on the needle-gun under his pillow.

'Pardon me, inquisitor,' she murmured. She moved no closer. No doubt she was aware of the gun.

'Are you somebody else's person?' he asked. 'Did Carnelian change your allegiance? Did he make you his?'

'No... Only yours. And mine own. And the Emperor's.'

'Why are you here?'

'You need solace, Jaq, relief from burdens. I need a different kind of exorcism to free me from what he did to me. While I was hooded I was dreaming of how to accomplish this. To kill him seems forbidden now, does it not? I must regard him as... an ally?'

'True. And you wish to know why. Exactly why.'

'No, I don't need to know why. I'm your instrument. You're the commander of death; I'm death's agent.'

She crept forward and reached out a hand with no digital weaponry on the fingers... though even her naked fingers could kill. She touched him lingeringly.

'Solace, Jaq. For you, for me. Your mind is troubled by impossible contradictions.'

Jaq's heart beat faster. 'Then one must purge those contradictions. Only the Emperor's way is true. We should pray.'

'Pray to be shown *which* true way is the truly true way? If you'll pardon me, I have a better idea. Am I not your mistress in masquerade... trader? The others won't know. And if they do discern, why, Grimm will only grunt, "Huh" while Vitali may compose a forlorn ode. Privately Vitali will feel relieved that his yearning can finally be classed as hopeless – that he need not spur himself recklessly to act in regard to me; and maybe die as a result.

'You're at a cusp of decision, Jaq. But you do not possess... perspective, to perceive which way to leap. I offer a different perspective than prayer.'

She gestured towards the hulk which hung outside *Tormentum Malorum*.

'Those new masters of yours will not expect you to adopt this perspective. They will expect you to bottle up your inner uncertainty, whatever it is about. And so to stifle it. They will expect *purity* to drive you onward. Be impure with me for a while. And seek your light.'

Slowly she began to strip off her clingtight black tunic, and so to become more visible. Soon she was tracing all his tattoos and he her scars.

As HE LAY beside her later, exalted and still alive, he thought of how he had previously denied himself this ecstasy.

Ah but no! Rather – for years – he had denied himself banality, as if disbelieving in the possibility of such physical transcendence. Truly, an assassin's body was well trained. Maybe she could have surfeited him with pleasure as surely as she could have overwhelmed him with agony. And his ecstasy had soon become her ecstasy, an electrochemical fuel that had ignited in her, burning away all the taint of that earlier false frenzy enforced on her by the Harlequin man.

'Meh'Lindi–'

'It can only happen this once,' she murmured.

'Yes, I realise.' He knew that. 'After climbing the highest peak, who would seek foothills?'

'I know what I see from my peak, Jaq. I see myself again: lady of death. I am purged of corruption.'

'With which Carnelian had infected you... Why did he do that to you? Why did he use pleasure as a weapon?'

From Jaq's own high peak, in his state of exalted altered consciousness, what did he see?

'Perhaps,' he said, 'Carnelian was sending you – and therefore me – two messages in one. Firstly, that if he could do so, he would rather bring joy than pain. Which is why he shot Moma Parsheen, in sheer rejection of her bitter vengeance.'

'And secondly?'

'Secondly, that the human mind can be utterly controlled by the users of the hydra. That message, delivered to you in Kefalov, may not have been a boast but a warning. Meh'Lindi, I need to confide what I learned in that conclave.'

ONCE JAQ HAD finished explaining all about the hydra project, she said, 'Zephro Carnelian must be a double agent. He's working for the Ordo Hydra, but also subtly against them. What he did to me... that was to show us how total a tyranny was being planned, so that I – so that we – would loathe it. Why do that unless he's secretly opposed? If we're right, he also loathed the complete destruction of Stalinvast – even though he co-operated with Obispal in kindling the hydra, a task that cost millions of lives.'

'So who else does he represent?'

'Are those High Masters human, Jaq?'

Jaq nodded. 'Yet maybe *they* obey hidden masters elsewhere, who may not be quite so human. Truly, the universe is a skein of lies, deceits, and traps.'

'Carnelian has shown a perverse attraction to you too, Jaq. Did he deliberately draw himself to your attention merely to involve you in this new Ordo – or because he hopes you might lance the boil of a conspiracy without him needing to show his own hand? While he pretends to foster it loyally all the while so as to stay in contact with it?'

'I don't know... Those servitors: they were like some suits used by traitor legionnaires corrupted by Chaos. You could almost employ such automatons as emissaries – or couriers – to the Eye of Terror itself... And where else could the hydra really have been spawned? Where else? In some great covert laboratory orbiting the outermost ball of frozen rock in some uncharted system? Am I supposed to believe that story?'

'The Eye of Terror, Jaq?' Did Meh'Lindi shudder beside him? Was even she appalled at the prospect he was unfolding? He stroked her again, while he still could do so.

The Eye of Terror... That great dust-nebula hid within it dozens of hellish solar systems which witnessed no stars, but only rippling rainbow auroras forever a-dance.

The legions of those who betrayed the Emperor during the Horus Rebellion had fled to the Eye and thereafter... had mutated vilely. For the Eye was a zone where truespace and the warp actually overlapped, braiding together in nightmare distortions.

Where else could an entity composed of blended matter and immaterium really have been conceived and forged but in the Eye?

Could the cabal be a conspiracy against the Emperor and *against all humankind* mounted by the denizens of the Eye, by those twisted bitter enemies of the Imperium?

Not a secret master plan on the part of the Emperor – but a dagger aimed at his heart? And at all human hearts?

'For us to head for the Eye of Terror would be to invite almost certain death,' mused Jaq. 'From the cabal, first of all. Even more so, from the twisted creatures that flourish in the Eye.'

Meh'Lindi gripped his hand. 'No, Jaq, that is not the way to think about this. One does not *invite* death. That is the way of fools and failures who plunge to their own destruction because a part of them has despaired and wishes to die. Thus doom accepts their invitation.

'Think rather that I am the lady of death and that you are the master of death! The Eye of Terror invites death into its own house. It invites *us* – as if calling upon a godly power which is its superior.'

'Aye, to blaspheme against it vigorously and violently, and consume it if it can.' Jaq sighed. 'We could simply flee.'

He was voicing a desire which he feared might only bring him Meh'Lindi's contempt – so soon after she had honoured and anointed him with her body. Yet this needed to be said. Flight was a possible avenue and he must not overlook any of their options.

'We could try to drop out of sight on some far world. We could defect to some alien civilization which might understand the hydra. We could seek exile on an eldar craftworld.'

'Indeed,' she agreed. 'The eldar should be grateful to know about this weapon which would one day be launched against them.'

'Long before the hydra could be activated we would have ended our days amidst aliens – or on some wild frontier world. Why, the galaxy is so vast that in the latter case I could continue to pose – and behave – as an inquisitor; though I would truly be a renegade...'

Even as he spoke, this avenue closed up in his mind's eye like a pupil contracting to a black point. That was why he had voiced this craven option; so as to witness it vanishing.

A different, vaster, sickly eye was staring at him and daring him: the glowing nebulosity where space and unspace wove together.

'No, we must go to the Eye to investigate,' he murmured.

If they survived, why, Jaq must then go to Earth to ask for guidance.

That undertaking would be fraught with enormous peril too. For they could trust nobody. Except themselves.

'Jaq–'

'Hmm?'

'Before one travels among people who are diseased, it's wise to seek an inoculation against their diseases. Before going amongst outlandish strangers, it may be sensible to camouflage oneself. In Carnelian's hands I was vulnerable to the hydra...'

'What are you proposing?'

She told Jaq, and he almost retched.

THE ADAMANTIUM TRUNK yawned open, the glassy coils lying immobile within.

Meh'Lindi had injected herself with the polymorphine. Now she recited sing-song invocations in a language Jaq had never heard before.

She flexed herself, she breathed spasmodically as if to confuse the natural rhythms of her body.

Jaq muttered prayers. '*Imperator, age. Imperator, eia. Servae tuae defensor...*'

Meh'Lindi reached into the trunk and lifted out a small tentacle, which squirmed as it left the stasis-field. Then she sank her teeth into that flesh which was not flesh.

Hastily she bit gobbets loose and swallowed them, bolting down a dreadful and disgusting feast. Those lips, which had so recently roved over Jaq's body, now sucked in the slithery tough stuff of the hydra with the same seeming hunger.

How could she do so without vomiting? The strength of her jaw, the blades of her teeth!

'It's nothing,' she mumbled, catching his expression. 'I was weaned on jungle-slugs. Our mothers squeezed them. Proteins and juices pop into the baby's mouth. The baby sucks until the slug is dry...'

Her foul meal completed, she sat cross-legged and concentrated, brow furrowed. This time, she wasn't metamorphising her own body by will power. In ways Jaq did not understand, she was studying and altering and neutralising the dissolving contents of her stomach, immunising herself to those through the mediation of the polymorphine.

After a long while she belched several times, then said, 'Maybe I'll be more resistant now. Carnelian won't play that trick on me again. Ever.'

Jaq gazed into the trunk. Where the consumed tentacle had rested a mist seemed to be congealing out of nothing as though the hydra was already replenishing itself. The immaterium did not heed all the laws of stasis. The entity remained inert within the trunk yet could still restore what was taken.

'Do you suppose that Carnelian and the cabal can have eaten this same terrible meal?' asked Jaq. 'Do you feel you can control – command – the hydra now, yourself? The way Carnelian does?'

Meh'Lindi brooded, then shook her head.

'I'm not a psyker,' she said. 'Immunity will satisfy me. Maybe if...'

'If I was to eat some too?'

'No, I don't think you should. You have never trained with polymorphine. You have never altered your flesh. It's a hard skill. We have no idea what rituals Carnelian may have used, if indeed he digested a meal of this stuff.'

Jaq felt profoundly glad that he had never studied in the Callidus Temple of Assassins.

'Maybe later I'll learn how,' he said. 'Meanwhile, let's wake the others. We'll leave right away. We'll sail to the Eye. And... thank you, Meh'Lindi.'

'My pleasure. Literally.'

TWELVE

TWELVE

THE EYE WAS five thousand light years distant from the area of truespace corresponding to that hulk adrift in the warp. Fifteen days warp-time, as it turned out.

Meanwhile, perhaps two years would have passed by in the real universe.

Stalinvast would long have been a scorched husk, its jungles rotted utterly by the life-eater, then cremated by firegas, only the plasteel skeletons of its empty cities towering above the barren desolation, dead reefs above a dried-out sea. Many cities would most likely have collapsed into tangled, fused ruins when the firegas exploded planet-wide. There would be not an atom of oxygen left in the now poisonous atmosphere; that too would have burned.

Jaq grieved for Stalinvast and dreamed of that holocaust.

As TORMENTUM MALORUM flew closer to the Eye, the warp grew turbulent, buffeting the ship. Googol navigated with grim concentration, dodging eddies which could pitch them light years off course, maelstroms which could trap them into an endless Moebius circuit until they starved, until even their bones became dust.

At times the beacon of the Astronomican was eclipsed. At other times writhing knots in the fabric of the warp smeared the Emperor's signal across a swathe of unspace so that its actual location became problematic.

Googol's third eye ached. Grimm chanted the names of ancestors by way of a lifeline to the more reliable external cosmos far from the Eye.

Meh'Lindi experienced nauseous tides within herself, which she quelled by means of meditation. Jaq felt the first nibblings of concentrated Chaos, Chaos blended with reality, Chaos with an evil purpose. Praying devoutly, he expunged these.

Finally, as they entered the fringes of the Eye, the Astronomican vanished utterly from Googol's awareness. But he had already fixed on the shadows of a dozen of the star systems that lurked within the great nebulosity, the imprint of the mass and energy of those suns upon the shifting, bubbling warp. Fingers dancing over a console, he conjured the pattern of these images holographically.

Jaq matched these traces with a holo-chart from the records of his Ordo, as stored in the ship's brain. Periodically the Inquisition sent screened nullships bristling with sensors racing through the nebula, probeships bearing psyker adepts who could spy on the madness of those who roosted on the cursed worlds within. Even the most loyal, best trained psykers might crumble under the assault of daemonic imagery. Traitor legionnaires could ambush such ships. Or the vessels would succumb to natural hazards. Yet some crumbs of information were retrieved.

'Where to, Jaq?' asked the Navigator. 'To which damned star?'

Jaq unwrapped his Tarot from the mutant skin. He laid down the High Priest card. The wafer of liquid crystal rippled as if static was disrupting it. Small wonder. The Emperor's influence was only negative within the Eye. Jaq wouldn't be surprised if all the cards he dealt were reversed. His face frowned back at him from the High Priest card, riven by stress.

He prayed, he breathed, and dealt.

Behind him... was the Harlequin of Discordia, reversed. Once again the figure which ought to have worn an eldar mask displayed instead the quizzical, impish features of Zephro Carnelian. Inertly so; immobile, frozen.

Accompanying Jaq... was the Daemon, a sinister, almost squid-like entity. Of course. And it too was reversed. Reversal might signify its defeat – unless the proximity of malevolent Chaos had turned the card around.

Impeding Jaq... was a warped renegade of Discordia. Likewise reversed. Which might portend the thwarting of such foes of the Imperium. Or, in the circumstances, might not. Jaq couldn't interpret clearly.

He dealt the last two cards.

And these were magical to such a degree that Jaq once more felt truly guided.

The Galaxy trump sparkled with stars. A starfish of billions of suns turned slowly, arms wrapped around itself, at once milk and diamond. In this grandeur the Eye of Terror was but a tiny flaw. The Galaxy card faced Jaq, affirmatively.

The final card was also positive. It was the Star trump. A naked woman – Meh'Lindi – knelt as she filled a pitcher from a pool in a rocky desert landscape. One intense blue star hung overhead. Arrayed around that first star seven other stars of varying degrees of brightness formed a trapezium pattern.

A pattern which matched Googol's holo; a pattern which framed that one particular blue sun.

This was a true astro-divination.

In spite of the tides of Chaos, the Emperor's spirit – enshrined in these cards – was still with Jaq.

'We steer towards the blue star, Vitali.'

The cards squirmed.

In the Galaxy, black threads spread like instant rot. From the pool where Meh'Lindi knelt, glassy tentacles surged. Spiked plants sprouted. The sky rained severed eyeballs that burst on the thorns. The Harlequin smirked and flourished a laspistol. Behind him, venomous figures capered, part scorpion, part human.

Jaq's own card began to simmer.

Hastily he flipped all the cards over to break the Tarot trance just in case – though this must surely be impossible! – a tiny bolt of energy might burst forth from the Harlequin man's gun and strike Jaq physically.

Averting his eyes he shuffled the pack, randomising it; recased and wrapped it.

'Carnelian is hunting us,' Jaq said. 'The cabal know I'm disobeying them.'

If Jaq's Tarot could so soon seem to turn against him, could the beatific divination have been true? Or were the cards warning him wisely into the bargain?

'Those cards are bugged,' said Grimm. 'Aren't they, huh?'

'I didn't hear Carnelian's voice taunting me on this occasion, little fellow. The cards may simply have been keeping overwatch for me. Whatever I asked them – which they answered! – they also needed to warn me about him. The Emperor's Tarot has a life of its own.'

What kind of powers must the Harlequin man possess, to be able to tap into someone else's Tarot without having even touched it?

'Plainly I can't manage without the cards entirely. How else could we have targeted the blue sun? I can't destroy my own Tarot. It's linked to me.'

'Exactly, boss! How about sticking it in the stasis-trunk? That might slow Carnelian down.'

'I think not!'

'Why not extract the Harlequin card and shoot a hole in it? Could you give our friend a headache?'

Jaq sighed. Grimm might be something of an adept with all sorts of engines, but he had very little insight into theological complexities.

'The Tarot is a unity, a web. You can't simply rip a piece out of the pattern and expect it to hang together as before. How long until we arrive, Vitali?'

'Maybe twenty minutes of warp time. Then days of ordinary flight, of course. We'll be deep inside the Eye. Could be debris everywhere. Our deflectors'll be working overtime.'

The ship juddered as a warp surge caught it, tossing it like a leaf.

'I must concentrate–'

VEILS OF SICKLY pigment draped the void in all directions, lurid, gangrenous and mesmerising, as if an insane artist had been set loose here to paint, on a cosmic canvas, the kaleidoscope of his mad, shapeless nightmares.

Scarlet, chartreuse, cyanotic were the gas clouds. Here was bile and jaundice and hectic gore, as the suns within the Eye excited the billows of gas and dust in a zone of space vexed and fevered by the pressure of the warp.

Only a handful of the very closest and brightest stars glowed faintly through rifts in the veils; and then only like distant lighthouses seen through dense fog. The blue sun ahead wore a livid halo as if space itself was diseased. Which it was.

Now that *Tormentum Malorum* was back in truespace, Meh'Lindi had taken over piloting. Vitali Googol recuperated in his sleep-cell from the stresses of the warp. Grimm was tinkering with the artificial gravity, causing moments of leaden heaviness, others of vertigo. Now that the warp-scope had nothing to display, other screens and some uncovered portals let Meh'Lindi and Jaq view the delirious spectacle outside and probe for planets.

Tormentum Malorum proceeded under full camouflage and psychic screening.

A sensor beeped; a display unit switched to farsight.

'Traitor legion raider,' said Jaq. 'Has to be.'

The other ship was shaped like a crab. An armoured canopy of dingy brown above and below, dappled with daemonic emblems. Two jutting, articulated claws that could probably tear through adamantium. Jointed, armoured legs, hairy with aerials and sensors, moved to and fro in unison so that the raider seemed to scuttle through space in search of prey.

Checking the scale estimate, Jaq realised to his horror that the other ship was huge. *Tormentum Malorum* was a shrimp compared to the traitor vessel. Those 'legs' were probably entire fighting craft in themselves. Were those making ready to detach themselves from the parent? Jaq imagined the crustacean vessel grappling with *Tormentum*, seizing and crushing their own shell, its horny mouth sucking tight to the opening it tore, and spewing merciless abominations through.

Meh'Lindi switched off all superfluous on-board systems including gravity.

'What's the big idea?' shouted Grimm from another crypt, offended.

'Whisper-time,' she called back.

Eyes on stalks telescoped up from the crab-like ship: observation blisters. Jaq invoked an aura of protection. He willed their own ship not to be sensed. Pouring his own psychic power into the artificial shields until he sweated, he thought: *invisibility*.

The crab-ship was still heading outward, away.

It turned over, so that its underbelly was facing in the direction of travel.

'It's getting ready to jump,' Meh'Lindi whispered.

In a rainbow implosion, the crab disappeared.

Off to another star within the Eye; or out of the Eye entirely, marauding.

Jaq relaxed; he hungered.

He ate marinated sweetmice stuffed with Spican truffles.

THE PLANET THAT hung below them several days later might have been swaddled in poisonous chlorine, except that the ship's sensors diagnosed a breathable atmosphere.

Here was where immaterium was leaking through gaps between Chaos and the real universe, polluting the visible spectrum with phantom hues of ill-magic. In part, mists of mutability were responsible, pouring through the sieve between the realm of wraith and this solid world below. Also in part, those on board *Tormentum Malorum* were viewing a psychic miasma hiding whatever vile sights lay underneath – red tell-tales on the instrument panel glowed, warning of daemonic signatures.

Here, if anywhere, the hydra might have been conceived, crafted by cunning psychobiotechnicians.

'I don't suppose we'll meet many pureblood people down there,' said Jaq. 'Long exposure to such an environment would change any living creature.'

Maybe the cabal needed to use those bone-sculpture automatons as go-betweens not merely to present an acceptably hideous face to the local inhabitants – but because such beings at least might not mutate before their mission was accomplished?

Jaq recollected that he had not *seen* the faces of the High Masters of the Hydra; though on the other hand he had sensed no foul taint.

'Just as long as there's some decent fighting to attend to,' said Grimm, to hearten himself. The world below did not exactly look inviting. If the mask itself was so plague-stricken, what dire countenance did that mask hide?

What price, Jaq asked himself, had the cabal paid to obtain the hydra? Suppose for a moment that the members of the cabal were honourable yet sorely misguided. Would Chaos collaborate in the eventual purging of Chaos?

Ah yes, it might. The scheme could appeal to the renegades who so bitterly hated the Emperor if it involved his replacement. Weren't the descendants of the cabal also likely to quarrel and jockey for leadership in the aftermath? One whole sector of the galaxy – controlled by one cabalist – might direct a mind-blast at a neighbouring sector. The psychic convulsion would be titanic. The rampant insanity. Human civilisation could collapse once more into anarchy, torn by psychic civil war. The majority of surviving human beings would by then harbour a parasite from the warp in their heads, a little doorway for daemonism.

If the Emperor had initiated the hydra plan, surely he must have foreseen just such a possibility?

Unless, Jaq reflected with horror, the Emperor himself was mad. Supremely dedicated in one aspect, yet in another aspect... demented. Perhaps one aspect of the Emperor did not know what the other aspect was thinking and plotting.

Though Jaq recoiled from this heretical thought, it would not leave him.

What if the High Masters of the cabal likewise knew that the Emperor was going slowly insane – and must at all costs be deposed, replaced? Their awareness of this must be the most terrible secret in the universe, one that they might not even dare to confide in their fellow conspirators. Hence the lie that the Emperor himself had originated the plan.

If it was a lie.

If the Emperor was even still truly alive.

Once again Jaq asked himself whether the denizens of the Eye could possibly have been duped into providing a tool for the destruction of the very powers that sustained and twisted them. Or at least duped into allowing the hydra to be conjured forth here in the Eye of Terror.

That would be a master-stroke indeed.

'No orbital monitors,' said Googol, consulting scanners. 'No satellites, no battle platforms.'

Even through the miasma, other instruments detected centres of energy use. Perhaps half a dozen such, scattered across the world.

Just as when, long ago, he had lain abed in the orphanage on Xerxes Quintus sensing the sparks of mental phosphorescence, only now in full mastery and able to guard – so he hoped – against any backlash, Jaq opened himself up to the world below, and let... filth... flood through him, fishing for the signature he sought, any awareness of the existence of the hydra.

'Open the trunk, Meh'Lindi.' He had told her the lock combination. 'Bring me some of the entity to hold–'

She did so, returning with a small coil.

Jaq was swimming upstream through a vast vaulted sewer filled with the excrement of deranged minds, searching for the shadow of an amorphous shape... Avoid those creatures that fed in this faecal torrent! Do not attract their attention!

The sewer branched six separate ways, each as large and as full as the combined cloaca downstream. Beware of the polyp that bobbed towards him!

Swim *that* way swiftly. Hint of hydra? *Maybe. Almost for sure.*

Jaq withdrew. He handed the coil back to Meh'Lindi, who hastened to restore that troublesome substance to stasis before more was propagated.

When she returned, he tapped the viewscreen gridded with reference lines.

'Here's where we'll land. Near this power source, though not too near. And we don't wish to stay too long. I don't believe any inquisitor has raided a world of the Eye before.'

'As you say, Jaq, they mightn't exactly welcome wholesome-looking types down there, might they?'

'They might not indeed.'

'Huh, so shall I pretend that you're my prisoners?' said Grimm. 'Shall I lead you about on a chain? I suppose you're thinking that I'll do nicely as a mascot of deviant abhumanity.'

'No,' said Meh'Lindi, 'you're comely too.'

'Comely? Comely?' The short abhuman flushed and blushed.

'You're a perfect squat, agreeable in appearance.'

'Comely? Huh! Why not ravishingly handsome, in that case?' Grimm twirled his moustache defiantly.

'Thou art as a wondrous warthog,' began Googol.

'Shut up, Three Eyes.'

'Shall I alter myself into the genestealer shape?' volunteered Meh'Lindi. 'I shall seem tainted by Chaos then, shan't I? What better protective coloration could we wish for?'

Jaq could only rejoice at her offer. He nodded in grateful admiration.

'Do it, Meh'Lindi. Do it.'

THIRTEEN

LIGHTNING FORKED ACROSS a jaundiced sky as if discharging the tensions between reality and irreality. Some clouds suppurated, dripping sticky ichor rather than rain. Clumps of clouds resembled clusters of rotting, aerial tumours. Some of the scene was lit biliously by a green-seeming sun filtering through that apparently chlorinous overcast. The sun mildewed the gritty landscape from which fretted spikes and spires of stone arose. The camouflage-screened *Tormentum Malorum* appeared to be but one more natural feature.

Illusions whirled as if attempting to solidify themselves, the way that milk turns to butter. Globular plants twisted hairy flowers that were all the hues of rotting flesh in the direction of those dancing wraiths, hungrily.

THEY WERE CHALLENGED to combat an hour later, in a fiendishly playful fashion.

A bull of a man clad in plate-mail led a dozen capering monstrosities out from behind a stalagmite-like tower of rock.

'Ho-ho, ho-ho,' bellowed the bull-thing. 'What have we here to divert us, my lovelies?'

Formidable horns curved from the sides of the leader's head, jutting forward streaked with dried gore. His armour was wrought in the contours of bones. Metallic bones were bent into hoops around his thighs. Bones welded to bones made runic designs. Leering alien skulls capped his knees. Giant toe and finger bones encased his boots and gauntlets.

An obscene codpiece of artificial bone bulged, encrusted with blood-stones suggestive of ulcers. He also wore a fine satin cape that cut a dash in the breeze, and a golden necklace with an erotic amulet. To Jaq's senses, the bull-man radiated an eerie, brutal sensuality. His gear seemed to say that even bones could copulate, that even metal could debauch itself... though not in any soft style.

Behind the leader trotted an upright tortoise of a man, whose squamous head poked out of a barrel-like shell spangled with iridescent stars and crescents as if he was a walking galaxy or a mad magician. Silk ribbons fluttered like streams of burning gas. Did he ever crawl out of his shell on to some couch at night, tender-bodied, squashy, all of his *plea-sure-nerves* exposed to the ministrations of some large, wet tongue? Jaq shook his head to clear that image away.

Another warrior wore a brass waistcoat and leggings glued with gold braid as if furry caterpillars crawled upon his armour; in place of his left arm he sported a sheaf of tentacles. On his head, an exuberantly ringleted periwig.

Yet another, who was visibly hermaphroditic, in plascrystal armour, thrust forth a great lobster claw studded with medallions. One thin tall small-breasted fighter, braced with a clanking baroque exoskeleton, bore the head of a fly, upon which perched a cockaded plumed hat. A brassbound ovipositor jutted from her loins. Her neighbour was a striding, slavering, two-legged goat in rut, with a starched organdie ruff fanning around his neck, lace ruffled at his elbows, and a velvet cloak.

Only one massive man appeared to be true human. He wore a night-mare parody of noble Space Marine armour, engraved with a hundred daemon faces, though disdaining a helmet. Great flanged pipes soared sidelong from behind his head as if copying the bull-man's horns in reverse. That head was of statuesque marble nobility, the hair bleached white and permed into waves. At the tip of his aquiline nose he wore an emerald ring that suggested to Jaq a drip of mucus. One cheek was tattooed with sword and sheath poised like lingam and yoni.

Alongside this Traitor Marine there danced a mutant woman who was at once beautiful and hideous. Her body, clad in a chain-mail leotard trimmed with rosettes and puffs of gauze, was blanched and petite, her hair blonde and bounteous. Yet her jade-green eyes were swollen ovals set askew in an otherwise sensual face. Her feet were ostrich-claws, ornamented with topaz rings, her hands were chitinous, painted pincers. A razor-edge tail lashed behind her plump buttocks. How like a daemonette of Chaos she seemed! Googol groaned at the sight of her, and took an involuntary step forward. Grimm gritted his teeth.

This band were armed with damascened boltguns and power swords, the shafts of which were inlaid with mother-of-pearl. They spread out in a fanciful skirmish line and paused to scrutinize the three figures attired in orthodox power armour – two full-sized, one dwarfish – their open visors framing natural faces.

Before disembarking, Grimm had sprayed their own great-shouldered armour a jaundiced hue to blend with the desert and to mask the counter-daemonic runes and devout red icons. Feeling a sense of disgust and deep unease, Jaq had daubed on some warped renegade emblems such as the Eye of Horus – sloppily so that they might have less efficacy, but could persuade at a casual glance. Jaq's weapons rack cradled a force rod, psycannon and a clingfire thrower tubed to a clip-on tank; in a steel sleeve-holster nestled an ormolu-inlaid laspistol. Grimm and Googol favoured boltguns, laspistols, shuriken catapults.

The band eyed three ambiguous, well-armed intruders... accompanied by a version of a genestealer. Oh yes, she was their safe-conduct, their guarantor, if anyone could be.

'Slaanesh, Slaanesh,' bleated the goat, and fluffed his ruff. The fly and the tortoise took up the chant. The fly doffed her hat sarcastically.

'Glory to the Legion of the Lust!' shouted that caricature of a Marine. Was he saying 'the Lust' or 'the Lost'? Or both? The man grinned mockingly.

Ice slithered down Jaq's spine. Slaanesh, lord of perverse pleasure and of joy in pain, might indeed preside over a planet where an entity could be forged that would tamper with the pain and pleasure centres in the brain.

This motley crew that barred the way – these chic abominations – seemed inclined to play some absurd if vicious game. The question was, could they be fooled? At Jaq's side, Meh'Lindi hunched as though about to rush into their midst with the lightning speed of a stealer.

She clacked her claws together; her savage equine head jutted forth. With a gesture, he checked her.

'As you can see by the shape of my companion here,' Jaq called out, 'we have spat on the so-called Emperor's face.' He clapped Meh'Lindi proprietorially on the shoulder. 'This is my familiar lover, my changed one who shows me bliss and agony.'

The bull-man gazed at Meh'Lindi. Did he truly perceive her as someone possessed? He licked his lips and turned to his band.

'We embrace *renegades*, do we not, my carnal companions?' He snorted mightily. 'Though of course first we must test their sense of ecstasy, hmm?'

Their thenth of ecthathy... The Imperial Gothic of these degenerates was decadently accented with lisps.

The fly giggled. 'Oh yes, an initiation is doubtless in order.' *Inithiathon ith doubtleth in order.*

Which, thought Jaq, it was doubtless important to avoid if possible. Adopting an air of lordly disdain, he gestured around.

'This is a sordid, dreary refuge. I seek more than a rocky desert watered with pus. I seek the home of the hydra. I'm an emissary from the High Lords of the Hydra.' Jaq plucked a strand of the entity from the containment pouch in his suit and threw it, writhing, upon the ground.

'Haaa,' the bull replied with a grin, 'those lovely cheating lords...'

Cheating? In what way, cheating? Had the cabal cheated the traitors on this world – or were the cabal cheating on the Imperium?

The bull-man called out, 'You must visit the delightful torment dungeons in our city, Renegade, for full appreciation of what this world has to offer.'

Was that an invitation, or a terrible threat? The thought processes of this champion of Chaos eluded Jaq, being in themselves... chaotic.

At that moment Jaq felt a powerful urge to divest himself of his armour and grapple with Meh'Lindi. If he should but demonstrate his boast before this audience of monsters, why, they would let him pass. They would tell him everything he yearned to know.

The malign insinuation blasphemed against all that he had felt was precious in their lovemaking on the ship. He was under psychic attack of a lascivious and perfidious kind.

So was Meh'Lindi. She hissed and clutched a claw to her midriff. Stealers did not possess reproductive organs other than their tongue that kissed eggs into victims. Yet now a pouch was forming below Meh'Lindi's belly, as if to receive Jaq. Her mind – the mind that controlled her false body form – was being manipulated. Not by the scrap of hydra that flopped on the gritty ground. She was immune to that. But by...

And the aim? Why, to divest Jaq of his power armour, to seduce him out of its sanctuary. The dozen mustn't exactly trust their own weapons and strength against power armour. Jaq snatched out his force rod and fired at the goat, who staggered back, his sly psychic attack neutralised.

'I shan't be cheated so easily,' Jaq shouted in defiance.

'Evidently not,' replied the bull. 'Graal'preen here misinterpreted me. As I said, we must test your ecstasy before we embrace you. This means that *your* loving champion must accost *our* paramour.'

The lovely and ghastly female shimmied forth, tail slicing the air, pincers clicking.

'Are they well matched? Perhaps not well enough. Our nephew – and niece – in debauchery, Cammarbrach, will assist her.'

The hermaphrodite with the giant claw and the power sword clutched in his/her true hand stepped forward, and bowed derisively.

'And, I think, Testood too. Though without his gun. We do not wish to be unfair.'

So the tortoise tossed down his boltgun and advanced, still armed with a power sword.

'Ah, but wait,' added the bull. 'We will draw a battle circle and enforce it with a little spell of containment. With which, lord psyker,' and he eyed Jaq venomously, lowering his horns, 'you will not interfere. Slishy, do it!'

The mutant woman danced at speed, dragging her sharp tail through the dirt. She cut a wide circle, leaving only one little gap unsealed.

Jaq calculated. Surely he and Grimm and Googol, being better armoured, stood a good chance of cutting down all dozen of these warped renegades?

Yet what would he learn then? Of course, they might succeed in taking the leader prisoner...

What use would Jaq's excruciator be against a disciple of Slaanesh who taught his minions how to revel in agony?

Meh'Lindi chittered. Grimm interpreted.

'Use subterfuge, boss. She's prepared to fight.'

Subterfuge was the better strategy. So therefore Jaq must seem to accept the challenge. Meh'Lindi must fight against three opponents, two armed with power swords. She wasn't a complete genestealer with four arms. Wouldn't her stealer crouch impede an assassin's acrobatic skills?

Meh'Lindi didn't wait for instructions but paced into the circle to join the other three. Slishy sealed the line with her tail. The air shimmered as if an energy dome enclosed the arena.

'I can't bear to watch,' muttered Googol.

'Go to it!' shouted Grimm.

Jaq reminded himself to remain wary of any psychic thrusts; he mustn't let the fight occupy his entire attention.

Rearing as high as she could, Meh'Lindi darted at the tortoise, who looked to be the most cumbersome of those who faced her. He swung his sword high. She threw herself flat. Rolling under the swing, she gripped his feet with her claws and tugged, sending him crashing backwards to the ground, head already retracted within his shell.

Instead of pressing her advantage by mounting her adversary, she immediately rolled in a different direction. Thus she avoided the down-sweep of

Cammarbrach's power sword – which sawed into Testood's shell instead, opening a rift, before the wielder reversed its course.

During that moment while the hermaphrodite and the tortoise man were tangled, Meh'Lindi leapt at the pseudo-daemonette. Claws grappled with pincers. The tail whipped round, slashing Meh'Lindi's horny skin. The mutant woman pivoted backwards in Meh'Lindi's grip bringing up both sharp-taloned ostrich feet in an effort to eviscerate her opponent. Talons raked across Meh'Lindi's toughened carapace. Already Meh'Lindi was tossing Slishy away, one pincer crippled. Meh'Lindi even caught an ankle in her claw, crushing quickly, releasing her hold while Slishy shrilled with what seemed to be elation.

Meh'Lindi wasn't seeking to kill any of her opponents outright. The extra moments involved in such a manoeuvre could have hindered her long enough for one of the others to surprise her.

Instead, she darted from one to the next, delivering a blow, a bite, a pinch of her claw... until the three who confronted her were tattered and tired.

Now Meh'Lindi paused a little longer with each. Batting Testood's sword arm aside, she ripped at his riven shell, wrenching it further apart. She snipped off Slishy's injured pincer. Wary of Cammarbrach's lobster claw, she tore armour from his/her sword arm – and returned to lacerate flesh and muscle; the sword fell.

Slishy died first, warbling deliriously.

In a moment of confusion, Testood slashed Cammar-brach; the lobster claw sagged, spasming.

Moments later Testood was disarmed. Meh'Lindi punched through the gap in his shell, crushing organs. The tortoise man collapsed. Cammarbrach fled, though only as far as the edge of the circle. Shrieking, he/she batted against the invisible barrier of force – until Meh'Lindi reached the hermaphrodite, whose neck she crunched with a claw.

'Ha!' cried Grimm.

'So we embrace you,' roared the bull-man. He pointed. 'That jelly thing is some powerful talisman.'

'You don't know what the hydra is, do you?' Jaq accused. 'Or who the High Masters are?'

'Maybe I do, cousin renegade. Truth is mutable in the Eye of Terror. All is mutable. You too will soon be mutable – if you're to win favour.'

'Cancel the force field.'

'The enchanted circle?'

'Psychic barrier! Whatever. Lower it.'

'You have destroyed our luscious deadly heart-throb. You must donate your champion to our group in exchange.'

'Boss.' Grimm was nudging Jaq's midriff.

From the east, scuttling from the shelter of one rocky column to the next, came Chaos spawn: dozens of spiderkin, hideous hairy unhumans with eight arachnid legs.

'Bastard's been playing us for time, boss.'

'I regret so.'

'What do those things do, you reckon?'

'Spin webs around us? Sting us?' Jaq levelled his force rod and discharged it at the circle inscribed in the grit. Meh'Lindi charged free and ducked out of the line of fire as Jaq shouted, 'Destroy the polluted!'

After which, he could no longer keep up any pretence of being a renegade. He and Grimm and Googol opened fire simultaneously at the devotees of Slaanesh.

Jaq's laspistol sewed silver lines across air and armour and parts of warped limbs that were exposed. Grimm's boltgun bucked and clattered, its little shells exploding percussively on contact or else winging away vainly to fall elsewhere – until, to his annoyance, it jammed. He too plucked free a laspistol to cross-stitch the scene. Googol had levelled a shuriken catapult resembling a species of miniature starship with its flat round magazine apeing an elevated control deck and its twin pod-tipped fins abeam of the muzzle suggesting thrusters. Their magnetic vortex hurled a swishing hail of star-discs with monomolecular cutting edges.

Most targets fell quickly. However, the big Chaos Marine charged, firing bolts. An explosive concussion against Grimm's armour knocked the abhuman over like a skittle. A similar hit winded Jaq, blurring his vision. Blinking, he slammed his visor shut and fired a stream of superheated chemicals at the bull-man who was charging thunderously too. All was happening within moments. The bull raced past, screaming rapturously, haloed with clingfire, trailing an odour of boiling gravy.

The Traitor Marine was singling out Googol. That statuesque bare head seemed impervious to weaponry, protected by some great hex. Googol's star-discs flicked to left and right as though deflected by a fierce magnetic or anti-gravitic field. Shurikens, that could slice bone like butter, only scratched the man's armour. Though the false Marine's boltgun had also seized up, he had pulled a power sword from a scabbard in his armour. That warrior was almost upon Googol when the Navigator dropped his catapult and reached inside his own open helmet. Googol tore the bandana from his brow and stared death from his warp eye.

At last that mighty blasphemy of a Space Marine sagged, drooled and fell, almost crushing Googol.

Jaq wrenched the ribbed, flanged, exorcistically garnished psycannon from his weapons rack and sprayed at the onrush of spiderkin. Those were summoned creatures. In the normal universe outside of the Eye summoned creatures were unstable, vulnerable to a psycannon beam. But here inside the Eye?

One burst followed another.

Googol writhed free. 'Don't look me in the eye,' he warned. Finding his bandana as first priority, he wadded the material across his brow inside the helmet. By now Grimm was on his feet again, lasering at the spiderkin, severing legs, though there were many legs to laser. As the rush arrived, Meh'Lindi leapt high to stomp down on the Chaos spawn with her genestealer feet. She crumpled bodies with her claws. Spiderkin keened. Their spinnerets gushed milky adhesive threads, which she dodged. Jaq reverted to laser. Googol joined in.

Presently, thwarted and leaderless, the remaining spiderkin scuttled away, scaling spires.

'We won,' said Googol.

'We lost,' Jaq corrected him. 'We learned nothing.'

They continued circumspectly through the desert of spires, Meh'Lindi ranging ahead as a scout.

FOURTEEN

LUMINOUS VEILS DRIPPED from the glowing soup of the night sky. The buildings of the city ahead were gross idols to corrupted pleasure.

Some of those buildings were modelled to represent lascivious deities: many breasted, many organed avatars of twisted lust. In the weird veil-light the hunchbacked shadows of dark gods seemed to brood everywhere. Spouts of flaming gas leapt up, adding further spasmodic illumination.

Other great buildings were giant mutated solo genitalia. Horned phallic towers arose, wrinkled, ribbed, blistered with window-pustules. Cancerous breast-domes swelled, fondled by scaly finger-buttresses. Tongue-bridges linked these buildings, sliding back and forth. Scrotumpods swayed. Orifice-entries pulsed open and shut, glistening. Some buildings were in congress with each other: headless, limbless torsos lying side by side, joined abominably.

Through his magniscope Jaq spied nipples that were heavy-duty laser nacelles, and lingam shafts that were projectile tubes.

The inhabitants were mere ants by comparison with this architectonic orgy. Eager, scurrying ants. Jaq's ear-bead picked up wailing music, drumbeats, screams, chants, and the throb of machinery. The city pulsed and palpitated flexibly. Somehow plasteel and immaterium were alloyed together. Thus buildings moved, butted one another, penetrated one another, crawled upon one another. Towers bowed and stiffened. The deity buildings caressed and clawed at one another. And the ant-like inhabitants swarmed within and around

185

and over, sometimes being crushed, sometimes sucked into vents, or spewed out.

Jaq turned away sickened, muttering exorcisms. Meh'Lindi's claw closed on his gauntlet and squeezed a couple of times consolingly.

'Are we to go into the body of that city?' whispered Googol. 'The *body*, aye, the body!'

'Huh, living in that lot it must be some relief to get into the desert!' said Grimm. 'You reckon the hydra was made there, boss?'

'Maybe... They do seem to possess a technology of immaterium in the service of foulness. Ah: party heading out this way, I'd say.'

'In search of their lost bedmates?'

Jaq's own band lay on a shelf of rock overlooking a road which wended away from the lascivious, living, cruel city. An anti-gravity palanquin – a cushioned platform sheltered by an awning – bore a gargantuan individual upon it. Four enormously long-snouted quadrupeds, striped blue and red as if wearing livery, pulled this palanquin along, hovering a metre above the road.

Probably the buoyant land-raft could have proceeded under its own power except that the monstrous passenger preferred this ceremonial charade. Or maybe the passenger's fingers were too fat to manipulate the control levers accurately – if she could even reach them.

Rows of tattooed breasts circuited her enormous trunk and belly; through each nipple, a brass ring. Coiling in and out amongst all those glistening, oily bosoms, squeezing its way between, was a long thin purple snake, its origin, seemingly, the woman's navel. A birthcord grown to hosepipe length, it bound her around like a rope, creasing and squeezing so that flesh flowed forth. The snake's flat venomous head wavered hypnotically alongside her cheek, caressing it.

The fat woman's face was bovine, with big oozy nostrils, large liquid eyes, floppy lips, and a jaw that seemed to chew cud, ruminating placidly. Her snake – her other self – did not seem so placid.

A dozen bare-headed Traitor Marines escorted her, encased in mockbone armour. They carried plasma and projectile weapons.

In the vanguard danced a dozen sisters of Slishy, lashing their tails, swirling their pincers.

The procession advanced almost to where Jaq's party lurked, then halted. The Slishy look-alikes pirouetted to the rear, to join the legionnaires. The creatures that pulled the palanquin crouched, stabbing their snouts underground through the very fabric of the road. The enormous, mutated woman faced out into the desert of spires, her snake swaying beside her.

'Boole!' the woman mooed mightily into the veil-lit night.

'Cover your ears, Meh'Lindi!' ordered Jaq. 'Visors down. Switch off audio. She will be deafening.'

'B-O-O-L-E! BOO-OOO-OOO-LEEEEE!'

Even with microphones deadened, the great noise seemed that of a starcraft at take-off. Her voice jarred and vibrated their very bones inside their suits. A stone spire shattered and fell. Meh'Lindi writhed, clutching her unprotected head. That voice was directional like a searchlight beam. Legionnaires and Slishy-sisters behind the palanquin merely rocked to and fro in the backwash of echoes.

'WHERE ARE YOU, BOOLE? I WISH TO BE HUNG UP BY A HUNDRED RINGS! THEN BY FIFTY LESS! THEN BY TWENTY LESS!'

Letting his psychic sense loose, Jaq was invaded by a vision of the massive, multibreasted, altered woman hanging suspended on many strong slim chains clipped to her many nipple-rings. Of her being joggled up and down on variable numbers of rings, moaning in distorted delight, while the bull-man served or slapped or kneaded her, or pricked her with his horns.

At such times, Jaq perceived, the woman's snake participated too, entering her by one orifice or another, completing the circuit.

The giant woman gathered herself again, her head turning in a different direction.

'BOOOOOOOOOLEEEE! BOOOOOOOOLEEEEE!'

Earth shook; another pinnacle snapped apart. Jaq lay stunned.

A muted roar of anguish answered the woman's call from out of the radiant, iridescent night.

The bull-man came pounding into sight. He was eyeless, faceless, burned to the bone. The flesh had crisped to crackling on his arms and chest. His very horns were black and twisted.

Her voice had called him back. Could she raise the dead with that shout? Or had he been stumbling blinded, half-cooked, in the desert, yet kept alive by daemonic protection? Through *her* protection, if she was possessed by Slaanesh.

She must – thought Jaq – be the mistress of this whole evil, animate city. If anyone knew the truth about the hydra, she should.

When Boole – the bull-man – reached the palanquin he collapsed and lay still. The woman's snake whiplashed free from amongst her bosoms. Unfastening itself at such speed that the friction must burn or split her unctuous skin, it arced out to taste the fallen body with a flickering twin tongue.

The woman quaked and howled.

'AIIEEEEEEEEEE! BOOOOOOOLEEEEE!'

The blue and red animals unplugged their heads from the ground and lurched widdershins, foaming at the mouth. The palanquin rocked and rotated. The woman's head swung from side to side. Her voice caught legionnaires and pseudo-daemonettes. Some ran around behind the gravity-sled to try to stabilise it. Others collapsed, gaping, eyes, bulging.

'AIIEEEEEEE! OHAAAAAAAA!'

The voice was reaching back to the very city. Buildings responded by wobbling and shaking. Some, like gargantuan snails, sought slow refuge behind others. A few shuffled slowly in the direction of the voice. Tongue-bridges tore. Breast-balconies bled white juice. The antlike inhabitants tumbled. Lasers started firing at imaginary targets amongst the cascading lurid veils.

Jaq banged Googol and Grimm on the shoulders while the voice was pointing away from them. He gesticulated with his gauntlet.

Their laser beams and bolts sliced and hammered accurately at the woman's escorts. Some of these returned fire, but the palanquin continued to swing around, dragged by the rabid-seeming beasts. The defenders dodged. Jaq targeted and killed, before crouching, gritting his teeth against the great noise. As soon as the stunning thunderfront passed by, Jaq popped up and shot the proboscis-beasts one by one. Their dead weight dragged the palanquin to a halt.

How to silence the monstrous woman, so that she could be captured? Puncture her windpipe, carving through the slab of fat that was her neck? That wouldn't help her to answer questions. He might even decapitate her unintentionally.

The snake part of her! Jaq thought of the soul-threads descending from living beings into the abyss of uncreation.

Could the snake be a materialization of something akin? A tendril of Slaanesh rooted into her navel, nourishing her umbilically with power?

The snake continued to arc out as though afflicted by rigor mortis – the mortis in question being that of Boole.

Muttering an exorcism, Jaq aimed psycannon with one hand and laser with the other, both at the serpent's neck.

When the snake's head hit the ground, it exploded in the manner of electricity earthing. Span by span from the front, the snake's long body detonated backwards like a firecracker, golden fire gushing out until the pyrotechnic display arrived at the woman's navel. Then whatever had been rooted in her burst forth in a spray of blood and excremental juices. Her bosoms closed the wound swiftly, compressing it shut. The thunder had stopped.

Meh'Lindi had scrambled to her knees, and was shaking her long snout from side to side as if she was a swimmer trying to dislodge water from her ears. Whether Meh'Lindi was deafened and stupefied or not, they must all act now. Her training must take over. An assassin should fight on, even if a leg and two arms were broken. Jaq threw up his visor, signalled Grimm and Googol to do likewise.

'Boss, buildings are heading this way.'

It was true.

'But not very *fast*. We must hijack the gravity sled, haul it into the wilderness–'

The four descended at speed to where the wounded lady squatted vastly on her floating litter, surrounded by dead and incapacitated legionnaires and Slishy-kin. Her injury seemed minor compared with her bulk. The woman's mouth opened and closed but she only lowed quietly in protest. Or maybe loudly; compared with earlier, her lamentations and vituperations didn't register as amounting to a din.

Slishy-kin were already rotting, dissolving. As Grimm delivered the coup de grâce to a lingering legionnaire who might use his last erg of energy to snap off a shot in the back, Googol cut the corpses of the proboscis-animals loose and gathered the traces to fashion a harness... into which Meh'Lindi began to slip herself willingly.

'No, no,' Jaq told her. 'I'm wearing power armour. You're not.' He attached himself instead.

'Boss: ugly customers boiling out of the city.'

Yes indeed. But two kilometres away. Beginning to haul, Jaq powered up the slope towards the maze of spires. As he overcame the inertia of the giantess on her raft, so he ran ever faster, and cast a psychic haze of confusion behind himself and his companions to hide them like a cloud of mental dust.

THEY WERE DEEP inside the desert, perhaps half way to the ship. Rock spires flashed by; Jaq had to calculate well ahead when to deviate the sled. Pursuit seemed nonexistent.

Grimm panted up alongside Jaq – even though the armour amplified their actions they were still doing the work of sprinting. 'Boss, boss, I've been figuring. We can only get her on board *Tormentum* – if we trim her down. Don't have a good enough medikit with us for that – without her expiring, do we?'

Grimm was right. 'Vitali, slow the sled!'

Googol applied himself to the rear of the speeding palanquin, digging in his heels to kill its momentum. The squat was a little too short to assist in this task, but Meh'Lindi soon caught up and pitched in. Presently the vehicle was hovering at rest. Jaq strengthened the aura of protection around the little group.

The woman glowered at them malignly as Meh'Lindi hoisted Grimm to peer over the lip of the litter. The little man evaded a sluggish, dropsical foot almost as large as himself and stabbed at a lever. The palanquin began to sink. The woman's nipple-rings clinked against each other as all her breasts heaved. A pig-size arm swung slackly at Googol, knocking the armoured Navigator over. Deprived of her serpent, though, she was definitely less than she had been. Swearing, Googol picked himself up as the litter settled. Grimm deactivated it entirely, and the mountainous woman slumped backwards shapelessly, suggesting that the sled had been providing other uplift too, a supportive corset of antigravity.

'We'll do what we have to do here,' Jaq unpacked his excruciator, a bundle of seemingly frail rods.

He telescoped out the spidery yet supremely strong device and slapped it down over the giantess. With much wrestling they attached its hoops to her extremities – more for the sake of holding those extremities in place and thus avoiding being swatted, he thought to himself. Where was the point in racking a person who enjoyed being dangled and stretched from rings? Many rings, then fewer rings!

Fumbling off a gauntlet, Jaq produced an ampoule of veritas to press against her skin. Bearing in mind her mass, he used a second and a third dose. The recommended Inquisition procedure was to induce extreme pain first of all. This, he reasoned, might be counter-productive, aside from the fact that the prospect nauseated him somewhat.

'Name?' he demanded.

The woman spat at Jaq, at least two handfuls worth of reeking drool, and he sprang aside.

'Jus' clearing my throat,' she explained. 'Seems as how I've lost my old voice.' ...*lotht my old voith.*

'What do you know about an entity called the hydra?'

'My name's Queem Malagnia. An' my beaut Boole just die. Never pierce me again with his horns after rousting against the Grimpacks.' ...*againtht the Grimpackth.*

'He was monkeying around with a daemonette,' Grimm said wickedly.

'Very little,' stated Queem Malagnia.

Was that said in answer to Jaq's last question, or was it a comment upon Grimm's remark? Had the fat woman been reduced to the condition of an imbecile by the amputation? Or was she prevaricating slyly?

'What do you know?' Jaq repeated sternly.

'I know something's missin' from me!'

'The serpent that possessed you is what's missing. Now let's get down to business. Tell me all you know about the hydra, or I shall kill you.'

'You wouldn't know nothin' then, would you? No, that ain't so. You'd know whatever you knew beforehand?' Her jaw convulsed. She could no longer hold back the truth – yet unfortunately he had given her licence to tell *all* that she knew. 'Why, hydra is a name,' she said slowly. 'Am not exac'ly a scholar but ah hazard it's spelled with a haitch and a why and a dee–'

'Stop. Was the hydra first made in your living city?'

'Aha! *First* made, now there's a question. What does first mean? Originally, primarily? Whatever made immaterium in the first place, if it's stuff that's essentially unmade? Ah take it we're talking about summat made of immaterium?'

Would pleasure perhaps hurt her? How could he define pleasure for such a person? In a well-equipped dungeon over a period of several days, oh yes. Yet on the spur of the moment? Jaq glanced askance at his companions.

Little Grimm stepped forward. He jiggled some of Queem Malagnia's brass rings, those that he could reach. Each ring was incised with miniature scenes of depravity. From a tool kit he produced a small pair of shears and held them up in Queem's line of sight. Since Grimm's earlier taunt had been aimed intelligently at unsettling the woman, Jaq let him proceed.

'Listen, you freak,' said the squat, 'I'm gonna steal all your stupid rings for my souvenir collection.'

He snipped and withdrew one ring from a nipple, gently, not tugging.

Queem gasped. It was as though Grimm had pulled a plug. The breast deflated, disappearing. The teat became a mere blemish, which quickly faded.

'Warp-stuff is bulking out her body!' the squat exclaimed. 'She's like a hydra herself. Each ring is a seal. Here goes number two.'

He snipped and slid the severed ring free. Another breast collapsed.

Queem whimpered.

Jaq doubted Grimm's mechanistic explanation. The small man had little instinct for the workings of arcane thaumaturgy.

Grimm stood up on tiptoe and smirked into Queem's great face. 'Huh, we'll soon have you trimmed down to size! You'll fit on board our ship.'

'Leave my lovely rings alone,' begged Queem. 'I'll tell you anything.'

'I don't wish to hear *anything*,' snarled Jaq. 'I wish to hear quite specifically... Grimm, cut off ten rings.'

Snip-snip.

'Nooooooo!'

Snip.

'Noooo–'

Snip.

'Please stop it–'

Snip.

'What's a hydra, anyway?'

'Do you *know* what it is?' barked Jaq.

'It's an entity,' she said viciously and that was all she said.

Blood erupted from her neck. She gagged. Her head lolled back, half severed.

'Don't anyone move!' cried a familiar, teasing voice.

FIFTEEN

FROM A HUNDRED metres away, partly sheltered by a spire of rock, Zephro Carnelian was covering them with a heavy boltgun. He must almost instantly have discarded the laspistol he had used so accurately on Queem Malagnia, so as to grapple with the more devastating weapon. Its brass-bound chrome glittered, reflecting the abnormal, sickly luminosities of night. In the midst of spying, had the Harlequin man actually taken some time out to polish the dust of the chase from that boltgun and burnish it stylishly?

Carnelian was wearing grotesque bone-armour with spurs and spikes, his impertinent face peering out of a flanged, horned helmet. One of the robots from the hulk flanked him, cradling a plasma gun.

'I just can't abide to witness suffering!' he called.

'I wasn't racking her, you fool,' Jaq shouted back. 'I wasn't intending to. How else do you pin down a megapig? Now you've killed her like you killed Moma Parsheen.' Pretend still to be an ally.

'How do you know what evil that woman consummated while she hung in her rings, Draco?'

'So you've been inside her boudoir! That settles one doubt in my mind.'

'Stop moving apart, you four.' Carnelian fired warning bolts to right and to left, causing the ground to erupt. 'I too can have visions, Sir Inquisitor, Sir Traitor. *You* are a blasphemer of solemn oaths, a despoiler of duty.'

'And you seem singularly at home in the Eye of Terror, Harlequin man.'

'Ah, but I'm at home everywhere, aren't I? And nowhere too...'

'The hydra was first forged here, not in some orbital lab.'

'Is that what you suppose? Did *she* say so?'

'You know she didn't have time. You stopped her.'

'I wouldn't believe much that a servant of Slaanesh says. Wouldn't she lie, to trouble your soul and confuse you, Jaq?'

'She was under the influence of veritas.'

'Veritas, indeed?'

Why didn't Carnelian and his servitor simply open fire? Gobbets of plasma and heavy explosive bolts could do severe damage to even the best armour; and never mind about the contents. Meh'Lindi, who was unprotected but for her chitin, would instantly be blown apart. Yet the Harlequin man continued to toy with Jaq.

'What is truth?' cried Carnelian. '*In vinculo veritas*, wouldn't you say? Truth emerges within the dungeon, in fetters. Yet if truth is chained, how can it be true? Is not the whole human galaxy bound with chains? Is not our Emperor manacled into his throne? Who will ever free him? Only death.'

'Idle paradoxes, Carnelian! Or are you threatening to dispose of the Master of Mankind?'

'Tush, what paranoia. Wouldn't the hydra set everyone free by binding them tight?'

'I ask you: whose hands will steer the hydra? Who are those masked Masters really?'

'Really? "Really" is a truth question. I thought we had just disposed of the truth. There's no truth at present, Jaq, not in the whole of the galaxy. You know very well, as a secret inquisitor, that such is the case. The truth about genestealers? Truth about Chaos? Such truths must be suppressed. Truth is weakness, truth is infirmity. Truth must be tamed as psykers are tamed. Truth must be soul-bound and blinded. Our Emperor has banished truth, exiled it into the warp, as t'were. Yet there *will* be truth. Oh yes!'

'When the hydra possesses everyone in the whole damn galaxy? If everyone thinks the same, I guess that must be the truth.'

Carnelian cackled hectically. 'Truth is a veritable jest, Jaq. The lips that tell the truth must also laugh. Laugh with me, Jaq, laugh!'

Carnelian fired another explosive bolt, well clear of Jaq's party, though dirt spattered them.

'Dance and laugh! Our Emperor has banished laughter. From us, from himself. Yes, he has exiled joy from himself so as to save us. He has outcast truth, for the sake of order. Because truth, like laughter, is disorderly, disturbing, even chaotic; and there can be no hilarity in the dungeon of lies.'

What did Carnelian mean? The Emperor if anyone should know the truth – about human destiny, about history; he who had reigned for ten thousand years! If the Emperor did not know the truth – was unable to know the truth – why then, the galaxy was hollow, futile, doomed. But maybe the Emperor no longer knew what the truth was; no longer knew why his Space Marines and his inquisitors imposed his rule with iron dedication.

As Carnelian smirked at Jaq under the lurid sky of this corner of Chaos, so Jaq's resolve to travel to Earth with his – admittedly ambiguous – evidence strengthened. If he could but escape from Carnelian's clutches!

Another bolt exploded, showering grit.

'Shall we try to take him, boss?' muttered Grimm.

How could they? Compared with Carnelian they were out in the open. The combat servitor held a heavy plasma gun. Meh'Lindi would probably be incinerated... though an assassin's duty was to die, if need be.

'Jaq: let me give you a snatch from a very ancient poem to riddle out during your last remaining moments. Which moments may refer to the immediate future right now, or alternatively to when you are a very doddery embittered old man looking back on your life before the light finally dims forever for you... In this snatch of verse a God is speaking. Perhaps he is like our own God-Emperor surveying his galaxy. Ahem.'

Carnelian cleared his throat, and recited:

'Boundless the deep, says God, because I am who fill
Infinitude, nor vacuous the space.
Though I uncircumscribed my self retire,
And put not forth my goodness, which is free
To act or not...

'Pretty words, eh? How they roll off the tongue.'

How they mystified Jaq. How the meaning escaped him, just as Queem Malagnia's confession had eluded him so frustratingly.

'Ooops!' shrieked Carnelian. He fired one bolt that clipped Grimm's shoulder. It ricocheted onward unexploded, since it hadn't penetrated. Even so, Grimm was punched sideways.

Jaq had no choice but to return fire; Googol too. In another moment, Grimm. Carnelian had already disappeared behind the spire, as had his robot.

Bolts hammered away and plasma gushed from the rear of the stone column – away in the opposite direction. Legionnaires in baroque bone-armour hove into view, darting from column to column, firing back as they came. Pincer-waving daemonettes and scuttling Chaos spawn accompanied them.

'Run for the ship!' ordered Jaq, summoning auras of protection and distraction.

They sprinted, abandoning the palanquin with its gross corpse and Jaq's excruciator, unused. He was glad he had lost it.

As TORMENTUM MALORUM rose on a tail of plasma out of the festering ionosphere, a couple of near-space fighters, hawk-ships, attacked but Googol outdistanced these and continued boosting outward in over-drive. The starship sang with the strain on its engines.

'Your tinkering seems to have been of some use,' Googol finally conceded to Grimm.

'Huh, tuned 'em good, didn't I?'

'For the moment ! You didn't recite a single litany. How can you expect an engine to perform properly if you scorn its spirit?'

'Its spirit,' said Grimm, 'is known as fuel.'

'Just don't let it hear you say so.'

'Huh, catch me talking to an engine.'

'Vitali's right,' said Jaq. 'Spirit pervades all things.'

'Huh, so I suppose you understand all that stuff our Harlequin man was spouting, about pervading infinitude?'

'The Emperor pervades. He's everywhere. Everywhere within the compass of the Astronomican, at least.'

Grimm shrugged. 'I'm a mite bothered why Carnelian let us go. With his fancy marksmanship he only clipped me. He was herding us back towards our ship, boss. Basically. He held those legionnaires off–'

'After attracting them by firing off a few bolts.'

'Why shoot at them if they're his allies?'

'Maybe,' suggested Vitali, 'with their first lady kidnapped and her escort wiped out the renegades were in a bad mood and would shoot anyone who wasn't from Sin City?'

'You're dense,' said Grimm. 'Maybe Carnelian killed that Queem woman to make us think the hydra came from that place, even if it didn't.'

'It must have originated here in the Eye,' Jaq said flatly. 'And on Queem's world too.'

'Hers no more,' said Googol. 'Good riddance. She wasn't exactly my prototype of fatal beauty.'

'Carnelian seems to have agreed with you,' observed the squat.

The thought of Carnelian herding them – towards Earth now? – irked Jaq extremely.

'I'm not quite so dense,' said Googol, 'when it comes to interpreting verse. The God-Emperor in that poem seemed to be saying that he had separated off part of his power. That part is elsewhere, independent of him, free to go its own way or fail to go its own way. Is that the good part? In which case the remaining part would be evil.'

'The Emperor cannot be evil,' said Jaq. 'He is the greatest man ever. Though he can, and must, be stern; without a smile.'

'A fact which Carnelian seemed to regret.'

'So that he could have the laugh on us,' jeered Grimm.

Truly I'm scurrying through a maze, thought Jaq; and maybe this maze has no true exit at all.

'Speaking of prototypes,' Grimm teased Googol, 'here comes yours.'

Meh'Lindi had returned to her true flesh, and now returned to the control crypt.

'So that was Chaos,' was her comment.

'No,' Jaq corrected her, 'that was merely one world out of hundreds where Chaos intrudes.'

'Do you know, I felt almost at home there in my grotesque body? Something appealed to my altered senses.'

Jaq was instantly alert. 'A taint of Chaos?'

'Something in the air. No, in the hidden atmosphere. I didn't feel the same way when I changed in Vasilariov. That was... a job. This was more like a vile seductive destiny.'

'Could changing your body be habit-forming?' the squat asked with concern.

'On a Chaos world, I think so. You would be trapped, becoming a monster and not being able to change back again. Chaos is the poly-morphine of the mad and the bad, of sick minds, of brains that crave without control. You become the content of your own nightmare, which starts as a delirious and enticing dream. Then the nightmare shapes your flesh. The nightmare possesses you. You still believe you're the dreamer. But you aren't. You are what-is-dreamt. I wonder–'

'What?' asked Jaq. Meh'Lindi seemed on the verge of some revelation – maybe akin to the false enlightenment of a drug fugue, when a crushed beetle seems pregnant with cosmic importance. 'What, Meh'Lindi?'

'I wonder whether a truly remarkable person could escape from the sway of Chaos by her own power. Or by his own power. Such a person would then be immune to Chaos, just as I'm immune to the hydra – or hope I am.'

'Would such a person be Zephro Carnelian?' Googol asked quietly from his Navigator's couch. 'At home everywhere, according to his boast! Able to romp across a Chaos world without contamination.'

'I hate him,' she answered vaguely. 'Yet... I've been touched by him deep within.'

More deeply than by me? Jealousy pricked at Jaq.

'I smell the reek of cults,' he announced severely. 'Of crusades and saviours. The human mind is very prone to cults. Stealer cults, cults of Chaos, cabals... But there's only one redeemer. He is the Emperor. Cling to that one strong chain.' (*Though how strong was it in reality? How strong did it remain?*) 'Let that chain bind you. Welcome its protective bondage.'

'In that case,' asked Grimm, 'oughtn't we to welcome the bondage of the hydra? If it'll really scour the galaxy clean of daemons and mutants and wicked aliens?'

Jaq glared at him. 'And of abhumans too, little one? Why not of anyone who diverts from the human norm? Until there is only that norm everywhere, in a galaxy of mono-mind.'

That was the positive face of the hydra plan; the flip side being... a galaxy boiling with Chaos spawn.

'I wasn't the norm, I recall.' Contradictions warred in Jaq's soul. He cradled his brow in his hands. He muttered prayers – to what, to a failing Master of Mankind?

'I was only asking, boss,' Grimm said humbly as if Jaq's anguish communicated itself.

'The whole galaxy *asks*.' And what answered the plea? A devious cabal of potential slave-masters? A trickster Harlequin man? Or the crumbling rock against which the tides of Chaos burst?

'Where shall we head for?' the Navigator wanted to know.

Aye, another iota was asking for guidance. And of course the hydra promised to bestow total guidance. If only Jaq could believe the cabal... but he couldn't.

'We're aiming for sacred Terra, Vitali. Where else? We shall sneak in announced. That should challenge your piloting skills.'

'I wasn't, um, especially requesting to be challenged. Not in that sort of way, at any rate! Not that I don't welcome opportunities... But Vitali Googol versus the whole of the solar system's defence network, um, right, very well...'

'This flight could become legendary,' hinted Grimm. 'You might compose a praise-song about your piloting.'

Meh'Lindi smiled bleakly. 'Alternatively, a suicide ode.'

'First,' said Jaq, 'we must jettison that trunk of hydra. Set it on a lazy course into a blazing sun. The blue one hereabouts should serve the purpose as well as any.'

'That's your only proof, boss. The hydra's your evidence.'

'Do you think I would dream of smuggling that into the heart of the Imperium? Imagine the hydra let loose in the bowels of our birthworld, in the headquarters of humanity. Impossible!'

Nevertheless, he reflected, some of the substance of the hydra would travel all the way to Earth notwithstanding. Some was subtly hidden within Meh'Lindi's own body, incorporated, neutralised.

He imagined Meh'Lindi confined in a dungeon of his Ordo. He imagined her stretched out and opened like a toad in a daemonological laboratory of the Malleus, being investigated, probed to destruction, first of her mind, then of her flesh.

His mind rejected this vision, though not before her troubled gaze had met his.

SIXTEEN

THE EYE OF Terror lay far out near the fringe of the galaxy, to the galactic north-west, in a region as lonely as Jaq sometimes felt himself to be these days. His spirits were hardly raised when Grimm almost deserted ship mid-way to Terra...

The squat had insisted that the distance was simply too great to attempt in one warp-jump with the fuel remaining in the tanks of the *Tormentum*.

He was undoubtedly right. Vitali Googol should have been the one to point this out. Indeed the Navigator insisted that he would have done so just as soon as their ship had left the system of the blue sun, just as soon as *Tormentum* was running, storm-tossed, through the warp once more.

Did Googol in his heart wish to obstruct their flight to Earth by limiting their options as to a refuelling stop – so that they might be obliged to call at some major base where awkward questions could be asked, or agents of the cabal could strike at them more easily?

Worse still, was Googol's attitude becoming cavalier? Did he not care whether they were marooned or not? The Navigator protested, in a hurt tone, at Jaq's semi-accusation.

From tortured snatches of verse that Jaq overheard subsequently, it seemed that the memory of that beringed giantess was preying on their poet's mind, eroding his romantic soul like acid, for reasons which Jaq only half comprehended and thought it wiser not to pry into. Had Queem Malagnia represented some sort of anti-ideal to Googol, some appalling pattern of sexuality which haunted him even as he tried to reject and purge it, failing to?

What romantic formula could he possibly fit Queem into? If he did not do so, how could he forget her? How could he come to terms with forsaking the dark lusts of that corporeal, living city – in the way that he had come to terms with never attaining Meh'Lindi?

This depressed Jaq.

They aimed for a lone red dwarf star named Bendercoot, a thousand light years inward towards Segmentum Sola. Records listed Bendercoot as parent to only four small rocky worlds, all uninhabited. The outer-most hosted a minor orbital dockyard for Imperial Navy and trader vessels. The gravity well wasn't deep: a mere two days to travel inward from the safe jump-zone, two days to travel outward again.

It was to be hoped that this dockyard hadn't been destroyed by alien attack or abandoned; records could be centuries out of date. Failing Bendercoot, the travellers had at least three other obvious options – ports on minor routes they could call at. Jaq hoped that Googol was navigating faithfully, and cursed himself for his doubts.

However, the millennium-old dockyard was still circling Bendercoot IV. An Imperial cruiser was moored upon it: a cluster of fretted, fluted towers linked by flying buttresses studded with death's heads. Also, a pocked, patched, bulbous old freighter.

Grimm, who had spent further long hours fine-tuning, then polishing, *Tormentum's* engines, went 'ashore' inside the orbiting dock to convey a satchel of rare metals for payment and to 'sniff the air,' so he said.

Came the hour for their departure, Grimm was still missing.

'Shall I go and seek him out?' asked Meh'Lindi.

Jaq stared from the porthole across a scalloped plain of metal bristling with gantries and defensive weapons blisters. Bright-lit towers cast groove-like shadows. This was a minor dockyard, yet doubtless it housed many kilometres of internal corridors and halls. The fuel and oxygen tubes had already snaked away.

'*Sapphire Eagle,* clear for departure,' crackled a radio voice. 'Human purity be yours.'

'Be yours too,' replied Jaq. 'We'll hold for half an hour.' To Meh'Lindi he said, 'If he's in any trouble, that could snare us.'

'He left the engines in good trim,' said Googol. 'I'll miss the little tyke.'

'Do you believe he has skipped ship, Vitali?'

'Maybe he doesn't feel much like diving down the throat of a tiger... I don't know much about the protocols of you inquisitors but you're probably posted as a renegade by now.'

The journey to the Eye and then the return to Terra, though measured in weeks of warp time, would have cost Jaq years of real time. Once it was certain that Jaq was heading towards the Eye with Carnelian in pursuit, an astropath could have signalled Earth instantly, using Malleus codes. Perhaps the Harlequin man even had his own tame astropath aboard *Veils of Light*. He had made sure that he murdered Jaq's starspeaker, Moma Parsheen.

Bael Firenze was powerful. Obispal, on the other hand... he could be netted and forced to confirm Jaq's story. Obispal might be anywhere in the galaxy.

They waited.

For fifteen minutes.

Twenty.

Twenty-five.

'Prepare to leave, Vitali.'

Jaq had valued the squat. Jaq had spoken in defence of abhumans... Now the squat was betraying him. Although this was only a trivial betrayal compared with the cosmic treachery planned by the cabal, yet it still stung.

Jaq himself might need to betray Meh'Lindi by handing her over to the Malleus laboratories. If Meh'Lindi suspected this, would she still remain loyal, girded by her assassin's oaths?

At the twenty-eighth minute Grimm bustled back aboard.

'Sorry, boss,' he said. 'Thanks for waiting. I met some brothers. We got to drinking. Hey-ho, hey-ho.'

'And off with them you thought you'd go?' asked Jaq sadly.

Grimm didn't exactly deny this, which at least was honest of him. 'I feel the tug of kin, boss. I'm the roaming kind, but still...'

'You thought you'd see whether our ship left without you, thus deciding the matter.'

'Launching now,' warned Googol. *Tormentum* began to pulse slowing away from the dock.

'Huh, so you *were* going to abandon me!' Grimm managed to inject a note of indignant reproach, at which Jaq couldn't help but smile wanly.

'Course, I also thought to myself: *Earth*. Likely never see Earth otherwise. See Earth and die, don't they say?'

How true. How many shiploads of young psykers arrived on Earth, only to die. By some people the Master of Mankind was dubbed the Carrion Eater. Would he likewise consume Jaq?

'Sorry, boss. Really!'

'You did come back, Grimm; that's the main thing.'

Squat, Navigator, assassin: which could Jaq be one hundred per cent sure of? He prayed not to fall victim to the paranoia of which Carnelian had accused him – or else his story, whenever he managed to tell it, might seem wholly unbelievable.

Was not paranoia a touchstone of sanity in this universe of enemies and deceit?

Trust no one, not even yourself, he thought, for you, too, may stray from the pure path without even realising it.

Jaq fasted.

TERRA.

All comm-channels burbled with vox traffic hours, minutes or seconds old. Astral frequencies would be quite as crowded with telepathic messages of even greater urgency, though such messages wouldn't be time-lapsed by the speed limit of electromagnetic radiation. Long-distance radar registered the blips of hundreds of vessels heading in-system or climbing the last shallow incline out of the deep gravity-well of the Sun.

To scan even the approaches to the home system from beyond the outermost challenge-line would seem ample confirmation that the hub of the Imperium could never falter. Yet Jaq hardly needed to remind himself how warp storms had formerly isolated the home system from the stars for several thousand years. The first flowering of human civilisation throughout the galaxy had wilted, rotting into the cesspool of the Age of Strife. That earlier heroic age was eclipsed so utterly that it was now whelmed in obscurity.

He hardly needed to remind himself that during the thirty-first millennium the possessed rebel warmaster Horus had laid waste to Luna and invaded Earth, breaking through to the very inner palace. The putsch was defeated, oh yes, but at what dire cost. Thereafter the wounded Emperor could only survive from grim millennium to grim millennium immobile in his prosthetic golden throne.

What Horus had almost accomplished by main force and using fighting machines of the Adeptus Mechanicus, Jaq hoped to finesse by guile – assisted by a lugubrious Navigator, a squat whose reliability was now in question, and an assassin whose thought processes increasingly puzzled him.

Jaq stabbed a finger at one particular blip on the radar screen. 'Display that one, Vitali.'

Googol fiddled with the magniscope and brought a flying, dark castle into sharp focus. He gasped. 'A Black Ship, inward bound, Jaq.'

'Match its course. We'll board it. Inquisition inspection.'

'Won't that be among the most vigilant of vessels?'

'It'll have been on tour for a year or so. If I'm on a black list of criminals I doubt that any resident inquisitor will know.'

Jaq spoke with a show of confidence. He was a Malleus man. Therefore let the Black Ship be carrying an ordinary inquisitor; this could work to Jaq's advantage.

Inquisitors frequently travelled on Black Ships while the vessels traversed the galaxy, harvesting fresh young psykers. An inquisitor was extremely useful to the officers of a Black Ship who needed to test their human cargo and root out any malignant weeds en route. As Jaq knew only too well; for he had been similarly rooted out, not as a weed but as a precious flower, transplanted, advanced to greater things. He remembered Olvia. Many such as Olvia would be crowding the dismal dormitories of the Black Ship, their prayers crescendoing as the ship dipped ever closer to Earth, their spirits focusing mournfully upon the impending sacrifice of themselves. The oppressive psychic miasma inside such a vessel would provide a useful protective fog for Jaq.

'What about *Tormentum*?'

'Program her to head away beyond the jump zone under ordinary drive towards the comet halo, then just to drift. We'll know roughly where she is, if we can ever rendezvous with her again.'

Googol nodded. Few ships strayed out beyond the jump zone. Ships were either in-system vessels, remaining within the confines of Sol space, or else they were interstellar – in which case they would dive into the warp as soon as they could. *Tormentum* could remain undetected, yet reachable aboard a conventional craft, offering an option for the unpredictable, dark future.

How *much* Jaq's companions knew by now! They knew of the Ordo Malleus, of the cabal, of the hydra, of the Eye and of creatures of Chaos. More, much more, than ordinary mortals ought to know. If Jaq's mission succeeded, his accomplices in it ought really to be mindscrubbed... Ought to be, as Marines were mindscrubbed after participating in a daemonic *exterminatus*; reduced to the condition of babies so as to safeguard their innocence and sanity. Or else honourably executed.

'Meh'Lindi, I'd like to speak to you alone,' said Jaq.

He walked ahead of her through the ebon corridor past twinkling niches to his own sleep-cell, which he cloaked in privacy.

Memories of that other occasion when they had been alone together teased him turbulently, even though he knew that there could be no repetition of that exultant night. Nevertheless he yearned to know her true feelings.

'Yes, inquisitor?'

'You do realise, Meh'Lindi, that you're the only repository of hydra hereabouts?'

'Just as I knew,' she replied, 'that you would need to travel to Earth and would feel obliged to jettison that adamantine trunk.'

'Was *that* why you ate some of the hydra? Not to protect yourself from it – so much as to preserve some trace?'

'An assassin is an instrument,' she said expressionlessly. 'A wise instrument; yet still an instrument in the service of greater goals.'

'You would give yourself to be tormented? Dissected?' There: he had said it. He had confessed his guilty fear to his one-time mistress.

'Pain can be blocked,' she reminded him, 'as it is when I alter my body.'

He knew that this was less than the whole truth. The pain of physical injuries could be blocked. Yet inside the brain was the centre of raw, absolute pain itself. It could be reached by cerebral probes. Did she know how to isolate *that* from her consciousness? Aye, and what of the terror of having one's very identity taken apart entirely? Must that not be agonising in the deepest possible way?

'If I could give you a gift, Meh'Lindi, what would it be?'

She considered for a while. 'Perhaps... oblivion.'

Now he understood her even less.

Unless... unless she realised – as Grimm and Googol undoubtedly did not suspect – that it was the sacred duty of the Ordo Malleus to erase the very knowledge of monstrous Chaos from human minds, lest this knowledge seduce the weak. Such knowledge must be obliterated.

Was Meh'Lindi forgiving him in advance for the possible fate of his companions, supposing that he *succeeded*?

That indeed was loyalty.

Jaq staunched the flash of anguished pride he felt. Loyalty to anyone who was not the Emperor was a dangerous commodity, was it not? As the hosts of Horus had proved.

Still, he promised himself then and there that he would do his utmost to save Meh'Lindi and Googol and Grimm. Even if this made him, in some small way, a traitor. Even if, in so doing, he denied Meh'Lindi the gift of utter amnesia she requested.

On the point of departure, she paused.

'I have much to forget,' she told him. 'Inside this body of mine lurks plastiflesh and flexicartilage in which is written the permanent memory of a certain evil shape.'

'Do you mean you feel as though there's a kind of *rune* of evil written inside you? Do you feel that you're somehow cursed? Rather than blessed by your wondrous ability?'

'An ability to become one thing and one thing only! When I use polymorphine now I can't adopt the appearances of other human beings. I will trigger the genestealer pattern within me. Thus I deny my chameleon possibilities. I ask you: is that *Callidus*? Is that *cunning*?

'So do you suspect you're false to the traditions of your shrine? Yet your shrine asked this of you.'

She nodded. 'It was done to me with my consent.' Perhaps she felt that her shrine had cheated her.

He hesitated before asking, 'Were you pressured into consenting?'

She laughed bitterly. 'The universe always applies pressures, does it not? Crushing pressures.' That was no real answer, nor had he really expected one. Would an assassin betray the secrets of her shrine?

'Yet on Queem's world,' he reminded her, 'you felt illuminated... about Chaos, and the possible nature of the Harlequin man.'

Meh'Lindi pursed her lips; those lips that had roved over his body once, those same lips that had stretched into a terrible snout.

'Darkly illuminated,' she corrected him. 'Darkly.'

And even so, he would not wish to extinguish her light.

SERPENTE

SEVENTEEN

'FRUITFUL TRAVELS, JOURNEYMAN?' Jaq asked a young bearded inquisitor who could almost have been his earlier self.

Rafe Zilanov wore some alien foetus pendants dangling from his ear lobes. The man seemed alert, though a little inexperienced. Whatever his special talents – however well honed those were to diagnose any daemonic contamination among the passengers – the moaning psychic static aboard the Black Ship provided just the level of astral interference that Jaq had hoped for.

'Fruitful? A net of eleven hundred psykers for the Emperor. I think that's fruitful. We were only obliged to eliminate half of one per cent. Five per cent seem worthy of advancement.'

And ninety-five per cent worthy of feeding to the cadaverous Master of Mankind to power his Astronomican. How long, how long, could the noble agony of the human galaxy continue? Maybe the cabal had the right idea, to replace this cannibalistic system – with the ultimate totalitarian control.

Oh no, they did not. And oh no, they were almost certainly not what they seemed.

Jaq grunted.

'Is something wrong?' asked the skew-eyed, brawny captain.

The lines on Captain Holofernest's ruddy face told of many years exposed to the psychic migraine of those he must transport. Here, thought Jaq, was an unsung hero of the Imperium. Not a Marine, not a Terminator Knight, but a hero even so. An ignorant hero, blessedly ignorant, his uniform hung with amulets. A hero to be browbeaten.

Tapestries of space battles cloaked the walls of the captain's cabin – permanent reminders of a more active destiny that might have been his?

Jaq noted faint ring-marks from liquor glasses on the captain's desk. Private drunkenness, while his Navigator steered through the warp, was Holofernest's solace, his consolation, anaesthesia – and his weak spot.

Jaq had activated his tattoos for Zilanov's benefit, so that the journeyman understood that Jaq was his superior in ways that the young man did not wholly comprehend, yet knew enough not to query.

Still, Zilanov reserved his opinion; as Jaq too would have done. The journeyman scrutinised Jaq's motley companions curiously. He appeared to have identified Meh'Lindi as an assassin.

'Wrong, captain?' drawled Jaq, as nonchalantly as he could. 'Oh, something is wrong. I'm investigating a certain matter. It relates to ships such as yours. Specifically, what happens when they deliver their cargo to Earth orbit.'

'Our passengers get sorted out a second time,' growled Holofernest. 'To double-check our own good work; and very wise too. Then shuttles convey the majority to the Forbidden Fortress for long Astronomican training followed by brief duty. What of it?'

'Whereabouts is that Forbidden Fortress, captain?'

'Hah! That information is forbidden to such as me. Very wise too.'

'Where do you suppose it is?'

'I shouldn't dream of speculating, inquisitor.'

'Very wise.'

The stronghold of the Adeptus Astronomica was inside the mountain range known as the Himalayas. One whole mountain was sculpted into the upper half of a sphere of rock that housed the Astronomican.

'You speak of *long* training and *brief* duty. Why do you add those details? Do I detect grievances? A streak of softness in your soul?'

Holofernest glanced at Rafe Zilanov for reassurance.

'Loose tongues!' snarled Jaq. 'Those are best torn out. I'm sure you'll be more discreet in future in your implied criticisms of the Imperium – unless of course *liquor* loosens your lips. But no matter. What concerns me is illicit slavery – namely the creaming off of a tiny percentage of comely psykers.'

Zilanov knit his brow, and the captain gaped. 'Who by?' And visibly wished he had not asked. 'Not that I'm inquisitive. Not that I–'

Jaq favoured Holofernest with the thinnest of smiles. 'I almost hesitate to say it. By perverted officials relatively high in the Imperial court.'

Illicit slavery, thought Jaq, as opposed to legitimate *dedication* to the Emperor... Would those illicit slaves of whom he spoke live longer in private hands? He rather doubted it. Their brief existence might be positively vile in the hands of connoisseurs of degradation. Admittedly no such connoisseurs *existed*, to the best of his knowledge, except in his own imagination. It was a good idea to believe one's own lies, then others might believe them too.

'I need hardly emphasise the peril of harbouring untrained psykers even in the outer palace,' he went on. 'Even if such persons are kept prisoner behind psychic screens, any one of these might still become a conduit for a daemon; especially since they will call out in their pain and misery for any form of assistance. If a daemon possesses just one slave, and that slave escapes inside the palace – consider the possible consequences!'

'Our passenger manifests are always accurate,' protested Holofernest.

'I don't doubt it. Yet what of the tiny percentage of passengers that every Black Ship needs to eliminate? Do you store their corpses to be counted and tallied too?'

'You must know that we scuttle such corpses into the warp.'

'What if that tiny percentage did not in actuality become corpses, but are held alive in stasis in some nook or cranny of a ship as cavernous as this?'

'Not on board mine, I assure you!' The captain glanced towards his desk where his liquor glass habitually would rest. He was yearning for it now.

'I make no personal accusations,' said Jaq. 'You have now received privileged information; that is all.'

'What do you want us to do?' asked Zilanov. The young inquisitor almost believed. Why should he not? The story was plausible enough to send a shiver down the spine of any Emperor's man. Why should a senior inquisitor be lying?

Jaq said, 'I need to be smuggled into the number three south-eastern port of the Imperial palace in exactly the way we suspect these illicit slaves are being smuggled, namely in stasis food chests. Myself, and my companions.'

'You'll be utterly vulnerable,' Zilanov pointed out.

'Until the stasis deactivates at a pre-set time, that's true. Do you suggest we should evade danger, when by risking ourselves we can lay a hand on the perpetrators of this crime?'

Zilanov believed completely now. No traitor would make themselves so utterly helpless or risk delivering themselves paralysed into the possible hands of enemies.

'This is an undercover operation of alpha-prime importance,' said Jaq. 'You are sworn to total secrecy. Now I'll explain the routing codes you must use for the caskets...'

AND STASIS CEASED.

Jaq cracked open the lid of the container in which he had lain cramped in an enforcedly foetal position.

He had felt no sensation whatever. He had expected to know nothing, either.

Instead, his consciousness had been suspended in a single quantum of thought; and that thought had been anxiety. Maybe the workings of his consciousness had progressed ever so slightly during the timeless interval of his encapsulation, as his psychic sense of protection attempted to lift the siege of anxiety. Yet essentially he had been suspended frozen at that point of dread – his whole being composed of apprehension and nothing else. No memories, no active thoughts, no sluggish dreams; only an impersonal distillation of anxiety occurring within the same endless ever-instant.

Now that he was Jaq again, he shook with accumulated fear. What if he had entered stasis already in a state of terror or of pain?

Ultimately, he hoped that his psychic talent might have soothed and opiated him, altering the nature of that ever-instant.

What if not? What if he had possessed no enchantments? He suspected that he had discovered a new and terrible torture or punishment. For at the height of torment a prisoner might be dropped into a stasis casket to experience that climactic moment for a year, for a century.

Jaq squinted up at massive rusty pipes beaded with condensation. Ah, those mottlings were not rust. Generations of pious runes had faded and been overpainted and had faded again. The mottlings were moving past a couple of metres overhead. He heard clanking, creaking, distant tintinnabulations of metal ringing on metal. His casket was obviously on a conveyor belt.

Just as it should be. Mastering the fear which had washed over him in the release from stasis, he stood up. The four caskets were indeed travelling slowly along a segmented steel belt through a dismal, seemingly endless downhill tunnel. Dull orange light ached from glowglobes. The air was frigid. No one, nor any servitor, was in sight.

Clambering to the nearest neighbouring casket, Jaq lifted the lid. Meh'Lindi sat up, a snake rearing to strike. She did not sting. She kissed Jaq fleetingly.

'Thank you for that taste of oblivion, master.'

'Master?' he echoed.

'We're pretending to be slaves, aren't we?'

'We can forget about that now. Any ill effects?'

'We assassins know how to blank our minds if need be, to induce hibernation. I became a blank, aware only of beloved nullity, the state before universe and Chaos came to be, when God existed, God the Nothing.'

She was, he suspected, harking back to some strange half-remembered cult of her long-lost home world. The true God, the ever-dying Emperor, eater of souls, beacon of suffering striving humanity, was almost within reach now, perhaps only four hundred kilometres distant through the palace.

Meh'Lindi in turn raised the lid of Grimm's casket, and the abhuman exclaimed, 'Huh. Huh.' As if uttering his own restored heartbeat.

Jaq opened the final stasis-box.

'Void,' whispered Vitali, 'endless void. The third eye did not cease to see. It ranged an empty infinitude. Did you know that there are degrees of nothingness? Shades of unlight?'

"Nuff of that guff,' said Grimm gruffly, popping up alongside Jaq. 'Quite like the old home caverns, this place, 'cept I don't see any stone. Don't seem much of a palace, though. Where is everyone? Sure we've taken the right route, boss?'

'Oh yes. This is an ancient deep supply tunnel, a tiny tendril far away from the heart. Even so, we've been rather lucky that no members of the Adeptus Terra are labouring down here right now.'

'Huh, now he tells us.'

IT MIGHT HAVE been winter in the outside world. Though truly there was little of the outside world in existence on Terra. All of Earth's continents – save for the south polar icelands, deep under which the Inquisition lurked – were clad, often kilometres high, in the labyrinthine sprawl of one edifice of state or another. Palace, ecclesiarchy, huge bureaucracies, virtually worlds unto themselves.

Generations could live out lifetimes within a single Imperial subdepartment, almost oblivious to the stars above except as notations on data-slates or in ledgers, never seeing a wan sun peer through a poisoned sky.

Presently the air began to warm and to catch foully in their throats. The belt was bearing them onward and downward towards intimations of noise and activity, towards distant stabs of light. Evidently their tunnel would soon debouch into somewhere vaster.

After heaving the stasis boxes off the belt, they took from them strap-on oxygen bottles and breathing membranes. Those membranes also served to shield their eyes from an increasingly gassy and acrid atmosphere. Whispers of oxygen refreshed their lungs now.

Behind them in the orange obscurity other cargo was looming. Collapsing the stasis boxes, they hid those in a dusty side chamber. They walked on, alongside the trundling belt.

In a vast pillared hall of plasteel, cyborgs and amputees bonded into machines ground to and fro on caterpillar tracks or clanked about on tarnished metal legs. The floor was awash with oily chemical spillage fitfully iridescent in the glance of shifting lights.

Some of the mechanised workers serviced cable-sinewed thudding engines. Others tore open crates from the belt with powered pincers, inspected bills of lading, and transferred the incoming cargo to a branching array of mighty, rusting pneumomagnetic tubes which despatched items in distant directions with a fierce hiss and thunderclap of compressed air and a sizzle of electromagnetic surge. Smashed empty crates disappeared into the maw of a furnace, a throat of fire which ruddied the sloshing wash of liquids around it. The hall echoed with rumble, hiss, clap and roar.

Even as the four intruders watched from a ledge of concealment, one of the tubes ruptured, spraying ochreous flakes. A welder-servitor trundled to repair the sprung plates.

Perhaps this kind of accident was a regular occurrence. Perhaps that automaton did nothing else but reweld tubes. Had those not burst from time to time, its monotonous life would have been empty. Jaq and companions were in a very minor oesophagus of an ancient, neglected, far fringe of the palace – or more properly, underpalace.

Did the cargo from the stars which arrived by this route ever reliably reach its intended destination? Perhaps it did. Just so, did much of the Imperium itself function, rupturing, then being rewelded. Yet at the same time, mighty energies were being deployed. And there was vigilance too.

On impulse Jaq removed his Tarot significator card, of the black-robed High Priest with the hammer. Surely Carnelian was far far away, hundreds, thousands of light years away, and couldn't intrude again...

Jaq's image was shading his eyes with the hand that clutched the hammer in the manner of someone peering from brightness into an obscure distance. The card twitched. It throbbed. Abruptly it pulled like a dowsing rod as though, should Jaq release the card, it would promptly fly away under its own impulse.

'Boss–' Grimm reached as if to catch the card, should it spring free, but jerked his fingers back. 'Are you doing that yourself?'

Am I? wondered Jaq. Is my hidden mind, in which all engrams of memory are recorded, prompting me to recall the safest route through the topographic nightmare of the palace? Or does some power unseen preside over this, our journey?

Whose power? That of the God-Emperor himself?

The card yanked urgently. 'This card will be our guide,' he said. 'We must hurry from this place.'

None too soon. Scarcely had they skulked through the vast hall from shadow to shadow, from pillar to pillar, sliding along in the slosh of foul liquid, avoiding the spotlights and scrutiny of the trundling servitors, than – staring back through his magniscope – Jaq spied a tall figure far away scrutinising the area around the conveyor. Boots, leather breeches, long black cloak... The ominous tall helmet was a three-tiered brazen skull tipped with crenellations from which antennae sprouted. The figure stirred the poisonous soup that hid the plates of the floor with the butt of a laser-spear.

'Who's that guy?' asked Grimm.

'Custodian,' murmured Jaq. 'Palace guardsman. Maybe we triggered a sensor beam.'

Just then a giant warty rat, its matted coat faintly phosphorescent, scuttled from the tunnel mouth. The custodian levelled his spear and lasered the creature.

Jaq spoke a conjuration of stealth. 'O furtim invisibiles!'

The Tarot card tugged gently towards one of several archways.

THEY DESCENDED THROUGH several strata of plasteel where whole rivers flowed, of dirty oil and chemicals, where torrents of effluent vented into lakes abrew with luminous algae. They dodged mobile machines, patchworked with stains, that might have contained human beings or at least the torsos and heads of cyberworkers. They slept in the cab of a derelict mammoth bulldozer half-sunk in glittering sludge.

AND NOW THEY climbed, by circular stairways hidden within the cores of columns, up into a twilit mall where scribes scrivened by electrocandle outside their family cells.

This mall stretched for a kilometre. Several hundred hooded scribes in black fustian laboured at penning data from implants in their brows into massive ledgers bound in skin, perhaps the skin of their fathers and grandfathers, lovingly flayed after death, cured and dedicated to the work that had occupied those bygone lives.

Other scribes were copying the fading penmanship of ancient, crack-backed dusty volumes into newer tomes. Tottering, spiderwebbed towers of codices rose from floor to ceiling, ladders propped against some. Many scribes whispered as they worked. A toothless crone of a curator in brown habit perched like some shrivelled mummy in a high chair. An antique alien manuscript lay open on the high desk before her, but she was more occupied in supervising her scribes through the mag-nilenses of a lorgnette. She pointed a rod that caused her target to twitch and sweat. Couriers came and went, some bringing data-chips, some carrying ledgers away.

'Who goes?' she cackled as Jaq and party approached.

'The word is powerful,' replied Jaq.

'Pass by. Pass by.'

WEARING STOLEN GREY robes of Administratum auditors – and Grimm the buckskin of a kitchen servant – they strode through a busy basilica housing arcane machinery. Sacred klaxons wailed. Tech-priests fiddled with vernier gauges. Sandalwood incense rose, sweetening a haze of acrid fumes.

Later they crossed a cathedral-laboratory. Icons marked with sym-bols of the elements dangled from internal flying buttresses. Sodium vapour flambeaux behind high false-clerestory-windows of stained glass painted patches of amber ichor, sap, and haemoglobin across the tessellated floor. Athenor furnaces glowed and alembics bubbled, purifying and repurifying rare drugs extracted from the organs of alien animals being vivisected by surgeon-butchers behind armour glass.

Trumpets screamed and brayed, drowning howls. Evidently such organs must be extracted live without use of soporifics for full efficacy. Orange and golden blood ran through tubes, pumped by scrofulous bondsmen chained to bellows. Lift platforms rose into view, carrying new specimens; and sank, bearing carcasses and offal.

A laser-armed tech-priest dressed in a cream robe accosted them. 'Your business? Your rank?'

'We're accountants for the synthdiet administration,' said Jaq, casting an aura of persuasion. 'I'm Prefectus Secundus of the Dispendium, the office of Cost and Loss.'

'I have never heard of that.' Yet this fact need not rouse the priest's sus-picions. If anything, the contrary! The estimate that ten billion people were involved in the administration of the palace perhaps erred on the miserly side.

Jaq nodded at Googol and Meh'Lindi. 'These are my Prefectus Tertius and Sub-Prefectus. The squat is a servitor. We suspect protein is going to waste in these experiments.'

'You call these *experiments*?' cried the priest indignantly. 'Some molecules of immortality for the Emperor's own use are extracted here.'

'Leaving much good meat,' groused Grimm.

'That's *alien* meat, you inhuman turnspit! It's indigestible.'

'Could be rendered into diet.'

'Rubbish, impertinent scullion. How dare a servitor address me thus?'

'Excuse us, I'm sure!'

'Wise adeptus,' interrupted a beige-clad novice.

The priest excused Jaq's party, wearing only a slightly puzzled frown. This might have deepened had he been able to concentrate on remembering that auditors had supposedly been about to commence an investigation – yet had vanished out of sight instead.

Their exit from that cathedral through a heavily guarded checkpoint was easier than entry would have been by that same route.

Yet beyond, a seemingly endless, grumbling queue of applicants twenty deep crept like some hugely elongated snail along a gloomy arcaded boulevard towards some distant office of the Administratum, seeking... what? A permit? An application form? An interview?

The most foresightful applicants hauled minicarts on which fellow applicants, who would return the favour, curled up snoozing. Hawkers of sweetmeats and glucose sticks and vendors of stale water toured the queue. Hunched sanitizers in khaki coveralls drove mobile lavatoria to and fro.

An Arbites patrol team was maintaining surveillance from parked land-cars, while a bus of shocktroopers lurked in reserve in case of riot. Jaq spied their plumed helmets through the blue armoured glass.

A team of armed monitors was working its way along the queue, using portable psychodiagnostic kits. Occasionally an applicant was arrested. One broke free and was shot.

'Out of the frying pan into the fire,' said Grimm. 'We'll never squeeze our way past that lot.'

The queue was growing restive now. The Arbites were readying their suppression shields.

Jaq's Tarot card tugged.

EIGHTEEN

If viewed from low orbit through the foul atmosphere, the continent-spanning palace was a concatenation of copulating, jewel-studded tortoise shells erupting into ornate monoliths, pyramids, and ziggurats kilometres high, pocked by landing pads, prickling with masts of antennae and weapons batteries. Whole cities were mere chambers in this palace, some grimly splendid, others despicable and deadly, and all crusted with the accretion of the ages.

Common sense – and the High Priest card – insisted that Jaq and company eschew the option of renting a vehicle and taking to one of the multi-decked roads that bored through the palace. At precinct boundaries scrutiny teams would surely demand to scan electronic tattoos.

Thus instead they must detour on foot through a sprawling, rearing tenement-conurb of densely populated shafts and conduits, of crumbling many-times-braced and scaffolded urban cliffs that crowded closer than canyon walls under a grey steel roof held up saggingly by a suspensor field.

Even the scaffolding was colonised with tin shacks, torn tents, tattered plastic bedrolls. Here, the basic protoplasmic rump of humanity festered and simmered, in this breeding ground of those whose greatest dream was that their brats might become the lowest of adepts, hereditary slave-workers. Starvelings haunted the walkways like wraiths, seeking for recent corpses. Tattooed gangs roamed, armed with home-made blades. The susurrus of people was a sea of sound, often sinisterly hushed.

They stole rags to cloak themselves, they evicted beggars from ventilator ducts in which to shelter, on guard. They filched food from the starving.

Meh'Lindi killed; Jaq killed; and Grimm too.

For a while they seemed to be more distant than ever from their goal, as if backtracking. As day followed day they even reminisced nostalgically about the cathedral-laboratory and about the mall of scribes. Always Judges seemed to be in the offing, exercising random vigilance; much less often, the proud elite palace Custodians.

'Becoming quite the little nomad family, aren't we?' puffed Grimm on one occasion, after they had fled and hid.

Jaq stared at him. Oh yes, they were more than mere companions now. Disloyalty might have hovered – and the greatest, needful betrayal might yet await – nevertheless they pursued this last, seemingly interminable stage of their enterprise as family, of a kind.

Of a kind.

A SPOTLIT ZEALOT of a confessor was screaming through a megaphone at an arena packed with humanity, under a coruscated domed ceiling. The glittering shimmer above twinkled hypnotically, now forming the Emperor's face, and now potent runes, as if this was a planetarium of devotion and self-incrimination. The shifting lights and the booming words combined to work a spell such that the audience surged within itself, thrusting elements of itself forward, expelling individuals as a sickly body sheds cells.

These body-cells were heretics, or people who imagined they were heretics, or whose neighbours believed – at least in that setting – that they were corrupted.

Purity squads hauled such individuals away for execution, or perhaps for excruciation and redemption.

Jaq and comapnions stood near a young couple who had, so they gathered, set out with two Imperial credits to squander on a visit to a column-top cafe where real coffee from a starworld was served and which overlooked a vista of floodlit factories and shrines. The young woman had turned aside into the arena, enchanted by the vibrant words. Presently she began shoving against her young man, whispering bitterly to him, until in despair he squeezed forward to denounce himself.

Meh'Lindi had to hustle Grimm away. Even Jaq felt the urge to betray himself.

Jaq had never liked zealots. That night, after killing a guard, they broke into the residence of the preacher who had purged so many hundreds of hysterics (as well as, yes, accursed heretics). Meh'Lindi nerve-blocked and heart-stopped the hapless man and his family. Jaq and party bathed away the stink of days, feasted soberly, prayed, slept deeply. They thieved new clothes before pressing onward circuitously, evading the vigilance that was ever more evident, as omnipresent as the Emperor's spirit – yet also seemingly purblind, foxed by the intricate, degenerate immensity of that which must be overseen.

ONE DOES NOT tell exactly by what route – and by what chicanery – an enemy might slip from the outer palace into the inner palace. Oh no.

Some secrets must remain secret. Almost, they must remain secret from those people who themselves know them.

The journey of Jaq Draco and his companions from the number three south-eastern port to the Column of Glory took as long as their flight from the Eye of Terror had cost them in warp-time, and more.

At one time they masqueraded as ciphers, servitors who had memorized messages of which they had no understanding, and who trotted along in a hypnotic trance.

At another time they disguised themselves as historitors whose whole career was to revise subversive records, and to forge more reverend versions. Thus Jaq and companions counterfeited themselves.

They adopted the camouflage of a returning explorator team, which, in a sense, they were.

Always lying, pretending, stealing – robes, insignia, regalia – and sometimes compelled to kill, acting as though they were some covert traitor terror squad pledged to deep penetration of the ultimate sanctum. Meh'Lindi, as a Callidus assassin, was invaluable.

They passed increasingly amidst priests, battlemasters, astropaths, scholastics, and the retinues and brood and servants of these.

Once, as an extreme ploy, Jaq pretended to be an inquisitor; and afterwards was shocked to remember that he was indeed one in reality.

Could they have tried – having come so far – to surrender to an officer of the Adeptus Custodes, thus to crave audience with a commander of those exalted warriors who guarded the throne room itself? Could they have revealed themselves?

The reach of the cabal might easily extend as far as an officer of those final defenders of the Throne.

Besides, their journey of penetration had by now attained a bizarre dynamic all of its own, an almost self-sustaining momentum.

Fatigue became an anaesthetic. Ever-present anxiety must needs be deposited in some increasingly constipated bowel of the soul, where it mutated paradoxically into a stimulant.

Jaq felt as if he was forcing his way down into the depths of an ocean, where pressure measured itself in tonnes. Yet he and his companions trod a shining path, in a state of mind which alternated between dream and nightmare, and which had certainly ceased to be ordinary consciousness.

This path was luminous to themselves, yet obscure to strangers – as though their track was detached by a hair's breadth from reality; as though they were stepping along some twisting corridor, embedded within the palace, that nevertheless ran parallel to the true world of the palace.

Jaq's Tarot card led him like a compass; and behind the High Priest with the hammer there now hovered in the liquid crystal of the card the shadow of a figure, enthroned, that was coming ever more closely to resemble the Emperor, as though that other card of the arcana was fusing with Jaq's own significator card.

'We're in a trance,' Jaq murmured to Meh'Lindi once, while they rested. 'A trance of guidance. A voice seems to say to me: *Come*.' He refrained from mentioning that other echoing voices – shadows of voices – seemed to disagree.

'We're pursuing the ultimate ideal assassin's path,' she agreed. 'The path of cunning invisibility. This is the peak of achievement of any assassin of my shrine. Its goal must be our deaths, I think. For the paragon of assassins would be she who, after a long and terrible quest of sly subterfuge, tracked down none other than herself, and slew herself impeccably.'

'Huh!' said Grimm, and spat.

Googol, for his part, hunched in a daze.

One does not describe the precise route they took, oh no! That would be wicked treason. It may be, it may just be, that the selfsame pathway they followed towards the Emperor's presence, that identical pattern, only existed for Jaq and his comrades during that particular slice of time, unrepeatable ever again.

Comrades. Four members of a strangely braided family... who had once been total strangers, and might yet become so again. Jaq the father who made true love only once. Googol the wayward junior brother. Meh'Lindi the feral mother who carried within her not a child but the implanted lineaments of a monster shape. Grimm the child-scaled abhuman.

HERE NOW AT last was savage grandeur. Here was the Column of Glory itself.

Under a vaulted dome so lofty that clouds had formed to obscure its frescoed arcs, a slim tower of multi-hued metals rose half a kilometre high. The suits of White Scars and Imperial Fist Space Marines, who had died defending this palace nine thousand years earlier, studded that column. Within those shattered suits their bones still hung. Their skulls still grinned from open faceplates.

Crowds of young psykers, robed as acolytes, prayed there under the watchful gaze of their instructors. Soon those psykers would be led onward to be soul-bound, agonised and blinded, and consecrated for service.

Squads of helmeted Emperor's Companions stood to attention vigilantly, armed with bolters and plasma guns, black cloaks aswirl around ancient, ornately carved power armour. Dissonant music – gongs, harps – boomed and twanged and rippled, matching the pulse of ancient, adored machinery. Incense reeked.

Jaq was currently wearing the robes of a secretary to a cardinal, Meh'Lindi was a battle-sister of the Adepta Sororitas, Googol was a cardinal's majordomo, while Grimm was a robed tech-priest.

Two immense Titans, embodiments of the Machine-God, flanked the great archway that led onward, serving as columns, one blood-red, one purple. High over the archway, in obsidian, the wide winged double-headed eagle of the Imperium was mounted. The bowed carapaces of these giant fighting robots sustained golden mosaic roofing in which, as Jaq knew, were buried the heavy macro-cannons and multi-launchers of the Titans, just as their great cleated feet were locked underfloor. Purity seals and devout banners dangled everywhere they looked.

By each side of the archway sagged a power fist which could seize and crush to liquid any unpermitted interloper. The other jointed arm of each Titan terminated in a massive, poised defence laser.

Inside the jutting armoured head of each Titan, rotas of warrior adepts of the Collegia Titanica had roosted on honour-guard during thousands of years. During thousands of years those two Titans had stood as columns, immobile, statuesque, awing all who approached. Yet in ultimate emergency their plasma generators could presumably power up rapidly from standby mode. Energy could flow through hydroplastics coupled to actuators. The electrically-motivated fibre bundles that served as muscles could tear their heaviest weapons free from the roof, bringing tonnes crashing down as a blockade. The god-machines could wrench their feet free. They could open fire devastatingly. During overhauls throughout the millennia the appropriate maintenance litanies would have been chanted faithfully.

Even on standby, Jaq suspected that those power fists might flex and pluck a body from the floor if the devotees in those vast metallic heads saw fit...

'How did we get here?' whispered Googol, aghast with wonder.

'*Per via obscura et luminosa*,' replied Jaq. 'By the shining, hidden path—'

Time twisted.

Time shifted.

Time was, and was not.

An eerie silver power flowed through Jaq, as though he had invoked it by those words. The power used his mind as its conductor. He sensed how the time stream itself was being negated and annulled.

Some psykers of the highest level could distort time thus. Not Jaq, hitherto.

Never Jaq.

Yet now...

Was he *possessed*?

By no daemon, certainly. But by the shining path itself. To his senses that path now appeared to be the track of a phosphorescent arrow through twisted geometries. The arrow had accumulated a charge at its point until that point could transfix the fabric of time itself, pinning time temporarily like a moth with a needle through its spine...

'Run, now!' cried Jaq.

Did he and his abnormal family flit like hummingbirds which seem to flicker directly from one point in space to another, passing in and out of existence? Afterwards Jaq believed they must have darted thus – across the static, time-stopped Chamber of Glory, past the frozen Companions, and through the Titan Archway between the motionless menacing colossi.

And still the lustrous arrow impaled the tissue of time.

THROBBING PIPES RIBBED the walls of the vast throne room beyond. The muscles of the room were thick power cables feeding stegosaurian engines. The air was spiked with crisp ozone and bitter myrrh, and ointmented with balmy, somewhat greasy fragrances. The holiest battle banners, icons and golden fetishes flanked the arena of dedication where psykers were soul-bound.

Squads of Emperor's Companions who guarded that vast hall, a mob of tech-priests ministering to the machinery, a gaudy Cardinal Palatinate and his entourage, a red-robed High Lord of Terra and his staff – not to mention great clusters of astropaths, chirurgeons, scholastics, battlemasters: *all were motionless*.

The immense, soaring, tube-ridged throne resembled some fossilised, metastasised sloth crafted by some mad master of the Adeptus Titanicus. And it seemed to Jaq, though he did not know whether what he saw was true, or mere delusion instilled by that same psyker-dream, that this enormous, sacred prosthetic device, more precious by far than any gold, framed the wizened, mummified face of the God-Emperor.

Who looked not; though he saw through eyes of the mind, saw far beyond his throne room and his palace and the solar system. Who breathed not; yet he lived more fiercely than any mortal, enduring a psychically supercharged life-in-death.

'WE ARE CURIOUS,' came a mighty, anguished thought which itself transcended time.

'WE HAVE FOLLOWED YOUR INTRUSION INTO OUR SANCTUARY, OUR ANTRUM AND ADYTUM.'

'My lord.' Jaq sank to his knees. 'I beg to report to you before I am destroyed. I may have uncovered a major conspiracy—'

'THEN WE WILL STRIP YOUR SOUL BARE. RELAX, MORTAL MAN, OR YOU WILL SURELY DIE IN SUCH PAIN AS WE ALWAYS ENDURE.'

Jaq breathed deeply, slowly, stilling the panic that fluttered under his ribs like a trapped bird. He surrendered himself.

A hurricane roared through his mind.

If the story that he had thought to relate were a tangled forest – and if each event in that story were a tree – then within moments all the leaves were stripped away from all of the trees, denuding them to bare wintry twigs, to a raw basic life without the foliage of memories.

He was drained of his story; that was sucked from him in a trice, all of those leaves whirling into the mind-maw of the Master.

Jaq gagged. Jaq drooled.

He was an imbecile, less than an imbecile.

He was less than a new-born baby.

He neither knew where he was, nor who he was – nor what it even meant to be a someone.

The inquisitor sprawled. All that was known to his body was distress, the gurglings of the guts, breath and light.

Light from afar.

ABRUPTLY, ALL MEMORY flooded back. On that instant, each leaf sprouted anew to recloak the forest of his life.

'WE HAVE PUT BACK WHAT WE TOOK AND TASTED, INQUISITOR.'

Trembling, Jaq regained his kneeling posture and wiped his lips and chin. The previous moments were a hideous limbo, unknowable, immeasurable. He was Jaq Draco again.

'WE ARE MANY, INQUISITOR.' The voice boomed in his mind almost gently – if gently was how an avalanche would sweep away a doomed village, if gently was how a scalpel might strip a life to the bare aching bones.

'HOW ELSE COULD WE ADMINISTER OUR IMPERIUM–'

'AS WELL AS WINNOW THE WARP–'

'HOW ELSE?'

The Emperor's mind-voice, if that truly was what it was, had dissociated into several voices, as if his great undying soul co-existed in fragments that barely hung together.

'SO DOES THE HYDRA THREATEN US?'

'IMPERILLING OUR GREAT AND AWFUL PLAN TO STEER HUMANITY?'

'DID WE OURSELVES DEVISE THE HYDRA?'

'PERHAPS IN A PART OF US, SINCE THIS HYDRA PROMISES A PATH?'

'SURELY A MALEVOLENT PATH; FOR HOW COULD HUMANITY EVER FREE ITSELF?'

'THEN WE MUST BE MALEVOLENT TOO. FOR WE HAVE EXPELLED OUR SENTIMENTALITY LONG AGO. HOW ELSE COULD WE HAVE ENDURED? HOW ELSE COULD WE HAVE IMPOSED OUR RULE?'

'YET BY VIRTUE OF THAT WE ARE PURE AND UNCONTAMINATED BY WEAKNESS. WE ARE GRIM SALVATION.'

Beside Jaq, the squat twitched as if he had heard himself named. At that moment did the voice resonate within the abhuman? Jaq felt that he was listening to a mighty mind-machine argue with itself in a way that no Imperial courtier had perhaps ever heard, and that no High Lord of Terra even suspected could occur. Were Meh'Lindi and Googol aware of the voices in the way that Jaq was? Or was he imagining it all, caught up in some warp-spawned delusion, yet another twist in this labyrinthine conspiracy? He sensed the fabric of time attempting to tear free, and guessed that not much longer of this strange stasis remained.

'NOTHING THAT SAFEGUARDS HUMANITY CAN BE EVIL, NOT EVEN THE MOST STRENUOUS INHUMANITY. IF THE HUMAN RACE FAILS, IT HAS FAILED FOREVER.'

Maybe Jaq was too young by hundreds, by thousands of years, and his intellect too puny to comprehend the multiplex mind of the master who was forever on overview, whose thoughts battered in his mind. Or maybe the master's mind had become chaotic. Not warped by the

Ruinous Powers it surveyed, oh no, but divided amongst itself as its heroic grasp on existence ever so slowly weakened...

'WHEN WE CONFRONTED THE CORRUPTED, HOMICIDAL HORUS WHO ONCE USED TO SHINE LIKE THE BRIGHTEST STAR, WHO USED TO BE OUR BELOVED FAVOURITE – WHEN THE FATE OF THE GALAXY HUNG BY A THREAD – WERE WE NOT COMPELLED TO EXPEL ALL COMPASSION? ALL LOVE? ALL JOY? THOSE WENT AWAY. HOW ELSE COULD WE HAVE ARMOURED OURSELVES? EXISTENCE IS TORMENT, A TORMENT THAT MUST NOURISH US. EVIDENTLY WE MUST STRIVE TO BE THE FIERCE REDEEMER OF MAN, YET WHAT WILL REDEEM US?'

'Great lord of all,' whimpered Jaq, 'did you know of the hydra before now?'

'NO, AND WE SHALL SURELY ACT IN DUE TIME–'

'YET SURELY WE KNEW. HOW COULD WE NOT KNOW?'

'ONCE WE HAVE ANALYSED THE INFORMATION WITHIN THIS SUB-MIND OF OURS.'

'HEAR THIS, JAQ DRACO: ONLY TINY PORTIONS OF US CAN HEED YOU, OTHERWISE WE NEGLECT OUR IMPERIUM, OF WHICH OUR SCRUTINY MUST NOT FALTER FOR AN INSTANT. FOR TIME DOES NOT HALT EVERYWHERE WITHIN THE REALM OF MAN. INDEED TIME ONLY HALTS FOR YOU.'

'WE ARE AN EVER-WATCHFUL LORD, ARE WE NOT? DID YOU HOPE TO GAIN OUR UNDIVIDED ATTENTION?'

'HOW ELSE SHOULD WE SOUL-BIND PSYKERS AND OVERVIEW THE WARP AND BEAM THE ASTRONOMICAN BEACON AND SUR-VIVE AND RECEIVE INFORMATION AND GRANT AUDIENCES ALL AT ONCE, UNLESS WE ARE MANY?'

'AND YET STILL WE MISS SO MUCH, SO VERY MUCH? SUCH AS THAT WHICH GUIDED YOU HERE.'

'OUR SPIRIT GUIDED YOU.'

'NO: ANOTHER SPIRIT, A REFLECTION OF OUR GOODNESS WHICH WE THRUST FROM US.'

'WE ARE THE ONLY SOURCE OF GOODNESS, SEVERE AND DRAS-TIC. THERE IS NO OTHER SOURCE OF HOPE THAN US. WE ARE AGONISINGLY ALONE.'

Contradictions! These warred in Jaq's mind just as they seemed to coexist in the Emperor's own multimind.

Was another power for salvation present in the galaxy, unknown to the suffering Emperor – concealed from him, though somehow partak-ing of his essence? How could that be?

And what of the hydra? Did the Emperor truly know of it or not –
even now? Might he refuse to acknowledge what Jaq had reported to
him?

The Emperor's voices faded from Jaq's mind as time tried to stretch
back into shape.

Grimm tugged at Jaq's sleeve.

'It's over, lord. Don't you understand?' Yes, Grimm must have heard
something – other than what Jaq heard; some simple order. 'We gotta
go, boss. We got to get out.'

'How can a minnow understand a whale?' Jaq cried. 'Or an ant, an ele-
phant? Have we succeeded, Grimm? Have we?' Jaq's own voice rose to a
scream in that holiest of chambers, yet somehow it was hardly audible.
His words echoed like a flock of screeching, ultrasonic bats.

'Dunno, boss. We gotta go.'

'Out, out, out,' chanted Meh'Lindi. 'Away-way-way.'

And then...

EPILOGUE

So HAVE YOU finished scanning the *Liber Secretorum*?' asked the black-robed master librarian.

'Yes indeed.'

The man with the hooked chin and piercing green eyes sucked his cheeks in thoughtfully. He too was robed and badged as a Malleus man, his face almost hidden by his hood. The two men were shut inside a dimly lit room that was fashioned like a skull. Save for twin electrocandles illuminating icons of the Emperor in the two niches that corresponded to sockets, only the scanner glowed greenly.

'Where and when was this recorded?'

'Lord, it was delivered under inexplicable circumstances to the then-master of our Ordo more than a century ago. That was soon after Jaq Draco was declared a renegade for his *exterminatus* of Stalinvast, and disappeared. As to where this was recorded... perhaps on Terra?'

'The assassin? The Navigator? The squat? What of them?'

'A Meh'Lindi certainly existed, as the present Director of Callidus Assassins can confirm. But that is all the Director will acknowledge; and that she vanished from view, presumed dead. The Officio Assassinorum will admit nothing regarding the experimental surgery. Maybe that proved to be a fiasco, of which they wish to obliterate all memory. Or maybe it has an extreme security classification. Thus supposedly nothing in their records links her to Jaq Draco.

'The Navis Nobilitate cannot, or will not, authenticate the existence of a Navigator by the name of Vitali Googol. They have too much independence, in my view! Maybe Googol was the person's poetical sobriquet. Maybe Draco invented the name, if indeed he did not invent everything, other than the *exterminatus* which certainly occurred. As regards the visit to the throne-room of His Terribilitas, no member of the Custodes reported anything. It is utterly inconceivable that such an event ever took place.'

'The squat?'

'Grimm is a common name amongst his ill-fated kind, and this squat was of no importance to the Imperium.'

'What of Captain Holofernest and Inquisitor Zilanov?'

'Why, Inquisitor Zilanov executed that captain for dereliction of duty.'

'For drunkenness?'

The librarian nodded. 'There was... trouble on board that Black Ship. A rebellion among the passengers, some of whom were possessed. Zilanov died too. Draco could possibly have known of this before the *Liber* came to our attention, and therefore before it was composed. If Draco composed this at all! Why did Draco avoid the first person in his story, unless he was lying? *Did he even compose it?'*

'Our Ordo denies that any such project exists under our own aegis?'

'All Hidden Masters at the time denied belonging to such a cabal. Baal Firenze, who declared Draco a renegade, volunteered for the ministrations of deeptruth, metaveritas. Nothing relevant was learned. Proctor Firenze became as a baby thereafter.'

'He was re-educated?'

'Oh yes, Hidden Master. He redeveloped a personality, anew. He was rejuvenated, trained all over again as a dedicated inquisitor.'

'Harq Obispal?'

'Aliens ambushed and killed him shortly after the events which the *Liber* purports to describe.'

'How convenient.'

'His murderers were believed to be eldar.'

'Ah? Indeed? That's known for sure?'

'No, not for sure.'

'Our Ordo has never discovered any trace of this hydra on any world?'

'None. We track down any distorted whisper, yet we gain no hard evidence at all. Naturally, if Draco's account is correct we could hardly expect to find *material* traces...'

'So the Liber may actually have been a weapon aimed at Baal Firenze by some unknown enemy – to discredit him, to sabotage his career and his very identity.'

'Aye, or to sow distrust amongst the Hidden Masters of our Ordo, and thus to undermine us all.'

'Or to... or to sow doubts about the Emperor himself, blessed be His name.'

'That too. Truly, all is whelmed in darkness and the Emperor is the only light. Of course, Draco's narrative isn't *only* of negative value. We do now use the stasis coffin as an adjunct to interrogation, where time isn't of the essence...'

A note of doubt crept into the librarian's voice. 'You are newly a Hidden Master, and naturally you must research the secrets of our Ordo now. Would you let me admire your tattoo just once again?'

The green-eyed man said, 'Why, certainly.'

When the visitor to the Librarium Obscurum drew back his sleeve, the librarian only had an instant to note the digital needle gun fitted to the Hidden Master's slim finger... before the librarian's face stung, and toxins convulsed his whole frame.

The librarian's body flopped on the floor, muscles pulling every which way. His bowels had emptied stinkingly. Blood poured from the old man's nose and mouth.

The visitor started to giggle hectically. He needed to bite on his sleeve to silence himself. His teeth ravaged the cloth as if a hound had caught a hare, or in the way that someone who was experiencing inner agony might seek to distract himself from a sensation or spectacle that he found abominable. The librarian was already dead; it was only a corpse that twitched.

The visitor left the first page of the *Liber Secretorum* displayed upon the dimly glowing screen. And beside it he tucked a Tarot card – of an inquisitor whose featureless face was a tiny, psychoactive mirror to whoever would next look at it.

Wrinkling up his jutting nose, he slipped away out of the skull room.

THE INQUISITION WAR had begun.

Though in another sense it had begun years earlier when Jaq Draco first uttered the words, *Believe me. I intend to tell the truth...*

WARPED STARS

WARPED STARS

On Jomi Jabal's sixteenth birthday he watched a witch being broken in the market square of Groxgelt. The time was the cool of the evening. The harsh blue sun had set a while since, however the night with its star-lanterns was a couple of hours away as yet.

The saffron-hued gas-giant still bulged hugely in the wispy sky, shouldering high above the horizon like some mountainous desert dune. Its light gilded the tiled roofs of the town and the dusty, hoof-printed street.

That golden giant in the sky seemed to be such a furnace, such a molten crucible. Yet, unlike the sun, it dispensed no heat. Jomi wondered how that could be, but he knew better than to ask. When he was younger a few whippings had deterred him from excessive curiosity.

His Pa's punishments had been well intended. Boys and girls who questioned were perhaps on the road to becoming witches themselves.

A trumpet would sound from the watchtower after the golden giant did finally sink out of sight. That braying screech signalled curfew at the onset of darkness. Thereafter, mutants were said to prowl the black streets.

Did mutants really roam Groxgelt by night, hunting for victims, seeking entry into the homes of the unwise? It struck Jomi as a convenient arrangement that the townsfolk were thus exiled to their houses during the cooler hours. Otherwise the taverns of Groxgelt might well have remained open longer. Workmen might have caroused till late, and thus be tired when dawn came, grumpy and lethargic at their labours during the hot day.

Oh but mutants certainly existed, without a doubt. Witches, hoodooists. Here was yet another one, bound upon the wheel.

Two hours till darkness…

'This witch uses a cunning trick,' Reverend Henrik Farb, the preacher, proclaimed to the crowd from the ebon steps of the headman's residence. 'He can hoodoo time itself. He can stop the flow of the time stream. Though not for very long… so do not run away in fear! Witness his punishment, and mark my words: the witch looks human, but in truth he is distorted. Beware of those who seem human, yet are not!'

Farb was a fat fellow. Beneath his black cloak, leather armour bulged in a manner that, had he been a woman, might have been described as voluptuous. Womanly, too, was the jade perfume phial dangling from one pierced nostril, intercepting the odours of manure and of bodies on which sweat had barely dried. The tattoo of a chained, burning daemon caged within a hex symbol writhed upon one chubby cheek while he spoke, guarding his mouth and porcine eyes from contamination. Usually the preacher wore loose black silks on account of the heat, which was only now draining away. For combat with evil, though, he must needs be suitably protected. A holstered stub gun hung from the amulet-studded belt around his rotund waist.

Horses snickered and stamped. Men patted their long knives for comfort, and the few who owned such, their rune-daubed muskets.

'Destroy the deviant!' shouted one fervent voice.

'Break the unhuman!' cried another.

'Kill the witch!'

Farb eyed the brawny, half-naked executioner who stood beside the wheel gripping a cudgel. As usual, the agent of retribution had been chosen by lot. Most townsfolk might sport wens, carbuncles, and other blemishes of their burnt skin, but few were feeble. Even if so, a puny executioner would only take the longer to perform his task to the tune of jeers and mocking cheers.

'Aye,' declared Farb, 'I warn you that this witch will try to slow down his punishment – stretching it out till nightfall in the vain hope of rescue.'

Spittle flew from the preacher's lips as if he was one of those mutants who could spit poison. Such a mutant had been rooted out a few months earlier, gagged, and broken in this selfsame square. The front ranks of Farb's audience pressed closer to the ebon steps, as if a drop of spray from the preacher's lips might keep their vision clear, their humanity intact.

Farb turned to the standard of the Emperor, which flanked him. The townswomen had painstakingly embroidered in precious wires an image copied from the preacher's missal. When Farb genuflected, his audience hastily bent their knees.

'God-Emperor,' chanted the preacher, 'oh our source of security. Protect us from foul daemons. Guard the wombs of our women that wee mites are not twisted into mutants. Save us from the darkness within darkness. Oh watch over us as we carry out your will. *Imperator hominorum, nostra salvatio!*' Sacred words, those last, powerful hex-words. Farb snorted through one nostril, spat saliva at the crowd.

Jomi gazed at the standard. That age-old Imperial face was a mask of wires and tubes, which the metallic embroidery persuasively evoked.

'Begin!' shouted Farb.

The wheel, which was powered by a massive, firmly-wound spring, started to turn. It carried the witch around, his limbs bent into a half-hoop. The executioner raised his club.

Nothing happened. The wheel stood still. The stalwart was frozen. Though forewarned, the crowd groaned. The spectators were outside the small zone of hoodooed time cast by the doomed witch; they could still move about – yet hardly a body moved.

'At this very moment,' Farb explained, 'the witch may well be calling out with his mind to some vile daemon – leading it here, showing the way to Groxgelt.'

Jomi wondered whether this was true. If so, why not slay the witch speedily with a knife as soon as captured? Maybe the preacher relished the ceremony for its own sake. Certainly such a spectacle riveted the crowd and dramatised their deepest fears. Otherwise, people might grow careless, no? They might fail to report suspicions of mutants in their midst. A mother could try to protect a child of hers who only seemed slightly twisted.

Though wouldn't the permanent presence of the wheel in the market square put such fear into hoodooists that they would try their utmost to hide their witching ways, and not betray themselves? Jomi puzzled about this.

The timeless moment ended. As the delayed cudgel descended crackingly, the witch screamed. Time paused once again in his immediate vicinity. Presently another blow fell, crushing flesh and snapping bone. Due to his futile evasions the witch did indeed take much longer to be broken, and would take longer to hang draped around the wheel, slowly dying in utter pain. Though what else could the wretch have done?

'Praise the Emperor who protects!' cried the paunchy preacher. '*Laudate imperatorem!*' His leatherclad breasts and belly quaked. He panted as he sniffed perfume, blood, excrement, and sweat.

Each time that a new blow fell, Jomi felt a fierce itch at a different location inside the marrow of his own bones, as if he was experiencing a hint of that excruciating punishment through the filter of a pile of pillows. He wriggled and scratched uselessly...

OVER THE COURSE of the next year a dozen more witches and muties died in the square of Groxgelt. A few of the more vocal townsfolk began to ask in their cups whether there could be some sickness unique to the human seed, which did not plague beastkind. Mares did not give birth to foals which developed strange powers as they matured, did they now? Jomi's father, who was a tanner of lizard hides, discouraged any such speculation under his own roof; and Jomi had long since learned to hold his tongue. Preacher Farb encouraged the townsfolk as well as terrifying them. He promised that the Emperor would not let his people drift into chaos.

On Jomi's seventeenth birthday, he dreamt the first dream...

It seemed that a mouth was shaping itself inside his brain. It was forming from out of the very substance of the grey matter within his skull. In his dream he knew that this was so. If only he could turn his dream-eyes backwards, he would see the lips deep within his cranium and, between them, the lolloping tongue that was responsible for the soupsucking sounds he heard in his sleep.

Terror gripped him in the dream. Somehow he couldn't awaken till those internal lips had finished their slobbery mumblings and shut up.

Over the course of the next several nights those interior sounds came more closely to resemble words. As yet these words were too blurred to understand, but they seemed to be coming clearer, almost as if adjusting themselves to the words that Jomi knew.

Jomi shared a poky garret room with his elder brother, Big Ven. Naturally he did not enquire whether Ven dreamed of a similar voice, nor whether Ven ever woke in the wee hours and thought that he heard a whisper coming from within Jomi's brain. Always the wheel stood in the market place as a warning. Jomi sweated as he slumbered. His straw palliasse was damp each morning.

'Am I becoming... *unhuman*?' he asked himself anxiously.

Maybe he was only experiencing nightmares. He dismissed any notion of consulting Reverend Farb. Instead he prayed fervently to the Emperor to dismiss the mumblings from his mind.

EACH BLUE DAWN, along with a band of fellow labourers, Jomi walked out of town to the grox breeding station and farm. Stripped to his loincloth and charm necklace, he toiled in an annex of a slaughter shed, sorting offal.

'You're lucky,' his short sturdy mother often told him. 'Such a soft job at your age!'

This was true. The big reptiles were notoriously vicious. If they had not provided meat that was delicious to eat and highly nourishing, and if they had not been so well able to nourish themselves on any rubbish tossed their way, even soil, any sane person would have steered well clear of them. Although the breeding specimens were kept sedated with chemicals, a beast might still go berserk. When penned alongside its fellows, that was the natural inclination of a grox. The meat-stock were lobotomized. When being driven to the slaughter, even these brain-cut brutes could prove fractious. Any grox-herdsman or butcher could lose a finger or an eye, even his life. Virtually all bore disfiguring scars. The rulers in Urpol, the capital city an unimaginable hundred kilometres away, demanded an endless supply of grox meat for their own consumption and for profitable export. Refrigerated robot floaters carried the meat to Urpol.

'You're well-favoured,' Jomi's mother had also told him, more than once. This was true too. Jomi was clean-limbed and clean-featured, unblemished by the cysts and warts which afflicted most of the population.

It was the farmer's wife, tubby Galandra Puschik, who had assigned Jomi his cushy billet. Madame Puschik would often wander through the offal shed to ogle Jomi slicked with blood and sweat. Especially she would loiter by the farm pond to leer at him when he was washing off after a day's work. Oh yes, she had her eye on him. But she was too scared of her bullying husband to do more than look.

Jomi had his own eye set wistfully on the Puschiks' daughter, Gretchi. A slim beauty, Gretchi wore a broad straw hat and carried a parasol to shade herself from the bright blue sunlight. She turned up her pert nose at most of the town's youths, though she favoured Jomi with a smile when her mother wasn't watching; and then his heart would beat fast. From occasional words he and she exchanged, he knew that Gretchi's sights were set upon becoming mistress to one of the lordly rulers in Urpol. But maybe she might care to practice with him first.

That day, while Jomi sorted grox livers, kidneys, and hearts, the mouth within his brain began to speak to him clearly, caressingly.

'Be calm,' it cooed. 'Don't fear me. I can teach you much you need in order to survive, and to gratify your young desires. Aye, to survive, for you are different, are you not?'

'What are you?' Jomi thought fiercely; and even then he resisted the impulse to speak out loud, and risk being overheard by a fellow worker. Was the languid voice male, or was it female? Perhaps neither...

'What are you, voice?'

'Before you can understand the answer, you need to learn much. Tell me: what shape has your world?'

'Shape? Why, it's all sorts of shapes. It's smooth and rocky. It's up and down – '

'Seen from afar, Jomi, seen from afar so that hills and valleys are as nothing. Seen by a bird flying higher than any bird has ever flown.'

'I guess... like a plate?'

'Oh no... Listen, Jomi, your world is globular like an eyeball. Your world is a big moon that swings around a giant world wholly made of gas, which is an even bigger eyeball. Your blue sun is the hugest eyeball hereabouts.'

'How can that be? The sun's so much smaller than the giant.'

'But hotter, hmm? Have you never wondered why it's hotter?'

'Sure I have.'

'But you thought it wiser not to ask, hmm? Wise, Jomi, wise.' How the voice fondled him. 'You can ask me without fear. Your sun is so vast that its own weight burns it. It's a star; and so far away that it looks like a thumbnail at arm's length. As I myself am far away from you, my Jomi.' The voice seemed to sigh. 'Indeed, much further than your star.'

Jomi continued sorting the slippery, reeking entrails into different trays. 'It can't be a star. The star-lanterns are tiny and cold.'

'Ah, innocent youth. The stars aren't lanterns. Let's take this step by step, shall we? Your moon and your sun and the giant and the stars are all spherical in shape.'

'Spherical?' What words this voice knew, such as the lords in Urpol might use.

'Circular. Think loudly of a circle floating in empty space.'

'I'd rather not!' A circle was the shape of a wheel, the terrible taboo wheel. No man must make any wheel, nor use one save for the punishment wheel, or else witches would triumph and rule the world.

'Calm yourself, sweet youth. The wheel is the beginning of knowledge. I will tell you why, if you will concentrate on imagining a circle. That helps me to... focus on you.'

'Focus?'

'To see you, as through a lens.'

'What's a lens?'

'Ah, you have so much to learn, and I will be your secret teacher.'

When Jomi washed himself later, Galandra Puschik stood with hands on giant hips surveying him as if he was the next day's dinner; and to his horror he overheard her thoughts...

She lusted to run her meaty hands all over Jomi. She yearned to kneed him like dough then bake him like bread in her hot embrace. Farmer Puschik would be going on a business trip away from the farm some day soonish. Then she would enjoy the boy...

Jomi could hear thoughts. It was as if the voice in his head was massaging muscles of his brain that had been puny as threads till now; was tickling sensation into nerves of his mind that had previously lain loose, causing them to knot and knit.

He could hear thoughts. Therefore he was a witch.

'Be tranquil,' the voice advised. 'Yet think loudly of the circle. Thus I can find you. Thus I can save you, my bewitching boy.'

For many days the voice told Jomi about the pleasures and beauties of the wider universe beyond his farming moon where there was only toil and sweat and fear.

The delights and glories that the voice described seemed somehow like memories of memories, echoes of echoes, as if the experiences in question had occurred too many years ago to count, and the voice no longer quite understood their nature, yet felt compelled to recount them even so.

IN THE CABIN of the space cruiser *Human Loyalty*, Inquisitor Torq Serpilian brooded about the paradox which had begun to haunt him. He keyed his coded diarium and spoke to it.

'It is a week since we emerged safely from warp-space, *benedico Imperatorem*. We are in orbit around the gas-giant Delta Khomeini V.' Beyond the quatrefoil tracery of the viewport the huge orange ball of storming hydrogen and methane held on an invisible leash the crescent of a single large moon that gleamed with atmosphere.

'*Propositum*: for millennia past our undying Emperor has defended humanity against psychic attack from the warp, so that – one far-off day – humankind can evolve psychic powers puissant enough to protect itself...'

Battle banners hung from ochreous plasteel walls which were the hue of dried blood. Bleached alien skulls and captured armour were mounted as trophies. For this was a ship of the Legiones Astartes, the Space Marines.

Yet aliens as such rarely worried Serpilian. Even the most devious of aliens were, after all, natural creatures born and bred in the same universe as humankind. Aliens were as nothing compared with the terrible parasites that dwelled in the warp. On Serpilian's home world a certain unpleasant wasp would inject its hooked eggs into the flesh of beasts and men. Warp parasites could lay their equivalent of eggs in human minds. Those 'eggs' would hatch into entities that controlled the body, consuming it and using it to spread contamination. Other warp creatures could seize human souls and drag them back into darkness to feast upon, slowly. And there were far mightier daemonic entities too.

Psyker-witches were beacons shining into the warp. They attracted parasites and daemons that could lay waste a world and make its people unhuman.

'*Subpropositum*: wild, unguided, wayward psykers must be sought out by our Inquisition and destroyed.'

'*Counterpropositum*: so as to nourish our Emperor, hundreds of fresh young psykers must daily sacrifice their souls – aye, gladly too – to feed his own huge anguished soul.'

Yes indeed, emerging psykers were sought out avidly and sent to Terra by the shipload. Those of high calibre, who could be trained to serve the Imperium, were soul-bound to the Emperor for their own protection, an agonizing ritual which generally left them blind. Exceptional individuals such as Serpilian were allowed to guard themselves mentally. The cream of such free psykers became inquisitors. Yet daily hundreds of those transportees to Terra, duly guided in the blessings of sacrifice, were yielding up their lives in the sucking gullet of the God-Emperor's mind. And elsewhere throughout the galaxy, untamable psykers were being exterminated as witches.

'*Paradoxus*: we root out as weeds what we cannot harvest. Yet whether we harvest or root out, the new crop is largely crushed, in so far as is within our power. How then can humankind evolve that independent future strength it so desperately needs?'

Serpilian imagined a meadow of grass being trampled repeatedly for millennia. He visualized new green blades struggling up into the light only to be flattened remorselessly lest they feed the malevolent creatures of the warp.

Would the Emperor eventually relax his crushing pressure by permitting himself to die? Thus allowing the grass suddenly to sprout up straight and tall and strong, a crop of superhumans?

Yet until that wonderful epoch, utter repression?

'Let me not become a heretic,' murmured Serpilian. 'I must not.' On reflection, he erased this last entry.

During Serpilian's career he had encountered situations sufficient to persuade him of the Emperor's wisdom. He had been a party to enough acts of harshness; had been the initiator of such deeds of necessary savagery – most recently at Valhall II, where enslavers had been invading from the warp and instigating a fierce insurrection against the Imperium.

'The universe,' he told his diarium, 'is cruel, savage, unforgiving. A battleground. And the darkest enemies hide in the warp, like tigers ever ready to pounce on the human herd. If one of that herd attracts the notice of a tiger, the rest of the herd may be ravaged – or worse, possessed and twisted obscenely into evil.'

Was not Serpilian himself thus forced at times to act like a beast, presiding over atrocities in the service of a tyrant?

Serpilian did not exactly pride himself on his independence of thought. He rather regretted such intrusions of doubt. Still and all, these qualities produced a certain flexibility and ingenuity, thus best serving the cause of the Emperor and of the human race.

His attire reflected that independent demeanour. He wore a long kilt of silver fur, an iridescent cuirass suggestive of the shell of a giant exotic beetle, and a blood-red cloak with high collar. On both forefingers he wore rare jokaero digital weapons, one of these a miniaturized needler, the other a tiny laspistol. Orthodox guns were always secreted about his person. Amulets jangled round his neck, making exorcistic music as he moved.

Serpilian was tall, dark, and lean. His drooping black moustache resembled some insect's mandibles. On his right cheek was the tattoo of an ever-watchful eye.

Long before the cabin door opened to admit Commander Hachard, Serpilian expected his arrival. The inquisitor was a powerful senser of presence, who knew where everyone was within a generous radius. An unusual offshoot of this sense allowed him to anticipate intrusions from the warp. That was why Human Loyalty had come to the Delta Khomeini solar system. Shortly after leaving Valhall II, Serpilian had dreamed of a sickly-sweet coaxing voice that was neither man's nor woman's cajoling a bright young mind far far away; and that young mind was... special, in a way that the young Serpilian's had been special, only more so, much more so, it seemed. Thus, even across the light years, and through the immeasurable fluctuating currents of the warpsea, Serpilian heard... something that resonated with his own psyche; that plucked at his instincts, as if threads of dark destiny bound him direly to that mind and to that eerie, seductive voice.

A casting of the runebones by Serpilian in tandem with a Tarot divination performed by the ship's Navigator had indicated the blue star that was fourth brightest in the constellation of Khomeini...

'We are in orbit around the parent planet,' Hachard reported respectfully, with only the merest hint of reproach, which he would hardly dare voice. 'I thought it diplomatic not to order our captain to orbit the moon itself till I had presented our compliments by comnet to the governor.' Scar tissue on Hachard's chin stood out whitely as though he had been punched. His cheek-tattoo was of a skull skewered by a dagger. His teeth were painted black as a signal that any smile of his was dark. A vermilion badge of nobility – a stylized power-axe – adorned his right knee-pad modestly so that, whenever bending to the Emperor's image during devotions, he should kneel upon this heraldic honour. His gloved hand strayed to the Imperial eagle emblazoned in purple on his lavender dress cuirass, as if to emphasize his unquestioning loyalty.

Serpilian knew that the commander would far rather have returned to the Grief Bringers' base after the action on Valhall II, to take their dead home and to renew their strength.

Even Grief Bringer Marines had been hard put to quash the enslavers disorder. Losses had been heavy. Only three platoons of the warriors remained. Perhaps the Valhall mission should best have been entrusted to one of the redoubtable Terminator teams, but none had been available. Truly, the resources of the Imperium were stretched thin. En route to Delta Khomeini, during a refuelling stopover at a high-gravity world, Serpilian had commandeered the services of two platoons of ogryn giants as a fighting supplement; also, of a lone, mechanically-minded squat, for the Grief Bringers had lost their tech-priest on Valhall II. It was an uneasy mixture.

'Yes, that's sensible, Commander,' said the inquisitor. 'And have you presented my compliments yet?' Thus did Serpilian emphasize his personal authority, at a time when he nevertheless felt beset by doubts.

'That I have, my lord inquisitor. Governor Vellacott felt obliged to mention that he maintains adequate planetary forces in case of alien attack, and that preachers on that moon root out any psykers fiercely.'

'Would you describe him as an independent-minded governor?'

'Not obstructively so. We are welcome to land and investigate.'

'Just as well for him.'

'He suggested that we wouldn't need too many Marines to cope with a moonful of farmers, where there isn't even any obvious threat.'

Serpilian snorted. 'The level of threat is for me to decide. The worst threat is often the threat that hides itself.'

'The governor suggested – most politely, you understand – that it might be beneath our dignity to blow human rabbits to pieces. I wonder whether he has any inkling that our strength is depleted? Perhaps his court astropath somehow eavesdropped on ours; though I rather doubt it. I suspect he has some guilty reason to fear for his dynasty.'

'Such as irregularities in Imperial taxes?'

'The Vellacotts control the finest grox farms in this celestial segment. Much of the meat and other produce goes to Delta Khomeini II. That's a barren mining world, producing rare metals for our Imperium. Perhaps there are secret financial arrangements.'

'Which are none of our concern.'

'I implied as much, without saying so.'

'Ah, a Marine commander needs many skills, does he not?'

'I thank you, my lord inquisitor.'

Serpilian felt obliged to ask, 'How goes morale?' For the Grief Bringers had also lost their Chaplain in action on Valhall II.

Hachard hesitated.

'Be frank. I will not be offended.'

'The ogryns... they stink.'

Serpilian attempted an injection of humour. 'They are famous for stinking. If one cannot tolerate some body odour, how can one bear the stench of scorching flesh in combat?'

'My men will fight alongside the abhumans, with honour. But they don't like it much. Having to share a ship with those Stenches. I suppose, my lord inquisitor, you insisted on pressing the ogryns into service because, being abhuman and frankly thuggish, they're more expendable.'

Serpilian winced momentarily. What Hachard implied was perilously close to unthinkable impertinence; yet Serpilian had invited the commander to be outspoken, had he not? The loss of so many brave fighters in the earlier action – however justifiable – was a slight blot on the inquisitor's personal escutcheon of honour. Marines would willingly sacrifice their lives. They were not, however, suicide-berserkers. To replace them with 'expendable' abhumans somewhat smeared the pride of the Grief Bringers, amounting almost to an error of judgement on Serpilian's part.

One did not polish a fine sword with mud, nor repair a broken one with wood.

Muttering a brief prayer, Serpilian unclipped a pouch from his belt. Breathing deeply and slowly to induce a light trance, he cast his rune bones upon a desk of polished black wood. Those finger and toe bones, minutely inscribed with conjurations, had belonged to a rogue psyker mage whom the Inquisition had executed five centuries earlier. Now these relics served Serpilian's psychic sense. They were a useful channel for his talent, a focus.

As he concentrated, the pattern of white bones against black swam till a foggy picture formed, visible to him alone.

'What do you see?' whispered Hachard reverently.

The thought drifted through Serpilian's mind, like some seductive siren song, that it wasn't totally unknown for an inquisitor to sicken of his harsh duties and flee to some lost world, some primitive pastoral planet or other.

Not one such as this moon, certainly! The inquisitor resumed his breathing routine.

'I see a strapping, comely boy. Though his face isn't clear. I see the circle of a portal opening from the warp, and coming through it is... abomination.'

'What species of abomination? Enslavers again?'

A sensible question. The warp entities known as enslavers could open a gateway through the very flesh of a vulnerable psyker and spill out – to do as their name suggested.

Serpilian shook his head. 'The boy's being given an aura of protection now to hide him. He's somewhere within a hundred or so kilometres of the capital city. He's becoming a powerful psychic receiver. Other psychic talents are sprouting in him. I think he's about to be possessed. Unless we reach him first.'

'To capture him, or destroy him?'

'I fear for his potential power. One day perhaps,' and Serpilian sketched a pious obeisance, 'he might be a little like the Emperor himself. Just a little.'

'Not a new Horus, surely?' What loathing crept into the commander's voice as he uttered the name of the corrupted rebel Warmaster who had betrayed the Imperium, and besmirched the honour of so many Marine Chapters, long long ago. 'If that's the situation, maybe the relevant quadrant of the moon should be sterilised... though that would include Urpol city and the spaceport, and many grox farms. Delta Khomeini II would starve as a consequence... And the moon has orbital defences as well as its surface troops, who would fight us... They won't have much battle experience. I think we could do it. I think. Perhaps with our last drop of blood...'

'Let us pray it doesn't come to that, Hachard, though your zeal is commendable.'

'What is finer than death in battle to defend the future of mankind?'

'If we are in time, this boy must needs be a gift to our Emperor, for His own divine wisdom to judge. Let us head for that moon as soon as our present orbit permits.'

Serpilian uttered a silent prayer that his inner eyesight might pierce the veil that now partially hid the boy.

'THINK OF THE circle,' crooned the mouth within Jomi's head. 'It grows larger, larger, does it not?'

The boy watched a floater of grox meat depart from Puschik Farm. The engine and cargo section were spattered with mystic runes to help hold the vehicle in the air and encourage the robot brain to find its way to the city. Those runes had recently been repainted. If runes faded or flaked off the hull, the floater might stray from its course or its chiller unit might fail.

Clouds of flies buzzed around a couple of sledges on which piles of scaly hides, some barrels of blood, and sacks of bones were setting out for the much shorter journey to Groxgelt, there to be rendered into glue, and sausages, and crude armour. Whips cracked, slicing through the aerial vermin to tickle the draught-horses into action. The runners creaked across stones worn smooth by centuries of such local transport.

No, thought Jomi, the floater would only break down if it hadn't been 'serviced' properly. The meat-transporter was only a machine, a thing of metal and wires and crystals, based on ancient science from the Dark Age of Technology.

Courtesy of the voice, Jomi knew now that former ages had existed, unimaginable stretches of time unimaginably long ago. The current age was a time of 'superstition,' so said the voice. An earlier age had been a time of enlightenment. Yet that bygone era was now called dark to the extent that so much had been forgotten about it. So the voice assured him, confusingly. He mustn't worry his pretty mind overmuch about foul daemons such as Preacher Farb prated about. Such things existed, to a certain extent, that was true. But enlightenment was the route to joy. The owner of the voice said that it had been captured by the storms of 'warp-space' long ago, doomed to wander in strange domains for aeons until finally it sensed a dawning psyker talent that was peculiarly attuned to it.

'You aren't a witch, dearest boy,' the voice had assured him. 'You're a psyker. Say after me: I'm a psyker, with a glorious mind that deserves to relish all manner of gratifications. Which I, your only true friend will teach you how to attain. Say to yourself: I'm the most lustrous of psykers – and remember to think of the circle, won't you?'

The owner of the voice would come to Jomi. It would save him from the entrail shed. It would save him from the crushing embrace of fat Galandra Puschik and from the terror of the wheel.

'Sooooooon,' cooed the voice, like the coolest of evening breezes. 'Always think of the circle – like a wheel rolling ever closer to you, but not a wheel to fear!'

'Why have we been taught to fear wheels?' An inspiration assaulted Jomi. 'Surely our sledges would run more easily if we used... a wheel on each corner? Four wheels which turn around as the sledge advances!'

'Then it would be called a wagon. You're such a bright lad, Jomi. Bright in so many ways.' Of a sudden, the voice grew sour and petulant. 'And here comes spurious brightness to cheer you.'

'Gretchi!'

Her slim limbs, mainly hidden by a coarse cotton frock, yet imaginable as fair and smooth... her breasts like two young doves nesting beneath the fabric... her chestnut hair hanging in ringlets, mostly veiling a slender neck... the huge straw hat shading that creamy complexion... the teasing eyes of a blue so much less daunting than the sun: how could such perfection have issued from Galandra Puschik's hips? Gretchi twirled her pink parasol coquettishly.

Did he gawp?

'Whatever are you thinking, Jomi Jabal?' she asked, as if inviting him to flatter her naively – or even vulgarly, to excite her.

He swallowed. He muttered the truth. 'About science...'

Gretchi pouted. 'Would that be the art of sighing for a girl, perhaps? Fine lords will sigh for me in Urpol some day soon, believe me!'

Could he possibly tell her his secret? Surely she wouldn't betray him?

'Gretchi, if it were possible for you to go much further away than Urpol–'

'Where's further than Urpol? Urpol's the centre of everything hereabouts.'

'–would you go?'

'Surely you don't mean to some farm in the furthest hinterland?' She wrinkled up her nose pettishly. 'Surrounded by muties, no doubt!'

He pointed at the sky. 'No, much further away. To the stars, and to other worlds.'

She laughed at him, though not entirely with derision. Perhaps this good-looking youth could tickle her fancy in unexpected ways?

Should he whisper in her ear, arranging a rendezvous after work to hear his secret?

'Remember the cruel wheel, Jomi,' warned the voice.

'When you come, voice, can I take Gretchi with me?'

Did he hear a faint, stifled snarl in the depths of his mind?

Gretchi simpered. 'Are you pretending to ignore me now? Are your feelings hurt? What do you know of feelings?'

He stared at the twin soft birds of her bosom, yearning to cup them in his hands. But his hands were soiled with blood and bile, the memory came to him of Gretchi's mother feeling Jomi assiduously in her foetid imagination, exploring and squeezing him, and out of the corner of his eye he noticed Galandra Puschik glaring from the veranda of the farmhouse. Gretchi must have spied her mother too, for she promptly flounced away, turning up her nose as if at some foul reek.

'Huh!' GRIMM, THE tough stocky red-bearded dwarf, said to himself. 'Huh indeed, a world that bans wheels! Strange and many are the worlds!' The squat pushed back his forage cap to scratch his bald pate, which was scarred from a battle wound on Valhall. As a result of this injury, his skull had been shaved clean, and he was trying out baldness as a style. Fewer nesting places for lice! Now he would be compelled to leave his beloved trike, mounted with twin cannon, in the hold of the Imperial ship.

Grimm scanned the cavernous plasteel dormitory through his dark shades. Imperial icons gleamed, each lit by a glow-globe, sharing wall space with cruder battle-fetishes of the giants, one of which was draped respectfully with a ram's intestines from the arrival feast the night before. Scraps of meat, hair, broken bones littered the floor, mashed into the semblance of a brown and grey carpet on which assorted insectoid vermin grazed, or lay crushed themselves. The dormitory had ceased to reek; it had transcended stench, attaining a new plane of foetor as though the air had transmuted. Stinks did not usually perturb Grimm, but he wore nostril filters.

'Huh!'

The ogryn, 'Thunderjug' Aggrox, quit sharpening his yellow tusks on a rasp.

'Woz matter, titch?'

Sergeant-Ogryn Aggrox was a BONEhead, who had undergone Biochemical Ogryn Neural Enhancement. Thus he was capable of a degree of sophisticated conversation. Could be trusted with a ripper gun too.

Grimm, natty in his green coveralls and quilted red flak jacket, surveyed the crudely tattooed megaman in his coarse cloth and chain mail. Several battle badges were riveted to the giant's thick skull.

'I suppose,' said Grimm, 'being forced to walk or ride draught horses keeps the peasants in their places, don't it?'

'Seems use floaters, though,' objected Thunderjug.

'Oh well, you need to hurry fresh meat to the spaceport and up into orbit to be void-frozen. In my not-so-humble opinion banning wheels is going a bit over the top. I like wheels.' Especially the wheels of his battletrike. 'I guess in this neck of the galaxy the wheel represents the godless science of the Dark Age…'

In common with all squats, Grimm was an instinctive technician. Watching Imperial 'technicians' sketch hexes against malfunction amidst their rune-painted machinery and hearing them utter incantations to an engine disturbed him mildly. In a sense his own race were in a direct line of descent from the obscure ancient days of science, when warp storms had cut the squattish mining worlds off, to evolve independently.

Oh my sacred ancestors! he thought. Still, everybody to their own religion.

Most of these thoughts were too complicated to convey even to a BONEhead ogryn.

The giant plucked a thumb-sized louse from his armpit and crunched the grey parasite speculatively between his teeth. Just then, ogryn voices bellowed.

Two warriors had bared their tusks. Seizing mace and axe respectively, they began to hack at one another's chainmail in a bellicose competition. Spectators roared wagers in favour of one combatant or the other, or both, stamping their great feet so that the steel dormitory rocked and groaned.

Thunderjug lowered his head and charged along the dormitory. He butted left, he butted right with his steel-plated skull. The quarrellers resisted, butting back at their sergeant, though not disrespectful enough to raise axe or mace against him. Finally Thunderjug seized the two by the neck and crashed their heads together in the manner of two wrecking balls till the fighters subsided and agreed to behave.

'Shu'rup all!' After issuing that command, Thunderjug ambled back, spat out a broken tooth, and grinned. 'Gorra keep order, don' I?'

Grimm removed his fingers from his ears, and combed some mites from his beard. Would he have been happier billeted with the true-human Grief Bringers? Undoubtedly more comfortable; less liable to be squashed by a reeling heavyweight. On the other hand, he had come to count on Thunderjug as something of a friend, a brainy bull among this herd of buffalos. Grimm prided himself on mixing with all sorts and conditions. He hadn't too much experience of Imperial Marines. There weren't all that many in the galaxy. But they seemed a shade cliquish.

Exemplary fellows, needless to say, but so devoutly dedicated to the traditions of their Chapters. A roving squat, who only gave nodding acquiescence to the worship of the Emperor, saw the universe from a slightly different angle.

From whichever angle, the galaxy was a fairly menacing sprawl of mayhem. Grimm decided to strip and clean his bolt gun; though without bothering to pray to it.

'You WERE BORN under warped stars, Jomi,' sighed the voice. 'Once, the warp seemed merely to be a zone through which our ships flew faster than light. Oh we were innocent then in spite of all our science! Naive and callow as lambs, such as your sweet self.'

Jomi shifted uneasily. Of late, a cloying stickiness had begun to creep into the accents of the voice at times. As if his informant realized this, its tone grew crisper.

'But then all over the galaxy that we had guilelessly populated, psykers such as yourself started to be born.'

'So there weren't always psykers around?'

'By no means to such an extent. When the powers and predators of Chaos took heed of those bright beacons, they spilled into reality to ravage and warp the worlds.'

'Those powers are what Preacher Farb calls daemons?'

'As it were.'

'Then he's right in that respect! You said I shouldn't worry my head about daemons.'

'Your sweet head... your puissant mind...'

From the low scrubby hillside Jomi stared towards the huddle of Groxgelt. At this hour the south pole of the gas-giant seemed almost to rest upon the headman's mansion and the Imperial Cult temple as though that golden ball would crush and melt the biggest buildings that Jomi knew. The sun's blue radiance ached. Due to a trick of light and wispy clouds, a bilious greenish miasma – the colour of nausea – seemed to drip from one limb of the hostile parent-world upon the town.

A skrak flew overhead, seeking little lizards to dive upon, and Jomi sat very still till the unpleasant avian discharged a tiny bomb of acidic excrement elsewhere.

'Ah comely youth, guard your skin,' came the voice, which could spy through his eyes.

'Does Chaos make our sun breed wens and carbuncles on our flesh?' Jomi asked.

'Oh no. Your sun is rich in rays beyond violet. You've been fortunate to resist those rays yourself. You'll be even luckier when I reach you.'

'How does Gretchi know to wear a wide hat and carry a parasol?'

'Vanity!'

'Does she have an extra sense to tell her?'

'If so, she needs it. In other respects she appears senselessly empty-headed.'

'How can you say so? She's so beautiful.'

'And presently she will sell what you call beauty, but only as a minion and a toy; only till she withers.'

'Beauty must mean something,' protested Jomi. 'I mean, if I'm fair and I'm a psyker... isn't there any connection, voice?'

From far away Jomi seemed to hear a stifled cackle of laughter. 'So you subscribe to the theory that body and soul reflect one another?' Heavy irony coloured the reply. 'In a dark sense that's often true. Should Chaos seize a victim, that victim's body will twist and warp... if body there be!'

'How can a person not have a body?'

'Maybe one day you'll learn – how the spirit can soar free from the flesh.' Was the voice telling him the truth? And how could that be the road to ecstasy, whatever ecstasy really signified? As if agitated, the voice began to ramble. 'I was one of the earliest psykers back in the epoch when true science gave way to strife and anarchy... Oh the madness, the madness... I was marooned. Our ship malfunctioned... it died in the warp. All through the dark aeons since, I've heard the whisperings of telepaths from the real universe. I've eavesdropped on the downfall of civilization and on its grim and terrible, ignorant revival... I could never escape. I lacked a beacon that cast a suitable light.'

'How long do aeons last?' Jomi still had very little idea.

For a period there was silence, then the voice answered vaguely, 'Time behaves differently within the warp.'

'Has your body been warped at all?' asked Jomi.

Again, that distant cackle...

'My body,' the voice repeated flatly. 'My body...' It said no more than that.

Phantom gangrene dribbled from the gas-giant.

SERPILIAN PRAYED. '*In nomine Imperatoris*... guide us to the golden boy that we may 'prison him, or rend him, or render him unto You, as You wish. Imperator, guard our armour and our gaze; lubricate our projectile weapons that they do not jam. Bless and brighten the beams of our lasers; *fiat lux in tenebris*...'

And cleanse my vision too, he thought. Pierce that aura of protection which cloaks the boy; and tear away any cataract of doubt.

The depleted ranks of Grief Bringers knelt cumbersomely in their bulging, burnished, insignia-blazoned power armour, which was principally a dark pea-green, with engrailed chevrons of headachy purple. Visors raised, they gazed intently at the inquisitor who wore borrowed vestments, of the slain Chaplain. Green chasuble; purple apron filigreed with the emblem of the Chapter. The long mauve stole dangling from Serpilian's neck to his knees was embroidered with aliens in torments. Amulets and icons chinked and clinked.

'I have decided I shall bless our ogryn warriors too,' Serpilian murmured to Hachard, who knelt beside him. 'Ogryns are men too. After a fashion. A blessing does not depend on the receiver but on the giver. Does a laspistol possess a brain, commander? A spirit, yes! But a thinking brain? Ogryns have spirits.'

Thus, at this sacred moment, did he condone his decision to dilute the strong wine of the Marines with the crude ale of the barbarian giants. Serpilian could guess what the commander might be thinking. 'Not on my ship they don't have spirits. A few bucketsful to drink, and the place would be wrecked.' Or maybe this was only Serpilian's own guilt speaking to him. That he, a survivor, should be wearing the vestments of a Chaplain who had fought the enslavers so fiercely.

The assembled Grief Bringers' eyes shone with pious dedication. All this, to hunt for one boy… Serpilian's instinct still told him that this mission mattered deeply. If only his vision was clearer! The very veiling of his insight suggested that he and the Marines faced a powerful adversary and might win a great reward.

To Hachard, he whispered, 'Ogryns and Space Marines must be as one body under your command. The former are not simply battering rams. If I do not bless them, we all fail in reverence.'

Would the Grief Bringers' slain chaplain have blessed the loyal, stout Stenches too? Hachard twitched, but of course made no objection.

'Benedictio!' Serpilian called out loudly. 'Benedictiones! Triumphus! Let your watchword for this mission be: Emperor-of-All.'

'Emperor-of-ALL!' the Grief Bringers chorused in response.

As Serpilian quit the assembly area, he vowed to redouble his exertions to sense the ambiguous presence of the boy. His rune bones continued to thwart him almost as if in conspiracy with the power that was aiming itself at the boy; almost as though those bones were enacting a five-hundred-year-delayed vengeance upon the Inquisition which had stripped the flesh from them.

Very well. He must dispense with their aid. He must use sheer mental discipline. He must attempt to put himself into the boy's frame of thought – for there was a link of destiny between himself and his quarry, was there not? He must detect the boy by that ploy.

He must forget all that he himself knew of the Imperium. He must erase all that he knew of the arcane wisdom of the Inquisition, garnered over millennia of terrible experiences and steadfast purity and, in Serpilian's case, some decades of duty.

He must imagine himself born on a farming moon. He must visualize his brain coming into bloom with bizarre petals – unseen by his fellow peasants – petals that served as esoteric psychic radar dishes, with unfurling stamens acting as antennae of the mind; each of these stamens tipped with pollen that would prove tasty to a daemon or a predator.

He mustn't ask himself: where precisely is this flower growing? Instead he must ask: how is this flower feeling right now?

He must identify with what he would pluck and present to the Emperor. He must imitate his prey. By that expedient he might dispel the psychic mist. Why, if he concentrated sufficiently well on pretending to be such a boy he might even distract whatever malign force was homing in – as though a heat-seeking missile were presented with a glowing decoy.

But first...

Serpilian had paused deep in thought in a corridor braced with mighty ribs and muscled with black power cables. Now he strode onward to the ogryn dormitory.

He ignored the stink, which was really no worse than the odour of many burst bowels; so he told himself. He disregarded the vermin underfoot, which were really akin to diminutive, edible pets.

'Benedico homines gigantes!' he cried out.

'Shu'rup ogryns!' bellowed the BONEhead sergeant, snapping to attention.

As Serpilian rattled through his litany of blessings and invocations all he received from the bulk of his congregation by way of responses were grunts and belches. These noises might, nonetheless, be signs of ogryn piety. The lone squat technician, clasping forage cap in hands politely, grinned sympathetically and zanily as if that little man felt some peculiar affinity for Inquisitors.

The engines of Human Loyalty were beginning to whine and its hull to wail. The cruiser was at last descending through the moon's atmosphere.

Concluding with a final resounding Imperator benedicat, Serpilian fled to his cabin and stripped off those chaplain's vestments.

Activating the viewscreen in its wrought-iron frame of death's heads and scorpions, he stared at the flickering, swelling vista of Urpol city below. The spaceport was a flat grey medal pitted with blast-pads. Spires sprouted like thickly waxed hairs. Suburbs were stubble, roads were wrinkles zig-zagging away into the sallow lumpy skin of the landscape. A snaking blue vein was a river, a lake was a haemorrhage, farms were bruises.

He knelt and thought: I am a strange flower growing somewhere in that land. My lurid, secret petals are ears that hear voices on the psychic winds. My pollen smells luscious to parasites…

He too had once been a strange flower, had he not?

Born into the salubrious upper tiers of the hive city of Magnox on Denebola V, young Torq had been torn between a taste for learning and a sensual nature. Both, of course, were facets of the search for new experiences.

Yet whereas a youth who seeks solely for madder music, stronger wine, stranger drugs, wilder girls, and for the thrill of danger may presently become a poet or a master criminal or some such deviant, he is much more likely to burn out, to run his adolescent course, and to settle thereafter into self-indulging conformity.

Whereas a studious youth may develop into a useful – even a brilliant – drudge.

Put the two together in one skin, though…

Torq's father was chamberlain to one of the noble houses of Magnox. So naturally, soon after puberty, Torq joined one of the fashionable and privileged brat gangs who rampaged and rousted in the latest glittergarb costumes, sporting black codpieces, grotesque jewellery, and plumed helmets fitted with krashmusik earphones. Who wounded and slew with power-stilettos which would spring a spike of vibrating, searing energy into the guts of a rival.

One night, during a raid on the lower tech levels of Magnox, Torq sensed for the first time the presence of ambush. A glowing, multi-dimensional map of human life-signs swam within his head, distorting, shot through with static, needing tuning…

Subsequently, in that mysterious multivalent map, he was to sense the eerie mauve glow of intrusions from the warp. He led the brat gang against a nest of psykers. These psykers were on the verge of being possessed by daemons. A rival gang were protecting them, and were making a playful erotic cult of them.

Had Torq's gang discovered those psykers first, events might have fallen out otherwise. Avid for thrills, the gilded youths from the upper tier might have made gang mascots of the psykers. Torq might have become a coven leader. Eventually, pursued by fervent witchfinders, he might have been forced to flee and hide among the scum of the under-city.

Yet events did not fall out in this fashion. Furthermore, Torq had stud-ied and he knew the lineaments of the Imperium rather better than his fellow brats. He thought he understood the strength of its muscles and the way those muscles pulled. His gang bested the patrons of those psykers, who had been pampered and abused by turns. Along with those captured playthings he presented himself to the Ecclesiarchy as a would-be inquisitor; whereby he would enjoy the wildest experiences, within a learned framework.

He hadn't by any means relished all of his subsequent experiences; and sometimes he was dogged by doubt that he was betraying kin-of-his-mind, all be it out of a dire necessity that became increasingly clear to him dur-ing his years of training. Piety had become his prophylactic against twinges of remorse. Faith was his pain-soothing pill, his vindication. Torq still dressed as a dandy, one devoted to terrible duties; and his superiors had smiled – in their thin, astringent way – at such evidence of honourable excess.

'I am a flower, a flower,' he droned, breathing in trance rhythm.

Torq had been somewhat of an orchid to begin with. Whereas the boy he sought was a wonderful weed infesting some flyblown farm. Could he identify? A mauve glow polluted his inner map every which way, refusing to condense into a single signalling spot. That glow masked the brash young hues of the flower.

A fortified palace stabbed upwards, tilted by the angle of the ship's approach: towers, spiked domes, laser batteries. Other chateaux within walled gardens drifted by. Factories, abattoirs. Then a plain of ferrocon-crete loomed.

Human Loyalty settled. The familiar throb of engines faded. A klaxon shrieked twice to signal the shutting down of artificial gravity. As the natural pull of the moon, which was a good twenty per cent weaker, replaced the generated gravity, so the ship creaked. The cruiser was at once relaxing and bearing down.

An inquisitor must bear down firmly without such inner relaxation. The gravity of this mission was, perhaps, extreme.

* * *

'I'M R-REALLY DEEPLY honoured,' stammered Reverend Henrik Farb. 'I never set eyes on a Space Marine before, let alone m-met a commander.'

And why should he have? If the Imperium comprised a million worlds, why, there were only a million Marines too.

Musky incense snaked inside the cavernous temple, wreathing icons and writing curlicues upon the air in what might have been the mad script of aliens. Farb, sweating, sucked in tendrils of that smoke like an asthmatic seeking soothing vapours to assuage a panic-stricken attack of suffocation. Candles flickered, contributing their own fainter odour of reptile grease.

This man, who had presumably terrified so many others, was terrified himself.

'Your respect honours our Emperor,' said Hachard. 'So does your dread. But now you must think clearly.'

The inquisitor had finally narrowed the likely area of search to a quadrant north of Urpol City. The Land Raiders that survived after Valhall II had sped forth on their cleated armoured tracks to the various towns in this zone, crushing the primitive roads, carrying Marines and ogryns. And it so happened that Hachard himself had come to this town of Groxgelt. If there was to be action, he wished to be as close as possible, not back at the ship awaiting reconnaissance reports.

How could he put this worthy preacher at his ease? 'Tell me,' he asked lightly, 'does the gelt in Groxgelt refer to cash, or to castration?'

Farb stared at his questioner as if he was being posed a riddle upon which his life depended. Could it be, wondered Hachard, that the preacher didn't understand all of his words? The man spoke decent Imperial Gothic; the dialect used on this moon was quite comprehensible.

'Never mind, Preacher. Tell me this: what lad in this community stands out as in any way different?'

Farb's gaze dropped to the Grief Bringer's protruding groin-guard, of a verdigris-smeared skull transfixed by a purple dagger.

'Castration, I think,' he mumbled.

'Concentrate!' snapped Hachard.

'Yes… yes… there's one boy – never caused any bother – prays in the temple here – good worker, so I hear…' Farb licked his fat lips. 'Attends witch-breakings, though they seem to make him squirm… Son of the tanner Jabal. The boy has no visible deformities; that's the odd thing about him. He looks,' and the preacher spat, 'so pure. Lately he has been… going places alone, I hear.'

'How do you come by that information?'

'The wife of the farmer who employs him... I, well, I cherish certain feelings for that woman... between you and me as man to man...'

Hachard forbore to sneer at this attempted comparison.

'Nothing illicit on my part, sir... She's... a woman of substance, if you take my meanings. Perhaps if her husband is ever gored by a grox...'

'What of the boy?'

'Why, Galandra Puschik keeps her eye on him, as a good employer should. The boy speaks differently. His tone seems less... local. He uses the odd word she does not understand...'

As THE GRIEF Bringer strode back to the Land Raider after interrogating the terrified tanner and Goodwife Jabal, who made a better showing, and the hulking stupid son Big Ven, he eyed the ogryn BONEhead and the squat sitting on the uppermost track of the vehicle. Zig-zags of pea-green and purple blotched the plasteel body and the track-walls, mounted with las-cannon ball turrets, of the Raider, less suggestive of camouflage than of a sickly infestation by some poisonous lichen. A cowed crowd of townsfolk were eyeing those who perched high upon the massive vehicle. The sprocketed wheels that moved the tracks were hidden from their superstitious gaze by the casings of armour.

For his men to have to mix with these scratching, farting, dumb-witted, sweating peasants. To have to try to tease some sense out of backyard gossip... After the costly victory over the enslavers – a perilous task that had almost proved beyond the Grief Bringers' reach – this present mission almost seemed designed as an insult, a reproof for losing so many comrades, however gloriously.

No, thought Hachard, that way heresy lies. I must trust the instincts of an inquisitor.

At least the fat preacher had understood well enough the power that Hachard and his men deployed, and the seriousness of the threat to humanity that must have brought such warriors here.

Hachard was fairly sure that he had located the prey they sought, while the inquisitor remained unable to pinpoint him. The commander permitted himself a slight, black-toothed smile, not of superiority but of grim satisfaction.

His return to the market square triggered a flurry in the gawping, fearful – and stupidly resentful – crowd. Yet most gazes flickered back quickly to the crudely clad ogryn and the squat atop the vehicle. The citizens of Groxgelt could see that the bulky Grief Bringer, with the visor of his helmet raised, was a true man. Did that passive mob of ugly specimens view the BONEhead as more intimidating than an armoured

Space Marine? Or, in their squinty eyes, was the grotesque, prognathous ogryn someone to whom they could more easily relate?

Hachard entered the hatch of the personnel den where techcrew and other Marines awaited. The comnet crackled alive as he fingered its rune-knobs, its spirit kindling faithfully.

'Lord inquisitor,' he reported, 'I have identified a possible suspect. Name of Jomi Jabal. Curfew approaches but boy has not returned home. Believed to be out by farm four klicks north-west of Groxgelt town...'

One boy. Against whom: Land Raiders, las-cannons, armoured Grief Bringers, and ogryns.

One boy... plus what else?

'I'm within twenty kilometres of you, commander. Am on my way. Don't let the noise of the Land Raiders alert our target. Advance the final four klicks on foot.'

'Understood.' Hachard switched automatically to battle code to summon the other Land Raiders to rendezvous at speed across country, just outside Groxgelt.

He would have to wait a while, so he stepped outside again. The setting gas-giant peered over rooftops like the disembodied eye of some enormous cosmic parent-creature which was slowly withdrawing its witness from this world so as to allow a cloak of gloom to descend.

'Do wish I had my trike with me,' the squat remarked conversationally from up top. 'Big battle-machines attract missiles and such. Zippy little trikes avoid 'em.'

Hachard recalled the dwarf's name. Grimm: that was it.

'Land Raiders protect little men like you,' Hachard said coldly.

'Huh. Don't know about this one. Armour's cracked. Needs welding.'

'You're supposed to be our technician. Paint another rune. Utter a charm.'

Grimm sniggered briefly; and anger flared in Hachard, at a time when he should be composing himself reverently for combat.

'Wretched abhuman!'

Sensing danger, Grimm gabbled, 'Apologies, Sir. Had me work cut out servicing the suits–'

'Silence! In any case we shall be advancing on foot to begin with; and that includes you, little man.'

Grimm goggled at the Commander's power armour, slapped his own quilted flak jacket by way of comparison, and muttered, 'Oh my ancestors.'

Thunderjug guffawed like distant thunder.

* * *

'Sooooon,' THE VOICE soothed Jomi. 'Welcome the circle into your mind.'

The voice had told him where to wait: by the biggest grox paddock. Jomi glanced anxiously at the sinking gas-giant. Already the last of the gloaming was upon the countryside. Soon the curfew trumpet would scream out in town, and no one human would be abroad but himself. He would have broken the law. If the owner of the voice did not come, what could Jomi do? Hide till morning? What, here where mutants might roam? For if muties did not enter the town itself, they might well haunt the open countryside.

Yet he was a mutant too. Why should other mutants be hostile to one of their own kind? Ah, but outcasts would surely be hungry. Jomi's flesh might smell sweet…

Sweet flesh reminded him of Gretchi. If nothing else happened tonight, he could stumble to the farmhouse. He might be able to climb to an upper window, Gretchi's, and tap for admittance. Surely she would admire his daring in venturing out at night to see her? Surely she would reward him suitably? He ached to cup those white doves in his hands, and to explore her private nest of hidden hair, which itself hid…

'The circle! Think of that! Or I may lose focus.'

He thought of Gretchi's mouth open wide. He thought of another part of her opening to him, a soft ring, of whose exact shape and dimensions he wasn't quite sure.

'Forget that foolish minx! She's worthless. I can let you glimpse such lust-nymphs as will make her seem trite and dowdy. I can conjure lubricious courtesans from memory – ayeeee!' Such a pang of anguish and frustration seemed to afflict the voice.

Glimpsing…? And conjuring? The voice had promised to introduce Jomi to delights, not merely show him, as if spied through a window of thick glass.

'You'll be broken on the wheel if I don't reach you,' the voice threatened.

The wheel… Jomi jerked back to reality. What else was his whole life on this damned moon but wretchedness? Entrails and heat and fear and Galandra Puschik's lusts which she would insist on satisfying one day soon, crushingly and disgustingly. He was about to leave all this vileness behind.

Don't think of Gretchi again till after the owner of the voice arrives! He forced her image from his mind. Wheel, circle; circle, wheel.

In the last golden light the horned, scaly, toothsome reptiles milled sluggishly in their corral. Each was the size of a small pony. Their claws clicked on the stony ground. Crop-land dipped away towards the river. Boulders, some the size of houses, punctuated the ridged oat-fields. Carried here by sheets of ice long ago, the voice had told him.

Jomi inhaled. He thought he heard whispers on the wind. He sensed minds: disciplined minds, almost completely shielded from him as if a firescreen stood in front of a blaze of grox dung. Yet some of the heat glowed through.

Could witches who were far cleverer than himself be creeping towards this place, attracted by the voice? No witches who had been broken in the square had ever seemed particularly clever. Of course, extreme pain reduced them to imbecility, to shattered bags of white-hot shrieking nerves, and little more than that. Could they ever have been clever to be captured? Compared with those wretches, Jomi had become educated... somewhat.

Maybe really clever witches had escaped and banded together in the furthest hinterlands far from farms and towns. Thus it had taken them months to trek here.

Jomi could also sense other minds nearby that were dull and slow and fierce. Was he hearing the thoughts of the groxen too? Surely not...

'Voice,' he questioned.

'Hush, bonny boy, I must concentrate. Oh it has been so long. Soon I will embrace you. Strive to see the circle in front of you.'

He mustn't fail the voice at the last moment; for thus he would fail himself. Nor must he scare it away by hinting at the presence of those other strange strong minds in the vicinity. Those, and the brutish minds. Obediently he imagined a circle and strained his eyes in the dimming light.

Yes!

A glowing hoop appeared, balanced upon the ground a few hundred metres away. Slowly it swelled in size, though it did not brighten. If anything, it grew dimmer, as though to evade scrutiny from elsewhere. Within the hoop was utter night, a darkness absolute.

THE FACT THAT the portal was coming into existence some distance away from the boy – and slowly – tended to rule out the activity of a warp creature such as an enslavers. Warp creatures of that ilk were usually impetuous in their attack.

Nor could the alien eldar be creating this opening. The eldar were masters of warp-gates and such; they hardly needed the type of psychic focus that the boy seemed to be providing. As though anything on this moon could possibly interest the eldar!

This portal was opening almost painfully – if such a thing could be. Almost creakingly, as if its 'hinges' had rusted during long aeons of time. Obviously a warp-portal didn't have hinges; but the analogy held.

Grief Bringers in power armour were spreading out under cover of the boulders. A gang of ogryns was lumbering into position in the almost-darkness.

'If we seize the psyker boy now…,' began Hachard, tentatively. 'We may scare whatever is coming. We must wait till the portal-maker steps through. We hunt for knowledge as well as prey.'

'Knowledge…' Did the commander shudder? 'In the Dark Age,' he murmured, 'they sought knowledge for its own sake…'

Serpilian said sharply, 'Only the Emperor knows what really happened during the Dark Age.' How the inquisitor wished that he too knew. Godless science had flourished back then. From time to time remnants were still found: precious, arcane techniques and equipment of utmost value to the Imperium. Long ago the human race had spread throughout the galaxy like a migration of lemmings – heedless of the beings lurking in the warp, for it was heedless of its own psychic potential. Innocents, innocents! Puppies in a daemon's den! Like a sudden storm, insanity and anarchy had erupted till the God-Emperor arose to save and unify, to control the human worlds, to calm the psychic tempest with utmost and essential rigour.

Here was a boy, of the possible future-to-be. Here was… what else? Serpilian extended his sense of presence, but mauve distortions dazed his vision.

A ROBOT HIGHER than any building in Groxgelt, a robot that bristled with what Jomi took to be weapons, lurched through the gate of darkness.

'Here I am, dearest boy,' exulted the voice in Jomi's brain. 'Don't fear this metal body. This is the shell that has sheltered the kernel of myself while I drifted alone for aeons in the warp in a derelict megaship. Now at last I can touch the soil of a world. Now I can hope to be a fleshly body once more. Oh the sweet endearing flesh, the senses that sing, the nerves that twang like harp-strings! And what song did they sing so long ago? Sooooon I shall remember.'

The robot took a tentative step towards Jomi. As if exercising limbs which hadn't encountered the pull of gravity for many millennia, the robot swept an arm around. Energies crackled from the tips of its steel fingers, gusting across the herd of groxen. The reptiles began to snort and hiss and rip at the soil of their compound, and butt their horns against the fence.

What fleshly body was the kernel of this huge machine hoping to be? As the juggernaut took another lurching step in Jomi's direction, he began to sweat. He crouched.

SERPILIAN SHOOK THE bag of rune bones at his waist so that he sounded like an angry rattlesnake, then switched on his energy armour. Beneath his cloak subtle forces wove a cocoon that clad his body, and his cuirass glowed faintly.

He too now heard that voice inside his own head, and shivered at the treachery which the ancient survivor must intend. It was hoping to seize control of the boy's brain and body, dispossessing his spirit, casting that into the limbo of the sea of souls.

The inquisitor stared at the giant gunmetal-grey relic, trying in vain to classify it. It was squatter than a Battle Titan, its limbs less flexibly jointed, nor did any obvious head protrude from the top of its chest in the way that control-heads jutted, turtle-like, from Titans. However, it looked almost as formidable. And what was more, it housed someone who had endured literally for aeons.

Serpilian knew of no mechanical system other than the Emperor's enormous immobile prosthetic throne which could sustain a person's existence during entire aeons.

What remnant of flesh and bone could possibly lurk inside that mobile juggernaut? Only the head and spinal column of the castaway? Only the naked brain, bathed in fluids? Or maybe – could such a thing be? – only the mind itself, wrought within some intricate interior talisman by ancient eldritch sorcery?

That robot was treasure.

Its occupant hoped to steal a human brain which housed such great psychic potential, to add to its own psychic powers...

Whosoever controlled such a boy...

Serpilian suppressed within himself a tenuous twinge of traitorous ambition. Was he being corrupted by proximity to this monster from the past?

'Tis ever this way,' Hachard commented grimly. 'A thin line confronts the foulest enemies. Yet, thank Him on Earth, that line is stronger than a diamond forged in a supernova. Permission,' he requested, 'to summon the Land Raiders?'

'Yes. Do so. But only as a reserve. I don't wish the robot destroyed utterly.'

Hachard radioed in battle code.

As the two men stood under a sheaf of stars, a voice piped:

'Sirs! Sirs!' It was the squat, accompanied by the ogryn BONEhead. 'Surely that's a robot from the early Age of Strife, sirs! The portal must lead to a space hulk in the warp, mustn't it? Where else could such a robot have lurked? That hulk could contain a wealth of ancient technology.'

'Yes, little man,' agreed Serpilian. 'I do believe that's so.'

At that moment the curfew trumpet shrieked from afar, as if that tocsin were the signal for battle.

'Commander, disable the robot. Shoot off its legs.'

Hachard rapped out orders. Almost immediately plasma and laser beams stitched the deepening night. Yet the beams glanced away, deflected by some shield – or even by an aura of invulnerability. For the mind within that machine was potent, was it not? Had it not had mad, lonely aeons during which to examine and hone its powers?

The robot's own inbuilt lasers and plasma cannon fired back, tracking the sources of the energy beams. At the same time a wave of confusion lapped at Serpilian's mind. The creature in the robot possessed psychic weaponry too, so it seemed.

Perhaps something else shared mind-space with the occupant of that plasteel refuge, something that one wouldn't exactly classify as human company...

Serpilian had seen to it that the Grief Bringers wore protective psychic hoods. Still, in that first onslaught two Marines broke cover impetuously, rushing directly towards the robot. Their suits glowed, then incandesced. The overload filter in Hachard's radio stole away their screams. Another brave man took advantage of the diversion to advance at a powered run from a different direction, clutching a melta-bomb. He was obviously hoping to sacrifice himself by detonating this against one of the robot's feet, thus destabilizing it. Plasma engulfed him; the night erupted briefly as the bomb's thermal energy gushed prematurely, liquefying his suit. The Space Marines quickly resumed more disciplined fire.

As Serpilian squinted at the flaring, stroboscopic scene, he could tell that the robot had halted, though it showed precious little sign of disablement. Beams simply slid off it, bouncing away into the sky.

A grim hill hove into view, then another.

'Land Raiders arriving on station,' said Hachard. 'If we aim their lascannons at one leg in concert we should bring it crashing down soon enough.'

'What if the shielding and the aura hold? Even temporarily? Fierce energies will recoil unpredictably. The boy may be evaporated in the backlash. If the lascannon beams do break through, the robot might explode.'

Couldn't Hachard guess at the value of this artefact from elder days? Maybe not. He only saw a present menace to the Imperium. Of all those present, save for Serpilian perhaps only the squat realized... The inquisitor could hardly confide in him. Indeed, he might need to silence the little man.

Once again, Serpilian felt a thread of heretical temptation insinuating itself within his soul, and muttered a prayer. 'Asperge me, God-Emperor. Cleanse me.'

'Permission, sah,' requested the sergeant-ogryn. 'My men... strong. We charge at the robot? Wrestle it on to its side?'

Hachard laughed; and it occurred to Serpilian that the wave of confusion might have affected the minds of the ogryns peculiarly. Unlike the Space Marines, the abhumans had been shielded only by their own dense skulls and by their brutish, if violent, thought processes. The confusion might only now be surfacing in their brainiest representative, the sergeant.

'Why not?' said the commander. 'Listen carefully, sergeant: send all your ogryns round to the north side. Yes, in that direction. Over there. Then you come back to report. As soon as my Marines cease fire, your ogryns must charge. Do you understand?'

'Yus, sah.' Thunderjug stomped over to his troopers and bellowed at them for a while.

'Couldn't one of them scoop up the boy?' suggested Grimm.

'They'd probably tear his head off by mistake,' snapped Hachard.

'Um... Commander, sir.'

'What is it now, abhuman?'

'Isn't a charge by the ogryns a mite suicidal?'

'Not necessarily,' intervened Serpilian. 'The robot replied to fire with fire. But the ogryn charge might confuse it. I take it that that's the commander's intention, rather than him implying that his hands are being tied.'

'Huh,' said Grimm.

Thunderjug returned and stood to attention.

JOMI CLUNG TO the ground in terror as the air blistered above him.

'They'll need to change their tactics,' advised the voice. 'A lull must come – and I think I can cause a diversion. When I say run, sprint to me as fast as you can, ducking low. I can take you inside this body. I can transport you back through the portal. Better the warp than death, don't you think?'

The sizzle of lethal beams almost convinced Jomi.

Almost.

'I shall save you, Jomi, save you. I am your safety…'

The voice began to drone hypnotically, bewitchingly. It promised joys, it promised lusts, fulfilments – yet seemed savagely bewildered as to what these might be. Did Jomi hear a background hint of crazed laughter? His body twitched, puppet-like. He threw up his hand reflexively, and a low, stray laser beam seared his wrist superficially. The pain jerked him free from the growing enchantment, plunging him again into a terrain of terrible fear.

'Are you man or woman?' he gasped.

'I hardly remember.'

'How can you not remember such a thing?'

'It became unimportant… Yet a ghost reminds me of the flesh! A goading wraith within. Ah, Jomi, Jomeeee, I know so much, and am so separated from all that I knew. My ghost cries for a body to caress and sculpt to its desire… Come to me soon, Jomeeee, when I call–'

FROM THE VOICE'S moaning words Serpilian gathered ample confirmation that its owner had been a psychic eavesdropper on millennia of war-torn history and even of hidden pre-Imperium history. How the inquisitor thirsted for its knowledge.

But the ancient survivor was also, he strongly suspected, possessed.

Possessed by a daemon of the warp.

This was an unusual species of possession, for the survivor plainly owned no body at all, other than the vast metal body of the robot. The survivor consisted only of mind, wrought within a talisman of crystal wafers or some other occult material, a talisman which strove to maintain the stability of that mind – strove with a fair degree of success, considering the awesome timespan, yet of necessity imperfectly. The daemon had no tangible flesh to twist and warp and stamp its mark upon. It could only lurk impotently, glued to the imprisoned mind, tormenting it spasmodically by stimulating memories and sensuous hallucinations. Maybe the goad of the daemon was what had prevented the survivor from lapsing into sloth…

The voice spoke of science. The truth was corruption. Conclusio: its science was heresy.

Serpilian must not thirst for that!

And now that the castaway's dark scheme to possess Jomi had failed – a cursed, daemon-inspired plan! – the survivor was intent on at least carrying the boy back into exile with it.

At Hachard's command the Grief Bringers ceased fire…

* * *

Just as the ogryn squad was commencing its assault, the robot aimed a plasma blast low at the grox compound, crisping several beasts yet also tearing a long gap in the fence. Serpilian sensed the aura of venomous intent which the mind in the robot – daemon-assisted? – directed at the reptiles to stir their blood lust.

Ripping at one another, groxen burst free of their captivity and rapidly were attracted towards the thundering giants. All plasma and laser fire had ceased. The psyker boy staggered erect and stumbled towards the robot; seeing which, Serpilian let out a cry of frustration.

'Catch that lad for the Emperor, Thunderjug!' shouted Grimm, as if he was a commander. 'And don't pull his head off unless you have to!'

No appeal could mean more to an ogryn. Tossing his encumbering ripper gun aside, Thunderjug Aggrox bared his tusks and pounded towards the distant youth. The dapper little squat sprinted after the ogryn, trying his best to keep up, panting, 'Huh! Huh! Huh!'

Careless of his own safety, Serpilian loped after them, blood-red cloak streaming, the very image of avenging angel. The boy must be stopped! A hatch was opening in the lower casing of the robot to welcome the lurching youth.

Just then, the stampeding groxen met the charging ogryns. The insensate animals leapt, clawed, bit, and gouged. They tore chunks of flesh, yet an ogryn hardly heeded such trivia. Ogryn fists smashed grox skulls.

However, the robot noticed the boy's pursuers and swivelled a weapon arm, opening fire with a raking of explosive bolts. Serpilian dived flat. Ahead of him, the ogryn's mighty legs pounded onward for a dozen more strides before the giant crashed to the ground. The squat darted past; his cap had fallen off, or been snatched away by a bolt. Then a blast grenade, launched from a tube in the robot's arm, exploded near him. The shockwave picked the squat up and threw him several metres.

Sprawled on the stony dirt, Serpilian stretched out his right arm, forefinger pointing the jokaero needler. One needle in the boy, and he would be paralyzed. The range was somewhat extreme for such a tiny, lightweight dart. The target was moving. The inquisitor strove to aim.

At that moment, when Jomi was barely twenty metres from the inviting hatch, he halted...

A psychic maelstrom of savagery and pain whirled around Jomi. The death-shrieks of those who had died, the berserker fury of ogryns as they fought the reptiles, the terror of all the energy beams and explosions...

these suddenly culminated. A lurid radiance seemed to flare in his mind, as if doors were flying open, behind which fierce furnaces raged, cauldrons of inchoate energy.

'Jomeeee! You've almost reached meee! Run just a little bit more and leap inside meee!'

Looking up at the towering machine, Jomi suddenly perceived it – by that blazing light from within him – not as a mountain of metal in approximately humanoid shape, but as...

...A VAST, NAKED Galandra Puschik looming over him lustfully. Her legs were squat trunks. The hatch was her secret opening. Her enormous torso, thick with fat, writhed with desire to entertain him. Her great muscular arms reached out...

'Jomeeee! My dearest delicious boy, my joy–!'

What confronted him was a robot again. Yet the light from within him did not cease. It changed hue and wavelength, so that he peered appalled into the world of what-might-be...

ASSISTED BY A *tentacle, he had leapt into a womb of steel, a metal pod barely large enough to stand up in. The tentacle withdrew, and he was thrown upon the floor as the robot rocked, starting to march back towards the portal, brushing aside the brawling bodies of brutal giants and rabid groxen. Its cleated feet crushed deep craters.*

The hatch was descending, to close him in.

Through it, while still open, by the resuming, spasming light of energy beams Jomi glimpsed a man in glowing breastplate and blood-red cloak – a thin, tall man with a drooping black moustache and a staring eye tattooed upon his cheek – sprinting frantically towards the decamping robot.

Jomi could hear the man's thumping thoughts. 'Even if I can paralyze him... too late to drag the boy out...! At least cling to some handhold on the robot... Don't lose it entirely, or all has been in vain... Accompany it, willy-nilly, through the doorway of darkness...

'Will there be air on the other side of the portal? Will all atmosphere have long since leaked out of the hulk? Will there be only vacuum, to boil my blood and collapse my lungs like empty paper bags? My energy armour will be no protection from that fate...'

The hatch closed, plunging Jomi into utter obscurity and silence. The body that carried him lurched and swayed.

Presently little lights winked on. Jomi hugged his own body protectively. How could he escape from this pod? Surely he couldn't live inside this miniature chamber even if the machine fed him? He imagined the narrow floor aswill with his urine, in which nuggets of excrement bobbed.

'Welcome to my kingdom,' the voice purred. Bitter mockery tinged the accents Jomi heard in his mind. *'Our kingdom, now–'*

('Mine tooo...') A malicious, disappointed echo seemed to haunt the voice, perhaps unheard by it, perhaps all too familiar. *('Failure, feeble failure... But here's a soft body at least...')*

The lid of a small porthole slid aside. Jomi pressed his face to the thick plascrystal as floodlight beams lanced from the robot. He stared at a great grotto of metal, from which several steel tunnels ran away into stygian gloom. Strange machines jutted from the plated floor and from the ribbed walls. A debris of loose tools and cargo floated like dead fish in a dank pond.

'There's one other such machine as mine on board,' the voice confided, as if oblivious of the soft, sinister echo that Jomi had heard. *'It has been inactive for millennia, lacking a person's mind to fill it, but I can revive it now. With my science, I'll put you into it. First, of course, I'll need to cut away your body–'*

('That'll be an exquisite hour or so...')

Jomi vomited in terror.

' – soon, before you use all the air I sucked in on that moon. Once you're activated we can play games. Hide and seek, for instance... You'll need to rely on the resources of your lovely mind. At least I'll have company now. Oh the madness, the madness. Maybe my imaginary companion will go away. Into you, maybe...'

A figure in a blood-red cloak drifted into view, out in the giant grotto. Its frozen arms stretched out vainly towards a vista which, prior to the flare of illumination, it couldn't possibly have seen...

WHAT-MIGHT-BE – and might still be – vanished.

Jomi still stood before the robot.

'Daemon, daemon, hidden daemon!' he shrieked at it. He spat. Reaching into his memory for an incantation, he recalled Farb's prayers, and howled:

'Imperator hominorum, nostra salvatio!'

'Jomeeeee! Do not betray meeee!'

The whitehot cauldron inside Jomi spilled over. The inner furnaces, so suddenly revealed to him, gushed psychic fire. Hardly knowing how, he sprayed a fountain of defensive mental energy, ill-focused yet incandescent, at the voice, which would have betrayed him.

'Nostra salvatio, hominorum Imperator!'

'Aiieee!' cried the voice, keening through his head like a scalpel blade attempting to severe the sinews of his new-found psyker ability, raw and unshaped as yet.

Recoiling, his brain in agony, Jomi nevertheless summoned another spout of hot repulsion to hurl at the robot.

THE BOY'S RAW power! And his piety too, all be it born of terror! Bathed in the backwash of inner light from the volcanic upheaval within the boy, with his own senses extended Serpilian had partaken of Jomi's vision of what-might-be.

As if an actor in Jomi's dream, the inquisitor had experienced the death-agony of passing through the portal. Of collapsing lungs. Of utter, absolute chill… He had also known Jomi's claustrophobic, dreadful dismay. Moments later Serpilian found himself still sprawled on the battlefield; and the battlefield was a blessed place by contrast.

Scrambling up, Serpilian signalled back towards Hachard, hoping that the Commander could see and would understand his gestures. Then he resumed his reckless run towards the boy who was holding the robot at bay, like a rat defying a bull. He no longer pointed his jokaero needler.

Casting his own aura of protection, Serpilian seized Jomi by the shoulder.

'In the Emperor's name, come with me to safety! Come swiftly, Jomi Jabal!'

HACHARD MUST HAVE understood. As soon as Serpilian had hauled the boy to some reasonable remove, and had ducked with him behind a boulder, the las-cannons of the Land Raiders opened fire. Shaft upon shaft of searing energy lanced at the robot. The Space Marine infantry added their contribution. Wounded ogryns scattered, abandoning the remaining groxen which had been preoccupying them.

Had the giants not engaged with the savage reptiles, by now one of those might have attacked Serpilian or the boy…

The robot launched jets of plasma and energy beams. A Land Raider exploded, raining hot shards of plasteel. Several Marines fell victim to beams and jets. The Imperial energies cascaded off the robot's shields, pluming into the sky, rendering the landscape bright as day.

Yet now the robot seemed confused. It backed. It lumbered. Perhaps the mind within was anguished. Perhaps, infected by Jomi's vision, it imagined that it had passed safely back through the portal, though the nightmare evidence was otherwise. Perhaps it was running low on energy.

At last an Imperial energy-beam tore loose a weapon arm. Another beam pierced the vulnerable hatch. Part of the robot's mantle flared and melted. Still firing – but falteringly now, seemingly at random – the great, damaged machine stomped back towards the portal. Land Raider beams focused in unison upon its back, so that it seemed to be propelled in its retreat by a hurricane-torn, white-hot sail woven from the heart of a sun.

As it entered the portal, the robot incandesced blindingly. A detonation as of a dozen simultaneous sonic booms rocked the torn terrain. Glaring fragments of the robot's carapace flew back like angry boomerangs, like scythes. The bulk of its disintegrating body pitched forward, out of existence, vanishing.

SERPILIAN DEACTIVATED HIS energy armour, and Jomi, smeared with dirt and stinking of sweat, wept in his arms.

'I shall,' vowed Serpilian, 'recommend you for the finest training – as an inquisitor yourself.'

The boy cried, 'What? What? I can't hear! Only the awful terrible thunder.'

'Your hearing will return!' Serpilian shouted into the boy's streaked face. 'If not, that can be repaired with an acoustic amulet! One day you will serve the Emperor as I serve him. I came a long way to find you!'

AFTER A WHILE, Jomi listened to Serpilian's thoughts instead and began to understand. This cloaked figure had come a long way to find him. Why, so had the voice; so had the mind, and the daemon, in the robot…

Jomi would be sent far away from the wretched moon, to Earth itself. He thought fleetingly of Gretchi; but as the voice itself had suggested, that kind of yearning seemed to have become extremely insignificant.

GROANING, AND RUBBING his head, Grimm ambled back to where the BONEhead lay sprawled; but it was undeniable that Thunderjug's whole skull, including the riveted battle honours, was missing. The dwarf patted the toppled giant consolingly on the shoulder. 'Huh!' he said.

Bilious-hued power armour loomed. Commander Hachard himself stood over the ogryn.

'I watched him charge,' said Hachard's external speaker. 'The other subhumans remain alive – I think so, by and large – but not their sergeant. The Grief Bringers are… honoured, by his bravery.' Ponderously, the Space Marine Commander saluted.

What about me? thought Grimm. I nearly got bloomin' blown to pieces. But he said nothing. It was Thunderjug who was dead.

Bending, assisted by the squat, Hachard dragged the ogryn's corpse into his powered arms.

As Grimm gazed up at the indigo sky, the stars stared back down at him blindly. The portal had disappeared a while since, yet a tremor seemed to twist the night air, warping the heavens. Or was the distortion due to moisture in his eyes?

HARLEQUIN

CLASSIFICATION: Primary Level Intelligence
CLEARANCE: Slate
ENCRYPTION: Cryptox v.2.1
DATE: 091.M41
AUTHOR: Tech-Adept Auralis Fo, assignum Ordo Xenos
SUBJECT: A bundle discovered
RECIPIENT: Tech-Magos Xandrus Har Lambetter, assignum Ordo
Xenos

My lord,

As the Machine God is my witness, I have been engaged upon my habitual duties of repair and maintenance. An hour or so before vespers yesterday, while invoking the Ritual of Rust Suppression in the eastern chambers bearing the outflow pipes from the Great Cogitatorum, I had cause to anoint the sacred unguent upon a deep section that has not been visited for many a century.

It was there, lodged between two ancient and holy effluent tubes that I discovered a dust-covered bundle. At the first, assuming it was nothing but the commonplace cadaver of one of the dust-rats that typically are to be found in these ancient chambers, forgive me, I struck it with my soldering lance, causing it to catch light and smoulder for a few moments. In that instant I realised that the item was not as I suspected, but a bundle wrapped in oil-cloth. I levered the package loose and extinguished the flames with my feet. Upon further investigation, I was able to unwrap the binding, to reveal a clutch of parchment and manuscript, cracked and creased with great age. The pages vary in material and dimensions, but the hand of author remains constant, leading me to ascertain that they form a journal, or possibly a fiction. May the Machine God forgive me, but I confess my inadvertent application of flames to the package did no more than destroy more than a handful of sheets and obscure a few dozen more with burns and scorching.

Lord, I am certainly no scholar, but these documents seem fearful old. From careful study of the records of the dates of previous rituals in these chambers, I have ascertained that they have probably not been disturbed for over seven centuries. Beyond that, I am unworthy to pass further judgement. That is plainly for our great masters to determine.

And thus I am despatching my discovery in all good haste to you, sir, in the expectation that you will decide whether these scraps are an important, long lost journal of great important to our Inquisitorial masters. If they prove to be mere trash and ephemera, I trust that you will forgive my imposition, and destroy them in any manner which you see fit.

Praise the machine!

Tech-Adept Fo

ONE
MURDERS

PLANET XENOPHON OF *the star Xerxes...*

A tree-fungus offered Inquisitors Rufus Olafson and Russ Erikson shade from the aching blue sunlight. Gunfire racketed in the distance. During the turmoil of the past few hours Rufus and Russ had become separated and had only just met up again.

Why was Erikson pointing a plasma pistol at his friend?

Olafson gaped at the gun's jutting hood with its ventilator holes like slanted nostrils, at the accumulator vanes like compressed vertebrae clamped in a vice inlaid with pious cloisonné runes.

He was bewildered not by the purpose of the gun – which was the discharge of superheated plasma – but by Erikson's stance.

'What in the Emperor's name?'

With his free hand Erikson reached to his brow as though to shade his eyes. As if transfixed by a terrible thought, Erikson dug his fingernails into his skin.

In one swift downward motion Erikson tore his face off – that familiar bulbous face – to reveal a second face beneath. A mask of pseudoflesh dangled limply from the stranger's fingertips.

No, not a stranger...

'Brodski? You?'

The face which now confronted Olafson was that of another inquisitor whom he recognised from a comradely encounter five years earlier.

'Where's Russ? Russ Erikson! What happened to him? Why are you here?'

It was as though Brodski had waylaid Erikson, scalped Erikson's face, and made a mask of it. Why was Brodski on this planet at all? Where had he come from, and how?

Nightmarish bafflement beset Olafson. Had the fierce blue sunlight dazed him with fever and hallucination?

'Display your tattoo, Brodski!'

The palm-tattoo, of identification. Inquisitor's credentials. Printed electronically upon the palm. Bid it to appear.

All that Brodski displayed was the plasma pistol.

And a grin.

Olafson's last sight could hardly be claimed to be the discharge of this pistol. That was a sight too blinding and all-consuming. Already the sun-hot plasma had vaporized Olafson's eyes, his face, his whole head.

A headless corpse lay supine, shoulders steaming. The killer laid down the exhausted gun to re-energize itself and, where a head had been, he placed the floppy false face of Erikson.

Then he removed a Tarot card from his robe and propped it against one of Olafson's boots. The card was of the High Priest, enthroned and grasping a hammer, surrounded by a frieze of wailing daemons. Blatantly the design proclaimed Ordo Malleus, one of the most powerful orders of the Inquisition, a secret wrapped within a secret.

The killer reached to his hairline again. Fingernails clawed. He tore off Brodski's face, balled the mask up in his fist, crammed it into his mouth, chewed and swallowed.

'INQUISITORS ARE BEING murdered,' confided the Master Inquisitor to the robed man who stood before him.

The Master was a black man. His hooded face bore concentric circles of ridged ebon scars around eyes and mouth. His original features eluded observation. Those scars drew one inward, downward, through cycles of darkness to pouting lips beaded with pearls, like wellings of creamy saliva, and to eyes which were mirrored lenses, and within which therefore one only discovered oneself in miniature. Lumps under his ornately purity-tasselled robe might have been adjuncts to his bodily organs – purifiers or glandular enhancers.

Cyborged servitors – mind-wiped snail-men – constantly cruised the black marble floor of his long, barrel-vaulted chamber, cleansing and laying down trails of scented polish behind them. The floor reflected the vault above as though the chamber were half flooded with dark liquid upon which one could nevertheless walk. A dungeon seemed to plunge below the surface.

The Master sat at an archaic work-desk inlaid with shimmery nacre and aglow with icon-screens.

'Murdered, so it seems, by fellow inquisitors!'

THE ICE-SHEET of Antarctica was over three kilometres thick. Carved in bedrock a further kilometre below that frigid shield was the most ancient of all the headquarters of the Inquisition.

If a hole opened up in the global pollution of the skies – as sometimes was the case over Antarctica – and if no blizzard was raging, then from space an observer scrying through a magni-lens would have gleaned almost no idea of the magnitude of those headquarters.

Admittedly, scattered across the ice-sheet there rose many great baroque edifices of molecularly bonded ice. Those would be visible to that privileged scryer in space principally by their long shadows; strange runes inscribed upon the dirty whiteness.

Shadows of bastions and towers and salients sheltering and servicing widely scattered space ports...

Hidden deep below the blank expanses in between were uncountable cubic kilometres of artificial caverns and vast tunnels and grottoes and antrums housing sombre labyrinthine complexes and whole cities of servitors and scribes. Of protectors and warders and functionaries. Of medics and tech-priests and repairers and excavators – for, yes, these headquarters must continue to extend, downward and outward, by the cutting of new dungeon-chasms and arched galleries, while older ones fell into disuse or were blocked by the accumulation of the ages.

Uncountable cubic kilometres! How many ordinary members of the Inquisition might know, for instance, the whereabouts of certain daemonological laboratories? Or even of the existence of those? Who might know where some of the highest officials hid their sanctums, or even the identities of those officials? How many ordinary inquisitors – powerful men, themselves! – were aware that beyond the already secret archives were *occult archives*?

Who could encompass, in his mind, the Inquisition? Could the Masters of the Inquisition even do so?

THE MAN WHO listened to this Master sported a scar across one cheek to which were sewn sapphires. An ormolu-framed lens occupied the socket of one eye. A perforated tube led up one nostril. The other nostril exhaled wisps of virtueherb smoke.

'An apparent attempt was made on my life recently,' confessed Baal Firenze. 'Yes, magister, here in the heart of our own headquarters! Or at least in a certain *bowel...*'

Why, the *heart* of the Inquisition was right here in the Master's quarters! How gauche to suggest that treachery might reach as close as here. Undoubtedly some decorative flourishes on the front of the Master's desk could gush plasma or a hail of toxic needles if the Master twitched a toe.

YES INDEED, A murder attempt had almost certainly been perpetrated in one of the many annexees to the archives...

In a certain dusty depository of memoranda undisturbed for several thousand years, back-up memoranda were stored, illuminated in ever-ink upon the permaparchment pages of great brass-bound tomes. Plasteel shelves towered in the obscurity. A thousand tomes were racked upon each section. Wrought-iron ladders climbed to a gallery.

Baal Firenze had lately been haunted by confusing dreams of exotic faces of exquisite grace and uncanny expressions. Alien physiognomies! Faces of the eldar...

He didn't know why this should be. It was a memory he had lost. Yet a faint hunch had directed his steps to this depository, which only a few glow-globes lit dimly, and which was deserted but for a solitary simian servitor. The creature shuffled about, its knuckles dangling upon the floor of polished rock. The servitor would climb a ladder and shelving to fetch a tome if anyone ever ordered it to. It, and its many antecedents, had burnished the floor in their aimless unoccupied meanderings for century after century.

Were some relevant memoranda about the eldar stored here? Had Firenze once known this to be so?

How should a servitor know? It would understand a command such as 'Shelf ninety-seven, volume seventeen!' yet nothing about the contents of what it was ordered to climb and bring down.

Why had Firenze thought of those particular numbers?

As he opened his mouth to summon the servitor, laser pulses flashed from the high gallery cloaked in deepest shadow. Air and dust ionized to a brilliant green. The pulses hit books, melting brass, setting perma-parchment ablaze.

Firenze had already thrown himself sidelong and was rolling, clutching his own laspistol, pointing it upward.

An ambush? Here in the headquarters?

He fired at the gallery, and molten iron sprayed.

He was already rolling again. From further along the gallery more pulses streaked, glancing off the stone floor, setting more tomes on fire.

The servitor was shrieking. On account of this outcry Firenze couldn't hear which way his ambusher was heading along that dingy gallery. He fired again – at the servitor, to silence it.

Instantly Firenze was deafened by multiple explosions. Air buffeted him. Tomes lurched from lower shelves to splay open upon the floor. Pages fluttered away like giant night-moths taking wing.

Grenades, hidden bomblets: a whole line of these must have been triggered remotely all at once! No devastating blastwave had swept Firenze off his feet. Consequently the tiny bombs must have been *krak* – their explosive effect concentrated, not dispersed.

And *crack* was what the cliff of shelves proceeded to do.

A gloomy precipice sagged. Brass-bound tomes cascaded. Choking dust billowed. Like a building demolished by mines, the whole structure settled with fearful momentum, ripping loose from stanchions and wall-bolts and clamps.

Frantically Firenze propelled himself away from under the descending avalanche. He scrabbled into a niche as great tomes raked and shelves concertinaed, shrieking and snapping.

Fire roared upward, to meet the buckling, collapsing gallery. Smoke roiled amidst dust which was aglow with flames. Cinders swirled. The very bedrock of the floor seemed to rock as wreckage impacted, tonne by tonne.

By now Firenze had scrambled into the doorway, just as the depository became an inferno.

Shelf ninety-seven, volume seventeen would never be consulted – if indeed it had possessed any relevance whatever. The ambusher would by now be roasted, if he hadn't already been hurled to his death or chopped apart.

A klaxon wailed. Firenze turned and sprinted – as a massive fire-door began a grinding descent which would block his exit from this annexe. The machinery was ancient and slow. A scurf of rust showered down as he threw himself under the descending barrier, to safety.

THE DARK MASTER seemed not to have heard of the minor fire in that minor annexe. Yet the incident was certainly symptomatic.

'I don't think this attempt was intended to succeed,' said Firenze.

How could the attack have been aimed *knowingly* at Baal Firenze? The unseen ambusher had virtually committed suicide. Wisely indeed, in view of the excruciations he would have suffered! But prematurely.

Within this guarded labyrinth beneath the southern ice-cap were other booby-traps waiting for inquisitors?

'The event fills you with doubt,' said the Master. 'And in a sense it casts doubt upon you too.'

Indeed. Could a target be a target for no reason?

'How is your latest rejuvenation, Baal Firenze?' enquired the Master, as if this was the true reason for Firenze's audience with the High Lord.

Firenze touched the jeweled scar on his cheek. 'I still can never recall the cause of this wound.'

'The immediate cause was our own surgeons who refreshed your body a second time. They slashed the new flesh and replaced your regrown eye with a familiar lens.'

'I know, lord.'

'This time they adorned the scar with sapphires rather than rubies because you are a new man once again.'

The Master spoke as if this rejuvenation had happened just the other day, not two years previously! What was such a jot of time compared with the ten thousand years of torment of the Emperor? Pain was timeless and eternal.

Time had both cheated Firenze and bitterly blessed him. Was it a cheat or a blessing to have lived yet not to know many things which must have happened to him in the past?

He'd been privileged to be told, under an oath of secrecy, that a century earlier he had returned to Terra to denounce a certain heretical inquisitor named Jaq Draco. Draco had declared *exterminatus* against the world of Stalinvast, which had already been thoroughly cleansed of genestealer infestation. As a result of the needless *exterminatus*, Stalinvast had been rendered lifeless and lost to the Imperium.

Since Firenze was somehow implicated in this disaster, he had volunteered – aye, volunteered – for questioning under deep-truth. The onion rings of Firenze's mind had been peeled one by one, and examined and wrung dry, until he was as a newborn baby, speechless, incontinent, and as innocent as any baby obsessed with its primal cravings.

The Inquisition had re-educated Firenze honourably for fifteen years. By then he was in his seventies. To amortize their investment, he was rejuvenated, in the process losing some of the memories of his second childhood. Thereafter, he trained as an inquisitor – and a devout and ruthless one he proved to be for decades, on many worlds, until he retired to train junior inquisitors. And then the Inquisition had ordered him to be rejuvenated yet again.

Firenze was being retained as a future key to some unknown lock.

The Master said softly: 'Most inquisitors who have been murdered would appear at some stage in their careers to have been involved in the *Eternity* project–'

'The search for immortal mutants–'

'Precisely. To destroy those deviants. So that there shall not be any heretical potential petty rivals to the Emperor.'

The Master displayed the palm of his left hand, and energized an *electro-tattoo* – of a daemon's head.

Firenze likewise held up his palm, and willed an identical tattoo to gleam.

He and the Master were no longer merely regular inquisitor and the Master of journeymen inquisitors. They were fellow members of the Ordo Malleus, hunters of the daemons of Chaos.

Firenze inhaled virtueherb and breathed out slowly.

The Master said, 'These assassinations appear to be carried out by members of our Ordo Malleus.'

Firenze hesitated. 'Or perhaps by masqueraders who know of the existence of our ordo?'

'Perhaps…'

'There are schisms in our ranks?'

The Master chuckled in a blood-stilling manner.

Was this High Lord of the Inquisition, whose very physical appearance seemed to evade scrutiny, also the Secret Master of the Ordo Malleus? Or was the true Master of the Ordo Malleus someone else? Someone who was perhaps *suspect*, and who was bent on undermining the morale of the Inquisition itself?

Such thoughts were a torment, and were perhaps best purged by the tormenting of the Emperor's enemies, an activity which Baal Firenze used to relish. Aye, prior to his retirement Firenze had relished this activity to excess at times – almost as if to emphasize an intensity of faith which, at some earlier period, had perhaps been less acute.

The Master said: 'There are rumours of eldar being sighted in some places where assassinations occurred. Harlequins…'

An image swam nauseatingly in Firenze's mind: of a man who had acted and dressed like a Harlequin. Somewhere, somewhen. The mental mirage refused to come into focus.

'There are reports of an eldar craftworld taking shape in orbit around Stalinvast–'

'Stalinvast!' exclaimed Firenze. The devastated world…

Briefly Firenze was perplexed. In the wake of *exterminatus*, not even a breathable atmosphere remained on Stalinvast, let alone any jot of life, however humble. Why build a habitat near such a globe? The purpose could hardly be colonization.

In the minds of the aliens the whole point must be the symbolic power of such total ruin. Proximity to an exterminated world would endow some dire alien ritual with a gruesome intensity. The eldar seemed obsessed with cataclysm, and Stalinvast was an emblem of vast calamity.

Firenze said, 'They must be preparing for some blasphemous rite.'

The Master nodded. 'Something sacred, in their estimation.'

'Only the Emperor is truly sacred.'

'Of course. All else is blasphemy.'

'Maybe,' suggested Firenze, 'these assassinations of our inquisitors are ritual sacrifices? Carried out by human agents of the eldar?'

The Master puckered his palm so that the daemon tattoo seemed to become animated. 'Maybe,' he said, 'the spectre of Slaanesh looms.'

Slaanesh, the daemon of wantonness… The Ordo Malleus suspected that the downfall of the eldar, which had occurred aeons ago and which had laid waste to so many worlds, had some connection with that Chaos god. Exactly what this connection was had eluded the most scrupulous investigations.

Global destruction – of a once-human world – was surely what was attracting the aliens to Stalinvast, there to perform whatever eerie rite was impending…

The Master licked his pearl-studded lips.

'We need to know more about the relationship of the eldar to Slaanesh.' Only a member of the Ordo Malleus could sanely learn of such things.

The Master blanked his palm-tattoo. 'If only our Imperium could gain access to the eldar webway! If only we could chart some of that webway.' Now he was speaking simply as a Master of the Inquisition.

Firenze nodded. The eldar could not steer directly through warp space in the way that human beings could, thanks to Navigators and by virtue of the Emperor's blessed beacon, the Astronomican. Nevertheless, the eldar had access to an arcane maze of immaterial tunnels through the warp.

Inside that mysterious alien construction orbiting Stalinvast, security might be marginally looser. Especially at the height of a festival.

'Lead an expedition there, Baal Firenze,' ordered the Master. 'Let the goal of this, your third phase of existence, be to seize these eldar secrets.'

Aye, and to determine in what respect the aliens might be implicated in the deaths of inquisitors.

Inquisitors, who had all supposedly been engaged in the Eternity project.

What if the eldar involvement was simply a deception?

Eldar faces haunted Firenze.

Had he been retained in Inquisition service so that at last he might himself exhume what metaveritas had failed to uncover? Certainly a journey to the vicinity of Stalinvast must be, in a sense, a journey of self-discovery for him.

Once there, he could cause torment. He imagined eldar children dying.

The dark Master flashed that daemonic tattoo once more.

'Call upon regular Space Marines, Firenze. Not upon our own Grey Knights. As yet there is no proof of a Chaos power at work.'

'What if there does prove to be any daemonic manifestation?'

The Master spread his hands serenely. 'Marines can be mind-scrubbed. Hypnosis will remove their memories.'

Aye, just as Firenze's own memories had perhaps once been removed by some unknown agency – so that not even radical mind-peeling had been able to recover those!

Eldar faces haunted Firenze – especially the foggy face of a Harlequin, who seemed to be human not alien. Eldar children would surely die, bringing grief to presumptuous aliens.

The overt aim of the expedition was to seize some of the secrets of the webway. Indeed, the Grey Knights wouldn't be called upon. Already Firenze was beginning to calculate logistics, requirements, requisitions.

A human snail cruised by, spreading polish, incapable of understanding an iota of what had transpired. Firenze knew that ignorance was the human condition itself. Let there be truth through torment.

PLANET ORBAL OF *the star Phosphor: Inquisitor Ion Dimitru used plasma to demolish a final doorway. Blast rocked him, and heat toasted him briefly. Imperial Guardsmen crowded behind him, their shaved heads tattooed piously with the ravaged face of the Emperor staring blindly upward, their protector. The Guardsmen clutched long-barrelled lasguns. Corpses littered the debris-strewn tunnel.*

Inside this final bunker must be the so-called Inquisitor Errant whose trail Dimitru had followed from world to world. 'Errant' signified roving or wandering. This was the very name chosen by the mutant who masqueraded as a member of the Inquisition.

'Errant' also implied error. Heresy and blasphemy!

'Errant!' bellowed Dimitru. 'Surrender to me!'

Aye, for excruciation prior to termination.

As the smoke cleared, a figure moved within the bunker; and Dimitru steadied a laspistol in his other gauntleted hand.

Yet the shots which killed Dimitru did not come from within. The shuriken discs flew from a ventilation grating in the ceiling, scalping Dimitru of hair and skull and slicing his brain apart.

'Fools!' cried a voice from above. 'He who led you here isn't a true inquisitor at all! Dimitru was an impostor! He who honours the Emperor must honour Errant!'

A Tarot card fluttered to the floor, settling near the corpse of Dimitru.

Two
Awakenings

Such total darkness. It was as though the whole of existence ended long ago. It was as though all the stars in all the galaxies had become dead ashes and frigid soot adrift in futile nullity for ever more. Dead in a waste of darkness.

It was as though the universe had ended.

Or as though *it had not yet begun*. As though the cosmos had not yet uttered its first anguished scream, nor commenced upon its festering agonized course.

Such darkness, such silence… But wait…

This darkness, as of a cave at the heart of a moon wandering dead in the deeps without world or sun within a hundred light-years, wasn't absolute. A single faint light glimmered dimly. A solitary electrocandle flickered.

Stare for a year and, courtesy of those feeble spasms of photons, you might begin to make out a terrible corpse-face enclosed in wires and tubes, the only blind witness of the nullity.

Stare for another year, and you might distinguish part of a soaring tortuous throne which encased the corpse, hiding from sight all but that ghastly visage.

Stare for a further year, and you might imagine that you detected a glint at the edge of what had once, long ago, been an eye. Could that minuscule welling of moisture be a tiny teardrop – or only a puny reflection of the electrocandle?

* * *

OF A SUDDEN – frightfully sudden amidst such nothingness – other stars kindled. Each revealed a snarling imp, vile and twisted. These monstrosities and abominations had been the lurking invisible spies upon that solitary witness of the nothingness, upon that haggard over-watcher who was sightless and paralysed and moribund yet who somehow perceived and endured.

Here, there, elsewhere, electrocandles brightened. Or at least they attained a degree of gleam which was brightness by comparison with the preceding darkness.

The original star-candle brightened too. Its light unveiled a bulkhead which was a great bas-relief of the Emperor of All. The bas-relief itself was not wrought in gold, but in black-lacquered adamantium. This effigy had been the blind witness, keeping the dark watch.

The imps were images of evil, set in niches. Reflections of the electrocandles writhed now in walls and ceilings of black glassy obsidian and jet, animating runes and sacred axioms carved therein, in cryptrooms and along narrow corridors. Here and there daemon faces leered: masks which covered the infrequent portholes. Gargoyles exhaled and inhaled silently, stirring the memory of incense burned a century ago.

Other lights blinked to life: indicators and tell-tales. None of these, separately or collectively, exactly conjured brightness. Rather, they accentuated the devout gloom of ebon and obsidian.

Nevertheless, the warpship *Tormentum Malorum* was reviving.

JAQ DRACO UNCURLED himself from the confines of the stasis chest. Its pre-set horologium had ticked off a hundred years. Its lid had risen. He was restored to the ache of life, to awareness.

Or rather: to ongoing awareness. For within that food chest, which would ordinarily have preserved unchangingly succulent steaks of groxen or a consignment of Spican truffles, Jaq had experienced one ultimate instant perpetuated eternally.

An instant of purity, of devotion.

Devotion to the Emperor whose effigy adorned the bulkhead nearby.

Jaq's limbs weren't numb. Yet by comparison with the purity which supersaturated his awareness after so long spent in stasis – and after, really, no time at all: null time – his body seemed to be obscene bloated meat, a gross anchor weighing down his spirit.

Smoothing his black, ornamented, hooded habit around him, and shivering, he knelt before the bulkhead and prayed.

For what, though?

He was already as pure as water distilled a hundred times. He was brimful with excess of purity.

A hint of scepticism intruded. Surely this sense of purity was too extreme – extreme enough to be a fault, a seductive weakness, consequently a crime against duty and clarity.

'Help me,' he begged, 'Father of Humanity, to endure being alive. Help me to wallow in the flesh once again.'

No such option was available to the Emperor himself, that living corpse fastened in an eternal casing more terrible than any mundane stasis box. All the agony of the human species perpetually impinged upon Him whilst He in turn sustained that agony by steadfast will so that humanity should endure, inhumanly, against the horrors of Chaos.

'And guide me, my God-Emperor.'

Guide whither? Guide wherefore? The air was arctic, yet this was not the only reason why Jaq shivered.

A shining path of occult consciousness and twisted time had guided Jaq and his three companions into the presence of the Emperor... or so it had seemed. Had their intrusion been sanctioned by the undying ruler – or merely discerned by Him? During those awesome moments of communication in the throne room, after Jaq had been soul-stripped, then restored again, he believed that the Emperor had manifested a multi-mind at odds with its own self. The Emperor's exalted consciousness had seemed as capacious and as sundry as the galaxy itself where no truth was to be trusted.

Had part of the Emperor ordained the creation of the hydra creature which would mind-bind humanity, wheresoever it infected? Maybe so that it could replace Him in his tormented weariness! Or was the Emperor oblivious to the conspiracy to spread that entity wrought from the warp itself?

'Guide me,' whispered Jaq, adoring that bas-relief of black adamantium.

Guide whither? The shining path had vanished long since. It had endured long enough for Jaq and his companions to flee, flee far from central courts guarded by the Emperor's ruthlessly dedicated companions; to escape through the great thronged cities which were the sprawling, soaring chambers of the palace patrolled by Custodians and Arbites; to flee for week after week through ten thousand tenements and foetid cloacae and labyrinths and libraria and shrines and massive bureaux of the Administratum, ascending and descending through malls and cathedral-laboratories, stealing new clothes and identities, lying, masquerading, compelled to kill, yet always eerily guided by

Jaq's twitching Tarot card of himself as High Priest with the hammer, a card now reversed. At one point during a riot which was almost a minor war, Grimm the squat had become separated; and Grimm remained missing.

Eventually Jaq and his two remaining companions had reached a minor space port just as another riot was erupting – a food riot, seemingly. A festering boil of human discontent had burst, spraying out the hot pus of bedlam.

The shining path had urged them through the vicious tumult, and onto a small cargo ship. This freighter was loaded with a merchandise of gourmet edibles. Only two crew members were aboard, and both of these were dead – recently killed by shuriken pistols. The pistols were still clenched in their hands. The whirling razor-discs had sliced each man's face to bloody ribbons, carving through the nasal and lachrymal bones, making porridge of their brains.

Had the two crewmen quarrelled and fired those pistols at one another simultaneously? Their faces were unrecognizable.

Would such men ordinarily have been armed with shuriken pistols to protect them in portside bars and brothels during shore leave? The weapons seemed to be of Martian manufacture, a copy of alien eldar weaponry produced in one of the factory hives of the Adeptus Mechanicus…

Evidently the freighter was bound for Mars, its cargo consigned to the tech-priesthood of the Cult Mechanicus. However, that cargo was no produce of Terra – where the poisoned soil was crushed deep under vast edifices beneath polluted skies. To land such merchandise upon Earth for trans-shipment onward to the factory planet seemed devious. Perhaps some high-ranking artisan or engineer subordinate to the Fabricator General was a smuggler?

Jaq's escape route stank of manipulation – of surveillance of his shining path, and of his Tarot card.

The route reeked of overwatch. By some part of the schismed mind of Emperor? So he prayed.

Or of intervention by some other agency?

Yet this was an escape route.

Transmitting appropriate codes while the riot raged, Vitali Googol had taken the freighter up into space crowded with vessels and orbital fortresses. They had boosted for Mars. Then they had strayed from their course. And strayed again. Jaq answered voxed challenges with lies about engine trouble, about mechanical litanies failing to massage the spirits of the machinery. Almost, he began to believe his own lies. When is a lie more plausible than when the liar himself is convinced that his deceits are nothing but the truth?

The fact was that the engines were responding perfectly to the invocations which Jaq chanted over them, in the absence of Grimm. Jaq missed the bluff, plucky abhuman engineer. Admittedly, Grimm himself would not have prayed to these engines. The creature had preferred spanners and vernier gauges to runes and orisons. The freighter had passed through the inner challenge line, through the central challenge line, through the outer challenge line.

By then all sense of the shining path had long since vanished. Jaq was loath to handle that haunted Tarot card again, in case some different presence manifested itself.

Finally, space was empty of traffic other than the billionfold burble of radio messages hours and days out of date. And of course telepathic communications too. However, there was no astropath on board who could eavesdrop on these.

The freighter had passed beyond that zone on the fringe of the planetary system where interstellar vessels jumped into warp space. Sub-stellar ships rarely had reason to venture further outward into the ordinary emptiness.

Interminably later, the freighter reached the comet halo.

For a long while already, the sun had been merely another bright star to stern, a shining point. How insignificant Earth's parent star had become. The freighter was still so very much closer to Sol than to even the nearest neighbouring sun in this star-island of billions of suns scattered across immensity! Nevertheless, Terra's parent star was already as nothing – a mere grain of brilliant dust amid so many others.

Earth's true parent was that living corpse in the golden throne whose psychic beacon, the Astronomican, could pierce almost all the glittering darkness of the galaxy.

The comet halo seemed empty too. A million jagged mountains of ice or rock circled in the frigid void on their millennia-long orbits. Yet most were as far apart from each other as Terra was from Mars. Starlight illuminated these orphans very faintly. Only if one mountain wandered near another and was perturbed and headed inward towards the home planets, would it finally form a visible tail of volatilizing vapour streaming in the solar wind. Then and only then would it become a comet as such: a dragon-mountain with kinetic energy a thousand times greater than any barrage-bomb or thermonuke.

Ach, everything in the cosmos was endowed with the capacity to destroy. Even dead things were.

Until such a time, the widely scattered comet-cores in the halo were virtually invisible.

Eventually Vitali Googol had found that portion of dark emptiness which *Tormentum Malorum* had been programmed to reach, there to roost.

From the freighter they had transferred many laden food-caskets, and three empty ones in which they could lie curled in stasis.

During the long outward journey to this region of nowhere, in the privacy of his sleep-cell Jaq had voiced into a data-cube his report. Coded for the eyes of the Masters of the Ordo Malleus, this *Liber Secretorum* would be the tiny cargo in the abandoned freighter aimed sunward again like flotsam down into the gravity sink of the home system. Would that liber be retrieved and reach its destination? Would the tiny cube have the impact of a dragon-mountain? Or would the empty freighter be destroyed at the outermost challenge-line?

Once aboard *Tormentum Malorum*, Googol had at last been able to navigate the warp again. The starship had jumped and jumped. Then it had paused, to drift in the void, over two light-years from the nearest star. To drift swiftly, perhaps. Even swift drift through ordinary space would bring the vessel nowhere near anywhere at all within the next several thousand years. Even so, *Tormentum Malorum* was shielded by camouflage force-fields and hexes and by an aura of protection cast by Jaq.

The ship had been powered down, internally, to standby. Jaq and the Navigator and the assassin had cramped themselves into the three empty caskets, preset to reopen a century later, three carcasses of living meat.

A century later was *now*.

Time had lost all meaning.

A protracted instant of purity: a century of purity! Now came the hideous demands of awareness.

Jaq shivered anew. The ventilation system had been set to begin warming the air a whole week before the caskets opened. Plainly a week had been too little time for comfort. Yet it had been long enough so that Jaq did not freeze to death as soon as he emerged from stasis.

Jaq himself, alone.

Those two other caskets… Meh'lindi's… Googol's… *Had those failed?* Within those boxes was there only bone and mummified skin and dried sludge?

To be alone here without a Navigator would be terrible. Even with the Emperor's spirit to sustain him, a man would surely go insane, tormented by the impotent knowledge that here he would remain until he died. His confinement would be more solitary than even that of a heretic sealed alone for ever in an automated dungeon of the Inquisition, in a bubble within solid rock beneath kilometres of ice. At least such a man might hope for interrogation, even for torment. The prospect of eventual excruciation might even become the prisoner's perverse solace.

Without a Navigator who could see into the warp, Jaq's ship could never jump away from this nowhere.

'Father of All, sustain my Navigator and my assassin–'

Before Jaq could nerve himself to open Vitali Googol's casket – and confront... a grinning skull? – the lid of the other stasis-box clicked opened, raised by an exquisite deadly hand.

Meh'lindi!

Her cropped raven hair, the smooth ivory of her face, those golden eyes.

How lithely she arose and stepped from the box, in her cling-tight black tunic and scarlet assassin's sash!

Though Jaq was pervaded by purity, yet in this moment of Meh'lindi's resurrection he could not but imagine fleetingly her hidden family of black tattoos, each of which masked a scar. Those scarabs on her breasts. That huge spider which wrapped her midriff. So very many scars – and a terrible scar, the most hidden of all, in her soul...

'Jaq,' she said quietly. She stood poised there, a touch taller than himself, even though he himself was tall.

A touch? *Her touch was death, if she so chose.*

Once, in his sleep-cell, she had touched him otherwise...

'Purity,' he said to her by way of greeting. Then, with a brusqueness masking hesitancy: 'What did you think of, a minute ago, and a hundred years ago?'

She blinked, and answered: 'Of nothingness. Of oblivion.'

Yes, that *would* be her reply. It proved she was sane.

She cocked her head quizzically. 'I suppose Vitali will have thought about the void.'

'I suppose he will have...' If Vitali Googol was still alive!

And if he were dead, to be alone here for ever more with this assassin and mimic courtesan! Alone for the rest of their lives...

What folly! They would only live until all the food taken from that freighter was consumed. A matter of a year, perhaps, until they starved.

Be of clear mind!

If Vitali was dead, then he and Meh'lindi must place themselves in stasis once again. Permanent stasis – until someone happened to find

Tormentum Malorum adrift. In another thousand years, or ten thousand tears. Or until the galaxy ended in raging chaos. Or until the triumph of light, which he could scarcely imagine.

Jaq was prevaricating. He didn't want to examine Googol's casket. Both Meh'lindi and Jaq hurried to that casket in the same moment. She reached it sooner. Such swiftness after a century of nothingness! Their hands brushed fleetingly as both seized the lid.

Vitali Googol lay foetally, drooling.

He drooled blood.

Blood ran down his chin.

Fresh blood.

Stasis had ended for Vitali while Jaq was praying, or even while he was staring at Meh'lindi. The Navigator hadn't pushed up the lid. Instead, he had bitten into his lower lip. His teeth still tortured the flesh.

'Vitali!'

Meh'lindi hauled the Navigator upright. Her fingers calmed his jaw. Blood stained her nails. She wiped him with a gathering of the fluted black silk which was Googol's favoured garb. She stroked the wrinkles of his face, so prematurely wizened by years of warp-watching. She checked that the black bandanna around his brow was firmly in place beneath his bald cranium. Let not his warp-eye be glimpsed for an instant!

Vitali gurgled.

'I–' he said.

Even this one word, of self-assertion, was such a balm.

Googol's teeth sought his lip again and he frowned, he flinched.

'The pain's so sweet,' he mumbled. 'The flesh, so sweet. I bit... to hurt myself. So sweet, and yet it's pain as well.'

'What did you think of in stasis?' demanded Meh'lindi.

'Father of All, strengthen this man,' implored Jaq.

'*What was in your mind, Vitali?*'

The Navigator's lips parted in a crazy grin, and blood flowed. 'I... made a little mistake,' he said. 'In a final moment of dread I thought about – I thought about what I would least wish to think about perpetually! For a moment I thought about Queem Malagnia–'

That Chaos-bloated monstrosity of sick sensuality! She with all the tattooed oily breasts, each with a brass ring through its teat, on the Chaos planet where the hydra may or may not have been devised...

'I thought of Queem Malagnia... giving birth... to Slishy!' To that hideous lovely mutant woman, her body so white and petite in its leotard of chainmail adorned with puffs of gauze and rosettes, her hair so blonde and bountiful, her face so sensuous. A veritable daemonette of Slaanesh, Chaos god of pleasure, Chaos god of torment. Slishy, with pincers of chitin for hands, with ostrich claws for feet, and a razor-edge tail sprouting from her voluptuous rump. Slishy, whom Meh'lindi had killed, and who died warbling delightedly.

Meh'lindi's breath hissed from her.

'Out of Queem,' mumbled Vitali, 'cometh Slishy, snipping her way with a claw…'

'Be quiet!' snarled Jaq. All sense of purity was sullied by the evocation of this vile parody. *'Esto tacitus!'* he added in the hieratic tongue. *'Silenda est!'*

Rime from their mingled breath was now settling on the obsidian of the walls.

'It's cold,' remarked Meh'lindi. Neither freeze nor bake ought to trouble her after the ordeals of her training. This was not the reason for her remark. 'I shall exercise,' she announced.

Oh yes indeed – so that Vitali might be distracted by her isometric grace, her acrobatic elegance…

Distract the Navigator's mind by a rival spectacle, sensuous and deadly as Slishy had been? Jaq nodded equivocal approval. In his ice-blue eyes was sceptical vigilance.

Meh'lindi commenced her exercises.

SOME WHILE LATER, spindly Googol lolled in his ornate Navigator's chair contemplating the warpscreen which was, as yet, inert. He was hung with amulets and icons. The air in the obsidian control room was still chilly. Smoke lazed from the incense sticks which Jaq had lit. The air reeked of Vegan virtueherb, for piety. Also of musty myrrh, the exudate of wounded desert bushes. Myrrh, to preserve and strengthen.

Aye, to preserve Vitali Googol's mind long enough for him to see his way through the warp to a sun and its worlds.

Quietly the Navigator recited to himself:

'Click of claws upon the hull,

'Sweet tendrils crawling in my skull–'

Googol shook his bald head in rejection of these images. His teeth sought his injured lip, but he refrained. He eased his bandanna up by a millimetre or so. He was sweating feverishly.

Vitali was trying his best to master himself.

Was his best sufficient?

Meh'lindi watched him carefully, ready to kill him instantly with a nerve-blocking fingertip, if she must. *Tormentum Malorum* was shielded against the intrusion of daemons from the warp. But what if the Navigator, whose mind reached out into the warp, were to invite a daemon? Or daemonettes!

Better to kill Googol and wallow here in the empty void. And if *Tormentum Malorum* had already entered the warp... kill Googol even faster, praying that daemonic forces would lose their focus.

Be adrift in the warp, hoping never to converge upon any derelict hulk, to become part of it...

Did Vitali understand that Meh'lindi might be obliged to kill him?

SHE WHISPERED IN mumblespeech, 'Inquisitor, our Navigator is half-way insane.' Hers not to question, nor to object. Yet she made this observation.

'Our hopes must ride on the other half of him,' Jaq replied; and she nodded. If another day passed, Googol might be two-thirds demented, not merely half-way mad.

They must reach a world. They must find an astropath. An astropath would eavesdrop for them on the torrent of psychic communications emanating from Terra in their direction and onward. Military transmissions, commercial ones, theological ones. From this thin segment of psychic sendings – yes, thin, yet a flood nonetheless! – the astropath would try to winnow what was happening a century downstream from Jaq's flight from Earth. A hundred years after his discovery of the hydra conspiracy, let there be some clue by now! Let his *Liber Secretorum* have reached the Masters of the Malleus. Let the ordo have acted in some way which Jaq might understand – even though none but a secret inquisitor might identify the signs.

Which world should they aim to reach?

While Meh'lindi kept much of her attention intently upon Googol, Jaq had taken his Tarot pack from its wrapping of flayed mutant skin. He prayed aloud that the Emperor's spirit should guide the divination.

Then he fanned the seventy-eight wafers of liquid crystal, with their fluid interactive designs.

Four suits: Discordia, Adeptio, Creatio and Mandatio. And the major arcana trumps.

Discordia was the suit of strife, though it could also signify authority. Discordia cards comprised enemies of the Imperium, aliens whether hostile or nominally friendly, and warp entities. Here was the terrible figure of a Chaos renegade from the Eye of Terror. Here was an eerily beautiful eldar, an aspect warrior.

Adeptio was the suit of vigorous work. Here was a Space Marine. Here was an assassin – and Jaq noticed that this card by now depicted a figure very like Meh'lindi.

Creatio, suit of fertility, embraced such persons as Navigators and astropaths. Here was an engineer, a squat with bushy red beard and forage cap and quilted flak jacket – so very like Grimm whom they had lost.

Mandatio, suit of stability, included the Inquisition, though Jaq's own significator card was the trump of the High Priest, enthroned, hammer in hand. That figure wore Jaq's face: rutted and scarred. Slim grizzled moustaches. A circuit of beard cupping the base of his chin. A single thin line of beard ascending to his lower lip. On his right cheek – in the card – glowed the electro-tattoo of an octopus clinging around a human skull, emblem of the hydra. Its spores would invade human minds. On some distant day, in some distant year, the conspiracy would knit all the minds of ensnared humankind into a terrible involuntary instrument of destruction, scouring away corrupted souls and aliens throughout the galaxy and even ravaging Chaos itself, harrowing the hell where daemons dwelled.

Supposedly purifying the cosmos.

Or else bringing about its devastation and the final doom of enslaved humanity.

The hydra tattoo on Jaq's own rutted cheek was invisible. He certainly wasn't willing it to show. As for all his other tattoos, of lurid daemons he had overcome, why, those were all hidden by his black garb.

Around the High Priest who was himself, he began to deal a star of cards.

And he shuddered.

For one was the Star trump indeed, with a pattern of stars around one star which was more prominent. Yet alongside it was the trump of Slaanesh – *in the form of a daemonette*! Something very like Slishy simpered and leered from the card. Next, was the Navigator card. It was reversed in a fashion which Jaq had never seen before. The Navigator hung upside-down by one foot from a scaffold. The solid black warp-eye in his brow, the eye which could kill, was exposed.

Jaq turned those two cards face-down swiftly.

'Protect us,' he prayed.

Finally he picked up the Star trump and thrust it toward the mumbling Navigator.

'Use *this* to seek our destination.'

THEIR VOYAGE HAD begun. *Tormentum Malorum* was in the sea of lost souls, racing through warp space. Eerie patterns swirled in the warp-scope, as of entities attempting to form and breaking apart.

Googol had chosen to wear jewelled gloves to manipulate the controls. The engines, which Grimm had tuned a century ago, wailed and throbbed just as excellent consecrated engines should.

'The Astronomican's so bright, so clear,' chanted Googol, an anguished rhapsody in his tone. 'So clear, so bright...'

Oh, clear enough to him who could behold the Emperor's beacon with his warp-eye. Not clear at all to Jaq. Nor to Meh'lindi who was poised to kill, at a word from Jaq. They only saw the swirling frogspawn of the warp.

And they heard a clicking on the hull...

A clicking of claws, a caressing scrape...

'Wait,' Jaq whispered to Meh'lindi. 'Wait.'

Sweat slicked Googol's face. Were it not for the gloves, his hands might have lost their clutch on the baroque rune-infested wheel and damascened levers and tumorous knobs.

Blessedly the scratch of Chaos against the hull-screens and protective hexes grew no louder.

STARS IN TRUE space on a screen! Vitali Googol had fainted.

Had his heart failed? No...

Jaq undogged one of the daemon-shields from a porthole.

Stars! Stars of varied hues! The yellow of pus and of jaundice; the angry red of blood; the cyanotic blue of suffocation.

'Kill him now?' enquired Meh'lindi. 'It might be a mercy.'

Jaq's voice was harsh. 'Does my assassin mention mercy?'

'I'm sorry, it was a figure of speech. I apologize.'

'All of one's words should constantly be scrutinized for heresy. Language is a tissue of lies. Metaphors, rhetoric... Pah! We might still need Vitali till we can find ourselves a reliable new Navigator.'

'Of course, of course. We are all only instruments.'

THE SUN THEY were heading towards was known as Luxus, and its habitable world was Luxus Prime. This, they presently determined from radio traffic while they were still several days away from the planet itself.

It also became evident that a war was raging on Luxus Prime. But war was perennial. War was a deadly bloom which flourished from one year to the next under another ten thousand suns.

For renegades such as themselves, war meant commotion and opportunities.

THREE
REBELLION

JAQ RAN ALONG the so-called Lane of Loveliness of Caput City, boltgun in one hand and force rod in the other.

This particular boltgun was plated with iridescent blue titanium inlaid with silver runes. The force rod was virtually unadorned, a solid black flute embedded with a few enigmatic circuits. The force rod was for use against whatever spawn of Chaos he encountered, to augment his psychic attack. The rowdy boltgun was for use right now – against a trio of cultists who darted from cover amongst giant broken potsherds which were the remains of one of the glazed ceramic buildings.

The cultists' eyes were glazed with frenzy. One fired a stub gun inaccurately. Bullets from the slugger pinged off a nearby wall of glazed terracotta. The second cultist was swinging a chainsword two-handed. Obviously he was unfamiliar with the weapon. The sword buzzed furiously as its razor-edged teeth spun round, cutting empty air. The third of the cultists was a burly muscular brute. From a hand flamer gushed a narrow cone of burning fuel. Heat scorched Jaq's face, but none of the fiery droplets had touched him.

Such a flamer was too compact a weapon to be worth firing from a distance, nor could its reservoir hold much pressurized fuel. Each blazing aerosol jet was spectacular but it extinguished quickly. You had to be close to your target.

Jaq's bolter yakkered. Several bolts erupted in the body of the flamer wielder. It was as though the man had been booby-trapped internally with packets of explosive. These now detonated. For a moment the cultist quivered like jelly. The muscle-bound envelope of his body actually seemed to contain the shock waves. Abruptly he burst apart, gutted thoroughly and bloodily.

A bolt from Jaq's gun caroomed off a great glazed potsherd, winging skyward into the haze of smoke which drifted across the city front fires. Subsequent bolts tore the gunman apart, then the swordsman too.

Jaq sniffed the sharp nitric aftermath of propellant which had ignited after each bolt flew from the muzzle.

'Noisy,' said Meh'lindi.

Yes, noisy. Yet with hardly any recoil. *RAAARK*, the gun would utter with each squeeze of the trigger. It hardly bucked at all in one's hand. With a plosive pop it would ejaculate a bolt. With a flaring swish, that bolt would ignite and accelerate away. Then there would come the thud of impact, followed by the blast of detonation.

RAARK-pop-SWOOSH-thud-CRUMP: this was the lingo of a boltgun. When it uttered several such statements, what a cacophony! The name of this particular boltgun, inscribed on the trigger guard, was *Emperor's Mercy*.

Meh'lindi held a laspistol in one hand and a toxic needle pistol in the other. Both weapons were delicately damascened. She had sprayed herself with black synthetic skin and wore her red assassin's sash twisted around her loins, various secrets concealed therein. The sash and her golden eyes were the only colours visible. Otherwise, she was a deadly black effigy of herself – supple and lithe. Even her eyelids were black as night. She had eschewed the digital weaponry which sometimes adorned her fingers like baroque thimbles.

Jaq wore lightweight mesh armour under his black habit, but Meh'lindi needed none. Her syn-skin would resist flame and flash and poison gas as well as honing her vitality. She breathed and spoke through a throat plug. She heard – acutely – through ear plugs.

She favoured the needle pistol. The bursts of energy from the laspistol tended to disperse over distance, especially if the air was hazy, as now. It appealed to her assassin's instincts to speed tiny toxic dartlets by laser pulse into some distant target.

Abruptly Meh'lindi pivoted. Without seeming to take aim she fired at a rooftop, twice. Two cultists convulsed as neurotoxins ravaged their nervous systems.

For Jaq, with his psychic sense, a vast shape seemed to brood in the smoke over the city. The shadow-figure wore a carnivorous, bullish head. How balefully its eyes gloated at all the killing which was in progress. Two mighty arms ended in serrated crab claws. A single female breast bulged obscenely. The presence came and went, a phenomenon of the smoke.

Could many other people than Jaq perceive that manifestation? 'Do you see it, Meh'lindi?' Jaq demanded, gesturing. 'It's up there again!'

She shook her head. Yet she believed him. She hissed assassin's curses – as if those curses might injure an aerial apparition which gallingly did not even register upon her senses.

Somewhere in the city a corrupted Cult Magus must be invoking and conjuring and sacrificing victims while praying to the cards of a Chaos Tarot.

Jaq pointed his force rod at the sky.

'Don't listen to me,' he ordered Meh'lindi. Yet how should an assassin fail to register every diagnostic sound in her vicinity? 'At least try not to understand me. Try to hear just noise.'

She began to chant some primitive outlandish barbarisms from her erstwhile jungle-world home which she would never see again, nor wished to.

'Avaunt, daemon,' yelled Jaq. *'Apage, O'tlahsi'isso'akshami! Begone, Slave of Lust! In nomine Imperatoris ego te exorcizo!'*

He discharged his weapon, and his psychic rebuttal, skyward. A pastel-orange glow ballooned. The phantom was gone. For the moment.

This was not the first occasion on this violent day that Jaq had used his force rod. Earlier, though through no fault of his own, he had used it too late. And Vitali had died in the embrace of a dancing daemonette.

A daemonette present in Chaos-flesh – and in Chaos-chitin!

Plainly this world needed Jaq for its salvation. Yet he must only linger long enough to find a new Navigator and to abduct a first-class astropath.

A higher purpose claimed him. Or was his quest an obsessed and futile one?

Vitali had died in that sweet and lethal embrace… How much better if Meh'lindi had killed the Navigator immediately after they landed at the besieged space port.

THE LANE OF Loveliness was a broad boulevard rather than a lane. It was far from lovely now. Its glazed ceramic buildings were cracked or wrecked. Debris and corpses littered the cratered tessellated paving.

A kilometre ahead, weaponry chattered and raved. A robed Judge was leading a team of dark-clad, visored Arbites against a barricade of burned-out vehicles. Upon the barricade was mounted a lascannon. Formidable! However, a lascannon was a poor anti-personnel weapon.

It took too long to recharge. It couldn't fan around. The Judge and his zealous warriors would soon seize that particular barricade.

The balance of loyal and rebel forces teetered to and fro, but the rebels appeared to be winning. The governor's Planetary Defence Force had been taken aback by the sheer number of cultists who were rebelling. Some of the governor's troops were insufficiently ruthless. Others mutinied. The forces of the courthouse, while fervently brave, weren't too numerous.

The recently arrived Pontifex Mundi of the Ecclesiarchy should have waited for reinforcement by Imperial Guardsmen before declaring that heresy polluted the planet, and trying to root it out. Yet an evangelical confessor had egged the pontifex on. This confessor had detected signs of Slaaneshi cultism amongst the population. Under the pretence of a so-called 'Goodlife Movement' people were addicted to the Chaos god of pleasure-pain.

Signs of laxity were everywhere: in the continuing beautification of the cities with mosaics and fountains, in charity towards beggars, in the peace and prosperity of the planet, in regulations for the benevolent conduct of brothels, in the ever-rising standard of cuisine, in the abolition of laws allowing the torture of suspects, even in the pronunciation of the local dialect of Imperial Gothic.

The new pontifex wished to establish his authority firmly. That pontifex was dead now. So was the confessor.

Luxus WAS A yellow sun, almost saffron: a rich yolk. Its name signified light but also splendour, with a hint of debauchery, and even riot.

Bathed in the light of Luxus, Luxus Prime was primarily a granary-world. Its single huge continent yielded vast harvests, reaped by giant mechanised harvesters. On surrounding lush islands ranches raised fine beef and lamb – a wealth of realfood. Some of this yield was exported to the hot, airless mining world which orbited closer to the sun and to its factory moon which was as large as Earth's Luna. Some of the produce travelled as far as Terra itself.

In the interior of the fertile continent, a great ring of mountains encircled a region of different grains: endless grains of sand.

Rains from the ocean could never cross the mountain range. In the enclosed desert, where poisonous sand-grubs excreted gems, the glazed glittering ceramic cities of Luxus Prime clustered.

By the standards of the Imperium these cities were idyllic places, elegant and amenable.

To the newly arrived pontifex, Luxus Prime must have seemed almost effeminate and innocuous, ripe for pious chastening, unlikely to offer much resistance to the rod of religion.

The pontifex had misjudged the situation – as had the Imperial Judges in Caput City.

No sooner was pressure applied than poisonous pus burst forth – to the amazement even of the governor. Foppish Lord Lagnost, so it seemed, had maintained his family's rule by default rather than by domination. His Defence Force was equipped with too many stunguns and not enough lethal weapons.

Oh, there were armouries, in case of raids by marauding aliens. No such raid had occurred for a thousand years. The rebels seized two of the main armouries. How many of these rebels there were! If the Goodlife Movement – at least in its higher echelons – had been a mask for worship of Slaanesh, other Chaos cults evidently existed too. Evil joined forces with other breeds of evil in a treacherous alliance.

Oh, but an affronted fop could summon up some savagery. Pontifex and confessor died. Yet Lord Lagnost managed to resist, holding onto the space port and the sprawling purple and golden faience pleasure domes of his palace.

A SMALL SQUAD of the Defence Force hove into view. Four men. Their mustard-yellow tunics were torn and dusty. Under the film of grime each man's cheek was tattooed with a small purple carnivorous flower resembling a birthmark. This was an affectation typical of Luxus Prime. These defenders of the state were 'Lord Lagnost's Flowers'. Three were armed with combat shotguns and one with a bolt pistol, the junior relative of *Emperor's Mercy*. The Flowers gaped at the tall black golden-eyed figure of Meh'lindi in her synskin. They whistled lewdly.

'Tall pushy cat!'

'Black pershine pushy cat!'

'Purr for ush!'

'Shurrender! Pull in your clawsh, pushy cat and keeper!'

A cat? What was a cat?

Ah yes: Moma Parsheen, the astropath of Stalinvast, had owned one such creature as a pet. She had stroked and pampered it so as to experience the scratch of its claws. Such a sensuous selfish egotistic animal – as selfish as Moma Parsheen herself, who had transmitted Jaq's message ordering the *exterminatus* of her whole planet even after Jaq had countermanded the message.

'Pershine' must be some kind of cat-animal with particularly glowing fur…

'Pushy cat, pushy cat!'

This aspiration of words was typical of Luxus Prime. People would say 'shunshine' for sunshine. This *aitching* of the ess sound seemed somehow connected with the aspirations – in the ambitious sense – of the Goodlife Movement. The mannerism was soporific, tranquillizing. It served a calming and hushing purpose, reassuring everyone that nothing harmful was happening.

Wasn't it sinister that people should refer to 'shunshine', as if light was to be shunned? As if illumination must not be cast too brightly upon the festering pus beneath the surface, underneath the lovely skin? Upon the filth which nourished the roots of the flower!

'In Lord Lagnosht's name shurrender, pushy cat and her keeper!'

Meh'lindi must seem like some daemon to them, and Jaq in his hooded habit like a magus.

'Assist us in the Emperor's name!' shouted Jaq. 'Assist us in His Name!'

Even as he called out, suspicion stung him.

Why should these men suppose that Meh'lindi was a daemon or that he was a magus? Even the bulk of cultists might be oblivious to the existence of daemons and unacquainted with magi.

Maybe the men had recently seen something as terrible as the daemonette which it had been Jaq's ghastly privilege to encounter.

If so, wasn't their attitude flippant?

Meh'lindi hissed…

…as two of Lord Lagnost's Flowers trotted forward, smiling and nodding. Without the least betraying signal the soldiers fired their shotguns at Jaq.

Two massive blows impacted in his chest, hurling him backward…

DURING THE INITIAL assault on the environs of the space port, cultists had rampaged through the Navigators' quarter, butchering any they could find – as Jaq had learned soon after a dangerous landing.

None of the extensive Navigator families maintained a formal chapterhouse on Luxus Prime. Yet numbers of inns catered to interstellar Navigators, as well as to ordinary in-system pilots. The armed mobs had trashed these inns. Reportedly some Navigators had fought back by tearing off their bandannas to expose the warp-eye in their brows, and darting the *killing gaze* at their attackers. Their assailants were too numerous. Very few Navigators had escaped, fleeing into hiding.

In the Mercantile district adjacent to that ransacked quarter, the mobs had lynched blind astropaths who sent commercial messages for the large food cartels. The cultists had assaulted the temple of the Imperial Ecclesiarchy and killed the astropath of the Adeptus Ministorum. That was when the pontifex and the confessor had also died.

Obviously the aim was to isolate the solar system of Luxus from the Imperium.

Embattled Lord Lagnost had warmly welcomed the arrival of an Imperial inquisitor at his palace, when Jaq displayed his electronic tattoo of the outer Inquisition.

Outer Inquisition, ha! In Lord Lagnost's view of the universe there was only one, almost legendary Inquisition. A planetary governor such as he – and many roving inquisitors themselves – knew nothing whatever regarding an inner Inquisition, the daemon-hunting elite of the Ordo Malleus who scrutinized the scrutinizers.

Ordinarily the Inquisition was much to be feared. Who in the whole cosmos did not have some cause to fear vigilant scrutiny? The attentions of the Inquisition were a cause for qualms. In the present extremity those attentions were very welcome.

If only Sir Draco had arrived accompanied by several shiploads of Imperial Guardsmen, or even (whisper it) *Space Marines!* Naturally Sir Draco was welcome to commandeer a unit of the Defence Force in defence of Lord Lagnost's devout and loyal dynasty...

THE OBESE WHEEZING Lagnost had worn robes sequined with the iridescent wingcases of beetles, by turns azure and violet and sapphire. On his head was perched a gem-crusted velvet hat in the shape of a half-size peacock with tail fanned erect. Breathing tubes, studded with jewels, arched from a collar of golden flexi-metal. Like tusks sprouting from his neck, these curved up around his jowls, and plugged his nostrils. His breath whistled in and out through grilles like gills inset into those tusks, assisted by miniature pumps. Below his tusks hung numerous amulets.

His palace was ornate with arabesque tile-work and tessellations. Its thick soft carpets were woven in silk mixed with wool of all the hues of green, as if intricate pathways of grasses and mosses covered all the floors. The ever-shifting sheen seemed constantly to reveal new routes.

Silk-clad boys and girls, young catamites and junior concubines, cowered from the crackle and thump of battle; but Lagnost had been wheezing perceptive orders to officers whenever one hurried into his presence to report.

Jaq had demanded to know the whereabouts of the governor's astropath.

Why, Fennix was calling astrally for military assistance from a safe deep location. So would be his counterpart deep beneath the fortified courthouse.

Assistance from an Arbites ship, if any was in the vicinity of Luxus. Assistance from a ship of the Imperial Guard – or even from a vessel manned by Space Marines.

Could one dream of assistance from Space Marines? Could any of those legendary warriors, bastions against so much more terrible foes, be spared to help restore order, even if any were within a hundred light-years?

Vast was the galaxy. Myriad the worlds. In any volume of space few were the forces of order. A star system could fall out of touch for decades – even centuries – before any heed was paid. Decades – or centuries – more might elapse before anything was done.

The governor's personal astropath was staying under seal. What help could be called upon, beyond what was already being attempted? What help but Sir Draco's own expertise? And that of his lithe, exotic woman companion!

Hardly the help of his Navigator. Googol had not been able to stop eyeing the governor's terrified junior harem. He recited dismayed verses to himself. He muttered copulatory couplets. His ravaged lower lip sported a grotesque displaced moustache of caked blood. Saliva moistened it.

JAQ CRASHED BACK upon a ruptured mosaic. Immediately he was hit, his mesh armour had stiffened. The web of woven thermoplas had become rigid to spread the double impact. Those shotguns had fired solid shells, not scattershot. Two sledgehammer blows at close quarters had knocked him off his feet. He must lie momentarily until the armour relaxed. But his forearm remained unimpeded. Already he was pointing *Emperor's Mercy* at his assailants, even as they swung their weapons to address the matter of Meh'lindi.

They assumed that the robed person on the ground must be dead. His black habit was torn open just where his lungs would be.

Should they pump shells into the tall black 'pushy cat' with the golden gaze? Or simply disarm her? Perhaps literally so! With shotgun and bolt pistol apiece, two Flowers were aiming at Meh'lindi's hands. Lacking hands, she would be much more amenable. They believed her to be more decorative than deadly.

Little did they know that even deprived of hands she could kill with her feet or with almost any other part of her anatomy. She could spit poison from a crushed tooth. Even crippled, she could kill, overriding any agony she felt. Small chance would they have even to discover their error in this regard.

Already neurotoxic darts from her needle pistol were causing two of them to convulse. Their muscles tugged every which way. Their internal organs waged war on their own liquefying tissue. Their brains were a-crackle with short circuits.

Already bursts of laser energy from her other pistol had melted the leering eyes and features of the other two Flowers–

–even as *Emperor's Mercy* began to utter its lethal opinion:

RAARKpopSWOOSHthudCRUMP
RAARKpopSWOOSHthudCRUMP
RAARKpopSWOOSHthudCRUMP
RAARKpopSWOOSHthudCRUMP...

Its opinion was hardly necessary. Two of its targets were already dead on their feet. The other two might still have some residual life in their scorch-blasted skulls.

Nevertheless, *Emperor's Mercy* blew three of the renegade Defence Force men apart. The stink of blood and guts, toasted flesh and excrement mingled with the nitric tang of burned propellant.

Jaq's armour had relaxed across his chest. He scrambled erect to examine the rips in his black habit. The thermoplas web showed through, as if his skin was scaly as some reptile's.

This ancient bodyglove of mesh armour had once been worn by an eldar. It had become a souvenir of the Inquisition, memento of that enigmatic species, one of whose females Meh'lindi had once impersonated.

She could never again hope to impersonate an eldar by injecting polymorphine to reshape her body. Not since her terrible experimental surgery at the hands of the Callidus shrine of assassins. Now she could only alter into that abomination, a genestealer hybrid. Compressed implants were within her. If her flesh became pliable the polymorphine drug would expand those implants tyrannically. Her own willpower would have no say in the matter.

A bodyglove of eldar armour – forged by that secretive species, some of whose most exotic members were known as Harlequins...

Wandering warriors and performers...

The *Harlequin Man*, who aped their ways, had led Jaq such a dance on Stalinvast. That crazy cunning human clown had subjected Meh'lindi to his will. He had lured Jaq to become involved in the hydra conspiracy. Zephro Carnelian had worn the garb of those fabled eldar Harlequins, doing his best to mimic the notorious quicksilver speed of an eldar. (He had almost equalled an eldar in his capers!) What statement had Carnelian been making? That he was fundamentally alien at heart? Alien to the human species? That the human species only deserved to be plied like puppets? Or that he was alien to those conspirators with whom he consorted?

Jaq's head ached with enigma and dismay. His chest was bruised too beneath the mesh armour.

He and Meh'lindi must find one of the surviving Navigators, wherever in this war-torn city one was hiding for his life.

He blew upon the muzzle of the boltgun, adding his spirit to its own, and hummed a quick canticle.

'Hesitation is always fatal,' he told Meh'lindi, reproving himself as much as her. Hesitation had been fatal for the four renegades. Hesitation had also been fatal in the case of Vitali.

'And yet,' he continued, 'rashness can be worse.'

Would they find a skulking Navigator by rampaging? She eyed *Emperor's Mercy*.

'Noisy,' she repeated tersely. In this city which had become a jungle she seemed to have reverted to feral tribeswoman in her jargon.

Needn't be quite so noisy, a boltgun. Bolts ignited after being ejected from the muzzle. Arguably the gun could simply say *pop-SWOOSH-thud-CRUMP*. And not roar *RAARK* as well. Noise was part of its impact, part of its message of shock and death.

Jaq had wished to be noisy – ostentatious and flamboyant, like an inquisitor of the stripe of Harq Obispal. Thus he would impress Lord Lagnost. Thus he would cloak his own secret agenda. Maybe he should have armed himself with a fiercely buzzing chainsword which would scream whenever its teeth bit into its objective. There had been neither chainsword nor power sword in the weapons lockers of *Tormentum Malorum*.

Meh'lindi was implying that the clatter of the boltgun must necessarily attract hostile attention. No sooner would one set of opponents be killed than others would hurry to confront the source of the cacophony.

These flowers who now lay converted to cooked manure hadn't been frenzied. They had been sly...

More spontaneity in killing Googol might at least have saved the man's soul!

* * *

AFTER HURRYING FROM the governor's palace with two squads of loyalists, Jaq had indeed rampaged along the fringe of the smoldering Navigators' quarter with Meh'lindi, Googol stumbling in tow.

Why would a Navigator flee, to hide himself? With that black betraying bandanna round his brow. Or with brow exposed, betraying the deadly third eye!

Jaq and Meh'lindi killed. Interrogated.

Why were they searching for a Navigator? This was the question which the officer attached to those squads finally nerved himself to ask. Jaq already had a Navigator. Evidently of dubious calibre and mental imbalance! Was Jaq truly here to bring salvation?

'Don't you understand?' Jaq had shouted at the officer. 'Naturally we must rescue any Navigators. Otherwise this world will be isolated from the Imperium!'

Were they searching for a particular relative of Jaq's own Navigator? For some member of Googol's own vast family?

'*Nefanda curiositas*!' Jaq had snarled at the officer. The man must obey an inquisitor without thought – even when their route was taking them away from the strife-torn vicinity of the palace and space port.

Then a sniper had shot the officer with a laser-guided toxic dart. Maybe it was as well that the officer was shot and could never report any of his impious misgivings to Lord Lagnost.

'Here dies a heretic!' Jaq had bellowed at the dead officer's men. 'Whoever doubts, dies. *Qui dubitat, morit.*'

How he loathed to use sacred words to reinforce a lie. Yet was not the deeper truth that this staunch officer was indeed a heretic in the vaster perspective? To dispute with any inquisitor was a blasphemy. How much more so when Jaq's vital need impinged upon the very future of the human species. It would be anathema to explain this. And impossible. And incredible.

Then Vitali had begun to spook the soldiers.

That spindly bald figure capered upon the glossy smashed tiles fallen from roofs. He swirled his fluted silks around himself. He sang out:

'*Heart-throb, heart-throb,*
'*Here am I, here am I!*
'*Oh I wink with my killing eye.*
'*What a day to die!*'

He tore off his bandanna.

Jaq had instantly averted his gaze; and Meh'lindi – she was writhing about on the ground. Was she a casualty?

Googol's warp-gaze ranged over the soldiers. One man's scream strangled as his throat constricted, suffocating him. Another man collapsed as if a hand had squeezed his heart. A third vomited blood. The eyes of a fourth man popped out because of the pressure in his skull.

Meh'lindi was scrabbling about for a piece of glazed tile suitable to use as a mirror – a mirror to mute the terrible reflection of Googol's eye.

That was really the moment when she should have launched herself towards Googol with her eyes closed tight, relying upon her assassin's instinct for location. She should have nerve-blocked the Navigator, killing him. However, Jaq had not given any such order.

Such a presentiment of imminent abomination violated Jaq's psychic sense. He fought to repel immaterial fingers from congealing into existence.

'He's gone gone gone,' chanted Meh'lindi.

Silks flapping, Googol had taken off along a winding lane as if hounds were at his heels or razorwings at his neck. He passed out of sight around a corner. To their ears came a fading halloo of '*Slishy-slishy-slishy!*'

A spasming hand caught hold of Jaq's boot as he passed a victim. He wrenched free. He called out to survivors, 'Stay here and kill the injured mercifully!' With Meh'lindi he raced in pursuit of Googol, readying his force rod as he ran.

Too late.

Far too late.

In a court of lustrous pink tiles inset with golden mosaics of dancing girls, Vitali had encountered the terrible object of his tormented longing.

A daemonette had materialized.

One of Slaanesh's she-creatures had actually come into existence – a Chaos-creature of perverse seduction and lethal consequences.

Her single exposed breast was divine. So were her thighs and loins. Yet hers was a malign divinity. Her cascade of blonde hair almost hid green eyes which were unnaturally elongated. Her lips, so lush. She was embracing Vitali. She was cooing, rubbing against him. No endearments could hide the scaly claws of her feet or the pincers of her hands – yet what did Vitali care?

The Navigator's exposed warp-eye certainly hadn't devastated the daemonette. Why should it, when she was herself such a warped denizen of that other dimension, roost of the Gods of Chaos? Vitali's warp-eye had surely summoned her all the more vigorously into existence. How she writhed against him. How her razor-sharp pincers sliced his silks, denuding him. Exposed skin was being sliced softly and subtly, inscribing upon him a slim calligraphy of blood which might in some arcane script be that daemonette's secret name, signed upon him so as to possess his soul.

An eddy of harrowing lusts rocked Jaq. Such sickening images assaulted him – of Meh'lindi lying naked with him on that single occasion in his sleep-cell aboard *Tormentum Malorum*. In his temporary hallucination all the tattoos on Meh'lindi's body were alive and squirming. The snake which climbed her right leg bared its fangs to bite. The scarabs and other beetles which masked her many scars were much larger, and hungry. The hairy spider which engulfed her midriff waved its legs mesmerically, to trap Jaq and suck him dry.

Meh'lindi wasn't human at all. She was a huge spindly wasp infested with parasites. All of those virulent bites and the suction would enrapture him hideously – until he expired. The delusion sullied all that he had experienced with her, of solace and exorcism. How it blasphemed.

Was Meh'lindi likewise experiencing a monstrous distortion of what occurred between them, once and only once, a negation of any fleeting tenderness and compassion?

If so, let it be! Tenderness was treason to duty, and delusion. Had he not blasphemed by consoling himself? Contrariwise, what ecstasy might yet be his if Meh'lindi strangled him slowly or sliced his flesh a thousand times?

Even as Jaq levelled his force rod, the daemonette parted her legs. A barbed tail slid through the gap. The barb jerked upward impaling Googol. Vitali rose on tiptoes as the razor-thrust penetrated deep within his bowel. In a delirium of agony and rapture Vitali screamed, '*Slishy*!' as Jaq's force rod discharged.

Energies coruscated around the daemonette. Auroras outlined her as if to highlight that she belonged not in this tiled court but elsewhere entirely – right outside of the world, outside of the natural universe. She shrieked shrilly. Her soprano outcry might have been one of exultation and glee.

Then the energies imploded. And so did she. She became flat instead of solid. She became a single angular line which seemed to stretch far away, distorting geometry itself. Swiftly that line shrank to a nauseous bright point. The point left an aching after-image.

Vitali's ravished corpse sprawled. Torn silk adhered to him like long, thin black leaves.

He was dead. Utterly dead. And surely the daemonette had stolen his spirit away – to continue that vile tormenting tryst elsewhere in immaterial phantom form forever while his ghost-lips gibbered.

Jaq prayed devoutly at the head of the corpse. Meh'lindi stood over the feet, crouched and predatory, in case the Navigator might yet twitch back to life, possessed by some zombie parody of life, to be killed anew.

'Bitter regrets,' she murmured.

'On my part too,' said Jaq.

When they retraced their steps to where dead soldiers and the officer lay, the survivors had fled. One victim still moaned. Meh'lindi mercifully snapped his neck.

SMOKE HAD DESCENDED to veil the Lane of Loveliness. 'Noisy,' repeated Meh'lindi.

No longer was she alluding to the boltgun, but to a throb of engines which became growl and then a roar.

From out of the dirty haze a trio of power-trikes came bouncing over the debris. Twin autoguns were mounted on the front forks of the trikes.

FOUR
ABHUMANS

THE RIDERS OF the trikes were compact little abhumans. They sported bushy red beards and outlandish moustaches. Jammed backwards or sideways upon their heads were forage caps. They wore quilted red flak jackets, green coveralls and big stumpy boots. Around their waists were belts of pouches. Steering one-handed, all three were waving laspistols. Slung across their backs were hefty axes.

Jaq's soul lifted. For these were squats. Tough, gruff squats.

They were hardly the kind to be corrupted by perverted lusts or seduced into cults organized by corrupt sybarites. Not that the appetites of squats weren't heady – but more along the lines of gobbling a gourmet banquet and emptying a barrel of beer until they belched!

Not for them an evil mockery of sexuality. Oh, by their honoured ancestors, how could they dream of polluting themselves? These must be mining technicians who were in town on Luxus Prime to spend their cash and perhaps take their beloved power-trikes for a race out across the desert.

Unusually, no hair sprouted from under the leader's forage cap, though the other two squats sported knotted ponytails.

The trikes skidded to a halt. The autoguns pointed in the general direction of Jaq and his athletic ebon companion.

'Boss!' bawled the burly little fellow who was foremost. '*Jaq*! It's you!'

The squat hopped from the saddle.

'And Meh'lindi. Meh'lindi!'

Surely he couldn't be…?

All squats resembled one another quite closely – squats were faithful to their blood and gene-runes. But those particular ruddy cheeks, that particular bulbous nose, those bloodshot hazel eyes which seemed now to twinkle, now to glower, could surely only belong to...

The dismounted biker tore off his cap and wrung it in his sturdy calloused hands in an excess of emotion.

On a shaven scalp blushed a crimped scar as long as a finger and a thumb. Some axe must have tried to cleave that thick skull in recent years. A certain squat engineer had never had a bald pate... *a century ago.*

'Grimm!'

Jaq and Meh'lindi both uttered the abhuman's name at one and the same moment. Grimm dashed towards them, then halted.

'Huh,' he exclaimed. 'Well I never!' Twisting and twisting his forage cap.

On closer inspection Grimm's scalp wasn't entirely denuded, except along the channel of scar tissue. Some gingery fuzz was sprouting. Evidently he had just recently abandoned efforts with a razor. A few crusted nicks of brown blood bore witness to how recent 'recently' was. With Caput City in turmoil, doubtless Grimm had been too busy to shave his head during the past few days.

To hug him would be demeaning to a squat – and to Jaq, and to Meh'lindi. It would be absurd.

'Huh,' repeated the little man. Perhaps his own expletive best summed up their reunion.

How did Grimm come to be here out of all the places upon all the worlds? Had the Emperor's spirit guided him? Imbued with grace, had Grimm consulted a reader of the Tarot? Truly, the little man could never have succeeded in using the Imperial Tarot on his own – not when he wouldn't even pray to an engine.

It was but a few months, from Jaq's point of view, since he and Grimm had become separated. From Grimm's perspective many decades must have passed – depending on how many time-compressing interstellar journeys he might have undertaken. Squats could live for centuries; and previously Grimm had been no more than fifty years old. Apart from his bare cranium and the scar, he looked much the same. How much time had yawned for him?

'Why are you here?' demanded Jaq.

'Huh, there's gratitude!'

A rattle of gunfire and an explosion reminded Jaq that he could hardly pursue his enquiries here in the Lane of Loveliness.

A wrecked, scorched shrine to the Emperor beckoned pitifully. 'Over there!' urged Jaq.

That domed building, clad in lustrous purple tiles, had suffered a tiny iota of what the Emperor himself forever suffered. Holes had been blasted in the walls. The gilded door hung askew.

Jaq felt utter rage at the sacrilege inside. The mosaic of Him-on-Earth was spattered with excrement. Purity banners had been torn down. Sacred relics were scattered about. A robed preacher lay eviscerated. His guts unwound like a greasy snake across the tessellated floor.

Otherwise the shrine was deserted. Smoky sky showed through the dome, as if that vault were a skull which had been crudely trepanned so as to scoop out the brain within.

Grimm's fellow squats blocked the doorway with their trikes, auto-guns pointing outward.

'Huh, took me the best part of three years to stow away to Mars, it did. Always work for a good tech there, I heard! Slaved me guts out for your Adeptus Mechanicus. Fifteen years I lived in a scrofulous factory hive. At least it kept me fingers nimble, even if I had to warble litanies while I was labouring. I don't mean literally I slaved me guts out. If so, some tech-priest would have cyborged me. Me top half would be plonked in a cyber-pram. Oh, my sacred ancestors!'

Grimm's tale spilled out of him hectically.

'Then it was out to the stars along with a consignment of Titans. Me by way of being an advisory engineer. What you might call a guarantee for the goodness of the goods. Any breakdown in the first month of field-testing those gun-goliaths, and you burn the guarantee! Flame him!' Grimm chuckled. He cleared his throat, and spat on the floor.

'I'll thank you to remember this is still a shrine,' Jaq reproved him.

'Oh, I'm sorry. I rip myself.' Grimm stooped hastily and cleared the phlegm away with his cuff. 'Jaq, I declare there's still Martian dust in me lungs.'

'That was long ago, unless you've been in stasis.'

'Well, after the business of the Titans, it was here and there for me, you see. This star, that star. Year here, year there. Sometimes longer. Working me way, but mainly biding me time. You see, I guessed if you got away, Jaq, then you'd go into stasis in the old *Tormentum*. I wanted to be around when you showed your face again, and it would likely be some-where in this region, 'cos you'd want to know quickly what was going on about you-know-what. Once the flood of years had allowed a fair chance for something to get going! Nowt's very quick in this universe.

Death's often quick – but that's about it. Sometimes,' with a wry glance at the gutted cadaver on the floor, 'it ain't quick enough.'

Indeed, a flood of years carried the debris of events along. The hydra conspiracy was conceived in terms of generations and centuries. The Emperor's response, if any, and the reaction of Jaq's ordo need not be swift.

'I even got married for ten years to a lovely squat lady–'

Loveliness! What was loveliness?

Was it that lane outside this shrine? Was it this speciously prettified planet, now riven by a Chaos cult? Was it what Vitali had perceived in his dying moments? Was it a dumpy dwarfess whose hips undoubtedly resembled a donkey's saddle?

Grimm wiped a tear from his eye.

'–but Grizzy was killed in an earthquake. Half of a factory collapsed on her. I dug and I dug but… never mind about it! Life goes on. Death goes on. I knew you'd be turning up somewhere some day. You, and herself,' this with a rueful nod at Jaq's assassin in her syn-skin. 'It's not just our own mortality we confront, Jaq, it's also our essential loneliness. We were by way of being a bit of a family, of oddbods – weren't we just? – on our way through your Emperor's palace. Now–' and quickly he wiped another tear on his phlegm-stained cuff, '–the family's back together again. Huh! So where's Vitali? Is he on board *Tormentum*?'

Meh'lindi replied softly through her throat-plug: 'A harlot of Chaos possessed Vitali and killed him just a few hours ago. A Chaos creature, another Slishy. She took Vitali's soul.'

Even as Jaq made a forbidding gesture, lest Grimm's cousins should overhear forbidden knowledge, the abhuman was sitting down and shaking his head and groaning.

'Oh, my ancestors…'

Jaq shrugged. 'It happened. This is a different hour. A later hour. Time never turns back. What we failed to say remains unsaid. What we failed to do remains undone. Though there is always… *revenge*, in the Emperor's name.'

'I couldn't revenge myself much against an earthquake,' muttered Grimm. He got back to his feet. He balled his sturdy fists. 'This, I can revenge myself against!'

'Even so,' said Jaq bleakly, 'there are other priorities.'

To help cleanse this world of corruption couldn't possibly be the main priority.

'Huh, Googol!' said the little abhuman. 'Him and his daft poetical pretensions. So much for composing that sort of lush morbid verse. He

ought to have listened to me about the virtues of our squattish ballads.
Not that he would ever have mastered the mode. Still, our ballads have
backbone – backbone long enough to reach from here to orbit.'

'Apart from getting married,' asked Meh'lindi, 'what else have you
been doing?'

'Uh, well, in recent years I've been hanging around with a few inquisitors. Not that those gents necessarily knew I was hanging around with
them! But I've been in their vicinity. Part of the personnel, I was hoping
I might overhear some word about you, or you-know-what. Did you
ever meet an inquisitor called Torq Serpilian?' he asked Jaq.

'Not unless he has been rejuvenated!'

Grimm looked blank. 'I dunno about that.' Was Grimm being obtuse?

'Otherwise I could hardly have known him in the past – considering
that a century has gone by!'

'Damn it, I'm forgetting. Real humans don't usually last as long as
squats.' Was there a sneer in Grimm's voice? A chip on his quilted flak-
proof shoulder?

'What about this Serpilian? What did he know of me? Or of,' and Jaq
lowered his voice, 'the hydra cabal?'

Grimm was wide-eyed with a protest of innocence.

'Nothing that I know of! Honest. He was just the most recent inquisitor I hung around with.'

Jaq asked piercingly: 'Did he oblige you with a Tarot reading to steer
you here to Luxus?'

'Huh. I was going to get on to that, boss. Yeah, obviously I did need a
spot of Tarot guidance, from someone who could pray to a pack o'
cards. It wouldn't have been very bright of me to spill the beans to an
inquisitor.'

Was Grimm merely saying what he hoped would seem most plausible
to Jaq? How chivalrous of the little abhuman to have hung around and
then kept company with inquisitors in the hope of rejoining Jaq's
bizarre and scanty parody of a 'family'. Jaq as tormented paterfamilias.
Meh'lindi the feral lady, pregnant with an implanted monster. Vitali the
deviant junior brother – whose ghost was now being ravished agonizingly and exquisitely by a daemonette.

How endearing of Grimm.

Even if the inquisitors with whom Grimm had consorted had been
secret members of the inner order, privy to some information about Jaq,
a squat could hardly have hoped to learn any secrets from them. The
whole logic of secrecy as practiced by the Inquisition, even more so by
its inner order, was that sometimes some secrets were so awful that these

must almost remain secret even from oneself, bound under seals of heresy.

Such a sealed secret might well be the existence of a seeming renegade who had travelled to a Chaos world in the Eye of Terror, and then had apparently penetrated the Emperor's throne room.

Small chance of any gossip on that score from Serpilian, or whatever the man's name had been!

The archives of the Inquisition were vast beyond belief, yet there was an Inquisition saying: *One does not scribble upon adamantium.* The meaning of this was that when a sculptor did scribe an inscription upon that hardest of all substances he should be economical with his words. An inquisitor's heart, likewise, must be of marble or adamantium. He did not unburden himself verbosely. Babbling was for charismatic confessors of the Ecclesiarchy who could word-whip a crowd to deliver up any heretics from amongst themselves.

Jaq understood secrecy. He knew he had erred by letting Meh'lindi learn of Chaos – and Googol too, and Grimm. But if he hadn't confided in them, how could he have accomplished anything? Yet had he truly achieved anything at all?

What real hope did Jaq have that by scrying the psychic babble of the cosmos a kidnapped astropath might be able to eavesdrop on any relevant hints or evasive clues?

When hope is gone, then one strives more ferociously.

'Um,' said Grimm, 'you see, I like being around inquisitors. Got used to it, with you. There's action.'

Grimm's story didn't ring quite true. Though what was true in this cosmos of darkness and lies? Only the shining beacon of the Astronomican! That beacon conveyed no actual information other than the inspiring and vital truth: here is Earth, heart of the Imperium. Here is the Emperor, still watching over all – for as long as a dying god can endure.

'Um, it was a lady poet who read the cards for me. Name of Johanna Harzbelle. A niece of the governor of Valhall, where there was trouble.'

Oh yes, such trouble as would likely have destroyed all records and testimony.

'That's where I got me scar, on Valhall. Johanna was psychic but she'd escaped the Black Ship 'cos of her connections. She lived in an apartment shielded with psycurium, so that no daemons would notice her. I managed to wangle a job as her caretaker.'

'Were this person's poems famous?' asked Meh'lindi.

Poems might well be famous in the frogpond of one planet. They would be unknown anywhere else. Even the most famous poems would be no more than a grain of dust upon a speck of sand in a desert ten thousand miles across. If on each of only half a million worlds only ten poets of genius flourished each century then after merely a thousand years no less than fifty million bards would have perpetrated their masterpieces. After ten thousand years, five hundred million bards. Simply to name each bard of genius once, allowing only two seconds per name, would occupy a calculator almost thirty-two standard years non-stop. Futility was the final fate of all endeavour. And Valhall, wherever it was, had obviously been trashed by war. Grimm would be quite safe in claiming fame for this... Johanna Harzbelle, shielded by her precious psycurium.

However, Grimm shook his head. 'She wrote for herself, in a private language she'd devised.'

'So she was her only audience.'

'But the poems *sounded* so lovely.' The little man wrung his hands in apparent anguish. 'Johanna had a cat-animal, like Moma Parsheen had. She recited her poems to it, and because she was psychic it seemed to understand. The cat had golden eyes, like yours, Meh'lindi. I knew if Johanna read the cards for me I'd have to snuff her – for your security, Jaq. So I hesitated. But then her cat-animal died of a tumour in its throat. Johanna was devastated, and so lonely. She was so grief-stricken by that little furry death, in this universe of death! She only wished to die too. And a war was brewing. After she read the cards I strangled her as a favour. That was our bargain, boss.' What distress Grimm was exhibiting.

Could a person read cards in an apartment shielded by psycurium? Cut off from the psychic flux? Or at least protected from evil consequences! Jaq could read his own cards when aboard *Tormentum Malorum*, shielded from the daemons of the warp. Grimm had seen Jaq reading the cards in such circumstances.

Grimm could have noticed – through the magnifying lens of an oculus – that *Tormentum Malorum* had landed at the space port. He might well have recognized the unusually sleek outlines of *Tormentum*. In the present conditions of strife the abhumans would hardly have headed for the palace, Jaq's most likely first port of call. They would soon have set out to scour the city since Jaq must be looking for something here on Luxus Prime.

Plausible, plausible. The story was plausible.

On board *Tormentum Malorum* – on board the *Scourge of Evil* – was a certain drug named veritas which could force a person to tell the truth...

'Enough!' snapped Jaq. 'Enough about your Grizzle and your Johanna! We've lost our Navigator. Googol's dead, or at least his body is–'

'We need a new Navigator, boss.'

We need a new one. The three of us. Wasn't this mockery of a little family now reunited?

'I know where one's hiding. I'd have told you sooner – but the news about Vitali ripped me up inside…'

And besides, Grimm had had his alibi to recount. 'In fact me and my mates helped him hide. We gave him a trike-ride out of the teeth of a mob.'

Meh'lindi asked through her throat-plug: 'Wasn't his warp-eye exposed to protect him?'

'He's weird about his warp-eye, this one is.'

Weren't most Navigators weird in one way or another? To stare into the warp thrust weirdness upon them, and wrinkled their faces even while young.

From the wrecked doorway of the polluted shrine the autoguns of Grimm's cronies erupted. Caseless ceramic shot flew along the Lane of Loveliness at high velocity. From out of the veil of smoke a gang of cultists were rushing towards the shrine – scores of frenzied marauders. They were being egged on by a blonde woman who wore thigh-high boots and a scanty leotard of black rubber hung with obscene trophies. She was waving a laspistol. Her hands weren't claws, but her eyes, lavishly framed by mascara, looked so slanted and oval that surely they were a mark of daemonry beginning to manifest itself. How else could she have been attracted towards this already vandalized shrine unless something evil had sensed the presence here of a psyker who had already exorcized a daemonette and who had discharged his force rod at the spectre in the sky?

Several cultists fell, ripped by shot. The woman shrieked: 'Who killsh him, enjoysh me! Who enjoysh me, killsh!'

Jaq had dashed to the doorway by now, Grimm had scrambled back on to his trike alongside his kin. Grimm swung the handlebars to and fro as he opened fire from the forks. All three squats cut swaths through those crazed devotees of corruption. Trike-mounted autoguns weren't an accurate or subtle weapon. Would anyone wish to confront a rabid mob with precision sniper rifles? Numerous onrushers survived – almost as if they were protected by auras of invulnerability. Bullets and scattershot were twanging off the ceramic portal, impacting in the dangling door, winging through into the interior of the shrine.

A squat shrieked and clawed at shrapnel in his eye. A bullet took him in the throat. Blood burbled. Gagging, he slumped from his saddle.

Jaq was firing over Grimm's shoulder. *RAARK-pop-swoosh, RAARK-pop-swoosh.*

The blonde in the boots and rubber leotard was way behind her wild enthusiasts. She wasn't advancing but dancing from side to side. If anyone wore an aura of invulnerability, it was she. Over the crackle and crumple of fire, and the screaming and the bellowing, she could still be heard shrieking: 'Killsh, enjoysh!'

Deranged faces loomed closer. The attackers' guns were spitting. The other squat tumbled, his face a ruin. Several bullets smashed into Jaq, ripping his habit, stiffening his mesh armour. Grimm crouched lower as he fired. Flush with the tiled door-jamb, Meh'lindi took aim at the blonde again. Because of that woman's unpredictable jinks Meh'lindi had missed twice already. What could be more galling for an assassin than to miss her target? Meh'lindi began to squeeze the trigger. Then she closed her eyes. She was willing upon herself a calming condition of firing-in-the-dark. It was as if millennia of tradition gathered around her in that moment. Her hand twitched. Her finger tightened. The gun launched its toxic needles.

And the blonde danced. Now her dance was one of muscles puffing every which way, of a body vibrating with lethal contradictions. The blonde's eyes bulged. Her mouth frothed. She was quivering jelly, sustained for a moment more by her rubber corset and her boots. And then the bag of jelly, hung with its scrotal fetishes, slumped.

The onrush subsided. It was if puppet strings had snapped. Some attackers stumbled onward almost in slow motion. Grimm's autoguns yakkered. Meh'lindi squeezed laser pulses one by one. *RAAARK-pop-SWOOSH-thud-CRUMP*, spake Jaq's boltgun.

A few survivors were scuttling away. Otherwise: corpses. Some fallen bodies shuddered with fatal injury, moaning, whimpering. Meh'lindi stepped past the trikes and terminated the injured with stabs of her finger into the neck.

'Buggers are blocking our wheels,' grumbled Grimm.

Meh'lindi was already hauling bodies to right and left to clear a path. She seized collars or hair. She yanked. All the time, she glanced about her in case a threat remained.

Grimm knelt briefly by his fallen kin.

'Huh,' he addressed one, as if the puff of his breath was sacramental. 'Go with our ancestors, and goodbye.' He didn't bother to close the squat's remaining, gaping, bloodshot eye.

'Huh,' he said to the other. Then he turned to Jaq. 'I guess this solves the question of transport to find your Navigator. Always supposing that you and herself can cramp your long legs up sufficiently to ride a squattish trike!' He eyed Meh'lindi. 'Course, she can dislocate her bones if she feels like it.'

This was perfectly true. Meh'lindi could distort herself to crawl through a narrow twisty tube. However, legs out of joint would hardly be very effective for riding a power-trike.

Jaq stepped astride a trike. He settled himself. He drew up his knees. 'I think we can manage,' he said. 'You're only a dwarf, after all, not a midget.'

Grimm puffed himself up. He cast around for his forage cap. Failing to find that much-twisted hat, he acquired a replacement from one of his fallen friends.

Jaq's ornamented black habit had by now definitely seen better days. Yet really, was this particular day better or worse than any other? Was any day anywhere, anywhen, better or worse? Throughout the Imperium millions of people were dying every second, so many were the worlds. Millions more people were being born, to die – in agony or anguish, in delirium or despair.

'Father of All,' prayed Jaq, 'how can you endure?'

'Huh,' was Grimm's response. He revved his trike, then he discarded his axe as too cumbersome. 'Let's find a fourth member for our godforsaken family.'

'No,' breathed Jaq, 'not forsaken. Not by Him. Never.'

Not until the paralysed anguished immortal Emperor failed at last, unsustainable even by the perpetual sacrifice of so many thousands of young psychic souls. Or until His multifold mind could no longer maintain its precarious equilibrium. Not until then!

Yet perhaps the demise of divine protection was inevitable – unless a hydra in the head of everyone made mind-puppets of the whole of humanity, save for a cabal of controllers!

Jaq could almost sympathize with the supposed purpose of the conspiracy. If indeed that was its true purpose! Which he doubted…

Ach, their plan was treason in the extreme. It would transform the whole human race into raging puppets. How easily that plan might unleash a new and murderous Chaos god more terrible than any other, so that the warp would overwhelm all the worlds rather than contrariwise.

Where was there any sure salvation?

Why, here in this boltgun named *Emperor's Mercy*!

And in the black force rod. And in Meh'lindi's needle gun, and in her assassin's sash. And in Jaq's psychic vigilance.

FIVE
WARP-EYE

SEVERAL BLOODY INCIDENTS punctuated the zig-zag trike-ride across Caput City to the street where Grimm boasted, in a few sidelong gruff yells, that he had 'cached' the Navigator.

Cached, indeed. As if this was an act of prudent forethought on Grimm's part! As if Grimm had anticipated that Vitali's verses might have predisposed the Navigator to destruction by a daemonette.

Undoubtedly the squats' assistance to that other Navigator hadn't been merely an act of charity. If the insurrectionists won – who could say that they wouldn't? – then more massacres would occur. Neighbouring cities must already be in a state of convulsion. Three abhumans could hardly have taken off into the desert on their trikes with any sure hope of survival pending an invasion by Imperial Guardsmen from some other solar system – in ten years' time, or twenty, or never.

If exports from Luxus Prime resumed, maybe the new regime could blame Lord Lagnost himself for the slaughter of representatives of the Imperial priesthood, and judges and arbitrators – irrespective of those psychic cries of crisis sent by his astropath. Maybe it was really Lagnost who had been in rebellion? Aye, rebellion against the Imperium. Maybe the cries for assistance had been a pretence. Maybe Lagnost had been attempting to set himself up as an independent ruler of his rich world.

Truth could be turned inside-out. Who other than Jaq was conscious of that brooding presence in the sky?

The rotten new regime – if capable of governing – would extend its tentacles and its daemonic claws to the mining world and its factory moon. If the three squats tried to return to the mines, why, they were witnesses of what had actually transpired on Luxus Prime. They would be snuffed out.

Their only escape route was to the stars. With most of the interstellar Navigators butchered, to have saved the life of a Navigator could serve the squats in good stead.

Cached, ah yes. Grimm had used the right word after all.

ARBITES IN DARK uniforms and reflective visors were advancing against a radio station. The building was faced in lustrous majolica mosaic. A frieze above the entrance spelled out piously in golden letters: VOX IMPERATORIS. This would be a religious radio station. However, the 'Emperor's Voice' must now be broadcasting falsehoods. Twisting towers soared overhead, corkscrews of orange and green enamelled tiling – the transmitter-aerials of the building. Sheets of plasteel barricaded the entrance.

Overturned vehicles littered the boulevard. The arbitrators availed themselves of these wrecks as cover. Those warriors of justice wouldn't be greatly concerned with their own safety – especially if those glossy ceramic corkscrews overhead were transmitting blasphemies. Yet there were only a score of the mirror-helmeted men. To squander one's life in such circumstances would be treason.

A shower of bullets and laser-pulses flew from the building. Several Arbites replied with krak grenades, fired from tubes clamped to the long barrels of lasguns. Pretty mosaic flew apart into tinier shards and sharp dust. Three arbitrators were wrestling a thermal cannon into position, bracing it in the wreckage of a limousine. That cannon was now close enough to the barricade to be effective.

Soon would come the sweet soft hiss of the cannon's beam super-heating the air in its path. Sheets of plasteel would begin to melt and slump. If any rebels exposed themselves, what a roar would arise as their bodily fluids suddenly vaporized.

Jaq and Grimm and Meh'lindi had skidded to a halt.

'Damn,' grumbled Grimm. 'The way's blocked.'

Mirrored visors turned in their direction. Lasguns with launcher tubes swung round.

'In the Emperor's name!' bellowed Jaq. *'Ego inquisitor sum!'*

Just then, a squad of men in mustard-yellow tunics came rushing from an alley. They were brandishing shotguns. Tattoos on their cheeks were scarlet, as if each had been bitten and lost a gobbet of flesh. The tattoo was of some bloody-hued bird of prey. *Lagnost's Hawks*, these ones! And covert cultists! They began to blast solid shells at the Arbites, and in the direction of the trikes. As the trio ducked, shells flew past.

Another mustard-squad with bloody cheeks arrived by a different route. Arbitrators fired las-pulses at those newcomers, killing a couple, before their true loyalties became apparent. This second squad weren't rebels at all.

From around the side of the radio station, there clanked a tracked vehicle mounted with twin autocannons. Faded runes and rust mottled its antique armour. Smoke belched from its exhausts. Its engine coughed. The autocannons were much more pristine. Their long barrels sported rows of vanes to radiate away the heat of rapid firing, vanes like the backplates of some saurian predator. Muzzles protruded from fanged mouths wrought of plasteel. The vehicle's cleats crushed tessellated paving. It swung to bear upon that thermal cannon in the limousine. Gunners upon the autocannon carriage let fly a high-velocity hail of shells. Shells ricocheted like stones skipping across a frozen river.

Evidently the rebels in the radio station had broadcast for assistance against the arbitrators.

The limousine erupted as fuel in its tank exploded. One arbitrator soared many metres through the air. The thermal cannon twisted upwards. Heedless of the blaze, another threw himself into the burning wreckage – so as to discharge the thermal cannon at least once, if the weapon was still capable of functioning. Even though the arbitrator's uniform caught fire, his visor and gauntlets offered brief protection to face and hands. His lungs must be roasting.

That sweet hiss…

High overhead, enamelled aerial spires intercepted the beam. Elegant beauty blotched and dripped.

And now a sleek transporter had arrived, with many wide fat tyres. Plainly it was designed for desert travel. The transporter was towing a thudd gun set on a tarnished tractor unit as elderly as the autocannon carriage.

That tractor unit's motor must have succumbed. Servicing rituals must have been neglected, litanies misspoken – if anyone had chanted those at all in the past century or two.

Amazing, really, that anyone had remembered where this weapon had been mothballed. Amazing that there was any such cumbersome heavy weapon on Luxus Prime. Some ancestor of the present Lord Lagnost must have acquired it to fire rowdy salvoes in his own honour out in the desert on his birthday.

'Oops!' exclaimed Grimm.

Laboriously the transporter wheeled the thudd gun into position. Why wasn't it defending the palace or space port? *Vox Imperialis* must be broadcasting appalling and seductive heresies.

Mustard-tunics were firing autoguns from the back of the transporter at rebel Hawks as the crew of the thudd gun hastened to ready it. Shells from the autocannon carriage ripped into the huge tyres of the transporter. Tyres deflated. The transporter sagged. It would be towing nothing for a while.

The first salvo from the quadruple launcher of the thudd gun flew high into the air. The shells fell far short of the autocannon carriage. Four closely spaced geysers of debris blasted from the street. The crew were either utterly inexperienced, or had been hoping to hit the remaining aerial-spires high above.

'We'd better double back,' advised Grimm.

The trio swung the trikes around. Taking sides here was futile.

THEY HAD POWERED their trikes into a square. Several hundred folk were dancing naked, waving knives and wailing a wordless psalm. Blood and sweat trickled down shimmying bodies. Footprints were pink. The dancers seemed to be trying to imprint a rune of evil power upon the glazed flagstones.

Autoguns firing, Jaq cut a path through the sacrilegious dance – though whether he hampered the ritual or contributed to it, who could tell?

FUGITIVES FROM THE fighting thronged an avenue. On a high majolica plinth from which a statue had been toppled, a demagogue shrieked at the refugees. Many of them paused. Others forced their way past. An awful parody of a righteous preacher, the tall gaunt man was promising bliss if enough people would join him to march on the space port.

'Blissh, blissh!' he bawled. He sounded like a psychotic sheep.

'Whoever diesh shall go shtraight to paradishe to enjoy the eternal embraces of nymphets and lushty lads–'

To *endure* those embraces, more likely! What could such nymphets be, but daemonettes of Slaanesh? The lusty lads likewise: daemons!

Many refugees were faithful to the Emperor. They called upon His name to preserve them. 'Emperor of Us All! God on Earth!' If the Emperor had once possessed an actual name, it was long forgotten even by Himself. Thus the pious called on a name which no one knew.

True believers began to rage at those who were swayed by that orator. Brawling was breaking out. Blood was being shed. The demagogue bleated on about bliss.

Meh'lindi gestured with her needle pistol at that mockery of a preacher on the plinth. Jaq shook his head brusquely. Too much of a long shot. Hers wasn't a needle rifle. To wade deep into a surging crowd would be folly.

Overhead, smoke writhed as if trying to assemble itself into some vast distorted drifting body. Dusk was coming on now. The street lamps of Caput City were out of action. The glow-globes upon their fluted ceramic columns remained inert.

Jaq and his companions detoured once more.

ONLY THE SKY-GLOW from scattered fires and the flash of spasmodic explosions lit the prevailing gloom as the trio finally arrived in a certain courtyard off a certain Lapis Lane.

Quieter, here.

Plasteel shutters covered windows. Buildings were pretending not to exist. This was the jewellery district. Here was where gems excreted by the poisonous sand-grubs of the desert – and other stones mined in the mountains – were cut and polished and set and sold. The district cowered silently. Within the workshop-dwellings lapidaries and their families would be cringing.

The insurrection was motivated by lustful corruption of the flesh, not by gems and gewgaws.

Yet perhaps, since gems were ornaments of the flesh, the jewellery area therefore remained inviolate and sacrosanct. Obviously no looting had occurred. Lapis Lane was quiet. The dark courtyard was deserted.

GRIMM POUNDED ON a door – THUMP, thump, thump; THUMP, thump, thump. He banged over and over in the same rhythm until a small security shutter opened. A frightened face peered from the darkness within – into a lesser though larger darkness which framed a bearded man in tattered black and a tall woman so inky that her eyes seemed to hover disembodied. On tip-toe, Grimm grunted, 'It's me, Mr Kosmitopolos. Open up.'

MEH'LINDI HAD PLUCKED a pencil-lumen from her sash. Mr Kosmitopolos blinked in its light. The tubby merchant was sweating. To be harbouring a Navigator at such a time! He began to stammer a question of Grimm. The merchant's accent wasn't local.

So he too hoped to be able to escape on a warpship with a bag full of the finest gems, if the need arose…

Grimm had chosen a good hiding place for the Navigator.

'Who are you?' Kosmitopolos gasped at the inquisitor. 'Who are you?' at Meh'lindi, black as ebon, almost invisible behind the glow of her lumen, a void-like silhouette.

'*Te benedico*,' Jaq said in the hieratic tongue, thus blessing the man for his contribution to a higher cause. 'The Emperor be with you always.'

Jaq nodded to Meh'lindi. Even in the darkness the hint was unmistakable.

Meh'lindi appeared merely to touch Kosmitopolos on the side of the neck. With a sigh of departing breath the merchant slumped to the floor.

'Huh,' said Grimm. 'I suppose I would have shaken him off more noisily! Wouldn't have robbed him, though, squats' honour.'

The beam of the lumen picked out a high wainscot of ornamental panelling, with tiles cemented above. As if the pencil light were a cutting laser Meh'lindi traced swiftly around some of the panels.

'I was about to *tell* you–' began Grimm. Meh'lindi clicked her tongue. Her fingers roved. She pressed the wainscot just so. A low door swung inward. The door, hardly high enough for a squat, was of plasteel, veneered on the outside to hide its nature.

The entire wainscot must be of plasteel with a decorative façade to disguise it.

Quite shrewd of Kosmitopolos to have located this hidey-hole near the front door. If intruders burst into the merchant's house to ransack it, their instinct would be to rush on into the interior to search for his treasures. If, forewarned, he was already in his hidey-hole, he would have a chance to escape while the intruders were otherwise occupied. The wainscot had betrayed itself to Meh'lindi by being excessively high, enough so to accommodate a concealed door.

A steep flight of stone steps plunged claustrophobically into absolute darkness.

Grimm called out softly: 'Azul! Azul Petrov! I'm with friends. Keep your bandanna on! We've come to fetch you. We're coming down.'

Meh'lindi was already descending, black and silent. To her, a claustrophobic plunge was an invitation. She averted her eyes in case the Navigator failed to heed Grimm's advice.

THE UNDERGROUND CELL pleased Jaq. How it reminded him in miniature of the catacombs of *Tormentum Malorum*. Illumination came now from a glow-globe, which previously had been doused.

A bunk. A table bearing some microtools and lenses. A small stasis chest of food. A large flagon of water. Trays of gemstones were stacked.

And here was the Navigator, perching nervously on a stool.

Walls were hung with faded quilted tapestry, to deaden sound. Those dim designs were of statuary on a lawn surrounded by high hedges. Marble men and women stood static and unmenacing.

PETROV HAD NEVER seen such a woman as Meh'lindi before, and kept staring at her golden eyes as if those were large living beads of amber.

His two visible eyes were a cool green. And large. His once-handsome face was wrinkled, just as Vitali's had been, by exposure to the warp. One thought of the frail grey gills of a fungus. The shape of that face was mantis-like, so that his eyes seemed those of an insect. His ear lobes were large and studded with tiny rubies as if droplets of blood were welling. Two similar rubies studded his nose. A larger one, the tip of his sharp chin. Yet another, his lower lip. He might have been a haemophiliac. To touch him would make him bleed.

But bleed *hard*. Bleed rubies. A Navigator needed strength to steer a ship safely through the warp.

Azul Petrov wore a grey damask robe hung with rune-embroidered ribbons. The moiré surface of the damask shimmered, hinting at blue or green. It could have been coated with a film of oil. There was an evasive sliminess to his attire, a muted chameleon quality. But mostly, a sense of slipperiness. It was he, after all, who had escaped from the massacre of his colleagues – albeit with the help of the squats.

Petrov darted glances at Meh'lindi, but didn't enquire about her.

With Jaq's role in the scheme of things he seemed conversant. He acknowledged the electro-tattoo on Jaq's palm as conveying authority. Navigators travelled widely; Navigators told each other secrets. He understood that Jaq was empowered to commandeer assistance and obedience in the Emperor's name.

Jaq interrogated, impatiently but not harshly.

Had Petrov spent his period in hiding down here studding his earlobes and lower lip and chin with choice items from the merchant's collection?

Oh no! Jaq must understand that the rest of Petrov's body was similarly studded with excrescences of crystal-blood. Petrov's navel, his nipples. Other parts too...

'In my warp-eye,' rhapsodized the Navigator, 'there are a thousand billion atoms, I believe. Atoms are so tiny! In the galaxy there are a thousand billion suns. I think that each atom in my eye must correspond to one of those suns! No one beholds a Navigator's warp-eye nakedly without dire consequences. Yet let me tell you, inquisitor, that it is black, solid black. Once, there was a pupil and an iris in that eye. But not now, oh no. My eye has become a sphere of jet, which can enclose the galaxy. It is a bio-gem. I have secreted my eye just as the sand-grubs of the deserts of this interesting world secrete other hues of gems. When I die, will my eye continue to see? Will I be within my eye, hung around someone's neck in a velvet pouch? If that someone is in danger, will they expose the eye at their enemy? My beautiful deathly orb of jet! If they are in danger of capture and torture, will they take my eye from the pouch, themselves to gaze at its black lustre – and momentarily behold the warp, and die?'

Well, this was all within the parameters of strangeness of Navigators! Vitali Googol, with his doomful verses... Petrov, with his fixation upon that organic gem in his forehead...

The Navigator leaned forward intently. 'It's said, inquisitor, that the eldar wear a special crystal in a pouch, into which constantly trickles their soul throughout their lives. When they die their soul is saved within that gem... Have you heard this, inquisitor?'

'Perhaps,' said Jaq.

THE INQUISITION FOREVER gathered such information, much of it of the highest secrecy, not suitable to be shared.

When Jaq had been admitted into the Ordo Malleus, he had learned more than most ordinary inquisitors knew about the tragedy of the eldar species. This topic abutted upon daemons, and upon a Chaos god – whose deluded human cultists were responsible, in fact, for the present strife upon Luxus Prime. Slaaneshi cultists! Worshippers of Slaanesh. Evokers of daemonettes.

The honour of Slaanesh seemed to dog Jaq.

The Chaos world which his little 'family' had trespassed upon in the Eye of Terror – the world which was supposedly the origin of the hydra creature – had been a planet under the aegis of Slaanesh, the daemon power of cruel lust.

That visit had sowed a poison seed within Vitali. Vitali had succumbed.

Once the eldar had been a great species. Their civilisation had spanned the stars. Now they were reduced to scattered remnants, inhabiting enigmatic 'craftworlds' lurking deep in the interstellar void. Even these remnants were puissant and proud and seemingly more perfect – at least in their own opinion – than the festering rag-bag of humanity which had supplanted the eldar across the ocean of stars.

Eldar could be as cunning as Callidus – and as relentless in pressing an attack as any assassins of the Eversor shrine or even elite Space Marines. The roaming artist-warriors of the eldar rejoiced in the name of Harlequins. Maybe they bitterly mocked themselves with this name!

Whatever had destroyed the eldar civilization was linked to Slaanesh. Yet in precisely what way? Or even imprecisely! Eldar were notoriously evasive in this regard. So quoth the illuminated Inquisition reports which Jaq had scanned. Some of those reports had been denied even to him, a secret inquisitor. Those were shut under a seal of heresy, access-locked.

Somewhere in the galaxy, so it was whispered amongst Inquisition, was the answer. Somewhere there existed – supposedly – a *Black Library*, repository of invaluable and ghastly knowledge about daemons and about Chaos. Eldar fanatics and terrible psychic barriers guarded that library.

Did even the Hidden Master of the Ordo Malleus know the full truth of all this? Or were those records of the Inquisition heresy-sealed so as to conceal a terrifying ignorance?

IF THIS NAVIGATOR were to accompany Jaq and Meh'lindi and Grimm, he would glean worse secrets than gossip about the eldar.

'Continue,' said Jaq.

And Petrov confided: 'It's said that the eldar journey afar by means of a webway through the warp. They possess no Navigators such as myself and my kin. Eldar ships don't jump through warp space. They themselves can walk through tunnels in the warp. They step through gateways and soon are elsewhere…'

'Perhaps,' said Jaq.

Meh'lindi was listening so attentively. Mention of the eldar stirred a bitter reverie. She had even masqueraded as an eldar female once. Never to do so again. Not with that alien beast concealed within her.

Was Petrov fascinated by the eldar – fixated upon those rumoured spirit-stones and upon that rumoured webway because of his own peculiar concept of the warp-eye in his forehead?

Oh, this was well within acceptable limits of oddity for a Navigator. Those limits must needs be broad ones, here and now, in chaotic Caput City! Compared with Vitali Googol at the terrible finale of his life, Petrov seemed positively sane and pure.

'Will you swear loyalty and obedience to me, Azul Petrov, in the Emperor's name and by the honour of your House and by your soul? And,' added Jaq, 'by your special eye, which I swear I shall pluck out and shatter if you betray me?'

Grimm nodded encouragement to the Navigator. 'That might sound a bit remorseless. It's just so we all know where we stand!'

Jaq glared at the squat. 'Do we know any such thing? Curb your tongue, abhuman! Do you swear by those things, Azul Petrov?'

The Navigator gave his word.

WHEN THEY REASCENDED those steep steps from the hiding place, the house remained silent. Nothing stirred.

The merchant's body lay where it had fallen. In the interior of his home, were a wife and children still stifling their anxieties at the knock on the door half an hour earlier? In another half an hour, would the wife nerve herself to creep out and discover the corpse? Then at least she would be certain that her husband had not deserted her.

The courtyard was pitch-dark. Gunfire crackled here and there. A flash lit the sky briefly. A feral animal, Meh'lindi sniffed the air. Extending his psychic sense, Jaq was aware of the turbid slosh of life and death throughout the city. What once might have seemed – spuriously – like a limpid lake of sweet water was now an agitated swamp. Foul mud had been stirred up; and worse: slimy phosphorescent creatures of the mud, aglow with corruption, homicidal, voracious. Ebbing and flowing, waxing and waning, a ghostly daemonic presence was yearning to incarnate itself.

The insurrection was evidently proceeding in spasms, in spastic paroxysms. In rabid convulsions punctuated by pauses. Lulls interspersed the fevered delirium, lulls from which the loyalists could take little comfort other than to grab some rest before another frenzied surge occurred, before another festering wave assaulted them.

When Jaq had discharged his force rod in exorcism at the coagulating presence, maybe he had impaired the co-ordination of the rebellion in some small degree. Doubtless he should be hunting for all manifestations of vile *otherness*, such as had seized upon Vitali Googol. Jaq should be expunging each such manifestation that he found, snipping off the feelers of evil.

Alas, there was no time for such sanitary ministrations. Those might cripple him. Might cause his death. Might cause him to be marooned here.

'There's a lull,' Jaq told the others. He was shielding the white spark of his own soul from the attentions of that inchoate Chaotic power brooding over the city. He was casting an aura of protection around his companions. Even so, they mustn't use the power-trikes again – irrespective of whether Petrov might have been able to ride pillion with Grimm. Too noisy.

It wasn't too far to the governor's palace, there to take callous advantage of this pause in the collapse of Lagnost's reign.

'We need stim-pills, Meh'lindi.'

From her assassin's sash, without asking for further clarification, she provided two.

None for herself. The synthetic skin she wore over her scarred and tattooed body provided booster chemicals, as well as protection and oxygen.

Grimm tossed back his pill, and belched quietly.

'Good square meal is what I'd prefer, boss. You always kept a good larder.'

Boss? Whose boss, genuinely, was Grimm's?

No pill for Petrov. He'd been resting until now. He mustn't become hyped and manic.

SIX

ASTROPATH

DURING HIS PREVIOUS audience with the governor, Jaq had sensed the whereabouts of that 'safe deep location' where the astropath was cooped. Although Jaq had never been able to detect persons as such at a distance, he was certainly sensitive to the sparkle of a psychic's spirit. An astropath sending out telepathic messages was a beacon as clear to him, in miniature, as the Astronomican to a Navigator.

The man named Fennix was four levels almost directly below the governor's audience chamber.

Half a dozen mustard-uniformed guards armed with laspistols were on weary duty in the audience chamber. Glow-globes were at half power while Lagnost slept. The guards became more alert as the ragged inquisitor entered, flashing his palm-tattoo.

Emperor's Mercy was holstered. Jaq was insisting that his three companions accompany him.

The gross governor was wallowing in a doze on a great divan, his weight crushing satin cushions. His young concubines and catamites clustered around him like so many silky cubs. His peacock hat was set atop a lacquered brass pillar inset with gems.

Did he suppose that if a murderer managed to rush into this chamber the intruder might mistake that peacock-perch for Lagnost himself and fire his single hope of a shot at the ormolu pillar instead of at the governor?

A genuine expert from the Officio Assassinorum would immediately have detected Lagnost's asthmatic wheeze.

What did such a man as Lagnost know of genuine assassins? What did anyone know – until one day they stared death in the face, for a moment or two?

The guards' cheek-tattoos were of fanged worms. An officer in peaked cap and braid, with a flower tattoo and a single carbuncle earring, was sitting on a pouffe. He cradled a long-barrelled lasgun while he awaited his lord's revival from slumber. This was sudden.

Lagnost peered.

'You've brought a Navigator with you, Sir Draco. And I suppose the squat is an engineer. Does that mean we must evacuate. Can the situation be so bad?' Lagnost gazed at the rips in Jaq's habit. 'You're wearing some sort of armour, aren't you? Won't you give it to me? The Emperor's loyal governor needs to survive.'

Indeed, the death of Lagnost would castrate the loyalists. The governor hauled himself laboriously upright scattering catamites and concubines. Air sighed through his breathing tubes.

'My lovelies,' he lamented, resigning himself to their loss. Aye, to become the playthings of Slaaneshi cultists, until each perished!

'The armour,' he repeated more brusquely.

'My lord,' said Jaq, 'I fear your girth is too ample for my undergarment. And an inquisitor does not strip himself! I need an immediate consultation with your astropath. I must send a message to my superiors.'

Lagnost blinked dubiously. 'Are you not superior enough yourself, Sir Draco?'

Once again Jaq displayed his palm, activating by a thrust of will the seal of the Inquisition.

'It is a sacred obligation to assist me, just as I assist you! Have the astropath brought here.'

Lagnost eyed the shimmery grey Navigator with those excrescences of crystallized blood upon lobes and lip and chin.

He temporized. 'I fear you must descend to the oubliette for a conversation with my astropath. Meanwhile the Navigator will be entertained elsewhere.'

The guards and the officer were keeping their weapons inconspicuously pointed.

To kill Lagnost would emasculate all piety on this planet. Yet by what other means could Jaq prevail?

Slowly Jaq said: 'I have a terrible secret to confide, my Lord. In the warp be it known there exist powerful daemons of Chaos. Chaos is the contradiction of all sanity and civilization, and of reality itself. These daemons can enter reality if they are invited by corrupt fools. The name of one vile Chaos god is *Slaanesh*. I regret to say there are worshippers of Slaanesh on your own world–'

And all of these words comprised an order of execution for all those who heard them in this luxurious room – as Meh'lindi well knew.

She only awaited the distraction of a nearby explosion. If none came before Jaq had done with enlightening this lord, and coincidentally his guards and his minions, why, she would still act, now that Jaq had deliberately voiced what she knew were forbidden topics. How could Lagnost not realize that he only had moments left to live? The governor was so intent upon the inquisitor's words, struggling to grasp them.

On three of Meh'lindi's fingers, donned before she entered the palace, were what might look to the unilluminated eye like three items of jewellery. Three baroque thimbles, or hooded rings. What jeweller in this whole city would have recognized these three items of bijouterie for what they really were? Meh'lindi had entrusted her laspistol and her needle pistol to Grimm, to stow in pouches round his waist. On her fingers now were rare miniaturized digital weapons so neat that they had easily stored in tiny pockets in her scarlet sash…

Crump. A massive detonation somewhere in town. The lull was over.

The guards flicked a momentary glance.

In that moment Meh'lindi crooked her fingers in different directions.

A sliver from the miniature needler stung Lagnost on the cheek. Within instants his corpulent body was at war with itself inwardly. His tube-tusks were hyperventilating. Oh, the strangled flute-mute of asphyxiation! One of Lagnost's fat juddering hands succeeded in tearing the jewelled tubes from his neck and his nostrils. This could only hasten his choking. Besides, he was already suffering a massive heart attack and stroke.

A thin jet of volatile chemicals from the tiny flamer, igniting in the air, had wreathed the officer's face in fire. Sucked into him, oxygen would instantly be blazing in the ovens of his lungs, forestalling even an out-cry of agony. The officer's very breath was being consumed.

A laser beam had cut the throat of one of the guards. He burbled qui-etly, choking on blood.

Yet the digital weapons were already forgotten. Those tiny devices could only fire once before requiring a fresh needle, a replenishment of chemicals, a recharge of the laser.

Meh'lindi had already launched herself. The edge of her hand jerked upward under a guard's nose. Her elbow jabbed another under the heart. Spinning, she kicked a third with her heel. Her other hand chopped the fourth.

Meh'lindi regulated her breathing.

Seven corpses lay in the audience chamber. No cry of alarm had arisen – though the huddled catamites and junior concubines were whimpering, wide-eyed, perhaps about to wail.

'Quiet, brats,' snarled Grimm. He waved Meh'lindi's laspistol at them. *'Not a peep out of you!'* How avuncular the ruddy-cheeked abhuman seemed. An uncle enraged at the wayward nephews and nieces.

'So what about this lot?' muttered the squat.

Petrov's stunned gaze ranged from the dead bodies to the living.

He said to Jaq: 'They won't understand–' He gulped. 'Won't understand whatever you said about,' and he whispered, *'warp things.'* He sounded almost as if he was pleading for his own life. Oh, he was quick on the uptake. 'I understand about things of the warp, a bit. Tentacles reaching out to brush my mind. Sometimes! Though not about…'

Not about… *Chaos gods*?

'You're in for an education,' said Grimm.

'Only,' snapped Jaq, 'if it's essential.'

'Anyway,' rambled Petrov, 'these dollies of his won't understand…'

'Yes, dolls!' echoed Jaq. 'Living dolls. Do you wish these to be played with by sadistic lunatics of lust?'

Petrov swallowed. 'We should show mercy to them…'

'Yes indeed. Indeed.'

'I'll do it, Jaq,' volunteered Meh'lindi.

She stepped swiftly among the dead governor's playthings, stooping. A stiffened finger here, a nerve block there. So swiftly. It was indeed merciful. Limp silken bodies lay unblemished all around Lagnost's poisoned corpse. A few more entries on the self-erasing list of death, that mumbling litany of a sickly galaxy offering up praise nonetheless to Him-on-Earth.

Already she was examining the arabesque tile-work of the walls.

'Four levels down,' she mused. Her fingers roved. She tapped. Four levels would have been four too many for such a fat man to have descended on his own, without recourse to a chair equipped with suspensors. Of such a chair there was no evidence.

'Ah…'

A faience knob turned in Meh'lindi's hand. A large panel of tiles moved inward and then slid upward, revealing a little room decorated with runes freshly gilded. An elevator.

Such pious gilding! Whatever the governor's private peccadilloes, he had indeed been devout. Despite his proclivities Lagnost must have been a man of fortitude not to succumb to pollution. Knowing of his tastes, had the secret Slaaneshi cultists condoned his governorship – until the new pontifex had inspired Lagnost to even more energetic piety?

A flaw in his faith had been his reluctance to surrender his astropath to an inquisitor. Yet should a governor be a *fool*?

Already Meh'lindi was slipping inside the elevator, mingling with shadows. Grimm jerked forward to follow her – as once the little man had trailed after her in Vasilariov City on Stalinvast. Jaq stayed him.

'We'll remain here, Grimm. She'll find her way into the dungeons and out again better without us.' Already the panel was sliding downward.

'*What is she*?' breathed Petrov.

'An Imperial assassin,' Jaq said simply.

Imperial – or renegade? Which? These days to be a renegade might mean to be truly faithful.

WHILE THEY WAITED, privately Jaq dedicated the deaths of the governor's youthful attendants to Him-on-Earth. To nourish the Emperor's soul many hundreds of bright young psychic lads and lasses each day surrendered their vital essence and their lives, consumed to feed His supreme yet lacerated spirit forever on psychic overwatch.

The bodies of those who were sacrificed were consumed in sacred furnaces, crewed and stoked by priests. The incense of burning flesh and evaporating fatty tissues was a plume piercing the pollution of Earth's atmosphere, sweetening the sulphurous acidic sky.

These other bodies here would simply lie on silk or woollen glade of carpet or against satin cushions until they were dragged by the heels to some foetid sump, their sacrifice uncommemorated.

Might Jaq's heartfelt prayer prompt their deaths to be registered momentarily and fractionally light-years away? From the Emperor's withered eye-socket, might a tiny miraculous tear trickle?

Sentiment, Jaq reminded himself, is the foe of sound judgement.

Out in the night, explosions were occurring more regularly. Glow-globes flickered, faded, then resumed their mellow partial radiance.

INEVITABLY ANOTHER OFFICER hastened into the audience chamber. He closed the door behind him before he really saw.

For a moment this officer could scarcely comprehend: the raggy inquisitor, the eerie Navigator, the abhuman with a laspistol pointing, and the bodies, the bodies, those young ones seemingly asleep. Blood. Burnt flesh – not much at all, really. The sprawled governor bereft of his breathing gear.

Grimm was about to shoot the officer when the man sank to his knees.

He wept such tears of loss, of devastation. For in that moment the officer had seen the future, and the future was empty of hope. With Lagnost's demise all hope was gone. The city, the world was lost. Through his tears the man gaped devastatedly at Jaq, the Emperor's inquisitor who had condemned Luxus Prime to be lost.

'I know,' said Jaq, almost gently. 'I know. I would weep too.'

'But… why?' whimpered the officer.

'You could never begin to understand. If you began to understand you would be doomed.'

Wasn't the man doomed, in any case? Wasn't he seeing his last sight in all the world – and that sight one of utter futility?

'At least let me kill myself,' the man begged.

Just as gently, Jaq shook his head. The man mustn't draw his weapon. He had been permitted enough grace.

Quietly: 'Grimm…'

Grimm lasered the officer through a tear-stained eye. Let the intense heat burn away that man's grief.

WHEN MEH'LINDI RETURNED, a green-robed figure lay limply over her shoulder.

Fennix would be blind, of course. When he was formally soul-bound to the Emperor his eyeballs would have curdled.

Should she have tried to guide him by the arm? Assuming that he accepted her guidance! In all likelihood Fennix possessed near-sense of his surroundings. How nimbly would he have moved? Assuming that he wished to shift from his place of supposed safety!

She had simply sedated him.

Fennix's weight seemed inconsiderable. His physique, slight. Meh'lindi could have been carrying a child over her shoulder. His face was hidden. There was no leisure for curiosity. They must leave, leave. Impeded by the body, Meh'lindi seemed like some black robotic machine, some mind-wiped porter bearing luggage.

Bitterly purified by his meditation upon the Emperor's tears, Jaq marshalled his psychic power. Using this power, he had fought against daemons on a score of worlds and more, before his life became less simple due to the Harlequin Man and the hydra cabal. The tattoos on his body bore witness to his successes. Nay, could any tattoo have borne witness to the contrary? If defeated, his very soul could have been consumed.

He must summon his power to enforce and befuddle whoever encountered their party on their escape from the palace. He must cast an aura of *conviction*. What they were doing would seem to be right and appropriate.

If the dead officer's grief-stricken reaction was symptomatic, premature discovery of Lagnost's death could swiftly topple the whole house of cards, of resistance – not to mention enfeebling the defence of the space port before *Tormentum Malorum* could take off.

It was highly unlikely that Lagnost had spawned an heir to the governorship. That heir would be some nephew or cousin – a situation rife with the prospect of civil war if a different kind of strife had not supervened.

What happened on Luxus Prime after Jaq's departure was of no account. None whatever. It weighed no more heavily than a feather in the balance. Jaq could only grieve impotently at the unfolding tragedy.

Stalinvast had been utterly destroyed subsequent to his visit to that world, because that cursed message of *exterminatus* had been sent.

Was Jaq becoming a destroyer of worlds? When word filtered to the Inquisition on Terra about the Luxus episode and the murder of the devout governor – if indeed word ever filtered to Terra! – would Jaq be branded doubly anathema?

In his own minor way Jaq partook of the Emperor's agony. This participation – this sour sacrament – strengthened him, even though the shining path had long since vanished.

Enforce, and befuddle, and convince...

But let not the brooding daemonic presence sense his exertions!

They left the governor's chamber, to confront, almost immediately, such innocent honest bustle and loyal activity. Jaq, in his raggy gown. A scowling squat. A shuddering Navigator. And a black machine-woman carrying a comatose astropath.

Jaq had displayed his palm-tattoo and brayed out: 'Lord Lagnost has been in communion with Him-on-Earth.' In a sense this was true, supposing that Lagnost's soul had ascended.

'He must not be disturbed at this holy moment. His Lordship is praying and conceiving a plan for victory. Alas, his astropath was traumatized by acting as the terrible channel between his Lordship and Him-on-Earth. We must take Fennix to our ship for treatment with special drugs to restore him. Lord Lagnost was in communion with our Emperor–'

How these dupes hoped this was true. They made signs, and kissed amulets. Would an inquisitor blaspheme?

'Spread the word! The Emperor's great soul is with Lord Lagnost, miraculously. Salvation is imminent–' Jaq felt like a zealous confessor rather than an astute inquisitor.

If you must lie, let the lie be so amazing that no one can doubt it.

AND PRESENTLY *Tormentum Malorum* had risen throbbing into space, leaving a doomed world behind.

THE FUEL WHICH had been pumped on board a century earlier at that dockyard orbiting the fourth world of the red dwarf star, Bendercoot, was three-fifths gone. If any safe reserve were to remain, the ship only now held enough for a few short warp jumps once the jump-zone was reached, or for a single medium jump. Luxus Prime had not been the place to refuel, nor could the manufacturing moon of the mining world be trusted.

In the short term only one short jump was impending – back out to nowhere, to a different part of the infinity of nothingness.

There, Fennix must trawl through the torrent of astral messages for however long it took – until some sprat of a clue could be netted, and then maybe another hint to couple with it.

For however many months this took.

It was as well that the larders of *Tormentum Malorum* were well stocked with stasis chests of gourmet victuals.

AS THE SLEEK funereal ship headed outward, Jaq refrained from eavesdropping on any vox traffic which would embroider upon the agonizing collapse of devout government in the Luxus system.

Fennix refrained from contacting his colleague underneath the besieged courthouse, if any courthouse still endured.

BLIND FENNIX WAS a shrunken little fellow, more monkeylike than human. His ears resembled a bat's, big and pointy, and his hearing was acute to a degree where loud noise caused actual pain. His preternatural hearing, of course, had nothing to do with the telepathic talent. If he had not kept his ears deeply stuffed with wadded cotton, his hearing might indeed have impeded his talent.

In retrospect, Lagnost's immural of Fennix in an oubliette located beneath dungeons (as Meh'lindi reported laconically) had been a wise and almost compassionate measure. It distanced Fennix from detonations as well as safeguarding him.

Remarkable, really, that Fennix had not been deafened as well as blinded during his soul-binding to the Emperor. However, his value would have been diminished if he could never hear a master's voice telling him what messages to send. Could his instructions have been painstakingly tapped on to his palm in code? Telepathic talent and hearing were both cursed blessings.

Although Fennix's limbs seemed withered, he was spry. The astropath was made of dried, preserved, toughened meat and sinew.

And he was a strange mystic, as it transpired.

Fennix believed that every telepathic message reverberated forever, and that within every message every other telepathic message past and future nestled as a silent indetectable sub-text. At the moment of death Fennix was sure that he would be bombarded by the totality of messages. He would be gathered into an infinite babel, achieving understanding and annihilation in the selfsame fatal seizure.

He also believed that no message was limited in direction. According to him, ghosts of all messages propagated in every direction through space and time. Yet the Emperor's Astronomican skewed each message so that it seemed confined in direction and duration.

Might Fennix be vulnerable to possession? Might his notion of unheard messages lead him to strain to hear them – and to open his mind to daemon voices?

Was he a genius, yet by that very token – and despite his soul binding – potentially dangerous to himself and to others?

ON THE FOURTH day of their outward voyage, Jaq had come upon Fennix secluded with Azul Petrov in an obsidian cell of stasis boxes.

Immediately Jaq had flinched back.

For Petrov had teased up his black bandanna to expose his warp-eye.

A Navigator took such solemn oaths never to do so unless his life was in deadly danger. Fennix seemed almost about to embrace Petrov. From very close the blind astropath was staring at the Navigator's wrinkled brow.

Jaq had averted his own gaze from any risk of seeing what Fennix could not possibly see, since Fennix was totally blind.

What strange communion was taking place between Petrov and Fennix?

FENNIX, OF COURSE, required motivating and briefing. Petrov would pilot the ship where Jaq required. Yet Fennix must understand the essentials of the astral quest he was soon to commence. What exactly to seek. What was the import of allusions which must otherwise mean nothing to him, and which even if forewarned might elude him.

'I thank you for kidnapping me,' he had said to Jaq.

The astropath's nearsense allowed him to discern the flavour and aura silhouettes of Jaq and Grimm and Meh'lindi. Meh'lindi's presence particularly caused him to shudder with a kind of horrified excitement.

'Aura within aura,' he had lilted. 'Monstrosity within the mistress.'

It wasn't merely that he gauged Meh'lindi's lethal musculature and grace. He was also perplexedly aware that her body masked those gruesome implants. Such mysteries he had been abducted into the midst of!

By now, of course, Azul Petrov had seen with his own eyes an entirely different transformation. Once they had lifted off from Luxus Prime, Meh'lindi had slipped away to her sleep-cell. Another woman entirely had seemed to return – a woman with ivory features, dressed in a gown of iridescent silk, arrayed in cool green emeralds, with curly-toed slippers upon her feet, the quintessence of an elegant courtesan.

Who else was this who shared the ship with them? This superb twin of Meh'lindi's, tall and chic! Sharing the same golden eyes, to be sure, and the same scarlet sash.

After dissolving her syn-skin, Meh'lindi had chosen not to resume her cling-tight assassin's black tunic but this voluptuous disguise instead.

Why, this stranger was none other than Meh'lindi herself. In her throat, hardly noticeable at all, was some flesh-coloured valve.

After much scrupulous thought and prayer – like a scattering of hot ashes upon his soul – Jaq had outlined certain details to Fennix and to Petrov too.

He explained the reason for Meh'lindi's double aura – and she had listened expressionlessly. He touched on the mind-invading hydra. He described secret inquisitors involved in a conspiracy. He named the Harlequin Man. He confessed to intruding into the Imperial palace. Names such as Ordo Malleus and Baal Firenze were on his lips... and even *Slaanesh*.

The simian astropath and the carbuncled Navigator had shivered as if the chill of space had invaded their bone marrow. Both prayed with Jaq. Meh'lindi prayed too, though she dedicated her prayers harshly to the shrine of Callidus. Only Grimm had refrained from prayer, taking himself off to anoint the engines with spittle and polish them.

PRESENTLY *Tormentum Malorum* had jumped – to the middle of nowhere, into a void which contained no midpoint since it possessed no boundaries. Stars were sickly jewels utterly distant, adrift in endless emptiness, vain pinpoints of light in domineering darkness. Nebulae were haemorrhages of blood shed in milk.

Daemon-hatches blanked the portholes, closing out that stygian gulf with all its remote pathetic lanterns and luminescent veils.

The five had feasted on grox tongues in aspic, upon caviar of Arcturan great-eels with embryo elvers curled in sweet juice inside the translucent eggs, on steaks of foetal whale from some waterworld, all washed down with gloryberry juice.

Such a menu was routine aboard *Tormentum Malorum*, yet upon this occasion the meal was ceremonial and sacramental. Jaq feasted to the glory of the God-Emperor, and for strength, and so that puritanical inhibitions should not impede whatever must be done. By now he was wearing a fresh black ornamented habit, replacement for the garment which gunfire had defiled. Grimm feasted to the glory of his gut. Meh'lindi consumed gracefully though indifferently. To her, a rat was as fine a source of protein as a ragout.

And at last, in that drifting catacombed chapel of jet and obsidian, Fennix had commenced his telepathic trawl.

SEVEN
RELEVATIONS

THE TASK TOOK Fennix almost three months. Daily he honed his telepathic sense and eavesdropped until he was exhausted.

Such a swarm of messages to attune to, upon so many wavelengths of thought. Swarm upon swarm. Commercial messages, and military and bureaucratic and theological. Streams of data. Requests, decrees and proclamations. Messages of hope and horror, desperate appeals...

It was, so he said, as though at every moment a million lights were shining into a vast mirror, as though a million glittering pebbles were forever being tossed upon a bottomless lake, radiating a shimmer of ripples.

To aim or receive a particular message, to establish a mutual mind-to-mind link, was simplicity compared with this godly overwatch which he was undertaking.

A mere twelve weeks seemed almost miraculously short a span of time – a tribute to Fennix's esoteric concept of astral telepathy. Of course, the assignment could never be completed satisfactorily. It could only be abandoned at a stage when several tantalizing inklings had been gleaned and correlated.

Fennix wasn't one of those ciphers of the Administratum who could memorize entire texts verbatim for mechanical recital without any comprehension of the words. Fortunately he understood the hieratic language in which crucial inquisitorial messages were often couched.

Item, urgent ongoing enquiries into the assassination of an inquisitor upon a certain world of which none present had ever heard.

Item, another similar assassination. Deep suspicions seemed to be stirring.

Might the Inquisition be at war with itself? Might the unnameable ordo (which Jaq understood to be the Ordo Malleus) be in conflict with the broader ranks of the Inquisition? The covert at war with the overt? (Not that the ordinary Inquisition was exactly *visible* – except when it chose to be flamboyant, often as a cover for more secret manoeuvres.)

Item, *Stalinvast*.

Disguised as drifting rocks, robot drones had been left behind to scrutinize that exterminated world. These had reported that alien ships were appearing in the vicinity. Eldar vessels.

Petrov commented from his own gleanings of Navigator gossip that for this to be so, there must already have been an entrance to the eldar webway somewhere within the Stalinvast system; an entrance – and an exit – large enough for starships. This gateway must have remained dormant and concealed for aeons during which human beings had festered upon Stalinvast. Had not the eldar been masters of the galaxy before their downfall and well-nigh obliteration?

In orbit around the corpse of Stalinvast the eldar had begun to construct a huge habitat.

Why there? What attracted the eldar to a totally devastated world where even the air had all burned in a planet-wide inferno of firegas begotten from the rot caused by the life-eater virus? Great resources were being brought to bear.

Item, a certain Baal Firenze was requisitioning an expeditionary force of Space Marines to raid that habitat and disrupt the aliens' blasphemous plans.

Baal Firenze! Unless a namesake, this was the very same man who had once inducted Jaq into the Ordo Malleus.

Proctor minor of Jaq's chamber. His superior, who had sent him to Stalinvast. Member of the hydra cabal. To be still alive and active, Firenze must have been rejuvenated at least once. Therefore Firenze must have been exonerated of conspiracy – unless the conspiracy had sunk its claws deep in the very heart of Jaq's ordo.

Or unless Jaq's book of secrets had never reached its destination.

The fact of Firenze's activity was precious information.

An eldar event was about to occur around Stalinvast. And Firenze was intervening…

Firenze was intending to use regular Space Marines. (How could one possibly call such warriors ordinary?) Apparently he wouldn't use a unit of the Grey Knights from Titan, such as Jaq had used on Zeus V. Was Firenze unable to avail himself of the ordo's elite Knights? Ah, but Grey Knights did not generally fight mere aliens. They were destroyers of daemons. Perhaps daemonic outrages were occurring all over the galaxy and the Grey Knights were fully occupied in a dozen far-flung theatres of horror. Firenze's mission might be a relatively minor one. Jaq's instinct said otherwise.

Those 'assassinations'…

Not perpetrated by Imperial assassins, surely!

Then Fennix had eavesdropped on a message of vehement urgency phrased in incomprehensible language. This message was being repeated over and over. Thus, though Fennix was no cipher, he was soon able to parrot snatches of it…

And Meh'lindi had stiffened.

For the message – which she proceeded to interpret – was in Callidus code.

'Confirm report of apostate Tarik Ziz hiding on third planet of Whirlstar! Planet Darvash! Confirm report of heretic surgeons…'

Ziz had been Director Secundus of Meh'lindi's shrine of assassins, deputy only to the Supreme Director. How could Ziz possibly have become an apostate, betraying his allegiance? Was there a war within the Officio Assassinorum as well as within the Inquisition?

What's more, Ziz was still alive. High officials did not always relish death for themselves. In common with Firenze he must have undergone some form of rejuvenation.

It was Ziz who had ordered the surgical experiment upon Meh'lindi.

Had Ziz done so without the Supreme Director of Callidus knowing or approving? Had the Supreme Director discovered and disapproved strongly? Maybe surgical implantation such as Meh'lindi had endured had been declared anathema, even if the technique had fascinated Ziz. That technique of specialized body implants restricted the range of options for an assassin. More sinisterly, it meant that a seemingly normal human being could physically become a monster in the style of someone possessed by a daemon, and yet still remain virtuous.

What if an assassin were to infiltrate the sprawling labyrinths of the Imperial palace, and there transform himself or herself into a semblance of a ravening genestealer or a tyranid? Such panic might ensue!

Why, a certain assassin – Meh'lindi herself – had already done the first of these things. She had entered the Emperor's throne room with the shape of a genestealer hybrid hidden within her.

Tarik Ziz had been disgraced. Or rather, he must have *fled*…

* * *

THIS MUCH DID they glean from three months of astropathic snooping. A few frail threads of inklings.

'Stalinvast,' Jaq said slowly to Meh'lindi. 'That eldar habitat in orbit there. It's significant in some way...

'Take some doing to get inside *that*!' piped up Grimm. 'Huh, eldar *snobs*.'

Oh yes, there was ancient animosity between the elegant eldar and the rough-hewn dwarfs. Grimm wouldn't wish to go near an eldar habitation, would he?

The squat scratched his head. As his hair grew back, his pate resembled a red scrubbing brush. He seemed to be massaging his brains. 'These *Harlequins*, hmm? Crazy guys who stage big song and dance ceremonies...'

'Exactly how much do you know about Harlequins?' asked Jaq.

'Well, I could recite one of our shorter ballads on the subject, if I could remember all of the hundred thousand words.'

Baal Firenze was – or soon would be – heading towards Stalinvast to interfere with the eldar ceremony. Wherever Baal Firenze went was germane to Jaq's own tormented quest.

From within his gown Jaq took his Tarot deck. He stroked the wrapping of flayed mutant skin. Yet he did not unwrap the cards. Nevertheless, in that moment much became clear to him – save for one aspect, which must wait for elucidation.

Inquisitorial analysts regarded the eldar activity around Stalinvast as a blasphemy. Why, so it was, in the simple sense that alien intrusion into a corner of the cosmos which had recently been inhabited by human beings under Imperial sway was a desecration.

A deeper blasphemy would be for the eldar deliberately to stage one of their own sacred ceremonies in such a venue, exploiting the catastrophe which planet Stalinvast had suffered.

In the past the eldar had suffered racial cataclysm. Their own home worlds had all been devastated. Stalinvast was an emblem of devastation – one which the eldar dared to venture near.

Eldar Harlequins were intended to perform a sacred ceremony concerned with the devastation of a whole world...

The secrets of the eldar and the anguish of the human race were converging, so it seemed. Firenze, apostle of the hydra, intended to wreck that ceremony. The cabal's stated desire was one day to rid the galaxy of aliens – and of Chaos too – by means of a psychic tsunami, a tidal wave of mind-fire. The eldar would be among the victims of this mind-fire.

Who else but Jaq himself had been responsible for devastating Stalinvast?

Jaq said carefully, 'When Firenze and his warriors attack the habitat there'll be mayhem. We'll have a chance to get inside if we seem to be prisoners of an eldar–'

'Of an eldar aspect warrior?' Grimm groaned. 'Oh, my ancestors.'

'Or if we seem to be collaborators with the eldar…' Jaq eyed Meh'lindi with harrowing intensity. 'If we're to succeed, we need someone who can mimic an eldar.'

Once, Meh'lindi could have done so – using polymorphine to alter her body. Once – before Tarik Ziz had ordered the implants of the gen-estealer physique in her. The whereabouts of Tarik Ziz and his heretic surgeons were now known.

'I serve you,' Meh'lindi said simply. In her face there was no clue to her feelings. 'The name of that sun is Whirlstar. The name of that world is Darvash.'

Previously, she had been wont to say, 'I serve'. Now she had said, 'I serve *you*'.

Jaq had been holding his breath. His breath sighed from him in an exhalation of pity.

'Oh no,' said Grimm. 'Oh no.'

'Yesss,' hissed Meh'lindi. 'I wish to be free of the alien beast inside me.'

Did she dream of avenging herself upon Tarik Ziz, who was no longer her Director Secundus, and who therefore no longer commanded her sworn loyalty?

On Darvash seemingly there were rogue surgeons who could dissect Meh'lindi alive again, to slice and scour out what had once been inserted into her. She had once sketched for Jaq, in privacy, a mere out-line of the surgical atrocity which had been perpetrated upon her. To go through that process again, in reverse, would be abominable. To go through it in dubious surroundings would be terrifying. To persuade – or to force – Ziz to comply would require such ingenuity, such guile; or perhaps such brutal violence.

'I serve,' repeated Meh'lindi. Had she ever really defected from her shrine? If Ziz supposed that she still served the Callidus shrine which was hunting for his skin, that would pose such a problem. Naturally she would need to seem to serve Jaq, not her lethal guild.

'Whirlstar,' she said tonelessly to Azul Petrov. 'Planet Darvash.'

The Navigator frowned. He hadn't heard of that sun or that world. Unsurprisingly so. If the place was well known, would Ziz have hidden himself there?

On an ormolu-framed screen Petrov summoned the Gazetteer of Known Worlds. His fingertips touched the little icons, to scroll through the illuminated entries. Celestial co-ordinates which hopefully would be accurate. Descriptive notes which in many cases would be sheer legend.

'Ahem,' said Grimm to Meh'lindi. 'You do *speak* eldar, don't you?'

Of course she did! Prior to her earlier imposture she had learned that lilting alien tongue with her head in a hypno-casque. No assassin ever erased a language from her mind. Languages were weapons. Was not almost everything potentially a weapon?

'Emperor be with us,' prayed Jaq.

Let Whirlstar not be thousands of light-years and weeks of warp travel distant, or because of time-distortion Firenze might already have arrived at Stalinvast long before *Tormentum Malorum* could put in an appearance.

Besides which, there was the question of fuel.

'*Darvash*,' said Petrov presently...

No, not too far. Only a fraction of immensity away from the nowhere where they now drifted.

A WEEK LATER *Tormentum Malorum* was falling down the gentle gravity gradient within the inner haven of the Whirlstar system.

That lurid orange sun was rotating so rapidly that it wasn't a sphere but an ovoid, flattened at the poles and stretched at the waist.

Darvash spun quickly too. Its day was only ten standard hours. It was a desert world, of rust and ochre, bronze and apricot: a citrus-fruit pitted with eroded craters. Coriolis forces whipped frequent sandstorms across the terrain, obliterating landmarks. Remarkable that such a world possessed an atmosphere which was breathable when not choked with dust. Filter masks and goggles might be *de rigueur* – and really this would be ideal for maintaining an incognito.

According to cryptic notes in the Gazetteer, the atmosphere was artificial in the sense that photophagic microbes in the sands – nano-orgs – manufactured oxygen and nitrogen, somehow transmuting elements.

Deep in the past, before the human race had ever spilled across the stars, something had apparently visited dead dusty cratered Darvash and had introduced these nano-orgs to begin the process of rendering the planet habitable.

THIS PROCESS HAD ceased at an early stage. Here and there on the world, great enigmatic buildings sprawled, of sand bonded molecularly, tough as adamantium, their vast internal spaces braced with arches. It was in the gloom of these ancient edifices – lit by mirrors and glass cables – that human townships sheltered, hive-like tiers surrounded by food-gardens of phosphorescent fungi and algae.

Darvash was home, seemingly, to the 'sand dancers'.

There was only a single space port. But a single space port did at least signify fuel.

BEFORE LANDING, THERE were two problems for Jaq to resolve. So he cloistered himself in his sleep-cell with Meh'lindi.

Ever since the decision to find Tarik Ziz, she had uttered hardly a word. Was she honing her spirit for the ordeal which awaited? (Let that ordeal at least await her – and not prove spurious and unavailing!) Was she anticipating the devout destruction of Ziz on behalf of her shrine, after he had been of use – and of abuse – to her? Was she recalling how Ziz, prior to his presumed rejuvenation, had been rated omega-dan in fighting skills? She had performed her exercises relentlessly in silence.

'My brave assassin,' murmured Jaq, 'shall we let our astropath live, knowing what he now knows about us?'

Fennix might transmit what he knew to anyone in the Imperium. Had not a previous astropath, Moma Parsheen, cheated Jaq?

Meh'lindi considered the question. She was still wearing Sirian silk and curly slippers.

That body of hers, which had once solaced Jaq, and once only! For it to be cut apart so radically, albeit to free her from a lurking monster! Would the reverse-surgery even succeed? To be... deprived of her company... would be unfortunate.

She said, 'There is a bizarre relationship between Fennix and Azul Petrov.'

'Eye to eye, as it were?'

'Oh yes: blind eye to warp eye!'

Black gem, to poached egg... Both she and Jaq had observed this.

'It's a perverse bond, Jaq.'

A bond such as Jaq and Meh'lindi experienced, though of a different sort? Thus did Meh'lindi touch upon her own relationship with Jaq, and his with her. Theirs was a bond which they could not express openly on account of other loyalties. Hers, to what she was. His, to the salvation of humanity, and to Him-on-Earth...

'Our Navigator might be distressed if Fennix died,' she said. 'Besides, Fennix is becoming addicted to our hunt for truth.'

Jaq nodded sombrely. 'So we rely upon addiction as a guarantee of loyalty.'

She almost smiled. Almost. 'Addictions of one kind or another often guarantee fidelity.'

Did she imply an addiction, on her part, to Jaq? In this universe of deceit, maybe this was the closest that anyone could come to an avowal of affection or trust.

'Anyway, Jaq, you might need Fennix urgently some time in future to send a telepathic message.'

A message to whom? To the vast schizoid multi-mind of the Emperor?

Jaq sighed. 'This brings us to the matter of our faithful abhuman.'

Oh yes, the puzzle of Grimm, turning up like a good penny on Luxus Prime...

'I hadn't wanted to confront this matter prematurely. Not until I had the measure of Petrov, and could be confident he isn't a stooge.' Jaq gestured at a small lacquered cabinet inlaid with hex signs. 'It was my intention to dose Grimm with veritas and question him. Now I find that the remaining ampoules of the drug have vanished.'

Meh'lindi nodded. 'Hexes would not deter Grimm.'

'So Grimm must be compelled to confess the truth by some other means.'

Must they now torture Grimm? He, and Meh'lindi! Jaq's collapsible excruciator had been lost on the Chaos world, but between them an inquisitor and an assassin could think of other methods.

'Oh, why did he dispose of the veritas? The absence of those ampoules incriminates him so! Did you study torture in your shrine, Meh'lindi?'

'I'm acquainted with pain,' she said simply.

'Aye, pain; and how to overcome it. Grimm won't know how, unless he was deeply tampered with during all the years which have gone by. In our Inquisition,' he confided, 'we study the history of torment. Really, the history of Mankind is the history of torment. Our Inquisition recommends the virtues of pain, even though speedy obliteration of heresy is generally our goal. The problem is that torment can elicit sheer fiction in the name of truth. A tormented victim will often invent anything he hopes will ease his physical agony. Torture frequently negates itself.'

'He must be tormented,' she said, 'in his imagination. His own fantasy must torment him.'

'Ah, you understand...'

'My own imagination tortures me, Jaq. The spectre of the beast within me – soon to be cut out! I never forget how I was tormented by pleasure at the hands of Zephro Carnelian. That was an ordeal I was never trained to resist! Yet,' and her voice sank to a whisper, 'you helped exorcize me.'

Jaq shuddered. Did she imply that on that unprecedented occasion when she and he had made love, as the expression was, she had experienced, cleansingly, the opposite of ecstasy?

'I don't suppose,' said he, 'that Petrov could have slunk in here and disposed of the veritas, for some reason that I don't understand?'

Petrov would first have needed to know what veritas was. He would have needed to know that Jaq kept truth in an ampoule – and to be scared of interrogation.

'How about me myself?' Meh'lindi asked him slyly.

Thus she reminded Jaq that no one could ever really know another person totally; and that doubt must always remain, festering amidst universal loneliness. Not even the Emperor had known His own self fully.

GRIMM WAS IN the engine room, mumbling some squattish ballad as he polished.

The barrel-vaulted chamber reeked of sacred oil and ionization and hot insulation, though not of incense. Electrocandles imparted a jaundiced glow to the fluted rune-painted turbines, capacitors and accumulators. Cables like the web of a titanic spider led to the cores of the great warp-vanes. Ornamented dials glimmered with icons. Since *Tormentum Malorum* was currently falling towards Darvash, the main engines barely hummed, on standby, though the gravity generator was droning.

Jaq sealed the adamantium bulkhead hatch behind them. No noise would reach the Navigator or the astropath.

He seized the abhuman in a grip which hardly permitted Grimm to move, though his heels drummed the deck.

'What's the matter, what's the matter–?'

From her sash Meh'lindi pulled some silk with which she blindfolded Grimm. Working around Jaq's shifting grip, she peeled off Grimm's flak jacket. Then she divested him of his coverall, and finally of grey calico drawers worn beneath.

Grimm was bare but for his red beard and the smaller beard fronting his loins.

'Oh, my ancestors!'

Meh'lindi's fingertips roved in a dire parody of the art of the courtesan.

THE SHEER EXPECTATION...

The imagination: a person's worst enemy...

She touched Grimm gently on a nub of nerves. How he shrieked. How he babbled. He confessed that he had poured the veritas into the fuel expansion basin, from which it had trickled to mix with the octanes.

'A little truth goes a long way, eh?' Jaq murmured into Grimm's ear.

At no stage did Meh'lindi actually hurt Grimm with her fingertips or teeth or tongue. Yet his fantasy excruciated him. Writhing, the abhuman screeched, and begged.

'I'M TELLING YOU, Jaq boss, Carnelian contacted me, no not on Luxus, before that, and he's really an Illuminatus!'

Whatever in all the worlds was an 'Illuminatus'?

'Carnelian was a psyker who was possessed,' gabbled Grimm, 'but he managed to throw off his possession through his own willpower and with the help of some eldar Harlequins–'

Ha!

'–as well as by the grace of the Numen!'

The Numen? What was that?

Grimm shrieked: 'The shining path! It's a force of goodness and strength that will congeal one day into a power.'

Another daemonic god!

'No, it'll be a radiant Power, boss, I swear, but it's only a foetal thing now, trying to grow, so Carnelian says, and it's the opposite of what'll happen if Homo Sap goes crash, and the opposite of what went wrong for the eldar, I think, though I'm not too sure, but Slaanesh is what went wrong with the eldar 'cos they were too snooty and sensual and got themselves addicted to all sorts of lusts–'

Grimm groaned with a great pang. 'Doesn't surprise me about those snobs! Their Harlequins keep an eye on outbursts of Slaanesh 'cos Slaanesh will consume them all if it can, I think they're terrified of that happening, says Carnelian, so they sometimes use people they've bought or persuaded to spy on cults, like I was doing on Luxus, only not spying for the snobs themselves, I'm a squat after all and proud of it, but for Carnelian 'cos he convinced me, and 'cos you might have shown up again somewhere in the vicinity, and Carnelian was leading you, leading you, 'cos rogue Illuminati are in control of this hydra caper, and inquisitors are mixed up in it, like we know, and they gotta be disrupted–'

Rogue Illuminati? How Grimm babbled. Was he about to commit suicide by asphyxiation? Would he hyperventilate himself to death?

'Yeah, you see the Illuminati are immune to powers of the warp, so they can manipulate warp energy safely, that's how they brought the hydra into existence, I mean that's how the rogue Illuminati did it, hoping to mind-fuse everyone in the galaxy some day and even tame Chaos and enslave it, but they're wrong about that 'cos *then* the Numen will never be born and the shining path will never shine, and what'll happen'll be the awakening of the fifth great Chaos god out of humanity's torment, that's what terrifies the eldar, says Carnelian, 'cos they know what it was like last time, when Slaanesh awoke, but this'll be worse, this'll be the end, there won't just be the Eye of Terror bleeding corruption into the galaxy but the whole galaxy will become Chaos from end to end, and what other Illuminati like Carnelian are striving for is for the Numen to be born instead. How's that to come about, you may be asking, why it's by finding and protecting all the Emperor's Sons what he conceived long ago long before his carcass got stuck inside the golden throne–'

'Beware of blasphemy, abhuman!'

'–'cos these Sons are immortal but they don't none of them know who their dad was, oh my ancestors–'

'Take care!'

'–and neither does his carcass know anything about them 'cos they're psychic blanks, which is how they've been able to hide out for so long–'

Captain Eternal… The wandering inquisitor… Folk-tales about certain mysterious figures who had appeared and reappeared throughout many millennia! Sheer folk-tales! Was this any verification of what Grimm was burbling?

Jaq reeled, dragging the squat a pace or so with him. He swayed, and Meh'lindi's fingernail did indeed scrape Grimm in a sensitive part so that the little man howled appallingly.

Illuminati… Emperor's Sons… Jaq had never heard of such persons. Did even the Ordo Malleus hold secret records about these personages, locked under a seal of heresy? How Jaq doubted it!

'–that's even though your blessed Inquisition hunts the Sons down, 'cos you inquisitors think the Emperor's Sons are just sinister mutants, so do the Sons themselves, but the Illuminati are seeking them out too and enlightening them, so that the Sons can join a special order of knights. The Illuminati call the wised-up Sons sensei, and these sensei are all becoming part of a long watch of knights who'll intervene when the Emperor finally succumbs and Chaos tries to flood in, then I think they'll take over from the Emperor because they all have His gene-runes in them, even though the Sons themselves are sterile, so you see there are all these offshoots of your Emperor scattered around the galaxy, that ain't all, 'cos when your Emperor fought the Chaos armies of Horus all those thousands of years ago before He was crippled in victory and put in His golden throne the only way He could win was to renounce all His soft tender feelings and purge these out into the psychoflux, into the warp, I mean, and these lost parts of Him are what's trying to come together as the Numen, to bring us the shining path, that's what the sensei knights will summon into being for salvation when the Emperor finally flakes it–'

Sensei knights! Jaq felt stunned. Before becoming part of the Ordo Malleus had he himself ever hunted down and extinguished one of those unacknowledged Sons of Him-on-Earth?

There had never even been a hint that such persons existed.

'–the Emperor mustn't ever learn about his Sons, the sensei knights, even if He could believe it when they're all a blank to Him, 'cos then He might relax His overwatch premature-like, and the sensei mightn't be ready enough, you see, so the Numen might be aborted in the flood of Chaos–'

Illuminati… Sensei knights… Was this a case of let the lie be so amazing that no one can doubt it?

'–the rogue Illuminati are impatient even though their own hydra scheme, is bound to take centuries, 'cos you scheme, Illuminati can be pretty fanatical after what they suffered at the hands of Chaos, getting possessed then managing to break free, and what scares other Illuminati like Zephro Carnelian is the hydra cabal succeeding disastrously and all too soon before the long watch is ready to take over, that's why the good Illuminati are trying to sabotage the hydra plot and stir trouble, specially as secret inquisitors are involved in the plot, which is why Carnelian led you that dance–'

'Enough!' Jaq bellowed.

Supposing that these Illuminati existed, and were capable of fanaticism on a cosmic scale, why then should one believe in 'good' Illuminati? In Illuminati of purity who were presiding over a long watch which would benevolently render Him-on-Earth superfluous? This might be an even more devious plot than that of the hydra cabal! Supposing that these unprecedented Illuminati existed…

In the absence of any veritas, verification was impossible. Had Grimm spilled the truth-drug into the fuel so that when he was finally forced to babble there could be no check upon his claims? No check other than by finding Zephro Carnelian again.

What the little man now believed wasn't necessarily the truth at all.

'When did you last meet Carnelian?'

Why, Grimm had already said. It was because of the eldar interest in Slaaneshi infestation of Luxus.

'How did the eldar learn about Luxus Prime?'

'Zephro said some of the eldar can see the future–'

Oh, so the Harlequin Man was 'Zephro' now, an intimate of Grimm's! Grimm had been willing to assist a human agent of the eldar even though with squattish disdain he viewed the aliens themselves as snobs.

'How did you communicate with Carnelian?'

There would be a human courier now and then...

'Did you know what the eldar are planning at Stalinvast?' (Aye, at *Jaq's* Stalinvast! The world he allowed to be destroyed.)

'No no no, boss, honest–'

Let Jaq follow his nose, and if he became sufficiently *illuminated*, then he might be worthy of another taunting, perplexing encounter...

If Grimm had told Carnelian all about Jaq, then veritas could have been mentioned. Jaq could almost hear the Harlequin Man's mocking voice: 'Oh, do get rid of any that's left, there's a good fellow, Grimm. Do bemuse our seeker for truth so that his wits will be really sharpened!'

Had Grimm ever told Carnelian about Meh'lindi impersonating an eldar? Adopting an alien guise sufficiently well to fool humans, at any rate... Futile to ask Grimm even under this devious species of torture!

'It's enough...'

Jaq released his hold on Grimm. He pulled the blindfold loose.

Grimm sagged, and almost fell. With his clumpy yet nimble hands he protected aspects of his nakedness at last. Then he peeped up and down himself, amazed to find that he was intact.

Meh'lindi stooped over him, so predatory.

'*Huh*,' she said delicately into his ruddy face. That tiny explosion of breath almost blew him over.

Grimm grabbed for his drawers and his coverall. His teeth chattered.

'It's all in a g-g-good cause, boss–'

A *good* cause? Good?

'The shining path, boss–'

Jaq sighed deeply. 'Oh, you naïve little man. The only cause is His-on-Earth's.'

The cause of the ever-dying God-Emperor.

Could Jaq truly believe that, either? In his incredulity was his belief. In his scepticism was his faith.

In the light of the electrocandles Grimm was florid all over. The smell of hot insulation seemed to be that of his own inflamed nerves and muscles and sweat. Grimm might have been reprieved from a roasting alive.

However, it was his recent tormentress whose flesh must soon be torn open. If fortune favoured her.

EIGHT

ASSASSIN

Flechettes zipped past the crouching trio.

Fleshettes might be a better name for these tiny darts. Their flanges spinning too fast to see, they would mince any flesh they met.

The gang which had ambushed Jaq and Meh'lindi and Grimm was at least twenty strong. They had pinned the trio in a crater by the base of a vast gritty column. All of the gang were using handbows. They had to reload their handbows after each shot. However, the ambushers were firing turn by turn from behind ruined walls, observing some sort of discipline.

A flechette had impacted in the back of Grimm's flak jacket, and had torn through the reinforcing metal fibres. Momentum and spin had been lost, but the dart's point pricked Grimm's back irritatingly. He fumbled over his shoulder for the shaft. Lucky shot, or duff part of the jacket. Damnably the dart seemed lodged. His groping fingers couldn't gain enough purchase. At least by now he could be sure that the dart hadn't been doped with a paralytic poison.

With his other hand Grimm loosed shots from a boltgun inaccurately in the direction of those ruined walls: *RAAARK-pop-SWOOSH*.

The boltgun, a twin to Jaq's, and plated in shimmery titanium embedded with silver runes, was named on the trigger guard: *Emperor's Peace*. It belched explosive bolts.

This gun and *Emperor's Mercy* – ancient, precious weapons, both of them must have been lovingly crafted long ago by some devout artisan of the Adeptus Mechanicus as part of a set celebrating the attributes of Him-on-Earth.

Before handing the weapon over to trustworthy Grimm from out of the armoury cell in *Tormentum*, Jaq had harangued the blunt-spoken squat lest he not treat the gun with appropriate respect.

A flechette had torn open Jaq's glove of saurian-skin. Blood dripped. He was firing *Mercy* left-handed, though economically. He wouldn't waste bolts on walls even if the explosions did blast out shrapnel and splinters. *RAAARK-pop-SWOOSH*. A flechette whined past his ear like an angry hornet.

Meh'lindi had caught a dart in her right arm. For several reasons she wasn't wearing synthetic skin. If she was spotted by the wrong eyes, syn-skin might be misinterpreted. It might seem that an assassin of the Callidus shrine was seeking Tarik Ziz with deadly intent. Another reason was that her exposed flesh was destined to be cut – if she was fortunate.

She wore a long grey cloak over her assassin's cling-tight tunic, and seemed to be some pilgrim.

The girth of the pillar by which they lurked was such that it could almost have swallowed *Tormentum Malorum* entire. Grainy in texture, and gloomy in the diffused light, the pillar soared upward two kilometres to a vault. There, mirrors were slung, reflecting distant daylight from optic tubes which originated outside the enormous building.

Other such columns marched into the distance. Many of these were hidden, except towards their summits, by the linked tiers of habitations braced around them. The vast shell within which the city heaped itself was a gargantuan cavern. Dilute illumination was leprous. Had light been brighter, the pillars might have shone golden. They were com-posed of sand – sand which had been bonded by some alien energy field of unknown nature. Thus had the cavernous structure sustained itself for ten thousand years. For a million years? No one knew.

The human city was named Overawe. All its people were parasitical, of necessity, within this unnatural cavern. Ordinary habitations in the open upon Darvash could be destroyed by sand tornadoes. The tech-knowledge and litanies for rearing independent hive-cities into the clouds did not exist upon Darvash. Consequently the hives of human-ity sheltered within abandoned alien colossi.

To the Darvashi people did these colossi seem like sanctuaries? Or more like traps, which might betray them? Fortresses of sand, which might suddenly collapse into tonnes of grains and grit! Some pillars, such as the one they sheltered by, remained uninfested by piles of sand-brick buildings. Jaq and his companions had already seen robed figures whirling around at the base of another such pillar, ululating and gash-ing themselves and each other with miniature knives worn as extensions to their fingernails. Those sand dancers had been performing a rite – in the Emperor's name – so that pillars and vault would maintain their impervious solidity…

Within Overawe, there appeared to be a peculiar etiquette to weaponry. Flechettes were acceptable. Handbows. Shuriken pistols. Weapons which fired darts or discs which spun swiftly just as the planet itself spun, and as its sun spun. Noisy explosive weaponry seemed to be taboo, as if violent shocks might disrupt the molecular bonds of the pillars and the vast roof.

When waylaid by this gang, what choice did Jaq and Grimm have but to use *Emperor's Mercy* and *Emperor's Peace*?

Were all visitors fair game, or did those gang members perhaps view the owners of such noisy weapons as impure? Other furtive masked figures were hurrying to join the attack, ducking along behind heaps of debris or trash.

The masks worn by the gangsters depicted great pouting lips the size of a face, with concealed eye-lenses and breathing vents. These lips would *consume* their enemies.

Meh'lindi tore the flechette from her arm. Blood welled. Already she was muttering a prayer of coagulation and constriction. She plucked Grimm's dart from his back, ripping a hole in his flak jacket. She squeezed a toxic needle on its way as Lips exposed themselves. Lips swallowed the needle. One of the attackers was whirling, whirling, arms flung out, spinning around. Then he flopped.

Jaq's head still hummed with arcane names.

Illuminati. Sensei knights. The Numen.

Put those out of your mind for now!

Or else die, at the hands of these Darvashi hooligans, who might regard themselves as devout.

THE LANDING FIELD had proved to be a broad mesa of rock rising steeply above the desert sands near the colossus. Great pits had been cut in that flat-topped table of stone, not by human hands but by those of the colossus-builders. If sandstorms threatened, massive stone lids on frictionless bearings could be swivelled to cap the berths for starships. In serpentine tunnels around the pits were servicing facilities and reservoirs of fuel.

The last stage of descent from orbit had been through moderate gritty winds which must be only a mild breeze for Darvash. Just prior to landing they had seen only a solitary freighter ensconced in one of the pits. In another silted pit there lay an ancient wreck.

On disembarking, Jaq had commanded refuelling in the Emperor's name. The port authorities, such as they were, had obeyed. In caverns presumed to have been carved by the colossus-builders were a subterranean promethium well and a refinery.

Petrov and Fennix had remained on board *Tormentum Malorum*. Perhaps right now they were gazing into one another's eyes, blind eye into warp-eye, warp-eye into blind eye. Perhaps they were murmuring to each other about the universality of telepathic sendings or about the way in which a warp-eye contained the whole galaxy within itself.

Anyone ordinary witnessing this warp-eye would instantly be destroyed. Did the sanction apply to Petrov himself? Oh, he was immune to himself, so he claimed. To stare into a mirror at the reflection of his own warp-eye wasn't an act of suicide.

Nor would it provide *him* with a revelation.

What if he stared into another Navigator's exposed warp-eye?

Petrov had refrained from answering. This was private to Navigators. Yet one sensed that Azul Petrov regarded his own warp-eye as uniquely special, blessed with an exceptional destiny.

For transfer by heavy crawler to Overawe, the trio had worn filter masks and goggles. In Overawe itself, such protection was despised. Nevertheless many of the denizens wore grotesque decorative masks.

How to know whether any of those masks hid agents of Tarik Ziz, keeping watch on arrivals? Anyone he had trained would be a master of disguise. Here, such mastery seemed almost irrelevant.

Jaq had decided that filter masks and goggles, worn inappropriately, would be more of a beacon than an incognito.

Who had informed the Officio Assassinorum of Ziz's whereabouts? Someone hiding behind a mask, even more stealthily than any of Ziz's agents?

Was Ziz aware that the Callidus shrine suspected his presence here? Jaq would need to gamble that the former Director Secundus did not know.

'If one of our assassins is here keeping watch,' Meh'lindi had assured Jaq, 'she'll be virtually invisible.'

'She, or *he*,' Jaq had reminded her. She had been too long on her own, with Jaq. A hundred years too long. In stasis, time had deposited itself upon her heart like a drift of dead creatures settling upon an ocean floor.

Through the stacked sombre markets and workshops and fungus gardens of Overawe they had pursued the discreetest of enquiries, exploring the crowded multi-tiered terrain of that artificial alien cavern, keeping their eyes open.

The local dialect of Imperial Gothic was a compressed rush of consonants. On this sandy world vowels had virtually dried up. Tarik Ziz's name would be 'Tuk Zz' – not that Jaq or Meh'lindi voiced that name, which the apostate would hardly be using. Imperium was 'Mprm'. It took a while even for Meh'lindi to mimic the compressions of the speed-speech. Jaq couldn't master it. If the space port, such as it was, had not employed several interpreters, how could it have functioned at all? The Darvashi seemed almost insectoid in their utterances, as if dry sticks rubbed together rapidly in their throats.

The trio had strayed too far in their investigation of Overawe. Flechettes said so. This area was derelict, a haunt for riff-raff.

RAARK-POP-SWOOSH, spoke Grimm's gun.

–*thud-CRUMP*.

Lips exploded, brain mushrooming through a mask. The attackers chittered agitatedly. Like a horde of rats, more had arrived.

The gravel trench around the base of the column was shallow, barely affording protection. Had a flamer been brought to bear, Jaq and his companions would have been roasted.

However, there was an etiquette regarding weapons – against which Jaq and Grimm were offending.

Jaq crawled closer to Meh'lindi.

'I want you to shout that we are going to empty our boltguns into this pillar behind us – unless they all pull back.'

'Hey, boss,' protested Grimm, 'it might collapse.'

Meh'lindi relaying the message loudly. *'Blt gns. Pllr!'*

A stridulant outcry arose.

Squirming around, Jaq pointed *Emperor's Mercy* at the vast column so close behind. He shut his eyes tight. He squeezed once.

–*thud-CRUMP!*

A ripple passed up the bonded sand to a height of fifty metres or more. A shock wave of distorted air was sliding up the outside of whatever energy-membrane maintained the sand in its density and permanence.

From the attackers came a howl of horror. In a trice the Lips – forty and more of them by now – had quit their cover. They came rushing pell-mell towards the crouching trio. Tossing their handbows aside as they raced, they dragged darts from their bandoleers to brandish as claws.

They raved insensately: 'G'DS L'G B' STR'NG! G'DS L'G B' STR'NG!' *God's Leg Be Strong...*

Let not the pillar give way! Let the sand stand firm!

Charging, they yelled at that pillar as if it were a limb of some giant elephantine deity in whose shadow they lived their lives. With bolts, with laser pulses, with toxic needles, Jaq and Grimm and Meh'lindi fired again and again.

Lips flopped, cut down.

Fifteen of them. Twenty.

Another five.

Three more.

Half a dozen of the Lips threw themselves into the trench, stabbing with darts. Darts impacted in Jaq's shoulder, ripping his gown, stiffening his mesh armour, barely missing his neck. Darts ripped into Grimm's flak jacket. Meh'lindi had tossed her first assailant aside, so that he broke his neck. Though a body bore down on *Emperor's Mercy*, Jaq fired the gun. He was rocked and bloodied by the detonation, as his attacker lost a leg. Grimm butted with his ruddy scrubbing-brush head and clubbed with *Emperor's Peace*. Meh'lindi chopped a wrist, then a neck.

And silence fell.

A few moans came from injured Lips lying at a distance, cut down but not killed. Otherwise: peace.

And then a tall cloaked figure, masked with lips, peered circumspectly from behind a broken wall. Of a sudden the person divested himself of the mask.

Jaq imagined that he was seeing the mocking face of Zephro Carnelian. That hooked chin, that long jutting nose, those green eyes like chartreuse and ice...

Yet though the man's features were angular, he wasn't Carnelian. His brown hair was close-cropped. His eyes were grey and unworthy of much attention.

He called out some words which meant nothing to Jaq.

And Meh'lindi called in reply, just as incomprehensibly.

A brief exchange of unintelligible dialogue occurred. The man moved into clearer view, pacing lithely and warily.

'He's a Callidus assassin,' Meh'lindi muttered in mumble speech.

It was assassin code they had been talking in. Once he approached, they were soon consulting in Imperial Gothic.

THE MAN DID not disclose his name. Nor did Meh'lindi confide her own. He remained extremely alert. Nevertheless, she had apparently convinced him that their shrine had despatched her to Darvash on account of Tarik Ziz.

If anything she said jarred slightly, that was because she had been placed in stasis by her shrine. She was one of Ziz's earliest experiments in implantation – which subsequently had been deemed anathema. In her body, activatable by polymorphine, was the shape of a genestealer hybrid...

The man had merely nodded. His nod was pregnant with understanding. The nod also betrayed, to Meh'lindi at least, that the man did not connect this self-proclaimed victim of Ziz with any bygone assassin who had vanished and might have become rogue. Her surmise was correct that Ziz must have erased records regarding her or concocted false ones. The archives of the Officio Assassinorum, as of the Inquisition, were steeped in secrecies, and just as labyrinthine.

To her, by the grace of the Callidus shrine, belonged the honour of terminating Ziz. Hers, the privilege of manifesting her terrible secret shape, and killing Ziz with his own tormented former tool, herself.

Jaq fully believed what she was saying. It was probably true that Meh'lindi would try to kill Ziz subsequent to surgery upon her, now that Ziz was an apostate. In this regard she would genuinely be loyal to her shrine. Jaq struggled to bear in mind that her truths were lies.

According to Meh'lindi, her shrine planned that she should pretend to be a renegade who had escaped from the shrine after long confinement in stasis. She would beg Ziz to reverse what had been done to her. Ziz would be challenged by the difficulty of this. The shrine had injected her with a long-lasting antidote to metacurare. Thus she wouldn't be paralysed during surgery upon her mutated body. Undoubtedly Ziz would observe this procedure at closer and closer quarters. By willpower she would block the pain of dissection. At a crucial moment, when her body was half-dissected and all Ziz's caution was dispelled, she would rear up and kill. Assassins could still slay with two arms broken, and a leg broken, could they not? Supreme effort, supreme vengeance! Callidus would be satisfied.

Was Meh'lindi a mite extravagant in her outline of this grotesquely ambitious revenge? Her supposed plan seemed on the very borderline of physical possibility – revoltingly so!

All the man said, drolly, was, 'Are you sure, sister, you are not on loan from the Eversor shrine?'

Eversor assassins boosted their bodies to superhuman exertion with a suicide drug, immolatin...

The man confided that Tarik Ziz was secluded within a hive-colossus named Sandhouse three hundred kilometres southward across the desert. There, he was known by the name of Jared Kahn. A rich man.

Very rich. (Had he not brought some of the shrine's treasury with him?) He was almost impregnably rich. (Though what was impregnable to an assassin?) He was never seen in public.

Why, enquired the man, was an inquisitor – for such Jaq must be – accompanying Ziz's avenging angel?

Grimm had been using *Emperor's Peace* to scratch a crease in his regrowing hair where his scar was. Tutting at his disrespect, Meh'lindi idly relieved him of the gun. Suddenly she fired a bolt, then another, and a third into the Callidus agent. The man was thrown backwards upon the rubble, already dying from internal explosions. Blood soaked through his cloak.

Warily, Meh'lindi knelt by him, the boltgun pressed against his face.

'I'm sorry, brother,' she said.

That face twisted with ultimate effort. The man seemed to summon a faint word before he relaxed into oblivion.

Meh'lindi lifted his left hand which had clenched. She prised middle and fourth fingers apart. Her tongue darted into the notch. She licked, she scrutinized. Then she cracked those fingers apart and buried her mouth in the cleavage to bite.

Rising, she spat a slice of the man's flesh on to her palm, and showed this to Jaq. On the skin which had been between the base of the two fingers was a tiny tattoo of an eyeball cupped inside a letter 'C' in Gothic script.

'The cunning eye of Callidus...' Her saliva had made the miniature tattoo visible. 'I shall show this to Ziz to prove that I eliminated someone who had accidentally stumbled on his whereabouts.'

'What did the man say finally, Meh'lindi?'

She frowned. 'He said *mistake*. Oh yes, he made a mistake. And yet... he seemed almost to be warning me of something – as one assassin to another.'

'Is Ziz not in Sandhouse after all? Isn't he going under the name of Jared Kahn?'

'I'm sure he is. I'm sure that's true. It must be something else that my colleague was holding back. You realize I had to kill him as soon as he began enquiring about you.'

'Of course you had to.'

'Something about my supposed assassination plan also jarred with him.'

WHAT MIGHT THAT something be? Something intimately connected with Ziz – something which they would not discover for another week – by which time they had reached Sandhouse by lumbering land-train across a desert swept by gales which whipped up blinding clouds of grit.

THOSE GALES WERE only moderate breezes for Darvash, no disincentive to a shielded land-train which was navigated by dead reckoning and by litanies and with the assistance of radar.

No bands of mutants roamed the deserts of Darvash, preying on transport as on so many other worlds. Any such mutants would soon enough have been scoured to skeletons by any stiffer squalls.

Grimm worried that they might be stranded in Sandhouse for weeks or months if the wind blew stronger, though indeed they would need to remain there for several weeks. Meh'lindi wouldn't be able to walk for a while after dissection and resection.

Determined to communicate more effectively with these speed-speakers, Grimm struck up a rapport with the master of the land-train by offering a hand at tuning the motors. The master reassured Grimm about the weather forecast by casting runes carved on the hand bones of an explorer who had once been caught in a hurricane and stripped of his flesh. These bones now pointed the way of the weather, and helped safeguard the land-train.

Prognosis: fair. For a fair while.

Jared Kahn? Oh yes, heard of him. Came to Sandhouse in a big transport machine years ago. Rich as rubies. No one ever sees him face to face. Keeps to himself in a huge fortress along with several peculiar secretive companions...

Oh, and guards too. Lots of those.

JAQ SPENT MUCH time brooding and praying about what Grimm had confessed under duress.

Enough time had gone by for Jaq to attempt to achieve perspective, in a rational reassessment. Sceptical analysis was one of an inquisitor's most prized tools, along with his weapons and his faith. All too many people lived their lives in a state of delusion. All too many of the pious were rabidly and fanatically devout to the point of delusion too, or delirium. To see clearly required a very special soul.

What one must understand above all, for the sake of sheer sanity, was that there must always remain some unresolvable mysteries – the very existence of which often must needs be concealed. Ach, the Inquisition understood this keenly.

If Grimm were to be fully credited – and the trenchant little abhuman had certainly been convinced! – there existed a whole new level of meaning, and of manoeuvre and machination, to the universe.

Ten thousand years earlier, before His Holiness the crippled psychopotent schizoid Emperor was maimed almost to death and enshrined in His life-support throne, in His rovings of the galaxy He had spawned immortal Sons unbeknownst to Him – and still unbeknownst to Him, for uniquely those Sons were psychic blanks to their Sire.

Nor did those Sons know their parentage – until the coming of the Illuminati, those secret psykers who had suffered daemonic possession, and then struggled free. Blessed with transcendent understanding, and possessed henceforth only by a loathing of Chaos, these Illuminati were gathering in the Sons, who would form a psychic battalion of sensei. When the Emperor's inner light finally flickered out, and when the forces of darkness surged from the warp, these sensei would unite to summon a new protective divinity, the Numen, the shining path.

Some rogue Illuminati were too impatient and fanatical to await this outcome. In conspiracy with certain associates in the highest echelons of the Secret Inquisition, they had used their power to mould the immaterium of the warp to create the hydra entity to infiltrate the massed minds of humanity and create a psychic doomsday weapon – which might backfire. If it backfired, a fifth and final Chaos god could emerge instead of the Numen. Chaos would submerge the cosmos.

The eldar were involved with the supposedly 'benign' Illuminati, such as that trickster Carnelian.

Certain eldar seers could reportedly scry into the future.

Stalinvast, and the ceremony to be enacted there, was a pivot of cosmic consequence, a stage for vaunting hopes and ghastly fears – which Baal Firenze would invade, because the hydra cabal hoped to purge the galaxy clean not only of the peril of Chaos but also of all aliens too…

Though how had Firenze contrived to retain the confidence of the Masters of the Ordo Malleus?

While the land-train proceeded through the desert, Jaq analysed and re-analysed until his soul ached.

NINE
DREADNOUGHT

THE MASTER OF the land-train had been accurate about the fortress.

Under the two kilometre-high vault of vast Sandhouse, Jared Kahn's (or rather, *Ziz's*) citadel sprawled upward for half a kilometre and more of brick-clad plasteel canted against a pillar and partly enclosing it. Gargoyles jutted; the tusky tooth-crammed homicidal visages of orks. Had green-skinned alien pirates descended upon Darvash and raided Sandhouse at some time in the past? Had this stronghold been a bastion of human resistance? The citadel seemed ancient. Here and there, where sections of façade had loosened and fallen, the metallic under-fabric could be seen.

Was that substance not plasteel, after all, but adamantium? Difficult to tell in the crepuscular gloom. The towering half-cone of the edifice could probably resist the attentions of a battle cannon – not that the Darvashi would dream of allowing such a destructive weapon inside any of the colossi wherein they dwelled as parasites.

The citadel was at the southern end of Sandhouse, far from the land-train depot and just two pillars away from the massive perimeter wall.

Notions of battle cannons were irrelevant. Deceit was the key to entering Ziz's citadel. Honest guile.

Soon they discovered wherein lay the error of which the dying assassin had gasped.

In a colossal fan-vaulted hall, lit meagrely by a few electro-flambeaux and almost a quarter of a kilometre above the gateway, Jared Khan granted his visitors audience.

Jaq had told the guards at the gateway that he had certain precious information for the ears of their master alone. Cryptically Jaq mentioned *an assassin wearing Lips.*

Why, of course the master was intrigued. Naturally he would grant an interview after his visitors surrendered their weaponry. Information was protection. These informants need never emerge from the citadel again.

None of the guards who escorted the trio lingered in that great hall. What need of guards? Ziz was his own guard.

When Meh'lindi had last seen the erstwhile Director Secundus of her shrine, he had been a short compact swarthy man, of Grimm's stature or even more stunted – a lethally dangerous dwarf. Rune-wrought rings upon his sinuous fingers had contained tiny doses of powerful poisons and hallucinogens and paralytic toxins. His natural teeth had been replaced with canines coloured scarlet and black. That pygmy body was omega-dan, by all accounts. No master of martial arts could match it, except perhaps the Supreme Director of Callidus.

What now confronted her and Jaq and Grimm was literally a killing machine.

A machine twice the height of Meh'lindi. Its towering hull was made of ceramite – in so far as one could see the actual hull! Upon that resilient casing were hung hundreds, perhaps even thousands, of petite blades. Tiny archaic knives, some of them no larger than a fingernail. These hung like some glistening secondary razor-armour of steel swarf from lathes.

On one of the monstrosity's metal arms was mounted a power fist. This could pick up a man effortlessly and wring him dry, compressing him to the width of his spine. The other arm sported an assault cannon with six separate rotatable barrels which might spit hundreds of shells every second.

Crystal lenses regarded the intruders. A synthetic voice issued from a grille.

'I appreciate your surprise...'

Meh'lindi seated herself in a double lotus position upon the reinforced plasteel floor. She averted her eyes respectfully or in a convincing semblance of respect. She observed the ritual of obeisance even if no human being nor even a genestealer with its powerful claws could realistically launch an assault on this armoured mass with a hope of scratching it.

Scratch it, indeed! Irrespective of the impregnable ceramite hull, anyone leaping at this prodigy would be sliced to pieces by those blades.

Meh'lindi well remembered Ziz's collection of miniature vintage knives. These had decorated one whole wall in his quarters in the Callidus shrine. Now they ornamented the prodigious machine which confronted her. A pair of slim steel tentacles were coiled like whips below the armpits of those bulky limbs which sported the cannon and the power fist. Surely these whips could unfurl, pluck any knife from its position, and toss it.

Evidently this fighting machine did not indulge in target practice with knives within this hall. The metal walls of the hall were pitted but neither by knife points nor yet by decorative hammering. The monstrous machine must occasionally loose off a salvo simply to enjoy the percussion of ricocheting shrapnel.

'Am I not formidable?' asked the voice.

'So you are, Secundus,' agreed Meh'lindi. She retained her submissive posture.

'Secundus? Secundus? What is this?' The power fist flexed its massive metal fingers. 'Am I not Jared Khan?'

'You are Tarik Ziz,' she replied.

The power fist crushed empty air.

'How can anyone be sure what is within this dreadnought?'

Indeed, it was a dreadnought such as the fabricators on Mars still strove to fashion after ancient designs for the Emperor's knights.

'But, master,' she said, 'it is ornamented with Tarik Ziz's special collection of tiny knives.'

'Ornamented? Are these mere ornaments? One of the whips uncoiled lazily. Its tip wrapped unerringly round the tiny haft of one petite knife. Would the knife fly towards Meh'lindi? What drug or toxin might there be on the burnished blade?

There was such subtlety in the flexure of that whip. Yet the dreadnought was so brutally bulky. It must weigh many tonnes. How speedily could it manoeuvre within the confines – however ample – of such a citadel? On a battlefield, no doubt. But here indoors?

Was this Callidus? Was this cunning?

One must not underestimate the agility of this machine!

'Indomitable dreadnoughts are rare even among the Chapters of the Space Marines,' mused the synthetic voice, as if in answer to the unasked question. 'If the mortal body of a Secundus were failing, yet he wished to avoid the risk of amnesia which rejuvenation often causes – and if he wished to retain his faculties intact! – and if Callidus were enough to obtain such a supremely protective device…!'

The power fist opened up again. 'In the womb within this dreadnought a body curls foetally, preserved. Now I am this dreadnought body; and it is myself. So puissant, so invulnerable; much more than omega-dan.'

'That is Callidus indeed,' said Meh'lindi. 'It must have taken real cunning to relieve a Space Marine Chapter of one of these treasures.'

'Aye,' agreed the voice. Did Ziz recognize Meh'lindi yet? Did he realize that she, too, had lived beyond her natural span? Ach, there came a point in time when the most cunning villain must boast of his villainy. 'Aye, it took years of planning. And the sacrifice of numerous loyal assassins. Who amongst all of the Adeptus Mechanicus knows how to construct one of these dreadnoughts perfectly today? Small wonder that the best are reserved for revered Space Marine heroes whose bodies were beyond repair yet in whom life flickered on indomitably, still striving to serve the Emperor – heroes who now survive to His glory within such a living machine as this!' His tone, though mechanical, was almost ecstatic in its smugness.

'Great cunning indeed,' murmured Meh'lindi.

'Aye, and great cunning demands great protection.' The tentacle caressed a blade. The power cannon rotated slowly, humming. Electro-flambeaux flickered as if in awe.

Plainly it was not only – nor even principally – the matter of the vile implants which had caused Tarik Ziz to flee into hiding. Ziz had used the resources of the Callidus shrine to finesse the theft of one of these sacred antique dreadnoughts from a Chapter of Space Marines! Somewhere in all the worlds, amidst the pandemonium of battle against some overwhelming enemy, a dreadnought had been downed. A skulking team of dedicated assassins had spirited the dreadnought away with them aboard a ship; all because Ziz had ordered it.

Had the heroic foetal warrior's body inside the dreadnought even been fully dead? Or had the crippled dreadnought subsequently been opened up to expose that great puissant posthumous foetus and extract it, so that it expired?

The blasphemy of this.

Was Jaq sub-vocalizing a prayer?

Ziz's private activities in preservation of his own life and memories had vilely injured a Chapter of Space Marines – did they but learn of this, ever! He must have corrupted some tech-priests too, to repair and refurbish and customize the dreadnought to his specifications. Small wonder that the Callidus shrine were patiently seeking for Ziz.

And they had found him, here on Darvash.

To wish to inhabit such a device so as to survive with all his memories intact, Ziz must truly be a megalomaniac.

To wear – or rather to be – such a dreadnought, Ziz must be supremely paranoid.

Perhaps justifiably paranoid.

* * *

'MASTER,' SAID MEH'LINDI. She rose lithely, though slowly and discreetly. She was holding the scrap of flesh and skin which she had bitten from the murdered assassin. The scrap had dried. She licked it, reviving the tiny tattoo of the vigilant eye – and held this up towards those crystal lenses looming over her.

'Master, in Overawe I killed a Callidus man. He was following a scent of a rumour. I was following him, for my own reasons. Now he is dead and he cannot betray you.'

Dead, yes. She had killed her colleague so spontaneously. Yet the man had never been wholly fooled by her – until that final moment. What, fooled by a tale of herself planning to attack this… dreadnought, while enduring dissection! The dead assassin had been trying to determine her true purpose. So as to gain additional information for Callidus, he'd been willing to expose himself. Even in death he had tried to correct her mistake about the nature of Tarik Ziz – in the hope that she might actually kill the apostate Secundus.

All this while, Jaq had kept his counsel. Now he said to the dreadnought: 'Tarik Ziz, we have an astropath on board our ship. Our astropath is primed to send a message to your former shrine reporting your presence here if we do not return safely within forty standard days. If anyone attempts to gain entry to our ship, which is sealed and shielded, the astropath will likewise report.'

A crystal lens scrutinized Jaq. Could crystal seem cunning – and psychotic?

'Forty standard days,' repeated the voice. 'What do you wish from me which will take so long? How can I be sure that you will not betray me afterwards, in any event?'

'I swear it by Him-on-Earth, Tarik Ziz. I swear it in His holy name. We have no interest in your quarrel with your former shrine. That is no more to me than a flea in the hide of a cudbear."

'You must have some momentous mission, *inquisitor.*'

Jaq hesitated. Then he summoned a bitter laugh.

'A mission from no one at all, Tarik Ziz! I'm as much of a renegade as you are. What is it which drives the engine of the galaxy?'

'Terror and death,' suggested Ziz. Perhaps he meant terror *of* death.

'Also,' said Jaq, 'hiding in the cracks of horror, just like a flea on that bear, there is love. Or should we call it obsession? I am in love with – I am obsessed with – this assassin here.' What a disingenuous avowal! Especially if love consisted in delivering Meh'lindi up to appalling surgery… What a denial, besides, of true fidelity to Him-on-Earth.

Though expressionless, Meh'lindi bowed her head as if in shame.

'Meh'lindi,' said the voice, acknowledging her at last by her name. 'My talented chameleon... You see, I do remember. My faculties are not merely intact, but sublimely amplified.'

His *chameleon*.

What a poignant identification of her! Ziz had been responsible for denying her the expression of that talent which had freed her from herself, allowing her to mimic other roles and thus be more truly herself. Ziz had locked her into one possible option, and one alone: to masquerade as a monster!

'You have worn well, Meh'lindi,' said the voice, with a hint of angry envy.

'She was in stasis,' said Jaq dismissively. 'What I require for my love – or else we betray you – is that you remove the implants from her body. I wish that by using polymorphine she can assume any form – the most beautiful, ravishing forms.'

Grimm uttered a quiet groan.

'True love, indeed,' remarked Ziz. 'Yours might be a romance of legendary proportion, inquisitor.' Both of the steely whips caressed razor-sharp little knives. 'How fortunate for you that I have kept up with my pastime of experimental surgery. To remove such embedded, organically fused implants will pose quite a challenge...'

Surely this hulking dreadnought would not itself attempt such surgery using its tentacles and knives! That would be butchery. When originally Meh'lindi had been operated upon, several specialists had laboured hard and long, using intricate equipment which required the knowledge of many litanies. There had been a radiographer-adept and a chirurgeon, a soporifer-adept and a medicus...

'A challenge to your chirurgeons,' said Jaq emphatically.

The synthetic voice gurgled in what might have been a simulation of laughter. 'Never fear, I brought my sacred toys here with me, and their devout operators.'

Those peculiar secretive companions of his... Yes indeed.

'Yet I think I shall assist in the surgery,' added the voice. 'Who else but I knows best what was originally done?' The dreadnought raised a massive foot and Grimm flinched back. The abhuman was afraid of being squashed like a bug.

'I am filled with exhilaration by this opportunity to complete my experiment at last!' declared the voice. 'Existence has been a mite tedious lately, even with all my knives to appreciate and their histories to recall. How shall I best demonstrate my enthusiasm? Have you had opportunity to admire the sand dancers of Darvash?'

The dreadnought began to turn.

It stomped around in a circle, picking up speed.

The reinforced floor reverberated thunderously as the killing machine whirled, stamping its feet. It was dancing gargantuanly and grotesquely. Its massive steel arms rose like burly wings. The power fist pointed one way. The assault cannon, the other. Let the dreadnought not open fire over the heads of the three stunned spectators while it gyrated around, or they would be deafened, then disabled by the ricocheting spray. Extended, the steel whips lashed the air. The dreadnought was a monstrous animated idol. Surely they must be its worshippers.

Perhaps this bizarre display was a warning that the dreadnought was by no means cumbersome. Or else it was proof that Tarik Ziz was deranged.

The dreadnought ceased its dance.

'Forty days.' The voice sounded calm and calculating now.

'As I recall, the original implantation took six painstaking hours. Even if we use liberal applications of sanitas balm to promote speed healing, we must allow a week for recuperation from dissection and for post-operative scrutiny. I also presume that you did not travel here from your ship in less than a week. What contingency plans do you have, inquisitor, should a hurricane delay you seriously?'

'It won't, your magnificence,' piped up Grimm. 'Our land-train captain tossed the bones.'

The dreadnought regarded the squat as a cud bear might eye a fire-ant.

Jaq said hastily: 'Our astropath is briefed for all eventualities.'

As he said this, Jaq even believed it. Just so, on an earlier occasion during their intrusion into the Emperor's palace, he had pretended to be an inquisitor and then had realized, to his wonderment, that he was indeed just that, and none other.

'Our astropath is remarkable,' he added.

'I DON'T THINK you oughta go through with this,' Grimm muttered to Meh'lindi, once they were in the chamber hung with silks and carpeted with furs which Ziz had assigned as their hospitality suite.

Jaq frowned at the draped walls and at the glow-globes, and tapped his ear prudently.

'I am but an instrument,' murmured Meh'lindi. 'An instrument… of love.' Indeed this was true. She was trained as a courtesan as well as an assassin.

Do they not say,' she added softly, 'that love is often a torment?'

* * *

NEXT DAY, IT was Meh'lindi's old nightmare revisited – replayed in the setting of a plasteel cavern so brightly lit that light itself seemed like a scalpel blade.

Wearing masks impregnated with frankincense for antisepsis, Jaq and Grimm watched from behind a screen of stained glass. This made what transpired within the operating theatre appear devotional, a sacred ceremony. Truly it must be so were it to succeed. The fragrant masks hid most of the expression upon Jaq's face, and upon Grimm's, except for the horror in their eyes. In Jaq's case this must, to an observer, surely seem proof of his supposed mania for Meh'lindi.

Jaq was determined to watch, to scarify his soul. Grimm made a gruff show of being technically minded. The squat kept his eyes on the operating machines and not upon the subject of their operations.

Robed and tattooed, a tech-adept sat high on a lofty examinator machine, wired into its circuits. Brass-banded snouts scanned Meh'lindi as she lay spread naked upon the grooved table. From lens-eyes sprang holograms of her bloodstream and nerve network and skeleton, and, fluorescently, the glow of her implants.

In an arachnid-like soporifer-machine sat a wizened adept. He was monitoring the trickle of metacurare which immobilized Meh'lindi and blocked all sensation in case she flinched.

With one natural eye squinting obliquely at the holograms, and a magnificatory lens-eyes peering downward at her flesh, a servo-gloved chirurgeon manipulated the laser-scalpels dangling from a gantry.

Incense lazed in the brilliant light like some vastly more diffuse and mutating hologram of what might have been Meh'lindi, grey with shock.

A medicus intoned a litany.

A cyborged servitor patrolled – once human, and now reduced to a brass snail-shell mounted on little rubber wheels with muscular neck and goggling head protruding. The servitor was devoted to sucking up, with its long tongue, discarded tissue or fluids which leaked from the runnels of the table.

In soundproofed glass cages at some distance crouched various subjects of ongoing experiments.

At the head of the table towered the presiding dreadnought. Its long customized tentacles each held a miniature knife with which it pointed out angles of incision for the chirurgeon.

The extrudable reinforced plastiflesh and the flexicartilage, which had been inserted into Meh'lindi a century and more ago, were not the main technical problem. The 'clever' pseudoflesh which would assume the genestealer shape whenever triggered by an injection of polymorphine had sent invasive neural fibres deep into her anatomy. These fibres must be dissected out microscopically. Extra glands had also been inserted high in Meh'lindi's chest to synthesize growth hormone at great speed, and then to counteract it too.

Stubs of flexicartilage had been grafted to her vertebrae, and to many bones in her limbs. Her tongue had been cored to insert a collapsed imitation of a genestealer tongue. Her nose had been invaded. Her frontal teeth had been drilled and the roots replaced with fangplasm. Her skull had been trepanned and her arms and shoulders transected.

In stasis-tureens there awaited compatible pseudoflesh and synth-musclefibre and nervewires to replace what must be removed; and toothpulp and elastic dentine.

The operation lasted for ten standard hours; and throughout Jaq prayed. Grimm recited to himself a squattish ballad, which lasted equally long.

WHAT WAS TO stick in Jaq's mind most from the subsequent days of convalescence (first in the surgery reeking of incense, then in the silk-hung hospitality suite where frankincense also smouldered) was the sound of Meh'lindi recovering the use of her tongue.

She did so by practising phrases in the eldar language.

'Da gceilfi an fhirinne, b'flieidir go neosfai breag–'

'What's that mean when it's at home?' enquired Grimm. The little man was most industrious in his attentions to her while she lay prostrate.

'It means,' she whispered, 'if the truth were hidden, perhaps a lie would be told.'

'That sounds indisputable,' agreed the abhuman. He promptly eyed the silk hangings, as Jaq had done on that earlier occasion, and sniffed suspiciously.

Jaq shook his head. *Don't worry about Ziz eavesdropping on a few alien phrases through hidden audio buttons.* Jaq hadn't the heart to deter Meh'lindi from getting her tongue around language again. If she felt that she was betraying vital secrets she wouldn't have indulged herself. Was it not useful for Ziz to suspect that Jaq's intentions somehow involved aliens, and that Ziz was truly of no concern? Jaq was defecting with a heretic mistress from the human Imperium to alien society, where he could hide with her!

'We'll soon be safe, my love,' he breathed. 'You'll be so splendid.'

'Perhaps a lie would be told,' Grimm echoed, and Jaq cuffed him hard.

'*Bhi se chomh dorcha gur cheapamair go raibh an oichie tagtha,*' Meh'lindi pronounced fastidiously. 'It was so dark that we thought night had come.'

Aye, the darkness of existence – which is always so close to extinction and eternal night.

Eternal night might be a blessing compared with the nightmares which stalked the sea of souls.

MUCH HELPED BY sanitas balm, Meh'lindi was recovering. Fresh scars marked her skin like some dire map of savage initiation. These scars conformed where possible to the pattern of her tattoos. Lying alternately prone and supine, she resumed some isometric muscle exercises.

At last she was redeemed from the alien beast which had been within her. Yet a grief seemed to possess her. With his head pressed close to hers, Jaq consoled her in the softest mumble-speech which surely no audio button could detect.

Her problem: how could she possibly kill Tarik Ziz in retribution for a hundred years of alienation from herself? That long exile from her perfect talent for the transmutation of her flesh! Paradoxically, that talent had allowed her to be truly herself by undergoing bodily alterations. Ziz had robbed her of that great consolation.

And now Ziz had restored her chameleon talent.

How could she kill him?

She couldn't – not when he was sealed within that stolen dreadnought.

Nor could Jaq.

'Lady,' mumbled Jaq. 'We cannot fulfill a certain dream. And that deed would only be an irrelevance.'

Irrespective of his oath to Ziz, might they nevertheless send a telepathic message from deep space to the Callidus shrine? That would hardly amount to a personal reprisal. Personal satisfaction was simply vanity – a distraction from purity. Jaq had promised Tarik Ziz continued anonymity in the name of Him-on-Earth! What other pivot, what other frail solidity, was there in this tormented galaxy than faith in Him-on-Earth? The paralysed Emperor was as true a god as anyone might ever know.

At least until the coming of the Numen, of which Grimm had bleated… At least until the coming of the shining path which had once briefly guided Jaq.

Jaq had indeed glimpsed that shining path. He had travelled it for a while. That path had *not* been of the Emperor's making. Then the shining path had vanished – and there remained only Him-on-Earth.

Beware of false enthusiasms! Beware of deceitful revelations!

THUS MEH'LINDI HEALED. Presently assassin and inquisitor and squat bade goodbye to that citadel and to Tarik Ziz. Ziz was indeed impregnable – omega-dan, and more.

Up until the hour of their departure there was always anxiety that Ziz might merely be playing with them. He might be allowing false hope to fester – before surgically eradicating it.

But no. They were truly to leave.

During a final audience with the dreadnought, Ziz presented Meh'lindi with a syringe of polymorphine. The syringe was a mere shiny splinter lying upon the steel palm of that power fist.

'This is a bridal gift,' the synthesized voice explained. 'Go with your renegade inquisitor and your dwarf to gratify him amidst aliens. I release you from your Callidus vows, my fine chameleon.'

Release her from her vows? Ziz had released himself from all honour and duty!

Meh'lindi bowed. Calmly and slowly she reached to take the syringe from the open power fist. Was this when that fist would close upon her entire arm, crushingly and inescapably? Ziz's steel whips simply riffled across his little knives, causing them to tinkle like silver laughter.

'Go amongst aliens...'

Ziz had assuredly eavesdropped. Could it be that a piquant erotic fantasy tantalized that preserved body locked within the dreadnought? If so, then Meh'lindi had succeeded in bemusing a past master of Callidus.

'Be your inquisitor's bewitching instrument, my feral Meh'lindi!'

Jaq's instrument... It was she whom Ziz addressed, as though she were the initiator of Jaq's corruption. Thus Ziz's blessing was an ambivalent one.

As THE TRIO rode a land-train back towards Overawe, winds had screamed and airborne sand generally obscured any view. However, this was still far from being a Darvashi storm. At the space port those stone lids would still be open.

Meh'lindi hid the syringe in the little lavatorium aboard the land-train. Did the bridal gift contain pure unadulterated polymorphine? She had no intention of testing it to find out. In her sleep-cell aboard *Tormentum Malorum* she still possessed several ampoules of the drug. If some future passenger of the land-train came upon the syringe and injected himself in foolish expectation of euphoria, a report might well reach Ziz – about someone's untrained anatomy fluxing chaotically in a somatic fugue. Then her former superior would realize how Meh'lindi spurned Ziz's frustrated fantasia.

THE NAVIGATOR AND the astropath still seemed quite functional. Left alone together for so long, they hadn't become mystically intoxicated to an incapacitating extent.

And so *Tormentum Malorum* lifted into orbit. The fast-spinning planet seemed to throw the ship outward like a stone from a sling, away from itself and away from the squashed orange furnace of Whirlstar, towards the deep, towards the dark.

FOUR NIGHTS AFTER their departure, on the eve of reaching the jump-zone, Meh'lindi came stealthily to Jaq's sleep-cell, as once she had come before.

She was captivatingly beautiful.

Attired in her courtesan's costume of iridescent Sirian silk, she was several centimetres taller. Her limbs were long and elegant. Her golden eyes were slanted, her features so refined, with an austere sensuality, a blend of the ascetic and the voluptuous which could only fascinate compellingly. Such grace was in her movement and her gestures – for one who had been dissected and put back together. The fluid motion of her body, and of the silks she wore, was more than gorgeous. It was almost arcane, unearthly. Her head, a-tilt and angular. Her ears, just slightly pointy. She had styled one of her clingtight courtesan's wigs so that her brow was fully exposed and a long coaly tail of hair spilled back from the centre of her crown.

She had accomplished the change by willpower, by concentration, and by polymorphine, alone in her cell.

'Eldar lady,' whispered Jaq. 'Our captor.'

'Jaq,' she murmured, 'I find that I need to achieve full sensual attunement so that I can move as gracefully and as swiftly as an eldar.'

'Are you not doing so already?'

'I must be erotic, then I must pass beyond eroticism to the ethereal. Will you sanctify me, my lord inquisitor? Will you consecrate this instrument?'

'Yes,' whispered Jaq. 'In His honour.'

Meh'lindi dropped her Sirian silks to the obsidian floor. By the light of the glow-globe Jaq saw how her tattoos of snake and beetles and spider had faded. Those seemed to be mere mottlings of sublimely muscled skin, dappled as though she stood naked in a leafy grove shafted by golden sunlight.

Soon, the heart under the neat high breasts pressing against him beat quickly. Her lips breathed into his ear, 'My heart must beat faster to be an eldar heart.'

Soon, due to their ecstatic exertions… sinuous on her part, blunter on his – it did beat more swiftly.

'I consecrate you,' Jaq gasped.

Now IT WAS the dark morning preceding the leap through the sea of lost souls.

Azul Petrov marvelled at Meh'lindi in her new 'aspect'. She was wearing those silks and a silverfur stole, though her feet were bare. An 'aspect' was the name for any of the warrior traditions which an eldar chose to assume. The metamorphosed assassin's countenance and bearing were such an eloquent, persuasive aspect of herself. Easy to believe that such a person could take prisoner a burly inquisitor and a wizened Navigator and a squat and a telepathic runt.

Grimm chewed at his hairy calloused knuckles.

Petrov smoothed the shimmery grey damask of his robe, then he touched the ruby at the tip of his sharp chin.

'You need a spirit stone to wear around your neck,' the Navigator said to Meh'lindi. 'I would donate one, but my rubies are too small. Likewise those items of your own costume jewellery that I've seen. None quite large enough.'

Grimm burrowed in a pouch and pulled out a speckled pebble. 'Huh! Will this do? I picked it up on Darvash to fiddle with. A worry-pebble. Here.' Grimm thrust the pebble at Meh'lindi. 'Shall I bore a hole and thread a thong? Where do you wear these things?'

'Against her chest, under her garments, I believe,' said Petrov.

'Against her heart,' Grimm said glumly.

Petrov eyed the glittery flecks in the stone. 'That looks suitable. Those speckles are like scintillae of soul. Some silver wire would be best, cradling the pebble rather than piercing it.'

'I'll look in the engine room.'

'You need to choose an aspect,' Petrov told Meh'lindi. How it fulfilled that cobweb-grey fellow, carbuncled with rubies, that here was a mimic eldar!

'I'm aware of that,' she replied.

'You ought to be a Dire Avenger. They are the least specialized, the most common, I believe. I have gleaned many rumours in my star-travels.'

Meh'lindi nodded. She said something in the eldar language, which might perhaps have signified that she was not entirely ignorant on the subject.

'You'll have to make do without the psycho-sensitive armour – unless or until you can steal some. Aspect warriors can dress ordinarily, I believe, unless at war. If anything eldar can be described as ordinary!' Petrov's look implied that she was already sufficiently extraordinary.

Jaq cleared his throat. Petrov's fixations seemed to make the Navigator imagine that he could pre-empt the planning, as though this journey were for Petrov's private fulfilment.

'We have a shuriken pistol in our armoury,' said Meh'lindi. Thus she forestalled the Navigator's next likely suggestion.

'What eldar name have you chosen for yourself?' he pressed her.

Her faint smile was ominous.

'Mile'ionahd,' she replied. 'Warrior of wonder, warrior of surprise.'

'Ah, and will you fool the eldar themselves, irrespective of fooling me?'

'You're impertinent,' she told the Navigator. 'Mile'ionahd will be Callidus.'

Jaq asked impatiently, 'Are we at the jump zone yet?'

Petrov's cool green gaze interpreted the navigational icons. He tugged on his studded ear-lobe. Then he nodded.

'So let us pray,' said Jaq. 'And then: *on to Stalinvast.*'

TEN
BATTLESHIPS

CAPTAIN LEXANDRO D'ARQUEBUS of the Imperial Fists stood with Terminator Librarian Kurt Kempka on one of the observation terraces of the Gothic-class battleship *Imperial Power*.

Fifty metres away, a senior ship's officer paused briefly. His heavy high-collared greatcoat was trimmed with silver fur. His sleeves and breast were adorned with honour braids, nobility brooches, ship's icons and medals. A power-cutlass hung from his belt.

The officer glanced respectfully at the two puissant Marines, but would not intrude.

Lexandro and Kempka were both wearing pus-yellow dress uniform. Fanged skulls within crosses decorated their knees. Their fur-trimmed cloaks of dark blue were embroidered with sunbursts and icons.

A line of five-lobed windows revealed, a kilometre below, the starlit deck of the battleship. Like some broad gargantuan spear-blade, this deck jutted fully four kilometres into space. Moored halfway along it, the Fists' own troopship seemed almost lost amidst the battleship's Cobra attack cruisers. Nevertheless, that troopship's sleek bulk housed assault torpedoes into each of which half a company of Fists could pack.

The cinquefoil windows also framed a sister battleship sailing in harmony with *Imperial Power*, gushing a wake of brilliant plasma. How splendid that celestial city of crenellated spires studded with great lasers and bomb launchers! How like an axe-head was the warp keel diving below.

Further off was an ancient ironclad, massively armoured.

'Praise be to *Him*,' remarked Lex, and Kempka nodded.

Aye, glory to Him-on-Earth. Glory likewise to the indomitable dead primarch who had founded the Fists.

Lex's own left fist itched. It often did so when a campaign was gearing up. This itch was within. Upon the very bones of his left hand he had once inscribed with an engraver tool the names of two battle-brothers who had been closest to him in all the universe, though he could only acknowledge this fact after they were dead.

To engrave his bones, he had first dissolved the flesh of his hand in caustic acid. *Pain is the healing, purifying scalpel!*

The chirurgeons of his fortress-monastery had rebuilt Lex's hand with synthmusclefibre and nervewires and pseudoflesh. True, he had been reprimanded and he had experienced punishment in the nerve-glove – which cloaked his whole body in simulated furnace-fire. Yet his gesture of devotion had perhaps been admired. Here he was, decades later: an officer, a captain, with six steel service-studs in his forehead.

Twelve studs decorated Kempka's forehead. However, the Librarian – a powerful psyker whom Lex held in comradely awe – was a military seer rather than a tactical commander. Lex could faintly smell the Librarian's superhuman hormonal secretions, like a sacred spice.

Lex's finger-bones tingled and prickled. They wished to be encased in a power glove, clutching a heavy bolter and firing it. To slay is to pray, is it not?

Yet not to fire heedlessly. A Fist was a planner and a thinker.

Thus Lex had only lost three of his company of a hundred men (and ten wounded) on the planet Hannibal, where the itch had most recently been assuaged in action against alien eldar warriors.

THE FISTS' VESSEL had been far indeed from the fortress-monastery which sailed everlastingly through void in the Ultimum Segmentum.

There had been a rumour of tyranid incursion deep into the Imperium, deeper than ever previously reported. Were those terrible creatures about to seize another human world so as to harvest its population and pervert people into freakish slaves of their bio-tyranny?

Hannibal was a human colony. Evidently due to a warp storm it had been out of contact for several thousand years until an exploration team of Terror Tiger Marines rediscovered it. That team had been destroyed. Before he too was killed, and despite suffering psychic damage, the Tigers' blind astropath had managed to send a confused message about terrifying tall, slender aliens with baffles of bane-white and fiery red who flourished some type of energy-sword almost too swiftly for Marines to see.

Those weapons sounded chillingly like the boneswords of tyranids.

Recently, the Terror Tigers had suffered a dire mauling in an attack by a mutant warlord upon their monastery world. Unlike the Fists, the Tigers were land-based. The Tigers had lost almost a quarter of their Chapter before eventual victory. Almost two-and-half companies destroyed! The Tigers' commander had decreed his own execution without honour.

Since the Tigers were so depleted, it fell to the Fists to send a company to Hannibal, under Lex's command and accompanied by a Librarian who could combat alien psychic malice.

How SWEETLY LEX remembered the final ground engagement which had driven the surviving alien trespassers back to a sub-light ship.

These aliens were certainly no tyranids bent on the vilest *bio-exploitation* of what they did not exterminate. No, these were arrogant eldar – and they had ordered the human population to quit Hannibal within a year or else be forced to leave.

Brown-skinned colonists had babbled to Kurt Kempka in a barbarous dialect of Imperial Gothic of how an alien spokesman had declared that the human scum on this world were themselves trespassers. Human beings were parasites upon this planet which aeons ago – before some unmentionable event – those selfsame aliens had supposedly terraformed with an eye to the distant future.

The eldar were not only arrogant but irrational. How could a disorganized population of millions go any place else? Hannibal had been their home for aeons. They had no ships.

All they had were the mammoth armour-skinned beasts native to Hannibal's jungles, beasts towering ten metres high on legs each as thick as the trunk of the stoutest tree.

And so the people had ridden these beasts against the eldar warriors, beasts which were the zoological equivalent of Titans manufactured by the Adeptus Mechanicus. These living Titans were not armed with plasma cannons, macro cannons, or multi-meltas – only with crossbows and muskets.

The alien warriors were so swift. Female warriors, they were. With their laspistols they blinded the pachyderms. With their power swords they hamstrung the armoured beasts, bringing them crashing down. The warriors' masks were screaming faces. From those came such mindshrieks as to stun the beasts' riders insensible and stampede the mammoths.

Those devil-women with flame-orange hair screeched and darted, easily butchering all opposition.

And then, like an answer to a prayer, from out of nowhere, unimaginable to most of the denizens of Hannibal, there had come that ship of the Terror Tigers, bringing knights in power armour.

Not nearly enough Tigers…

With only light losses, the superior force of alien banshee-bitches had destroyed the Tigers. Next, the eldar had begun a methodical massacre of the human population. The arrival of those Tigers had annulled the useless year of grace.

To exterminate millions would take a long time. Meanwhile, the colonists could always evacuate their world – if only they could teach mammoths to fly into space and learn to breathe vacuum.

During the extermination the Imperial Fists had landed. A whole company of a hundred Marines. Soon, inspired by prayers to their primarch, the Fists were making headway with insignificant losses.

The banshee-bitches seemed to have lost their sense of judgement. They had become obsessed with the dance of death they performed, like vulpine predators in a vast shed of chickens, crazed with killing.

In the final action, Lex and Kempka and the ten squads with their sergeants had advanced in their power armour through a devastated jungle where titanic corpses of mammoths rotted.

Had the mammoths stampeded to escape from the stings of lasers? Smashing trees in their panic, uprooting other trees in their agony?

Every few minutes, several masked banshee-bitches would rush from behind the shattered bole of a tree or from behind a mountainous cadaver. They would howl their amplified mind-shriek, but the Space Marines' helmets incorporated psychic shielding. A wave of nausea was the usual consequence, disorienting but not disabling.

Blue mists lazed through the jungle, as if serpents of smoke or gas had been born from the dead pachyderms.

How agilely and how swiftly the alien bitches moved. They fired laser pulses. They dodged bolter fire as if foreknowing where an enemy would aim. They rushed in upon a chosen Marine, swirling their power swords. Their armour was the colour of bleached bone. The helms of some were of bone-hue too. Other helms were blood-red. Plumes were flame-red.

The sheer rage which emanated from them! Their uncanny deadly dexterity! If the bitches had all attacked at once, they really might have harmed the Fists. Yet these shrieking aliens seemed to be challenging themselves to isolated exhibitions of reckless daring – as though they had become frenzied puppets in a fatal drama.

Two warriors had raced from behind an armoured hill of decaying mammoth tissue. They pranced towards Lex. The screams were sickening in their vehemence.

His bolts missed the jinking attackers. The aliens might almost have been distorting space itself by their ghastly gymnastic antics. Their power swords veered to left, to right, to touch the speeding bolts and twitch them on their way. Co-ordinated laser pulses had incandesced upon the pauldron protecting Lexandro's left shoulder. The doubled energy blast bored inward searingly. Briefly, he tasted the spice of pain. Diagnostic icons flickered on the readout projected within his visor. The injury was minor, a tender caress of combat.

A Banshee was so near! During the fleeting distraction of those icons, the alien had reached Lex. Her power sword was swinging to slice into his armour.

Bolts from Lex's gun pierced the armour of her belly. Within her, they erupted. Even so, the sword impacted against his breastplate. With a raucous screech and a spray of sparks, the power blade sheared a few millimetres into his eagle-plastron.

Unable to bring greater force to the blow, her alien entrails torn and mingled, the wielder of the sword was already dying. The sword's power failed.

Briefly Lex had stared at the scream-mask. Stretched lurid lips seemed about to kiss him upon his snout-visor. About to ravish his tough helmet with a bite.

What agonized face hid behind that mask? Oh, he knew well enough what kind of face. With their power gloves his men had ripped the psycho-masks from several earlier corpses.

A female face! Intoxicatingly lovely. Strange. Alien.

Truly Lex had forgotten about females of his own species – who were just as alien to him. Ach, of course he had seen womenfolk since entering his fortress-monastery. He had killed some, but never come so close to one. Servitors who had dwelled for generations aboard the fortress-monastery necessarily included females to generate more servitors. But those were beneath a Fist's notice.

The faces beneath the masks had slanting eyes and sloping cheeks – a lethal, otherworldly loveliness.

Still masked, still projecting a fading fury, the banshee-female had fallen dead.

The other Banshee!

Even as Lex swung his heavy bolter, bolts from other armoured knights had caught the second alien.

The style of the aliens' attack had become so frenzied and spectacular – and, provided one wasn't intimidated, so self-defeating. These aliens were no longer reasoning beings. They were mere masks, shells of armour equipped with weapons.

THUS LEX'S COMPANY had fought its way through the jungle, driving the seemingly suicidal eldar back, until trees gave way to a low plateau of bare granite. Upon that plateau towered a slim, graceful sub-light ship. Its iridescent fins could have been those of some exotic fish. A cordon of warriors wearing black armour guarded the ship. The surviving Banshees were now sprinting across the granite.

Voxing his men to pause in the shelter of the jungle's fringe, Lex willed the optic sensors in his visor into telescopic mode.

The input into the visual node of his brain showed those black warriors to be armed with missile launchers. That coal-dark armour of theirs was crafted of interlocking plates embossed with metal skulls. It looked heavy, not flexible as were the suits of the banshee-bitches. The inky cuisses and greaves protecting thighs and calves were particularly sturdy, to steady the wearers against the recoil of those missile launchers. Vanes in the helmets might be equipment for locking on to a target. An antler-like bracket supported arm and missile tube.

Banshee-bitches were streaming towards the ship, and towards the cordon too. The aliens would block the path of missiles for about another thirty seconds – unless the black warriors fired irrespective.

This was a risk which Lex could only spare a couple of seconds to assess. Praying that he was making the correct intuitive, transcendent calculation – and not leading his men into a salvo – he ordered, 'Switch to grenade launchers, and charge at will!'

With bulky gauntlet, Lex deftly threw the catch on his gun to deactivate the regular firing mechanism. His manipulation was fastidious, as befitted a Fist who could engrave minuscule scrimshaws upon a dead battle-brother's finger-bones.

Ten squads of Space Marines with their sergeants powered their way from out of the trees, the pumping motion of their legs amplified through the fibre bundles which controlled their suits. Now that the auxiliary grenade tubes were primed, the guns could no longer fire bolts. Maybe it seemed that the Fists were rushing forward without loosing a single shot because they were now intent on capturing the aliens rather than killing them. Unimpeded now by jungle, already Lex's company had covered half the terrain between themselves and the retreating Banshees.

'And fire!'

Almost as a man, the Fists came to a halt – just as the black warriors were galvanizing into action, clasping their launchers.

Almost a hundred frag grenades roared toward the fleeing Banshees and the cordon.

Lex prayed as he adjusted his gun to rapid fire again.

Eruptions. Detonations.

The impacting grenades exploded and fragmented in a myriad of directions. The hot rush of splinters peppered armour whether bone-white or black. Even those aliens who wore the stronger black armour weren't entirely encased, as were Space Marines in their power suits. Splinters ripped flesh and bone. Banshees and black warriors were sprawling, juddering, dying. One warrior fired a missile – but upwards, into a dreary sky. The projectile fell far away.

Boltguns resumed their regular activity – then quit, since this activity was unnecessary.

Superheated gases began to billow from the vents of the fish-ship – roasting the dead and dying, surging against the Fists' battle suits, harmlessly as yet. Some crew members inside the ship were about to boost it away from this place of disaster.

Lex powered towards a fallen rocket launcher. He snatched it up in his amplified grip and raced clear. A couple of sergeants retrieved other launchers. Blessedly, or due to stout craftsmanship, the launchers seemed largely undamaged by the spray of lethal fragments.

He and the sergeants withdrew to five hundred metres from the ship. One of the sergeants yielded the launcher to Librarian Kempka.

'Everyone else back to the trees,' Lex ordered, and the Fists decamped.

Kempka studied the lustrous bulky weapon, encased with alien runes. Since the firing tube was no longer in synch with its operator, arcane icons flickered incoherently in a display panel. There was a morphological logic to weaponry, just as there was an evolutionary necessity in the anatomy of a living creature – unless that creature were warped by Chaos. Kempka pointed a gloved finger at a jewelled intaglio button, and indicated elsewhere too.

As the fish-ship rose on a surging tail of heat, Kempka and Lex and Sergeant Kurtz raised their launchers. The ship was fifty metres aloft. A hundred. It was beginning to speed up.

Let that ship rise a little further – so that momentum would carry its wreckage away from the vicinity of the Fists.

Where had the ship come from? A sub-light vessel! Librarian Kempka considered that it had come to this solar system through some sizeable warp tunnel. Perhaps its warriors had been exploring at random. Perhaps they had been prompted by some ancient archive.

Bracing themselves, locking armoured legs and torsos in position, the three men fired their missiles.

Recoil jarred Lex as his missile screeched upward. A bright little fireball bloomed against the ship. A second explosion immediately blossomed – and a third. The sky itself seemed to erupt.

The shockwave from the disintegrating ship knocked the sergeant and the Librarian off their feet, and almost tumbled Lex too.

Even in his power armour he was bruised. Trees were bending their crowns. Molten metal was raining. The main mass of devastation was plummeting downward a full kilometre away.

The granite apron rocked on impact... Then there was peace.

AND THE PEOPLE of Hannibal had been blessed.

After long separation, they were a part of the human Imperium once again. In due course preachers would come, and judges. Psykers would be hunted for extermination or pressed into service. The cult of the God-Emperor would flourish. The jungles and mammoths of this world would serve a purpose, not merely endure a stupid existence.

This had been work well done.

Lex's finger-bones itched for more such loyal work.

AT LAST, THE robed inquisitor had joined Lex and the Librarian beside the windows which framed that awesome, serene sight of battleships.

Sapphires were sewn upon a scarred cheek. A tube puffed incense into a nostril. A lens in the socket of one eye reminded Lex nostalgically of Sergeant Huzzi Rork who had recruited Lex as a lad so long ago on Necromunda.

The captain of the Fists scrutinized this Inquisitor Baal Firenze courteously. In the inquisitor's one natural eye there seemed such a callous, wily regard. As must needs be with a man who must clearsightedly and ruthlessly detect and unmask evil! By comparison, to be a Space Marine was virtually to be an innocent – no matter what slaughterous sights each mission brought. To be an Imperial Fist was to experience a constant purity of heart. An inquisitor, by contrast, must forever be assailed by impurity. Hence, Firenze's nasal tube of virtueherb.

What did that shrewd scrutiny reveal to Baal Firenze concerning Captain Lexandro d'Arquebus?

Lex's complexion was olive, nicked by duelling scars. A tattoo of a skeleton fist crushing a moon which dripped blood adorned his cheek.

Through his right nostril was a ruby ring. How dark and lustrous his eyes. How pearly his teeth. His crewcut hair was dusky. Those shining studs on his forehead...

With his enhanced musculature and ceramically reinforced bones Lex massed twice the bulk of Baal Firenze. Lex stood so graciously. A paladin!

Firenze wheezed. 'Captain, your first name, Lexandro, signifies *man of law*. Your second name, d'Arquebus, alludes to an ancient firearm. With your boltgun you impose the Emperor's will.'

How true.

Firenze continued: 'We must impose our will upon a blasphemous alien construction in orbit around a once-human world. We must wrest secrets. We must bring grief so that the grip on secrets slackens. The greatest grief to most living beings is generally caused by the destruction of their children before their very eyes.'

The two Space Marines exchanged a fleeting glance of misgiving.

Blithely Firenze continued: 'The alien construction in question will be hosting a baleful festival. Children often attend a festival. Do not hesitate to destroy the spawn of the eldar, who are already a dying race! Thus we will put these aliens and their construction to the *question* in the rigorous inquisitorial sense of *quaestio*, an investigation conducted by means of torment unto death. In this I represent the Emperor's will, and you are the Emperor's own Fists which execute that will.'

Firenze's breath hissed as he exhaled odour of virtueherb.

Librarian Kempka had stiffened, and Lex felt a squirm in the guts. Why should this inquisitor refer to the annihilation of alien brats as if the pre-echo of their screams were a personal hymn of devotion? As if anticipation of their burning ashes were a kind of incense in his virtueherb-plugged nostril! Lex had certainly once participated in the eradication *ad ultimum foetum* of a rebellious governor's family. On that occasion the killing of the whelps had been a vital necessity. Where was the urgent necessity here, amongst so many more pressing matters? Simply to demoralize? What a waste of the precious time of Marines!

A Space Marine was a warrior of honour. He was the cutting edge of the Emperor's sword of valour. Where was the dignity in slaughtering defenceless juveniles? To be a superhuman Space Marine was the most virtuous of destinies. To scourge rebels and aliens with death. And to suffer in so doing.

Oh, the *lure* of pain! This was a flaw in the gene-seed of the Fists – praiseworthy in that it made Fists stauncher, yet seductively suspect too.

Pain, enjoyed within oneself: that was almost a virtue. Yet not pain enjoyed by proxy, in the agonies of others. Could that be Firenze's flaw?

Necessarily Lex must obey this inquisitor, or else Lex would be a heretic! Yet to be led by a sadist was so at variance with a Fist's most precious secret sentiments.

Perhaps Firenze was simply being effusive? The inquisitor proceeded to discourse about eldar warp-gates and about other matters – with a hint, just a hint, of possible abominations which brave Space Marines might encounter and for which Lex must prepare his men without corrupting them by so doing.

THE LIBRARIAN HAD stiffened anew – and Lex was minded to say that he himself had once encountered the sort of abomination to which Firenze alluded, and that he had been privileged to retain his memories, unexpurgated. Aye, memories of the corruption of a certain Lord Sagromoso by a deity known as Tzeentch…

A distate for Firenze disinclined Lex to confide such matters in the inquisitor.

Were Lex's men being led by Firenze to confront something daemonic?

Firenze had merely alluded. Perhaps he was testing Lex's fidelity. Such matters were forbidden secrets.

FIRENZE REJOICED DARKLY. *A company of hardened veterans who had recently fought eldar warriors – with sublime success. Accompanied by a powerfully psychic Librarian, should there be any Slaaneshi manifestations… Men of a Space Marine Chapter with a strange furtive relish for pain, according to Inquisition archives… Ideal!*

'YOU ARE PRECIOUS men,' Firenze told Captain d'Arquebus. 'And I am accompanying you all the way, of course. First in the troopship. Then in one of the boarding torpedoes–'

Naturally Firenze would accompany the assault force. '–since perhaps we will not return here.' His statement implied much to a wise battle veteran.

It implied that if need be, this battleship, *Imperial Power*, and those two other combat-cathedrals visible in the void nearby were… expendable. Sacrificeable, along with their tens of thousands of engineers and officers and pilots and gun crews and servitors. The three battleships would stage an attack upon the alien construction and whatever vessels guarded it, not so as to destroy the construction as swiftly as could be, but to provide a massive distraction whilst the Fists carried out their penetrating questioning surgical raid.

Afterwards, the battleships would be at liberty to destroy, to the extent that the ships remained spaceworthy.

By that time, thousands of casualties might have entered the sea of lost souls.

Thus, at least, the galaxy did not overfill to bursting point with people! Nor with aliens, either. War forever weeded the Emperor's pastures.

The two other battleships seemed by now like ivory cameos displayed upon black velvet in a reliquary of night studded with diamonds which were stars; and Lex's twin hearts – the one he'd been born with, and the extra one implanted by Imperial Fist surgeons – were tranquil.

FIRENZE HAD TAKEN his leave, to consult with the captain of *Imperial Power*.

Kempka confided to Lex, 'I am troubled.'

Lex nodded. 'Aye, and perhaps with good reason. If this inquisitor reiterates such remarks to our battle-brothers at large about slaughtering alien brats, I fear the brothers will defy him.'

'Justifiably defy him, by Dorn!' Kempka's hand formed a fist, then relaxed. 'Maybe Sir Baal was merely being effervescent. But I suspect that a huge number of mortal lives are shortly to be sacrified by way of diversion in order to place us in position.'

'Yet never the lives of our brothers, unnecessarily,' growled Lex.

Kempka hesitated. 'The inquisitor seemed to hint that there may be a vile occult element in what awaits us.'

'I understand you, Brother Librarian. Believe me, I do. Such a thing, I have endured and survived in the past. All of our men will be shielded. Ach, is this inquisitor deploying us as part of an – *experiment*? With highest authority, to be sure!'

Kempka frowned. 'That cannot be. The Emperor's will is wise. His gaze sees far.'

Lex lowered his voice. 'Sir Baal may be deranged.'

The Librarian gazed out into the void. 'Inquisitors,' he said, 'are a breed apart.' His tone firmed. 'As are we, by the grace of Dorn!'

ELEVEN
ILLUMINATUS

ZEPHRO CARNELIAN STARED through his spread fingers at the farseer. Ro-fhessi's robe shimmered iridescently. The eldar's high masked helm evoked some bleached equine skull set upright upon his shoulders. Crystals studded the helm. From within twin cavities eyes gleamed, seeming crystalline likewise. From Ro-fhessi's waist dangled a pouch in which would be rune stones. A jewelled holster housed an ornate shuriken pistol.

'We meet again,' said Ro-fhessi. 'I have woken. I have walked.'

Led by a vision, the farseer had evidently walked through the webway from far Ulthwé craftworld, so close to the Eye of Terror.

Zephro laughed softly. How like a child he felt, peeking through his fingers at this farseer!

Ro-fhessi laughed too. The farseer mimicked the exact cadence of Zephro's mirth – as if he were testing that mirth for any taint of hysteria and madness.

Zephro was peering through his fingers because they were webbed with gossamer. Tiny sparkling warp spiders had emerged from one of the wraithbone ribs which supported the huge amphitheatre, upon the rim of which he stood.

Beneath the soft-seeming terraces of viridian moss was the *quasi-living* skeleton, stronger than adamantium, which had grown outward from the initial core of this habitat. Akin to a craftworld – although of lesser size – this habitat boasted no vast sails to propel it slowly through the void on a frail plasma breeze of its own production. It had been grown in orbit around a planet. That planet now hovered in holo-projection over the heart of the amphitheatre, a diseased eye hideous to behold.

That phantom world was one on which Carnelian had once walked – and had skipped and pranced – and for which he grieved.

Stalinvast.

The entire land surface of that world, beneath a veil of storm-blown ashes, was scoured rock and cinder desert. Its seas were poisonous sludge. Former cities would resemble dead shattered coral, if indeed any cities had outlasted the worldwide firestorm of exploding rot-gas. Not a microbe would be alive. Even the life-eater virus would finally have consumed itself.

The psychic webs of the warp spiders tickled Zephro's hands pleasantly.

Really, there was no need for Ro-fhessi to test the quality of laughter – that purgation of horror. If the least residue of Chaos – other than a dire memory – had lurked in Zephro's spirit, many more of the tiny spiders would have crystallized out of the wraithbone to swarm all over him. By now they would be melting their way into his body to devour the evil and perhaps the host as well.

The spiders had chosen to investigate his hands. Had Ro-fhessi summoned the glittering mites? No longer was the farseer in a trance, in a longdream of communion with the wraithbone of his craftworld, uttering oracles. He had woken; he had walked. Ro-fhessi wore a shuriken pistol. Only in time of crisis would a farseer of his calibre involve himself to this degree.

From behind the projected semblance of that leprous orb of Stalinvast, flying warriors began to glide: Swooping Hawks. Their lightweight blue armour was hard to see against the deeper blue of the dome which arched above the amphitheatre. That dome's sombrely luminous substance conjured an illusion of sky in which a ghost sun swam and where a few of the brightest stars were faded motes. The soft radiant light was partly captured from Stalinvast's sun, and was partly wraithbone energy. A hint of a road, leading away beyond the false sky, was actually a spire which jutted far into space.

The feather-plates of the Hawks' wings vibrated so swiftly, hardly visible except as blue blurs. The fierce shrill of their beating was easily audible. Down they swooped to meet streamlined jetbikes which were rising from the bowl of the amphitheatre.

Those flying craft bore Dire Avengers. Flexibly armoured in blue. Dragon banners flying from their helms. Suspended from the front carapaces of the Avengers' bikes were shuriken catapults.

Hawks were cradling long lasguns from which pennants fluttered.

Engines howled as the flying craft climbed steeply to intercept the plunging Hawks. Hawks and Avengers appeared about to joust in mid-air. Surely they were on a fatal collision course.

With impeccable aerial agility the two teams of warriors flew in between one another. Jet-bikes looped gracefully over to begin a descent upon the Hawks as the Hawks soared upward again from out of their dive.

Manoeuvres continued, expressive of such delight, such fervid anticipation of genuine combat. Oh, the stimulus of warfare.

From where Zephro stood he could see across most of the elegant city underneath an adjacent sky-dome. In the shrines of that city, many other eldar would be adopting their chosen warrior aspects. Exarchs, forever bonded within their ritual armour – studded with the spirit-stones of all previous wearers – would be performing rites before altars of the Bloody-Handed God.

You would need to climb one of the space-spires and peer through a lens to see, as yet, the light of plasma torches which were propelling Imperial battleships inward towards Stalinvast from the jump zone. In two more days those titanic fighting ships would be closer.

'Is the impending battle to become part of the ceremony?' Zephro asked Ro-fhessi. 'Or was this not foreseen?'

Irrespective of the approach of Imperial battleships, preparations for the Commemoration of Cataclysm were continuing – at the same time as aspect warriors were donning their armour and their military roles in expectation of bloodshed.

A troupe of Harlequins were rehearsing gymnastically. They leapt high. They somersaulted backwards. They jinked hither and thither, almost too fast for a non-eldar eye to follow.

The Harlequins' bright costumes were boldly zigzagged, or checked or striped or spotted; sometimes all of these in one kaleidoscopic outfit: a bizarre motley of designs. How many buckles and belts and scarves and sashes and ribbons each Harlequin wore! As yet they had not switched on the visual disruption effect which would let each assume a whole illusory repertoire of costumes. Even so, each Harlequin's mimic-mask forever hid the wearer's true face behind a shifting sequence of feigned identities, some exquisite, others horrific.

Watching this masked ballet from a distance was a lone Solitaire in chequered gold and silver clothing. His or her mask was a grin of voracious lust.

Roaming spectators and other Harlequins avoided glancing at the Solitaire. Much less would they have dreamed of addressing him or her.

(What dream would that have been but a *nightmare*?) The Solitaire would never speak to a soul, lest that soul be cursed.

The Solitaire's presence signified that the ultimate horror was due to be evoked beneath that palsied eye of a devastated planet. Evoked, and exorcised in the name of the Laughing God. May the exorcism also apply to the doom which menaced the crude rabid race of so-called 'human' beings. The warp was groaningly pregnant with their own as yet unimaginable Lord of Chaos. Stalinvast was so potent an emblem of the wanton destruction which would overtake a million worlds if so-called 'humanity' fell – just as ten aeons earlier the eldar had fallen from vainglorious bliss.

That was when the Eye of Terror had opened within the material galaxy. If stupid crass humanity fell too in an all-consuming mindfire, the great ocean of Chaos would overflow to drown the whole galaxy. The material cosmos would be no more, engulfed by tormented nightmare eternally.

At times, Zephro felt ashamed of his human heritage – no matter how versatile and quicksilver he tried to be in emulation of an eldar Harlequin.

Zephro was wearing a suit of dark red and green triangular patches symmetrically sewn with yellow edges. His was a shadow figure seen through intricate stained glass. A white ruffle around his neck – indented by his hooked chin – supported his head as though upon a soft plate. A minimal black mask framed his green eyes. He could have been some nocturnal lemur-animal. From a gold-edged tricorne hat of black rose an ostentatious crimson plume suggestive of some aspect warrior's helm. Was Zephro perhaps no more than a mockery of an eldar, a tolerated pet?

The eldar had failed. They had failed themselves. Their former self-indulgence – their crying out for madder music and darker wine, their unbridled excesses – had allowed Slaanesh to come into existence.

Whereas, some thread of hope remained for the human race. If only the hydra scheme could be aborted. If only enough of the Emperor's Sons could be sacrificed to Him-on-Earth, in the moment of His demise, to bring into existence the redemptive Numen rather than a ravaging Chaos god.

All those innocent sensei… Oh, that seductive illusion of a long watch of knights pending the ultimate psychic battle. Despite their immortality, the sensei were oblivious to so much.

Principally they were innocent of how the Illuminati, out of necessity, intended to immolate the Sons on the mind-altar from which the Numen would arise.

Swooping Hawks and Dire Avengers plunged and soared. Harlequins leapt and pirouetted. Small streams of elegant spectators were heading away out of the amphitheatre. By the time of the rite, would the entire potential audience have donned their bloodthirsty aspects and armour?

Would that be an essential component of the rite, not merely a reaction to the approaching battleships?

The entire audience? Surely there would be time for children to slip away with guides through the webway. If not, then maybe Slaanesh would triumph over the Laughing God.

Were the eldar gambling their own offspring because of a farseer's vision of what must be, so as to deflect something infinitely worse?

'Was this not foreseen?' repeated Zephro. He nodded towards the faint silhouette of the space-spire, and by implication those incoming Imperial battleships. 'Was this theatre created deliberately to lure the Imperium on to its stage?'

'All theatres,' replied Ro-fhessi, 'are theatres of war. War must needs be theatrical.'

Indeed. Harlequins were players as well as warriors of flamboyant yet subtle skills. Zephro had studied those skills assiduously under their patronage. Admittedly, Harlequins might stand aside from conflict with Imperial forces. That was their privilege.

How could Harlequins intervene, and also enact the upcoming ceremony?

To any eldar, when he or she put on an aspect, war immediately became spectacular.

'I have been in a long trance of divination,' announced Ro-fhessi. 'You, Zephro Carnelian, have several times been to a Crossroads of Inertia.'

Zephro took off his hat and bowed ironically. 'I have been elsewhere too in between whiles, farseer.'

The eldar webway linked craftworlds and a multitude of natural planets as well as unnatural places which were closed off by powerful prohibitions and psychic seals. As a privileged initiate, Zephro and certain other Illuminati had learned to traverse at least some of the labyrinthine webway, so as to search for the Emperor's Sons, and to bring confusion and grief to inquisitors who hunted for those mutants, and to try to foil the extremist cabal of Illuminati who were fostering the hydra plan to melt the massed minds of humanity.

At certain rare intersections in the webway, time itself slowed or was even annulled. Travellers could be trapped in stasis. A forewarned psyker could pass safely through these nodes – or he might choose to linger, while in the ordinary universe a year flew by, or a decade or even a century. The Theory of *Uigebealach*, the philosophy of the webway, hinted at the necessary existence of one particular node where time actually flowed backwards. The Great Harlequins who wandered the webway, and who alone knew the location of the Black Library, had undoubtedly searched for that crossroads.

To find that node! To return to the time before the eldar fell and to warn their ancestors of their doom! To avert that doom so that the eldar might still be the laughing lords of the galaxy, their civilization preserved! And the gross human species still hamstrung by warp storms! Those storms had only calmed when the festering boil of Slaanesh burst open.

Maybe only the Laughing God knew the location of that crossroads where time reversed, if any such crossroads existed at all. Maybe the Laughing God refrained from revealing its whereabouts to his wandering Great Harlequins – or even hid it from them. Its discovery might result in the foulest triumph of Chaos. Ten thousand years of blighted history would unravel, becoming only a phantom of events. Quadrillions of anguished lives would become unlives. How wildly Tzeentch, the Chaos Lord of Change, would revel in this deconstruction.

By lingering now and then at a Crossroads of Inertia, Zephro had not been evading responsibilities. In between his interventions he had leapfrogged through time, as a long journey through the warp by jumpship speeded up the passage of time for its crew, relative to the time experienced in normal space. Only, much more so in his case.

The name of the present moment was crisis.

Ro-fhessi said to Zephro, 'This habitation, and the ceremony, were ordained by Eldrad Ulthran.'

Eldrad, the foremost farseer of Ulthwé.

Ro-fhessi's mentor...

Also the agent – over a century previously – of Zephro's own salvation.

If a supreme farseer of the calibre of Ulthran declared that an enterprise should occur, that was because the farseer had dreamed the runes of futurity. The enterprise would be undertaken – whether it be a seemingly suicidal raid upon an Imperial stronghold, or an attack upon a squat warlord who seemed of no consequence to the eldar, or an expedition to a Chaos world. The farseer had scried the skein of probabilities. He had glimpsed how such an action could produce a cascade of significant happenings. One of these happenings would very likely avert a disaster elsewhere and elsewhen. Perhaps it would promote a success unachievable otherwise. Even if his oracle made no apparent sense or even seemed utterly perilous, the eldar would heed a farseer.

Consequently eldar actions often seemed capricious to human beings. On a deeper level the contrary was the truth. It was owing to one such oracle that Zephro Carnelian himself had been saved and had become an Illuminatus...

ON ACCOUNT OF its proximity to the Eye of Terror, Ulthwé was the craftworld most closely menaced by Chaos. Frequently throughout its history, warbands of Chaos Marines and other warped entities had attacked Ulthwé, to be repelled only with tragic losses. Ulthwé was sailing away from the Eye, yet only at sub-light speed. Thousands more years would pass before the craftworld reached any region of dubious safety.

Abandon Ulthwé's domes and docks and space-spires? Evacuate in ships by way of the swirling webway portal held in stasis to the stern of the craftworld? Flee through the webway portals within Ulthwé itself?

The eldar could hardly afford to lose any craftworld, any sanctuary in the endless night. Let not the name of Ulthwé fall out of the sad litany of survival: of Biel-tan and Saim-hann, of Alaitoc and Ulthwé and Iyanden...

Iyanden? That once-vast craftworld was now much devastated due to attack by tyranids. Its yellow-uniformed guardians still defended their ruined home. Iyanden was still a part of the litany. Let Iyanden be named for a while longer. Let Ulthwé be named forever.

From time to time, Ulthwé's domes and spires and keel were damaged by ferocious onslaughts of Chaos minions. Even so, wraithbone slowly regenerated itself. Ulthwé was quasi-living. Within the infinity circuit of its wraithbone structure were all the souls of bygone inhabitants. To abandon those would be an abomination.

From Ulthwé had come Striking Scorpion aspect warriors and Eldrad Ulthran himself and the Warlock Ketshamine to purge Zephro's world and rescue him from *horror*.

TO SAVE HIM from the quintessence of horror, from horror in its most primary embodiment! And from the planet Horror too, from a world which was ceasing to be of the ordinary universe and was being polluted by rheum from the Eye.

Zephro's world had once been called Hurrah by its human colonists in their sheer jubilation at reaching it and in joy at its lush fertility.

Thereafter, a minor warp storm had isolated that world for several thousand years, but had not condemned Hurrah to barbarism or savagery. On the contrary, the arts of civilization were cultivated to a pitch which even the eldar might have acknowledged as above contempt. Perhaps this was Hurrah's doom. If only the planet had been more brutish, forcing a pious puritanism upon its people. When the warp storm finally calmed, corruption began to attend the cultured pleasures of Hurrah, like mould upon a sweetly rotting fruit.

And Chaos was nearby.

Zephro could still recall the blooming of his own psychic talent. He could conjure sensual phantasmagoria out of thin air. He entertained friends, then eager audiences, with voluptuous pageants. He could even render temporarily tangible some nymph conjured from his throbbing imagination, producing a seductive physical presence, a succubus. Zephro became rich and celebrated, lord of revels who could tune his body to experience prolonged exquisite delights, and who could bestow this orgiastic capability upon those around him.

Soon, pain entered into pleasure as a seemingly necessary spice.

A little sprinkle of spice at first.

Then more.

The erotics of cruelty were burgeoning on Hurrah – which was becoming Horror.

Fantasy torture-parlours became fashionable. Zephro himself became an exquisite illusory torturer, much in demand. He conjured imaginary pageants of pain. These seemed almost innocuous at first. Only visionary victims were involved. The phantoms, in any case, seemed to relish agony.

Then tangible succubi were used; and these also seemed to relish torment.

Then certain men and women volunteered. Finally victims were being kidnapped or bought or otherwise coerced.

The transition had been so subtle and insidious. Each stage seemed to lead naturally towards the next; indeed, to *demand* the next.

One day, Zephro experienced a paroxysm of revulsion – an appalled recognition and rejection of evil. In that very spasm he was suddenly robbed of all control over his own body. A spirit which was not his usurped the governance of his limbs and his lips and his loins, all, all of him. It was a fierce, squirming, lecherous, bloodthirsty entity. Slaanesh, Slaanesh, was the throb in his ears and the pulse in his veins.

Within his brain, a maddening lisping voice was whispering over and over unearthly words which curdled his imprisoned mind.

Q'tlahs'itsu'aksho.

Q'qha'shy'ythlis…

Q'qha'thashi'i...

What were these foul things which were being invoked?

He soon knew. He dreamed of them.

By night or by day he dreamed, whenever his possessed body was too fatigued to move around any more with his mind as its impotent passenger.

Which was worse? The vile actions undertaken by his body – or the dreams?

He dreamed of luscious lethal daemonettes. He dreamed of poisonous fiends which were half human and half scorpion. He dreamed of ostrich-horses with voluptuous legs and lashing blue tongues, upon which daemonettes rode.

It seemed that soon those daemonettes and fiends might try to rip their way into the world through his very own flesh – which was his own no more. They might tear a gateway open in his bowels. They might emerge through his anus and then expand to full-size.

How his mind fought against this hideous prospect.

The entity which possessed him met its first resistance.

Could Zephro regain control of part of himself? With all his psychic power he fought harder. Frequently his body lurched and drooled, convulsed by tics and coursing with sweat, feverish and incontinent. Still he could not oust the entity which directed him.

That entity took him to all those places of painful pleasure where he had performed previously. He presided over the entertaining torment of prisoners. But now each pang which he inflicted rebounded upon himself, excruciating him until his mind screamed. He would have succumbed to gibbering insanity, except that he knew that thereby the entity hoped to defeat him utterly and swallow his soul forever.

Somehow he endured – fastened in the torture dungeon which his usurped body had become.

The struggle lasted for weeks. For months. His waking hours were a nightmare more agonizing than his dire dreams.

While stumbling through the streets of the capital city of this world which was now Horror he did indeed spy daemonettes on their steeds, and fiends too – should the entity which was controlling him jerk Zephro's head in their direction in acknowledgement. Evidently such creatures had emerged from other victims of possession. He would glimpse an eviscerated corpse, torn open by the abominations it had hatched. The city – to the extent that he could notice it – was increasingly ravaged and despoiled. He was in the midst of a vile war, a helpless participant.

At last, in a piazza where fountains gushed blood, Zephro had found himself aligned, with caterwauling devotees of pain and daemonettes upon their steeds, against the remnants of true humanity. A jagged sword writhed in Zephro's grip. In vain he strove to restrain it, and restrain himself.

The devotees' eyes were distorted and aslant. They were armed with saw-toothed swords alive with flickering green fire. Heedless of any minor wounds, even relishing them, they stormed barricades of rubble and overturned carts manned by musketeers and pistoleers and archers.

Fiends were running forth, some on all fours, some with their segmented burnished pastel bodies upright. The intoxicating musky perfume of these creatures! If one of them reached a defender and touched him with its long tongue, the man was stunned with a desire which became hysterical obsession – until the poisonous tail lashed him into toxic spasms. To the rear of the melée, tattooed daemonettes in tightly provocative chain-armour capered on their mounts. They flourished their pincers. They kicked with their clawed feet. They summoned fiend after fiend into existence from out of columns of dense, scented mists.

But then the eldar had come.

THE STRIKING SCORPIONS had seemed, at first sight, to be a new and terrible manifestation of the evils which already haunted Horror.

Their insectoid armour and sloping helms were green, with bands of black – which Zephro was to learn was the funereal black of Ulthwé. They wielded buzzing chainswords and pistols coupled by flexible tubes to their arms. From the cheeks of their helms jutted pods like mandibles, an insect's biting mouth-parts.

These green warriors did not join the devotees and daemonettes and fiends, except in a deadly duel.

What a swift, lethal duel this was. Although clad in rigid plates of armour, how rapidly and limberly these Striking Scorpions moved. The buzz of a chainsword rose to a wail as the razor-edge monomolecular teeth carved through chitin and bone. What a scream those teeth vented whenever they met metal. The pistols fired little spinning discs too fast to see, until they had exited from a body shredded by their passage.

Those mandibles… A Scorpion paused in front of a fiend, as if dazed by its odour. As the fiend flicked out its tongue and began to swing its tail, minuscule needles sprayed from the mandibles. A flash of light – and plasma was boiling where the slivers had impacted. The fiend's horned head was ripped open. Its tail still swung. The chainsword sliced through it.

Most of the daemonettes dismounted to be able to attack with their two-toed clawed feet and sharp tails as well as with their crab-claws. Their steeds pranced forth, lashing out abominably long tongues. A Striking Scorpion was ensnared from two directions and pulled from his feet. As he fell, a daemonette fastened a claw upon the Scorpion's armoured wrist, grinding and wrenching. Another daemonette turned tail. Exposing luscious tattooed buttocks bulging from a chainmail leotard, she back-kicked at the fallen warrior's groin. Ripping armour loose, she drove the fang of her tail into the gap. The warrior convulsed, firing discs at a sullied sky, his mandibles spitting needles in vain.

More fiends were emerging. The fiends and the mounts seemed bestially unintelligent compared with the daemonettes. Yet with their odours and stings and tongues they caused havoc.

Another Scorpion succumbed to a passionate drunken desire to embrace abomination. What illusions might he be seeing? Was vision itself a paltry blur compared with the pheremonal imperative, the primal fragrance which assaulted the most ancient and deepest part of the brain? A daemonette's claw closed around the deluded victim's helm, crunching into it.

With their toothed swords, scores of devotees were flailing at these green-clad newcomers. Green fire dripped from armour as though that armour were dissolving gangrenously.

Zephro fought to stay still, to tame his writhing sword. How he struggled not to swing that sword at any Scorpion warrior – even though torment inundated his nerves.

'Kill me, kill me!' he shrieked at a Scorpion, who ducked away from him swiftly.

AND HERE AT last came the one whom Zephro would come to know as Eldrad Ulthran. An elaborate staff was in Ulthran's left hand, a long sword with richly embellished hilt in his right. The crest of his helm resembled a serrated axe-blade. Ulthran's black cloak was a banner for bold yellow runes. Power shimmered around him – and potentials. With his sword he pointed at Zephro.

Accompanying the farseer was a skull-masked companion. Runes the length of an arm decorated the vast sleeves of a skirted costume. The runes were ships of light questing through darkest night. A tail of hair swirled from a topknot knob on his helm, like pitchy smoke.

Later, Zephro would learn the name of this warlock – Ketshamine. Ketshamine gripped a witch blade almost as long as he was tall. Runes decorated the flaring blade in high relief. Rings and loops adorned the triple-guarded hilt.

With this blade the warlock pointed at Zephro as Zephro quivered in his tormented, palsied defiance of the daemon within him.

Twisting blades of ice seemed to slice through Zephro's body, lifting skin from muscle and muscle from bone, grooving the very marrow of the bones and the tissue of his brain, searching and seeking and surgically excising all the immaterial tendrils of the entity within him.

Power, so cold that it blazed, scalpelled at his very essence, peeling and coring him.

The entity within was squealing in anguish.

Zephro pushed inwardly. He might have been attempting to give birth to himself – since he sensed that this thrust of his own stark will was vital to rid himself of the terrible parasite.

'Begone, begone,' he screamed while the warlock observed him through that merciless skull-mask.

The witch blade was a bridge of icy mind-energy between the two of them. If Zephro could not redeem himself despite such reinforcement, then he must be destroyed, torn apart. Despite the madness and agony of months, Zephro squeezed at his daemon, experiencing unbelievable pangs yet accepting and using them.

Of a sudden, though he may have looked unaltered, Zephro gave birth to himself indeed – as if he had turned himself inside out. Such coolness balmed and anointed him. He was free. The daemon had dissolved. He owned his body once again.

The sword in his hand was his slave. He hurled it at a daemonette. The blade impaled the daemonette against the succulent thigh of a tongue-lashing steed. Zephro dived for the shuriken pistol dropped by a slaughtered Scorpion. He fired at a devotee, lacerating the man's sword-arm to scarlet ribbons, the dangling streamers of a toxic jellyfish.

Human musketeers and pistoleers were climbing from behind their barricades. Desperate hope was upon their exhausted faces as they discharged their guns, then used their spent weapons as clubs.

Lightning-swift, the Scorpions were striking and striking.

ZEPHRO HAD REGAINED more than himself. He had gained illumination. It was as though, despite his psychic gifts, milky cataracts had previously covered his eyes – and the eyes of his mind. Through these veils he had peered only dimly at reality. Small wonder that he had squandered his gifts upon summoning shadows. Daemonic possession had imposed tyrannical lurid lenses over those eyes of his. Salvation from possession had stripped away the lenses, and had razored away the cataracts too, and had seemed to him even to shave away the jelly of his eyes so as to strip the retinas bare – and likewise the retinas of his mind – so that he perceived reality raw and flayed and primal.

Thereby he had acquired a bright, icy inner shield against Chaos, which would reflect Chaos back upon itself.

Later, in Ulthwé, mercurial flamboyant alien Harlequins would teach him more, focusing his purified vision on the hidden depths of the cosmos upon which the froth of raging events swirled.

This galaxy of so many starclouds, so many billion suns, so many worlds pullulating with life, was a frail raft afloat upon the immaterial warp of festering mind-essence. Four terrible Chaos powers had already congealed, the fourth of these – Slaanesh – when the eldar fell through overwhelming self-indulgence. These anti-gods lusted to overthrow reality by violence or disease or lust or mutability, inaugurating a reign of mutating. metastizing, brawling nightmare forever. Already the Eye of Terror was a tumour of vile disruption in the fabric of the galaxy.

The human race had almost fallen, once, when the Emperor's bosom comrade, Horus, had been corrupted by Chaos. To defeat Horus, the Emperor had sacrificed almost all of Himself that could properly be described as 'human'. What hope was there henceforth but in brutal repression? Repression – until the paralysed Emperor Himself would finally fail; and the human race, deprived of its beacon, would succumb in a psychic nightmare which would give birth from the sludge of tormented souls to its own terminal Chaos god.

Yet there *was* a hidden hope.

Of a shining path.

Of all the forsaken goodness coagulating into a radiant being of light and wonder.

Of the coming of the *Numen*, a deity for New Men, for transformed and transfigured humanity.

If only the Emperor's unacknowledged offspring could be found and brought together – by those who had achieved illumination.

Zephro would learn of other such extraordinary Illuminati as himself, who had been possessed by Chaos yet who had endured and who had purged themselves either by their own will or else by help of exorcism.

VIVID BANNERS WERE planted around the tiers of the amphitheatre. The spectre of Stalinvast hung overhead. Swooping Hawks and Dire Avengers continued their mimic combat. Other aspect warriors were beginning to practise upon the terraces: Striking Scorpions and Howling

Banshees. Under the gaze of the silent Solitaire the Harlequins continued their rehearsals.

Zephro said to Ro-fhessi, 'I suppose the desired outcome of this ceremony and the Imperial attack it provokes mightn't become apparent until another decade or even century.'

The farseer replied mildly, 'You can always linger at the Crossroads of Inertia again, my illuminated friend.'

Friend?

Was Zephro really a *friend* of any eldar?

Oh yes. No doubt.

To a certain degree, to a certain extent.

Though, in the present crisis, any eldar of his acquaintance who put on the aspect of a warrior would override any past sentimentalities, becoming a perfect killer and survivor. As any Imperial invaders would soon learn to their cost.

To what extent had Zephro constantly been steered in his errands by farseers whose cryptic vision of probabilities must elude even the most illuminated human being?

Illuminati such as he gathered in the Emperor's Sons and stepped up their campaign of confusion to the Inquisition. Renegade Illuminati continued to infect untold worlds unawares with the hydra entity, seducing power-hungry inquisitors to their perverted cause. Were the eldar farseers genuinely concerned for the survival of the human species?

To Zephro's grief, most eldar viewed the human race as irredeemably brutish, a teeming plague of pox-flies whose maggots fed on a million worlds. Humanity's downfall would be a disaster of galactic magnitude. How could a Numen, a shining path, arise from this infestation? Or would the shining path only be akin to ignis fatuus glowing over a foul swamp, a will-o'-the-wisp?

Zephro must believe that a Numen could arise! He must believe that New Men would emerge everywhere, men and women like himself, illuminated, and shielded against Chaos.

'Ro-fhessi,' said Zephro, 'what is the probability of Jaq Draco arriving here?'

Draco had served the purpose of the Illuminati so usefully, and unknowingly. If Draco had survived, and stored himself away, Stalinvast must be a hideous beacon to him – supposing that he had been able to learn of the impending ceremony of Harlequins. A tiny fraction of the reason why Eldrad Ulthran had ordained the Stalinvast Rite of Cataclysm might be to lure the moth of Draco to this flame. Draco could only become an Illuminatus if he suffered – and survived – the atrocity of possession by a daemon…

Ro-fhessi shrugged.

'One cannot *speak* of probabilities. One cannot utter them nor assign a percentage. One can only envisage lighter and darker shades in the aching spectrum of *B'fheidir*.'

Aye, in the sickening swirl of *maybe* and *perhaps* which only a farseer fathomed…

This habitat orbiting the cinder of Stalinvast continued to prepare itself simultaneously for sacred ceremony and for slaughter.

TWELVE
TRESPASSERS

A BATTLE IN space is largely invisible, as well as silent. On battle-screens, aglow with icons generated by devoutly anointed cogitator machines relying on radar and deep-scannings, the ebb and flow of conflict is generally comprehensible.

Not so comprehensible for the majority of participants.

The speed of ships and the vast volume of void in which they manoeuvre frequently makes an engagement between whole fleets appear to be a matter of isolated spasmodic duels interspersed by vast longueurs. The unique blend of terror and tedium could sometimes cause gunners to fire at phantoms of the imagination; they would be punished by induced pain – though leniently, since gunners in their armoured flash-gauntlets and their boom-hoods were respected specialists.

Perhaps to be punished thus was preferable to the stress of awaiting a breathless excruciating demise which might come now or never.

Much of the Battle of Stalinvast – that fight of futility – was characterized by terror-tedium. This was especially true since the Imperial Fleet was on a rein known only to its fanatical admiral and to his highest officers. Many of the orders – to break off, to veer, to neglect a damaged enemy vessel – must have seemed insane or even treasonable to anyone not privy to the logic behind those orders.

How many participants could comprehend the full picture, or even a fraction of the facts?

Thousands of men immured in engine halls or galleys or repair shops or arsenals might have had little idea that any engagement was even taking place – until, perhaps, death deeply breached part of the hull in their vicinity.

The cacophony of machinery, the shriek of steam gushing from ruptures, the crackle of electric discharge from generators: these were like the very air one breathed – until an alien missile might impact and plasma would gush, and air would rush away. Then at last convulsing victims might momentarily know the silence within which the true events were occurring.

Of course, most of the crew would have heard combat klaxons – or a devout address by a chaplain broadcast from a gargoyle-speaker high up a sculpted internal tower. Nevertheless, many hundreds of technicians in the bowels of the battleships had long since been rendered stone-deaf by the perennial din. These communicated entirely by hand signals. Would they even hear the roar of a power-shaft when laser cannons fired from the decks? At least they would feel the shuddering vibrations...

THOSE ABOARD *Tormentum Malorum* scrutinized screens for hours. Fennix eavesdropped on the astropaths aboard the battleships. Meh'lindi scanned through the vox traffic. This was sometimes hectic, sometimes mute. Periodically Jaq stared through a magni-lens at remote flashes of light. Then he would swing the oculus towards the distant thin sickle of Stalinvast. From this celestial angle, the pus-yellow sun scarcely lit one-tenth of the planet.

'Huh!' was Grimm's frequent gloss on the developing situation.

FROM THE DECK of a Gothic-class battleship Cobra destroyers had flown to engage several eldar wraithships. Though the Cobras could boost quickly and turn tightly, this squadron seemed disinclined to push to the utmost – whilst wraithships could tack with such bird-like elegance, flexing the solar sails on their towering bone-masts.

A Cobra's vortex torpedo ran beyond one wraithship before exploding. The explosion disrupted the very fabric of space. The wraithship yawed. Yet it wasn't drawn into the disruption. Laser pulses raced from a second wraithship at the Cobra. Screens absorbed the energy. A third wraithship fired plasma cannons. The Cobra's screen flared in apparent overload before dying. Those shields should have accepted much more load. Had the generators not been properly blessed? Had the captain lowered the shields prematurely to bleed off the excess?

A final laser fusillade caught the stem of the Cobra. Its engines exploded, blasting the broad bows forward even faster amidst a meteoric shower of wreckage, unsteerable ever again. Already the wraithships

and other Cobras were diverging vastly, leaving behind fading plasma
and a shuddering wrinkle in the void.

A GREAT IMPERIAL ironclad powered implacably towards a cluster of
wraithships, shedding its flotilla of support vessels like chaff. Ordinarily these minnows would ransack neighbouring worlds and planetoids
for ore or fuel. If they remained upon the ironclad's decks, many were
certain to be destroyed.

The ironclad was an armoured mountain range of peaks and plateaux,
as pitted and scarred by previous battles as a moon by meteor strikes.
This ancient battleship possessed no screens. Giant plates of adamantium, tens of metres thick, were its protection – if not to those who
manned its laser turrets and plasma cannons.

An Eldar Shadowhunter jinked nearby. It pulsed laser bolts at the
ironclad. It raked the adamantium with blooms of energy. Craters were
punched, fleabites on a cudbear except to the crew in the immediate
neighbourhood of impact.

That Shadowhunter was here. It was there. It was a dancing cloud of
fragmentary kaleidoscopic glimpses. When it accelerated, its presence
was a mere shimmer, a nausea amidst the stars.

Its holoscreen was no energy shield, however. The ironclad loosed a
massive broadside at the Shadowhunter. The eldar vessel's masts and
sail disintegrated, though not the great shark of the hull.

Wraithships dispersed as this armoured bull of planetoid size charged
towards them, spewing superheated plasma from its rear.

The Imperial forces were closing in upon Stalinvast – yet so circuitously. Cobras and support vessels were all over space. Many seemed
to present themselves as deliberate targets to challenge the eldar vessels.

'THERE'S NO SENSE to it,' said Grimm. 'That ironclad alone – if it is an
ironclad – could probably ram its way inward and burst the orbital hub
wide open. I know it ain't a Tyrant ship with an energy ram on the prow,
or a Dominator with an inferno cannon. But it could, I'm sure it could.'

Grimm was so proud of his tech-knowledge of ships.

Mile'ionahd, their supposed eldar captor, said to him curtly, 'Obviously this is all a diversion to confuse my people while a surgical
intrusion occurs. I believe our wraithships can cope with a frontal
assault, though.'

'Huh to that.'

* * *

Tormentum Malorum WAS in stealth mode. Aboard the ship, for hours, it had been whisper time. The gravity generator was switched off. Jaq had conjured an aura of protection, injecting his psychic power into the energy shields, willing invisibility. May their vessel be a blank to all observers and all instruments.

'*In nomine Imperatoris: silentium atque obscuritas,*' he prayed profoundly.

More of the ravaged planet was discernible now. The bleached skull was blessedly veiled in poisonous cyclones.

The eldar habitat was also visible via magni-lens.

Behold a tiny intaglio upon the invisible ring which was its orbit. A scalloped disc was studded with spires and with nodules which would be great domes. Even as Jaq watched, a wraithship swooped past the habitat, seeming to shimmer in and out of existence, and sailed onward to join the battle.

DECOYS SPIRALLED THROUGH the emptiness, piloted by devout men of noble families and ancient tradition who had no idea what their orders signified in any wider scheme yet who would carry out those orders for the sake of their admiral and their heritage and out of utter commitment to His Divine Terribilitas on Terra and His representative, agent of His Inquisition.

Despite the flimsiness of the Emperor's hold upon so-called human space, despite the hundreds of thousands of worlds where His writ was merely nominal, the Imperium could still muster vastly many more machines and fighting men than the remnants of eldar civilization. Despite all ravages of war, humanity still bred faster than it died. The Imperium could afford to spend its currency of people.

Looming into sight on a trajectory which would bring it quite close to Stalinvast, came the greatest of decoys. A Gothic-class battleship was firing salvoes at the high-finned sharks of wraithships.

Co-ordinated laser and plasma fire from the eldar vessels seethed at the base of one of the battleship's spires. Metal boiled. Gas plumed sternward, a comet's brilliant tail. A shield amidships must have failed. Had the shield been lowered momentarily to spill energy? In this perilous moment were its operators taken unawares by death, and a generator destroyed?

The kilometre-high spire of the combat-cathedral was fretted with gables and pinnacles, with lancets and cusps and balustrades, with buttresses and trefoil tracery and crocketed turrets.

The spire snapped.

Like some vast ornate javelin it swung away from the course of the battleship. That javelin was heading towards a wraithship.

No doubt the eldar crew were mesmerised by the magnitude of what was occurring.

The adamantium tip of the spire, and two hundred metres more of it, impaled the wraithship. Wraithbone ribs opened like those of a cooked fowl speared by a skewer. Sheer momentum carried the eldar vessel aside.

Small cannon fire continued to pour from armoured men on balustrades of the spire. The fire spat down into the pierced belly of the wraithship, aggravating the terrible wound in the wraithbone.

Then the wraithship exploded internally – even while the amputated spire still pushed the wrecked vessel on its way. From fractures in the spire spilled a dust of men-mites.

Another wraithship was pouring fusion-glare into that bubbling cavity in the battleship, such a terrible convulsion of energies! If the eldar continues to press their advantage, the battleship might split in half. Its deck would soar onward forlornly or perhaps dive into Stalinvast. Its rump might attempt to manoeuvre away.

Such a wonderful distraction was this agony of the battleship.

Tormentum Malorum DOCKED unobserved on magnetic grapples in a great vacant hangar at the base of the habitat. The hangar had possessed no doors – either to open, or to close so as to flood the dock with air.

Almost as soon as Petrov had extinguished the screens and Jaq had allowed the aura of stealth to evaporate, an eldar voice clamoured on the vox. It must have seemed as though the sleek vessel had appeared out of nowhere.

Who were they?

What were they?

How RELIEVED JAQ was to relax his psychic exertion. This had endured for so very long.

In view of the lack of air in the hangar they might be obliged to wear power armour to leave the ship. Four suits were aboard. One of these was even Grimm's smaller version from so many years ago. Four suits, but not five. By this reckoning Fennix would have had to stay behind.

Jaq was determined that everyone must go inside the habitat. He couldn't risk abandoning the astropath. Fennix was a resource whom Jaq had decided he might dearly need – should a renegade inquisitor such as he feel obliged to contact Imperial forces. Jaq mistrusted that he might ever see trusty *Tormentum Malorum* again.

Did supposed prisoners wear power armour? Ach, none of them could wear any armour! Meh'lindi especially – or rather, Mile'ionahd – must be visibly identified as an eldar. This was hardly possible if she was encased in black metal of Imperial manufacture.

WHO WERE THEY?

What were they?

Mile'ionahd was talking swiftly in the eldar tongue over the radio. Lying fluently.

PRESENTLY A SEGMENTED tube, big enough to allow the passage of a modest vehicle, flexed out from the wall of the dock to lock against *Tormentum's* hatch. As they quit the protection of their ship, to step along that enclosed glowing passage, Jaq's plan seemed almost suicidal.

A radiant path, indeed! Lenses would be scanning them. Eldar eyes would be watching them, derisive at the paltry pretence. Maybe the guardians of the dock would be more curious than alarmed, too puzzled to kill prematurely.

Was it for this – to infiltrate a robed man and a whey-faced Navigator and a blind runt and a vulgar abhuman – that the Imperium had sent three battleships laden with Cobra fighters? Impossible!

Demurely, as if cowed, four persons preceded the eldar woman. Although Fennix possessed nearsense, Petrov guided the astropath by the arm, exhibiting a strange protectiveness which Fennix appeared to appreciate.

Mile'ionahd brought up the rear, a haughty and elegant spring to her step. She pointed a shuriken pistol at the backs of her prisoners. With this pistol she had supposedly seized an Imperial ship – after stowing away – and had disarmed its occupants. Sight of Fennix and Petrov and the slouching abhuman lent some credence to the possibility. Jaq let his shoulders slump as if he were in despair.

Their captor wore Sirian silk over her clingtight bodysuit, her scarlet assassin's sash a graceful adornment to the silk. Her torso was hung with an armoury fit for a squad of warriors. All those confiscated weapons... *Emperor's Mercy* and *Emperor's Peace*; needle gun and force rod; two laspistols and a clip of grenades.

THE PASSAGE DEBOUCHED into a long soaring hall of achingly beautiful proportions, tiled in pale pastels. Corridors led away. Several transit tubes housed what appeared to be monorails. Perched on one rail was a streamlined car decorated with enamelled runes and images of multicoloured wings. Another on a further rail was embellished with heads of dragons from whose mouths gushed zigzag fire.

Cloaked in brindled fur, over light pearly armour with bold runes upon the breastplate, several guardians were waiting by the dragon-car. Alertly they cradled long-barrelled lasguns.

Five guardians for five uninvited visitors.

Should Mile'ionahd move aside from her prisoners now? Should she fire the shuriken pistol, and snatch the needle gun from its holster to pump toxic slivers at the eldar?

These weren't men. They could be faster than her. She was Callidus. Had she transformed herself so dazzlingly and undergone radical surgery simply to gain a minor advantage and squander it forthwith? Supposing that other guardians were keeping watch on what transpired in this hall! Maybe none were.

The population of eldar wasn't large compared with the human race. Tiny, really.

In many human environments, such a hall as this would have been crowded. Whole families would have lived in it. There would have been tech workshops and dens. Vent gargoyles would have forever sucked in the odour of bodies and exhaled recycled air.

The eldar might build extravagantly, yet there wouldn't be a festering rabble of them aboard this habitat. Most of those who were aboard must be vitally engaged elsewhere.

Grimm was mumbling to himself, 'Bloody eldar. Still, I don't want to mess with them.'

Quite against the grain, for an impulsive squat! Of course Grimm had been suborned by the Harlequin man and had acquired a new perspective upon the eldar.

Illuminati. Emperor's Sons.

The tallest of tall tales? Or the most crucial secret in the segmentum? And one in which the eldar meddled!

Mile'ionahd called out, Jaq knew not what.

A guardian responded – but then broke off. Glittering motes were falling upon the guardians. Mites seemed to scuttle over their pearly armour.

The eldar were cocking their heads in a way which suggested to Jaq that they were harking to some telepathic cue.

A guardian came darting along the hall, calling out. She was a female, with a pluming top-knot of hair. She leapt lithely into the dragon-car. Ignoring Mile'ionahd and her prisoners, four of the other guardians joined her in a trice. The car was already accelerating away. A lone guardian remained to cope with the abhuman and the runt and the three other intruders.

Oh, the arrogance of the eldar. That one of them should be the equal of four humans and an abhuman.

Before the car quite vanished from sight Meh'lindi – no longer Mile'ionahd – had already fired her shuriken pistol at the guardian.

The hand which had held a lasgun disintegrated bloodily. Promptly the guardian damped the stump with his other hand, squeezing tight. Blood leaked between his strong graceful fingers. Meh'lindi shouted at him. He made no further move at all, merely eyeing her with deadly enquiry.

Jaq had seized *Emperor's Mercy* and Grimm was clutching the boltgun's twin. The squat rummaged a laspistol loose and thrust it into Petrov's hand. 'Damn well take it!'

Meh'lindi reported: 'The female guardian said "Come quickly" and "Disable their clumsy legs".'

So that Jaq and his companions would have remained in this hall for later questioning, no doubt.

Elsewhere in the massive habitat, some dire distraction had occurred. One could make certain guesses as to its nature.

Shuriken pistol pointing, Meh'lindi strode towards the bloody-handed guardian. She kicked the fallen lasgun aside then picked it up. Her shuriken disc hadn't damaged it; flesh and bone had served as a cushion.

The mimic and authentic eldar exchanged words.

'Grimm and Azul: unclothe him,' said Meh'lindi. 'I want his armour and his cloak.'

Blood had spattered both items. The eldar shut his eyes. He must be concentrating upon staunching the flow of blood by willpower.

More blood was lost as the abhuman and the Navigator manoeuvred the injured eldar out of his guardian's armour. Now Jaq was pointing his boltgun at the alien's head.

Meh'lindi shed her silk and assumed pearly armour and cloak. She said quickly, 'Let's leave him as he is. I told him, "Mercy to the eldar". I am an eldar myself, aren't I?'

'Huh, mercy. And now he has one hand–' Grimm licked blood off his own hairy hand. 'Yuck.'

'He said to me, "Now I am nearer to God the Bloody-Handed." That's their war god.'

Meh'lindi was soon dressed as a guardian – one who had been involved in some sanguinary action.

The eldar began singing to himself, and swaying.

'We'll leave him alive,' agreed Jaq. 'There's no reason for us to alienate the eldar unnecessarily.'

'They're already alien enough,' said Grimm with a gruff flippancy which disavowed anxiety.

'He'll get inside our ship,' protested Petrov. 'He'll drip all over it.'

'I'm not sure,' said Jaq, 'that we'll ever see *Tormentum* again. I have a feeling–'

At that moment a psychic itch assailed Jaq. He realized that his Tarot was vibrating inside a pocket of his robe in a quite extraordinary way – demanding to be consulted.

Scarcely time to do so. To linger could be fatal as well as futile. They must leave this hall behind as soon as they could.

Jaq, Meh'lindi and Grimm hastened to the remaining car and climbed in. Grimm was muttering over a joystick as if resorting to prayer. Petrov hauled the blind astropath towards the winged car. Was Fennix going to prove an impediment? Needing to be abandoned? Needing to be euthanased by boltgun on account of what he might reveal? The car was throbbing, straining to move. The Navigator heaved the astropath aboard the car, and leapt in himself – then the vehicle was accelerating.

'Hey, I didn't do a thing,' yelled Grimm.

The car sped along a tunnel through arcs of rainbow light. It tilted to left, to right. It changed track of its own accord where the rail branched. The slim rail was of a seemless creamy bony substance evidently of great strength, with supports of even slimmer bone.

Jaq's cards, in their wrapping of mutant skin, were still throbbing. He sensed that the car was riding along part of a great intricate skeleton which reached everywhere in and around the habitat. Wraithbone. *Psychoresponsive*. The energy to propel the car came from the wraithbone itself. If he were an eldar he would be choosing the car's route. Since he wasn't an eldar, the bone rail was determining a psychically significant destination – abetted by his own cards? If he could pull out his significator card and focus upon it, he might be in control.

An image assaulted him of all his cards flying from his hand into the car's slipstream, the runes of fate fluttering away in disorder back along the tunnel, bursting into flames wherever they touched the bone rail.

'My warp-eye aches with *absences*,' Petrov shouted in his ear. 'Can you sense the absences?'

Aye, absences. Such a habitat should contain gardens where trees of wraithbone grew above the crystals of dead souls – whereby those souls became part of the network of the quasi-living milieu. If this were a craftworld that would surely be the case.

There exist morphic forms, insistent shapes which configure realities. Runes are such. Likewise, the gene-rune which delineates an embryo out of protoplasm. Strange awarenesses were leaking into Jaq. Among the eldar there must be bonesingers – mages who could manipulate the growth of this wraithbone to build ships and furnish habitats. Here in orbit around Stalinvast they had built not an abode for souls but a theatre of horror. Or at least this was a place with a potential for horror – horror to be catalysed by the Imperial attack.

Fleetingly Jaq visualized this vast structure as a trap for a Chaos god to be summoned here, then isolated in a psychic cage. A bone-corset would close crushingly around the malign force. The cage would tumble out of orbit down on to the world of nullity which Stalinvast had become, where not even the soul of a microbe endured for evil to possess. Could the wraithbone cage survive impact, twisted but unruptured? Jaq imagined an incarnated Chaos god gibbering within the bone bars as poisonous cyclones scourged it.

A waking dream, this... or a nightmare!

Surely no living beings could achieve such an imprisonment and punishment of part of Chaos – the inverse of what happened when a daemon possessed a living victim.

The desire to do so perhaps existed. The hydra conspirators themselves desired something similar. Ach, futile treacherous dreams!

Maybe Jaq was hallucinating.

At one point in their journey, the car slowed almost to a halt as if inviting its passengers to descend. A short side passage became a misty tunnel, blue and glowing.

'Oh the warp, the warp,' groaned Petrov.

Here was a pedestrian portal into the eldar webway.

During this pause Jaq pulled the mutant-skin package from his robe. When he had last wrapped his Tarot away, the High Priest card had been on top, dominating the pack. No longer. Cards had shuffled themselves.

Warily, Jaq stared at the Harlequin card. Here was a moving image of Zephro Carnelian attired in a suit of red and green patches, a plumed tricorne hat on his head. The man was minimally masked yet it was certainly he. He was capering, giggling, beckoning. Faint wild music skirled.

Jaq laid his fingertips on the card. The liquid-crystal wafer twitched and pulsed of its own accord, just as when his own significator card had led him along the luminous path slightly adjacent to ordinary reality, towards the Emperor's throne room. Now he felt like a fish with a hook in its mouth, being hauled inexorably through contrary currents.

Hastily he bundled the pack away. The car was picking up speed again. Tube and monorail began to spiral upward. The tube was a conduit now for the sound of combat, for the crackle and whistle of weaponry.

Suddenly the car emerged from confinement. Abruptly it braked. Meh'lindi caught hold of Grimm by his flak jacket just as he was about to fly out of the vehicle. Jaq managed to brace himself bruisingly. Petrov's head and shoulders impacted in Jaq's back, yet at least the Navigator had clutched Fennix to himself. Damn the quicksilver pace of the eldar! The car had halted on a grooved bone circle. Presumably this would rotate to swing the car around for a return journey. A cowl arched over the bone circle, as gaily painted as some carnival booth. Blood trickled from the Navigator's nose as if his rubies had melted and multiplied.

This was the least of the blood being shed furiously in the vicinity. Beyond the carnival-cowl was a great amphitheatre of tiered turf.

An arena of bedlam – and pandemonium. A stadium of homicidal madness.

Jaq growled like a beast, and prayed for enlightenment.

Thirteen
Invaders

The scene which met Jaq's eyes eluded immediate comprehension.

A bowl of green moss several kilometres wide. Looming in mid-air above the bowl: the corpse of Stalinvast, its weather systems churning like seas of maggots.

Vertigo assailed him. He felt as though he were falling upward towards that malign vision. Maggots, maggots, a looming eyeball of maggots.

'Emperor's tears!' he cried aloud.

No, that sight was an illusion. It was only a holographic projection, part of the alien pageant.

Bursting from out of the phantom planet, like glittering insects from a swollen carcass, flew vibrant blue warriors. These swooped down over – yes, over Imperial Space Marines in power armour. A squad of the Astartes was advancing across the bowl.

Their armour was the colour of pus; their chest-plastrons were blazoned with spreadeagles. The invasion was already under way. This theatre of death was hosting a violent performance.

Las-bolts lanced from the long-barrelled guns of the fliers. Patches of turf vaporized around the Space Marines' great boots. One staggered as the cuisse protecting his thigh seethed. The servos of his power armour righted him, even if his leg had been wounded. The Marines fired clattering streams of bolts upward.

How the eldar fliers' wings shrilled as they jinked to avoid the lethal hail from below. A flier convulsed, hovered feebly for a moment, then dropped from mid-air. The winged alien's fall was a long dripping smear of blurred blue and blood.

Aspect warriors on flying bikes were attacking another squad of Space Marines. Shuriken stars ricocheted off a suit. Stars spiked a Marine's right arm like so many baneful badges. Other stars must have torn their way inside the armour. The arm hung limp, its cables severed. But he still retained the use of his left. A bike disintegrated in a fireball. A shattered body plunged.

From beyond the rim of the amphitheatre came the crump of a distant explosion. In that direction graceful towers arose. Under an adjacent sky-dome was a small city. Dirty smoke plumed upward, undoubtedly from infernos caused by other Space Marines.

Scores of gaudy structures stood about in the amphitheatre. Stiffened pennants jutted like tongues of chemical flame. Some structures seemed real. Others were surely illusions. In some places low black walls wrote networks of runes upon the slopes of moss. These angled walls were serving as cover and firing positions for guardians and for gaudy warriors.

Several Marines had stormed one of those runic redoubts. By seizing it, did they acquire power over the symbol as well as over its physical embodiment? A richly ornamented battle banner rose tauntingly, depicting a mailed fist wreathed around with skulls.

Fists? *Imperial Fists*? Jaq had most certainly heard of the Chapter. Ten thousand years ago the Imperial Fists had been stalwarts in the desperate defence of the Emperor's palace against the hordes of Horus. He remembered how the armour of dead Fists killed in that battle was embedded illustriously in the Column of Glory, their skulls grinning out of open visors.

ELSEWHERE, IT WAS as if a war and a sacred rite – or a bizarre pantomime – had intersected absurdly like two contradictory holos crisscrossing one another.

Armed Harlequins in multicoloured costumes were darting about with prodigious energy and speed. They leapt. They whirled. They keened strangely melodious chants. They touched one another, they rushed apart. They were here. Already they were somewhere else.

As the Harlequins cavorted, those holo-suits and masks of theirs underwent a whole repertoire of changes – from brightly variegated Harlequin to monstrous predator, from lusciously enticing androgynous harlot to a horrific daemonic semblance.

A Harlequin seemed to be a Space Marine in yellow. Then the same Harlequin was an animated skeleton.

Another vanished. It became merely a vague ripple as it rushed away – to reappear elsewhere. How these Harlequins disordered the senses of the beholder! What mercurial mirrors they were for one's own phantoms and fears!

They fired laser pulses and streams of shuriken discs.

Skull-masked and decorated with blanched bones, a supremely agile figure of Death lithely manoeuvred a great flanged gun. From the fluted muzzle sprang a misty cloud. The cloud flew towards an Imperial Fist. On impact, that cloud became a writhing mass of thinnest wire, tearing at the Marine's armour, trying to find any chink or cranny.

Another Harlequin jerked out his forearm, to which a tube was strapped. A similar wire leapt almost a hundred metres towards a Space Marine. The wire was so fine as to be almost invisible. Yet its tip pierced some ancient weakness in the Marine's gauntlet. The warrior's whole arm hung limply. Inside the armour was there now only jelly?

A Marine with only one sound arm was still a Marine with a *fist*. Marine armour was supremely puissant – usually. Injured Marines could frequently fight on, courtesy of their armour and reinforced bodies and hormonal boosts. An eldar might easily match himself or herself against several Imperial Guardsmen – but hardly against a Space Marine. The invading force was making inroads without sustaining too many casualties.

WHO WAS THIS person in massive heraldic Terminator armour, armed with storm bolter and power glove? Surely a Librarian, escorting an exhilarated inquisitor. The latter wore a golden carapace breastplate and groin-shield under a flaring black cloak. His blunt head was bare. A lens in one eye. A tube up one nostril. Sapphires were stitched across one cheek.

'Purge and cleanse and seize!' the inquisitor was shouting at the advancing Space Marines – as though their own captain were not present to give orders.

FIRENZE HAD SCORNED the wearing of armour. Naturally he couldn't wear a power suit of the Astartes variety. He lacked an artificial carapace beneath his skin, and input sockets. If the mission proved protracted, too many pieces of carapace armour could have slowed and fatigued him.

To be directing fully armoured Marines without the benefit of much personal armour made this inquisitor appear almost superhuman, an effect which Firenze devoutly desired. He wielded a power sword and a laspistol.

Purge, and seize... The instructions were almost schizoid.

Massacre – and capture Harlequins who kenned the webway! Seize a Great Harlequin who could open portals upon the secret route of the eldar through the warp.

And annihilate opposition.

Firenze was effervescent with righteousness in a way which must surely be inspirational.

CAPTAIN LEXANDRO D'ARQUEBUS felt renewed qualms. Imperial Fists did not need their loyalty to be cranked to fever pitch as if by a rabid preacher. Their sense of duty was perpetually honed by contemplation of Rogal Dorn, their primarch, their progenitor, their angelic intermediary with Him-on-Earth.

This disagreeably charismatic Baal Firenze had already swayed the emotions of at least two sergeants and numerous battle-brothers. When the Fists finally returned to their fortress-monastery these men would need to pray devoutly for purity.

Ideally a Fist's life was one of sublime simplicity. Differences of view between Fists were resolved courteously by a duel. This Firenze was a seething maelstrom of complexities, as though his overt mission was not necessarily his real mission, and as though he did not entirely know who he himself was, and hoped by coming here to enlighten himself in some arcane fashion.

Maybe such complexity was only to be expected of an inquisitor? Lex still felt serious qualms, as he fired his boltgun.

As yet Sir Baal had not reiterated, to the men at large, his effusions about the slaughter of alien youngsters – perhaps because none were to be seen, or perhaps because he had indeed noted the tacit disgust of Lex and Kempka. Had he repeated such sentiments, sergeants and battle-brothers would have lost their respect for him.

How OPPRESSIVELY THAT phantom holo-world hung over the battle-ground. Might that image presently resolve itself into a rapacious daemon enwombed in that ghastly sphere? Even as Firenze glanced aloft, a shape of lust and cruelty seemed to swim momentarily within that globe. Perhaps these were simply his own emotions.

'Where are the alien whelps?' bellowed Firenze.

Ah, now he was verging upon the obscene.

'Which portal did the whelps flee through?'

But now the question seemed a rational one.

During the rampage through the fringes of the city, Firenze had come upon a shimmering foggy blue tunnel within a building. To enter such a tunnel uninitiated would be to stride to an unpredictable wherever.

'Snatch a Harlequin, my fine men! I'll reward you richly in the Emperor's name!'

What was this talk of riches? Why, what reward should an Imperial Fist require but simply to know that he had served the Emperor as well as he could? Was this inquisitor regarding Marines as akin to Imperial Guardsmen?

A Fist was rich when he hurt in the pursuit of a crusade dedicated to the memory of Dorn.

'I'll see you honoured!'

Battle honours were bestowed not by an inquisitor but by the commander of the fortress-monastery. How dare this inquisitor trespass upon sacred prerogatives?

Baal Firenze's word was law. It was *lex imperialis*, the dictate by proxy of the Emperor.

Yet Lex's own name meant *law*. Firenze himself had said so. Lex's word was law for ten sergeants and ninety other battle-brothers. Somewhat less than ninety by now, in fact.

Lex activated the disposition readout on his faceplate. In the burning eldar city and in this amphitheatre of hell eighty-two Fists were still alive, though a dozen had suffered significant injuries. Dietrich, Volker and Zigmund were among the dead. Brave men, brave.

Compared with the triumphant campaign on Hannibal against the Banshees, this was... unfortunate. Even agonizing.

Yet it was acceptable, in the way that agony often was acceptable.

Greater numbers of aliens had died here.

On Hannibal those Banshees had behaved with abnormal frenzy. Their behaviour had seemed demented, as if they could no longer view their activities objectively. Frenzy was the foe of rational tactics.

These gaudy Harlequins and aspect warriors and guardians of the habitat were hectic in a far more dangerous and versatile fashion.

Imperial Fists were still superior.

Lex dearly wished that he could consult again with Librarian Kempka privately on the command channel about the matter of Firenze. But the inquisitor wore master communicators dangling from both ear-lobes. He would hear any words which might seem to him to reek of heresy – and which might indeed be heretical.

Dorn, dawn of my being, scald me with sanctity so that any impurity peels from me...

Lexandro fired at the blue blur of a Swooping Hawk. He rejoiced to see feather plates spray from a damaged wing. The Hawk still flew, though less skillfully. The anti-gravity lifter and jet-pack of its harness remained undamaged. Lex fired again. His gun simply clicked. The magazine was empty. Such negligence was heresy. Quickly yet scrupulously, with his sturdy gauntlets, he ejected and reloaded.

Jaq saw a Harlequin pop up from behind a zig-zag rune-wall. No, not an eldar Harlequin at all – but the *Harlequin Man!* Zephro Carnelian, in a plumed hat! He was here!

Carnelian beckoned with a laspistol. The suit he wore flickered spectrally, a motley of shifting colours. It was him, it was him. The hooked chin, the long jutting nose. Doubtless he wore mesh armour under his holo-suit as did Jaq under his hooded robe.

Carnelian, possessor of the secrets of Illuminati and Emperor's Sons... Jaq's bane...

'Sir Zephro!' Grimm bellowed before Jaq could hush him. 'Sir Zephro!'

The Harlequin Man vanished – except for a crimson plume and a taunting grin. Then these, too, ducked out of sight.

In the spectral sphere overhead, figures were forming. What had been a phantom world was now a globular stage which dwarfed all occurrences below – or which reflected and magnified these, augmenting the significance of the bedlam in the wide arena.

Upon that global stage, giant aerial Harlequins were pirouetting and somersaulting. Death was stalking victims – to toss these at the feet of a gibbering monster of lust and cruelty which one hardly dared to glimpse. A Laughing God nimbly evaded the attentions of this monster. Behind and within that vast evil presence was a seeming infinity of screaming delirious eldar. Psychotic eldar composed that Chaos god's body. Wherever the Laughing God trod, a road of bright light leapt forth, launching lightning at the malign spectral daemon.

Down below, real Harlequins were vanishing. Their holo-suits merged them prismatically with their surroundings. They seemed to leap up into the air, to become one with the terrible pageant above.

'It's an evocation of Slaanesh!' snarled the Librarian.

Lex sweated coldly in his power suit. Thank Dorn that his men and he wore psychic shielding inside their helmets.

'These aliens must be insane,' exclaimed Kempka.

Firenze swayed as he stared upward. Froth flecked his lips. He licked the foam fastidiously.

'What a bloodily stupid and evil undertaking. Our crusade is blessed.' Firenze almost sounded pleased. He squinted through his lens at the stage in the sky. 'Now I see how the eldar fell. Those imperious besotted fools gave themselves over to delirious delights and self-indulgences. Their wild lusts erupted into existence as a Chaos entity. All of their own deities died except for that laughing spirit, that mockery of deity–'

'Don't speak of such things,' implored Lex.

HOLO-SUITED IN darkest night asparkle with stars, and rictus-masked, a Solitaire was gazing upward.

His was the loneliest of existences. No spirit stone enshrined his soul. When he died his soul was forfeit to Slaanesh, unless the Laughing God could play a splendid trick. A strong eldar soul did not dissolve into the sea of souls at death, dissipating in the way that weak human souls did. Its integrity survived. The dead Solitaire would be the toy of cruel lust for ever more. In all probability.

A Solitaire lived alone. He wandered alone. He killed alone.

Could this rite of cataclysm possibly redeem him?

The Laughing God should triumph today. In all probability. Probability was a province of farseers, not of a Solitaire.

The Solitaire danced the cursed role of Slaanesh, capering towards a Harlequin who evaded him.

Pivoting, he fired his shuriken pistol at a distant Space Marine. Yes, this was a true dance of death today.

One thought disconcerted the Solitaire. Wasn't this rite, imbued with such bloody realism and murderous verisimilitude, all too reminiscent of the fatal excesses of the eldar of old?

Eerily sang the Solitaire who must speak to no one alive.

VAPOURS WERE COILING up from the moss, obscuring swathes of the landscape, though not the holo projection above.

A masked Harlequin appeared before Meh'lindi. Before the blood-stained guardian Mile'ionahd.

Grimm's pebble had been pressing into Meh'lindi's chest under the creamy breastplate. She had pulled the pebble out. It hung loose on its wire thong.

Miming, the Harlequin invited her mockingly to dance.

Before Meh'lindi could decide how to react, the Harlequin snatched at her pebble. The move was lightning-fast. Wire bit into the back of Meh'lindi's neck like the momentary kiss of a garrotte. The thong snapped. The Harlequin dissolved into a blur of light. It was running away with her forgery of a spirit-stone. Petrov fired his laspistol vainly – light in pursuit of light. Meh'lindi rubbed the back of her neck.

A guardian had spied this incident. With bounding leaps he sprinted towards them, crying out and pointing a lasgun. Meh'lindi brought the guardian down with a stream of shuriken discs.

JAQ COULD HAVE sworn that he was drugged and in a hallucinatory fugue. The confusing colours of the Harlequins! The soul-aching music that he heard. The racket and whine and percussion of weaponry. The intoxicating tide of high emotions which impinged on his psychic faculty.

Would his senses overload? Would they fracture into madness? Or would they transcend to a new vision of reality? A perception of a rainbow mad?

Weaponry seemed like so many surgical instruments for performing psychic surgery upon consciousness rather than upon flesh. Laser pulses were the firing of neurons. Nerve signals flashed along death-kisser filaments. Explosions were thunderous new concepts, quakes as world-views shifted.

'Clarify me, my Emperor!' he cried.

Clarify? He-on-Earth was of many diverse minds.

Vapours roiled from the moss, drifting and obscuring.

This battle was the catalyst for the transfiguration occurring up in the holo-sphere. That aerial stage seemed to suck souls and bodies upward into it. Jetbikes and Hawks sped into the maelstrom of gods and avatars and jesters in conflict, to pern and spiral there. Surely some revelation was at hand.

High beyond the holo-globe and beyond a faint silhouette of a spacespire, a craft swooped by on a tail of plasma.

'Cobra,' commented Grimm. 'That one came close.'

Jaq had almost forgotten that battleships were burning and wraithships disintegrating. The ongoing combat in space seemed even more irrelevant than previously.

Just at this moment, a bolt shell ripped *Emperor's Mercy* from Jaq's glove. The shock almost broke his fingers. His hand throbbed, paralysed. A las-bolt sizzled past, ionizing the air. Ozone reeked. An aspect warrior was firing at any strangers. Meh'lindi, in her guardian's armour, cried out eldar words which well might have signified, *No, don't, these are our friends*. As the warrior hesitated, explosive bolts hit him from another quarter, throwing him aside, dead or dying.

It was a Space Marine who had fired the bolt from out of the midst which disarmed Jaq. A captain, by his regalia.

The captain was accompanied by a Terminator Marine and by two other battle-brothers in yellow armour.

Behind these, brandishing power sword and laspistol, came a robed, bare-headed man – one of whose eyes was a lens and whose cheek glittered with sapphires.

'*Firenze!*' cried Jaq.

Grimm had retrieved Jaq's boltgun. Jaq flapped his numb hand to restore some finesse to it.

The amplified voice of the captain came, in stern Imperial Gothic: '*None of you shall move!*'

'Heretic!' Firenze shouted at Jaq. A shower of radiance from the spectacle on high caught Firenze's lens. That lens winked and flashed as Firenze goggled at Jaq's exquisite armoured female companion.

'Consorter with aliens!' Firenze bellowed. 'What did your eldar allies do to my mind a hundred years ago?'

Jaq had no notion what Baal Firenze was talking about. Ignorance ached within him.

Ignorance was often a blessing for the mass of human beings in the galaxy. Blessed be those who are oblivious – of daemons, and of genestealer monsters, and of the Emperor's schizoid decrepitude, and of so much else!

For such as Jaq, ignorance was a kind of sacrilege.

What had the eldar done to Firenze's mind a century previously? Assuming that Firenze wasn't lying or deluded.

Would it be eldar Harlequins whom Firenze accused? Harlequins acting in consort with Zephro Carnelian? Or perhaps manipulating Carnelian? Using the Harlequin Man?

Jaq threw caution away. 'Don't you remember your part in the hydra conspiracy, Firenze?' he called. 'Conspiracy against the Imperium!'

Firenze looked haunted and insane.

'Renegade!' Firenze retorted, yet without passionate conviction. 'Did you really dictate the Book of Secrets which implicated me?'

All this while, the four Space Marines and Firenze had been moving forward, but very slowly, as though the words which were being exchanged were ponderous leaden weights – or bombs primed to explode if tilted.

How veiled the groundside scene was by the thickening mist. But for the spasms of percussion and detonation and the occasional glimpse of an airborne warrior, this confrontation might have been taking place in some private domain detached from the field of battle. Yet war was sometimes thus: a medley of isolated encounters, the participants divorced from the totality in personal hells.

LEX SHUDDERED. HIS suit magnified his spasm until he stilled it.

What was this about a conspiracy against the Imperium? And who was the conspirator? Faith itself was being questioned in this encounter. Even Librarian Kempka might be out of his depth. If only a battle chaplain were here to advise.

A chaplain would surely insist on unquestioning devotion to duty in the Emperor's name, illuminated by the inner light of Rogal Dorn. But was that sufficient guidance?

This rival inquisitor, so unexpectedly encountered! Surely he was irrelevant to the Fists' mission. Their mission was the capture of eldar Harlequins and the seizure of keys to the legendary webway. Their mission was to disrupt this terrible ceremony being enacted by illusions overhead and by kaleidoscopic alien warriors below.

The brave actions of Lexandro's company of Imperial Fists seemed almost to be contributing to the bloody ceremony. It was as if his men were sacrificing themselves, and even their enemies, in some arcane cause which was not their own cause at all.

Serve without question.

A Fist did question. Especially a captain of Fists should question. He must never squander his battle-brothers. No matter how puissant each Space Marine might seem, no matter how invincible a company of fighting knights, there were really so few to withstand all the dire threats to the Imperium. When any Space Marine died the sacred glands of geneseed must be harvested if at all possible, so as to kindle new brothers to replace the dead.

Could it be that battleships and tens of thousands of crew and Fists too were being expended here because of some vendetta between inquisitors?

Could it be that the Battle of Stalinvast and the invasion of the alien habitat were being staged to weaken the Imperium?

As IF TO mirror the confusion in Lex's mind, commotion erupted. A Space Marine appeared in the mist to the right: a fog of yellow.

Another to the left. Other figures were moving nearby.

Those weren't, those couldn't, be Fists. Imperial Fists were broader, much heftier in their armour.

Lex pined to see in infra-red.

They were eldar Harlequins in those damnable chameleon holo-suits of theirs. One wore a mask mimicking the helmet of a Space Marine.

Briefly the mask became a terrible laughing alien face. Next moment it was a death's head. And then it was a helmet again.

The other Harlequin wore no mask nor semblance of helmet. His face was bare, or it seemed to be. The face was more human than alien – beneath a tricorne hat with a high plume. How that flimsy hat mocked the helmets of real warriors.

In a spooky affected voice the Harlequin Man called out: 'Come this way, Sir Jaq!' He fired a laspistol.

Firenze screamed with pain and rage. The inquisitor's right arm was on fire. His laspistol had fallen. Firenze swept his power sword to and fro as though he might attempt to amputate his own injured arm at the shoulder. One of the Fists was already squirting extinguishing froth at Firenze. White lather coated the top of Firenze's golden breastplate. Firenze seemed to be foaming at the mouth.

Librarian Kempka was firing his storm bolter – at a target which had vanished.

Shuriken discs hit the other battle-brother's armour. The Fist continued firing his boltgun. A shriek came from the mist.

One of the other persons with so-called 'Sir Jaq' was a Navigator. Around his brow, above his wrinkled insectoid face: a bandanna. That Navigator crammed a laspistol into the hand of a bat-eared, monkey-like fellow, then he picked up the monkey-man in his arms. The monkey-man flung his free arm round the Navigator's neck to cling tight. Staggering, the Navigator was carrying the monkey-man away – to what he might imagine was a place of safety. The laspistol dangled unused in the monkey-man's grip.

Another associate of 'Sir Jaq' was a short abhuman in a flak jacket. The squat was clutching two boltguns and stamping his foot in nervous frustration. To fire? Not to fire? To fire at whom? Wouldn't it be suicide to fire at Space Marines?

To fire at Firenze: that's who the squat wished to kill. Therefore this squat knew Firenze from once upon a time; and loathed him. Another mystery! Another riddle!

Overhead, and invisibly all around, the vaster riddle of the alien rite was in sickening, mind-assaulting progress.

MEH'LINDI MADE HER move. She swung her shuriken pistol towards the awesome figure in embellished Terminator armour. It wasn't he who had ordered Jaq and his companions to submit. It was that captain who had spoken the command. But the captain seemed curiously indecisive – in so far as one could read body language when the body in question was fully armoured.

The ornate Marine was the dangerous one. Was it possible to cripple him or neutralize that storm bolter so that Jaq could escape? Decamp as Petrov had already done, with Fennix in his arms, like a child being saved by its mother! Petrov was trusting in the advice of Zephro Carnelian, who had so humiliated Meh'lindi once...

No doubt the Space Marines would kill her.

Fire was incoming through the mist. Laser pulses seared the air. A glittering filament flew past, then retracted quickly with a tremulous twang, for it had hooked and gutted nothing alive, had failed to kiss and kill or maim.

As SHE FIRED the first stream of discs, Jaq shouted, 'No!' Without thinking, Meh'lindi obeyed him.

Meh'lindi mustn't sacrifice herself. Not so soon after she had painfully recovered her true self. If she died now, Jaq's quest would seem so futile.

In whom else could he confide? In Grimm, who had been enticed by Zephro Carnelian? In the Emperor's shattered spirit? In himself alone? He would be the loneliest person in the galaxy.

He who confides in himself alone is a lunatic, prey to delusions, prey perhaps to Chaos too.

MEH'LINDI MERELY HELD the shuriken pistol pointed, inert. The captain was aiming his boltgun in retaliation. The Librarian's armour was grazed but only trivially damaged. He had noted the captain's intention of killing the eldar woman. Presuming that she would be dead in a moment, the Librarian resumed firing at glowing phantoms in the mist.

Jaq could have fled. Firenze was still preoccupied – and too far away from Jaq for that power sword to serve any purpose.

By his order Jaq had condemned Meh'lindi to death. If her death were to be the diversion he required, she was accepting this. He distrusted her alien armour. He knew that she wasn't sprayed with an assassin's resistant synskin.

As the captain squeezed his trigger, Jaq threw himself in front of Meh'lindi, howling 'No!' once again.

Two bolts smashed into Jaq's ribs, and detonated.

FOURTEEN
LEXANDRO

An explosion of pain expanded across Jaq's side. There would be such a purple bruise, the breadth of his outspread hands. Despite the mesh armour Jaq was sure he had cracked a couple of ribs. It felt as though the pickaxe of a broken rib had punctured a lung. A blow from an exploding bolt was different from that of a stubgun shell.

He had been thrown against Meh'lindi. He sagged momentarily, gasping. Tears had squeezed from his eyes. She sustained him with a strong grip.

How much greater pain must be endured by Him-on-Earth to cause a minim of moisture to well in the desiccated eye-sockets of that immortal cadaver! Jaq's hurt was so trivial by comparison.

Meh'lindi's other hand still held the shuriken pistol. Superficially, she may have seemed to have taken Jaq hostage.

This captain was no superficial witness. He had only fired two bolts. Short on ammunition – or long on intelligence? He had desisted the moment that Jaq interposed himself to intercept the bolts.

'Why,' came his amplified voice through a hailer in his helmet, 'protect an alien warrior? Why give your life?'

Did the captain imagine that Jaq was mortally wounded?

Jaq righted himself. Gently he pressed a hand to his side where his robe was torn asunder.

'Is it true what Inquisitor Firenze says?' demanded the captain. Aye, Firenze with the foam-dotted arm and the power sword swinging to and fro, its blade a-crackle with that hazy blue energy field. Firenze was keeping his distance, wary of that pistol in Meh'lindi's hand.

Was it true what Firenze had said? About Jaq being a renegade and a heretic and an ally of aliens? Why, the evidence was there before the captain's eyes.

Yet the captain posed the question.

In so doing he questioned Firenze's word.

The Librarian had quit firing his storm bolter and seemed to be listening vigilantly.

Meh'lindi called out: 'Captain, I am an Imperial assassin mimicking the appearance of an eldar in order to infiltrate this place.'

'Lies!' yelled Firenze. 'She's lying.'

'She speaks Imperial Gothic fluently enough,' observed the captain deferentially.

'A trick! An eldar can speak our language, especially if associating with human renegades.'

'But, Sir Baal,' purred Meh'lindi, 'surely you know me perfectly well from aboard the hulk in the warp, where you captured us, and had me hooded – you, and your fellow conspirators of the Ordo Hydra!'

Did Firenze's jaw sag as he gaped at that seeming alien while he raked the ashes of memory?

Firenze had seen Meh'lindi only briefly in her regular human form. He had ordered her head to be draped in a null-sense hood for privacy whilst he was instructing Jaq in the mysteries of that conspiracy so appalling.

'When I assigned Jaq Draco to Stalinvast, doing my duty as proctor,' declared Firenze, 'I did arrange for an assassin to accompany him. Oh yes. But the assassin in question…' He paused, perplexed.

'But,' said Meh'lindi, 'the assassin in question had received experimental genestealer implants which limited her splendid ability to alter her appearance. How, therefore, can she be mimicking an eldar now?'

Firenze chewed at his lip, fretting at failures of memory and at memories which might be false.

Meh'lindi sang out: 'The surgery was a secret of the Officio Assassinorum, Callidus shrine, my shrine. You have evidently scanned the Book of Secrets which implicated you in treason. So you know the consequences of my surgery. So you disbelieve my present guise.'

If Firenze had not been so set on rooting out personal enigmas he might have screamed at the captain or the Librarian for her to be silenced. He merely clutched the hilt of his humming sword ever more tightly.

Meh'lindi continued, while Jaq was regaining an aching composure. 'Sir Baal, you believe that the wily eldar interfered with your mind. You must be right – since you quite failed to recognize who it was who set your arm on fire a few minutes ago!'

'What?'

'It was your fellow conspirator, Zephro Carnelian!'

Who – according to Grimm – was no fellow traitor at all, but an infiltrator of the hydra cabal bent on sabotage.

'That's a lie! I never knew any such person. Probing by deep-truth failed to expose–'

'That was after eldar mind-seers had rearranged your memories. You ought to be grateful to those eldar, Sir Baal. But for their tampering you would have been excruciated and executed by your own Inquisition. Are you really the most suitable inquisitor to come here leading Imperial forces into their web?'

Oh, Meh'lindi was being Callidus indeed. She seemed truly to have exposed the reason why Firenze had been meddled with, somehow, somewhere. Carnelian, or his eldar mentors, had wished it so, for the sake of confusion and disinformation.

'Their web,' cried Firenze. 'Their webway. That's why we're here.' He jerked his gaze at the awesome drama overhead. 'And also to abort this abomination!'

'Oh no,' she contradicted him. 'To contribute to it, I think! To donate the blood of Space Marines – and of eldar warriors too. Carnelian set your arm on fire,' she mocked, 'and you didn't even recognize him. How he must be laughing.' Her derision was tinged with a private rage at that Harlequin Man.

She was tugging Jaq purposefully. 'Grimm,' she whispered, nodding her head.

Elsewhere in the mist: such cries and explosions. Some were real. Some might be simulated, the work of Harlequin performers who were both fighting and enacting groundside aspects of the rite.

The las-blasts burning through the mist were actual enough.

THAT RIVAL INQUISITOR and the mimic woman and the abhuman had run off into the drifting vapours without Lexandro himself firing or calling upon his companions to fire. Nor had the Librarian presumed upon Lex's prerogative.

What was the truth? A captain of the Imperial Fists ached to know.

The battle must certainly continue to a victorious conclusion. Would it be desertion of his men to try to pursue that trio, and the truth? To pursue them at least briefly? To force more information out of them?

Lex imagined snapping that exotic woman's neck, cracking her skull open with his power gauntlet, and eating some of her brain so as to know her innermost thoughts. His implanted omophagea organ would permit him to know her in this way. She claimed she was an assassin. His second stomach would detoxify poisons. Maybe an assassin's grey matter might be permeated with some bane which could kill even him or disorientate him so as to protect her secrets. Aye, some passive brain-venom concocted in the laboratories of the fabled Officio Assassinorum.

Better to feed on the inquisitor's brain instead.

'Stop them!' shrilled Firenze. 'Catch them, destroy them, capture them!'

Schizoid orders, again. Nevertheless, this was what Lex wished to hear, so as to exonerate him.

'Brother Kempka,' he transmitted, 'kindly take command of the sergeants.'

A HALF-DOME canopy made of that wraith-material, decorated with gaudy rune-pennants. Near the entrance, one of the Swooping Hawks lay bloodily dead in a heap of crumpled blue wing-plates. Bolts had torn its armour open, revealing to Lex's momentarily enhanced gaze the texture of that armour. It was as porous as the bones of a bird. Compared with Lex's own armour it must weigh so little. Here a fierce bird had fallen from the artificial sky.

To a Space Marine, his powered armour also weighed little. Lex had arrived here at an enhanced swift pace.

Inside the half-dome, a tunnel of wraithbone descended in a curve. A voice came faintly from beyond the camber of the bend, and Lex amplified his hearing.

An anguished grieving voice cried: 'My friend, my friend, we saw eye to eye!'

Another voice spoke Imperial Gothic with a squattish accent: 'Oh ancestors, leave him, Azul! Put him down! You can't lug a corpse around or soon you'll be hauling half the cosmos with you.'

'He saw into my secret eye with his blind eye!'

'Sawed into your eye, did he? That must have hurt a bit. In future I suppose you'll see the warp all decorated with fretwork.'

'You deliberately misunderstand me!'

'Oh, aren't we all misunderstood! Squats especially, us being shorties. Tell me: when you Navigators want to make a baby Navigator do you and the lady keep your bandannas on? Or do you do it eye to eye?'

Gruff abuse continued, with an apparently therapeutic intent. A third voice belonged to that bearded inquisitor. 'In the Emperor's name, come now, or we'll leave you–'

'Not necessarily alive,' warned that exotic assassin creature. Evidently she and the abhuman and the inquisitor had caught up with the Navigator hereabouts. En route, the monkey-man must have met with some fatal accident. Maybe the runt's heart had failed in terror!

These weirdly assorted people seemed almost as loyal to one another as brother Astartes. Such mutual fidelity from an inquisitor and an Imperial assassin? Lex could hardly imagine a similar fastidiousness in Baal Firenze. Such sentiments might indeed be heretical, a mark of corrupt waywardness. These people seemed to behave almost like brothers – including the female warrior, in her alien armour, with her exquisite alien features, which an artistic Fist could appreciate… and pulverize, if need be.

Lex's fist itched.

That was on account of the derisive allusion to sawing an eye. Lex imagined bringing his engraving tool to beam not upon bone but upon such an organ.

One heard such tales about Navigator's warp-eyes. Hard as basalt or vitrodur, those eyes in the forehead were said to be.

The downward tunnel confronted Lex. Eldar were a tall species. He in his power armour loomed quite as tall, though broader. Ample headroom, ample sideroom. Here was hardly a confined space, an armour-scraping space such as he and the owners of those names writ on his fist-bones had manoeuvred their way through in the abhuman warrens of Antro years ago. Lex could be dainty in his approach, and stealthy – to the extent that the impact of his boots would permit. Noise from the amphitheatre should mask his tread.

IT HAD BEEN a stray shuriken disc which sliced into Fennix's head. Azul had been about to stagger with Fennix into the shelter of the half-dome, having just glimpsed that Harlequin Man beckoning again.

A disc from the mist. A token of random futility tossed in their direction as blindly as Fennix himself was blind. A razor-edged coin from the currency of ruin.

The astropath had lurched, and then sighed – almost in relief.

All the noise of battle had been such a confusing torment. No matter how deeply wadded with wool Fennix's bat-ears had been, the recurrent hubbub of bolt fire and the eerie skirling music had been an agonizing misery. As for the amplified voice of that armoured knight: cacophony.

Fennix might as well never have bothered to keep his body spry. Despite his nearsense he was so disoriented. Were it not for Azul he wouldn't have known which way to head. Azul had cradled him. Now Fennix would re-enter the dark womb of disintegration – or the infinite illuminating babel of his own inner creed.

The disc had torn into his brain. Thought and life lingered for a while.

'I'm dying, Azul,' he had managed to mouth. 'Soon I'll hear all the messages that ever were or will be... all at once... one gigantic blaring utterance, one mega multi-word that is the name of–'

Of destiny? Of cosmic history and futurity? Of arcane mystery?

Then the astropath had died – and either knew momentarily, or did not know.

AZUL HAD CONTINUED to carry the corpse further. He crooned to it. Blood and tissue stained the shoulder of his grey moiré damask robe where the astropath's head rested.

Descending, Petrov had entered an oval chamber. The chamber had three subterranean exits into three passageways which soon became filled with swirling blue mist. Azul's warp-eye ached at those glimpses into the webway. Would that his warp-eye could weep for Fennix, tears squeezing from its black marble substance.

Three archways were decorated with mosaics of eldar runes – perhaps cryptic instructions for those who were conversant with the webway?

Petrov stared dazedly along one passage. To gaze along an energy-channel through the warp and nowhere glimpse the signatures of distant stars nor the beacon of the Astronomican was vertiginous. All familiar orientations were absent.

It occurred to him that the webway might possess no readily map-pable linear structure but rather a quasi-random interconnectedness. To walk unknowingly along such a passage into the blue mist might lead to fearful surprises. Small channels, these ones were, suitable for persons. There would be larger channels, through which spaceships could sail.

The webway was like a haphazard psychic bloodstream. It possessed major highways: arteries. It possessed veins. And thin capillaries such as these.

Blood soaked into Azul's shoulder as he clutched the limp astropath. He grieved until Draco, Grimm and Meh'lindi arrived.

GOADED BY GRIMM, Azul was at last laying Fennix down upon the floor of wraithbone. A few sparkling spiders oozed from the floor, to scuttle over the corpse. Azul grinned wildly at Jaq, to disavow the horror of bereavement. Grimm was right. Do not seem disabled! Do not seem fragile!

'Will the spiders spin a shroud for Fennix?' he enquired.

'We must hurry,' insisted Jaq. 'If the eldar lose the fight there'll be such a rush of aspect warriors evacuating the amphitheatre. If we're in the way they'll not feel too many scruples. Which way did Zephro Carnelian go? He did come here, didn't he?'

Which capillary had the Harlequin Man chosen to enter? Azul hadn't seen.

Just then, yellow armour hove in view. A boltgun was pointing.

UNEXPECTEDLY THE CAPTAIN of the Imperial Fists swept his visor open. 'I want to talk with you,' rumbled a bass voice.

An olive skin, scarred neatly by nicks. Lustrous dark eyes and pearly teeth. A ruby ring through the right nostril. A cheek tattoo of a winged fist crushing a skull. Steel studs were inset along the man's forehead. How startling to behold the man within the intimidating ancient armour.

'I am risking psychic assault to show myself to you.'

Ah, that snouted helmet must incorporate psychic shielding. It was open to the air now, and to possible mental pollution. The captain held his gun unwaveringly.

'My name is Lexandro d'Arquebus. My orders came from the headquarters of the Imperial Inquisition. The orders were accompanied by the correct codes.'

This mighty man harboured doubts! Or at least he was capable of rationality.

'Imperial Fists are scrupulous thinkers, not just bringers of death,' he added.

Jaq heaved a painful breath. 'Are you aware,' he asked, 'that the Inquisition is at war with itself? Or that there is a secret Inquisition within the Inquisition?'

Jaq displayed his daemonic palm tattoo. 'Do you recognize this?'

The captain gaped. Of course he did not know the emblem of the Ordo Malleus – nor even of the existence of such an ordo.

'Or this?' Jaq willed the hydra tattoo on his cheek to show. 'Has Baal Firenze showed you this mark of abomination and conspiracy upon himself?'

Lex blanched. He made a warding sign with his gauntlet. 'Tell me not of heresies.' Yet he had demanded conversation. 'Inquisitor Firenze does not entirely seem to know who he is. Or was,' he conceded.

'So I have gathered, Captain d'Arquebus! Once, Firenze was a participant in the direst conspiracy in the galaxy. This knowledge was evidently
taken away from him. Firenze forced me into this conspiracy – which is
why I wear its secret sign. I rebelled against these heretics and their
secret leaders. I even travelled into the Eye of Terror to try to unmask
their treasons–'

'You went where?' In the captain's tone there was awe and dread.

'I encountered a mutated Marine, and we killed him.' Vitali Googol
had been the instrument of that bullman's death. Now Googol's soul
was a plaything of daemons...

'I swear this, captain, by the Column of Glory which I have beheld
with my own eyes.'

'That's true enough,' said Grimm.

'*The Column of Glory*...' breathed the captain. Awe beyond awe...

'In the Emperor's palace,' added the squat helpfully. 'That column.'

'Of course an Imperial Fist knows of the Column of Glory! To be able
to make a pilgrimage there! So very close to the throne room of our
God-Emperor!'

'Which we entered, and left again,' said Grimm, plainly. 'We can
hardly be heretics. Or at least not your regular heretic – like Firenze was
before he was washed and hung out to dry.'

'Be quiet, you impious abhuman,' snapped Jaq. 'Do you think I trust
you especially?'

'I'm hurt,' muttered Grimm. Meh'lindi hissed ferally at the stocky
quasi-human silencing his grumbles.

With evident reluctance the captain enquired, 'What manner of conspiracy was Firenze involved in?'

Jaq shook his head.

'What is its aim?' repeated the captain. 'Who are its leaders?'

'Such knowledge could destroy you.'

'Aye. Perhaps it could.'

'Besides...' Jaq gestured impatiently up the tunnel toward the
amphitheatre of war. 'We need to go into the webway before it becomes
crowded. We must find the Harlequin Man.'

'That was my mission, and my men's,' said the captain. 'To breach the
webway. To capture some Harlequins.' Bitterly he added, 'And to purge
and cleanse because Inquisitor Firenze does not know his own true purpose! Do I know yours? My military allegiance should be to Inquisitor
Firenze.'

Meh'lindi's comment was even more bitter: 'Just as mine should be to
the Callidus shrine of the Officio Assassinorum.'

The captain gazed at her. 'You are so strange…'

On account of being a woman? Or seeming to be an alien?

'Huh,' grunted Grimm. 'Do we have another potential devotee of our Lady of Death?'

Jaq said firmly, 'We are about to enter the webway, captain.'

The captain would be obliged to kill Jaq to prevent this.

'How will you find your way?' the captain asked slowly.

'By my Tarot, I hope! By the grace of Him-on-Earth. By the light of the luminous path, if it illumines me.'

'What is that luminous path? I only know the radiant light of Rogal Dorn.'

Jaq made no reply.

The captain surveyed the three archways leading from the chamber.

'Which path will you take?' He did not intend to prevent Jaq's little group from departing.

Jaq also eyed the three misty blue tunnels. He reached to remove his Tarot pack.

However, the puzzle of which route to follow was about to be simplified. From out of the shimmering mist along the middle passageway came an armoured predatory figure, glowing a bilious green.

FIFTEEN
WEBWAY

THAT FIGURE WAS an Imperial Fist Marine. The blue fog of the webway had temporarily made his armour appear of a different hue.

In salute to his captain the Space Marine clashed his gauntlet across his plastron. The boltgun in his other gauntlet shifted to and fro. Now it was veering towards the alien guardian, and now towards the squat who was armed with two boltguns. Especially towards the alien female. What in the name of Dorn was the situation here?

Crisply the Marine reported his own situation on the comm-channel.

'Lord. Sergeant Wagner led us on an exploratory thrust into a portal in the city. These hazy tunnels sometimes branch without the fork being obvious. I became separated, sir. I apologize to our Chapter.'

'No need, brother,' said Lex. 'Your information is valuable. Be at *battle-ease*. These four people aren't detainees.'

Stockman regarded his captain's open visor with respectful wariness. The captain's explicit order had been for suits to remain sealed until the company regained its boarding torpedoes and until those were well on their way to rendezvous with the troopship. Stockman's report might have been squeakily audible to the four strangers through the captain's open visor.

A runty corpse lay on the wraithbone floor. Recently shot – with a shuriken disc, so he judged. Shot, therefore, by the female eldar woman. A human shot by an alien.

Nevertheless, Stockman assumed battle-ease, stifling his impetus to kill.

'These are agents of the Imperium, Brother Stockman. The female is an impersonator of aliens.'

That open visor...

'With respect, lord, is theirs a separate mission to ours?'

'You might say so.'

'With respect, lord, have they come here through the alien webway?'

If that was so, then what sense did the massive deployment of battleships and Cobras make? All of it so that the Imperial Fists could breach the eldar habitat. What sense, if the Imperium already knew of a more cunning and stealthy route by which to enter?

Was the Fists' brave deployment within the habitat a deliberate diversion – a footnote to the activities of this robed and bearded man and the female impersonator, the Navigator and the abhuman? Was Inquisitor Firenze merely orchestrating an additional diversion which was costing the lives of his battle-brothers as surely as the battle in space was expending thousands of lives of more ordinary mortals?

And had Captain d'Arquebus known this all along?

Misgivings were implicit in Stockman's dutiful query.

'You think clearly, Stockman,' said Lex. 'But have faith.'

The secret inquisitor spoke up. He must have judged the probable reason for Lex's words.

'We came here in a shielded ship, captain, not through the webway. Who but the eldar understand the ramifications of the webway?'

'Are the other men of Sergeant Wagner's squad lost in this webway now?' Lex asked Stockman.

'My lord, I do not know.'

'I shall attempt to locate them. Stockman, I have transferred command temporarily to Librarian Kempka. Remain here and hold this place if possible. Try to deny it to the enemy as an evacuation route. If hard pressed, retreat by the way you came. Do not squander yourself. Report my decision to our Librarian. Time presses.'

THE CAPTAIN WAS intending to accompany Jaq's party. To escort them!

The lone Space Marine stood a fair chance of interdicting this chamber to the eldar. If Stockman heard eldar beginning to descend from the surface he would fire up the tunnel. His bolts would ricochet wildly, lethally. Needless to say, Stockman must also watch his back in case enemies came through the webway. Equally, Sergeant Wagner and his squad might come.

Was a squad of Fists really lost in the webway? A devout captain would do his duty. If he became lost too, this would not be desertion or dereliction...

JAQ HAD TAKEN out his Tarot, unwrapped the mutant skin which swathed it, and removed the Harlequin card. Carnelian's face was clear enough. His clothing, however, was constantly changing. It underwent a flux of styles and hues. Hectic hilarity was almost audible.

The card jerked leftward.

The captain consulted an instrument on his wrist as if loath to be guided by a Tarot card. He shrugged massively. Muttering a prayer, Jaq restored the other cards to his gown.

Almost as soon as they began to make their way along the leftward passage, they heard Stockman opening fire behind them. Eldar must be coming already. The RAAARK of bolts became muffled as glowing blue mist swirled. Then the noise was inaudible. Whatever occurred behind them could have been a world away, in another reality.

HOW DISCONCERTING TO tread this spectral path, perhaps only a frail energy-membrane away from raw increate warp where daemons roosted!

Or were the energy-walls of the webway as firm as adamantium?

Azul Petrov, aficionado of the eldar, had opinions which he began to voice compulsively. Either his garrulousness was due to anxiety, now that his curiosity was at last being satisfied. Or he spoke to distract himself from agonizing about the dead astropath.

Maybe regions of the webway fluctuated, and could become thin – permeable to Chaos?

Was the webway a creation of bygone eldar mages? Or was it simply a discovery of theirs? Surely the former must be the case. Yet perhaps the network also grew spontaneously, of its own impetus. The eldar of today could not know all its ways. This webway was an immaterial equivalent of the wraithbone from which they crafted their artifacts by psychic engineering. Perhaps it also possessed its own autonomy.

Was it a shining path? No, it was a maze of mysteries – where Harlequins capered, masters of various of these mysteries, but probably not of all of them.

Despite Petrov's garnering of hearsay, what did he really know? Despite Meh'lindi's ability to speak eldar, the essence of the aliens still eluded her. Language supposedly allowed insights into world-views. This was true only if one appreciated the secret significances hidden within words and syntax. Otherwise, essentially one parroted noises. Effective noises, admittedly; but noises nonetheless.

During their brief and hectic sojourn in the alien habitat, what had Jaq, or Meh'lindi, learned of the eldar or their Harlequins? Why, hardly anything! What had they learned of the ceremony which had been under way? What of the aliens' protégé, Carnelian? They had gathered precious little beyond what Grimm had already revealed. Grimm's had been a vast enough revelation.

If it was true. Or even half-way true. And thus half-way false.

What truth in this universe was absolute and undeniable?

The Emperor's immortality and perfect wisdom? No! The vile threat of Chaos, the hungry clamour of evil bedlam? Yes... That could not be gainsaid. Should one's faith then be in Chaos? Small wonder so many seduced souls succumbed!

All else was appallingly relative. Deceitful. Deluded. Whelmed in darkest shadows, or in brutal pious zealotry.

'You're injured,' the captain remarked to Jaq.

'My ribs. A bruise. It's irrelevant. I can soothe myself psychically to some extent.'

'I regret those shots. However, they showed me your sincerity.'

'Huh,' said Grimm. 'A few extra shots could have demonstrated total credibility and righteousness.'

Jaq held the card in one hand and *Emperor's Mercy* in the other, otherwise he might have cuffed Grimm.

'I apologize for my companion, captain. Squats are forever brusque and blunt.'

'Aye, blunt as a pencil-stub that's half worn down.' Was this Space Marine officer hazarding some humour? He must be feeling radically strange. Divorced from his command, from his company, from his Chapter.

'Kindly call me Lexandro. No, just Lex. That's quicker.' They might need to react very quickly.

Did Captain Lex consider himself to be in command of this expedition, in any sense? How could he, when he knew nothing of Jaq's objective? By inviting these companions to use his private name, he disowned his authority, and in a sense his status too, lest the Imperial Fists be dishonoured. Qualms must be bubbling in the breast of this versatile and thoughtful soldier – boltgun in his gauntlet and laspistol holstered on his cuisse.

Petrov held a laspistol too. Grimm toted *Emperor's Peace*. Meh'lindi, still carrying Jaq's force rod upon her eldar armour, cradled her shuriken pistol in one hand and her needle gun in the other.

The hazy passage had branched numerous times.

Sometimes the mist divided like some amoeboid creature splitting apart into two new individuals. At other times two branches fused into a single one. Odours predominated at intersections: cinnamon, musk, hot oil, putrefaction. Each direction possessed a characteristic aroma, a perfume or a stink of which one was barely aware whilst en route, yet which might well assist an adept of the webway to orientate himself.

Twice, Jaq was aware of psychic obstacles along certain routes, as of forbidding alien runes hovering within the mist.

Once, their route verged upon a nebulous void. This must be one of the major channels of the webway, an avenue vast enough to accommodate a wraithship with its sails.

For some time thereafter their route resembled a capillary attached to a great artery, only a membrane away. If a starship sped by through the foggy blue gulf, might they be sucked into its wake, scraps of flotsam fluttering through the webway until somewhere they were vomited out into the zero-vacuum of the void to gasp their lungs out while their eyeballs burst? Their route veered away from this awesome highway.

Maybe such a conjunction of wraithship and webway wayfarers could not have happened.

Jaq sensed fleeting presences, as of ghosts in transit. Initially he feared that these rushing auras might be those of daemons.

But then Petrov queried the absence hitherto of any other travellers. Was the webway vacant save for themselves?

Perhaps, suggested the Navigator, travellers who commenced a journey at a particular time were 'out of phase' with other travellers, and occupied a unique time-slot of their own. They might pass other users of the webway, yet not interact with them. They might always be a minute or an hour earlier or later in time while nevertheless briefly occupying the same location.

This was a twisted echo of Fennix's notion that in some greater reality all telepathic messages, past and present and future, existed simultaneously. Petrov expatiated inventively on the idea. All journeys through the quasi-organism of the webway might occur in some meta-time, where the present possessed no absolute existence but rather was scattered, as light by a lens into different adjacent spectral bands.

Yet, to their eyes, the mist was always blue.

Sense of duration had certainly evaporated. Lex's chronometer recorded a lapse of an hour, a lapse of a month, a lapse of only two minutes. Dreamtime, this! Time, smeared as if by Chaos. The blue mist might almost be hallucinogenic, affecting not only the mind but instruments as well. It seemed only moments since they had quit that chamber and Brother Stockman. Or was it only moments since one remembered quitting that chamber? Had they recalled the selfsame moment several times already, imagining that each successive memory was the reality?

Wasn't it said that on some Chaos worlds in the Eye of Terror time had ceased to signify? There, Traitor Marines from the era of Horus existed in a state of everlasting daemonic timelessness.

The webway seemed a luminous counterpart of that dark destiny. In bringing it into being – if indeed they had done so – had the ancient eldar perhaps taken the first step towards catastrophe? They had writ a vastly complex and potent rune in the Warp – a pattern of power, a presence, a multifold channel.

Ruinous Chaos powers had congealed like perverse distorted reflections of this rune.

Maybe the webway was ultimately sinister in a way which no eldar could ever understand or acknowledge, such was their dependence upon its galactic network.

Yet it also held Chaos at bay, and was the roost of their Laughing God whose acolytes were the Harlequins.

A minute, an hour, an age, a few seconds: how long had they been in the webway?

Eldar seemed to live at a more accelerated rate than human beings. Their reactions were so quicksilver-swift. Maybe they experienced time-shifts in the webway differently from more sluggish human mortals…

The Harlequin card continued to pull Jaq onward – until, of a sudden, the blue mist thinned.

THE RIBBED WRAITHBONE walls of an immense dome rose sombrely upward. Across the zenith stretched a lake of night. A vast sky-light or energy-field excluded yet also revealed the void of space.

That funereal lake was polluted by diseased lurid gases. Hues of jaundice and gangrene and blood and bile stained those billowy shrouds. Suns within the sickly veils ached feebly. The nebulae were diseased nightmarish wraiths of gas, and of vile corruption, of a cancer spreading through the void.

It was the Eye of Terror – where Chaos spilled into reality. Where warped worlds of unnatural geometry orbited furnaces of nauseous light. Where daemons ruled.

To behold the Eye again – so nearby, in cosmic terms – sickened Jaq. Was the contaminated region larger than a hundred years previously? Impossible to say.

'Oh, ancestors,' muttered Grimm.

Azul Petrov retched a thin bitter gruel. He wiped his lips. At least, at last, he could sense far away the glimmer of the Astronomican, the Emperor's beacon.

Lex studied the phenomenon beyond the huge skylight with loathing. 'It's the Eye, isn't it? We've come such a long way…'

Far, far from Stalinvast. Far to the north-west of Earth, towards the edge of the galaxy. Close to the lair of Chaos Marines – and of even less endearing entities, all bent on spreading the plague which infested reality and sanity.

'Well now,' said Grimm to Petrov, 'ain't the webway a better means of travel than hauling ships through the warp for days or weeks on end?'

'No,' murmured the Navigator. 'No, it isn't. It's too close to the immaterial. It's too facile.'

'Huh, you're just worried about being out of a job.'

'What Azul means,' Jaq said to Grimm, 'is that the webway is too lordly and proud a marvel, like the eldar themselves. It's a sort of hubris, an arrogance. It indulges.'

'It's not painful enough,' muttered Lex. 'Not arduous enough. It's only by struggle and constant self-control that we survive.'

Petrov nodded agreement. 'The eldar know enough tragedy and pain, so I've heard. They fight with a sort of self-induced psychopathy. Yet formerly they must have been a luxurious people. I think the webway epitomizes this luxury. Even if their aspect warriors use it as a military highway! Even if their Harlequins use it to run rings around the Imperium…'

Lex growled his disapproval of this notion.

Grimm gestured at the shattered landscape. 'They ain't so proud everywhere…'

'Craftworld, this,' said Lex. 'Isn't that so? A genuine craftworld. I never thought my eyes would see such a place.'

Few human eyes could ever have beheld an eldar craftworld, though their fabled names were prattled now and then by such as Petrov.

'It must be Ulthwé,' said the Navigator. 'So close to the Eye of Terror. Still hanging on to existence by a rope or two.'

The sheer endurance of Ulthwé! Certainly Traitor Marines had invaded and ravaged this place. Meh'lindi pointed, and Lex sucked in his breath.

Amidst the weed-infested ruins, scum-covered pools, and jagged fractures of wraithbone, there jutted a cleaved, baroquely armoured suit such as Lex had hoped never to see.

They picked their way cautiously through rubble. The suit was ornamented with horns and brazen daemon-heads and blasphemous
badges and a necklace of foetuses in amber. The face-plate had been
ripped off. Tiny spiders had spun webs across the majority of the skull
within, masking it with phosphorescent tissue.

The lower jaw gaped open, showing sharpened steel teeth. Lex
reached down with his gauntlet but reconsidered. Bulges in the web suggested that the majority of the skull had become radically abnormal.
Horns may have sprouted from the brows, bony spurs or crests from the
cranium. Spiders had softened these grotesque deformities, eroding the
marks of Chaos.

Beyond the crepuscular dome of destruction into which the travellers
had emerged – with that awful lid revealing the sickening Eye – was a
distant brighter dome. There, graceful fluted towers and tall slim pyramids rose amidst great trees of jade and emerald foliage.

To Jaq's eye, this craftworld in its entirety might be no more ravaged
or sullied than a great number of human worlds which plagues of people had ransacked and poisoned in the sheer process of exploiting
resources. To the eldar, no doubt, the ugliness in the immediate vicinity
was hateful. A warren of human beings could easily have inhabited, rat-
like, this war-torn wasteland.

When he heaved a sigh, was it from pain in his lung or in his soul?

Grimm urinated into the open helmet of the Chaos Marine. Sizzling
softly, the webs became a gingery mat clinging to horrid contours above
that gaping metal-fanged jaw.

From one of his pouches Grimm produced a bar of marzipan and
began to gobble.

Lex snapped his visor shut to scan data and diagnostic icons. When he
opened it again, he announced, 'My waste storage unit may be malfunctioning somewhat.' He murmured a prayer to Rogal Dorn.

Grimm cocked his head. 'Does that mean that your mighty metal legs
will start to fill with muck?'

Lex's gauntlet lashed out. He stayed the blow before it could pulverize Grimm's face.

'I can recycle and detox my own waste for two days, abhuman. This
suit is ancient,' he declared. 'Reverently repaired.' His groin-hauberk had
visibly been renovated with a damascened silver engraving of a potent
warrior firing a storm bolter.

'Breastplate's a bit scraped,' muttered Grimm. Was he determined to
test the limits of a Space Marine's forbearance and flexibility?

The spreadeagle on Lex's plastron was indeed scarred.

'An eldar Banshee caressed me with a power sword.' Lex glanced away towards Meh'lindi with a haunted fascination. 'Aye, just as she was dying. We haven't been back to our fortress-monastery since. Baal Firenze's mission pre-empted our return.' His scrutiny shifted to Jaq. 'I think you should undergo some medical examination. I'm no medic, but I do have a certain amount of expertise. A Space Marine's body is his temple, therefore one must know the appropriate canticles. I'm willing–' But he glanced at Meh'lindi. 'Unless an assassin-courtesan is also well acquainted with anatomy, so as to kill… or delight, or both.'

Meh'lindi nodded. 'Forgive me for not considering this sooner, Jaq. Pain means so little to me.'

How can it be so, Lex mused to himself? It sounded as though Meh'lindi were devoid of a fundamental awareness, of an entire sense. How alien she was indeed.

'Except,' she added, 'for mental anguish.'

'Well now,' said Grimm, 'I suppose that's mostly rinsed out of your system since you were dissected.'

'You aren't too comfortable being in an eldar environment, are you, my little fellow?' she enquired. 'Even if the Harlequin Man's your real hero.'

As Meh'lindi approached Jaq, he tossed *Emperor's Mercy* to the squat, who caught it by the handle. ('Huh, trust me, trust me not!') Then Jaq yielded to her ministrations.

His ragged robe came off. With the tips of her fingers she stroked the woven thermoplas of the armour, which was as squamous as lizard skin. Softly she probed the side of Jaq's chest. He grunted. Now she was massaging with such gentle pressure, murmuring Callidus incantations.

Lex's gauntlets were flexing as though fire-ants roved the flesh within them.

Grimm seemed determined to tease that robust knight. 'Huh, I've hung around with Astartes before – but I never had a chance to find out what's under the groin-hauberk. Never shared vibroshowers with our potent warriors. If you don't mind me asking, are you… ahem… modified, in what one might call the genial part?'

Lex was almost too preoccupied with the intimate massage by alien hands to take offence.

'One hears talk of gene-seeds,' hinted Grimm.

'That's a sacred matter,' growled Lex. 'Those are in our progenoid glands.' He slapped his chest and his neck. 'Here, and here.'

'You do have a lot of extra organs. I was wondering if any regular organs get deleted to make space.'

'Kill a Marine and find out!' snapped Lex. How dare this stunted thing interrupt his concentration upon the massage. 'Our progenoid glands create germ cells corresponding to our special organs. Thus new implants can be cultured. Does that satisfy you, abhuman pest?'

'Actually, I was wondering how much you oughta be told about what's what – with Jaq's approval. Or whether you might be a bit unstable, pardon the expression, with all your superhuman hormones and no regular outlet, as it were.'

Meh'lindi loosened the mesh armour, exposing a livid purple bruise and frightful tattoos on Jaq's torso.

'What are those *marks*?'

'These are emblems of daemons he defeated in the past.'

Lex shuddered at the sight. Of course the greave protecting his own right shank was quartered and augmented, similarly, with honours.

'Hear me,' Lex said to Grimm. 'We Fists supremely sublimate our animal urges by means of *art*. By the art of war.'

Presently Meh'lindi finished her nursing. Jaq's tattoos were once more hidden by the scaly, supple, finely-woven chainmail.

'Mesh armour's a useful corset,' she said. 'A good flexible truss for a fracture. You'll be almost as mobile as usual.' Jaq resumed his robe. He scrutinized Lex and Grimm.

'I think,' he said to the squat, 'that you should probably tell Captain Lex what you told us, under duress. Yes, illuminate him. Strip the secrets bare.'

Grimm puffed himself up. 'Oh well, if you insist.'

The little man tugged the forage cap from his gingerbrush head, thus to make a more eloquent and winning speech to the looming armour, the lustrous eyes, the pearly teeth, the steel long-service studs.

'It's like this,' he began. 'Your beloved Emperor, when He had the use of his legs and loins once upon a time, sired hundreds of immortal Sons – without ever realizing. That was because His offspring were all psychic blanks to him, so He could never detect their existence…'

GRIMM HAD FINISHED babbling. Lex mulled over the tale he'd been told. Inquisitor Draco seemed to regard this account of *Illuminati* and *sensei* with a sceptical passion. A long watch of sensei knights preparing for the final cosmic battle.

A Chapter of more-than-Marines! Of more-than-Grey-Knights! Utterly secret from the Imperium.

Yet associated with the eldar…

Rogue 'Illuminati' were attempting their own awful conspiracy... rogues who corrupted inquisitors... Oh, to be able to discuss all this with Kurt Kempka in a secluded reclusiam aboard the fortress-monastery, surrounded by sacred relics and trophies!

Were the foundations of Lex's faith shaken? No. The light of Rogal Dorn illuminated him. The names writ on the bones of his left hand lent strength, as if he were three-in-one. He bowed his helmeted head, terribly privileged to endure such knowledge – or such falsehoods.

Truly, the universe was a morass of glutinous mire which could suck a man under so easily. An Imperial Fist must stand firm. Perhaps it was time single-handedly to storm those fluted towers of the eldar in the distance and to yield his life in glory.

This opportunity was to be denied to him.

FROM AMONGST THE ruins close by, figures rushed. Some were dark as night, though with golden helmets. Some, in the gloom, were the colour of cinnabar such as a wounded Space Marine's swiftly coagulating blood would become. One was a kaleidoscope of shifting hues.

Funereal guardians of Ulthwé: their back-banners displayed a rune of a baleful weeping eye. They brandished rotund guns with splaying nozzles rather than muzzles.

And Banshees too. Predatory mandibles adorned their helms. Laspistols and power swords.

And a Harlequin warrior.

The amplified screams of the witches stunned Lex. His hand wouldn't move to slap his visor shut and exclude those mind-wrenching shrieks. Grimm had dropped his boltgun to clap hairy hands over his ears. Petrov's knees buckled. Even Meh'lindi screeched in an effort to drown the screams, to return them to their source.

The guardians discharged their guns. Squirming fluid gushed from the nozzles. No, not fluid at all – but bundles of mesh!

Clouds spun towards the stunned humans and the abhuman. Surely those were the ghastly guns which fired a wad of writhing mono-filament wire which would whisk all flesh to soup if any part of the body was exposed.

The expanding clouds engulfed Lex and Jaq and Petrov and Grimm.

SIXTEEN
DUEL

THE CLOUDS SPARED Meh'lindi.

Or rather, *Mile'ionahd*. In the eyes of those guardians of Ulthwé –
those golden-helmed eyes – she too was a guardian. She stood stock-
still, assessing. Only her eyes flicked. Her companions seemed to be
wrestling with themselves. Wrestling in vain. Tripping, tumbling
over.

Lex wasn't falling. Bolts were spurting from his gun, but those bolts
were hitting the ground well short of the black guardians and the blood
red Banshees. Rubble erupted as bolts detonated uselessly.

Still upright in his armour, the captain was trapped in a tightening
web of thin fibres. Those eldar guns had discharged a type of tangleweb
rather than monofilament wire such as would have torn flesh and guts
and bones asunder. Jaq and Grimm and Petrov lay on the ground,
enmeshed and incapable. Resistance merely served to tighten the tendrils. In their case, to lie still was to survive.

Lex in his power suit was resisting more mightily. As his muscles
flexed, so the servo-fibres of his armour copied his movements. Lex may
as well have been suspended in the stiffest of glues. His gun-hand simply couldn't rise higher. Could he even uncramp his gauntlet from the
trigger? He lurched, he swayed, he wrestled in slow motion: a great cara-
paced yellow beetle attempting to wade through treacle.

The magazine of his boltgun had emptied. Only now did guardians
and Banshees and that shimmering Harlequin continue their advance.

'Bravely done!' Mile'ionahd called out in eldar.

The Harlequin bowed ironically. The mask showed a laughing godly alien face.

How clearly could the Harlequin see her, in her eldar aspect and her armour? It was so gloomy under this dome. Illumination leached from the neighbouring dome, and sickly hues radiated from the Eye of Terror. Spider webs contributed some phosphorescence.

Banshees stood over Jaq and Grimm and Petrov. The mandible weapons of their helms jutted downward. Power swords poised, as if prior to an execution. Other Banshees formed a loose circle around Lex. He was lumbering steadfastly yet so slowly, baring his pearly teeth. The eldar could have been about to bait a tormented bull.

'Well escorted through the webway, Guardian of the Rite,' the Harlequin said to Mile'ionahd. Ah, so in his or her eyes she fulfilled some special function. She wasn't a regular craftworld guardian but was a recruit to the ceremony ordained by Harlequins.

'And yet,' continued the Harlequin, 'the arrival of an Imperial warrior puzzles and provokes these mournful guardians of Ulthwé.'

Lex's presence was a conundrum which those guardians had resolved by tanglewebbing all human intruders, irrespectively.

Inspired, Mile'ionahd nodded in Jaq's direction.

'This one will be a fine recruit – to serve the purpose of illumination.'

'How much does he know?' was the reply. This gave her momentary pause. Her own status was ambiguous. She was a guardian; yet more than a typical guardian. She had come through the webway. Yet she wasn't a Harlequin. *How much was she herself supposed to know or not to know?*

Risk all, gamble all! Banshees with their swords and laspistols outnumbered her by six to one. Those black guardians still kept hold of the webguns, but lasguns were slung across their backs. It would only take seconds for the guardians to discard the webguns and seize the lasguns. Could the acrobatics of an assassin extricate her from amongst such nimble fighters? Unlikely! Only Callidus could. Only cunning and calculation. And sheer luck.

'This inquisitor knows about the long watch of sensei knights,' she stated.

'Ha, that illustrious illusion! That delightful delusion!' *Illusion? Delusion?* Had she understood the proper meanings of the words *seachmall* and *seachran*?

She was fooling this Harlequin, though, face to face. Her falsely elongated face confronted his or her mask of laughter.

Carefully, she said, 'He believes in the delusion.'

'Aiee!' shrilled the Harlequin. 'Do you not believe in the Rhana Dandra?'

She ransacked her memory. Rhana Dandra? A final battle, yes, between Chaos and the material universe... Rhana Dandra: that was the phrase for it. She had never understood more than the general sense of the phrase.

'The sensei knights will take part in the Rhana Dandra,' she said ambivalently.

The Harlequin's mask smirked. 'Only the Phoenix Lords will take part in the Rhana Dandra, if ever it comes! If it comes, both Chaos and the universe will be destroyed. Mutual annihilation is preferable to the triumph of Chaos.'

Phoenix Lords, Phoenix Lords? If only she could consult telepathically with Petrov! If only she were a telepath, and Petrov too.

'The sensei knights *think* they will take part in the Rhana Dandra,' Mile'ionahd equivocated.

'Naturally their illusion is modelled on our Rhana Dandra.' The Harlequin's tone was brusque.

'Whereas...' she said suggestively.

The Harlequin shrugged impatiently. 'The moribund human Emperor's will will finally fail. The human Illuminati will feed all the sensei into that climactic psycho-vortex. Dying Emperor and sensei will all fuse into a new and potent incarnation which Great Harlequins of the Laughing God will supervise. And the Rhana Dandra can be delayed. Did you not understand the Rite of the Ravaged World?'

So *that* was the truth.

The eldar were willing for this resurrection of Imperial power in a new guise to occur – under the guidance of Illuminati whom the eldar manipulated...

The eldar could never recover their once-proud suzerainty over swaths of the galaxy. Their civilization had been too shattered and scattered. The crude human race had supplanted them. Humanity seemed set to crash into Chaos too, bringing galactic cataclysm. Through the sacrifice of the sensei, apocalypse could be averted. The eldar would secretly have their hands on the new levers of power, swinging the new wheel of fate.

How like the hydra conspiracy was the Illuminati plot! The hydra conspirators aimed to sacrifice the mental liberty, such as it was, of the whole human race. The 'good' Illuminati *merely* intended sacrificing all of the Emperor's Sons.

The Harlequin cried intoxicatedly: 'Similarly does the Young King approach the throne of the Bloody-Handed God. Similarly is the Young King consumed in holy agony so as to kindle the Avatar!'

Maybe Petrov, with his eldar-mania, would have fathomed the meaning of this!

The Harlequin's mask had become one of horror.

'Maybe the Rhana Dandra is closer than we think. Phoenix Lords are said to be stalking the webway now. Did you glimpse any Phoenix Lord on your journey here?'

'No,' said Mile'ionahd.

'Heeding the summons of cataclysm the Phoenix Lords are leaving the Crossroads of Inertia where they lurk while centuries elapse!'

Meh'lindi's brain was a hive of bees, a-buzzing. Phoenix Lords? Great heroes, obviously... A phoenix was a bird of some fabled world which was supposedly reborn from its own ashes.

Eldar aspect warriors seemed to become possessed by their armour in a way which a Marine such as Lex never was. Phoenix Lords must represent a peak of this phenomenon. Ancient armour worn by some bygone hero must dominate the wearer, resurrecting the personality of the ancient hero time and again. By means of spirit stones! Of course, by means of those crystals and pebbles which enshrined an eldar's soul!

What had it signified when a Harlequin had snatched Mile'ionahd's spurious pebble from her?

Had one purpose of the terrible rite enacted in the habitat orbiting Stalinvast been to summon these Phoenix Lords from wherever they lingered while time elapsed in the ordinary universe?

'Ah, the Crossroads of Inertia,' she echoed. 'Those crossroads in our webway where time stands still.' This was the most likely meaning of inertia. She hazarded rhapsodically: 'Where time shifts sideways, where time twists backward.'

'*Uigebealach*,' whispered the Harlequin. 'If Great Harlequins have discovered the place where time twists backward, is that location now encrypted in the mutable *Book of Rhana Dandra* in the Black Library? When the Rhana Dandra comes time itself must rupture.'

'The secret place,' she mused, 'where what has been can be again.'

Could it be that some eldar mystics hoped to regain their past glories by turning time itself backwards, in a cataclysm where reality was utterly disrupted? Was that the purpose of this mutual annihilation of reality and Chaos known as the Rhana Dandra? The annulling of history? The abolition of aeons of elapsed time?

Lex continued to struggle massively. His suit groaned and creaked as he tried to thrust the tightening fibres apart. From his arms, from his legs. The fibres could not prevent him from exerting himself within the suit. Was he trying to compel the tendrils to tighten so much in response to his amplified movements that finally strands must snap? Lex may as well have been encased in solid rock. He might force the suit beyond its design limits until its systems failed.

Of a sudden, many things happened.

THE HARLEQUIN'S MASK became a pearly blank, cutting Mile'ionahd off from all communion with him, or her. Its chameleon suit was aswirl with all the sickly lurid hues of the Eye of Terror. The Harlequin was pointing a laspistol at her head...

From away across the rubble other black guardians came bounding, guardians with golden helms – and also a kaleidoscopic Harlequin with the all-too-familiar human features of Zephro Carnelian.

'Brother Harlequin, don't kill her yet!' Carnelian shrilled. He was swinging what appeared to be a primitive sling such as Meh'lindi had known on the feral world of her childhood.

Guardians and Banshees were now utterly alert. Any leap which Meh'lindi might have undertaken would surely have resulted in her immediate death. Swiftly guardians had discarded their rotund web guns for their long-barrelled lasguns.

In amazement Meh'lindi recognized exactly what that sling was. A sling? It was none other than her stolen thong with her speckly pebble attached to it!

Carnelian halted. He surveyed webbed prisoners and the webbed Marine who still strove ponderously – and he surveyed Mile'ionahd.

His laughter was a pealing bell.

'This time it isn't you who are ensnared, my dear!' he mocked her, in Imperial Gothic.

How she wished to spit poison at this person who had entrapped her once in the coils of the hydra and who had ravished her with enforced ecstasy within her very brain, stimming her pleasure centres unbearably!

He tossed the pebble dismissively at her.

'Your gewgaw, I believe.'

She caught it. The thong had been reknotted. She slipped the pendant over her head to rid herself of it. Foolish Carnelian! He had prompted her to use her hands. Now she could make other movements without inviting instant death.

'Your stone was stolen for a soul-tasting,' Carnelian explained. 'It didn't taste of much soul at all, let alone of any eldar spirit.'

So that was the reason why the pebble had been snatched away – to discover whether she was genuine or fake.

Meh'lindi retorted: 'And now I know that you and your Illuminati aren't very genuine, either, in your claims.' She spoke in Imperial Gothic for Jaq's benefit, so that he would learn what the eldar Harlequin had divulged. Jaq couldn't move, but at least he could hear. 'The long watch of knights is a hoax, Carnelian! You mean to use those immortal Sons in the same way as sprightly young psykers are fed to the Emperor. They're all to be sacrificed and consumed.'

Down on the ground Grimm heaved a groan – and came close to choking as fibres cramped him even more tightly. Grimm had discovered his own gullibility.

'Is this true, Carnelian?' came Jaq's voice. His lips hadn't been sealed by tangleweb.

'True?' shrieked the Harlequin Man. 'What a futile question, *true*! I thought you were worthy of becoming an Illuminatus!'

'And I thought,' retorted Jaq, 'a qualification for *that* was to be possessed by a daemon.'

'And to survive possession. With or without assistance.' Carnelian leered at Jaq. '*You* would have had assistance.'

'Emperor's tears,' murmured Jaq in horror. *The Illuminati, who loathed daemons so utterly, would have contrived that his soul and body might be possessed for a while – for a week? for a year? for a century? – so that later he could join their ranks.*

'Why me?' Jaq breathed.

Frustration and exasperation goaded Carnelian.

'Because Eldrad Ulthran saw this,' he raved. 'Because it is written in the Black Library in the mutable *Book of Rhana Dandra!*'

'Emperor's testes…' Oh, an oath of such sacred mystery.

'His testes, eh?' Carnelian sneered. 'Why, those testes must have been full to bursting once. His prodigal secret Sons are so numerous! I tell you, together the Sons will form his Son. The Numen, the light to New Men! To renew humanity, to thwart all daemons, when the Sons are sacrificed in the bonfire of transcendence! I speak as one illuminated by pre-vision of that bonfire of souls. Sir Jaq, you would have understood this wonder after being possessed and purged.'

'You,' he snarled at Meh'lindi, 'you're such a damned distraction!'

ZEPHRO TRIED TO calm himself. He must not appear possessed in front of his mentors whose mannerisms he aped as the sincerest form of gratitude and admiration.

His mentors were quicksilver by nature. He had needed to cultivate hectic affectations as an equivalent to their rush and dazzle.

Seeing one of his long-term projects undermined due to this assassin
– who must certainly abominate him! – his reactions had become
unstrung.

Did the insanity which had once possessed him haunt him anew in
his frustration at the spoiling of a cherished plan? A plan for Jaq Draco's
own benefit!

Once Draco had been redeemed from possession and become illuminated he would have appreciated Carnelian's long-term wisdom!

Now, damnably, Draco was deterred… thanks to the assassin, and to
his inquisitorial programming regarding daemons and the tarnished
rotting glory of that wretched Emperor. Emperor's testes, indeed! Draco
should have learned better by now!

Zephro must calm himself.

CARNELIAN SPOKE IN eldar to Meh'lindi. 'Let your pistols drop, *imposter*.
Prepare for an exhibition of your paltry skills.'

A Banshee skipped forward. Holstering her laspistol, she cried out in
a harsh voice, 'I challenge. I claim the honour!

Meh'lindi had little choice but to discard her weapons. Even so, she
was herself a living weapon.

The aspect warrior flourished her power sword. Her armour was the
hue of blood except for the round poleyns protecting her knees. Those
were bone-white. And except for the golden helm. Her mandible-
blasters jutted from that helm, deadly pods, scorpion-stings. A mane of
black hair waved behind the helm, the lacquered tentacles of a medusa.

How close did the Banshee have to come to an enemy to use those
helm-pods? Would it be part of her Banshee code to use them against
an apparently unarmed opponent? From the way in which the Banshee
swished her power sword it seemed that her main desire was to decapitate Meh'lindi with a single swing dealt whilst dancing. Or perhaps
mockingly to slice off one hand at the wrist, and then the other hand,
before delivering a coup de grace.

'Traitor!' cried the Banshee.

'No, *imposter*,' Carnelian corrected her. 'A human transformed by a
metamorphic drug. A mimic.'

'Aieeee!' How offended the Banshee sounded at this impersonation
by an alien of an eldar.

The genuine Harlequin was cursing himself for his earlier credulity.
He, a supreme performer! True, he had grown suspicious – even before
the arrival of this human ally in Harlequin gear. To have been duped
even for a while was detestable.

'Sister Banshee,' he called out, 'kindly slice off her nose first of all.'

Lex had quit moving. He appeared to have abandoned any attempt to snap the web. While guardians and Banshees were distracted by the one-sided duel, would Lex make one further supreme effort to wrench his powered arms apart, to reload his boltgun as quickly as could be, and to use it? Meh'lindi must survive as long as possible.

'Don't I get a sword as well?' she asked.

Carnelian considered this, as did the Harlequin.

'*Honour*,' prompted some guardian of Ulthwé.

'Honour,' echoed another.

'In – deed,' said the Harlequin slowly.

'She's fairly dangerous,' warned Carnelian.

The genuine Harlequin was not to be instructed by a protégé. However, he did pay some attention.

'Let her have a disabled sword,' he decreed.

'Her with a dead sword against two Banshees–'

'I am insulted,' the challenger snarled at Carnelian.

One of the Banshees ejected a tiny power-pack from her sword. She tossed the inert weapon at Meh'lindi's feet. Meh'lindi did not pick the sword up quite yet.

'I prefer to fight without this clumsy armour,' she said. Thus she wasted a little more time. In actual fact the eldar armour was far from clumsy. Might she inject a sting of self-doubt, a mite of inadvertent clumsiness, into her opponent! Probably not. More importantly, without the pearly armour, in this sombre gloom in her assassin's black tunic Meh'lindi would be a little less visible.

Carnelian was making an error in allowing her to continue living even for a little while longer. Sentimentality could hardly be a factor, merely because he had once ravished her so ecstatically and insultingly. Being himself only a kind of cadet Harlequin, plainly he must take account of eldar sensibilities. She would surely die within the next few minutes. She also intended to kill – Carnelian, if she could. Carnelian was withdrawing himself to a judicious distance.

What distance was far enough away from a Callidus assassin? Slowly Meh'lindi unpeeled her armour until she stood in her clingtight tunic.

'The red sash! She mustn't wear that! It's full of tricks–'

Digital weapons. Toxins. A garrote.

'She must drop the sash–'

So be it. She could always snatch the sash up again.

At last Meh'lindi picked up the inert brass-hilted sword. She hefted it to test the balance. Her opponent's sword blade shimmered with a hazy blue energy which could cut through her own dead sword blade – which at least boasted a razor-edge.

'Begin,' said the Harlequin impatiently. His mask, now, was a skull with pools of blood in the eye sockets.

The Banshee howled. Meh'lindi screamed back at her with all of her voice. They circled. They feinted. The Banshee leapt ballet-like, twisting in mid-air, slashing.

Meh'lindi had already ducked and sprung sideways. She touched the ground with her spread palm. She pivoted in a different direction. The Banshee sliced the air where she had been.

Again the Banshee howled. Again Meh'lindi shrieked as if she had been lacerated. Briefly she had indeed been stunned. However, Callidus reflexes sent her somersaulting one-handed. The tip of her sword struck the Banshee's bone-white poleyn – a visible target and the blur of scarlet. The knee-hood brushed off the disabled metal. Yet it was a strike.

Meh'lindi's hilt was against the hilt of the Banshee's power blade. The blade hummed in front of Meh'lindi's face. The scream-mask confronted her so closely. The Banshee had been almost faster than Meh'lindi could match. Would the mandibles discharge whatever they were loaded with? Meh'lindi threw herself aside. She rolled. She was about to bounce to her feet.

The Banshee was already beside her, judging her swing. Oh yes, the aim was to slice off Meh'lindi's nose first. To graze the tip of her nose with energy. Any closer, and half of Meh'lindi's face would tear off, bare to the bone.

As the power sword swung, Meh'lindi could only parry the stroke. With a crackling shudder the power blade met her own sword. Meh'lindi's blade ruptured apart. How the vibration jarred her wrist. Now she held only a hilt and a jagged stump. Diverted, the power sword swung by, caressing Meh'lindi's nostrils with ozone rather than with amputation.

And in this moment Meh'lindi stabbed upward elastically into the Banshee's armpit where shoulder-joint met breastplate. The toothed stub of her sword penetrated. It must have severed an auxiliary muscle. The power sword flew from the Banshee's grasp, and bounced upon rubble, inactive as soon as she had lost hold of it. Meh'lindi scrambled to seize the weapon, to restore its energy – no, not to kill the Banshee but to settle scores with Carnelian.

A skull-numbing howl hammered Meh'lindi as her fingers closed on the hilt. She sprawled prone, a bird of prey beaten down by a thunderous gale.

This sprawl might well have been the saving of her.

In the air there was another kind of thunder.

RAARK RAARK RAARK CRUMP CRUMP

RAAARKARAAARKACRUMPACRUMPACRUMPA

Boltguns!

Though a guillotining by power blade might have been her fate, she craned her neck.

Almost a full squad of Imperial Fists, wearing wonderfully welcome pus-yellow armour, were powering forward, blasting at guardians and Banshees.

Taken by surprise – even astonishment – Banshees and guardians were being ripped apart by exploding bolts.

The Fists were already so close. Banshees howled, but the Marines had their visors down. A jet of clingfire gushed from one exotic gun held by a guardian. Fire wreathed a Fist. Las-bolts impacted on his suit. The suit was blasted open. The blazing torch which was the Space Marine careered onward for a while before crashing into a broken rib of wraithbone.

Guardians and Banshees were fleeing for their lives. Carnelian and the Harlequin had disappeared. Marines were overrunning this place where Lex stood enmeshed and where the prisoners lay. Others were forming a defensive cordon.

Lex was shouting, 'Careful, brothers! The female on the ground is one of us!'

IT WASN'T LONG before Meh'lindi had looted spray-tubes of solvent from the corpses of two fallen guardians who had earlier wielded those web-guns. If they had hoped to march prisoners away instead of being obliged to carry bodies, a supply of solvent was inevitable.

It wasn't long before Lex was free. Then Jaq and Grimm and Petrov. How they panted to replenish their stifled lungs. How agonisedly they rubbed life back into their cramped limbs.

A Marine sergeant gaped at the vast skylight or energy-field displaying the ghastly veils of irreality.

'Where are we, my captain?'

'We're in Ulthwé craftworld, Wagner. You're beholding the Eye of Terror up there. How did you come here? How did you find us? How did you follow us?'

'The Eye of Terror…'

'Report, sergeant, report!'

* * *

EARLY IN THE raid on the city in the eldar habitat, one of Wagner's men had sustained damage to his helmet. Shuriken discs had razored Brother Goethe's helmet open, without more than nicking its wearer's skull. A formidable eldar had sprung forth, an eldar with a swirling mane of coaly hair, dressed in a black robe with a single silver rune as big as a squat embroidered on the fabric. This warlock had pointed a long potent blade at Goethe. The blade discharged energies which sent Goethe reeling. The warlock had hurried into some building.

Shortly thereafter, Goethe had begun to suffer what Wagner feared were hallucinations. Phantom perceptions, intuitions.

Because of the damage to Goethe's helmet, his psychic shield had been breached. The energy blast from the rune-wearer had leaked through. Some latent psychic sense had been rudely awakened, so it seemed. Goethe was coping, even so. And now Goethe was alert to sensory inklings which eluded his comrades, notwithstanding their enhanced senses and instrumentation. Far from being a casualty, it was as though Goethe were enriched.

This was one reason why Wagner had ventured to lead his squad into the webway.

When the squad became lost in the blue haze-maze, at one fork Goethe had claimed to smell Imperial Fist hormones ahead of them. Wagner's men had followed Goethe as he pursued the scent like some hound hunting a prey. If Lex's visor had not been open, Goethe might never have been able to follow Captain d'Arquebus through the webway.

'Goethe will be a Librarian one day,' proclaimed Lex.

Wagner gestured at that motionless lone suit, still lambent with white flame, impacted against wraithbone. Goethe had been the recipient of the alien clingfire.

'Sergeant, quench him quickly and harvest his precious progenoid glands.' Aye, perform this sacred act before they even thought about withdrawing – to where, and how? 'Foam and las-scalpel and stasis box, sergeant.'

'Yes, yes, of course.'

'Use one of the eldar power swords to cut the armour open. Do it now.'

MEH'LINDI WAS SWIFTLY speaking to Jaq about all she had learned from the Harlequin. Grimm was buffeting his own head in a passion of infuriated sell-reproach.

'That charlatan! The sensei all to be sacrificed? What a scam!' A whine of self-justification crept into Grimm's contrition. 'Still, if it brings about the Numen and the shining path–'

The eldar – or some of the eldar – hoped to control the galaxy again by proxy…

Some other eldar hoped to twist time itself backward! Could that really be so?

Phoenix Lords were walking the webway.

'Those are supposed to be ancient war-cult fanatics,' jabbered Petrov. 'So I've heard! No home or shrine of their own. Wearers of such armour become archetypal, almost wargods. They wander, they vanish for ages. They must lurk at those Crossroads of Inertia! I've heard names whispered. Karandras, the sinister Shadow Hunter. Jain Zar, the Storm of Silence. She throws a triple blade that always returns to her hand–'

A Young King sacrificed to the Bloody-Handed God.

'The iron Avatar sits on a throne in a shrine,' gabbled Petrov. 'When war comes, the Avatar becomes furnace-hot. A chosen aspect warrior enters the shrine stark naked. Those outside hear such screams of agony. So it's whispered–'

The Book of Rhana Dandra *in the Black Library, repository of prophecies. A mutable book; a book which could change as probabilities shifted… A book with Jaq Draco's name written in it, according to Carnelian.*

Petrov said, 'Well, isn't there a bond between Harlequins and inquisitors, Jaq Draco? Both being enemies of Chaos! Haven't some inquisitors been admitted to the Black Library, blindfolded and closely guarded?'

Shocked almost beyond belief, Jaq demanded harshly: 'Where did you come by this information?'

Jaq was a Malleus man. He *had* been a Malleus man. He had never known of such contacts between inquisitors and Harlequins.

Under a Seal of Heresy, such records must have been kept. Aye, under the *Inquisato Relinquo* prohibition! Jaq felt nauseated by his own ignorance.

'How did you come by this information?'

'It isn't… information. It's rumours, whispers. Navigators' hearsay which I've pieced together. I didn't dare broach any of this… You'd have executed me for heresy. I know what happens.'

How Jaq moaned.

Had eldar Harlequins, through the go-between of Zephro Carnelian, been testing him all along? At the same time as they used him to cause confusion to the Inquisition and to the Ordo Malleus? Was another aim of theirs truly that he should suffer the terrible fate of daemonic possession so that he could become illuminated to serve their cause?

Jaq pounded a fist upon his palm. 'If only we could find the Black Library and this *Book of Rhana Dandra!*'

'And steal it,' piped up Grimm. 'That'd show the snobs. Huh, Rhana Dandra. Sounds like the *Book of Dandruff* to me. The scurf of seers falling upon the pages, making lotsa runes. Course, finding the Library's one thing–'

And reading a book scribed in eldar runes was another matter.

'I don't read eldar,' said Meh'lindi. 'I can only talk it. I could learn to read from an informant.'

Grimm cackled bitterly. 'A friendly informant such as Zephro Carnelian, who wanted your head cut off?'

'I've looked at eldar runes,' said Petrov. 'They're difficult. Thousands of different shapes. I don't speak Eldar. I just know some names. And rumours. I don't know much.' The grey-faced Navigator almost whimpered.

'If only we could find the Black Library, even so!' Jaq reached for his Tarot pack, then restored it to a pocket. What pattern of cards could he possibly use? What prayer to the Emperor would assist him? Would he glimpse the shining path once more? Now was hardly the time to try, in cursed Ulthwé, after fighting off guardians and Banshees. *The eldar would be back soon, in greater numbers.* An intrusion by devout Imperial Fists might be as welcome as an assault by Chaos Marines.

SERGEANT WAGNER HAD returned to his captain. An odour of charred meat drifted with him.

'Foam won't extinguish the clingfire, sir. It's outside and inside the suit. Goethe's roasting. I can't harvest his glands.'

'We must leave him, then. We must find our way back to the habitat.'

Supposing that the habitat, thousands of light-years away across the galaxy, was still in existence. Supposing that the rest of Lex's company were still there. Supposing that Chaos hadn't engulfed the ceremony. Supposing that an Imperial battleship hadn't finally blasted the habitat out of orbit to crash upon deadly Stalinvast.

'What of these civilians?' asked Wagner, about Jaq and his tiny entourage. They were hardly civilians, yet a sergeant might think so in time of stress.

'We'll come with you,' said Jaq, 'to settle with Baal Firenze.'

'Oh, surely you'll come,' rumbled Lex. 'You must reverse your Tarot card and hold it backwards, to guide us.'

Would that work, even with prayers to the Emperor whose spirit permeated the pack – corrupted as that pack was by Carnelian?

An inverted card might lead to disaster. It might conduct them to a Chaos world in that gruesome Eye up there.

Yet they must leave. They must leave this ravaged sector of fabled Ulthwé.

As they were about to file into the tunnel-mouth amidst the ruins, a black guardian frisked from behind a wall of broken spider-haunted wraithbone.

That clingfire gun was in his hands.

The weapon sputtered. Instead of hosing, it spat spasmodically – a spittle of bright globules.

Even as exploding bolts tore the guardian apart, a screech arose from amongst the fugitives as if a Banshee were in their midst.

Liquid fire had wreathed Azul Petrov's forearm. Half of his right arm, from his fingers to his elbow, blazed. The oily damask of his sleeve fell away in writhing tatters. Clingfire wreathed the bare flesh.

The Space Marine nearest to Petrov foamed him so that at least the rest of his robe and its embroidered ribbons would not catch fire.

But nothing could extinguish the fire which ate into his flesh and his nerves – consuming ever so slowly, like lingering sticky acid.

Petrov's scream rose shrilly, ragged and soprano in its torment.

SEVENTEEN
CHAOS

HOW FEEBLE MOST men were, mused Lex, compared with a Space Marine. Could this wrinkled Navigator have tolerated ten seconds in the pain-inducing Tunnel of Terror back in the fortress-monastery? Could he have endured ten seconds' punishment in a nerve-glove? A nerve-glove immersed the whole of one's naked anatomy in simulated furnace fire – not merely a forearm.

Lex's left fist itched at the memory of how he had once held it staunchly in a bowl of acid until only the bones remained for him to scribe honoured names upon.

And Inquisitor Draco, impaired by a bruise! By now Jaq Draco seemed to have recovered his agility. Maybe the fibres which had clutched him so tightly had reset a rib.

The Navigator's shrieks continued. A hulking battle-brother was holding him upright by his uninjured arm. Petrov was hyperventilating. He might lapse into a coma of shock and be blessedly quiet until the cling-fire had consumed the affected half of his limb – until two charred twigs, of ulna and radius bones, fell off and his misfortune had finally run its course.

How frail men often were. Petrov could perceive the warp. He could endure that aching vision.

How desperately Petrov screamed.

'You gotta do something!' shouted the squat. 'Tear his arm off with your power glove!'

Transfer some clingfire to the gauntlet?

'I'm gonna go back for a power sword–'

Lex caught hold of Grimm before the little man could dart away. He lifted him off the ground. Couldn't the abhuman think more clearly than that?

'Sergeant,' ordered Lex, 'use your las-scalpel above the elbow. Slice through the humerus.'

'I grieve for the loss of Goethe's progenoids, lord.'

'Use your scalpel for this lesser purpose–'

Laser pulses hit the arch of the tunnel, blasting out shards of wraith-bone. A hideous howl arose. Lex clapped his visor shut. Banshees were in the offing.

'Not yet, Wagner! We need the confines of the tunnel to protect us. Everyone into the blue!'

Lex carried Grimm with him single-handedly. Wagner carried the shrieking Navigator.

Soon they were all inside the blue mist, protected from the warp by the mighty – or fragile – psycho-energy membrane of the webway.

To the rear, three Space Marines stood shoulder to shoulder. They blocked the tunnel with their bulky armour, ready to fire streams of bolts hindward at the slightest movement within the mist. Two other Marines were ahead, on point.

Petrov's forearm was a bright candle of combusting tissues and fats upon a wick of bones. Did Lex's acoustic sensors detect a positive note to Petrov's shrieks, an affirmative note?

'Now,' ordered Lex, and Wagner kindled his las-scalpel.

THE RESIDUE OF the Navigator's forearm, luminous with flame, lay on the floor of the tunnel. It might serve as a derisive offering to any eldar who should come in pursuit – a little token of the sacrifices which mankind was willing to make. Sign, too, of a defiant refusal, in this case, to euthanase and abandon a casualty, even though the casualty was no Space Marine.

Petrov hung, gasping, in a Fist's grip. The las-scalpel had cauterized the stump of his humerus and its sleeve of flesh in a sanitary way which no stroke of a power sword would have achieved, nor any snapping and wrenching by a gauntlet.

Azul Petrov began to babble–

–so *blessedly*, stunning Lex with awe.

And Jaq too.

* * *

HERE IN THE entry to the webway, so close to the warp, and in the grip of appalling pain, Azul had experienced a vision. An epiphany. A transcendent revelation.

The spirit of Fennix had seemed to visit Azul – Fennix in that dying moment when the monkey-man had striven to apprehend the telepathic totality, the Word, the Sign of Everything. From the sea of souls, dead Fennix was answering Azul's plea.

Upon the vision of Azul's third eye had appeared an eerie, complex rune.

An eldar rune. *Rune of locating, rune of unlocking,* so Fennix's voice seemed to cry from afar.

Intuitions of great brass-bound, hex-stamped alien tomes, brittle with age, infested Azul. Sensations of arcane incunabula and palimpsests and chained libers. Of ranks of daemonic codices and opuscules – the very words of which might melt the eye to keep the brain from imbibing what was writ. Impressions of labyrinthine ebon passageways and inky halls and chambers and cubicles wherein books themselves were luminous, phosphorescent. Impressions of a maze so extensive that an ignorant wanderer might well leave his bones there. Of terrible immaterial guardians of these macabre archives. Could those brooding presences be chained, tamed daemons, embodiments of formulae inscribed within certain volumes locked in arabesque cages?

Black… Library. Black… Library…

'I CAN SEE the rune in my warp-eye!' Azul cried. 'Like a twisted grid, like a zigzag lattice overlaying my warp-sight. It corresponds to a route through the webway. It dictates a route. He who follows it, arrives. It's a key as well. Only Fennix saw eye to eye with me. Oh thank you, Fennix my true friend!'

'It is an agony vision,' whispered Lex wonderingly. 'Like the light of Rogal Dorn…'

Petrov's voice faltered. 'Is it fading a fraction… already? Will we have time to follow it? How can I fix it in my mind?' The Navigator shut his ordinary eyes in concentration. 'Ah, much brighter now. Yet I fear, I fear the fading of the light!'

A Fist was a thinker; and Lex thought hard.

He thought as hard as ceramically reinforced bone. Hard as the shrunken black jewel of a warp-eye.

He declared. 'With my graving tool I shall scrimshander that rune upon your warp-eye, under your instruction, Azul Petrov! Then you shall always see it!'

Were there pain-nerves in a warp-eye, which would cause Petrov to flinch and spoil the design? To be unable to describe it lucidly, even if held immobile?

'Will your warp-eye sense pain if carved by my graving tool?' Lex demanded.

Petrov's head shook, maybe in denial or maybe in terror. His teeth chattered.

'I don't know... I don't think so. No.'

No to the artistic operation, or no to the question of pain?

To behold a Navigator's third eye directly is deadly,' warned Meh'lindi. 'I've seen the consequences. '

'Fennix was *blind*,' said Jaq. 'That's how he could look Azul in the warp-eye. You'll destroy yourself, captain.'

'Ah,' rumbled Lex, 'but I shall not behold his warp-eye directly. I shall not have my visor open. A Marine's visor isn't equivalent to a window. Imagery is transmitted by impulses through the suit's calculator to slim the visual centre of my brain. Thus I cannot be blinded even by the flash of a thermonuke. With my visor shut my regular vision is in abeyance.'

'Lord,' said Wagner, 'I volunteer to test this out.'

'Nay, sergeant,' Lex said courteously. 'I am fairly positive that my suit's inanimate calculator can draw the sting of the deadly gaze. The matter is urgent—'

Urgent indeed.

The rearguards opened fire. The corpse of an eldar warrior, the like of which they had not previously seen, tumbled out of the mist. Ahead of it skidded a sleek yet substantial weapon.

That alien wore heavy black armour. From the red rune-marked helm jutted flanges resembling squared-off upturned ears. Those might well be rangefinders. The red weapon was the heftier on account of a long cone-shaped nozzle. Surely a rocket-launcher!

'Uh-uh,' grunted Grimm, 'here come the heavy brigade.'

Heavy indeed. The detonation of a rocket in confined quasi-space might easily put paid even to Space Marines in power armour. Those who wore no armour stood little chance. Might such congested explosions destabilize the webway wall? Causing a local rupture? A sealing-off of the rupture? The plummeting of bodies into increate warp?

That eldar warrior surely had companions close behind him.

Lex bellowed, 'Carry the Navigator, Wagner. All of us run for it, at the pace of the slowest.'

Since Grimm's legs were short, Lex carried the abhuman by the collar of his flak jacket.

'Oh, ancestors! Did I ask for a ride? You're shaking me guts–'

A TRIPLE BRANCHING of the blue. Head left at random. Almost at once, another branch. Head right.

Jaq sensed a nauseating immaterial barrier. Had they not been fleeing pell-mell he would have cried halt. They were already through the uncanny obstruction. It was a flimsy obstacle – as if it had been sapped psychically from the far side, weakened by sedulous thrusts. Beyond, the blue mist thinned suddenly. Other sickly light welled forth.

They had emerged by way of a cave. Hardly even a cave. A concavity in rock too shallow to accommodate more than a couple of armoured Imperial Fists at once.

A dreary slope of great boulders, poised on scree, extended downward into murk. Upward likewise. In the upward direction rococo metallic towers were visible. A small fleet of grotesque vessels might have impacted in the terrain. Evilly flamboyant, those towers were canted at absurd angles to one another in defiance of gravity, yet they were linked by eerily wrought bridges along which prowled tiny figures.

In a bilious sky hung an hourglass sun. Two suns were joined impossibly at the waist like a double yolk within a glutinous pulsing albumen-womb of glowing gas. This absurd sun made the eyes and the spirit ache. How was gravity thus defied? That double-sun should have cohered into one sun aeons ago. Two such celestial bodies could not exist side by side.

'Chaos,' breathed Jaq in horror.

Six battle-brothers had formed a picket circle facing outward. Just then, the whole terrain began to tilt – horribly to the sense of balance. What had been downward was rising. Soon the land became level. The rounder of the boulders began to roll across the scree as *upward* asserted itself. Irregular blocks slid.

The direction-quake, the quake of orientation, ceased.

Might the terrain sometimes become vertical, shedding its boulders and scree and inhabitants? No – or how should those leaning towers have endured? Those haunts of Chaos creatures…

This must be deep in the Eye of Terror here, deeper than when *Tormentum Malorum* had landed on a Chaos world. There, at least, gravity had not been a mere whim, as now.

Activity was increasing on those tortuous bridges. Had the intrusion by the Imperial Fists been noted? Sniffed psychically?

How frequent were balance-quakes? What if this cursed land tilted sideways while Lex was engaged in his delicate work? And would his power gauntlets impede his dexterity by amplifying the slightest movement?

Wagner sat Azul Petrov down. Kneeling on the potent skulls which embellished his poleyns, the sergeant held the Navigator inflexibly – though Petrov must, of course, co-operate willingly.

Lex was obliged to ask Meh'lindi to delve in an external pocket of his armour for his cherished power-stylus. Who could have imagined that he would need to have recourse to the engraving tool in a combat situation?

She placed the tool, activated, in Lex's powered fingers. Unbidden, she handed Jaq his force rod. Resolutely she looked away.

Jaq also averted his eyes, stroking the rod gravely as he gazed towards those leaning towers.

Lex knelt bulkily before the Navigator.

He scrutinized the large cool green eyes in the insectoid face. That ashen face seemed all the frailer from shock and the loss of half an arm. Rubies upon the ear-lobes and nose and lower lip and chin might almost have been guidance markers preliminary to radical facial surgery – to the excision and unpeeling of Petrov's physiognomy. Lex reached to raise the Navigator's brow-bandage with a single powered finger.

'I'll never be able to navigate again,' whispered Petrov tragically, and closed his ordinary eyes.

Indeed not. Hereafter he would always behold through his warp-eye the domineering pattern of that rune.

The warp-eye, exposed, was a glossy node of darkness. It resembled a nodule of vitrodur. Death had not come to Lex, nor even nausea. The calculator in his suit superimposed a curved grid upon the magnified orb.

'Begin,' murmured the Navigator. 'South declination seventy, ascension twenty-five.'

Azul Petrov was an adept of celestial co-ordinates, and an eye was like a sphere of space.

Upon the grid in Lex's field of vision a tiny telltale cursor blinked.

Stifled by Wagner's gauntlets, the Navigator shuddered only slightly as the tip of the graving tool touched the surface of his inky eye.

'Ascension twenty-four...'

With unshaking power-steadied touch, Lex began fastidiously to carve the evocative eldar rune upon the atrophied yet potent eye.

* * *

NIGHT ROLLED TOWARDS them like a velvet curtain, or like a negative of an aurora. It hid from view those leaning towers. In the sickly sky an eclipse was eating swiftly across the leftward sun.

This was not how night fell in any sane reality!

The curtain of darkness halted before it reached them. Within that darkness flapped moth-like shapes, faintly phosphorescent, visible in violet.

More such moths swiftly gathered. They massed to form a giant humanoid figure bestriding the shrouded land. The hulking figure gained substance by the moment, as Lex continued to engrave Azul's eye.

On the shoulders of the figure were mounted what appeared to be plasma cannons. Great grasping powerhands dangled. Around the ankles of that solidifying ogrespook capered shadows – reminiscent of that horned spiked suit of armour which had lain in Ulthwé.

The ogre was a parody of a Titan, of one of the colossal fighting machines of the Imperium. This was a Chaos Titan, congealing out of immaterium. Or maybe the Titan did possess an actual existence, and had advanced within that curtain of night, camouflaged by the dae-monic moths.

Those tinier shadows were dire Chaos Marines, come from the lean-ing towers which must be their citadel. They were assembling to attack.

Sergeant Wagner was praying, but Lex could not allow his attention to veer.

Jaq was sighting his force rod tentatively at the looming colossus, muttering prayers of his own. Just then an extremely low moon sailed into view. Astride the capsized crescent sat the vilest of creatures, as on a saddle. Such saucer-eyes, such a parrot-beak. That tentacled fiend resembled some kraken from the deeps of an ocean. Its tentacles trailed down, becoming vastly long threads. With these, it began to fish. A thread adhered to a boulder. The thread drew the stone upward, then dropped it.

How far away was the kraken? Or how close? How close, or far, was the crescent moon which was its vehicle? Distance and size had lost all meaning. Here was nightmare incarnate. Another thread snared a Chaos Marine, plucking the armoured brute from out of the darkness. 'That ain't no helmet,' exclaimed one of the Imperial Fists, 'that's his head–'

To the amplified horror-struck gaze of the Marine it was evident that the grotesquely metamorphosed Chaos warrior was guffawing with insane delight as he was drawn up to share that surreal perch with the daemon.

One of the suns had disappeared. The other sun began to wink. It strobed so that the mockery of a Titan and the warriors around its feet vanished and reappeared, advancing jerkily, unpredictably.

Even with a floodlight beaming from Lex's shoulder, to finish scribing the rune upon Petrov's eye demanded such concentration and detachment.

'Declination thirty-one, ascension forty-three. Yes, yes, just a little more–'

A battle-brother cried out. In the spasming of light and darkness, so disorientating, a whip-thin tendril from on high had found him. The tendril wrapped around the stabilizing jets and reserve air bottles and purificator and intake pipes behind his shoulders. It heaved him from the ground. He was rising, rising, all the power of his suit rendered futile. In the strobing flashes of illumination the tangled Space Marine seemed to be ascending at an accelerating rate – doomed to become prey to that daemon, or else to that Chaos Marine up on that cock-eyed sickle of a moon.

'Wait!' cried Jaq, before the sergeant could order his men to fire upon their captured Fist.

Jaq pointed his force rod upward. He summoned all his hatred of daemonry into a psychic thrust. Then he discharged the rod at the angler in the sky.

The moon crescent rocked. A boat pitched upon invisible waves. The kraken-creature howled. Discarded, the Chaos Marine was falling from a great height towards boulders. The true and devout Marine was still being reeled in. His arms were flailing. His legs were pistoning uselessly.

Jaq growled bitterly. Which was worse? For the man's colleagues to blast him with bolts while still they could? If the victim's staunch spirit went into the sea of souls here, deep in the Eye of Terror, and did not disintegrate, what torment might await it! If his life were prolonged by whim, he might be vilely corrupted.

'Sergeant, kill the man to save him.'

Wagner barked an order. Bolts flew upward at the diminishing target. The bolts all seemed to veer. Their trajectory was bent by the twistedness of unreality which plagued this place.

Useless. Fruitless. Conserve ammunition.

Maybe there had been a single lucky hit at the limit of range...

Maybe the puissant Marine was merely injured by that hit, to add to his impending torments.

Meanwhile – *strobe, strobe* – the mass of Chaos Marines were leaping forward, jerky as grotesque insects.

Jaq swung his rod. Summoning an excoriating exorcistic fury, he discharged the rod at the Chaos Titan.

The colossus lurched. It stamped its way forward drunkenly, crushing at least one of its minion Marines beneath a massive cleated, clawed foot.

The Chaos Marines opened fire. Unnatural bolts flew from their weapons. Buzzing like robotic bees, these bolts swarmed towards their targets. They seemed to steer themselves to a limited extent. Maybe they were following oscillations in the warped space of this unreal world. A boulder erupted, spraying stone shrapnel at Grimm's flak jacket. A Fist's helmet erupted too.

Less than half a squad now fired back at the strobing onrush of figures in misshapen armour. Jaq gestured with his force rod, confusing the bee-bolts. A trio of these swooped at a Fist's groin, nevertheless, blasting his girdle-guard open. The Fist stooped right over. His gauntlet grooved the ground briefly until drugs abated his agony. How he strove to straighten himself. A bolt impacted on the vambrace of his forearm. Other bolts penetrated his ruptured groin-guard. He toppled.

From Petrov, in a terrible whisper: 'The rune's complete—'

'Withdraw, withdraw!' bellowed Lex. So total had his attention to the graving tool been, that for a couple of seconds he pointed it at oncoming attackers as if the stylus itself were a weapon.

And then they were all crowding through the recess in the rock, back into the blue, the three surviving Fists preceding, Lex and Wagner bringing up the rear, shielding their unarmoured companions.

A lurid comet of plasma streaked from the Titan. The Imperial Fists and those they protected were far enough into the blue, by now, to survive. Maybe lingering plasma would deny Chaos access for a while.

THE ENERGY BARRIER tugged only momentarily at Jaq. The psychic obstacle had not been intended for inhabitants of the sane universe, but for denizens of abreality, unreality. It was weak, though, weak. Weaker still, since they had violated it. This hymen had been stitched across the passage in the webway which had led to a world perhaps once bountiful – before it was swallowed by Chaos. Soon Chaos Marines and other daemonic familiars would flood through again, howling in anticipation, towards ravaged Ulthwé.

The fate of Ulthwé did not matter. Guided by the Navigator, the journey of Jaq and his companions was leading elsewhere.

EIGHTEEN
DEATHS

IT WAS LEX who recommended that the group must catch some sleep en route to the legendary Black Library.

Primo, he argued, Petrov had no idea how far away through the webway the Library was. Nor by what devious or dangerous ways. Petrov's rune-scribed eye – safely hidden now by his bandanna – led the Navigator onward without revealing the length of the journey they were undertaking. The entrance to the Library might only present itself after hours of travel, or days. Equally, it might present itself soon and suddenly.

They would need all their wits and alertness and stamina. Stamina must be measured by the weakest amongst them. Surely the weakest was Petrov himself, still shocked by the amputation of half his arm under less than ideal circumstances. Arguably that amputation had pre-empted the full impact of trauma which the engraving of his warp-eye might otherwise have induced. Nevertheless, the fellow must be existing on his nerves, fuelled by the revelation he'd experienced. He mustn't burn out.

All nerves were frayed, even those of the Imperial Fists. Their numbers were now reduced to a captain, a sergeant, and three battle-brothers. To have fought in the Battle of Stalinvast, and then in the skirmish at Ulthwé, and, then to have encountered daemonic Chaos was sapping of vigour and sanity. No brother should have had to endure what these had experienced on that perverse world in the Eye.

Lex feared that a gibbering psychopathy might be lurking in the Fists' souls. Even in his own! A psychopathy suppressed by faith, yet if new stress befell too soon, capable of undermining discipline.

Secundo, the Library was said to be fiercely and frightfully guarded. Though they were furnished with a key, with a talisman, would this suffice?

Tertio, according to Petrov the Library was vast and labyrinthine, all but unknowable..

Jaq Draco still moved sorely. After use of that rod against the monster-in-the-moon and against the Chaos Titan and the bee-bolts, his psychic reserves must be depleted.

This ill-assorted team must rest. Though hyped by action, they must recuperate.

PRESENTLY THEY CAME upon a cul-de-sac of the webway. A side-passage shrank to a vanishing point, braiding in upon itself like some umbilical cord.

Had the webway been twisted shut here by psychic power? Or might this be a place from which the webway might grow a new extension, spontaneously connecting up with some other part of itself?

If the webway resembled a bizarre nervous system, suave and commodious, was the Black Library the brain of the webway, where hideous knowledge was stored?

The cul-de-sac seemed more defensible than a stretch of open misty tunnel. A Space Marine could sleep alertly in a split-brain trance. One side of the brain would become dormant so that fatigue poisons could be purged, while the other cerebral hemisphere would remain aware of circumstances.

Before any sleep involving either half of the brain or the whole of the brain, nourishment and hygiene were a priority...

THE MARINES SHARED concentrated food with their four guests. Grimm proffered some tastier delicacies from the pouches and pockets of his flak jacket. Water came from pressure-flasks incorporated in the Fists' armour, and from similar vessels strapped to the legs of Grimm and Jaq and Petrov. Heavy-water, so called.

If this journey *did* last for several days, they might be obliged to quit the webway temporarily so as to raid some unknown world or craft-world and replenish their food and drink. Such a detour could prove doubly dangerous. On re-entering the webway, might the travellers once again be as far away as ever from their elusive destination?

'A joint of meat wouldn't go amiss,' Grimm groused. With morbid jocularity he added, 'We could all have gnawed on a well-cooked limb, eh Azul? Shouldn't have tossed that away.'

'Too well cooked,' lamented the Navigator. He seemed to appreciate the gruff sally. Here was squattish sympathy. Meh'lindi had already inspected Petrov's elbow-stump. She had found no sign of morbidity. The amputation had been righteously sealed by the sergeant's las-scalpel.

'There'd be nothing but charred bone left,' sighed Petrov.

'Oh, and a smear of hot marrow.'

'What use will I be in future? Supposing we succeed? I'll only be able to see my way to a Black Library – and to nowhere else.'

Grimm spoke more softly. 'Listen, Azul, be warned. You'd be of a vast amount of value to a certain Ordo Malleus. That ordo would give its eye-teeth to have that eldar rune in its pocket. Jaq Draco's all right, as inquisitors go. In fact, as inquisitors go, he went right off on his own! Other inquisitors would be, well… ruthless ain't the word for it.'

'The rune – *in its pocket*?' repeated Petrov. 'Do you suppose my eye could be used without me?'

'Azul, when this is over I'd advise you to ask the sergeant to cut your warp-eye out with his scalpel. Give it to Jaq to keep. Then you'll be safe. No one'll want to hunt you down.'

'Armless, and eyeless… Cutting out the eye might kill me. It's part of my brain!'

'Oh it's a risk, Azul. But then you can lose yourself on some backward planet.'

'Delightful!'

'Won't the other Navigators protect you? Those Navis Nobilite bosses?'

'I suppose so…'

A SQUAT'S WHISPER wasn't particularly inaudible. Jaq had overheard.

If he did reach the Black Library courtesy of that engraved eye, conceivably he could win rehabilitation with his ordo. Charges of heresy would be annulled.

Ah, foolish temptation! The Inquisition was divided against itself. Even the Ordo Malleus had been corrupted – as witness Baal Firenze. If Jaq succeeded in gaining entry to the eldar library, he would simply become the most estranged person in the galaxy. The most isolated! Were it not for the company of Meh'lindi. And to a far lesser degree, of Grimm.

Did he love Meh'lindi in some self-tormenting fashion? What a blasphemy such fondness must be. What impiety such ardour must be, when balanced against duty.

Yet in which direction did true duty lie?

* * *

MEH'LINDI ASKED THE captain of Fists, 'Does your Chapter possess any dreadnoughts?'

Courteously, Lex answered this strange exotic person, this woman in an alien guise: 'Aye, we treasure four Furibundus-class Destroyer dreadnoughts and three Contemptor-class dreadnoughts. Such a holy heritage, those!'

In his youth Lex had spent noble and blessed hours in the scriptories of the fortress-monastery, studying schematics of those dreadnoughts. On some future day as a highest battle honour might his mangled truncated body be enshrined in one of those, surgically and neurally synched with the machine? Enwombed in sustaining fluid within injection-moulded ceramite, itself veneered with adamantium shaped in some vast plasma-centrifuge of the Adeptus Mechanicus orbiting Mars!

Oh, the synchronized double dual boltguns of the Contemptor. Oh, the boltguns and lascannon of the 'Fury'. Oh, its mighty combustion fuel manifold and exhaust, oh, its rotary actuators.

A tear almost welled in Lex's eye at the thought of the paradise of potent piety which was the fortress-monastery of the Imperial Fists. Its scriptories and librarium, its halls and its foundries and gymnasia, its surgeries and firing ranges – and the Chapel of Dorn.

Would he ever behold that holy home again?

What was this strange, brave female's interest in dread-noughts?

'Are any of those fitted with a six-barrel assault cannon, captain?'

'Nay, lady, neither the Contemptor nor the Furibundus sport such a weapon–'

'Damn.'

'–though they could be so fitted.'

'Tell me, Lex, disregarding hits by heavy weapons, what is the most vulnerable feature of a dreadnought?'

Meh'lindi was still thinking of ways to disable Tarik Ziz.

Lex considered. 'If the cooling and exhaust systems are damaged, heat will build up inside the dreadnought – supposing that it continues to exert itself. The internal actuators might melt or even ignite. This would heat up the amniotic fluid which cushions the pilot. In extremis, this would boil the pilot alive. Signs of this will be black smoke venting from the dreadnought. The internal micro-bore hydraulics sometimes begin to leak. This reduces the dreadnought's strength and mobility.'

'Can cooling and exhaust systems readily be blocked by simple things such as torn-up clothing?'

Lex chuckled. 'Only a lunatic would contemplate attacking a Contemptor or a Fury with rags. I admit this would be unexpected!'

Meh'lindi persisted. 'What filters protect the air intake from poison gas or toxins?'

Grimm butted in drily. 'All you need to do, Meh'lindi, is perform a striptease in front of the dreadnought to over-excite its pilot. Keep hold of all the veils you strip off. When the pilot is intoxicated leap on to its back with your legs round its neck. Plug the vents with your veils. After half an hour of lumbering around, trying to dislodge you, it'll overheat. You'll know, 'cos by then you'll have hot thighs.'

This discourtesy offended Lex.

'Be silent, abhuman!' he rumbled.

To Meh'lindi he said, 'Well duelled, by the way, back in Ulthwé, lady.' The unaccustomed mode of address was becoming less awkward for him, though hardly effortless. 'Your style was flamboyant and sweaty, perhaps. We Fists fight our duels with our boots fixed in duelling blocks so that we cannot ever flinch.'

Meh'lindi eyed Lex dubiously.

He added: 'Your duel of alien words with that Harlequin was particularly effective. A Fist thinks. A Fist respects nimble thinking.'

She nodded, accepting the captain's commendation.

'Do you realize,' Grimm asked Lex. 'that you just paid her a compliment? Beware of making Jaq jealous.'

'You are absurd as well as abhuman!' declared Lex. 'I suppose many ordinary human beings, let alone abhumans, must be jealous of the Astartes with our purity and our reinforced bodies.'

'Huh, that's it. Don't forget the physique.'

'Shut up, Grimm,' said Meh'lindi. 'You're babbling. I am Callidus.'

'Inquisitor's consort,' he mumbled, with a hint of unrequited though cordial envy.

She asked all of a sudden, 'Did you really ever have a wife called Grizzy?'

'Yes!' he yelped. 'I did! Sure as I'm standing here right now.'

PRESENTLY JAQ WAFTED incense from a tiny pressurized thimble almost as if fragrancing a bower for a mistress.

'Let us pray before slumber,' he declared. 'Balm for the soul disperses nightmares.'

What a hollow prayer this might be, addressed to a schizoid husk in a golden life-support throne!

Nay. That husk must be rekindled for salvation's sake! It must be reborn as the Numen, to lead New Men. How might that come to pass? In a Rhana Dandra bonfire – of Himself-on-Earth and all His Sons?

From which might arise, phoenix like, a more potent, less agonized deity? One in liege, unbeknownst, to eldar Harlequins?

But still Jaq prayed; and though he was no battle chaplain, the Fists who survived reverently appreciated his prayer. Maybe his words were routine and orthodox, yet they were wearily impassioned. Then the travellers lay themselves down to sleep – or to half-sleep with visors open.

Lex murmured quietly to Sergeant Wagner, imparting his opinion of Baal Firenze.

Azul Petrov crooned to himself softly about the miracle of Fennix's message from the sea of souls. His murmurs were a private lullaby.

Then all was silence, save for the sigh of breathing.

JAQ JERKED AWAKE.

In the blue mist loomed massive red armour embellished in gold. On the great shoulder pauldrons were gilded fylfot crosses and tassels, on the knee-protectors skulls, and on the groin-hauberk a golden scarab.

Rising behind the shoulders: a blood-red bat-wing double-axe. The face which peered was grizzle-bearded. The sensual lips were twisted bitterly. And the melancholy eyes were ice blue.

It was Jaq himself, armoured as he had never been armoured before – almost in Terminator attire.

Was this a vision of himself illuminated?

'Turn back!' proclaimed his own voice from the armour. 'Do not go onward! You must not! I swear this by–' such anguish in the voice– 'by Olvia.'

Olvia?

As though a seering nub of phosphorus had ignited in his soul, Jaq remembered…

…the Black Ship which had taken him to Earth long ago, a naive young psyker.

…and that doomed wench with whom he had consorted aboard that terrible vessel a-throb with psychic turmoil and dread and tormented dedication.

Olvia. Yes. Just a girl.

The only other woman with whom he had ever been at all intimate, briefly – prior to Meh'lindi.

He could hardly even recall Olvia's oval face.

Why should this armoured doppelganger mention her? If not to prove that by knowing of this private bygone affair he was truly Jaq himself?

'Go back!' repeated the phantasm.

Jaq sensed psychic assault, a plucking at the roots of his willpower in an effort to dissuade him.

Surely this must be one of the snares which guarded the route to the Black Library. To encounter an illusion of one's own self, menacing and malevolent!

'Ego te exorcizo!' he cried, and discharged his force rod.

With a cry of despair that mighty red armour flew away from him, dwindling, vanishing.

None of Jaq's companions had stirred. How could they not have heard?

He was awake. He must have just awakened this very moment. The armoured doppelganger had been a dream, a nightmare. The depths of his own mind, appalled at what he was undertaking, had constructed that mirage to intimidate him.

If the spook had come from his subconscious, surely it would have sworn by Meh'lindi? Not by Olvia long ago. It had been a deceitful geist, a psychic ambush.

He must try to sleep again.

THE MARINES HAD become fully alert.

Meh'lindi, although comatose, had registered the change in respiration – and then its absence as visors were closed.

She had raised her head.

Outside the entrance to the cul-de-sac an alarming figure stood hunched. Such a snow-white coiffure surmounted a bone-white stasis – until the moment when a devastating shriek might erupt. A mask with golden crest! That mask seemed like ferocity held in lithe body was clad in black armour. The golden greaves upon the calves seemed about to caper, goat-like. Was that a long white tail? Gripped mid-way by a blood-red torque?

This apparition clutched some kind of power-spear. A blue scalpel-blade as long as an arm. In the apparition's other hand was a smaller weapon with triple blades of blue, resembling a rotary saw. Surely this was some she-creature akin to the eldar Banshees.

An archetype of them, an epitome. Being only armed with blades, that figure seemed almost primitive, yet even more lethal – a primal, elemental heroine.

How silently she held her deadly poise.

Meh'lindi was conscious of such an intensity of scrutiny. Fists shifted fractionally. Armour grated gently. Boltguns rose slowly.

At once that triple blade flew from the apparition's hand. It was a spinning disc, aglow with energy. Already it had sheared into a Fist's visor. The protective snout shattered like glass. The weapon was already speeding back to its mistress's gauntlet as if its blades were wings, as if it were some horrific hawk-bird. She caught it. She flickered out of phase even as a Fist's gun began to vomit bolts.

'Hold your fire!' The attacker was gone.

A Fist had slumped. Lex tore aside the remaining fragments of his brother's visor. He directed his shoulder-light within.

The blade had sliced through the Marine's brow. Bloodstained brain tissue had oozed. Already it had congealed.

The brother still lived. But he would never think rationally again. Drool flowed from his lips. His eyes were moronic.

'Phoenix Lords are said to be walking the webway,' murmured Meh'lindi. 'That's what the Harlequin said. Phoenix Lords – and a Phoenix Lady too!'

'I think we've just been warned to abandon our journey,' suggested Grimm.

And Jaq held his peace...

Meh'lindi disagreed. 'Oh no! If so, the Phoenix Lady would have sliced Azul through the brow, don't you see? Thus destroying the rune! How could we ever find the Black Library without the rune?'

'Are you implying,' Grimm whispered, 'that she didn't much care for our escorts? Unfit to enter a prestigious library?'

'Maybe we're all undesirable company except for Jaq and Azul'

'Huh, that makes me feel happy. Eldar snobs. I suppose you're desirable company for Jaq! Maybe a squat isn't even worth swatting.'

Lex cleared his throat. His hearing was acute.

'Marines, undesirable company? If only more of my company were with me! There's no other sane course but for the four of us to accompany you. We Fists would be lost in the webway on our own. I am going to behold this Black Library,' he vowed, 'even if I am cursed for it. We'll need to be more vigilant against surprise attacks.'

A spinning triple blade which could return to its owner after smashing the ceramite snout of power armour... This was surprise indeed.

Jaq placed his hand on Lex's vambrace. 'In the eyes of many,' said he, 'we're all already cursed. Yet we must endure, as He-on-Earth endures.'

'Aye, endure.'

'He mentioned four Fists,' mumbled Grimm. 'By my count there's five.'

Lex had not included the lobotomized brother with the line of hardened cinnabar blood and brain across his brow.

'Shall I euthanase and extract the progenoids?' Wagner asked respectfully.

A few moments' anguished hesitation later, Lex said, 'No, we must set out immediately.'

Did he no longer believe that he and the sergeant and the two Fists would ever return to their fortress-monastery drifting serenely through the void far away? Therefore it was futile to harvest any glands? Lex collected a spare clip of bolts from the Space Marine, who had been named Webern – and who was still called this but who no longer knew it.

With profound regret, and with a bolt in the brain, Lex euthanased Webern.

WEBERN'S TWO SURVIVING battle-brothers were Stadler and Scholl. Scholl was the next to die, a while later.

A storming shape came rushing from the mist. A baneful stunning scream confounded even protected ears. If Banshees shrieked abominably, this wail was even more intense. It transcended mere noise. Almost, sheer sound became a paralysing silence. It overloaded one's faculties. For fatal moments it paralysed trigger fingers. On the shock wave of the storm, like some lance poised on a tsunami, sped a devastating blade.

Scholl was toppling. The storm had already passed by.

A little blood trickled from unprotected ears.

Lurching, Lex knelt by Scholl.

Scholl's plastron was riven open. Ponderously Lex turned the inert armour over – and found a corresponding rupture. An exit wound, in armour.

The power-scalpel of the Phoenix Lady had lanced right through Scholl's plastron – through his carapace, through his fused, ceramically reinforced ribs, through his chest and his toughened spine, then through his back-plate and exhaust pipes.

The long-shafted scalpel had flown onward, to be snatched by the storm, and borne away.

Scholl had no spare bolt-clips remaining. The sergeant ejected the clip from Scholl's weapon. Three bolts remained within it.

THEN STADLER DIED.

Out of the mist came spinning that three-bladed sickle. The weapon swerved off the wall of the webway.

A Space Marine's shoulder-armour rises level with his helmeted ears. Often he seems like some mutant whose head is sunk into his chest. Forewarned by instinct, Stadler had turned. The whirling blades sheared through the flexible gorget joint, within which his helmet was seated.

Briefly the blades clung and cut, like some rabid razorwing. Crackling energy encircled Stadler's neck. The weapon swooped away, boomeranging back whence it had come.

The brother's helmet and head slumped askew upon his eagle-plastron, as though in shame. Between his looming ceramite shoulder-pads a brief gush of blood arose from his exposed severed neck to harden grotesquely in a trice. Upon that protruding cinnabar spike rather than upon rings of cervical vertebrae, his slumped head appeared once to have been mounted.

The suit swayed. It collapsed forwards. On impact, helm and head rolled aside.

'Next time, next time we'll take her!' vowed Lex. Sergeant Wagner echoed him righteously.

How could one fight such a swift stunning storm? Such a nimble hurricane! Her three-blade could sever armour. Her spear could pass right through a Fist's suit.

Banshees were but a pale imitation of that elemental force. Could even a superhuman mortal defeat a demi-goddess such as she?

Lex stooped over the decapitated corpse in its coffin of armour. How fervently he prayed to Rogal Dorn, primarch, progenitor of Fists, paladin supreme. Let the sublime Dorn infuse him so that he might become as puissant as the Founder – who would surely have been equal to the terrible alien Phoenix Lady.

'I FEEL WE'RE getting close,' said Azul.

The fabric of the timeless webway was becoming complex. On either side, and ahead and above and below too, the blue mist was textured with ghosts of warped architecture which defied geometry. The luminous mist had thinned, allowing vaster perspectives of vision. It had also condensed to form those columns and floors and vaults – of arcades and colonnades, of buttressed naves and transepts, of bridges over yawning voids. Without the guiding rune how easy to lose oneself forever in Möbius routes which curved back upon themselves.

Here was a spectral city, twisting at all angles to itself. Ascents and descents and deviations were pregnant with hidden horror for anyone who strayed. Devilish faces floated, always just out of the corner of one's eye. Giant hands. Claws. Tentacles. Bulging disembodied eyes the size of domes. To choose a route which brought those shapes into focus – into material existence – would be to court annihilation or tormented captivity.

Could it be that the Black Library did not possess any distinct identifiable doorway guarded by dedicated warriors or machines? Did the webway gradually mutate into the library, along one safe route and only one? Maybe without the rune in Azul's eye they might have beheld different surroundings, different psychoactive architecture. They might have seemed to be maggots inside a fossil whale in which worms had burrowed out a hundred thousand contorted passages. They might have seemed to be inside a vast ruined space hulk huger than any agglomeration of derelict vessels ever reported. So Jaq surmised, as they advanced.

The phantom blue architecture was slowly becoming violet; and, soon, the mauve of a menacing thunderstorm cloud.

They were attaining the suffocating limits of light and existence. The mauve hue was becoming purple. But now a globe-nebula of stars shone in the darkened distance – as if far ahead some window looked out upon the ordinary universe.

Along a crazily slanted sombre colonnade the Phoenix Lady appeared.

She stood poised on one goatlike golden-booted foot, about to skip aside. She vanished, and a moment later she was closer. Again she disappeared, and of a sudden was closer still. In another few instants she would be in their midst, scything with her long and lethal blade, reaping lives. Her black armour all but dissolved into the purple background. Her mane plumed upward from her feral mask so that her head seemed enormous, almost afloat. The mask emitted not a screech but a long trilling warble, provocative and mocking.

Maybe the attrition of his squad, from several battle-brothers down to none, had finally frenzied Sergeant Wagner. Maybe he could not bear the inevitability of her approach – and must meet her, and his likely death, directly. He bellowed like a goaded bull. He charged at full power, leaving the path of the rune.

The Phoenix Lady flickered away.

Huge hands materialized. Hands with great grasping fingers. Upon each fingertip was a face of lunacy. From gaping mouths protruded tongues as long as Wagner's arms, as beaded with sticky syrup as the leaves of a carnivorous plant.

Occult guardians of the library…

Those fingers closed around Wagner, jostling for purchase. Finger-tongues were wrapping around his armour. He was being hoisted – pulled in four or five directions.

Unbelievably to Lex, Wagner's armour slowly began to stretch. The liquid of the tongues had softened ceramite itself. On the comm-channel Wagner groaned like some armoured Land Raider when its cleated tracks and sprocketed wheels are bogged in a stiff quagmire. As his armour elongated so did he within it, socketed and synched to it. Wagner's racked torment intensified.

Should Lex cut the comm-channel so as not to intrude on his suffering?

In his extended agony maybe Wagner was perceiving the light of Dorn, as a Fist rightly should. Maybe he was approaching an epiphany – an exaltation which would transmute his last moments into transcendental joy.

Yet for an armoured Fist to be torn apart slowly by such vile unnatural hands, like a spider by playful children!

'Dorn be with you!' cried Lex. He fired.

The bolt hit Wagner at the base of his weakened back-plate. It penetrated and exploded within. The armour budded outwards.

Wagner simply burst apart. His arms flew in opposite directions, clutched in those hands. His legs, likewise. His torso ascended.

Just when all attention was upon the disintegrating sergeant, the screaming storm was amongst them. In the hand of the storm whirled the triple blade. It sheared into Lex's armour, spraying fountains of sparks. Here. There. Elsewhere.

The storm was rushing away. Meh'lindi had spun, firing her laspistol *phut-phut-phut*. Only light could be fast enough to catch that storm! Did the goddess's scream modulate momentarily into an enraged squeal – of affronted injury?

Lex wasn't wounded in his body. Diagnostic runes blinked red and faded. An appalling dead weight anchored him as if his limbs were of solid lead. The blades had severed control cables and connectors and fibre bundles. His suit wouldn't heed the flexing of his muscles. His armour was dead. Ponderously, as if hoisting a log, he raised his gauntlet to force his visor open.

'Abhuman,' he bellowed, 'help unsuit me!' Deafened by the Phoenix Lady's scream, Grimm gaped at Lex's mouthings. Meh'lindi understood Lex's need. She gestured. Soon she and the mechanically minded squat were wrestling with Marine armour, unclamping, unscrewing. Neither was a battle-brother nor an armour specialist, so the task took a while.

LEX STOOD NEARLY naked but for some body-webbing: a muscular giant with a medley of old scars mottling his skin as tough as leather.

On one buttock was a tiny brand mark, of a clenched fist, demure compared with the spinal sockets which had synched Lex to the suit. Grimm's gaze roved impertinently over Lex's anatomy. Should he admire such a robust mountain of sinew and brawn?

'Huh, you're a bit smaller without all the armour-plating!'

Smaller? Why, Lex still overtopped Jaq and tall Meh'lindi. Nor, exposed though he was, did he appear particularly vulnerable.

On Meh'lindi's former barbaric homeworld he would have been a champion of champions, a snapper of backbones over his knee. Indeed barbarism seemed to have embraced Lex now, although he still held a boltgun. The long-service studs decorating his brow could have been the most primitive of initiation souvenirs.

'An ox with a gun,' muttered Grimm.

A ghostly smirk, suggestive of aristocratic disdain, flitted across Lex's olive-hued duel-scarred countenance. His free hand flexed itchily.

He yelled with lordly contempt into the deep purple shadows: 'Lexandro d'Arquebus of Necromunda at your service, lady!' Regardless of whether the lurking Phoenix Lady understood Imperial Gothic, Lex's tone conveyed his message.

To have found Ulthwé and invaded its grim mysteries! To have fought in the Eye of Terror and to have travelled through the webway almost all the way to the most secret redoubt of the eldar. In the annals of the Imperial Fists, what exploits could compare?

He had lost all his men. He had lost his hallowed armour. He had lost his command, and his way homeward. This declaration of identity was his defiant accommodation to such ruin.

Lex retrieved his treasured graving tool, and a laspistol and a last clip of bolts, all of which he tucked tightly under webbing. Had he been able to equip himself with any more gear he would have resembled some giant semi-nude servitorporter, bred without brain to carry burdens.

'It is the Library!' cried Azul. 'The black parts are like a giant collection of keyholes which the rune in my eye fits perfectly!'

The nebula-window had become a labyrinth of darkness and of innumerable lights like stars. It was a maze-wheel at right angles to their approach. They might have been approaching a spiral galaxy from above, heading for the hub. Countless aisles and corridors and chambers of the library extended above them and below them and to either side, entirely roofless and dark. The myriad phosphorescent volumes were the source of the illumination.

Soon, in this no-space, the travellers' orientation must surely undergo a ninety-degree shift, a rotation of balance. What seemed like a labyrinthine city set on end, into the heart of which they were descending, would of a sudden be all around them, occupying the same plane.

Maybe the Black Library could only be approached thus, at right angles, vertically. Perhaps anyone who approached the periphery horizontally would be making an appalling, fruitless, and fatal error. One must approach, instead, as in a dream – or in a nightmare. One must heed a different logic, occult and arcane.

Were it not for the rune, Jaq surmised, they might be experiencing a different manifestation of the library. Or else the phenomenon might disorientate them utterly, pitching them into insanity.

This must be the most clandestine library in existence. Or ought one to say *adjacent* to existence? It was protected not only by the intricacy of the webway but also by its own enigmatic structure.

Vastly the library loomed: above, below, alongside. They were scarcely a dozen steps away from entering it, still at right angles to its presence.

With a sickening skew, orientation began to shift.

And with a stunning scream the Phoenix Lady appeared amongst them. She thrust her long power blade into Meh'lindi – may indeed have wounded that elemental being in her body or in her pride.

Meh'lindi swayed, transfixed through her stolen aspect armour and through the gut. She had grasped the hilt tightly in both hands to deny it to the shrieking Phoenix Lady. Otherwise, that long blue energized power-scalpel and shaft would have passed right through her body – causing terrible injuries to be sure, but perhaps, perhaps, sparing her heart, her spine?

Halted by her, the lateral motion of the weapon became rotary. Blood and tissue sprayed from the entry wound. That great scalpel was spinning within Meh'lindi, mincing her inwardly.

Meh'lindi's palms burned as the shaft rotated.

By force of willpower – of ebbing tenacity – Meh'lindi still clutched it, as it slowed, and as she fell, backwards or sideways, for which way was true?

The Phoenix Lady had vanished. Meh'lindi lay supine. The black shaft of the power-lance was a mast, erect.

Her assassin's fingers relaxed. There was no life in her eyes any more, only the glaze of death.

NINETEEN
LIBRARY

TILTED BETWEEN THE webway and the library, Jaq shook with shock and utter desolation.

'You should have torn your bandanna off!' Grimm snarled at Azul. Grimm shuffled. He stamped a booted foot in impotent fury. Tears welled in the squat's eyes.

Jaq was too desert-dry – too utterly deserted – to weep. How did one weep in this universe of grief? Enough tears had been shed to quench stars. To weep would be to trespass upon the divine sorrow of Him-on-Earth.

'If I'd fired a bolt,' muttered Lex, 'I would have gutted her.'

'Her?' demanded Grimm. 'Which her?'

'Meh'lindi…'

'She is damn well gutted, musclemind.'

Jaq sank to his knees beside Meh'lindi. He was her tombstone. 'You gotta leave her, boss!' urged Grimm. 'And fast. Be practical.'

Yes, leave this vertiginous chimera of a lobby, this antechamber where different planes of eerie geometry collided.

'She's still eldar,' mumbled Jaq – as if in some way Meh'lindi was cheating him. 'She is Another.'

Could it be that *she* hadn't really died here, but only a mimic?

'She must have some polymorphine in her sash…'

If he injected her now that she was dead, might she revert to her human form? Might he behold her essential self and features one last time? He touched the long inky tail of her wig as if he might rip it from her head.

To have died in alien guise.

Yet the essence of her own yearning had been for that strange freedom to be gained by impersonating others, chameleon-like, almost Harlequin-like.

If Jaq had been able to inject polymorphine *before* she died, with her whole body in flux might she have been able to repair her injuries by willpower? She had died too quickly for such a ghastly experiment – which Jaq realized that he *would* have attempted. Aye, he'd have attempted almost anything to save her!

Lex's voice rumbled sympathetically. 'I understand loss, Sir Jaq.'

Loss?

Jaq had long since lost his holy office. He had lost the fellowship of his ordo. He had lost his cherished funereal ship, which might well have been blasted to pieces in that eldar dock by Imperial forces quite incidentally. Now he had lost his... helpmate.

'Reckon we can steal this hyper-lance?' Grimm asked Lex. 'Can you *use* it? Must be ancient and revered to be so powerful. Shall we pull it free? Reckon that's wise?'

'*No-oh-oh-oh!*' Such a howl burst from Jaq's throat, a howl of universal rejection and misery. Pull the great blade from Meh'lindi's ravaged ribs and homogenized entrails? 'No!' he cried. 'She shall not be treated like some harpooned sea-beast!'

None of them should plant a boot or bare foot upon Meh'lindi to brace her while they heaved – even though the Phoenix Lady would dart here subsequently to retrieve her death-lance with similar ignominy.

Jaq glared balefully at Grimm. Grimm had at least galvanized Jaq's attention, weaning him from utter submergence in sorrow.

'We gotta get moving, boss – or our lady's sacrifice will be in vain.'

Jaq spat contemptuously. 'Sacrifice! I curse this festering cosmos!'

'Oh, my ancestors! Don't do that, Jaq. Who knows what's listening? Look at it this way. You wouldn't ever have known Meh'lindi if the cosmos weren't the way it is.'

'Death is everywhere,' remarked Lex comfortingly. 'Everyone dies except Him-on-Earth.'

'And except for His supposed Sons,' snapped Jaq. 'Supposedly! Where in the cosmos do those sensei knights keep their long watch? Where do the Illuminati ferry new recruits to? Is it to some world of the Eastern Fringe beyond the reach of the Astronomican? To some space hulk adrift in the warp?'

'Search me, boss.'

Jaq seemed to be reacting like an inquisitor again, unless he was merely outgassing empty words.

'Maybe,' suggested Grimm, 'there's a clue in the *Book of Dandruff* in this here library.'

Jaq moaned: 'Which of us understands the eldar language now that my... now that my... now that she's dead? What is the point in my finding this *Rhana Dandra* codex?'

Petrov seethed. 'Why else did I have my warp-eye *vandalized* – except to lead you here to that excremental book?'

The vandal, who was Lex, controlled himself. 'Examples of my scrimshandering are displayed in reliquaries in the fortress-monastery!'

How many thousands of light-years away was that?

'Oh, I'm privileged.' Azul's tone was bitter. 'If we don't enter the library now, my whole life is a mockery.'

'Rhana Dandra, Rhana Dandra.' Jaq muttered the words in incantation. 'Crossroads of Inertia – where maybe Phoenix Lords and a Lady linger to let the centuries pass by!'

If Phoenix warriors were to participate in the Rhana Dandra, the book might contain data about those crossroads – even some hint about that other mysterious place in the webway...

'–where time turns backwards!' Jaq exclaimed. 'Back to before Meh'lindi died!'

Grimm shuddered. 'That place is just a legend even to the eldar, boss. It's absurd, absurd! You can't reverse time and history.'

'Just a little way! Back to the moment when Meh'lindi was still safe!'

Had Jaq become insane?

'If only I were illuminated...' Jaq groaned. 'Knowledge is the key. Occult knowledge.'

'My vandalized eye's the key to *that*, damn it!'

As if in a belated show of respect for the dead, Grimm anxiously tugged the forage cap from his head. Who was Grimm to complain about someone deluding himself? Delusion was a key to Jaq's salvation at the moment – until the major pain of bereavement died away.

'Azul's right,' gabbled Grimm. (In Lex's throat was a grumble of warning...) 'Not about vandalism, oh ancestors, no! I mean about the *Book of Dandruff* and time turning tail. That's the ticket, boss.'

Grimm reached warily to pluck at the bearded inquisitor's sleeve. He was a grotesque hirsute child hoping to raise a stricken father to his feet.

Jaq resisted the pull. Was he about to gather Meh'lindi up in his arms to carry her? Even with the cumbersome shaft of the lance protruding hugely from her? Instead, he stooped and kissed Meh'lindi upon her hand, which still loosely lay against the haft.

Gently he unwound her sash with its assassin's secrets – her garrote and finger-weapons and poisons and toxins. He tied it around his own waist under his unkempt robe.

'Keepsake, huh?' muttered Grimm. 'Huh, you're keeping it for her, aren't you? For after you find the time-place.'

Finally, Jaq removed the speckled pebble from around Meh'lindi's neck. If she had truly been eldar, and if that pebble had been a real spirit-stone, her soul would now be enshrined in its matrix. Alas, it was only a worry-stone which Grimm had picked up casually to rub between his fingers. Nevertheless he kissed the stone, and hung the thong around his own neck. Then he struggled to his feet.

'I cannot,' he snarled, 'submit to sentimentality. Not when the cabal still sows its hydra! Not when Illuminati conspire! Yet I shall treasure the sash and the stone for ever... And now,' he cried, 'to rob the Black Library!'

With what main motive, though? With devout or with profane intention? With Him-on-Earth in mind? Or in Meh'lindi's honour, as a demented requiem?

WITHIN, THE LIBRARY was much as had been revealed to Azul in his agony-vision. Maybe this was why these intruders perceived the Black Library to be thus, rather than otherwise.

The entire fabric of the library was psychoactive. Wrought of webway substance, it configured itself to what Azul expected to see; as Jaq could sense now with his psychic faculty. Azul had been vouchsafed a visionary initiation, albeit not by any Harlequins.

Alternative parallel libraries might have presented themselves to the uninitiated. There might have been libraries where the books were of solid stone. Or where they were of sheets of furnace-hot metal.

Serried ranks of great rune-chased tomes of parchment and everplastic and thin adamantium and stiff silk – libers and eldritch leabhars and bibloi and codices and volumens – were bound in brass and wraithbone and leather and in what might have been daemon-hide. Filigree cages wrought of adamantium held certain volumes.

Books glowed with their own occult light while the surroundings were of stygian ebony and jet. Texts might be perused by this intrinsic illumination. Tomes seemed almost radioactive, as if whoever touched them might risk contracting rot of the fingers.

In places the dust of millennia lay along neglected expanses, and the glow was smothered. Such volumes, once revered, must later have been deemed to contain nothing but errors and foolishness. Conceivably some vital document might be hidden under dust.

Black corridors and halls and naves receded, harbouring cells and scriptories and descents to crypts. Embellishments were everywhere – scrolling volutes and latticework and arching spandrels, cusps and entablatures and friezes – but only darkly visible. Ceilings of inky mosaic loomed now, zeniths of night and obscurity.

Lights of libers glimmered in the sooty depths and distances.

DARK SHAPES BEGAN to move within the library. Negative auras. Silhouettes. The place was at once deserted yet occupied. Those presences were out of phase – as if Azul's rune distanced the figures from this precise moment in time.

What were they? Great Harlequins?

Those presences had been alerted by the intrusion into this secret place. They could not fully appear. They were almost here and now – but not quite. Each moment in time seemed sliced into subdivisions. Several timestreams flowed simultaneously, superimposed upon one another. Within one time-stream Jaq and his companions forged further into the library. Within another time-stream the custodians of the library strove in vain to prevent them. Custodians were merely shadows through which one could walk.

A Great Harlequin blocked their way. The figure barely possessed the substance of a cobweb – which parted, then reformed.

Once, they glimpsed a robed and bearded inquisitor, who was blindfolded. Some exceptionally privileged member of the Ordo Malleus! Evidently human, he was being escorted by shimmering Harlequins. Inquisitor and escort were a time-mirage from some earlier era.

So it was true that Harlequins and inquisitors shared – or *had* shared – a common bond in daemonic research. Secret inquisitors had previously visited this place, with vigilant alien escorts who controlled what such visitors saw.

Unlike Jaq, whom no one controlled...

'The rune in your eye led us here,' Jaq murmured to Azul. 'That rune seems able to trick time itself in certain ways, at least here in webway. Time is sliced and respliced.'

If the engraved warp-eye could trick time, could it help Jaq later to find a certain crossroads? Hardly, when its tropism, its whole bias, was towards this library and towards a certain book within.

* * *

'WE'RE HERE,' BREATHED Azul. 'This is it. My eye recognizes it.' Inside an arabesque cage, upon an ebon podium, lay a bulky volume. The binding was encrusted by gems a-glitter with the inner light of the book; with sapphires and emeralds, topaz and tourmaline.

Diamonds picked out runic lettering which must surely spell *Rhana Dandra.*

Harlequin-shadows flitted, agitated and vehement. These silhouette-figures were no impediment.

Petrov had navigated to his one and only possible destination. Now he rested his hands upon either side of the cage to gather his strength. Then he heaved. Whether the cage had previously been sealed by wizardry or tech, or by both, the lid arose now, unlocked by his shrouded rune-gaze.

Nearby stood a tall lectern as dark as coal, with outspread carved wings evocative of a Swooping Hawk aspect warrior. An ancient faded banner hung down the front of the lectern, depicting a scorpion above a field of bendy sable stripes. Jaq lifted out the heavy tome and laid it upon the ebon wings.

He opened the liber and turned the vellum pages.

These were covered with a diversity of illuminated rune-scripts, annotated and footnoted minutely. None could he read. Even as he glanced, a line of runes shifted, dissolving and reforming into a subtly different text. Aye, the future was multifold. The book was mutable. Its contents could alter. Carefully he closed the volume and stroked the jewels. Were any of these gems the spirit-stones of bygone eldar seers, embedded in the binding?

'That's a fortune in gems,' muttered Azul. Was there avarice in his tone? 'There's a fortune here.'

'Huh,' grunted Grimm, 'well, it *is* a Book of Fate.'

Harlequin-silhouettes jostled like great fretful bats. Frantic shadows.

'We may need a fortune,' said Jaq. He activated his inquisitorial palm-tattoo then banished it dismissively. 'I can scarcely draw upon Imperial funds ever again.'

'Such a book,' observed Lex, 'may take years to decipher and master.'

Grimm spoke searchingly. 'You big chaps live a long time, don't you?'

'Unless we're killed! As my brothers have been killed coming here, their glands left unharvested like carrion for any crows of the webway!'

Lex calmed. The real implications of the squat's question had broken upon him. 'I shall continue to accompany you,' he said. 'You lack a strong protector now that your assassin is dead–'

'Squats can look after themselves! Jaq's no slouch at slaughtering, neither. But yeah, I guess we'd be obliged. Indebted. I guess.'

'I welcome you. Lex,' Jaq said with heartfelt emphasis. 'I would be honoured.'

Lex nodded gravely.

'Too much is left unresolved. A crusade is not complete until the angelus is rung at dusk in honour of Dorn.' Plainly this was a potent metaphor to an Imperial Fist. 'Am I deserting my Chapter if no means exists to rejoin it? My fists itch with a sense of obligation – towards yourself, for the sake of Him-on-Earth. Yet which is your true aim, I wonder, Jaq Draco? To serve *Him*? To investigate vile conspiracies and abort them? Or somehow to regain a lost–' Lex sought for an unfamiliar word– 'a lost concubine. No, a lover. A comrade.'

Jaq struggled to control himself. 'Maybe,' he faltered, 'the quest for illumination and the quest for her will not prove too contradictory – for a sorcerer! Such as I must become!'

Grimm was agitated. 'With this book you'll be a sorcerer, right? A real one? You ain't gonna fall in with that scheme of, um, you becoming possessed?'

'I shall take Chaos itself in these hands,' vowed Jaq – aye, in the hands which held the *Book of Rhana Dandra*, 'and I shall bend it backwards till the spine of time snaps, if need be.'

'Oh, my ancestors. I'd feel safer if we wrap that book.'

'Until I find the luminous path again, the via luminosa–'

'Let's wrap the book, huh?' In the carbon darkness of the library more silhouettes were looming.

'Wrap?' repeated Jaq. Had he been intending to bear the volume blatantly before him, a great glittering talisman?

'Wrap it.'

A squat did not willingly shed his trusty flak jacket, even to steal a *Book of Dandruff*. Lex, apart from webbing, was basically in the buff. This left Jaq's torn robe, or Azul's shimmery slippery garb…

All this while Azul had been eyeing the jewelled tome.

'I'll tuck it under my damask,' the Navigator volunteered.

Grimm shook his head. 'Jaq's the psyker, not you.'

'Is not a warp-eye a psychic organ?'

Such a plea fell on deaf ears – even though hearing was well restored since the final assault of the Phoenix Lady.

'At least let me touch those stones for a moment before you hide them away out of sight!'

Once away from the Black Library, would the volume continue to emit light? Whether it did or didn't, it would require shrouding to hide it from eyes covetous of the mere exterior of such a tome, encrusted as it was with a ransom opulent enough to buy from pirates the freedom of any planetary governor's kidnapped daughter.

Azul's fingers lingered on topaz and tourmaline. Almost sacramentally, he touched the ruby on his chin.

'Uh, boss...' muttered Grimm.

Would the binding of the book prove to be an unbearable temptation to the bereft Navigator? Jaq appeared disconnected from such practical notions as the risk of pilfering, which might imperil the funding of his quest. He was almost ethereal in his own caress of the tome. (What was he now but one of the foremost thieves in the history of the galaxy?)

Petrov's free hand was straying towards his black bandanna to forge a link between the desecrated black gem in his forehead and those jewels of the tome, some of which might be spirit stones.

Balancing the book upon his arm, Jaq pulled Meh'lindi's speckled pebble from the neck of his robe. He compared that common stone with those jewels. In proximity to such occult gems might the pebble begin to scintillate with sparkles of her soul?

Lex had been noticing disconcerting symptoms in the Navigator. A Fist was a thinker, honed to notice and interpret and act upon betraying signs in hulks and hives, in natural jungles and in jungles of humanity.

As Azul's hand brushed his bandanna, Lex raised his boltgun and fired.

RAAARK-CRUMP

Reverberations echoed through the inky book-lit labyrinth. Great bats seemed to flap their wings.

Azul lurched backwards against the now-empty lectern. Blood soaked his slithery robe. Briefly the scorpion banner gripped the Navigator, as if claiming him in its pincers. Then the lectern toppled backwards. Its outspread wings formed a stretcher for the dying man, soon to be a bier.

Jaq was aghast. Were it not for the burden of the book he might have jerked *Emperor's Mercy* towards Lex.

Incoherently: 'Azul's eye. His eye! If he dies—'

How to use the rune again – should Jaq ever need to do so? Azul Petrov was dying, if not already dead. To Lex, in accusation: 'You're Firenze's man!'

'Nay—'

Before Jaq could commit a folly, Grimm seized a wrist.

'No, he did good, boss! He did right! Petrov was gonna petrify us with his warp-eye.'

A wisp of propellant fume lazed in front of Lex's gun. The giant nodded.

'I fear Grimm's right, Jaq.'

'But–'

'Those jewels were too much for him.' Brusquely the little man booted the dying, or dead, Navigator. 'Ain't it so. Azul? Thought you'd snuff us all with your gorgon-gaze and walk backwards out of here with treasure for the future.'

Petrov's chest was shattered underneath his bloodied robe. Thus no reply came.

'His warp-eye!'

Lex said: 'Such a hard gem does not decay. With our eyes closed tight we shall harvest it. We shall wrap it tightly in the bandanna.'

From inside his flak jacket Grimm produced a knife. He unfolded the blade and slapped it into Lex's hand.

'How can we ever use it without looking at it, though?' Lex pondered. 'Petrov's eye may serve as an unexpected weapon to guard the book. The gem that kills the would-be thief. Of course I am no lapidary.' He scowled at Grimm. 'Yet it seems to me that if one shaves the eye at the rear it may make into a monoculus lens which can be worn.'

'A lens forever showing the way back here, where I'm sure we'd be welcome!'

'Perhaps the rune will have other uses?'

'Oh yes, to a sorcerer!'

Jaq was shuddering. 'Petrov was Fennix's friend. More than that, perhaps. The rune-eye may prove to be a curse...'

'Maybe the monoculus will attach to the living eye, warping your vision and killing anyone you see–'

Jaq grinned insanely. 'Maybe it will protect me from a daemon, even though that daemon imagines it possesses my soul – until the day when I stare in a mirror!'

'What do you reckon, Azul?' Grimm kicked the Navigator again, but Petrov appeared to be entirely dead.

AND SO LEX performed the excision of the eye, the ophthalmectomy. He kept his own eyes shut tight, praying that with Petrov dead this stratagem would protect him as effectively as visor and calculator had protected him when the Navigator was alive. He operated delicately by finger-feel and point of knife.

Presently the engraved eye was wrapped securely in the black bandanna.

'We can all look again.'

Lex offered the tiny bundle to Jaq. Jaq shook his head. 'Keep it in one of your pouches, Grimm. We must trust one another.'

'Yeah.' The little man turned to Lex. 'If we reach a world with astropaths in residence, you mustn't coax one of those to send any messages regarding your whereabouts to that fortress-monastery of yours.'

'I shall not do so for ten years,' vowed Lex. 'Dorn be with me.'

Jaq laid down the book. He shed his torn robe. The squamous mesh armour beneath made him appear to be some lizard-man, mutated by Chaos.

He wrapped the liber in his robe, extinguishing its light.

Grumpily Grimm eyed the fallen Navigator one last time.

'Huh. Trail of corpses, that's what.'

No, NOT A complete trail.

Was this the same place as where they had entered the library? It seemed to be. Meh'lindi's body had disappeared. Taken away as a trophy by the Phoenix Lady, along with the scalpel-lance? No blood smeared the area. Maybe this was another place.

To say goodbye to her once again might have been unbearable.

THROUGH THE WEBWAY many worlds lay before them, worlds where the eldar had established portals openly or secretly.

Where to choose their hiding place? The choice was hardly theirs, where they might first emerge. Chance was their guide. Not Azul's eye. Nor the *Book of Rhana Dandra*, indecipherable as yet.

Side by side, with weary steps, with weapons at the ready, from the Black Library Jaq Draco and a near-nude giant and a stocky dwarf took their lonely way.

Perhaps anguish was a closer companion to Jaq than either Grimm or Lex d'Arquebus.

CHAOS CHILD

CLASSIFICATION: Primary Level Intelligence
CLEARANCE: Granite
ENCRYPTION: Cryptox v.2.21
DATE: 093.M41
AUTHOR: Adept Prestre Rhan'hei, Adeptus Ministorum
SUBJECT: Intercepted communiqué
RECIPIENT DESIGNATE: Inquisitor Halfadru Memphos, assignum
Ordo Xenos

My lord,

Subject to your instructions, I have been tailing Adept G— for fully nine weeks now. As you predicted, his palsy grows more and more severe, and his eyesight continues to deteriorate. It has been relatively easy for me to sift through his data-scrolls while his attention has been distracted. I have managed to lay my hands on a variety of items that will interest you (which can be collected from drop point Hyrax in five rotations) but felt I would risk sending you this one directly, as it is relatively succint, and will be of especial interest to you, given your interest in that exotic race, the eldar.

I hope that the latest batch of information will serve to fulfil my 'obligations'. In any case, my wife's health is now so poor that she is not expected to last more than a few days. Shortly, you will have no further hold over me; my own life means nothing to me. Believe me, if I never hear from you again I will die a happier man.

Rhan'hei

[Transcript begins:] My great friend, I would need have words with you. I have foreseen events of import far beyond this place in time, events that furthermore may yet bring knowledge of such things as had previously been lost.

I am Athenys, of the craftworld [censored] of ill-favoured fortune. And thus I am of the kin of Farseer Eldrad Ulthran. His oft-related saga of the renegade human inquisitor known to us as Jaq [tr: dragon?] and his motley band of associates has, for so many generations, been regarded as without conclusion. His disappearance from the sacred and most secret Black Library, taking with him one of our most precious books of fate, the [tr: tome?] of Rhana Dandra.

Some revolutions past, as I lay in my [tr: leafy glade?], contemplating the myriad waft and weft of the webway, contemplating all the possible futures which may yet choose to present themselves to our kind, my senses chanced upon a twisted trail. It was woven within such a [tr: confused ball of string?] of possibilities that my first thoughts were that it was somehow the trace, not of an event which was [tr: spiny-finned fish?] to come to pass, but of something that had never happened. How this ??? [transmission failure periodic] before that terrible moment.

And yet... within it all, beating almost like a living heart, was the defiant energy-pattern of this Jaq [?]. By following the traces of this spirit within the webway and beyond, I could follow this lifeline to its very end, and reveal a conclusion to his saga. A conclusion, however, that may yet prove to be nothing more than a [tr: layer of low-lying cloud?] laid by the Great Enemy.

Knowing the great wrong that this human is said to have perpetrated upon all of our kind, I fervently believe I cannot just dismiss this [tr: carpenter's boring tool?] as a mere fancy. All my senses tell me that this inquisitor and his deeds are little more than a myth, a ??? [transmission failure] rather than any true reality. Yet my spirit insists to me that these deeds, so long hidden from us, may well have been acted out in such a fashion as I espied.

And thus you see a little of my quandary. I owe it to my kin and my craftworld to seek the true way in all this. I would hope that your own great skills can aid me in my [tr: peering, close-work?]. Let us meet in the [tr: Hall of Raised Hands?] when the declining hour is upon us, and I will tell you all the parts of my dilemma. [End transcript]

ONE
RUNES

'YOU FAILED,' THE Harlequin hissed at Zephro. 'You weak human fool.'

The expression upon the Harlequin's chameleon mask was one of contempt and ridicule. Even the alien's kaleidoscopic costume, so buckled and belted and beribboned, seemed to mock Zephro Carnelian in his own mischievous motley garb of green and red triangles, which had seemed so harlequinesque to him.

In his tricorn hat with its ostentatious crimson plume, was Zephro merely a clown? Merely a human monkey who aped the scintillating quicksilver eldar?

'So you are "illuminated", are you?' jeered the Harlequin.

Zephro winced inwardly. Should he appeal to Farseer Ro-fhessi, his patron, his friend? (Hopefully still his friend, if indeed Ro-fhessi had ever fully been that!)

If his friend had overheard, no attitude was evident. The horse-like visor of Ro-fhessi's crystal-studded helm hid the farseer's expression. This was no time to intrude on Ro-fhessi – not when Ro-fhessi's mentor Eldrad Ulthran was about to cast the runes. All thoughts should be upon the impending divination. Zephro should rejoice that he was privileged to watch – whatever the outcome might be. Hostility from one of the group of Harlequins was understandable, acceptable.

Maybe Zephro's presence wasn't so much a privilege as a woeful necessity – due to his role in the fiasco which required this divination. Fiasco? No... *catastrophe*.

* * *

SEEN FROM SPACE, Ulthwé craftworld resembled an ornate coral-like cathedral with the dimensions of a major moon, though horizontal, not globular. Embellishing its surface, like gems studding a serrated golden shield, were domes. Nowadays many of those domes were dark. Others glowed with only ghostly light. Given several hundred years of peace, the psycho-plastic wraithbone of Ulthwé would repair itself entire and empower itself anew until the shield gleamed and the gems shone.

Peace was tragically lacking.

Immediately astern of the craftworld there floated a swirl of brightness and murk. Held in stasis like some baby spiral galaxy, that swirl was Ulthwé's major gateway to the webway. Through there, wraithcraft could reach far stars. That swirl was no propulsion system for the craftworld itself. Soaring ether-sails propelled Ulthwé into its flight away from a vaster and more terrible eddy several scores of light years further astern. These days the Eye of Terror seemed to be expanding more quickly than Ulthwé could outrun it.

Here in this interstellar gulf the harvest of energy was tiny. The craftworld could only sail slowly.

How soon would extreme jeopardy compel the digging up of spirit stones to be implanted in the metal combat-bodies of wraithguards? If those artificial bodies were destroyed, the spirits temporarily enshrined in them would be lost irrevocably.

How soon must the Avatar of the War God be awakened? The Avatar's berserker fury would wreak havoc upon foes – yet equally upon the whole terrain where a battle was fought; even if that terrain was precious Ulthwé itself, already so often ravaged.

ELDRAD ULTHRAN LAID down his staff and his long sword. He removed his helm to bare his head. Silver streaked his hair. Each of his movements was so stately – in keeping with a sacred moment, to be sure, yet nowadays Eldrad was always slow. It was as if Eldrad Ulthran was wading through an invisible syrup of time before coming to a final halt.

From a pouch at his belt Eldrad took the rune stones. He threw one of these upon naked wraithbone. Then he formally announced the subject of the divination, which was simply the latest in a grievous series upon the same theme.

'Inquisitor Jaq Draco!' Eldrad declared. 'Draco who penetrated the Black Library!'

Aye, such a fiasco; such a catastrophe.

* * *

ELDRAD − AND RO-FHESSI and Zephro Carnelian and the Warlock Ketshamine and half a score of Harlequins − were in the Dome of Crystal Seers.

Due to raids by the forces of Chaos all too many zones of Ulthwé were devastated wastelands, hideous blotches of ruin. Such gloomy wildernesses were of use only to the black guardians and aspect warriors as combat training grounds.

Other regions still retained their sublime elegance − slender pyramids and fluted towers rising from amidst groves of trees which seemed sculpted of jade.

This Dome of Crystal Seers was a place of especially sacred beauty and daunting power. It was here that the wraithbone core of Ulthwé was exposed nakedly underfoot, that gold-flecked creamy wraithbone. Elsewhere in the craftworld the psychopotent, quasi-living core was cloaked by loam and turf, or by marble or mosaic floors… or else by rubble and ruin.

Here, from the naked essence of Ulthwé, rose millions of trees of wraithbone. Each towering tree had grown from the spirit stone of a dead citizen, to unite their souls with Ulthwé's very being. In glades throughout the Dome numerous crystallized bodies also stood rooted. Those were farseers who had become totally attuned to this place − as Eldrad Ulthran would soon become. It was several years since Eldrad had left the Dome itself. It was several decades since Eldrad had last travelled out of Ulthwé on any such expedition as had rescued Zephro from the clutch of Chaos, well over a century earlier.

The most ancient and tallest of the wraithbone trees actually grew through the dome into space. That pellucid air-retaining dome was a hybrid of substance and of energy. It easily tolerated piercing by the trees. Topmost limbs of trees were tendrils questing outward from a transparent and softly luminous shell − into the black lake of the void.

Within that dark lake above, stars were tiny lamps. Many had been swallowed aeons since by the lurid gangrene and bile and jaundice of the Eye of Terror, which was all too visible through the dome. Nightmarish irreality was engulfing ever more suns and mutating ever more worlds into habitations for monsters and daemons.

If invaders from the Eye finally overwhelmed Ulthwé, not only would its defenders die but the wraithbone forest would be shattered. Ten thousand years of heritage and afterlife would disintegrate − yet not into pure oblivion, oh no. All the spirits of the dead would be sucked into the psychotic torments of Chaos.

* * *

'DRACO FOUND AND he entered the sacred Black Library!' declared Eldrad.

Indeed, indeed. Hidden in the webway itself, guarded by terrible forces, its location known only to Great Harlequins, that repository of knowledge about daemons should have been forever secure unless a guide led the way. Draco simply could not, should never, have been able to find the Library unaided, let alone enter it.

Yet he had done so.

Even worse, Draco had robbed the Library.

Warlock Ketshamine leaned his lofty, alien frame upon the hilt of his witchblade so that its point pierced the naked wraithbone. Ketshamine's mask was a bleached skull, awful and inscrutable. The warlock's swirl of hair was dark as coal. His flaring black sleeves and tent-like skirt displayed huge prints of runes such as were writ on the stones. Ketshamine too had once been a farseer who scryed the shifting flux of probabilities. Ketshamine had eschewed the study of prophecy in favour of the more lethal uses of psychic power.

'Draco stole the *Book of Rhana Dandra!*' called out Eldrad.

Aye, the mutable Book of Fate itself: it was missing. It was gone from the Black Library in the webway – because of damnable Jaq Draco.

It was Zephro who had involved Draco in the affairs of the eldar.

Not without good reason! Not without approval and guidance. Not without Draco's name being present in the Book of Fate.

'Did Draco steal the *Book of Rhana Dandra* to rehabilitate himself with the Imperium? Where thus did he take it? What will occur?'

So saying, Eldrad threw all the other stones. He stared at their pattern on the wraithbone, and at the shapes of the runes themselves. The farseer was entering a trance. Already the runes were beginning to glow as they became channels for energy – not only the energy of the psychic ocean which enfolded material reality, but also the spirit-energy of bygone seers, by virtue of this direct contact with the wraithbone.

The runes were warming. As they warmed, so their shapes shifted subtly.

Heat began to radiate from those stones.

Orange heat. Red heat.

In a high eerie voice Eldrad cried out: 'In robbing the Black Library Draco suffered a tragedy – a tragedy so terrible that he may likely become insane!'

A tragedy? This was new knowledge, sieved from the psychic ocean.

'What kind of tragedy?' The question burst impulsively from Zephro.

Ro-fhessi waved an impatient hand at his human protégé to silence him. Eldrad was peering into the web of future probabilities. Draco's 'tragedy' was responsible for the likelihood of him becoming insane. Thus his tragedy figured in the flux of cause and effect. Of the tragedy itself, which had already occurred, only the fact that it had happened could be gleaned, not its precise nature.

DREAD CLUTCHED ZEPHRO. It had been the eldar's dire plan that Draco should be ensnared by daemonic possession – and then led to salvation. Draco would become illuminated, like Zephro himself, and immune to Chaos.

Draco would become an Illuminatus, he believed. As such, he would help seek out and gather together the human Emperor's undisclosed Sons. The Emperor had sired those Sons before He was crippled and encased in His golden throne ten thousand years previously. He did not know of their immortal existence. Those Sons were psychic blanks to Him. Nor did the Sons understand their own nature until Illuminati enlightened them.

The Sons would become sensei knights, forming the long watch. When the Emperor finally failed and when Chaos surged to devour the cosmos, those sensei knights – all of whom were aspects of the Emperor – would fight the last fight. Or so they believed.

The eldar's name for the last battle between reality and Chaos was *Rhana Dandra*. In the eldar Book of Fate it was written that the outcome of this final battle would be cosmic cataclysm, the mutual annihilation of Chaos and reality. This at least would be preferable to the triumph of Chaos.

Chaos! Four major Gods of Chaos already existed, like malign rival monarchs amidst the countless potent entities of the warp. When the proud star-spanning eldar civilization collapsed in psychotic spasm ten millennia previously, the foul deity Slaanesh had coagulated into existence.

If the feebler human race collapsed, a fifth great Power of Chaos could emerge, finally to unhinge reality and sanity.

But there was an alternative…

In the psychic ocean of the warp, fed by whatever was noble in mankind, a force of goodness could coalesce: the Numen, the luminous path, the light for New Men, to renew mankind.

Such a frail hope! Eldar farseers had glimpsed that the Numen could emerge when the Emperor finally failed – if his Sons were fused in mind-fire, if they were consumed to give birth to a phoenix of salvation and renewal. Thus the apocalypse could be averted. Farseers would steer a luminous numinous renewed cosmos. The eldar would regain a measure of glory.

Supposedly Jaq Draco was to play some small yet crucial role in this process. Alas, the exact nature of that role was shrouded in mystery.

Now Draco had stolen the Book of Fate.

Maybe he did so out of sheer revenge! Draco had discovered the plan to engineer his possession by a daemon, and his subsequent purification. He had reacted very negatively.

If Draco were now to become insane – why, madness was only a membrane away from daemonic possession. Madness was an open doorway for a daemon. Draco was unsupervised. He had with him the precious potent *Book of Rhana Dandra!* Such a catastrophe, such a disaster.

Terrible doubt assailed Zephro. What if the eldar did not *really* control the majority of the Illuminati – and thus the Emperor's Sons? Zephro owed his very salvation to the eldar – as did other Illuminati. Yet it was a fact that renegade Illuminati were trying to create a psychic doomsday weapon with which to lash out at loathsome Chaos and at aliens alike.

Those renegades were busily infesting worlds of the Imperium with an insidious psychic parasite. The Hydra parasite would lie dormant for centuries. At some moment in the future it would suddenly fuse the human race into mind-slavery. The slaved minds of trillions of hosts would lash out in a lethal paroxysm – the most likely result of which (so farseers feared) would not be a purifying purge but the unleashing of the fifth Chaos power.

To sabotage this dangerous plan, Zephro had infiltrated the Hydra conspiracy.

What if he was only a catspaw? What if other secret Illuminati existed unknown to him – who had purged themselves of Chaos, and who were also trying to gather in the Emperor's Sons to create a true long watch? What if the activities of the eldar, and his own activities, were merely a travesty of that genuine search by illuminated individuals, a genuine search which was indeed nudging the Numen closer?

What if the intoxicatingly persuasive eldar were so sure of the inevitability of the Rhana Dandra apocalypse that their aim was merely to consume the Emperor's Sons in the hour of cataclysm – so that the mutual destruction of Chaos and cosmos should be absolutely guaranteed, and nothing whatever survive?

He, Zephro, must not give a place in his mind to such doubts! He was feeling alienated because of the Draco disaster. Because some Harlequins now despised and blamed him.

Ro-fhessi did not blame him. Surely not.

RUNES FLUXED AND shimmered. Stones glowed white hot. Energy was surging through those stones, from warp into wraithbone, from wraithcore into warp. Even the trees of wraithbone shivered. Away in the groves the crystalline statues of Seers would be vibrating.

'Where might Draco succumb to insanity?' shrilled Eldrad. 'Where in all the worlds?'

A thunderclap came – an ear-piercing *crack*.

For a moment Zephro imagined that one of the rune stones had exploded.

No! The sound had come from above – from the dome itself.

Up there, where one particularly titanic tree pierced through into space, a vessel had impacted. The ship's contours were shifting weirdly. One moment it resembled a scarab. The next, it seemed like a crab. Coruscating with malign energies, its frontal claws were ripping at the substance of the dome.

Beyond it drifted another incoming ship.

Moments earlier those vessels hadn't been there. Or rather, they had been. They had been cloaked in invisibility. They had been veiled from eldar lookouts by sorcerous shielding.

As the first ship burst through the dome, plasma gushed from its snout. Gobbets of compact superheated gas incandesced against one massive tree, and then another. Shattered trunks toppled upon shorter trees, snapping them. The scream of escaping atmosphere might have been the agonized voice of the ravaged trees.

Already the shriek was dying to a whistle as the dome resealed itself – only to be ripped open a second time, by the following ship.

Slowly the first intruder was descending. Rotating upon its axis, it jetted plasma in every direction other than where the divination had been taking place...

...and where it was still taking place! Never before had Chaos mounted a raid upon this place of power. Yet for a while the urgency of the divination outweighed the demands of the violent intrusion. Pray that enough guardians and aspect warriors responded to the intrusion. Eldrad shrieked at the stones: '*Where in all the worlds? Show me! Show me!*'

WHERE INDEED? As soon seek a needle in a haystack, or a bug in the coat of a cudbear. Draco's possession of the Book of Fate seemed to block perception, blinding the farseer to the infernal inquisitor's whereabouts...

From the Black Library, Draco would have fled through the webway, that maze of energy-tunnels through the warp. Many exits and entrances existed on human worlds, unknown to their inhabitants.

* * *

'SHOW ME!'

What was shown was something else entirely.

Nausea assailed Zephro – and with this came a fleeting vision. He saw a nightmare landscape of volcanoes and plains of lava and jagged crags. In a sombre sullen sky lightning of many colours flickered: incessant discharges of unnatural energy. From a precipitous peak there rose a skyscraping black tower. On top of that tower glowed a great crystalline eyeball.

Oh, but this brand of nausea was all too familiar to Zephro. It was the sickness of daemonic influence. With a surge of will Zephro dispelled it.

Had the others seen the same vision? No longer could they delay reacting to the attack. Warlock Ketshamine discharged bolts of energy from his witchblade at the descending ship. Those eye-searing pulses reached the vessel. Immediately they were deflected into the forest, as if from a sling, harming the wraithbone.

The ship was going to land upon the great scar it was creating for itself.

Harlequins plucked shuriken pistols and laspistols from holsters hanging amidst all the belts and scarves and buckles of their tight bright cling-suits. Those suits were gyrating with rainbow hues.

Black guardians had emerged in the distance, cradling long-barrelled lasguns. Their golden helmets were the heads of bees attached to the bodies of upright ebon warrior-ants. On their back-banners was the rune of the eye shedding a tear of passionate vitriolic grief for the sufferings of Ulthwé.

Spiders were swarming from out of the naked wraithbone. Those tiny white spiders materialized out of the very substance of the bone itself. Thousands of spiders, tens of thousands, in psychic defence of the craftworld! A carpet of these spiders rippled – towards the white-hot rune stones.

Of course! The stones were acting as a psychic beacon. The rune stones were in such an intense state of activation that they had guided raiders to the Dome of Crystal Seers.

Spiders surged over the stones, sizzling into steam. More followed. More again, to quench the runes. The divination was certainly at an end. How appalling that it had attracted not the hoped-for truth but disciples of Chaos instead!

An urgent sending assaulted Zephro's sensitised consciousness – and an image: of a domed abandoned wasteland elsewhere in Ulthwé. Of intrusion through a webway portal – by armoured Chaos Marines! Chaos warriors were spilling forth, attended by deadly daemonettes, the creatures of Slaanesh. Emergency, dire emergency!

A second attack was underway – conducted by vile perversions of human warriors who had once been so proud and noble, but whom Chaos had subverted ten millennia previously, and who were now the timeless standard-bearers of vicious depravity.

The battle-standards rising from the backs of those erstwhile Marines were so grotesquely obscene as to sicken witnesses of the intrusion. And Zephro shared their nausea.

The profile of the foremost vessel had stabilized. That ship had become rectangular – with razor fins, with pincers at the bows. The following ship was still fluctuating as it descended, wreaking more havoc upon the sacred forest.

High above the dome, a third raider swam into view. But out there in space a wraithship of Ulthwé was sailing to the attack. The wraithship's high sails tacked in the thin ether. Ether, ha! To a large degree it was radiant pressure from the Eye of Terror itself which the wraithship used to propel itself and manoeuvre. Upon its deck a fusion cannon opened fire dazzlingly.

A moment later the third raider ballooned with a light so intense that sudden shadows of trees were like physical blows from great cudgels impacting all across the beloved terrain. After-images wrought bars of darkness and blinding streaks upon Zephro's vision.

So much psychic surge! In stroboscopic flashes he was glimpsing that wasteland, elsewhere in Ulthwé.

ASPECT WARRIORS WERE responding to the invasion. Howling Banshees, in their white and red armour, were advancing. Imbued with the spirit of their shrine, those females would be uttering stunning mind-shrieks. Their masks were screaming feral faces. Energy pulsed from their laspistols. Their power swords would be humming in anticipation.

Daemonettes rushed at the Banshees. Oh, those daemonettes so desirable as regards the swell of thigh and bosom and curve of loins, so lethal in other respects! How jealous of the Banshees they were. How eager to rip the eldar females apart with the pincers of their hands. How keen to impale a Banshee upon the barbed prongs of their tails.

Behind came the Chaos warriors. Crustacean codpieces jutted from their armour. They toted such obscenely shaped boltguns. And those banners! Displaying such gross bizarre erotic icons!

Scorpion warriors of Ulthwé were attacking on the flank. Striking Scorpions! How nimbly they darted. Agility was their defence against the explosive bolts which ejaculated from the boltguns of the Chaos renegades. Agility, and strong green armour banded with funereal black.

Scorpions fired shuriken stars from their pistols. Stars glanced off
Chaos armour. Those Striking Scorpions were so alert for a chance to
rush in and deliver their sting. Once they were at close quarters the pods
in their helmets would discharge stunning psycho-conductive needles.
The final coup would be by chainsword.

FROM THE GROUNDED vessel, yet other Chaos Marines were emerging
accompanied by a mob of beastmen.

These Marines were burdened with heavy bolters and lascannon. How
angular their power armour was. Shoulder pauldrons were rounded, yet
as for the rest – such cruel angles! Above their helmets jutted vanes like
axe-blades. Their very stance was angular. They sported blasphemous
totems which would have wrenched at the mind of any devout Imperial Marine – mockeries of honour, mementos of foul victories over
former battle brothers.

'Renegades of Tzeentch!' cried out Ro-fhessi.

The beastmen were swifter than the Chaos Marines. Shaggy-legged,
they only wore light armour. From their brows twisty horns jutted forward. Clawed paws clutched boltguns. From scabbards at their waists
they pulled cutlasses. Their hooves were stamping marks of Chaos upon
the bare wraithbone. Oh yes, these were creatures of Tzeentch – of the
Power of Mutability, of Change the Destroyer.

'I glimpsed the watch tower,' Zephro called out by way of extra confirmation.

Aye, Zephro's psychic vision had been of the Tower of the Cyclops.
Zephro had recognized it from horrific sketches which Ro-fhessi once
allowed him to see. That tower stood upon the Planet of the Sorcerers
in the Eye of Terror. That planet was the stronghold of magicians dedicated to the Lord of Change. Those had once been true Marines.
Nowadays their foul master peered through the warp by means of that
cyclops eye. He spied upon the realm of reality, greedy to find arcane
trophies… such as sacred rune stones.

Those other Chaos Marines who had invaded the wilderness were blatantly servants of Slaanesh, the lord of Perverse Lust. Was it by
coincidence or by malign collusion that both groups had chosen the
same occasion to attack?

Black guardians fired their lasguns at the beastmen and their masters.
Marines of Tzeentch responded by discharging lascannons and heavy
bolters. Many bolts hit trees. Penetrating deep, the bolts exploded. Mighty
trunks quivered from bole to crown. A guardian was blasted apart by a
bolt. Another was burnt open by a lightning spear of laser energy…

The defenders of the wilderness – those Banshees and Scorpions – were all close-range fighters. Where were the airborne Swooping Hawks who could drop grenades from above?

IN THE WRAITHBONE forest Harlequins shimmered from place to place. Once in motion, they were virtually invisible. Pausing briefly, they fired las-bursts and streams of tiny razor-stars. So few Harlequins!

Where were the aspect warriors? Where, where? Were they diverted by that other assault far away?

Where were the anti-grav platforms for scatter-lasers? Terrible though the use of such weapons would be amidst the sacred trees!

Where were the shuriken shrieker cannons? Where were the wraith-cannons?

Harlequins darted. Harlequins vanished and reappeared.

TZEENTCH YEARNED TO unleash destructive tidal waves of change throughout the cosmos – to unhinge continuity itself.

The daemonic lord of the Planet of Sorcerors must have sensed the loss of the Book of Fate. He must have detected earlier divinations carried out by Eldrad Ulthran. His Chaos raiders had certainly been guided in their final approach to Ulthwé by Eldrad's latest and fiercest effort to locate the *Book of Rhana Dandra* and its thief. Oh, fate was cruel.

Those shapeshifting ships had arrived here through the warp. They had emerged into ordinary space very close to Ulthwé indeed, so as to take its defenders by surprise. Wraithships were forever on patrol around Ulthwé. There was no star nearby to bend space so that incoming vessels must emerge billions of kilometres short of their goal. A raider might materialize suddenly above the craftworld itself – especially if guided by such a psychic beacon as Eldrad had been obliged to light.

Those other Slaaneshi Marines had come by breaking into the webway and following some psychic scent. Upon their world there would be a gateway from long ago. That gateway would have been sealed. What could have weakened the seals? What could have laid the trail of scent?

An earlier intrusion which had produced that wilderness had come from a Chaos world which tilted crazily to and fro like a rocking plate. Aspect warriors had driven the surviving Chaos Marines back to their roost there. They had witnessed a landscape of lunacy. In the sky of that world they had spied a daemon of malign delight perched upon a low sickle moon.

Surely the present Slaaneshi invaders came from that selfsame world. An eldar adept had sealed the rupture. What could have re-opened the webway to Chaos but an intrusion into their world from *this* side of the seals?

The trail led back to Ulthwé. The meddlesome intruder must have been Jaq Draco himself when he had fled away from the craftworld to find the Black Library. Through malice or through stupidity Draco had breached the seals.

Damn Draco and damn him again. He wouldn't have lingered long on that world with its daemon-in-the-moon. Just a fleeting visit. Oh, the damage he had caused!

PRECEDED BY BEASTMEN, the Marines of Tzeentch were making headway through the glades. They were aiming for where the rune stones lay extinguished under a mat of spiders, the divination aborted. If lascannons had been able to recharge more rapidly, progress might have been even speedier.

Picked off by Harlequins, beastmen were dying. Spiders were trying to dissolve into those beastly bodies through the fur and hide, distracting the beastmen's attention. Chaos Marines seemed almost indomitable in their advance. Shuriken stars and laser fire veered off those enchanted angular suits. The Marines' loudspeakers brayed a hideous skirl of *Tzeentch, Tzeentch*. And then a roar of *Magnus, Magnus, Sons of Magnus!*

Oh yes, Magnus had been their founder and their primarch. Nowadays he was their sorcerer-king in the Tower of the Cyclops. These were some of his self-styled Thousand Sons.

The eldar plan involved the dying Emperor's biological sons, who were unknown to Him-on-Earth. Here came savage sons of another stripe. Oh, the bleak loathsome irony of it! Eldrad Ulthran pointed the Staff of Ulthmar, summoning and focussing its energies. Ketshamine discharged his witchblade once more. Psychically, Ketshamine was messaging for support. Where were the aspect warriors? Where were the anti-grav floaters with heavy weaponry?

Damn Draco forever. May he go mad and become the plaything of a daemon.

No, but he must not. He must be found.

Yet how, when Ulthwé itself was so assailed?

Other craftworlds would join in the search. The loss of the *Book of Rhana Dandra* was a calamity for the whole eldar race. Spies would search. Harlequin players would rove through the webway to human world after human world, risking their lives and staging spectacles as a pretext for their presence.

Zephro sighted his laspistol at a lumbering beastman who waved a cutlass. Zephro was preparing to kill and to be killed himself.

Into view, at last, came an anti-grav platform. The platform jinked its way amidst the soaring trunks. Behind it flew Swooping Hawks. Their wings shrieked through the air, a blur of hues.

There was hope! Forlorn hope.

Two
PILGRIMAGE

A WILD REGION of a southerly continent of the planet Karesh consisted of boulder-strewn goat pastures. Beneath those rugged pastures were limestone caverns. In a certain cavern was an exit from the webway.

Below ground, phosphorescent lichens flourished. From the other side of the cavern the misty blue glow of the webway might have seemed to the casual eye to be merely a more intense patch of natural luminosity. Thus was the terminus camouflaged.

In any case, why should anyone have come down from the surface to search? Such caverns were huge and spooky and dark. Idle curiosity was rarely wise.

Evidently some goatherd had intruded at one time or other. Maybe he had been searching for one of his animals which fell down a shaft or strayed too far into a cave. Facing the opening to the webway was a cairn consisting of three billygoat skulls. The horns poked defensively at the blue tunnel, as though to impale whatever might emerge.

The skull-cairn implied that the locals were primitive folk. Lex suggested re-entering the webway to find a more advanced world. Jaq was still deep in shock at Meh'lindi's death, and felt unable to make a decision. Lex and Grimm debated the issue.

To re-enter the webway would be to take such a random risk. They needed food and drink and rest. They had to hide. They had to think. In their hands was an alien Book of Fate – written in inscrutable script in a language which none of them knew, not now that she was dead.

530 *Ian Watson*

The book was a key to so many secrets. This business of the Emperor's Sons, for instance! Since the book supposedly contained prophesies about the final apocalypse, there must be details about those Sons in this book – if the Sons genuinely existed. One only had a Harlequin's word for this, and Zephro Carnelian's too. Both parties could have been lying. This book was the proof. The proof couldn't be read.

Nor could they risk contacting any Imperial authorities. The Inquisition numbered in its ranks profound experts upon the eldar race. Those would have sacrificed an arm to be able to scan this book. Alas, the Inquisition was infiltrated by conspirators and at war with itself. Jaq had been branded a heretic and renegade.

What of the place in the webway where time supposedly could turn backwards? Back to a time when Meh'lindi was still alive? Better not think of that! Not even Great Harlequins knew where that place was – if it existed at all. Only someone supremely illuminated might be able to find such a place. An extraordinary magician…

Such as… a master of this Book of Fate? Such as… someone who had undergone daemonic possession, and redeemed himself?

'You're still in trauma,' Lex told Jaq sternly at the mere mention of such matters.

'I shall pray for clarity,' said Jaq numbly. He didn't pray.

'Listen,' said Grimm, 'I once visited a farming moon so superstitious that even wheels were banned. 'Cos wheels represented godless science. Perils of witchcraft, hmm? Even on that moon there were anti-grav floaters and a swanky capital equipped with a spaceport.'

KARESH PROVED TO be a similar planet. Not that wheels were prohibited – but the rural peasantry were whelmed in ignorance and dread.

Finding one's way out of the cavern took a while. Half an hour after surfacing, they had spotted a goatherd. The fellow fled at sight of the trio. An hour's trek brought them to a hamlet of dry-stone hovels.

Stunted peasants were in awe of Lex's superhuman stature. Was that mighty chest of his – with the ribs beneath his muscles all fused into solid bone – a human chest? What were those sockets in his spine? (Aye, through which his lost armour had once interfaced with him!) The peasants were leery of abhuman Grimm. They were dismayed by stern Jaq, and by his scaly mesh armour. However, their dialect was comprehensible – so this world could not be too detached from the Imperium.

Dimly the peasants remembered tales of a team of powerful strangers roving a neighbouring province once upon a time, equipped with dreadful weapons, rooting out deviants.

Psykers were feared hereabouts. The sign of the horns was used to ward off evil, which must not otherwise be spoken about too much. Offerings must be made to a nameless menace, which was at once terrible – yet also benign, in so far as it kept its distance. Was this menace the Emperor himself, dimly understood? These peasants eased the trio on their way in the direction of 'the city' with offerings, including a new beige robe for Jaq, and a great loose homespun vest for Lex, which had been the property of a local prodigy, a farmer of grotesque obesity.

The 'city' proved to be a tatty town, although furnished with a landing field. Peasants would drive surplus goats there for slaughter. Far away across a sea, goats' brains were much in demand by gourmets. It was in this town that the trio finally discovered the name of the world they were on – a detail which had been beyond the goatherds' ken.

Planet Karesh.

Its capital was Karesh City. Once a fortnight, chilled brains were flown to Karesh City from this province. Otherwise, the region might have been even more isolated. The next such flight was due only a couple of days later. In exchange for bed and board at a hostelry near the landing strip, Grimm reluctantly surrendered a finely tooled silver amulet depicting one of his ancestors.

With one of the smallest gems prised from the cover of the *Book of Rhana Dandra*, Lex bribed the pilot of the cargo plane.

ANOTHER TINY GEM bought them lodgings in Karesh City. There it fell to Lex and Grimm to scrutinize the register of interstellar shipping due to call at this world. Jaq continued to be riven by grief for his dead assassin-courtesan. Was he obsessed by the quest for the luminous path and for truth – or for the supposed occult place where he might snap the spine of time itself and bring Meh'lindi back into existence? Sometimes it seemed to Grimm and Lex that the latter might be the case. Surely this was just the consequence of bereavement. Having encountered an inquisitor of the stripe of Baal Firenze, Lex respected Jaq's tormented loyalty to truth. Since Meh'lindi had died serving Jaq, some of that loyalty had become symbolised by Meh'lindi for the time being.

Lex understood all too well how deeply the death of close comrades could affect a person. Inscribed repetitively upon the bones of his left hand, from which he had once dissolved the flesh in acid, were the names of two fellow Space Marines who had died decades ago.

Yeremi Valance and Biff Tundrish, from Trazior Hive, upon distant Necromunda.

The chirurgeons of his fortress-monastery had grafted new nervewires and synthmusclefibre and pseudoflesh in the aftermath of Lex's self-imposed penitential ordeal. Decades later, Lex's hand still itched inwardly with the memory of those names.

THE INTERSTELLAR MERCHANT and passenger ship *Free Enterprise of Vega* seemed suitable as a route out of Karesh. According to the register its captain held an ancient hereditary free charter. This captain ought to be a man of honour, unlikely to murder passengers if he suspected that their baggage was valuable. The captain wouldn't wish to lose his Imperial charter to trade freely where he chose without too much obligation to the merchant fleet administration. An enterprising spirit such as he would surely want a huge ruby such as could buy half a dozen interstellar trips. He would be discreet.

What clinched the matter, for Jaq, was the destination of the ship: Sabulorb!

Meh'lindi had once walked upon Sabulorb. Three years prior to meeting Jaq, that very planet was the scene of her bravest and most harrowing feat. In the gruesome guise of a genestealer hybrid Meh'lindi had infiltrated a genestealer nest. She had killed its patriarch. She had escaped alive.

To walk where she had walked, albeit with horror in her heart. To see what she had seen. To be where she had been!

IN THEIR HOTEL suite, its windows plasteel-shuttered for privacy, Grimm raised a possible objection.

'Look, boss, I agree it's over a century since she was there, 'cos of all the time you spent in stasis. Sabulorb might still be infested.'

Genestealers were furtive. They tried to establish their control by guile. To penetrate society from behind the scenes by using normal-seeming hybrids as a facade was their goal. To prey on society until it could be monstrously transformed.

The plasteel shutters were embossed with floral motifs. Fragrances seeped from any grilles set in the hearts of the metal flowers. Walls were richly brocaded, and topped with a frieze of blossoms. A painting framed in filigree depicted a gauze-clad nymph dancing provocatively and inviolably upon a venus mantrap in a steamy jungle.

'Do you reckon,' asked Grimm, 'that her killing the patriarch resulted in any kind of public exposure of the menace? She went there in secret, remember.'

Oh, indeed. Her visit had been a cruel experiment on the part of the Director Secundus of the Officio Assassinorum. Meh'lindi had wrought some havoc, but clandestinely. She had reported back only to the Director Secundus of her shrine.

'That genestealer coven could still be patiently beavering away under another patriarch and another magus,' Grimm pointed out. 'They could have covered up the harm she did them. Huh, there might have been other covens in any case. What's the chain of authority for anyone intervening?'

Lex pondered. Untold hours of study in the scriptories of the fortress-monastery had been devoted to the traditions of the Imperial Fists, his Chapter. He had also familiarized himself to some degree with the intricacies of Imperial organization. Very few people could possibly grasp all of those in any great detail.

'As I recall,' said Lex, 'the shrine ought to have notified the Adeptus Terra. It should have informed the Administratum. The Administratum ought to have mobilized a Chapter of Space Marines.'

In a galaxy so vast, with so many urgent demands upon less than a million Space Marines – and with billions of officials involved in the Imperial bureaucracy alone – decisions might be delayed for years, dire though genestealers were. The outcome could take decades.

Grimm scratched his hairy rubicund cheek. 'That director – Tarik Ziz, damn his soul – could have suppressed her report, not wanting his nasty experiment to be known. Nothing might have happened yet. Taking up residence on Sabulorb could be risky.'

Jaq grimaced.

To walk where she had walked!

GRIMM AND LEX visited the captain of the *Free Enterprise*, on board his vessel at the spaceport, to enquire about commercial prospects on Sabulorb and its political stability, with a view to booking passage there. Alternatively, they might wish passage to a different world aboard his ship. The magnificent ruby which Lex showed to the captain spoke volumes.

Lex himself did not speak much at all, leaving this to Grimm. Already, back in the tatty town an ocean away, with Grimm's assistance Lex had torn the long-service studs from his brow with pincers. Lex retained the studs in a pouch. He must become incognito. Surrender of the studs had been painful to Lex's soul, if not physically daunting. Was not an Imperial Fist able to endure most pain? Did not a Fist privately relish pain?

Lex's sheer musculature might nevertheless proclaim his calling to anyone who had ever encountered the legendary warriors or who had watched devotional holos. That tattoo on one cheek, of a skeletal fist squeezing blood from a moon, might identify his actual Chapter to an aficionado. This hypothetical person, observing the eight livid puckers disfiguring Lex's brow, might even conclude that he had been discharged in disgrace. If even better informed, this person might wonder why Lex had been released from his vows at all, instead of being sentenced to experimental surgery, and his organs harvested for pious use.

Lex was most unlikely to meet such a totally knowledgeable person. With his coarse vest and groin-cloth, and great bare leathery legs, Lex seemed to be a barbarian slave owned by Jaq, whose trusted factotum Grimm was.

Should anyone ever spy the patchwork of old scars on Lex's trunk, where potent extra organs had been implanted by Marine chirurgeons, those marks would imply that Lex must have been savagely whipped to make an obedient servant of him – after his capture from some feral world, probably. If anyone caught a glimpse of those spinal sockets, why then, at some stage the slave had been used as a servitor cyborged to some bulldozer or crane.

As to the injuries in his brow, Lex must have been impaled in the head with a multi-toothed cudgel, and his thick skull had survived the impact.

To further the barbaric image, in public Lex suppressed his fluent and gracious command of Imperial Gothic. He parodied the scum lingo of the lower levels of his erstwhile home-hive on Necromunda. He was a Fist, a thinker. He could pretend cleverly.

Grimm and Lex learned from the spry elderly captain that Sabulorb was most certainly politically stable… nowadays. There had been – whisper it – alien vermin on that world. Blessedly, Space Marines had cleansed the planet around seventy-five standard years earlier. Space Marines, no less! Ultramarines, by name! The captain plainly made no mental connection between those Marines and the barbaric giant who stood in his cabin.

'Uh, did any of those Ultramarines stay on?' asked Grimm. 'To set up a recruiting base?'

They had not done so. The cities of Sabulorb had required a good deal of repair before the economy got back on track. Much devastation had occurred, and many deaths. Be assured: that was all in the past. Sabulorb had passed through its phase of reconstruction into relative prosperity once more. Moreover, this was Holy Year on Sabulorb. Pilgrims were flocking there with fat purses.

How perfect for the trio that Sabulorb expected many visitors from other worlds.

How predictable that there should have been so much damage and death three-quarters of a century earlier. That action by Ultramarines had occurred twenty-five years after Meh'lindi visited Sabulorb. Hardly a rapid response by the Imperium – though speedier than some responses. Had a clerk mis-routed a report? Had Tarik Ziz suppressed the information? Had intelligence about the infestation come from some other source?

Whatever the reason, twenty-five years had allowed the covens to become much stronger, and their response to a challenge correspondingly more violent. Yet even so, Sabulorb was clean.

THE JOURNEY FROM Karesh to Sabulorb consisted of an initial plasma-boost outward to the jump-zone on the periphery of the Karesh system. This took over three days. Then came a jump through the warp, of only seventy hours, yet bridging light years. *Free Enterprise* emerged on the outskirts of the Lekkerbek system, a prosperous port of call.

Inward, once again for several days. Outward, once again for a few days more. A second similar jump took *Free Enterprise* to the edge of the Sabulorb system. Since Sabulorb's sun was a massive red giant, the journey inward required almost a week.

In all, including a stopover on Lekkerbek, it was a journey of almost three weeks.

DURING THE WHOLE of this time Jaq remained secluded in the suite of three connecting cabins. Lex preferred not to show himself. But Grimm roamed the ship, as a mechanically-minded squat would. Amongst the passengers already on board were scores of pilgrims, and scores more boarded at Lekkerbek. All were agog to be present at the unveiling of the True Face of the Emperor – a ceremony which occurred only once every fifty standard years, in Shandabar City on Sabulorb.

So as not to disabuse pious fellow passengers, Grimm refrained from enquiring too specifically into the nature of the ceremony. Plainly many pilgrims had saved for half a lifetime to afford the trip. To behold their deity's true face would bless them utterly, guaranteeing peace everlasting for their souls, and bliss. These fervent folk presumed that Grimm and his reclusive master and his seldom-glimpsed slave were on the same pilgrimage.

In private, Grimm was sarcastic enough about pilgrimages in general to merit a warning snarl from Jaq.

'Would you appreciate your own squattish ancestors being mocked, little one? Those are your object of reverence. We cannot gainsay these people's devotion!'

Lex nodded agreement to this reprimand. In his own area of the suite Lex was often praying to Rogal Dorn, Primarch and progenitor of the Imperial Fists – those Fists whom he had, some might say, deserted. Through Dorn, by proxy, he prayed to the Emperor on Earth.

Lex also spent time studying a scanty *General Guide to Sabulorb*. The captain sold copies to the pilgrims, but he had handed one gratis to Grimm since the ruby was so spectacular.

The *General Guide* contained hardly any information about the Holy Year ceremony itself. Pilgrims would already know all about it. Mainly the guide discoursed about the planet; and this was of compelling interest to Lex, who was accustomed to assessing the vital statistics of a world thoughtfully prior to combat.

To circle its giant sun took Sabulorb ten of Earth's years. Each season lasted for three whole years. The inhabitants counted in standard Imperial years.

'That's sensible of them,' remarked Grimm. 'Otherwise, imagine asking anyone's age! Gosh, I'm almost two years old; I'm getting married. Oh dear, I'm eight years old; I'm dying.'

Due to the small tilt of its axis all the seasons of Sabulorb were similar: cool. Its sun was huge but diffuse. It did not radiate a great deal of heat.

Much of the three great flat continents of Sabulorb was covered by cool deserts (and permanent ice-caps shrouded the poles). Deserts of grit abutted on deserts of pebbles or of sand; and one must beware of the pernicious powder deserts. A circulatory system of rivers stretched long irrigating limbs throughout those continents, from freshwater sea to freshwater sea.

One might imagine that those rivers had been dug as giant canals at some time in the distant past – and that the basins of the seas may have been blasted out by unimaginable explosions. Debris had formed the deserts. The basins had been filled with water pumped from within the planet's crust.

Here and there on land were what might be ancient ruins, eroded to stumps. Or were those natural formations? In the seas, according to the guide, algae and vast weed-mats yielded oxygen. The waters teemed with fish and froggy batrachian creatures which lived on the weed-mats. On land, herds of camelopards grazed belts of vegetation along the rivers. Those quadrupeds sported humps and snaky necks. Scaly-sided sand-wolves preyed on them.

'Huh,' said Grimm, 'life's too simple on Sab–'

Where was the biological link between the amphibians of the seas and the grazers on land? What's more, the balance of camelopards and sand-wolves – of prey and predator, which must constantly seesaw up and down – was too simplistic in a cosmos which generally indulged itself in a fester of pullulating life-forms preying upon one another in a chain of ravenous consumption.

'Somebody or something kitted the planet out–'

No such life-forms could have arisen on Sabulorb of their own accord. A red giant became a giant by expanding. Once, that sun would have been much smaller and hotter – and Sabulorb would have been a frozen world far from its luminary. While expanding, that sun would have swallowed any warmer inner worlds. Faced by impending destruction, intelligent creatures on one of those doomed inner worlds may have prepared Sabulorb for habitation. Or perhaps, with its rumour of ruins, Sabulorb was akin to Darvash, the desert world where Tarik Ziz was in hiding. (Oh, to boil Ziz alive in his dreadnought suit! That would be incense to Meh'lindi's soul.) Aeons ago, Darvash had undergone some preliminary planetary modification at the hand of some elder race. The ancient edifices on Darvash had been huge and intact – not weathered away to stubs, as on Sabulorb.

'I think inscrutable aliens visited Sabulorb vastly long ago,' suggested Lex. 'Hence the batrachian creatures in its seas…'

Jaq cared nothing at all about such speculation or about the origin of Sabulorb, although Grimm had listened with interest to Lex's thoughts.

'Quite a bright big brute you are,' Grimm had commented. Lex had merely chuckled ominously, and relapsed into his mockery of scum lingo: 'Hrunt grunt. Bigman hear 'im. Bigman hunt 'im.'

'Oh, I shiver in me boots,' said Grimm, though not quite so cockily.

THEY ALSO ABSORBED the dialect of Sabulorb through a hypno-casque, provided as another bonus by the captain. Other passengers were obliged to pay.

The Sabulorbish language was full of –*ings*. 'Be giving me alms.' 'Be riding this camelopard.' Everything was larded with present participles as if partaking of sacred time – or of eternal timelessness.

FOREVER MEH'LINDI WAS in Jaq's thoughts, unshakably, agonizingly. Whenever he lit incense in his sub-cabin, the smoke writhed, hinting spectre-like at the silhouette of his Lady of Death.

Surely his devotion had undergone a bias for which he would once have scourged himself on grounds of heresy.

Had he lost his clarity?

Or was it the case that by allowing the memory of Meh'lindi to haunt and torment him, and by letting this obsess him, he might crank up obsession to a perfervid state of mind – aye, of psychic mind! – which would transcend all ordinary bounds? Dared he invite possession by a daemon of deadly lust so as to conquer the daemon within him, and thus become illuminated – immune to Chaos, able to scry and use the secrets of the *Book of Rhana Dandra* in the service of righteous duty? And maybe to bring Meh'lindi back as well. He must not think of this possibility! He must not let Captain Lexandro d'Arquebus of the Imperial Fists, his barbaric slave, suspect that his former wild words still haunted his thoughts.

He must purge such thoughts. He must lock them up in a private oubliette. Truly the notion of retrieving Meh'lindi from beyond death was an impossible and demented fantasy!

Jaq recalled the two occasions on which Meh'lindi had wrapped her lethal tattooed limbs around him, ecstatically – though for a higher purpose.

Meh'lindi had served him well, and thus the Imperium, so excellently. Let her image in his mind (and in his very nerves!) continue to serve obsessively as a means of whetting his consciousness – as a personal icon, a fetish, feeding him energy in a manner akin to Lex's bond with Rogal Dorn! Aye, inspiring Jaq tormentingly to strive to the very bounds of sanity, and perhaps beyond – and beyond again, into purity sublime.

This would not be heresy, but true fidelity and consecration, in the service of Him-on-Earth.

Alone, Jaq toyed with the speckled pebble on a thong which he wore around his neck – Meh'lindi's bogus spirit-stone. It hadn't fooled the eldar for long. Eldar souls might indeed suffuse into stones, but human souls did not. The stone was only a pretty pebble.

Might it serve, nonetheless, as an amulet for Jaq? As a focus for his own psychic consciousness, to imbue that faculty with agonized passion?

If there was any actual resonance with Meh'lindi, this surely resided in the Assassin card in Jaq's Tarot pack. That card from the suit of Adeptio had once come to resemble Meh'lindi closely. Did it still do so? In the wake of her death, had the resemblance faded?

From his robe Jaq removed his Tarot in its insulated wrapping of flayed mutant skin. Closing his eyes, by feel and by concentration he stripped open the cards, and cut them.

There she was: Assassin of Adeptio. The cropped raven hair, the golden eyes. The flat ivory planes of her face. She was bare to the waist. Tattooed beetles walked across her dainty breasts, decorating old scars. She was so lithe, such a wonderful weapon. Jaq's eyes could have bled. Her image in the psycho-active liquid-crystal wafer was so waxen and stiff. Her eyes were so empty. She was death itself now. She was oblivion.

The cards! Oh stupidity! Zephro Carnelian's mocking image must still haunt the pack, an infiltrator in their midst in the guise of a Harlequin! Carnelian might be able to snoop on Jaq through the card.

If the trio were to hide successfully, that Harlequin card would have to be destroyed, not merely insulated. Why hadn't Jaq thought of this until now? Ach, his capacity for analysis was askew because of the tragedy.

If a single card was destroyed, the integrity of the pack would be impaired.

Before wrapping the cards again, Jaq slipped Meh'lindi's image into an inner pocket. He had no need of protection and insulation against her. The Assassin card was the perfect icon, and fetish, and memento mori.

FREE ENTERPRISE was due to make its second jump through the warp. Jaq, Lex and Grimm were waiting for the warning klaxon in the little lounge connecting their cabin-cubicles. Let passengers and crew only think the purest thoughts while the ship was in transit through the sea of lost souls – where predators lurked!

Jaq removed the thong, and pebble, from around his neck. He held the speckled stone over the mouth of the disposal chute for Lex and Grimm to see.

'I must cleanse myself of distractions,' he said.

'Aw, don't, sire,' protested Grimm.

However, Lex nodded solemnly. 'Aye,' said the giant. 'Just as I removed my service studs.'

Jaq let the stone fall, to be incinerated, and the ashes voided into space.

'More distressingly,' Jaq went on, 'I must also destroy my Tarot pack, in case Carnelian can trace us through it.'

Just then the klaxons wailed. *Free Enterprise* was entering the grey realm of the immaterial, awash with psychic currents. May they not be assaulted by gibbering entities, scratching at the hull. May they not be trapped in a maelstrom, to become a lost space hulk in which drifted mummified corpses.

Where more appropriate for Jaq to dispose of the cards? Probably the ashes would not pass directly into the warp, due to the ship's energy shields; but rather would disperse into vacuum once the *Free Enterprise* emerged into reality again.

Down the chute Jaq rid himself of his own significator card – of the high priest enthroned and gripping a hammer. Ice-blue eyes. Scarred, rutted face. Slim, grizzled moustaches and beard. Might he become as blank to scrutiny as any of the Emperor's fabled Sons were to their paralysed sire.

The Emperor's spirit imbued these cards, which He had once allegedly designed. If the fervent pilgrims could only have seen Jaq consign to ashes the Emperor card itself, that grim blind face encased in the prosthetic Golden Throne!

Jaq rid himself of the Space Marine card. Let Captain Lexandro d'Arquebus be anonymous. The card had begun to duplicate Lex. An olive complexion, notched by duelling scars. Ruby ring through his right nostril. Dark lustrous eyes and pearly teeth.

Jaq dropped the Squat card down the hole.

'Oops,' said the real abhuman, as if a queasy flutter had upset his stomach for a moment. Whether the card had resembled Grimm or not was a moot point. All squats looked much alike with their bulbous noses and chubby red cheeks, their bushy red beards and prodigious handlebar moustaches. Grimm's ruddy head of hair had grown back by now with typical vigour.

Most squats who travelled outside their home systems – usually to serve the Imperium – dressed similarly, in those beloved green overalls of theirs, and quilted red flak jackets, and forage caps and big clumpy boots.

JAQ BARELY BLINKED at the contaminated Harlequin card. Into fire, into ash, into void. Away, away, quickly.

Many more cards flew down the chute.

The Daemon card from the suit of Discordia presented itself. Jaq hesitated, because it was flickering.

'What you seen, boss?' Grimm also saw, and groaned.

In the past, this card had adopted the semblance of the hydra: a writhing knot of jelly tentacles, due to cross contamination from the Harlequin card. Now it was a daemon pure and simple – if such a thing were ever simple. Snarling fangs, cruel claws reaching out. It flickered.

Of a sudden it was altering. The hideous face was puckering. The neck was shrinking. The head sank low into the chest. Curved horns shifted.

Instinctively Jaq cast an aura of protection. But he still held the card.

'Dump it!' squawked Grimm.

The daemon's body fluctuated so! Mocking faces were appearing all over its skin, only to vanish again. Lips were opening as if to speak.

Cruel thin lips. Fat slobbery lips. Twisted lips. Opening and closing. Opening again elsewhere.

Lex gasped at the sight – in a way which suggested *recognition*.

'In Dorn's name, destroy it!'

Jaq knew the image well enough from restricted codexes he had once scrutinized in a shielded daemonological laboratory of the Ordo Malleus.

This was Tzeentch, the Changer of the Ways, the would-be Architect of Fate. Recollection of studying that image once upon a time on Earth, in the bosom of the inner Inquisition, brought to this malign mirage almost a twinge of nostalgia as well as of horror.

Tzeentch embodied the path of anarchy and mutability and turmoil, whereby to unpluck the threads of events. Was it Change itself with which Jaq must risk meddling perilously, rather than rampant Slaaneshi desire?

To seek a route to the place in the webway where time and history might twist! Where Meh'lindi might still be un-dead! From which she might be summoned back!

Anguish gripped Jaq. Lex seemed paralysed by the image he witnessed, as if his strength was enchained. Grimm almost gibbered but the little man's babblings were as froth; babblings about the danger of summoning a daemon whilst in the warp itself...

That froth was bothersome.

'I already cast an aura of protection,' snarled Jaq. 'I have my force rod ready!' He stared at the card.

Might Tzeentch preside over the first stage of his transfiguration en route to illumination? One of Tzeentch's greater daemons, some cunning playful uncaring Lord of Change? Was this the meaning? Nevertheless, Jaq would keep a hidden kernel of his own spirit intact.

Oh, temptation.

Smoke formed uncanny patterns around the daemon's head, pregnant with revelations, with visions.

The card could be a litmus of the perils besetting Jaq. A gauge of his progress. A warning signal.

Sanity reasserted itself. Grimm was right. If this situation continued, instead of pure thoughts horrors might coagulate around *Free Enterprise*. Were those horrors already suckering to the hull, scritty-scratching at the welded plates, cackling, seeking entry? Pink, long-armed blurs would rush through the ship. So it was written in the *Codex Daemonicus*.

But to incinerate this card!

To whom might he pray for guidance now that he had burnt the Emperor card, director of the pack? To His Lady of Death, perhaps?

Lex uttered a strangulated grunt. He lurched slowly towards Jaq as if tearing chains of adamantium loose from rock.

'Hear me!' Jaq cried. 'As I am your lord inquisitor!' Lex paused, perhaps glad not to approach closer. 'If I'm ever to use the *Book of Rhana Dandra* I must meddle with some occult forces. I'm fully trained to cope. This card can warn me – like a radiation monitor.'

Jaq wrapped the Daemon card securely in the mutant skin which had formerly protected and insulated the whole pack.

'There, it's safe–'

All of the remaining cards he consigned to oblivion.

A regular captain of Space Marines such as Lex might rightly be appalled by a glimpse of Chaos. He wasn't a Terminator Librarian, a psychic specialist. Yet he had staunchly endured a brief sojourn on a Chaos world. The glimpse of Tzeentch had seemed to ravage Lex inwardly, as if kindling anew some ancient nightmare. With horny fingernails Lex scratched at his huge left hand as if he might tear away the flesh and lay bone bare. Or else to inflict some pain upon himself?

Lex was detaching himself spiritually from this brief episode. Jaq could hear the giant praying softly: 'Light of my life, Dorn of my being.'

Lex eyed Jaq with composure. Some trauma inside of Lex had been contained. Not to be voiced.

'I'm guided by your knowledge,' he told Jaq.

'I shall be very careful in all we do,' vowed Jaq.

Aye, careful that he did not alienate his companions.

As to prudence… why, a man could stand on a clifftop eyeing a maelstrom down in the sea for hours, calculating every twist of its swirling currents. As soon as he leapt from the cliff he would bid farewell to all solidity and stability.

After a further interval the klaxon sounded again. *Free Enterprise* was safe in the far outskirts of the Sabulorb system.

In a dream, the spectre of Chaos haunted Jaq…

The harem of Lord Egremont of Askandar had occupied a hundred square kilometres at the heart of the vaster metropolis of Askandargrad. Until two days before, the immense harem had been a walled Forbidden City within the greater city. Half of this Forbidden City was now in ruins. Fires blazed. Smoke billowed into the sullied sky where two suns shone, the larger one orange, the smaller one white and bright.

From north and from west, twin swathes of destruction cleaved through Askandargrad to converge upon the ravaged prize of the harem.

Astride the massive, much-breached wall between harem and metropolis, formerly the only point of entry, Lord Egremont's sprawling palace was an inferno. If he were lucky, the lord-governor of Askandar was dead.

As were so many hundreds of the elite Eunuch Guard. As were thousands of soldiers of the defence force. As were many of the maidens of the harem. If they were lucky.

In the ruin of what had been a splendid bath-house, Jaq crouched with three of the Eunuch Guards. Burly men, the Eunuchs were bare-chested save for scarlet-braided leather waistcoats. Golden bangles adorned their muscular arms. The belts of their baggy candy-striped trousers were home, on one side of the waist, to a holster for a bulky web pistol, and on the other side to a scabbard for a power sword.

Sufficient unto the policing of the usually peaceful harem, these weapons! The web pistol, to entangle any intruder or rebellious resident. The power sword, to decapitate if need be.

Sufficient, until now...

The Eunuchs' uniforms were soiled and torn. One had lost the top-knot of hair from his shaved skull to a near-miss by a flamer. His scalp was seared pink. Another nursed an obscenely decorated and contoured boltgun lost by an injured invader.

The ivorywood roof of the bath-house had fallen in upon the perfumed waters of the long white marble pool. Timbers and tiles had crashed upon naked bodies. Some bathers had died instantly. Some had drowned. Once-lovely bodies were broken and submerged. Some victims still whimpered, injured and trapped by wreckage yet able to gasp air.

A stretch of side wall had partially collapsed. Through the resulting gap, from behind a baffler of marble debris, Jaq and the Eunuchs were witnesses to vile revelry in the once-delightful plaza outside where terracotta urns of floral shrubs lay shattered.

Were the screaming tethered female prisoners hallucinating while abominations were perpetrated slowly and perversely upon their flesh? The Slaaneshi Chaos Marines had certainly used hallucinogenic grenades – as well as boltguns and meltaguns and terrible chainswords, and heavier weaponry too. Were hallucinogens intensifying the already appalling sight, and the implacable cruel touch, of pastel-hued armour exquisitely damascened with debauchery upon the breast plates and the shoulders? Was that which was already monstrous being multiplied far beyond the brink of sanity?

A few tormentors had shed items of armour, exposing grotesquely mutated rampant groins, their organs of pleasure bifurcated and more, with squinting eyes sprouting from them, and with drooling lips.

Others had no need to shed armour. Chaos Spawn had materialized: wolf-sized creatures with legs of spiders and bodies of imps, with questing tentacles and phallic tubes. Jaq himself almost believed that he was hallucinating. A snake-like umbilical cord connected these spawn to the swollen groin-guards of their master – who stood back, roaring and whinnying with delight, as they guided the spawn in the ravishing of their captives, soaking up the sensations of these roving external members.

Corralling other hysterical captives were beastmen slaves armed with serrated axes. A Chaos Tech-Marine monitored these slaves. His armour was studded with spikes. Each shoulder pauldron was in the shape of giant clutching fingers. He wore a nightmare helmet shaped like a horse's head, eyes glowing red.

One of the shaggy beastmen drooled and dropped his axe. The beastman reached out a paw to caress a particularly voluptuous captive.

Immediately the Tech-Marine adjusted a control-box strapped to his forearm.

The disobedient beastman's metal collar exploded, severing his head. The head fell. It bounced and rolled amidst the captives even as the beastman's body was tottering.

Two Eunuch Guards lay maimed. An Apothecary in fancy armour opened up one of them with a long knife and pulled out the writhing wretch's entrails to sort through. The medic snipped a gland loose and deposited it in an iron flask bolted to his thigh. From that gland some drug would be extracted, to induce deranged ecstasy.

This sight was too much for one of Jaq's companions.

'Hasim!' he moaned. 'My friend!'

Before the man could be stopped, he was scaling the barricade of broken marble, web pistol in one hand, power sword in the other.

The energy field of the sword blade shimmered, a blur of blue. The pistol was cumbersome with its cone of a nozzle and its underslung canister of glue. Blundering forward, the Eunuch fired the pistol. His aim wavered. A murky mass of tangled threads flew from the nozzle. The mass expanded in the air. Even so, the cloud of stick threads missed the medic – and wrapped around the Tech-Marine instead, clinging and tightening.

The Apothecary had grabbed up his chainsword from the ground. The sword whirred. It buzzed like furious killer bees. The sharp teeth throbbed into invisibility as they spun around. With seeming delight, and with one hand behind his back, the medic met the Eunuch.

How shrilly the teeth of the chainsword screeched as they met the energy field of the sword. An electric-blue explosion of power ripped teeth loose, spitting them aside. The medic's metal-sheathed arm was vibrating violently as if it might shake apart. No doubt such sensations only pleasured the medic. The guard of the chainsword had locked against the power blade.

From behind his back the medic swung his long surgical knife. He drove the blade into the belly of the Eunuch. The sword fell from the Eunuch's hand, suddenly inert. The web pistol tumbled too. That former guardian of the harem staggered backward, clutching at the hilt of the knife.

He tripped. He fell. He squirmed to and fro. The medic roared with satisfaction. Such an injury wouldn't bring quick death – but plentiful opportunity to operate upon the man while life endured.

Of course, other mutated Marines were heeding the place from which the Eunuch had come. Abandoning their pleasures, they were bringing boltguns to bear.

Meanwhile the contracting web had tightened upon the Tech-Marine's armour. Threads cramped one of his gauntlets upon that control box.

Maybe the Tech-Marine sought to activate the frenzy circuit, to goad the beastmen into a killing rage directed at the wrecked bath-house.

A collar exploded. A shaggy head was blown from its neck.

A second collar exploded.

A third. A fourth...

JAQ WOKE FROM the memory-dream, sweating coldly.

THREE
RIOT

AT SHANDABAR'S LANDING field, after much queuing, Grimm was able to exchange a minor gem for a bag of local shekels. Pilgrims thronged the port, which served long-distance aircraft as well as offworld traffic. These pilgrims were merely the latest arrivals, many from other continents of Sabulorb.

Since many of the pious preferred to conserve their funds for lodgings and the purchase of relics, it proved possible to hire a steam limousine with fatly inflated tyres and dark windows for transport into the city. Destination: any bureau specializing in the long-term leasing of property. Jaq had no wish to stay in one of the crowded caravanserais such as Meh'lindi had once used, pretending to be a governor's daughter from another solar system.

Shandabar was a dusty, chilly metropolis of considerable size. Even so, it was packed. According to the driver of the limousine the regular population was perhaps two million. Right now the number had swollen to at least six million.

Along the northern fringe of the city flowed the two kilometre-wide River Bihishti, the water-bearer. To the south was the Grey Desert. Dust and grit frequently blew across Shandabar, though it was rare for a storm to deposit more than a few centimetres' depth of granules. Still, by custom, tyres were balloon-like – both on cars and on the multitude of carts pulled by morose camelopards with long snaky necks and splayed feet.

From armoured vehicles, police kept an eye on the surge of humanity: the robed pilgrims and touts and pickpockets, beggars and jugglers, slaves and artisans and missionaries, zealots who preached to the passing crowds, porters and hucksters and couples foolishly in love. The sky was a copper colour; the red sun was vast. Many buildings were domed and arcaded.

AFTER VIEWING HOLOGRAPHS of several suburban mansions, Jaq chose that which seemed the most secluded and well fortified. A great diamond was perfectly acceptable as a deposit upon a ten-year lease. Doubtless the property agent rejoiced in the inflated commission which he would finesse.

By the time the driver had taken them to the quiet southerly quarter, the great red sun was beginning to set, protractedly. A curved maroon lake of sun still bulged up into the sky. Several stars already showed.

THE BOUNDARY WALL of the property was topped with lethal wire. The limousine halted outside wrought plasteel gates. Half a dozen cloaked fellows armed with autoguns were passing by.

They paused to eye the limousine.

The driver seemed unperturbed. 'Being vigilante patrol,' he explained.

Grimm demanded the keys to the vehicle before he and Lex and Jaq stepped out, to be challenged by the vigilantes.

The little man introduced himself as the new majordomo of this mansion. He gave his own name, which was common amongst squats. The name of the grim new master of the house he gave as Sir Tod Zapasnik, which was how Jaq had decided to be known in Shandabar. The hulking barbarian slave merited no introduction.

The leader of the vigilantes condescended to inform the new residents that, during the time the mansion had been empty, the lethal wire on top of the wall had apparently lost its power. A few days earlier, a party of fanatical pilgrims had climbed into the grounds to roost in tents overnight, when the temperature would become bitter.

'Not breaking into mansion itself, great sir,' the man said to Jaq. 'Cutting precious bushes for kindling, and felling trees for logs. Previous owner neglecting payment to our virtuous patrol.'

Jaq snarled at Grimm. The little man distributed shekels to the vigilantes. In bygone days Jaq might well have cursed their leader for his blackmail and his blasphemy. What did such a person know of virtue? Virtue was dedication, virtue was consecration. Virtue was an assassin-courtesan who had only ever embraced him twice, and on each occasion for an excellent reason.

However as new residents of this district, the trio should not provoke needless antipathy – but rather, respect.

'Being well able to protect ourselves and our property, however!' Jaq advised. From within his own cloak emerged *Emperor's Mercy*.

Eyes widened at sight of that precious ancient boltgun, plated with iridescent titanium inlaid with silver runes. Only two explosive bolts actually remained in the clip, but Jaq had his laspistol too, fully charged.

Grimm toted *Emperor's Peace*, with a single bolt remaining in it. He loosened the holster of his own laspistol.

From the webbing on his back underneath his vest, Lex pulled the bolter which still had a full clip. He transferred a laspistol to the multi-purpose holster which by now was strapped to his thigh. Hitherto the holster had remained mostly empty. With several compartments, it was such as a slave might carry tools in.

During the couple of weeks they had spent on Karesh, Grimm had failed to obtain any extra ammunition for the boltguns. Their bolters could still speak once or twice before falling silent. Quite a few times, in Lex's case. The laspistols would serve well.

Gloom was deepening. Shadows stalked the streets. The driver of the limousine coughed impatiently.

Tucking *Emperor's Peace* away after this demonstration, Grimm unlocked the gates. He thrust them open to admit the vehicle, and returned the keys to the driver. After glimpsing such guns, he surely wouldn't dream of revving and absconding with luggage.

'Be waiting just inside,' the little man ordered gruffly.

As the chauffeur complied, the chief vigilante was eyeing Lex's bare legs and scant attire. He pulled up the collar of his cloak. He shivered.

'Getting cold already,' he observed.

Lex snorted contemptuously. He was trained to endure extremes of cold, or of heat. His anatomy was modified accordingly. Under his skin was the quasi-organic carapace in symbiosis with his nervous system, enabling him to interface with power armour via the spinal sockets. The carapace also served as insulation. What did these mundane fellows know about cold?

The slave flexed muscles such as few could have seen before. 'Soft bods,' he sneered in scum lingo.

The vigilantes were all shrinking well out of the way. Was this in awe?

No! Brown shadows flitted mansionward along the street. A dozen shadows. A score and more. Of a sudden a chant arose, of 'His Face, True Face, His Face, True Face.'

'Who blocking the path of His true pilgrims?' cried a frenetic voice. 'Pilgrims returning to their tents with holy relics! Moving aside, moving aside – in His name!'

Grimm's eyesight was acute. Squats had evolved in gloomy caves and tunnels where lighting had once been scanty and power was strictly rationed. 'They only got stub guns, boss,' he said.

Handguns which fired ordinary bullets were the hardware of a commonplace low-life gang. Notwithstanding, Jaq called out: 'Warning you! Circumstances changing. Throwing down guns. Removing tents peacefully from this property!'

Needless slaughter was not the Imperial custom. All too often, circumstances might compel bloodshed to sustain civilization and stability and sanity and faith, but it was always a matter for regret. Sheer carnage was the style of lawless heresy and of Chaos.

The reply to Jaq's warning was a crack-crack like the snapping of twigs underfoot. Slugs whined past. A shot pinged against the open gates. Others ricocheted off the boundary wall.

Intoxicated with expectations of the coming religious spectacle, the devotees were besotted with a sense of personal righteousness.

Then even more righteous boltguns spoke.

RAARKpopSWOOSHthudCRUMP!

RAARKpopSWOOSHthudCRUMP!

A bolt ejected. It promptly ignited. Propellant powered the bolt on its way. The bolt impacted. It tunnelled and exploded. Flesh and bone or a vital organ erupted. It was ever this rowdy way.

By contrast, laspistols were silent in operation. If the aim was inaccurate, the scalpel-blade of energy soon dispersed. Whenever a las-pulse met its target: such a lacerating flare-up, such a scream of agony, if the victim still had the breath and lungs and heart to scream.

PERHAPS TEN OF the pilgrims had fled. A score more lay dead or dying, almost all thanks to the laspistols.

Quite a minor massacre.

The vigilante leader returned. In the dying light he eyed those boltguns with a sort of devotion.

'Being Space Marine weapons, great sir, not so? Grandfather telling me of when Space Marines were coming, him just a kid. Purging the aliens in our midst. Pilgrims collecting relics, right enough!'

From around his neck the man pulled a thong. Momentarily Jaq twitched. Yet what dangled from the thong was a burnished bolter shell – which the vigilante proceeded to kiss.

'Where getting that?' demanded Grimm.

'Being sold here in Shandabar, as relics.'

The Space Marines must have left unused clips of bolts behind, items compelling adoration.

'Gimme that,' demanded Lex. 'Belonging here.' He slapped his gun.

Surely the vigilante would refuse to surrender his talisman. By what authority other than muscle did Lex presume to make such a demand?

But no; a mesmeric sense of seemliness appeared to overwhelm the vigilante.

'To be seeing such guns fired...' he murmured. Reverently he handed over the shell. He gazed at the litter of corpses. 'Sending a sanitation squad in the morning, great sir.'

'Being grateful,' said Jaq. 'My slave will be using the pilgrims' tents as body-bags, and dumping them here in the street.'

Most of the sun had sunk by now. Stars were brighter. Sabulorb possessed no moon. If it had, seas might have spilled far inland every day, so low was much of the land. The power propelling the slow flow of the rivers must have been centrifugal Coriolis force due to the planet's rotation. Good citizens would not wish to corrupt their minds with such arcane matters, the province only of tech-priests.

According to the *General Guide*, the holy city boasted three major temples, in addition to countless lesser shrines to the great God-Emperor. Each temple was sited near where an ancient city gate had once been, during the early millennia of the colonization of Sabulorb.

It was towards the easterly Oriens Temple that the trio set out on foot early on the following day. Later they might buy a balloon-wheeled vehicle. Jewels from the *Book of Rhana Dandra* would easily make them shekel millionaires many times over, should they sell those all at once, which only a fool would do. Walking was the best way to understand a city, even if hours of tramping were necessary.

Oriens was the temple where Meh'lindi had been. Oriens was where she had found the genestealer coven. They must walk in her footsteps. They must seek for more relics identical to that which the vigilante had worn.

On their way to the Oriens temple they spied, far along a great boulevard, a massive edifice quite out of keeping with the local architecture. In place of domes and arcades: soaring buttressed battlemented walls and a central spire.

'Looks rather like a courthouse,' said Grimm with a qualm.

No such institution was marked on the meagre city-map of Shandabar in the *General Guide*.

Nor had they noticed any minor-masked Arbites patrolling the crowded streets hitherto.

'Better take a look later on,' suggested the little man.

As THE TRIO approached the place where the Oriens Temple ought to be, buildings became flattened ruins. A whole neighbourhood had been devastated, and nothing done by way of reconstruction. Even so, pilgrims were converging through the dusty rubble. Soon, what a swarm of touts there were! Not to mention beggars and fortune tellers, souvenir sellers, and vendors of savoury titbits such as stuffed mice or mulled wine. Booths and stalls and kiosks mushroomed all over, as if a fair was being held upon a former battleground. Amidst the devastation, trade was thriving. Customers were legion. Touts buzzed like wasps around juicy fruit. Would-be guides accosted visitors.

To prevent pestering, they hired a guide – a skinny middle-aged fellow whose very appearance seemed something of a deterrent. Due to some overactive gland the guide's eyes bulged. At some time a knife slash had cleft his upper lip. Perhaps he had been operated upon ineptly because of a deformity. As though as a consequence of his cleft lip, words spilled out of him volubly. Samjani was his name.

'Thanking for hiring, three sirs, coming here to Shandabar to be beholding the Divine Visage!'

'Yours not being too divine, eh, Sam?' commented Grimm. 'Business being slow for you compared with the other guides?'

Samjani grinned hideously. 'Normally no one bothering about facial beauty, not here at Oriens.' He leered hideously. 'Not here where deformed hybrids were once lurking!' To what fine dramatic effect Samjani used his split lip and bulging eyes, to suggest the half-human spawn of genestealers. During normal times he would be a fine, frisson-inducing guide.

'Conceding, short sir, that my looks are jinxing my luck a little when pilgrims being mainly intent upon the Holy Face.'

Indeed, the face of Him-on-Earth would be unveiled two days hence at the Occidens Temple.

Clarification about the nature of that ceremony could await a visit to the Occidens. Meanwhile, here they were at Oriens where Meh'lindi had once been.

Yet where was Oriens amidst all this ruination?

Samjani led them up a mound of rubble.

'Being before you!'

Amidst the detritus, across a wide area, vents gaped. Those vents evidently gave access to a subterranean maze of tunnels, catacombs, chambers and crypts. Debris had been cleared from below ground. Ladders led down into those tunnels which had once been infested by the deformed coven – their heartland, which had finally been cleansed by armoured Space Marines, a legend come to life. Of course this was a rightful place of pilgrimage. Though why had the Oriens Temple never been rebuilt?

'Priests of Occidens not wishing rebuilding of Oriens, sirs.' It transpired that there had always been rivalry between Occidens and Oriens. Although lesser in status, Oriens had grown rich because it hosted a giant jar containing clippings, it was claimed, from the Emperor's fingernails. He-on-Earth was immortal. His spirit reached throughout the galaxy. As if still joined to His person, those nail clippings continued to grow slowly. Priests of Oriens would shave off parings from the divine fingernails, set those in silver reliquaries, and sell them to devotees.

Whereas the Occidens Temple could only display the True Face once in a holy year, every fifty standard years.

The coven had subverted the entire temple administration of Oriens. Their foul magus had become high priest. When all the coven were slaughtered by the Space Marines, and the temple razed in the process – along with much of the neighbourhood, which the temple had owned – no administration existed any longer.

The local Pontifex Urba et Mundi should have appointed a new high priest for Oriens. However, during the uprising of genestealer hybrids this dignitary of the Ecclesiarchy had been assassinated in his palace. By virtue of seniority, his rightful successor should have been the high priest of the Imperial cult of the Occidens Temple.

'Comprehending me, three sirs?'

The elderly high priest of Occidens had refused to appoint a new high priest to Oriens. However beholden an appointee might be to begin with, new power would soon banish old allegiances. Piously the high priest of Occidens had insisted that first of all his own elevation must be properly ratified by higher authority. His argument was that if ungodly monsters had polluted one of the major temples of the holy city, how could the high priest of any other temple be worthy to elevate him?

'Years being spent compiling a heresy report...'

Finally this report was dispatched thirty light years to the office of the Cardinal Astral, who was responsible for a diocese many hundreds of cubic light years in volume. Since the report had not been properly submitted by the office of the Pontifex of Sabulorb (he being dead and unable to sign), a clerk returned the report, according to Samjani's gossip.

In the meantime the scrupulous high priest had died of old age. His acting successor resubmitted the report along with a request for his own formal ordination as senior cleric – which was rightly the business of the vacant office of pontifex on Sabulorb.

Thus the decades passed by.

The ruins of Oriens proved as worthy of pilgrimage as the erstwhile Hall of the Holy Fingernail. Beneficiaries were the guides and vendors – who all paid a hefty tithe of their takings to the supervising Occidens Temple.

'Ultramarines wuz here,' said Lex.

'Indeed, big sir.'

'Aaah…'

Lex could not quite sustain the role of uncouth barbarian in such a context. He must examine certain relics on vendors' trays.

The majority of these relics proved to be forgeries: mere solid models of bolt shells – with no armour-piercing tip, nor propellant, nor mass reactive detonator, nor explosive.

After careful scrutiny, Lex advised Grimm to purchase two genuine explosive bolt shells. The proposed price was ridiculously inflated, steep as the sky. Lex was lofty too, and massive. The vendor dared not refuse Grimm's offer after Lex flexed himself and growled about counterfeits and blasphemy.

Finally they came to the exposed crypts.

As JAQ GAZED down from above into one such crypt, his lips formed the name *Meh'lindi*.

In the guise of a monster she had crept through that very chamber which was now vulgarised by gawping sightseers, none of whom knew a scrap about her anguished bravery, no more than any of these guides did, nor anyone else on Sabulorb apart from Jaq himself and Grimm and Lex.

Such vulgarity! Jaq could have leapt down into the crypt with a scourge. He could have flailed about him to cleanse these ruins of infatuated tourists. How dared they obliterate her dusty footprints of long ago with their own trivial tread?

'Descending now to be viewing the monsters' lair?' prompted Samjani.

Deep in his throat Jaq growled at their guide, who was one of these selfsame instruments of vulgarity. Why should he not growl like a beast? Might he not need to wind his desolate passion up to a pitch of frenzy and temporary surrender of his own rational will?

Hastily Grimm intervened: 'So what happened, Sam – I'm meaning, what was happening to that jar of fingernails, eh?'

'Smashing and scattering during fighting, abhuman sir. His holy nails still turning up amidst rubble, often difficult to be identifying.'

'I bet they are,' agreed Grimm.

'Keeping a nail for oneself being punishable by flogging. All surviving nails being in safe keeping of Occidens. Half-shekel fee for finding one here!'

'Nails still growing, eh?'

'Nails under lock and key at Occidens, never being on display.'

'You amazing me.'

'During time of my great-grandad many bloody brawls were occurring between the disciples of the nails and followers of the True Face...'

Jaq wandered from vent to vent, pausing to gaze down in lengthy bitter reverie. Lex attended him silently.

FOR LEX, TOO, this was a place of potential purity despoiled by thieves. Here was a place where noble Space Marines had fought valiantly and victoriously; and where some had no doubt died, their progenoid glands to be harvested respectfully by medics.

The blue-hued Ultramarines had come; they had cleansed; they had gone – leaving behind seeds of legend and by no means as many unused explosive bolts as the trade in relics suggested.

How it would have heartened Lex to obtain a whole satchel of ammunition clips. Yet might he not then have felt himself to be all the more an impostor? Someone aping a Marine on account of his brawn – when he truly was a Marine in reality! Aye, a renegade knight who had torn the service studs from his brow... Let Rogal Dorn, the dawn of his being, remain with him through this time of self-imposed exile, for a greater good.

Despite Grimm's best efforts, at this meditative moment Samjani suddenly scurried to accost Lex. Goggling and leering enthusiastically, he exclaimed, 'You could almost be pretending yourself an Ultramarine, big sir!'

Pretend? How so? By leaping down into a crypt, wearing no armour at all? By dashing through crowded tunnels, fighting his way through all those thieves and beggars!

Pretend to be an Ultramarine – when he was rightfully a Fist! Lex's hand swept back reflexively, the broad bat of his palm about to swat Samjani.

Grimm interposed. 'Sam! There's a courthouse in this city, ain't there? Being a courthouse, being a courthouse!' he babbled.

Lex withheld himself. The courthouse, yes indeed. Oh. if he broke their guide's neck – if he knocked his head off – this wouldn't matter one whit to a courthouse. Yet that a courthouse should be here, where none had been mentioned by Meh'lindi: ah, that could be a nuisance.

Mundane crimes were of no concern to an Imperial courthouse. Murders and robberies? Let the local police take care of those. Crimes against the Imperium were the business of a courthouse. What were the trio seemingly involved in, but terrible covert treason?

Did Samjani realize the narrowness of his escape? Impassioned pilgrims who hired him might often be volatile in their behaviour.

'Being a courthouse, certainly,' chirped the guide obligingly. 'Construction commencing just a few years after the Ultramarines were visiting.'

It figured. The subversion of an important temple of the Imperial cult by sly inhuman hybrids – and the corruption of this world's administration – was proof of laxity. Laxity was a crime.

According to Samjani the hereditary governor of the time, Hakim Badshah, had been absolved of heresy along with his family. The Badshah dynasty could continue. Massive fines upon the Badshahs paid for the precinct courthouse, which took ten years to complete, and for its maintenance.

Samjani mentioned that the gates of the courthouse were generally closed. Those judges within seemed mainly involved in their own affairs and intrigues.

Jaq was paying attention by now.

'Are the marshals of the court leading no regular patrols through Shandabar?'

Not to Samjani's knowledge.

'Are the Arbites sending no execution teams in search of offenders?'

Samjani seemed not to know what an execution team might be. 'People killing themselves readily enough,' Samjani said. He refused to elaborate. Perhaps he was merely alluding to the religious rivalries and brawls.

PRESENTLY THEY LEFT the crowded wasteland, and their informant, to walk across the city in the direction of the Occidens Temple, by way of that courthouse, so as to study it. The trek could take two to three hours, if one paused to admire lesser shrines or the great fish market or the camelopard stockyard, with its vista of the governor's palace not far beyond.

* * *

WHEN THEY CAME close to the immense courthouse they watched for a while from the far side of a broad, thronged thoroughfare.

The looming sprawl of the courthouse occupied a whole city block. Evidently several hectares of buildings had been demolished to make way for such an edifice – unless those buildings had already been casualties of the genestealer uprising.

Stout walls soared upward, inset with hundreds of lancet windows which were too slim for any human body to squirm through yet which would serve excellently as firing slits. Bastions jutted. Buttresses were fortified. Grimacing gargoyles poked from beneath crenellated parapets and pinnacled turrets. Surmounting the central spire was an orb in the shape of a grinning skull. All along the upper reaches of the courthouse, an imposing frieze ten metres high bore the repeated motif of a jawless skull interspersed with the motto *PAX IMPERIALIS – LEX IMPERIALIS.*

The Emperor's Peace, the Emperor's Law.

For Lex to see his own name coincidentally writ high and huge seemed such an indictment of his own desertion of duty – as though that frieze were displaying the names of notorious criminals!

'Huh, well my own name ain't up there,' joked Grimm. 'They ain't looking for me yet.'

Were the judges looking for anyone in particular? True to Samjani's account, the great ornamented plasteel main gates were firmly closed.

This could be due to the sheer crush of pilgrims during the holiest time of a holy year. Judges in residence might not wish a paste of people to be squeezed through their portals willy-nilly into whatever great courtyard lay behind those gates.

The reason could also be, as Samjani implied, that this courthouse had become preoccupied by its own internal politics, since Sabulorb seemed genuinely pacified.

JAQ RECALLED A courthouse he had once visited, on a warmer world. Its gates had always been wide open. Vigilant Arbites had scanned the crowds within its courtyard. That courtyard had supported a whole community of arguing petitioners who might have been camping there for weeks or months on end, and of caterers who served herbal teas and spiced cakes to the petitioners, and of cooks who brewed and baked, and of clerks who took depositions, and of legal counsels who coached petitioners in the phrasing of their depositions, all of which concerned niceties of Imperial decrees which had been delivered hundreds or even thousands of years earlier. Some petitioners might spend half their lives in that great guarded yard, which was only the outermost region of the courthouse. The most devout supplicants might even become recruits to the ranks of the warrior-Arbitrators, their original legal case no longer of any significance to them.

Here on Sabulorb it was otherwise. The court was closed.

Jaq said to his companions, 'There's a lot to be said for acting under the very eye of the law.' Pious hubbub almost drowned his words. No one else nearby could have overheard. 'The law's gaze ranges far. It may not notice what is beneath its very feet.'

Grimm nodded at a towering viewscreen mounted on a gantry at the next intersection. Beneath, offerings were raining into a great bronze bowl, their tinkling quite inaudible. At present the viewscreen was blank. Now they noticed that many other viewscreens were mounted at regular intervals.

The abhuman accosted a pilgrim for information. It seemed those viewscreens had no connection whatever with the courthouse nor even with ordinary police surveillance.

Six million people could not reasonably hope to witness the unveiling of the True Face directly. To behold the unveiling on screen anywhere in this holy city was deemed equivalent to being a direct eye-witness. Spectators would even gain a clearer view on a screen.

'I don't accuse the judges of laxity,' said Jaq. 'But perhaps they're more interested in their own splendid power than in rigorous investigations. This is sometimes the temptation. A courthouse can seem a world unto itself.'

Behind those gates, beyond whatever courtyard, would be an immense labyrinth of halls and dungeons, armouries and barracks, firing ranges, scriptories and archives, warehouses and kitchens and gymnasia and garages. A courthouse wasn't unlike a fortress-monastery, a sovereign domain where the robed judges presided over the marshals of the court, and those marshals over the well-armed dedicated Arbites who would enforce the law of the Imperium, were it to be violated.

'I presume,' said Jaq, 'that the present Lord Badshah hatches no plots, no more than that Hakim Badshah did. Why should he? He can pay for the upkeep of this courthouse through taxation. The local administration was purged of hybrids years ago. Judges must consider their mere presence a sufficient curb upon treachery. This is wrong, wrong – yet it suits our purpose. We might be more conspicuous in a smaller city. Anyway, we ought to remain near the spaceport – unless we can detect an unknown opening to the webway buried under desert sands!'

To detect such an opening, by using Azul Petrov's amputated rune-eye...

The dead Navigator's warp-eye had been imprinted with a route to the Black Library which was in the webway. Might the eye somehow signal the presence of a webway portal?

Yet how might the lethal eye be used, except to deliver a killing gaze? And why should any hidden opening even exist on Sabulorb?

THEY HAD ONLY proceeded a hundred paces more – bringing them near to that great bronze bowl beneath the viewscreen – when a hectic babble arose from ahead, far louder than the regular hubbub. Like a storm-wind an outcry rushed through the host of people, in a medley of divergent dialects:

'Displaying the True Face early!'
'Dey dizblay dze Drue Face!'
'Prieshts shtarting dishplay Hish fashe!'
'Ostentus vultus sancti!'

It could only be a wild rumour. Those viewscreens remained blank. The priests of Occidens couldn't possibly be unveiling the True Visage in public two days prematurely.

Such a rumour was readily believed by pilgrims who had travelled from the far side of the planet and from other planets of other stars. To miss the crucial moment would be intolerable, excruciating. To miss out, after fifty years! Rumour spread like a firestorm.

Here came a variation on the rumour, which seemed to lend it a crazy logic:

'Being private viewing for those who are bribing!'
'So many bribing, private viewing being public!'
'Being classed as public viewing!'

The viewscreens remained ominously blank.

The consequence was sheer panic. The crowd was surging. From side avenues, pilgrims stampeded into the surge. A tide of bodies heaved and thrust and clawed and screamed. Jaq, Grimm and Lex fought for refuge in the lee of the bronze bowl. Even when empty, the bowl must weigh a tonne.

Part of the mob alongside the courthouse began to appeal dementedly. Fists battered on the courthouse gates. A thousand voices demanded justice.

'We paid!'
'We were paying!'
'Pious pilgrims petitioning!'

Was this supposed injustice within the jurisdiction of the courthouse? Not at all. Of course it wasn't.

A violent affray at its very gates was of vital concern to a courthouse. Fists thumping on the plasteel gates were engaged in criminal assault. From high lancet windows lasguns soon were pointing downward. Clamped to the long slim barrels were tubes.

From loudspeaker-gargoyles a voice boomed forth: '*CEASING AND DESISTING FROM THIS ASSAULT ON THE GATE OF A COURTHOUSE, GOOD CITIZENS AND PILGRIMS! REMOVING YOURSELVES PEACEFULLY IN THE EMPEROR'S NAME!*'

Yet the assault continued.

Again the gargoyles blared: '*DESISTING AT ONCE! NOT DASHING YOURSELVES AGAINST THE ROCK OF A COURTHOUSE, PILGRIMS! DISPERSING! BE NOT COMPELLING LETHAL RESPONSE!*'

The appeal was in vain. The battering at the gate persisted.

Moments later it seemed as though the unseen Arbitrators above were scattering large silver coins upon the crowd. Coins by way of a token refund of the costs which pilgrims believed they had incurred in vain. Coins by way of additional offerings to the Emperor, which pilgrims might pluck up and toss into a bronze bowl.

The coins began to explode amidst the crowd.

'Frag grenades!' exclaimed Grimm, ducking low.

Fragmentation grenades, no less. Those tubes coupled to the lasgun barrels were grenade launchers.

Each grenade was shattering into scores of zipping razor-sharp slices. These tore through clothing. They lacerated flesh. They severed arteries and windpipes. They maimed and blinded. They slashed runes of blood upon upraised hands and cheeks.

Such a slipping and a screaming there was. Such tormented frenzy, as of goaded beasts. Quite a few pilgrims carried about them some weapon other than a simple knife or studded brass knuckles. Only a fool walked any world without some protection. Stub guns appeared. Handbows. Even some laspistols. What were people who hadn't yet been injured or blinded to do? Should they wait for more grenades to rain down? Wait for pulses of las-fire? Running away was almost impossible. Too many other bodies were in the way. Upright bodies. Staggering bodies. Collapsed bodies.

Armed pilgrims fired back at those lancet windows. They fired bullets and mini-arrows and laser pulses. Small chance of scoring a hit, or even of aiming straight. Yet now the very courthouse, and justice itself, were demonstrably under attack.

Smoothly the main plasteel gates rumbled open – and the crowd heaved.

Inside of the gateway, further access was blocked. Three armoured vehicles stood alongside one another, wreathed in engine fumes.

On two of these vehicles heavy stub guns were mounted. On the middle one, an autocannon. The roofs of all three vehicles were platforms for a team of Arbites. Eerie reflective visors rendered them featureless. How dark their uniforms were. They were so many ebony automatons with mirror-screens instead of faces.

From grenade launchers popped such a cocktail of frag and choke-gas and flash-flares. Then the serpent-mouth muzzle of the autocannon blazed solid shells. From the big stubbers clattered a storm of heavy bullets.

Shells and bullets reaped a swathe through the dazzled, gasping, bleeding mob. Another swathe, and another. Heavy bullets ricocheted off the bronze bowl behind which Jaq and Lex and Grimm were sheltering.

This courthouse was like a cudbear pestered while hibernating in its den. Or a nest of death-wasps.

FOUR
MAYHEM

WITH EACH IMPACT of a stray bullet the bowl rang like a bell. The note did not linger. Nor did the trio wish to linger. Yet except in the ever-widening killing zone around the courthouse gateway hardly any open space existed. Everywhere else there was an undulating herd of hysterical humanity.

Those guardians of justice need not have opened the gates. Their gates were of plasteel. Their walls were massive.

Any assault upon a courthouse, however misconceived or provoked, was such a snub to Imperial authority. How could the Arbites have stayed ensconced in their stronghold in the face of defiance? Perhaps the conduct of the pilgrims wasn't really tantamount to rebellion. Yet if there was no overwhelming response the incident might lead on to worse defiance. Moderation on the part of the courthouse could so easily be misinterpreted.

Had some judge been poring over books of precedent for months in anticipation of some such incident? The holiest of days was at hand. This city was packed to the seams with fervent visitors. Shandabar was no hive-world city, but right now its population seemed similar in density. Judges rejoiced in a proud tradition of launching shock troops against rioters. Order could so easily tumble into disorder beyond the capacity of the local police to contain.

The autocannon and the heavy stub guns fell silent. Arbitrators leapt down from the vehicles. Firing energy packets from their lasrifles, they fanned out. At first they hardly bothered to aim into a seemingly limitless host of pilgrims. Due to the lumpy carpet of corpses, the Arbites' footing was unsteady, and their progress leisurely. Their helmets filtered the lingering choke-gas, which had not drifted in the direction of the crouching trio.

In hope of escaping death, many pilgrims began to throw themselves face down. This exposed the armed resisters in their midst as targets for more precise surgery. Energy packets flew further, causing more distant pilgrims to dive.

So it happened that for their own safety more and more pilgrims further and further away prostrated themselves. Prostration quickly gained a momentum of its own. A tidal wave of kowtowing spread outward. Bodies forced other bodies down willy-nilly.

Where the trio sheltered, all bodies bowed low in the general direction of the Occidens Temple – as though in abject adoration of Him-on-Earth. Such limitless homage filled the whole locality. Pictures of this scene could have been included in devotional holos, were it not for all the blood and untold hundreds of trampled corpses in the background. A picture in sepia might have disguised the bloodshed.

The Arbites had ceased fire. They were stepping across a field of limp or grovelling flesh – like some invigilators of prayer whose duty it was to punish any worshipper who raised his face.

Thus was the human cosmos righteously controlled for the salvation of souls. Thus was disorder curbed. Thus was the superfluity of humanity pruned. In defence of law and stability the harshest measures were often, tragically, mandatory.

At this spectacle of governance exercised to such potent effect Jaq felt a spasm of heartfelt reverence. He experienced such a poignant nostalgia for simplicities – not that his career as an inquisitor had ever been simple, but long ago it seemed to have been so lucid in its purity by contrast with the tormenting dilemmas which now beset him.

Yet a moment later a frisson of horror at the carnage shook him. How much death could be justified by the demands of discipline and stability? But he knew the answer. The alternative – of cosmic anarchy – was infinitely worse. If the Imperium failed – or when it failed – the cruellest Chaos would reign, and reality itself would fall apart.

'Now we get going!' declared Grimm.

Across the stepping stones of ten thousand sprawling pilgrims.

'No!' Lex called out, too late. His hand missed clutching Grimm to drag him back behind the bowl. The little man was bustling on his way, shoulders ducked, big boots bounding across living bodies. Away, away, before the dark faceless Arbites came close in their tour of inspection.

Probably Grimm was right, and Lex was wrong in this instance. Without another thought, Lex hauled Jaq into motion.

'Run, Jaq, run!'

The impact of Lex – even of Jaq – upon prostrate bodies was more momentous than Grimm's had been. Bodies squealed and writhed or reared in injury or protest. Injured or offended pates were too slow to delay Lex's dash, or Jaq's.

'Halting, in His name!'

'HALTING NOW!'

Arbites had noticed the decamping trio, which was what Lex had hoped to avoid.

An abhuman – and a giant, and another man: what made them act so guiltily? That absconding squat might have been overlooked. He wasn't a big fellow. Squats weren't worshippers of the Emperor. Their technical skills were merely useful to the Imperium. The squat must have been caught up in the confusion by chance.

A decamping giant as well? And another robust individual too? A trio was more than coincidence. Could this be a case of ringleaders?

Arbitrators were giving chase. Three of them. One for each fugitive, should the three split up. Merely to shoot the fugitives in the back would be to lose a source of intelligence under interrogation in the dungeons of the courthouse. Thus it was as a snatch squad rather than an execution team that the three Arbites pursued.

How it went against the grain for Jaq or Lex to run away as though they were criminals! Those mirror-masks were keeping up a nimble pace across backs and buttocks and heads. The fugitives had a good start and were even gaining distance.

A side alley hove into view – a lane crowded with hectic pilgrims. These ecstatics seemed to imagine that a viewscreen, which they couldn't see frontally, had lit up with the Unveiling. This must be why the mass of worshippers were cringing in adoration. Ignorant of the truth, the pilgrims elbowed and clawed.

Grimm hurled himself amidst them upon hands and knees. He was a grotesque child scuttling and scrabbling his way through adult legs.

Lex barrelled into the jam of bodies. All of his weight of muscle and ceramically reinforced bone carved a path. Jaq was immediately behind him.

'STOPPING THOSE MEN!'

Now there was more elbow room – and even open space, merely confined by alley walls. Some pilgrims were still plunging in the direction of the boulevard. Lex cannoned into several deliberately to knock them over. Grimm, up on his feet again, tripped a couple with his big boots. Fallen bodies writhed on cobbles.

The trio turned a corner and raced.

They had entered a cul-de-sac. They skidded on animal bones and offal. A dead dog lay butchered and trussed. Over a fire of coals, a second dog was roasting on an improvised spit, left deserted. The proprietors of the barbeque had dashed off towards the boulevard. Had they supposed that the distant detonation of grenades was the popping of celebratory firecrackers?

At first glance, there seemed little choice but to turn tail and collide with the Arbites.

FOR GENERATIONS GANGS of children had scribbled their graffiti in this appendix of an alleyway. Names and obscenities in rotund script rolled across the stone walls – and also across an iron door, which they almost camouflaged.

A second glance sent Lex rushing shoulder-first towards the door. Any external handle had long since been broken off. Lex crashed against the iron. Rust cascaded. The door groaned.

A second time he hurled himself. The door yielded with a screech of snapping hinges. He forced it open.

Within was a dingy warehouse. Protected by gratings, some small dirty skylights provided meagre illumination.

What lay piled along all those ranks of plasteel racks? Oh, those were saddles – and bridles, and reins, intended for camelopards. Glance back: lasguns at the ready, the mirror-faced Arbitrators leapt around the corner, into the cul-de-sac. Jaq and Grimm were hardly through the doorway before Lex was heaving a rack of saddles over as a blockage. The Arbites responded by opening fire. Packets of energy exploded against plasteel shelves and tumbled saddles – and winged inside the warehouse too. Outbursts of energy lit the interior stroboscopically as the trio hastened, ducking behind racks, towards a more massive door with a wicket set in it.

This wicket was sure to be locked. Manual bolts secured the greater door. Who would expect anyone to want to break out of the warehouse? Lex heaved a floor-bolt upward, hauled a roof-bolt downward. From behind came the sound of Arbitrators clambering over or through the obstruction.

Give them some pause for thought! Tugging the boltgun from its hiding place behind his back, Lex fired a single shot along an aisle: *RAARKpopSWOOSHCRUMP.*

Arbites were highly trained, zealous men. They ought to recognize the characteristic noise of a bolter. Surely this merited a few moments' reflection. Was that gun a relic of the Ultramarines' visit decades ago? Was it contraband from off-world? Had some local gunsmith succeeded in jerry-rigging such a weapon?

Perhaps Lex's action only increased the zeal of the Arbitrators. The trio fled into a road seething with pilgrims who seemed enraged. As Lex fought a way through a torrent of persons, the furious buzz was of murdering mirror-heads – or of mirror-heads murdering. The babble was so confused.

Jaq reeled and clutched at Lex.

'Somewhere in this mob there's a telepath. I can sense him! A psyker. He's terrified. He's sending out chaotic images–'

Aye, muddled images of the massacre, which had assaulted that psyker's senses with so much pain and so many death agonies. Pilgrims who possessed any trace of psychic sense were picking these images up. Everyone was already so highly strung. In this road there was none of the desperate mass prostration, as there was on the main boulevard. Voices cried dementedly:

'Murder!'

'Mirror-heads!'

Those who shouted could have no clear idea whether 'mirror-heads' were engaged in murder, or whether it was essential for themselves to kill anyone who fitted such a description. Hysteria was becoming ever more rampant by the moment, infecting almost everyone, whether remotely psychic or not.

LEX CRANED HIS neck. He glimpsed the masked Arbites emerge from the warehouse. Jaq and Grimm only heard the howl of the mob. For several seconds the trio were borne backwards by a homicidal tidal surge towards the Arbitrators. Then they were free.

They escaped along a less crowded lane which forked and forked again.

They ran and then jog-trotted until they came to Shandabar's fish market, where all seemed normal.

A host of stalls occupied several dusty hectares, arcaded on three sides. Under the vast red sun trade was brisk. Fishmongers were bawling the virtues of the harvest from the broad Bihishti and from the nearest freshwater sea – fresh or dried, salted or pickled. A glutinous tangy reek pervaded the chilly air. Of the panic and deaths near the courthouse there was no realization here, no more than there was awareness in any of the glazed bulging fishy eyes peering blindly from slabs and boards.

Grimm panted.

'Oh my legs! Reckon... that mob... minced the mirror-heads?'

'Probably,' said Lex. He scratched at his fist in frustration. 'It wouldn't have been right for us to kill representatives of Imperial justice. They were just carrying out their duties. I ought not to have fired that bolt. I apologize.'

'Why?' asked Grimm.

'Those Arbites could have reported the use of a bolter. Could have started an investigation.'

'With Arbitrators visiting every rental agency on the off-chance of tracing us?'

'I don't suppose we really drew much attention to ourselves, considering the mayhem. I've noticed big guys on the streets as well as little squirts.'

'Squats,' Grimm corrected him tetchily. 'I've spotted a few of us as well. Engineers off starships, probably. Us squats like to travel and see the sights. If I do run into one of my kin I shan't be doing any hobnobbing, let me assure you. Us three don't really stand out – not with all these pious lunatics around.'

'Devout souls,' Jaq corrected him.

For a brief while the little man hyperventilated. 'In my book,' he resumed, 'there's generally summat weird 'bout most pilgrims. Grossly fat, or got a squint, or a goitre size of an apple on the neck. Or a skin disease, or webbed toes kept well hidden. Bunch of freaks, if you ask me.'

'Our book,' said Jaq, 'is the *Book of Rhana Dandra*.'

'Which we can't read, 'cos it's written in Eldar, and the script's impossible.'

Jaq shrugged. 'I wonder how much local animosity there is towards the courthouse, aside from sheer dread of the judges? What happened back there was a mere reflex action of goaded animals. I'd guess that the marshals of the court will feel the need to show more presence now. As Grimm says, there's a whole haystack of people, even at normal times – and only a few needles to probe it with. I rejoice bleakly in the religious rivalries here. Those will sow confusion.'

He pondered. 'We may need to make contact with criminals – to integrate ourselves, and protect ourselves from the attentions of the courthouse. Crime, after all, is everywhere. We ourselves are similar to criminals.'

Grimm grinned. 'Cosmic jewel-thieves, eh?'

Jaq was eyeing Lex, who nodded soberly.

'Transgressors against the Imperium, my lord inquisitor. Seemingly so. Temporarily. Until we understand. Until we can report back to trustworthy authority.'

'If the Inquisition is at war with itself, Lex, what authority can we trust?'

'I realize that! My own Chapter is beyond reproach. Yet our Librarians could merely report to the Administratum.'

'Which would notify the Adeptus Terra. The Inquisition would intervene. But which faction of the Inquisition?'

Lex bowed his head briefly, as if praying privately to his sacred primarch.

So AT LAST they reached the vast sandy area outside the complex of domes which was the Occidens Temple. A few thousand expectant pilgrims were already camping. Thousands more milled. There was a heady aroma of incense and of grilling fish kebabs – no sooner cooked over braziers than sold – and of spiced wine, and of bodies. Acrobats performed atop tall poles for all to see. Fortune tellers fanned versions of the Imperial Tarot. Cripples begged for alms.

It was possible to wend one's way to the fore, in a slow journey of well over a kilometre. This the trio did.

AROUND THE TEMPLE stretched a strong plasteel crush-barrier manned by armed deacons. An elevated walkway draped with rich brocades ran from the top of the temple steps out to a splendid platform overlooking the barricade.

At a gate in the crush-barrier, a deacon was soliciting sumptuous offerings for the opportunity to enter the temple – which was otherwise closed to worshippers now that the unveiling was imminent. An armed sexton would guide those who paid lavishly. These privileged persons would behold the actual sacred aumbry cupboard where the True Face was kept.

Tomorrow – on the eve of the unveiling – offerings must be twice as sumptuous as today.

Here was the origin of the rumour which had caused hundreds of deaths and injuries. Someone had misunderstood; and the misunderstanding had been compounded.

A fat bald man, accompanying his squint-eyed daughter, had handed over a fat purse of shekels, which were being counted. For most pilgrims the cost of admission was too steep, whatever special virtue might accrue.

Jaq was consumed with curiosity – with an inquisitor's desire to know, and know. From a pocket he produced a small emerald of the finest water.

Rather than spiriting Jaq's offering away out of sight, the deacon held it up to the light. Did he suppose such a jewel was false? Even in the dull light of the red sun, the sparkle said otherwise.

Grimm dragged on Jaq's sleeve. Amongst the crowd a tall woman, grey-gowned and hooded, was peering intently.

'Meh'lindi…' gasped Jaq. It was her. Her ghost. Within that shading hood the face was–

No, that was not Meh'lindi's face. He mustn't delude himself. The features merely bore a resemblance. And the height, the lithe stance. Already the woman had turned away so smoothly that she might never have been watching at all. She was distancing herself amongst the throng, losing herself. Already she was gone from view.

'That lady was eyeing our sparkler,' said Grimm.

'Forget her,' Jaq said distractedly. The woman hadn't been Meh'lindi at all. Of course she hadn't been. Meh'lindi was dead, gutted by the power-lance of a female Phoenix Warrior. As to the resemblance, why, there were only so many possible permutations of physical appearance amongst human beings. Billions of variations certainly existed on the human theme – yet in a galaxy of a million populated worlds trillions and trillions of people seethed. Somewhere in the galaxy there must be several people who appeared to be identical twins of Meh'lindi. Dozens more people must bear a striking resemblance to her.

No one could truly match Meh'lindi. No one!

THE SEXTON WHO guided the trio was a wiry weasel-faced elderly man. A laspistol was tucked in the girdle of his camelopard-hair cassock.

'On entering our temple, first of all you are encountering–'

A portico crowded with the carved and crumbling tombs of previous high priests, hundreds of them.

In a huge colonnaded atrium beyond, a forest of incense sticks burned soporifically. Sweet smoke ascended through vents in the domed roof. This chamber resembled a colossal thurible.

Further beyond was the basilica, patrolled by armed deacons.

'Fifty side chapels being dedicated to fifty attributes of Him-on-Earth–'

Innumerable candles were burning. Millennia of smoke had deposited a coating of soot and wax on most surfaces. The great hall was a place of light, yet because of the soot the dominant impression was of darkness crowding in upon effulgent lumination to quench it.

'Paying attention, travellers, to the great wall-mosaic depicting our blessed Emperor's defeat of accursed Horus the rebel–'

This mosaic was actually kept clean of wax and smoke. It had been cleaned so many times that its details had almost been erased. That fat man and his squinty daughter were gaping at the mosaic, while their escort waited impatiently.

Next was an oratory for private prayers. Jaq and Lex only bowed their knees briefly. At the rear of the oratory hung an ancient curtain interwoven with titanium threads. That curtain was so frayed, save for the tough titanium, that one could see through it mistily into the sacristy beyond.

Through the curtain, and through a resplendent grille-gate.

'–being of arabesque tungsten, the grille.'

In the sacristy, by the light of many candles, an aumbry cupboard was foggily visible. The cupboard was so gorgeously decorated in silver and gold as to dazzle any spectator who did not view it thus through a veil. Armed sacristans stood guard alongside the aumbry, softly chanting a canticle.

'That holy aumbry itself being triple-locked. Within is reposing a rich reliquary. Inside that reliquary is resting the True Face of Him-on-Earth–'

That precious treasure was only ever exposed to injurious sunlight in Holy Years. In the interval between such rare public exhibitions, the Face was occasionally shown briefly by candle light in the sacristy to munificent donors, for half a minute or so.

'No such private viewing being permitted during Holy Year–' But lo: high above the veiled entrance to the sacristy there hung in shadows a gold-framed picture executed in ink upon camelopard vellum. A picture of a lean and rueful though glorious face.

'Travellers: that being a copy of a copy of the True Face of Him!'

Inside the sacristy, two indentured artists were labouring painstakingly to produce similar copies.

'Being expensive to buy?' asked Grimm nonchalantly.

Why, two priests known as the Fraternity of the Face were always selling such copies in one of the chapels of the basilica. The sexton would guide the trio by way of that chapel on their return.

More than ten thousand years in the past, enthused the sexton, when the sacred Emperor had roamed the galaxy in the flesh, one day He had wiped His face upon a cloth. His psychic energy had imprinted that cloth with His visage. After so many millennia the original cloth was frail. That was why the artists copied from a copy.

'A copy being shown to the crowds?' enquired Grimm.

The sexton's expression darkened. His hand brushed the butt of his laspistol.

'The True Cloth being shown!'

JAQ STARED UP at the dim face on the vellum.

When he had seen – or believed he had seen – Him-on-Earth in the huge throne room athrob with power and acrackle with ozone, amidst hallowed battle-banners and cherished icons, the face which had been framed in the soaring prosthetic throne was that of a wizened mummy. Such potent soul-stripping thoughts had issued from the mind within that mummy that Jaq had almost been annihilated. How could a mite comprehend a mammoth?

Would Jaq ever return to that throne room, illuminated within himself?

How dared he contemplate allowing any daemonic power access to his soul, in the hope of exorcising and illuminating himself?

The trio declined the offer to purchase a copy of the Face.

'Already giving our only real valuable for a squint at the sacristy,' lied Grimm.

WHEN THEY WERE heading away from the barricade through the host of pilgrims and tents, a scrawny liver-spotted hand clutched at Jaq's hem.

'Charity for a registered cripple,' croaked an elderly voice.

Smouldering thuribles of incense dangled on chains from a gibbet-like frame. Backed up against the base of this frame was a rickety cart with small iron wheels. Upon the cart crouched a ragged crone. Her face was wizened with age. Her stringy long hair was white. Yet her rheumy blue eyes were keen with a light of tense intelligence. In those eyes was a quality of anticipation for which expectancy of coins alone could hardly account.

Grimm scrutinized her circumstances. The thurible-gibbet protected this cripple from being trampled accidentally. A handle jutted from the rear of her cart. It might be pulled or pushed. Here she crouched under the cool red sun, begging.

'No respect for the elderly on most worlds!' grumped the little man. He fished in one of his pouches for a half-shekel. 'Oh, your legs being all withered away, mother.' This was plain to see: two brown sticks were folded unnaturally. Was Grimm about to shed a sympathetic tear? The crone's cart smelled of urine.

Grimm withheld the coin temporarily. 'Who's wheeling you away at nightfall, mother?'

Aha. Had her legs perhaps been broken by her own greedy family so that she could serve as a source of income?

'Temple servant pushing me into a shed,' she replied. 'Servant assisting me, kind sir.'

'Was the temple breaking your legs, mother?' Surely the Occidens Temple did not need to create and exploit cripples, pitifully to swell its coffers.

The crone rocked forward, as if in sudden anguish from a cramp of the bowels.

'Oh yes, it was breaking my legs!' was her reply. 'Yet not in the way you're meaning.'

Grimm hunkered down by the cart. Soon so did Lex, and Jaq.

THE CRONE'S NAME was Herzady. One thing she had never been was a mother. Defiantly she declared her age to be eleven years old.

Who else upon Sabulorb would dream of counting their age in local years? She had lived long enough to arrive at double figures. She had endured more than a hundred and ten Imperial years – the vast majority of them spent in this cart. Grimm was impressed by Herzady's longevity, even though to a long-living squat a century was rather small beer.

'Pretty impressive for an ordinary, unenhanced human being, particularly in such reduced circumstances!'

A century earlier, as a young girl, Herzady had attended that Holy Year's unveiling in company with her pious parents. During the bedlam which ensued, her mother and father both lost their lives. Herzady's legs were permanently crippled. A compassionate priest had taken pity and provided this cart. For decades Herzady had awaited the next Holy Year. When the unveiling came again she was watching from a safer place than on the previous occasion.

Bedlam?

Oh yes. At the unveiling fifty years later there had been homicidal bedlam again, due to the hysteria of pilgrims intent on seeing... what could not be seen.

Could not be seen? What did she mean by this?

Why, Herzady had been all ears and eyes for decades. She knew that the Visage had faded, aeons since, into invisibility. On the climactic day of Holy Year when the high priest of Occidens in splendid procession carried the reliquary out along the walkway, briefly to open the sacred container, what he would expose to the gaze of hundreds of thousands of pilgrims was a cloth which was blank, apart from a couple of stains vaguely located where eyes might have been.

'Pilgrims are glimpsing almost nothing, sires! How they are straining and struggling to see!'

Consequently a vehement riot would cut short the ceremony. What about those copies?

Ah, the earliest copy had been made by laying sensitive material upon the precious faded cloth until a psychic imprint was transferred. This imprint was then piously embellished.

'Huh,' said Grimm. 'In other words, invented!' This account of the invisible True Face filled Jaq with an eerie sense of awe at the sheer devotion of so many of the Emperor's subjects. What did it matter if pilgrims were besotted? What did it matter if they would die or be injured just to catch a fleeting glimpse of the cloth which had once wiped His Face? Their agonies were as nothing compared to the eternal agony of Him-on-Earth. The veneration of pilgrims would pass into the psychic sea of the warp, flavouring it with benediction.

Kneeling beside Herzady's cart, Jaq found that he was able to pray. For a while.

Gently he said to Herzady, 'Being crippled, crippled because of adoring him, you are partaking in His vaster malady.'

'I am waiting,' she replied bleakly, 'for many more persons being crippled and killed the day after tomorrow, as surely must be happening. Then I am dying contentedly.'

It was to witness this calamity that Herzady had endured indomitably throughout the five decades since the previous holy year! The crone's persistence was pathological. Her lucidity was madness.

Futility flayed Jaq's briefly-boosted faith, as surely as the gulf of time had erased the True Face. He rocked from side to side.

'That courthouse, hmm?' Grimm said to Herzady. 'You been overhearing talk 'bout the courthouse? Involving itself much in the life of this holy city?'

Did Grimm suppose that they might wheel the crone away in her cart to their mansion in the suburbs, to become their informant about matters Sabulorbish?

The little man prompted her: 'Hundreds of people dying outside that courthouse earlier on today. All imagining the True Face being unveiled early – and panicking.'

Galvanized by shock, the crone sat bolt upright upon her twisted shrivelled legs. She gasped tragically. 'Herzady missing so many deaths...'

Her wizened face spasmed in pain. A thin spotted hand fluttered to her chest. She slumped over.

Lex checked her pulse. In his hefty hand her wrist looked no wider than a pencil. Herzady was dead. Of a heart attack, of a broken heart.

It was Grimm who reached to close the crone's gaping empty eyes.

'Huh,' he said, 'saved meself half a shekel, anyway.'

TWO DAYS LATER, of an afternoon, they struggled to a position at the very rear of the great square.

Although Grimm had been reluctant to come to the unveiling, Jaq was intent on studying the pious madness of a multitude possessed by rapture to the point of derangement where injuries and deaths would be as nothing. There were lessons to be learned about passion, obsession, possession. About derangement of the senses and the soul.

How untypically warm and foetid it was in the square this afternoon due to the exhalation of so much breath and the closeness of bodies rubbing together.

How many people in this press had already fainted or asphyxiated during the hours of waiting? What a roar arose as – presumably – the True Face was borne forth at long last. How the spectators convulsed. It was as though that sea of people was a vast pan of water which had reached boiling point. Or perhaps a pan of hot oil.

'Oh, my blessed ancestors!' yelped Grimm. The little man was crushed between Jaq and Lex. Exerting his enhanced musculature, Lex forced wailing pilgrims aside, perhaps cracking ribs in so doing. The long, high sandstone wall of a nearby house was indented with shallow niches – as if a line of statues had once kept vigil along there, or as though that ancient wall had been squeezed and rubbed into that crinkled shape by the sheer pressure of people during so many similar unveilings in the past.

Lex tore pilgrims loose from a niche. He was a massive bulwark against the heaving tide of frenzied humanity. He offered partial shelter to Jaq and Grimm in his lee.

Grimm huffed and puffed to replenish his lungs. How many chests were being crushed in the crowd? The little man squawked disgustedly. Grimm could, of course, see nothing whatever other than the nearest bodies.

Jaq was inhaling odours of hysteria. Lex alone could see clearly over heads and hoods and hats bearing True Face badges – although the focus of his vision was a full kilometre away.

'Priest's opening the reliquary,' he bellowed. A greater roar came, briefly drowning his voice.

'Crowd's surging against the baffler...'

* * *

INEVITABLY THAT BAFFLER would have given way soon, and the walkway would have come crashing down, were it not for the guardian deacons in their white surplices.

At first, the deacons used humane stun-guns to subdue the excesses of enthusiasm. Pilgrims who had camped to the fore had merely guaranteed themselves a stunning into unconsciousness upon their flattened tents. A rampart of stunned bodies arose all along the barricade.

The rampart rose higher as frustrated pilgrims climbed up over bodies, and were stunned in turn. Soon that rampart of bodies was imperilling the security of the barrier. By now the resplendent high priest had shut the reliquary and retreated. Pilgrims still pressed forward.

Deacons discarded their stun-guns. Probably those guns had run out of charge. The deacons must resort to autoguns and shotguns. Now they fired high-velocity caseless shot and low-velocity fragmentation shot. The giant red sun which filled a quarter of the sky grew even ruddier as though soaking up the blood which was being shed. Dust stirred up by thousands of milling, stamping feet might be to blame for the deepening of the sun's hue.

IT WAS ONLY WITH difficulty, and with bruises, that the trio eventually extricated themselves from the edge of that square.

In spite of all the deaths in the vicinity of the temple, many pilgrims' eyes sparkled brightly. Their eyes might have been doped with belladonna. Many were weeping with joy. Some warbled to themselves, 'Oh the True Face!' – even though they had seen next to nothing.

THAT NIGHT JAQ dreamt his dream of Askandargrad again.

One by one, all the collars of the beastmen had exploded – and their heads had been shorn from their shoulders.

Some of the squealing maidens were tethered to one another. Some, to shrubs jutting from shattered urns. Some tethers hung loose upon the ground. If only some of the maidens might escape their fate while they were temporarily unsupervised. If only one of them might escape – and not fall foul of other marauders, and hide herself somewhere in the ruins.

Help was on the way. Just days prior to the invasion by the renegades of Chaos, Space Marines of the Raven Guard had refuelled on Askandar and their ship had departed for the jump-zone. Messaged by astropath before the governor's palace was destroyed, the Ravens had now turned back. They would reach Askandar in another two days. Potently armed, black-armoured Raven Guards would hurl themselves against the raiders. Pray that the daemonic sights they saw did not require battle brothers to be mindwiped subsequently, to save their sanity.

It was almost as if the powers of Chaos had deliberately planned to taunt the Ravens.

If only some captives might escape! But the din of exploding collars had swung attention toward the maidens.

'In the Emperor's name, fire that weapon!' Jaq ordered the eunuch beside him. Suiting deed to word, Jaq peered over the barricade and discharged his own boltgun at one of those terrible parodies of a righteous knight.

RAAARK–

The male and female rune of Slaanesh was emblazoned provocatively on that Chaos warrior's knee protectors. Unlike his accomplices, his obscenely moulded armour was enamelled in purple and gold – a sardonic flaunting of the ancient colours of his Chapter before evil perverted it.

The bolt hit the left side of his breastplate. It penetrated at least some way. CRUMP. It exploded. The warrior swung around, arms flailing.

RAAARK–

The eunuch also fired. The vambrace shielding the target's forearm intercepted the bolt. CRUMP. An arm was crippled. Pray that sufficient damage had been done to the invader's reinforced chest to collapse a lung! The renegade was still swinging around, almost as if dancing a solo waltz. Pray that this was a dance of death.

RAAARK. RAAARK. Both men fired again, then ducked a moment before a torrid hiss gushed across the marble barricade. Air was being superheated by a beam from a meltagun. Moments later: a terrible roar! The beam had caught the upper ends of some fallen roof-timbers jutting from the bathing pool. The moisture in the wood had vaporised. The timbers exploded. Daggers of wood and splinters flew like quills discharged by an enraged hystrix beast.

The other eunuch shrieked. Several jagged darts had struck him in the shoulders. He reared, clutching at those goads. *Shwooosh…* The beam from the meltagun caught his exposed head. In a trice his eyes vaporised, and his chubby cheeks, and all of his face. It was as if his head had been sprayed with an instantly acting acid which stripped his head to a skull – a skull within which the brain liquefied and boiled, grey steam surging from his ear-holes and bursting upward from his rupturing fontanelle. The dead eunuch sprawled upon broken marble.

Resin in the stumps of timbers had ignited. Flame capered above the pool clogged by debris and by bodies, some of which were still alive.

From outside came such callous laughter. Jaq clawed at the surviving eunuch.

'We must get away!'

The eunuch stared at Jaq, madly.

'You shouldn't be here in a maidens' bath-house!' he bellowed. Sanity had deserted him.

Oh, what the eunuch said had once been true. Just two days earlier the harem had been forbidden to all full men, except for Lord Egremont.

And except for a young Imperial inquisitor – here to investigate rumours of a perverse Slaaneshi cult in this guarded inner city of women. Lord Egremont's grand experiment in benign population control had bred certain mischievous frustrations. Egremont was an idealist, and his reign had been genial, if eccentric. Askandar had thrived.

Oh fools, to espouse such a cult! For now the consequences were all too painfully apparent. Agonizingly so! Corrupted Chaos Marines had come to reap the harvest of idle folly, laying waste to Askandargrad and sadistically ravishing the harem.

The Eunuch glared at the obscene boltgun in his hands. He began to turn it around. He moved the muzzle towards his mouth.

'Help will be here in two days,' hissed Jaq.

Laughter! So close, outside! To risk a look would be to lose his life. To stay any longer would be suicide. Swiftly Jaq withdrew, scrambling past timbers and spreading flames, keeping low.

Behind him: *RAAARK – CRUMP*. The Eunuch had shot himself. By doing so perhaps he had saved himself from a death more abominable and prolonged.

ONCE MORE, JAQ woke shivering.

FIVE
THIEF

THE MANSION WHICH they had rented consisted of three storeys. A dozen rooms on each. Extensive cellars below. Furnishings were ebon. Floors were of black slate. In some respects how like the funereal interior of Jaq's lost starship was this mansion! Lamps stood everywhere, reminiscent – at least in the way that their light reflected glossily – of the electrocandles in icon niches aboard *Tormentum Malorum*.

Jaq wished all curtains to remain permanently closed, blanking off the view of surrounding leathery shrubbery, tracts of silvery gravel, the great red sun, the high perimeter wall, and a neighbouring rooftop.

From room to room there now scampered a little bearded monkey. It was like an imp, bright-eyed and brindle-coated. Grimm had bought this miniature parody of a human from a street vendor. That was because Lex had remarked, on noticing the creature perched on the vendor's shoulder, 'As a Marine is to a squat, so a squat is to that monkey.'

'Huh, well I'm sick of being the short-arse,' Grimm had said. Jaq made no objection to the purchase.

The busy solitude of the animal struck a chord with Jaq. The monkey had no mate of its own kind. Yet it constantly quested, as though around the next corner or in the next room it might surely discover a partner. How exasperatedly the creature sometimes chattered at its vague reflection in shiny surfaces.

THE MONKEY WOULD try to groom Grimm's bushy red beard, hunting for lice or fleas. He didn't bother to give it a name.

A week after the day of the unveiling it was this monkey whose squeaking and scuttling to and fro upon his bed woke Grimm in the dark chilly early hours.

The abhuman still recalled dreaming about a fire-fight inside some caves. He and a few bold squat comrades were taking on a horde of orks. Those raucous, messy green-skinned alien brutes were armed with thunderous crude blunderbusses. The gaping mouths of the barrels spewed nuts and bolts and showers of sparks and plumes of fumes. With decent boltguns Grimm and his cronies were busily accounting for those alien thugs. *RAARK, SWOOSH, CRUMP. RAARK, SWOOSH, CRUMP.* This was a battle of systematic versus disorderly noise.

Grimm wished to resume such an entertaining dream. He was about to swat the pesky pet aside – when a dark figure loomed. Lex. Just had to be Lex. Using only two fingers, Lex picked up the monkey by the neck, squeezing slightly to silence it. Leaning low over Grimm, Lex murmured, 'Carry on snoring just as you were. Do so, and listen to me.'

Snoring? Snoring? Had that been the source of the dream!

'RAARK,' said Grimm, sounding like a carrion bird with a sore throat. 'SWOOSH,' he breathed out slowly. 'CRUMP,' he uttered.

As Grimm strove to imitate what must have been the sound of his snores, and as Lex held the monkey dangling, still alive, a chagrined squat listened.

'There's an intruder in here somewhere. Gone down to the cellars, I think–'

Lex had detected the intrusion with his Lyman's ears, which replaced the ordinary internal arrangement of tympanic membranes and auditory ossicles and spiralling cochlea. Thus to protect a Marine against motion-sickness. Hearing was also enhanced. Irrelevant sounds could be filtered out.

Lex had been asleep. Yet a Marine only ever slept with half a brain. The other hemisphere remained on alert standby. Lex was roused. He had been monitoring the progress of the prowler. In spite of Grimm's rumblings, the monkey must have heard faint noises too.

'RAARK,' repeated Grimm. Dressed only in his calico drawers, he slid out of bed. He took his laspistol from beside an empty pot of beer on a side table, and emitted a final strangulated *SWOOSH* – of someone whose snores had either stopped naturally or who had succumbed to asphyxiation.

Nude apart from his webbing, Lex held a laspistol in the hand which was not busy with the monkey. He could hardly release the animal: it would resume a frantic squeaking. Should he simply snap its neck?

Perhaps it had been trying to serve a pathetic kind of purpose. Still holding it, the giant padded softly with the little man in search of circumstances down in the cellars.

A SOLITARY NIGHT-LAMP burned half way along a stone passage. The door to one of the cellars stood open. That door was the stoutest of any down here. That cellar was the one in which the jewel-encrusted *Book of Rhana Dandra* was kept, in a locked iron chest chained to a wall. The faint light of an electrolumen glowed from within, dimming and brightening – in motion, evidently in somebody's hand.

A lock was grumbling softly, slowly. A lid was creaking open. Grimm was first through the doorway. Ducking low, he fired his laspistol at the roof of the chamber – so as to startle and distract. The packet of energy blossomed against the fan-vaulting. Like a flower of phosphorus briefly it illuminated stone tracery, intercurving ribs. It lit up the ebon lectern which Jaq had bought so that the enigmatic volume could be examined conveniently, if not understood.

And in that brief flash: an inky silhouette was stooping over the opened iron chest. A figure dressed in such darkness that reality might virtually be absent there – excised and cut out. That absence was already straightening, turning lithely. The face was inky. Only eyes to be seen. Yellowy, feline eyes. How tall the dark silhouette became.

Could it be an eldar, come to recover the Book of Fate? Could the black figure somehow be an Imperial assassin?

Having dazzled, light died. Nor did the electrolumen any longer shine. Darkness was doubled. A rushing passed by Grimm, wafting at his hirsute skin.

Of a sudden the doorway was blocked by something as sturdy as any reinforced door. At the same time a frantic squeaking was scuttling past Grimm's horny bare feet. Lex had discarded the monkey so as to seize the interloper tight. Fighting, writhing, kneeing were all in vain. Who could break free from such a muscle-enhanced, ceramically-reinforced embrace? Not the black shadow-person.

'I got him! Light lamps, squat!'

Yet it wasn't a him. It was a *her*. The blackened face was a woman's. A human woman, not an eldar. So very like Meh'lindi's after she had sprayed synthetic protective camouflage skin over her features! No filter-plugs in the nostrils, though. Her garb closely resembled an assassin's costume. No red sash was around her waist to conceal a garotte or toxins.

Recognition dawned upon Grimm. 'It's *you!*' he accused. 'You were in the crowd outside Occidens. You were goggling at our emerald.'

Of course it was her. That tall lithe woman had exchanged her grey gown for a black body-stocking – which was almost identical to the clingtight garb which Meh'lindi had formerly worn. How appropriate for a thief – who hoped to steal through the night unseen so as to steal... treasure.

Jaq's torn old robe had wrapped the Book of Fate. The wrapping had been opened up by the thief, exposing all the glory of jewels which crusted the binding. Resting upon the book was a little black bundle. The thief had just begun to open this bundle when she was interrupted. The bandanna was loose, but still hid its contents.

The woman remained passive in Lex's grip, which he did not make the mistake of slackening.

'Quite an uncommon thief,' said Lex to Grimm, 'to have circumvented the alarms, and to have found her way down here, and to have picked so many locks.'

'For a moment,' the little man exclaimed, 'I thought she was an eldar or an assassin!'

The woman's eyes widened. Lex growled at Grimm for his indiscretion.

The woman asked, 'Why should there be an alien or an assassin in your cellar?' She spoke the same standard Imperial Gothic as theirs.

'You ain't from Sabulorb, lady. Who sent you?'

Lex shook her.

Lips pursed, the woman considered Grimm's question.

'How close are you to death?' growled Lex. 'That's what you're thinking. If you say that no one sent you, then no one will ever know what happened to you.'

Yearningly her gaze strayed towards the jewelled book.

At that moment the monkey leapt upon the lip of the chest. It stared at all the gems, sparkling in the lamplight. It reached, yet those jewels were all firmly fixed. Took a knife to prise one out, not tiny monkey fingernails! With quick motions the animal's little hands completed the unwrapping of the black bandanna. Chattering to itself, it burrowed. It lifted a bauble inky as night.

'*Don't look there!*' Averting his own gaze, Lex shifted a hand to cover the woman's face.

The bauble rattled into the bottom of the chest. It had struck iron, and so was out of sight. Lex restored his hand as a fetter upon the woman's arm.

The monkey shrieked piercingly. It clutched at its head. A moment later fur and fragments of scalp and skull and brain sprayed the fan-vault and the stone walls. The animal's head had only been the size of a large grape, yet flecks hit Grimm and Lex and the woman.

Grimm rubbed his soiled brow. 'Just as well I didn't bother giving the damn thing a name! Now at least we know that Azul's eye works. I thought the whole point was to let would-be thieves find out for themselves, by the way, big fellow?'

'We can't interrogate her if she's dead,' snapped Lex. He hauled the woman deeper inside the cellar as if proximity to what had killed the monkey might be useful as a means of persuasion.

The woman said hesitantly, 'If I had opened the black wrapping would *my* head have exploded?'

'Not necessarily,' Grimm said darkly. 'You might have choked. You might have swallowed your tongue. Your eyes might merely have popped out of your head.'

'Toxin?' she asked. 'Assassin's toxin?'

'Nah,' sneered Grimm, 'a dead Navigator's warp-eye. Now the eye's somewhere in the chest and I'll have to feel around with me own eyes shut tight.'

'What are you people?' she breathed.

'Who are you, knowing about assassin's toxins, eh?'

'I'm a thief,' the woman said. 'I came to Sabulorb for rich pickings because of the Unveiling and all the pilgrims. I was watching at the temple to see who seemed wealthy. I followed you. I observed this mansion, avoiding the local vigilantes. That's all–'

Grimm licked some monkey tissue from his moustache. He spat upon the floor.

'What's happening?'

Jaq had come wrapped in his beige robe, laspistol in hand. As soon as he saw the black-clad woman he lurched and moaned. The exclamation 'My assassin!' escaped his lips.

'No she ain't, boss,' said Grimm. 'She's a thief. She was trying to rob us. My poor monkey took the brunt of the booby trap 'stead of her. Azul's eye worked a treat. Mistress of thieves she has to be, to get in here! She knows about assassins – somehow!'

Jaq glanced at the headless animal, its stump of neck gory.

He said, 'I must find a lapidary who can pare a monocle from the warp-eye carefully – for me to wear with a protective patch!'

The captive stared at this newcomer in dread – which she did her best to mask. What were these people indeed?

Jaq demanded of her, 'How did you come by assassins' clothing? Why are you wearing it?'

'For camouflage in darkness,' the woman protested. 'To blend in. Why else, why else?'

'You really are quite like her,' he mused. 'And yet, not close enough. A caricature of her!' Jaq was pointing his laspistol at her now. He would not fire while Lex still held her. 'You would have stolen the book just for its jewels. Now you know that it's here.'

She burrowed within the encompassing custody of Lex. 'I don't know what it is!' she cried. 'Yes, I do know about assassins!'

So the thief talked, to save her skin for a while longer.

HER NAME WAS Rakel binth-Kazintzkis; *binth* signified that she was the daughter of a father named Kazintsk. Rakel's wild homeworld was where black-clad assassins obtained the raw material for the drug which enabled trained assassins to alter their appearance by willpower. On Rakel's world postulant assassins and initiates would practise shape-shifting and predatory stalking and slaying amongst its primitive population. On Rakel's world people knew assassins well. Though not as acquaintances or friends.

That drug came from a lichen. Psychic shamans of her world would boil the lichen and drink the juice. Then their own appearance would change. They would take on the guise of spirits of the dead.

Grimm grunted approval at this honouring of ancestors.

Those spirits were wise and harmonious guides – yet Rakel had begun to doubt their effectiveness after her brother had been killed and impersonated by a black-clad practitioner.

To Jaq it sounded as though those local shamans risked attracting daemons rather than benevolent forces. Maybe not! Otherwise, would the assassins – who were clearly of the Callidus shrine, Meh'lindi's very own! – have used this world as their secret bailiwick, source of polymorphine and practice turf?

The inhabitants of Rakel's world couldn't help but breathe in spores of the lichen at fruiting time. A weak form of the drug pervaded their bodies, and the bodies of local animals too. All could alter their appearance temporarily to a certain extent. Yet not to the extent that assassins achieved!

What the assassins did was harsh and terrible. They refined the lichen, distilling it time and again in their laboratories into a pure product of enormous potency.

A female assassin could become a male, and vice versa. Much training was involved: deep concentration, and pain as well, though assassins seemed almost immune to pain.

Assassins would sometimes capture native inhabitants for fatal and agonizing experiments.

This was normal practice, Lex understood. Devout Space Marine surgeons must experiment upon mind-slaved prisoners and failed cadets in their unending programme of research into the capacities and shortcomings of those organ implants which rendered such a man as Lex superhuman.

Assassin scientists studied the stability of metamorphoses. A captured inhabitant of Rakel's world would be injected with the pure drug and forced to alter – and sometimes even released, attended by a swarm of spy-flies which would watch his doomed struggles to retain his new shape. Being untrained to assassin standards, unable to focus and control sufficiently – and because the drug was pure – sooner or later the experimental subject would go into agonizing flux, his body distorting, organs and limbs softening and reforming terribly till finally he dissolved into protoplasmic jelly.

This much Rakel knew about assassins.

One day a rogue trader's ship had set down upon her world. It landed near to her nomadic home. Rakel had ingratiated herself with the captain so that when his ship departed in haste, warned off by her tales of the black-clad users of this planet, he had taken her with him in gratitude.

After learning many useful tricks while travelling from star system to star system, and becoming a skilful thief, Rakel had deserted her captain. She had been in Shandabar now for several months, consorting with criminals and preparing to rob pilgrims. She had never dreamed that she would set eyes on such a treasure as lay in the chest.

How had she located it in this large mansion?

Thief's instinct. People often thought that cellars were the safest place. Head for the stoutest door with the toughest lock.

'JUST AS WELL you didn't open the book looking for pretty pictures,' said Grimm, 'or you might have become one of the pictures, for us to stick pins in.'

He was improvising. The *Book of Rhana Dandra* contained no such pictures. If Rakel were by any chance spared, she would avoid the book now.

Jaq nodded. He kept his laspistol pointed at their captive.

'Useful informant on criminals, her?' muttered Grimm tersely. 'Useful contacts?'

'Are you sorcerers?' she murmured to Lex, limp in his grip.

'Far from it!' he growled.

Was Jaq so far from pursuing such a course? With his free hand Jaq pulled from an inner pocket of his robe a folded red sash. Meh'lindi's sash. Did Rakel see the sash as a tether for her hands? As a gag? No, she recognized what it was.

'Assassin's sash,' she hissed.

'Yes,' said Jaq, 'and tucked inside this sash is an ampoule of polymorphine...'

'Poly–'

'That's the technical name the Callidus shrine of assassins call the pure drug by. The drug you've been talking about.'

Rakel squirmed ineffectively. 'I told you the whole truth! I swear it! I don't have any confederates, only some business acquaintances. Receivers of stolen goods. Shoot me dead with your pistol,' she begged, 'but don't inject me with *that*.'

Jaq nodded to Lex and Grimm. 'We need to consult together privately. For the moment we shall lock her in the adjoining cellar. Fetch some plasticated wire, Grimm. Scurry! Lex, kindly bring her next door.'

GRIMM SOON RETURNED to the neighbouring cellar with flexible black-coated wire.

'Frisk her for lock-picks first. No, what's the use of that? You probably wouldn't find them all. Nor any hidden digital weapons, nor poison. Even a body has its hiding place. Remove all her clothing first before you tie her hands and feet.'

Did Rakel misunderstand their purpose? Did she imagine she was to be violated by this near-nude giant and this hairy dwarf and the bearded, crease-faced man – before her body was injected and thrown into agonizing flux?

While Grimm stripped off her body-stocking, Lex shifted his grip from limb to limb. How attentively Jaq studied their captive's anatomy, analysing the cusp of the breast, the flexure of flank, the crease of buttock.

'Clean her face and hands,' he ordered. Because of the camouflage paint her features now contrasted bizarrely with the creamy whiteness elsewhere.

In a corner of this cellar stood a basin and ewer and rags, deposited by Grimm after the washing of the lectern on its arrival. The water was stale and dirty, but it served.

At last Rakel was left in darkness; and Jaq led his companions away from the door.

'I regret our rough discourtesy,' he told them. (Would Meh'lindi have even flinched at such treatment?) 'There'll be worse if she's to survive. I must not care about her too much.'

'You want to inject her with polymorphine,' Grimm said. 'You want to make her into an exact Meh'lindi. But how?'

From his gown Jaq produced the Assassin Tarot card, which was the perfect representation of Meh'lindi.

'With this as psychic focus, little fellow.'

'I thought you burnt 'em all apart from just the Daemon card! So you kept hers after all...'

'We can employ this to save a life, at least for a while. We can make use of an expert thief. If I'm ever to understand the book we need to lay hands on an Eldar language programme for a hypno-casque. If there's such a thing on this world, I would say it'll be in the courthouse.'

Judges were mainly concerned with internal security, yet it was a fact that the eldar sometimes meddled in human affairs. Somewhere in its data store it was just possible that the courthouse could have the means to interpret alien language messages. It would indeed require an expert thief to sneak into that battlemented citadel, evading the mirror-masked Arbites.

'That lady deserts people,' Grimm reminded Jaq.

'That's why she must be bound to us – so that she will never dare desert me. That's why we shall force her into the exact mould of Meh'lindi.' Such torment was in Jaq's voice. 'She must believe that only by regular psychic reinforcement of her new appearance, using the card in my keeping, does she escape going into agonizing flux.'

Grimm asked softly, 'Is it true she would go into flux?'

Jaq lowered his voice. 'I insist that it is true.'

'I see...'

'Bear in mind,' added Jaq, 'that some criminals may well have sources of information within the courthouse, however pure the judges and Arbitrators are themselves. I must pray for guidance. I must meditate. Then we shall act.'

Jaq took himself off along a dark side-passage towards a little crypt.

'What you reckon, big fellow?' whispered Grimm. 'Will having a living replica of Meh'lindi around here be good for the boss's mind?'

Lex considered.

'I think,' he said finally, 'this may divert Jaq from futile obsession. No matter how exact the duplication, the mind in the body will never be Meh'lindi's.'

'Yeah, wean him away. That's what I was thinking myself.'

* * *

IN THE STYGIAN crypt, Jaq knelt, eyes closed.

If he were ever to lose the image of Meh'lindi from his mind, he would be discarding an epitome of duty and dedication, of bravery and perfection.

And what about desire? Desire which could bring frenzy, especially when frustrated!

Surely he must court frenzy if he were to pass beyond delirium into illuminated purity. Would not that woman, Rakel, in her transformed body, frenzy him by her sheer physical presence – and at the same time frustrate him profoundly by her essential difference from Meh'lindi?

Desire! Cousin to lust, to the Slaaneshi passion! An inquisitor should rightly avoid the experience of desire. Had he truly desired Meh'lindi? Her beauty had been bizarre. Though not in the dark. Her tattoos hadn't phosphoresced. Her tattoos weren't luminous like an electrotattoo, when one willed one of those to shine. In the dark there had simply been the twisting alphabet of limbs, to be read as a blind person reads.

What words had Meh'lindi's limbs spelled in the darkness? Desire was something beyond language and beyond reason. Was this merely another way of saying that desire was a state of madness? Desire operated without analysis or explanation. It functioned in a space devoid of explanation – in a veritable void of logic. In that void the most powerful superstition could arise, overthrowing the familiar parameters of duty and sanity. To lose guidelines was to become chaotic. It was to court a kind of Chaos – out of which what new sort of order might arise?

Beauty, pah! What was mere beauty worth?

Could Jaq be said to have loved Meh'lindi? Hardly! How could he respond to her with love – were she even alive! In his thwarted desire, foreshortened by death, lurked deep mystery and paradox... and thus a route to illumination.

Probably it was sheer fantasy to imagine that, even if illuminated, he could ever find the legendary place in the webway where time could reverse – thus to call Meh'lindi back into existence in her own living body from before the time she was slaughtered. Hadn't Great Harlequins searched in vain for that rumoured place for thousands of years?

Yet could he accept that Meh'lindi's fierce spirit had simply dissolved into the sea of souls when she died? Hardly! If he became illuminated, and led Rakel into the webway – so close to the warp! –

yes, led her, transformed by polymorphine into the absolute twin of Meh'lindi in body, might not Meh'lindi's spirit be attracted irresistibly to that duplicate body? Might not Meh'lindi regain flesh and blood?

Mind and body would melt together. The consciousness which had been Rakel binth-Kazintzkis would be displaced – like some lesser daemon, exorcised! Meh'lindi would be Meh'lindi again, entirely.

It's a curious phenomenon that people generally look exactly the way their personality suggests that they ought to look. Or to put it another way: that a person's personality is utterly appropriate to their appearance. To explain this phenomenon some ancient poet wrote that 'soul is form, and doth the body make'. So therefore if a body became perfectly Meh'lindi's, Meh'lindi's soul must surely heed the call – the compulsion of identity.

Should Jaq have scourged himself for harbouring personal concerns and personal passions?

Not when he must energize himself to frenzy in the service of truth!

Thus Jaq meditated.

LAMPS WERE LIT, and Rakel was untied.

Hunched naked upon a flagstone, she listened with wide-eyed horror to Jaq's explanation of what must happen to her – as an alternative to her demise by laspistol. Death was no longer an option for her, unless the transformation failed.

'The transformation will not fail!' vowed Jaq. He entrusted the Assassin card to Grimm to hold constantly before Rakel's eyes throughout the agonizing process of metamorphosis. 'Rakel: you must focus on this image the whole time. I shall guide you as regards tattoos upon the body. Those are blazoned eidetically upon my mind–'

Likewise upon his heart.

Meh'lindi had been richly tattooed in black, to disguise and embellish scars. A fanged serpent had writhed up her right leg. A hairy spider had embraced her waist. Beetles had walked across her bosom. Her surface was tattooed – and hair-trigger lethal. Rakel must imitate that surface perfectly. What of the depths? Why, Jaq had twice been admitted to those depths, to purify and consecrate Meh'lindi; with Meh'lindi's full consent, and with more than consent.

Assassins were trained to tolerate pain, to banish pain. Rakel wasn't trained. If her concentration failed she might go into flux.

'Be staunch, female!' Lex advised her. 'Pain is the teacher and saviour. *Dolor est lux.*'

Rakel gritted her teeth then managed to say: 'Women do give birth, you know–'

'Have you given birth?' enquired the giant.

A shake of the head.

'Well then,' said Grimm, 'you're about to give birth to yourself, to your brand-new self.'

NOW AND THEN a scream tore its way out of Rakel's throat as her body remoulded itself.

'Concentrate! The serpent's neck bends leftward–'

Often Rakel whimpered, like a beast caught in a bone-crushing trap.

'The voice: a little less husky–

'Now the right breast smaller–

'Golden eyes: think golden–!

'Flatter, the face–!

'More muscle in the calf–

'Just a fraction longer, the legs!'

What a litany of invocations. Rakel's whimpers were the responses. Somehow she managed to keep her gaze fixed upon that Tarot card which Grimm held out before her, while her own flesh and bone racked her, there upon the flagstones.

AT LAST A counterfeit Meh'lindi stood unsteadily in the cellar, supported by Lex. In Jaq's eyes was a harrowed awe and a kind of appalled adoration. Almost, idolatry. What else was Rakel but an animated idol of his assassin-courtesan?

Jaq retrieved the Assassin card from Grimm. The card was hotter than the warmth of Grimm's palm could have caused.

'Rakel!' Jaq addressed her harshly. He resisted the self-beguilement of calling her Meh'lindi. 'Rakel, this card is the one thing you may never steal. Without my psychic boost you could never use it on your own.'

As he was restoring the card to an inner pocket of his robe, the card met resistance. An obstacle sprang free. Liberated from its wrapping of flayed mutant skin, another card fluttered to the floor. A tiny flat Daemon of Change leered at Rakel's metamorphosis.

Lex shuddered. He gulped. He lurched, letting go of Rakel. She staggered against a wall, but supported herself. In reflex Lex stamped forward to tread upon that terrible image – with his huge bare foot.

'Dorn, light of my being–' he chanted.

'Get back!' Jaq threw himself against Lex. 'You could brand yourself!'

Grimm was on his hands and knees, battering at Lex's tough toes. Lex yielded. Gingerly the little man seized the Daemon card. As if it were a burning coal, he restored it instantly to Jaq. Jaq wrapped the card tightly, and hid it.

'You are sorcerers, aren't you? That jewelled book! I'm so hungry I feel I'm con-con-consuming myself!' Rakel's teeth chattered. The idol was shivering violently, as if she might wobble apart.

'Feed her!' snarled Jaq. 'Feed her with the best in the kitchen, Grimm! Open a stasis chest. Heat foetal lamb and tongues and kidneys. Find a blanket for her, anything to cover her.'

Lex cast around. 'Where's her black costume?'

'I need to examine it.'

'I'll bring a blanket from a bed.' Did Lex wish to be alone for a while?

'Grimm can see to blankets as well as food. You stay here with me, Lex.'

JAQ AVERTED HIS eyes as Grimm led Rakel away. Lex eyed that transformed anatomy with what seemed more than mere curiosity.

'Will she stay stable?' he asked, anxiety in his tone.

'I'm sure she will. The Assassin card stabilizes her. Yet your reaction to that Daemon card, both now and aboard the *Free Enterprise*, compels me to put an Inquisitorial question to you, Captain d'Arquebus.'

Briefly Jaq willed the electrotattoo on his palm to display its daemonic face. 'I speak now as an inquisitor, of the Ordo Malleus, whose primary concern is daemonic activity,' he said solemnly. 'In your past career as a Space Marine, have you ever had acquaintance with the Power known as,' and Jaq lowered his voice, '*Tzeentch*? Have you ever had contact with, or knowledge of, this Power? Confess to me, Lex, if you have. Confess to me. In the Emperor's name tell me. *In nomine Imperatoris!*'

That mighty man blanched. He knelt.

'Yes,' he murmured.

Haltingly the story came out.

IT WAS MANY decades earlier, long before Lexandro d'Arquebus became an officer. It was in a cavern of a mining world inhabited by squats loyal to a rebel lord named Fulgor Sagramoso. Lord Sagramoso's followers had captured Lex and his companions. The captive Space Marines had been chained down. They were to be sacrificed to the Changer of History. The corrupted Lord Sagramoso himself underwent vile bodily changes. Such disorienting nausea had plucked at the very foundations of Lex's being. He had witnessed daemonic possession. He had known the sickness unto death.

Blessedly, Terminator Marines of the Imperial Fists in lustrous armour had come blasting their way into the cavern, storm bolters blazing with salvation.

Because of their bravery and endurance Lex and his two surviving comrades had been judged worthy to remember their experience rather than being mind-wiped to ensure their sanity. Lex and Yeremi and Biff had sworn never to tell any of their other battle brothers about the phenomenon of Tzeentch.

Lex had not sworn not to tell this to an inquisitor. That memory from the past still disconcerted him hideously.

'You endured a close encounter with Chaos,' Jaq said respectfully, absolvingly. 'You understand how tortuous our cosmos is, and thus how ingenious – even devious – the champions of truth must sometimes necessarily be.'

As devious as Jaq himself?

Was this confession of Lex's another indicator to Jaq that the route to illumination might well be through Tzeentch rather than through Slaanesh? Through mutability, rather than through lust?

Was it possible to balance the two Powers so that a person became simultaneously possessed by both, and therefore fully by neither? Could there be jealous conflict between rival daemons? A war in one's very soul! Thus daemons would mutually disable one another, allowing their intended victim to squirm free to salvation and immunity! Could it be?

From inside his robe Jaq drew his force rod. He kissed its tip sacramentally.

'With this instrument are daemons dispelled...' He offered the rod to kneeling Lex, also to kiss.

'If I was ever... possessed,' mumbled Lex, 'could your rod save me?'

'Or slay you. Or both.'

'And I you, likewise?'

Jaq frowned. 'Only a powerful psyker may use this rod.' A psyker, untrained, was a potential magnet to daemons. If a trained psyker such as Jaq were to abuse his training and subvert his own sanity, what might he conjure?

'What became of your two comrades?' asked Jaq.

Lex scratched fiercely at his left hand.

'Biff died fighting tyranids, ' he said simply. 'Then Yeri died too. Everyone's destiny is death.'

Jaq frowned. 'Except for those supposed immortal Sons of the Emperor! If they truly exist. Supposedly their destiny is death too, in the bonfire of souls which kindles the Numen!'

If those Sons existed. Wherever they might be.

SIX

ROBBERY

Away from the mansion it wasn't too difficult to remember to call Jaq *Tod* or *Sir Zapasnik*. Inside the mansion itself, however, the moment inevitably came when Grimm referred to the boss as 'Jaq' in Rakel's hearing.

'Jaq,' Rakel said tentatively as the foursome sat at table later, 'the food in your house always seems to be so wonderful.'

They were eating purple Sabulorb caviar and medallions of yellow *mahgir* fish poached in spiced camelopard milk.

Rakel's voice was really quite like Meh'lindi's. Meh'lindi would never have made any such remark. To Meh'lindi it had always been a matter of pure indifference whether she ate a raw rat or a ragout to fuel herself. Jaq's knuckles whitened as he clutched his plasteel fork.

'Huh!' blustered Grimm. 'Never call the boss that in public! And it's me who's the chef. Anyway, you shouldn't seem to enjoy your grub so much.'

'No, I sympathize,' Jaq said to Rakel with an effort. 'You've had your body altered by the thing you most fear – so that I can safely trust you rather than kill you. How much trust do I bestow?' He glowered briefly at Grimm. 'Rakel: my name is indeed Jaq, and I'm acting under cover. Deeply under cover. I am an inquisitor. Do you know what an inquisitor is?'

She did know. She paled. She had visited numerous worlds. On one of those planets an Inquisition purge of heresy had been underway.

They had allowed Rakel to return to her former lodgings, with Lex as escort, to retrieve her stolen valuables and to bring those back to the mansion to keep in her new room on the second floor. Rakel's accumulated treasure was trivial compared with the jewels still encrusting the forbidden book in the cellar.

Jaq insisted that Rakel must exercise gymnastically. For this purpose Grimm had obtained a range of equipment, now housed in a chamber adjacent to hers. Bars, pulleys, beams.

As a nimble thief, Rakel had never neglected her body. Now she must hone herself supremely. She would become a fitting shrine for Meh'lindi's spirit! Yet Jaq did not tell her this. The nominal aim was to keep the false Meh'lindi occupied and exercised and expend her surplus energy.

Rakel had fretted that such strenuous activity might disrupt her new body. But no, reinforcement was the goal, so Grimm assured her. In the curtained house, Rakel was adjusting to her new companions, bizarre though their own mysterious goals might be. The atrocity which had been inflicted on her was... surmountable. What other choice did she have than to align herself with this trio?

As majordomo of the household Grimm could always find ways to busy himself, especially in the kitchen. Lex also exercised solo, observing the proper Astartes rites. Nevertheless, Lex craved more than exercise and prayer. To Grimm, who had been preparing spare ribs of camelopard in a spiced sauce at the time, Lex had confided his mounting urge to scrimshander. He yearned to inscribe a fine image upon a bone.

The little man suggested using a camelopard rib after Lex had sucked it clean. This provoked Lex to fury. Did the abhuman not understand that Lex could only engrave scrimshaws upon the bones of fallen comrades? Maybe he might honourably decorate a bone of someone who had belonged to another devout Chapter. Alas, no corpses of Ultramarines had been buried on Sabulorb. All who fell would have been returned to their fortress-monastery.

Did Grimm, with his supposed reverence for ancestors, not understand this?

Lex was frustrated.

Grimm had mentioned this matter to Jaq.

'THIS WORLD WAS once infested by genestealers,' Jaq told Rakel at the dinner table. 'Do you know what those are?'

Yes, her criminal contacts had told her about the infestation by Old Four-Arms.

'Not all hybrids may have been destroyed,' said Jaq. 'The courthouse does not seem to be exercising enough diligence these days. I do not suggest that the courthouse is contaminated. However, an inquisitor must always harbour many suspicions – and often act secretly. You may have seen an inquisitor storming about on that other world you visited. The best work of the Inquisition is often pursued unseen, until the crucial moment. That book downstairs contains secrets about genestealers and their origin.'

Did it? Did it not?

They're bred by tyranids, Lex almost said; but he kept silent.

In the tyranid hive-ship, in that evil leviathan shaped like a snail, Biff and Yeremi had died…

'To read the book I shall need something which is probably stored in the courthouse. I must not reveal myself prematurely to the Arbites. So your arrival is timely. However, you must be tested. We intercepted you, after all.

'I'm told,' Jaq continued, 'that the Oriens Temple was once home to the ancient thigh bone of a Space Marine, housed in a reliquary.' The real Meh'lindi had told him this. 'I wonder whether that thigh bone survived the destruction of the temple? I wonder whether the Occidens Temple sequestered that bone, just as they have done with the Emperor's fingernails. Find out, Rakel, find out from your criminal contacts! If that femur is hidden away in Occidens I want you to steal the bone and bring it here for Lex to ornament with his graving tool.'

'Oh yes indeed,' said Lex. 'Oh yes!' His fists opened and closed as though already grasping the revered bone.

Why Lex should wish to engage in such an activity was not to be confided. Rakel knew Lex's name – but not his identity.

'Ask about illegal cults as well,' continued Jaq. 'Is there any cult devoted to metamorphosis – or to revolutionary change? Is there any cult devoted to lust and wanton pleasures of the flesh?'

Rakel ventured to ask: 'Is that why I should not praise the food we eat, no matter how fine it is?'

'Not at all! We eat well because austerity narrows one's perspectives.'

Grimm tilted his pot of ale. 'You used not to allow any alcohol aboard the good ship *Tormentum*, Jaq.' These days, Grimm had been allowed to provision the larder with beer and wine and even some of the strong local *djinn* spirit. Jaq himself still drank no alcohol. For Lex, with his supplementary preomnor stomach and his purifying oolitic kidney, indulgence would be futile.

'Alcohol disorders the senses,' Jaq explained. 'I may need to exploit disorder. You, Rakel, in your new assassin shape, should not express sensual preferences regarding food. It isn't fitting.'

Jaq placed the assassin's sash upon the table. From the sash he removed three small hooded rings, baroque thimbles.

'Wear these on your fingers, Rakel.'

With a professional, if puzzled, eye Rakel was assessing the possible value of these supposed items of bijouterie.

'You crook your finger suddenly just so,' Jaq mimed. 'These are rare digital weapons of jokaero manufacture. One fires a toxic needle, the next a laser beam, and the third is a tiny flamer. Each will fire once. We have no means to replenish these. They are only for use in case you are cornered, with no other means of escape.'

Rakel eyed the three digital devices, and the three other persons seated at table.

'See how we trust you!' sneered Grimm.

'You would not defeat me,' Lex growled at her, 'not with toxin nor flame nor laser burst. Even blind, I would break your back.'

'And your body would soon go into flux,' said Jaq.

Nodding, Rakel slid the three digital weapons on to different fingers.

'You're perfect,' Jaq said bleakly.

The abhuman dabbed a stubby finger in the spiced milk and sucked as if on a teat. 'Huh, this sauce is getting cold!'

RAKEL WAS NO longer a free agent. No longer was she even herself, physically. But then, what did freedom signify? What value was there in the freedom to tote a valise of stolen gems and drugs and Imperial credit tokens and such from star system to star system, paying bribes and sweeteners in the process? What value was there even in a self, in this cosmos of untold trillions of selves? If anything defined her 'self', it was thievery, the purloining of material aspects of other people with which to embellish in private her own identity.

In this mansion she had attained, inadvertently, a whole new counterfeit identity, forged upon her very flesh. Wasn't this a perverse kind of triumph? Now she had a mission and a mandate to steal, bestowed by a clandestine inquisitor. Wasn't this a perverse kind of recognition?

She proved to be a useful intermediary. Her main contacts were the Shuturban brothers, two dark moustached men whose father, now elderly, had been a camelopard driver and smuggler. Chor Shuturban was sly, she explained. Mardal Shuturban was rash and quick-tempered.

The Shuturbans had been most intrigued by the alteration in Rakel's appearance since last they had seen her. Indeed, at first they had been quite sceptical that Rakel was Rakel – until she reminded them of previous illegal dealings known only to herself and the brothers.

So had she undergone major surgery at the Hakim Hospitalery – and recovered already? She was obliged to tell Chor and Mardal – exaggeratedly – about the lichen juice of her homeworld, and how this made her people masters and mistresses of disguise. She had actually been in disguise prior to this – so she claimed, with a twisted smile – and now they beheld her true self. She spoke of shape-shifting chemicals in her blood. Chor had muttered darkly about wizardry.

Chor Shuturban did indeed know the present whereabouts of that thigh bone. It had been retrieved from the ruin of Oriens in its severely damaged golden reliquary when a tunnel was cleared of debris during his father's time. Occidens' deacons had been supervising the excavation. Shuturban senior had made it his business to learn where so much crushed wrought gold was taken. The reliquary had been locked inside an altar in one of the side-chapels in the basilica of Occidens.

While the elder Shuturban was musing about the future of that gold, a tetchy camelopard had kicked him in the gut. His pain wouldn't subside. Some organ must have been ruptured. It was only when he went to Occidens to pray in that particular chapel, and when he vowed never to desecrate it, that he was healed miraculously.

The reliquary must still be there to this day. Due to religious rivalry, how long might the relic remain out of sight, unexamined – and maybe in time become forgotten? No pledge prevented his sons from disposing of the gold if someone else should choose to loot the altar.

Fifty side chapels were in that basilica. Some of the altars were of adamantium. One was of ivory, dedicated to the Emperor's teeth. The majority were of plasteel. In exchange for a half-share of the precious metal Chor Shuturban would tell Rakel which was the chapel. Rakel had promised to consider this offer.

'Logically,' Jaq declared, 'it should be the Chapel of His Thighs…'

Rakel had already arrived at the same conclusion. Occidens was open again to the public, after the paroxysm of the unveiling. On the way back from the Shuturbans' premises she had visited Occidens to pray her way around the so-called Stations of the Emperor, as hastily as was compatible with decorum.

Many body-bags of camelopard hide cluttered the basilica, unclaimed, the odour of decay almost masked by the prevalent sweet incense drifting from the atrium. Because pilgrims had died in adoration of the True Face, they merited a time of display in the basilica. Body-bags were all tied at the necks, exposing to scrutiny the head or remains of a head. This was for identification – yet also so that a miracle could be recognized. A corpse might remain uncorrupted, demonstrably blessed by Him-on-Earth. Invariably there were one or two such miracles. These miracles vindicated all the deaths which might otherwise have seemed, to a heretic, to mar the climactic ceremony of Holy Year.

In the basilica, unfortunately, there was one chapel dedicated to His Left Thigh, and another chapel to His Right Thigh.

'Do we flip a shekel?' asked Grimm after Rakel had delivered her report.

Jaq scowled at this irreverence. 'It will be the chapel sinister where they hid the bone. The left-hand one. Leftward is the side of formulae, occult science, guile – and secrets.'

Lex agreed. It was on the bones of his left hand that he had inscribed the names of dead Biff and Yeremi.

'The priests wouldn't disregard the customary symbolism,' Jaq stated.

RAKEL'S BEST ROUTE into Occidens would be through one of the apertures in the dome of the atrium, through which the smoke of incense vented. Clad in black, she would descend on a thin strong rope like a spider on its silk, then drop cat-like to the floor. At night, when the temple was closed, no armed deacons might be on patrol in the atrium of the basilica. She had noted that residents of the temple – as opposed to visitors – rarely glanced upwards. Upwards was wreathed in smoke.

From the atrium she would proceed silently into the basilica. Apply lock-picks to the plasteel altar. Heave out the reliquary, heavy with gold.

'Heavy on account of the femur too,' insisted Lex. 'Space Marine bones are big, and reinforced.'

Rakel glanced at him curiously, but did not question.

Next: open a body-bag.

'Hide the corpse away inside the altar?' queried Grimm.

'No,' said Jaq. 'That would be sacrilege.'

Put the reliquary inside the bag along with the body. Tie the bag up again. Return to the atrium. An accomplice would let down the rope for Rakel's retrieval.

'Am I to be on the rooftop?' Grimm demanded. 'What sort of solo test is this?'

Rakel smiled wanly. 'There'll be other ways into the temple. Sewers, for instance. I'm sure Chor Shuturban will tell me if we promise enough gold. Wouldn't we prefer to amaze him?'

She wasn't Meh'lindi. Meh'lindi would have found a way in through the sewers, contorting herself and dislocating her limbs if need be. Yet Rakel was cleverly analytical.

The morning after robbing the altar she would present herself at the temple accompanied by a burly slave. She would identify a head poking from the bag. She would weep with mingled grief and joy. The slave would help her carry the burden away.

And if the reliquary proved too large, even in its crushed state, why, the night before she would cut off the head of the corpse, hide the headless body, then fasten the head to the top of the reliquary. The reliquary would substitute for the body.

'Hide, where?' demanded Jaq.

'I'd hoped to make use of the altar,' Rakel said humbly.

'Sacrilege. Blasphemy.'

'Indeed,' said Lex.

'I suppose,' grumped Grimm, 'this means I might have to haul up this rotting headless corpse on the end of the rope after you've climbed it?'

'A thief uses every means she can,' said Rakel.

Jaq said sternly. 'You're attempting to manipulate us to compensate for what has happened to you.'

Rakel shrugged. 'I serve you,' she said flatly, 'in whatever way I best may.'

Jaq's eyes widened at this echo of his dead assassin-courtesan.

'It's a plausible plan,' he acknowledged.

'Just so long,' jeered Grimm, 'as you don't fasten yourself inside the body-bag as a way of getting out of the temple! Even with verdigris and cosmetic slime on your face the priests might decide you were uncorrupted, and a miracle. Ach, that prompts a thought. Don't you reckon a corpse that's getting a bit high might fall to pieces en route to the roof?'

'I shall take a net with me,' explained Rakel. 'A net with a narrow mesh. Plenty of suitable fishing nets are on sale in Shandabar.'

'A net with a corpse in it,' muttered Grimm. 'What a haul.'

'I feel corruption gathering around me,' Jaq murmured sombrely. He added very softly: 'As I suppose it must gather.'

'Cults,' continued Rakel. 'I was to ask about cults. There is a private society of lust in the Mahabbat district of Shandabar. Aphrodisiacs, orgies. Mardal Shuturban attends its debauches. And his brother has heard rumours of a cult of "transcendental alteration". Evidently some people aspire to evolve beyond our human condition.'

Grimm asked: 'Do these dental alterationists by any chance file their teeth to points so they look like genestealers' fangs?'

'Mardal has only heard vague rumours. My startling change in appearance seemed to explain my interest.'

'Could be a remnant of genestealer hybrids, boss.'

'Or else unwitting disciples of a certain Power, who foolishly imagine that evolutionary change is virtuous! Oh, the courthouse is surely all too lax in its investigations,' declared Jaq. 'Praise be that there is an inquisitor here, to test just how lax.'

THE NEXT NIGHT, two hours after midnight, Jaq and Lex were lurking amidst the piled-up wreckage of vendors' booths which had been demolished during the furore of the unveiling.

It was that hour when body and spirit are at their lowest ebb, the hour when people most frequently die in their sleep. This nocturnal ebb seemed especially melancholy in the great space fronting the temple. By now the flood of visiting pilgrims had quit the city. Where a throng of tents had been, only scattered beggars slumbered, their bodies fully covered against the cold, dead to the world. Maybe in the Mahabbat district vigorous beggars were still holding out hands to drunks departing from brothels, to lucky winners leaving gambling dens. But not here. Here, the inert shrouded beggars seemed to epitomize the exhausted *tristesse* of the city in the aftermath of the frantic climax to Holy Year. No one stirred. Not even a cough to be heard.

The sky-wide stipple of stars only feebly illuminated the temple square and the looming domes of Occidens. Deprived of his power armour and interface with its calculator, Lex could not see telescopically. No magnified image fed directly to his visual cortex now. He strained to perceive the obscure tiny figures of Grimm and Rakel upon the temple rooftops. Maybe he wasn't even seeing them at all, but only a trick of darkness and starlight. Maybe Grimm had already propped the ultra-light telescopic ladder against the dome above the atrium so as to reach the lowest vent. Maybe Rakel was already descending into smoky darkness, relieved only by a myriad pin-pricks of burning incense. Lex kept his enhanced ears alert for any outburst of gunfire.

How his hands itched to caress the thigh bone and to power up his graving tool. Such meditative peace of mind that would bring; such reverent serenity. Let the theft not fail. Theft, indeed! It was the restoration of a sacred bone into the rightful hands, so that Lex could honour whoever that Marine had been, dead for millennia perhaps. The exploit must succeed.

'With your permission,' he whispered to Jaq, 'I'm going up on to the roof in case there's trouble.'

'I shall pray there isn't,' was the reply.

A great shadow departed swiftly.

* * *

GRIMM'S EYES STUNG and watered as he peered down into the atrium. The rope had gone slack in his hairy hands. He had pulled it up a good way, in case some insomniac priest went a-wandering and noticed. The end of the rope was highwayman-hitched to a spur of stone with a knot Grimm had learned on a world of nomad herdsmen where highway trails were beaten out by hooves across vast grassy steppes, and where steeds were tethered thus for quick release. A steed could tug on its tether until it was blue in the face. A rider need only jerk on the end of the rope for the knot to collapse.

Even with keen squattish eyesight Grimm could hardly make out the grossest shapes below. He might have been peering through a porthole upon a smoggy fuming dark nebula in which tiny dimmed stars burned feebly at a vast depth. Mustn't silhouette himself too much, even so! Might seem like a voyeurish gargoyle. Bit like keeping watch down a chimney. Grimm suppressed a ticklish urge to hawk and spit phlegm.

IN THE BASILICA a thousand candles burned. Light waged its perpetual doomed war with darkness. Light must eventually fail, for darkness was a fundamental condition.

In such an array, inevitably many candles were guttering. Their flames leapt and faded, leapt and faded. Shadows quivered like insubstantial night-creatures infesting the side-chapels. Rakel, in black, was merely one such shadow.

An eroded legend read: *FEMUR SINISTR-- BENEDIC---*

Silently Rakel lifted from the altar a crystal monstrance resembling a supernova outburst. Next, some altar bells. Finally, an iron candelabrum in the shape of an upright battleship. She pulled away the altar brocade.

This plasteel altar had only been locked for a few decades. Tumblers yielded to her lock-picks. She raised the heavy lid.

WHAT A BURDEN the battered reliquary was! To shift it she had needed to climb inside the altar, then heave with all her might, using the lip of the altar as a fulcrum. But not before she had dragged a malodorous body-bag into position to act as a cushion to deaden the fall. Otherwise, the din of impact upon a flagstone would have rung throughout the basilica.

Now that the reliquary lay upon the floor, she scrutinized the dead woman's head. She memorized for the morrow the rictus of teeth and shrunken sunken eyes. She unknotted the throat-thong. She unpeeled the camelopard hide from the abused body. Although ten days deceased, the corpse seemed unlikely to fall apart yet.

With a monomolecular blade she severed the dead woman's head at the base of the neck. Grimm had contrived a hooking device.

One hook would anchor inside a gap in the reliquary. The other would lodge within the decapitated head of the corpse. Thus to fasten the two together.

Rakel had scarcely begun to thrust a hook up through one of the artery apertures in the base of the skull when a voice called out, 'Who being there?'

There in the chapel she crouched. She froze.

Sexton? Deacon? Priest? Footsteps were padding close.

'Being you, Jagan the Wakeful?'

Rakel had a laspistol. Firing the gun in itself would be silent. A hit would result in a bright explosion. If only the night had been thundery; but it wasn't.

What choice was there but to use the miniature needle-gun? This would fire a tiny sliver doped with powerful toxin. The target's body would convulse. He would choke and suffer stroke and heart-attack all at once. Hopefully he would fall with no more than a thump.

Why, now she was an assassin! As the snooper entered the chapel, she crooked a finger at his silhouette.

Instead of a noiseless mini-needle, a jet of chemicals spurted from the baroque ring. Igniting in the air, the volatile liquid wrapped the intruder's chest in flames – and he screamed. How he screamed. She had mistaken which digital weapon the needler was. If she had fired higher, her victim might instantly have sucked flame into his lungs and been unable to shriek.

Head thrown back, he howled in agony as he tried with seared hands to tear a burning cassock loose. He was a shrieking torch – a screeching illuminated alarm, capering away from her.

Time almost stood still. Each moment seemed so prolonged. Adrenalin was racing in Rakel. Discard the body-bag plan! Separate the relic from the bulk of the reliquary! Three seconds were becoming four. Already she was clawing with Grimm's hook at the once-glorious gold, prising and ripping. No one was responding to the screeching yet. Four seconds becoming five. How much longer, how much longer?

'OH MY ANCESTORS, how could I be so stupid!'

At the first ascent of that scream Grimm had let the gathered rope drop. A moment later he was over the lip of the vent. He crammed himself through the aperture. He slid down the rope at high speed, braking perfunctorily with his boots. If his hands hadn't been so calloused, he would surely have suffered ropeburn. What if he'd met Rakel ascending from the incense-pricked gloom? Some collision! However, she wasn't in the way.

He had crashed to a standstill. He had dashed across the colonnaded atrium. Immediately he spotted the screaming torch. He pounded past it.

He knelt beside Rakel, helping rip the reliquary apart, bless his tough hairy hands.

'Oh my grandsires, how could I be so dumb!'

Screeching only spasmodically now, the torch fell over. A lambent aura spread around him as though some psychic energy had come into play. Reflection of the flames from the flagstones?

'Ach!' At last the great femur came free from its ruptured golden container. Bit bulky, that bone, but far easier to shift on its own.

Here came trouble, in the shape of numerous scurrying figures in various states of dress and undress: temple personnel brandishing stunners, autoguns, shotguns, laspistols. Beware of those stunners especially. Priests might not be prepared to blast off shells and fragmentation shot amidst holy chapels.

That aura around the burning sexton! Why, the floor itself was softly on fire! Grease and soot deposited by generations of candles had ignited. Higher up the walls of the basilica there must be an even thicker skin. Dumping the thigh bone temporarily, Grimm fired his laspistol over the heads of the oncomers. Swivelling, he fired in other directions.

Las-fire bloomed dazzlingly upon the walls. With a soft whoosh, a lustrous and almost gentle flame rolled outward from the site of each explosion.

'Run for it, Rakel! Keep low!'

The temple-dwellers had halted to goggle up at this phenomenon which was spreading swiftly around the interior surface of their basilica. Those who held stunners were themselves stunned with awe. The whole edifice was becoming radiant as if itself it were a candle. Everywhere candle-flame glowed yet did not consume. Surely this was a miracle. Surely what had ignited it – its wick – was the dying sexton who still writhed. Him, and those other outbursts of psychic fire! Was this some visitation from the Emperor's spirit, some wondrous and unexpected epiphany for Holy Year?

As the miraculous flame spread across the great ceiling, in majestic yet seemingly undamaging fashion, beads of molten wax began to drip. The faces of those below were stung. A deacon wailed as hot wax hit his eye.

Realization dawned.

'Being fire!'

'Being arson!'

'Incendium!'

Grimm and Rakel reached the archway to the atrium. They were spotted. Heedless of damage to columns, someone opened fire with high-velocity shells. Reason deserted many minds. Were they all not now in a vast oven, beginning to be basted?

GRIMM AND RAKEL reached the rope. No time to unfold a fish-net for the relic.

'Climb, lady, climb!'

She began to ascend, hand over hand.

How could Grimm possibly shin up a rope with a great bone under one arm? Impossible!

The bone was far too big to clamp his teeth on to.

He limber-hitched the end of the rope around the bone. This was a scaffolder's knot for hoisting a spar. No sooner done than he began climbing after Rakel.

Wondrously, the rope was rising as he climbed. It was being hauled up powerfully, by a familiar superhuman winch which loomed over the vent above.

PURSUIT HAD ARRIVED among the forests of smoking incense-sticks. The disappearance of the fugitives bewildered the searchers briefly. Some dashed towards the oratory.

Could the intruders have taken wing? At last someone stared up into the smoke. *Something* was on the point of disappearing through a vent.

WARMTH WAFTED UPON Lex's face as first he hauled Rakel clear. He inhaled greasy combustion. Then Grimm came through the hole, followed by a tail of rope on which a great bone waggled to and fro. Shots followed soon after. Several shots winged through the vent, and skyward. Others exploded within, the lip of the vent serving as shield, and shrapnel sprayed downward. Reverently Lex unknotted the bone.

They left the rope, still hitched for quick-release. No point, now, in removing evidence of the means of access. Let furious deacons fix plasteel grilles across the dozen vents. Away across the rooftops they scrambled, to commence a circuitous descent.

JAQ HAD HEARD gunfire, muffled and faint. Armed men spilled from the portico. They were gesturing to one another to head around the side of the temple complex.

He aimed his laspistol from within the wreckage of the booths. Subvocalizing a prayer of forgiveness – since those people were the loyal disciples of Him-on-Earth – Jaq fired surgically. A modest energy blast toppled a target, though the man still squirmed and writhed.

Jaq fired again, and another man fell.

A high-velocity shot crashed into the timber near him, spraying splinters. Jaq withdrew. Ducking, he darted away through the darkness. Deacons and sextons would be busy for a while, shooting at wood.

A COUPLE OF hours later, they had rendezvoused back at the mansion…

Lex sat upon a black slate floor with the thigh bone across his lap. That bone was pitted with antiquity. Lex's fingers roved over it as though it were some musical instrument which had lost its strings. Before he could begin engraving he would need to sand the bone finely then immerse it in hot paraffin wax to seal its pores and thus prevent the ink of the designs from bleeding. Meanwhile, he caressed this sacred femur with a sense of serene inner joy. Might it even once have belonged to an Imperial Fist, several aeons ago? Rather than to a Blood Angel or a Space Wolf or whomever else. Probably not. Yet no matter.

'I'm obliged to you,' he told the false Meh'lindi.

'And I to you,' she said, 'for pulling up the rope so quickly.'

'Huh,' said Grimm. 'Took three of us to steal a bone, and no gold at all. Besides setting fire to the temple.' The little man shrugged. 'Set fire to a chimney to clean it!' The flames had been superficial. That sooty grease must have consumed itself or been extinguished by beating. Otherwise, the night sky would have glowed with the bonfire of Occidens.

Deacons would have found the ripped reliquary, empty of its relic. This must seem to have been a religious, sectarian raid. Staged by whom? By Oriens loyalists? Hard to imagine who those might be! Not after genestealer infestation, and thorough cleansing, and all the subsequent decades. So was the raid mounted by the Austral temple? That's where the finger of suspicion might point, provoking a bitter and futile religious feud…

Had Rakel been tested sufficiently? Had the robbery proved to be partly a fiasco? Brave endeavours were often derailed; yet all four participants were safe, and remained incognito.

'Tomorrow,' Jaq said to Rakel, 'you will go to those Shuturban brothers bearing a ruby more precious than gold, prised from our book. Tell those Shuturbans that you found the ruby along with the reliquary. Say that the gold was merely gilding over soft copper. Buy any details about the courthouse, especially where data is stored. Local builders were employed.'

Grimm grinned encouragingly. 'Best plan once you're inside the courthouse might be to knife an Arbitrator and steal his black gear and mirror-mask. You'd better practise your exercises, mock assassin.'

Jaq was staring at the counterfeit woman with such bitter wistfulness. Of course she must assassinate some official while inside the courthouse! What other course of action would a devout inquisitor require to galvanize judges in their duties? What else would sow confusion and paranoia amongst them?

DURING THE NIGHT, yet again, Jaq dreamed of Askandargrad, ravaged and ravished...

Raven Guards, in their black power armour, were advancing through smouldering ruins, their boltguns ready to fire at whatever moved. Many brothers were also armed with chainswords.

Whatever moved could only be an enemy – whose joy was to kill, but especially, and lustfully so, by rushing in close with power sword or chainsword. Lethal close contact was the delight of these devil-Marines – an erotic, sadistic impulse which sometimes impelled them to berserk recklessness.

So long as a Raven kept calm, these assaults could be ideal opportunities to kill or cripple a renegade.

How could one keep calm? Chaos spawn scuttled, spiderlike, over the smoky terrain. How nauseating if these creatures leapt at a Raven, to cling to his armour. They could hardly harm a Marine in armour, but they could disorient. Worse, and far more sickening and dangerous, were the daemonettes.

Their exquisite single breasts. Their lush thighs and loins. Their green eyes – uncannily elongated – and their manes of blonde hair. The razor-sharp pincers of their hands! And the barbed tails which sought to impale!

To be assaulted by such a creature was sickening, dizzying, destabilizing to a devout Marine. Daemonettes materialized as accomplices of renegades. Daemonettes were manifestations of the vicious lusts of the Chaos brood.

Along with a captain of the Raven Guard, Jaq wearily surveyed the advance from the low roof of a warehouse. Hooded ventilators were like monkish sentries to Jaq's eyes. He hadn't slept for fifty hours or more. Neighbouring buildings had collapsed, forming ramps of rubble. The destruction was disproportionate. Numbers of the iniquitous legionnaires were now hosting daemons, daemons with powers, whose joy was to destroy people if possible, but people's property too, so it seemed, so that their victims should be as nakedly vulnerable as could be, utterly defenceless. To the Legionnaires of Slaanesh the battle was an orgy of foul delight.

The captain had been scanning rune displays within his visor of the disposition of his own men.

'The Emperor's Children!' he exclaimed bitterly to Jaq. Those renegades had been merely a dark item of history to him, until now. 'How dare these fiends still call themselves by such a title! Our Emperor protects the innocent.' He whispered hauntedly, 'Daemons are in their ranks. Such hideous blasphemy!'

Was this superbly trained man approaching snapping point? Badges of honour upon his inky-black armour told of past heroism. A scorch mark blistered his shoulder pauldron. His back-banner had been shot to shreds.

'We will win,' the captain assured Jaq. 'We *must* win.'

For if not, then his badges and those of his men would be taken as trophies; and worse, far worse, organs and hormones would be extracted from the corpses of the Ravens to create drugs of delirium.

Shrieking, a daemonette pranced up the ramp of rubble ahead of…

…that must be a *chaplain of Chaos!*

The armour was rampantly adorned with male-and-female runes of Slaanesh, and with obscene hermaphroditic insignia. That armour shimmered unnaturally, wreathed in baleful energies. This wasn't only a chaplain of Chaos, but a chaplain possessed. He had given himself as host to a daemon, or he had summoned one. The chainsword in his hand shrieked as if in sweet torment. His boltgun jutted phallically and spat a bolt. The bolt penetrated a ventilator column close by the captain. It ripped right through the backside of the shaft, swooshing onward before exploding belatedly in mid-air.

Forcing himself to ignore the onrushing daemonette, who was now so close, the captain fired back at the perverted chaplain. Those energies which cloaked the chaplain seemed to catch the bolt and sling it far away.

Praying and summoning his psychic power. Jaq aimed the sleek black force rod, in the use of which he had quite recently been trained. Embedded with a few arcane circuits, the force rod was a solid flute, virtually featureless.

'Begone into the warp!' Jaq yelled.

The flute discharged.

The daemonette pitched forward. She wrapped herself into a ball – of buttocks and barbed tail and clawing arms, hugging herself. The knotty ball of daemonic anatomy bounded up the rubble, bounce after bounce.

Of a sudden the ball was shrinking, ever so swiftly.

Only something the size of a pea bounced towards Jaq's boot – and he crushed it.

Another bolt from the captain of Ravens failed to penetrate the chaplain's defences. Waving that chainsword, the chaplain came onward. He did not trouble to fire another bolt. His rabid desire was to carve through the captain's armour intimately, not kill from a distance.

Jaq directed his force rod. Could he summon another discharge of sufficient power so soon after the first? He prayed to the Emperor. He exerted all his will.

The rod throbbed.

An orange glow, as of a ship entering atmosphere, engulfed the chaplain. Billows of orange hue swept away behind him, curling and coiling and evaporating. His armour was being stripped of its devilish occult shield.

The captain fired, *RAAARK, RAAARK.*

CRUMP, CRUMP. The bolts impacted, detonated.

The chaplain lurched. He reeled.

Dropping the rod, Jaq snatched up his own boltgun and added his fire to the captain's.

The chaplain's breastplate had burst open. Scarlet blood welled. The blood did not harden to cinnabar, as was the way with a regular Space Marine's blood. It coagulated into bright wobbling jelly, as if polyps were emerging from that mutated man. The chainsword fell from one hand; the bolter from the other. The armoured monstrosity toppled, crashing upon rubble.

'We *will* win!' vowed the captain.

JAQ AWOKE, DISORIENTED. Night pressed upon him, dark as Raven armour.

Ah. Sabulorb... Shandabar...

So far in time and space from Askandar.

The Raven Guards had indeed ousted the Emperor's Children from that city, and from that world. At much cost.

There was always cost. Casualties were often appalling in the brave struggle to hold dissolution at bay. The fight could only be waged savagely. Anyone who had witnessed the rape of Askandargrad could imagine the universal horrors – multiplied a million-fold – if Chaos were to ravish the whole galaxy with slaughter and plague and depravity, with anarchy and mutation.

Closing his eyes again, Jaq meditated wretchedly about the Emperor's Children, tools of Slaanesh. They were no children of Him-on-Earth now! Biologically they never had been, except in the sense that the Emperor's scientists had created their gene-seed. As for the Emperor's true children – his immortal Sons – *did they even truly exist?*

SEVEN
ORGY

THE SHUTURBAN BROTHERS were duly impressed by the ruby. Word had already reached them of a fracas outside the Occidens Temple – and undoubtedly within as well, and perhaps involving a fire, so it seemed. Two residents of the temple had been shot outside its walls. Searchers had climbed up on to the rooftops. In the morning the sextons hadn't opened the temple doors as usual. Worshippers had queued in vain.

Evidently one of the beggars who lived in the vast courtyard had been alert enough to make his way across the city to the Shuturbans.

Rakel the Thief now wished for certain details about the Imperial courthouse. Was there no limit to her enterprises?

The Shuturbans' source had noticed a robed man fleeing from the vicinity of Occidens; while another beggar had told the same informant how he had spied a giant and a dwarf in the vicinity that night…

Details about the courthouse were possible – such a fine ruby was persuasive. However, Chor Shuturban insisted on giving such information to Rakel in the presence of her mysterious patron – whose existence she could not reasonably deny. Chor wished to meet this new sponsor of crime. The new-style Rakel had left her former lodgings in a hurry. A wagging tongue said that a giant slave had escorted her away.

The meeting should be on neutral ground. Rakel had been curious about cults of lust, hadn't she? Therefore the neutral ground should be a certain building in the Mahabbat district a week hence. Rakel's sponsor, and herself, were invited to an *entertainment*.

Chor assured Rakel that there was no obligation to join in the frolics physically. Entirely up to herself and her patron! The giant and the dwarf could come too. Those two might be amusing performers.

'CHOR SHUTURBAN HOPES to unsettle our minds,' said Jaq, 'so that one of us may be indiscreet.'

Yet did he himself not wish his sanity to be unsettled and deranged?

'My mind is staunch against carnal temptations,' declared Lex. Now he had the thigh bone to caress if need be. Already Lex had begun to prepare the femur for scrimshaw, by sanding and waxing. While he worked he would pray to Rogal Dorn, silently in case Rakel overheard his prayers.

Grimm pouted. 'Huh, that a squat like me should join in some orgy with regular human beings! Slim chance. If there were some sturdy females of my kind I might be tempted.'

To WAIT A whole week was frustrating – though it would take the Shuturban brothers a week to marshal the information which Rakel had requested. In the meanwhile, though, there was much to be done.

Rakel filched a hypno-casque from the Mercantile College in the southerly Saudigar district. This posed no special challenge to her talents; but a casque was needed. The data-disc in this particular casque was programmed with standard Imperial Gothic, for the use of exporters who intended to travel off-world. Jaq discarded the disc.

Next, Rakel stole a laser-scalpel from the Hakim Hospitalery. Grimm bought certain equipment in the industrial district. Lex rigged up an imaging system so that he could observe Azul Petrov's warp-eye without looking at it directly.

Might the eye still be lethal to the beholder when viewed on a screen? Proof was provided by a leper whom Grimm led blindfolded by a roundabout route to the mansion on promise of fifty shekels which would buy the wretch consecrated ointments at the same Hakim Hospitalery.

This leper wasn't one of those whose disease had begun to attack his nerves painfully. Hitherto, the leprosy had robbed him of almost all bodily sensation – which he prayed that the ointment might restore. Did the leper fear ill treatment at his unknown destination? His hosts, if ill-intentioned, could hardly make him suffer greatly, since much of his necrofying flesh was already so numb.

Within an unseen room a large hood was put over his head and the blindfold removed. Before the leper's eyes, sharing the vacancy within the hood, was a small display screen. He was simply told to stare at that screen, and to describe what he saw.

'Being a black ball,' the leper had said. 'Being held in a clamp. The front of the ball being carved with a shape, with a rune–'

'Continue staring into the ball.'

After ten minutes of staring without apoplexy, the leper was blind-folded once again, and led back to the vicinity of the Hospitalery, and released – with fifty shekels in his mutilated paw indeed.

Evidently the dwarf who had accosted him had been a miraculous intercessor in his destiny.

Out of curiosity, Grimm had hung around the entrance to the hospi-tal. Half an hour later a hideous leper, now naked but for a loin cloth, had lurched out, shrieking, screaming for water to be thrown over him, crying to anyone that his body was on fire. The consecrated ointment must certainly have stimulated his numb flesh and nerves. In default of water the leper writhed in the chilly dust of the street to cool himself in vain.

While the thigh bone was soaking in paraffin wax, Lex set to work on Azul's eye with the laser-scalpel. Lex had no calculator to assist with gra-dients and curves – and he had to study the process on screen, not directly – yet his beefy hands were dextrous and fastidious. It would have been a wonder to stand by and to watch him – if an accidental glimpse of the actual eye might not have ravaged the observer's nervous system or killed him outright. Lex himself wore blinker-goggles so as to prevent any inadvertent glance aside.

For the sake of symmetry of the lens, the rune on the front of the eye must needs be pared away. What of it? That rune was a guide to the Black Library in the webway – to which they did not wish to return.

Ah, how Jaq's ordo would crave to possess such a guide.

The Inquisition and the Ordo Malleus must needs be disappointed – though before commencing Lex did take the precaution of copying the rune on to camelopard vellum. If in future some other Navigator was willing to sacrifice the broad spectrum of his warp vision, a replica might be made upon that volunteer's eye.

Surely no one in the cosmos had ever before made a monocle out of a Navigator's warp-eye!

The resulting lens should be slim enough for Jaq to see through, if need be. Finally enough material had been shaved away from the obsid-ian-hard eye for a murky lens to be slotted inside a fat monocle frame, with thickly enamelled covers hinged at front and back.

Would the killing gaze of the warp-eye be greatly diminished by the removal of so much substance? Or would the lens prove to be a quintessence, a lethal concentrate?

'Doubt if we can bring the same leper back here,' Grimm remarked. 'Probably drowned himself in the Bihishti by now. Still, I 'spose it has to be a person we expose, just to be sure, not another damn monkey...' The little man scratched his head and grinned. 'No need to do it here at home, though. You and me, Jaq, we should go for a walk in a dodgy neighbourhood and await some trouble. Then it'll be the fool's own fault.'

Not a walk in company with Lex. His physique would be a big deterrent. A walk with Rakel, on the other hand...

Thus it was that the three had set out for the industrial area, the Bellagunge district. Jaq wore his mesh armour under his robe. Grimm trusted as ever in his quilted flak-jacket. Rakel wore a shimmery silken blue gown over a clinging thermal undergarment. *She* would not be an immediate target for knife or bullet. For attempted abduction. For outrage. But not instantly for murder.

Jaq strolled arm-in-arm with Rakel, flaunting her like some seigneur with his courtesan. Grimm trailed a little way behind, a stunted dogsbody.

The smoky factory slums of the Bellagunge district were home to hundreds of thousands of souls. Any little factory producing a component for vehicles would be habitation to the whole family who worked there. The street immediately outside would accommodate another family busily manufacturing nails by cutting and sharpening wire. Around the corner would be a dozen other enterprises, busily soldering or laminating or dipping wing-nuts into noxious fluids to galvanize them. Each sweatshop jealously guarded its cluttered territory. Inside and outside the rickety buildings, equipment rumbled and thumped and throbbed and vented smoke and fumes. Conversation was conducted in shouts. Coughing was endemic. Sellers of water and sherbet and fish pasties contributed to the hubbub.

For someone obviously rich to saunter through this ants' nest of industry was to invite attack sooner or later.

The giant sun hung above the fumes like a red-hot lid. Indeed, because of all the spewing fumes and hectic machinery, Bellagunge was a few degrees warmer than the rest of chilly Shandabar. Many labourers would habitually strip off their calico *dungris*.

Presently, in an alley, four skinny fellows accosted Jaq and Rakel and Grimm. Those waylayers had been trailing after the trio for a while. Now they had taken a shortcut to bring them ahead.

Stub guns emerged from the rags of two of the opportunists. The two others produced gaudy swords shaped like meat-cleavers. Evidently the sword blades were of plastic – sharp flexible plastic, its substance dyed a streaky blood-red in the manufacture so as to convey a menacing impression of butchery. One red blade bore the motif of a green snake's head poised to strike. On the other was a baleful green eye.

An eye. How auspicious. How appropriate.

Grimm laughed.

Did Jaq's hooded monocle lend him a foppish rather than a sinister appearance? 'If being wise,' he drawled, 'getting out of my way.'

'Your way ending here,' was the reply, 'unless that woman accompanying us for sale in Mahabbat.' The speaker had been chewing blood-nuts. He spat a scarlet splash into the dust.

'If being wise,' warned Jaq again.

Another man waggled his sword. 'Being blind in *both* eyes?' he enquired.

The first man had tired of dialogue. He fired his stub gun at Jaq's chest, that being the broadest target.

Under Jaq's punctured robe his mesh armour had stiffened instantly, absorbing and spreading the impact. Compared with a hit from an explosive bolt the blow had been almost trivial. The squashed bullet fell at Jaq's feet.

Another slug hit Jaq as he drew his laspistol and fired. The erupting energy packet threw the gunman backwards. The other dumbfounded gunman fell to a shot from Grimm. Snakeblade turned tail, and was hit in the back. One remained: the man with the eyeblade.

'Not moving! Or lasering your legs!'

And thus becoming a cripple.

For a moment the man glared at Rakel as if he was tempted to hurl his sword at her to deny the silk-clad woman to the rich trespasser, or at least to deface her.

'Dropping your sword!' bellowed Jaq.

The man complied. Kneeling, he babbled for mercy. Grimm moved behind the fellow. He knelt on his calves to pin him. He clamped the man's wrists behind his back. Then he shut his own eyes as if it were the squat who awaited execution.

Jaq knelt in the rubbish-strewn dust in front of the captive. One-eyed, Jaq stared at the shivering subject of their experiment.

At this stage Jaq did not intend to look through the lens which had been Azul Petrov's warp-eye. Such an extremity must be reserved for a time when, possessed, he must gape at himself in a mirror and either purge a daemon from his mind, or else die in the effort. He simply flipped up the front cover. Of course the captive stared to see what such a cover had been hiding.

A gurgling arose from deep in the man. It was as if his very soul was being heaved loose from somewhere in his belly – along with all the breath from his lungs. The man's eyes bulged, haemorrhaging pinkly. A death-rattle choked into silence as he swallowed his tongue. His face became puce. His scrawny frame spasmed.

Jaq lowered the lid over the lens. He removed the monocle and slipped it inside his robe.

'You can look again, Grimm.'

Grimm released the man's wrists, and the body fell forward. Then Grimm picked up the eye-blade and thumped it into the dying man's back, almost up to the hilt.

'Looks more natural this way.' The little man nodded towards a small knot of spectators further along the alley.

They departed from Bellagunge without hindrance. Jaq no longer linked with Rakel. Yet she still walked alongside him. The blue gown she wore must be hateful to a thief. It was so revealing.

'Tod Zapasnik the sorcerer,' she muttered.

'You know very well,' he said sharply, 'that it was merely the nucleus of a Navigator's warp-eye which killed the man.'

'Merely,' she echoed. She shivered despite her fight thermals. 'What sort of merely will there be when we go to Mahabbat where I would have been sold by those ruffians?'

'Listen, Meh'lindi,' he told her, 'we shan't be participating in the debauch.'

He realized how he had addressed Rakel. His expression anguished, he strode on in silence.

To TRAVEL TO the Mahabbat district, they had hired a limousine. Security men in cheap grey flak armour mingled with the crowds outside the pleasure houses, of gambling and gourmandizing and lust and drugs. Illuminated signs flashed.

COMING TO MAHABBAT, COMING TO DELIGHT!
HYGIENIC EUNUCHS HERE!
JOY-JUICE JUST FIFTY SHEKELS A JAG!
WINNING A MILLION!
HAVING SPECIAL NEEDS?
HEAVENLY HUSSIES!

Copper-skinned, with piercing blue eyes and hooked noses, those security men all seemed to hail from the same clan or tribe. None were particularly young. All wore their black hair gathered up in a topknot, like a big shiny button upon their crowns.

'Armour looks like a job-lot of cast-offs from the Imperial Guard,' opined Grimm.

Sabulorb, of course, contributed its tithe of a regiment of its best fighters to the Imperium: specialists, in this case, in cold desert warfare. The Sabulorb regiments would be elsewhere in the cosmos. These men must have served their term of duty and returned to their homeworld. The branch-office of the Departmento Munitorum which supervised recruiting wasn't here in the capital but on another, harsher continent to the north. There in the north was the main base for the planetary army, which Lord Badshah preferred to keep well away from the capital. In case of emergency, troops could be airlifted to reinforce the garrison in Shandabar. Meanwhile the bulk of the army suppressed various recalcitrant warring tribes, and press-ganged new soldiery, the best of whom would be sent off-world.

The private patrolmen toted autoguns but they smiled at passing patrons. They smiled at Jaq's party when the four alighted from that limousine with tinted windows. Evidently interstellar experiences had accustomed these former Imperial Guardsmen to the sophisticated pleasures of a city, although none of them could have been soft men to have survived their military years.

The domed edifice to which the Shuturban brothers had invited Rakel and her sponsor was known as the House of Ecstasy. A fat, gold-braided flunky escorted the visitors into the main chamber. Erotic holographs shimmered languidly amidst the clientele seated at drinks-dispensing tables. Upon a central dais male and female acrobats performed suggestively. The air was heady with musk and patchouli.

Through this main chamber they passed, onward to the Sensuality Suite, which was reserved for special guests and private parties.

The floor of this suite was of rosy velvet padding, cushioned and supple. Soft low couches bulged, as much a part of the floor as a bosom is of the anatomy. Upon these velvet bosoms there lolled some fifty expectant pleasure-seekers dressed in multicoloured silks. Most were men of middle years. A few were mature women. Lighting was dim and rosy. A nymphette whose limbs and torso were painted with black spirals circulated, carrying a luminous tray of inhalants. Each step she took across the flexible floor made her body seem to pulse, spring-like.

'Please be discarding shoes and boots, good sirs...'

Lex had no boots to remove. How different this sybaritic den was from the plasteel decks of a fortress-monastery.

How different, save for the crepuscular lighting, from the funereal interior of Jaq's lost *Tormentum Malorum*.

'Didn't wash my feet,' mumbled Grimm, embarrassed, as he hauled off his big combat boots.

'Ah,' breathed Rakel, 'there are the Shuturbans–'

Two men arose from a soft divan. Both had curly dark hair, broad brows, large liquid eyes, snub noses and gleaming grins. Several teeth were of gold. Extravagant moustaches separated grins from the bantam noses.

'Chor's the stouter one.' The sly one. On Chor's right cheek was a tattoo of a camelopard which seemed to trot on the spot whenever he flexed his facial muscles.

His quick-tempered brother sported a scar on his right cheek. Sewn to the scar was a large deep-red fire-garnet. This carbuncle seemed like a permanent eruption of lava from within him.

'Be relaxing with us,' invited Chor.

Jaq and the giant and the abhuman and the thief-lady in her blue silks were soon ensconced in a half-circle of supple divans, along with the two Shuturbans. On behalf of his party Jaq refused inhalants from the springy nymphette. Lex restricted any responses to gutter-grunts. Grimm eyed the nymphette derisively. No girth to her!

'Robbing the Occidens Temple of a sacred bone belonging to Oriens,' probed Chor.

Jaq nodded dismissively towards Lex. 'A bone for my mastiff to be chewing on. We were testing Rakel's skills.'

'She being quite altered from when we were first knowing her.'

'Home world being planet of shape-shifters.'

'So she was telling us.' Chor leaned forward. 'You being magician of change? Rakel asking us about transcendental alterationists.'

'Those being whereabouts?'

'Identity still being whelmed in mystery, Sir Tod.'

'A fine ruby buying much information.' As Jaq glanced at the garnet on Mardal Shuturban's cheek, a surge of fury seemed to course through the brother. Did Mardal suppose that Jaq was comparing the garnet unfavourably with a ruby? The brother seized a bulb of inhalant from the passing nymphette and crushed it under his nostril, breathing deep.

'Coming here to be relaxing,' Mardal remarked. 'Discharging tensions.'

Chor probed some more. Jaq riposted. Chor waggled a ringed finger. Upon the ring, like a signet stamp, was a half-shekel-sized data disc. Evidently the plans of the courthouse were recorded in that disc. Before surrendering the ring Chor wanted to know more. Yet he seemed in no great hurry.

A door irised open – and the waiting hedonists sighed as an attendant pushed a balloon-wheeled cage into the chamber.

Squatting in the cage was a blind mutant woman. As the contraption rolled forward onto the springy floor, she clutched the bars to steady herself. Her body was scaly. Its texture was that of the mesh-armour which Jaq had worn again tonight. Maybe that woman was actually dressed in a tight body-stocking of lizard-skin fabric rather than her skin itself being squamous – for her white face was smooth. Hard to tell in the dim light.

Then it became evident that the woman's legs were fused together below her hips. Snakelike they curled and tapered around her, seemingly made only of muscle without bone. Her eyes were balls of boiled albumen – very like an astropath's who had undergone soul-binding! Glittering bangles adorned her arms.

'Lamia, Lamia!' the clientele greeted her.

Why was she caged? So that she should not squirm out amongst them? So that the clientele should not invade her personal space? So that she might keep a grip on herself, assisted by bars? What was her role?

She swayed to and fro hypnotically.

The mutant woman must project erotic illusions into people's minds! Was this how she had escaped being smothered at birth when her worm-body emerged? By seducing her parents she had survived... Was this also how she had escaped being killed by neighbours or priests or mutant-hunters? When she grew to adolescence, had she actually been acquired for astropathic training despite her deformity? Had she even been soul-bound, resulting in her loss of eyesight and enhancement of her telepathic talent?

Jaq strove to imagine her functioning as a regular astropath, transmitting and receiving coded messages or streams of commercial data.

Compelled from her earliest moments to sway minds sensually in order to survive, yet with physical gratification forever denied her by the frustrating fusion of her legs, what a powerhouse of libido she must be!

'Lamia being here,' the snake-woman called out in a sinuous and caressing voice. 'Letting all your secret desires loose. Becoming tangible to your nerves.'

Oh, she was no caged and exploited freak, this snake-woman! Not at all. She was a veritable madame, a queen bawd of the inner sanctum of the House of Ecstasy.

'That's Bhati Badshah over there,' confided Chor with a nod at a lascivious-looking fellow sporting large hooped silver earrings. Dangling gymnastically from those hoops, one could just make out miniature nude manikins of a shining iridescent icy blue – crafted of titanium, no doubt. 'One of our lord governor's nephews...'

High society indeed!

This was not to be the debauch which Jaq had expected. It was to be a mind-debauch. To refrain from participating might not prove so easy at all. Jaq could resist the snake-woman's sendings psychically – if he chose to. What of Grimm, or Lex, or Rakel?

Already, the sexual séance was beginning. Under Jaq's clothing fingers seemed to rove over his flesh, caressing him. It mattered not that he wore a corset of mesh-armour. Those immaterial fingers were not deterred. How did they know so cleverly which nerves to tease and stimulate? Why, because he himself knew. He had been touched thus by Meh'lindi, trained courtesan that she was – as well as assassin.

Was it Meh'lindi who was now communicating dumbly with him from beyond the grave – in a tactile wordless language, imperative and enchanting? Was her succubus hovering only a membrane away from him? Would total surrender to her embrace drag her closer to existence once more?

Or could this open the way to possession by a daemon of lust? Aye, right here and now. Jaq had seen Vitali Googol succumb to Slaaneshi possession. Jaq had been within the doomed Navigator's aura when a daemonette ravished Vitali. Oh to become possessed right here, raging with lust – and yet somehow to stagger to a mirror, to pull the eye-lens from within his robe, to uncap it, to stare his possessed self in the eye, withering the daemon, banishing it back into the warp! Thus to become illuminated! Might this be possible?

Phantom fingers roved all over Jaq so sweetly and tormentingly.

He began to pray in the hieratic language. '*Veni, Voluptas! Evoe, oh appetitus, concupisco lascive!*' Such a prayer he had never prayed before. It was the opposite of any devout prayer to Him-on-Earth in His everlasting suffering. A summoning of lust personified.

All around him, celebrants in this obscene rite were moaning. Most were oblivious to one another. Several had rolled over and were writhing upon velvet couch or soft velvet floor. Others lay back, panting as imaginary bodies of delight conjoined with them.

Dimly Jaq understood that the snake-woman in her self-appointed cage was soaking up the feedback of fevered fantastical sensations. The cage served to restrain her from squirming forth futilely amidst the wallowing bodies, losing control of her own psycho-erotic energy. If this were to happen, daemons of lust might very well heed. They might speed here to this beacon. They could displace the succubi of one's own imagination with materializing daemonic forms, given substance by the conversion of that energy. Jaq was on the very verge of invoking this, as he extended his psi sense in monstrous invitation.

Rakel was squirming in her own delirium.

Grimm was gasping, 'Grizzle, Grizzle!' That dead wife of Grimm's must have been genuine, after all.

Lex's left hand was slapping his face violently. His lips resolutely framed the name: *Rogal Dorn!*

Mardal Shuturban was grinning and drooling with joyous abandon. His brother Chor was still alert.

Of a sudden Lamia shrieked out:

'One is here who has known no woman ever since he was transformed into a superhuman! Another is here who lusts for a Lady of Death–'

How Chor Shuturban harked to Lamia.

Aspects of the Chaos God of Lust were gathering. They were on the verge of seizing a channel – and of manifesting in the flesh. In Jaq's flesh? Or in someone else's?

Wretched sanity clawed Jaq back from the brink. Resisting the immaterial fingers, he drew the force rod from within his robe. Too late.

Within her cage Lamia reared. She mewed loudly and lewdly. The snake-woman was being possessed! Because Jaq had resisted, the powers of Chaos were entering the vortex of Lamia's psycho-erotic energy.

Sighs of ecstasy were changing pitch to cries of painful pleasure as if sharp fingernails were raking bodies now.

Lex was shaking Rakel like a rag doll to restore her senses. Then he belaboured Grimm, sufficient to bruise though not to break bones.

Lines of blood appeared upon the silks of the pleasure-seekers, as unseen razor-claws stimulated their bodies with a delicious perversity. Blood was beginning to soak silk and velvet.

The garnet of Mardal Shuturban's cheek was aglow. Passions overwhelmed him. In a paroxysm he launched himself at his other self – at Chor. Mardal's thumbs thrust at Chor's eyeballs. Chor screamed in agony, too devastated by pain to know how to resist. Mardal was frothing at the mouth. He kissed his brother in a crescendo of vile rapture. His thumbs were pressing harder, to break through into the brain, into the ultimate communion with another.

Lamia was about to burst from her cage, to try to walk upright upon her mutant tail.

Lex seized Chor's flailing hand. He failed to pull the ring loose. Unwilling to snap off the data-disc in case he damaged it, Lex bowed his head over Chor's hand. When Lex raised his head moments later, Chor was lacking a finger. Lex had bitten off finger and ring. Chor's mutilated hand was limp. Chor was dead by now, or had been reduced to imbecility by the squashing of brain tissue. Mardal roared, enraged. His thumbs were trapped in the bony bloody orbits of his brother's skull.

Summoning heartfelt revulsion, Jaq discharged his force rod at the cage. Energies coruscated. A wild flashing of lurid rays illuminated the velvet chamber and jerking bodies stroboscopically. A caul of jagged lightning surrounded Lamia. Then it imploded inwards to swallow itself, and her soul.

Rushing shapes of light remained loose in the padded chamber. Bright dancing silhouettes!

Jaq discharged his rod again, more weakly. Lex was hauling up Rakel and Grimm, one in each hand like marionettes. The motion he imparted taught them to stagger, then to regain use of their limbs.

The main door had opened. The same gold-braided flunky gaped disbelievingly into the Sensuality Suite. Sprawling moaning bloodstained bodies seemed to be proof of attempted massacre rather than massage. A glowing silhouette rushed at him. The servant shrieked in alarm.

The silhouette popped out of existence.

As Jaq and Lex, still lugging wobbly Grimm and Rakel, burst past the flunky into the main chamber, silhouettes followed them. As moths to candle-flames the silhouettes flew towards the posturing erotic holograms. The holograms altered. Eyes were slanted and swollen and green. From gorgeous rumps barbed tails sprouted.

Panic erupted. Tables overturned. A bell began to clang.

This alarm quickly brought a pair of the copper-skinned security men with those big black buttons of oiled hair on their craniums.

Such a melee there was in the House of Ecstasy! Such horror at the floorshow! Leaping onto tables, and bellowing, 'Down, down!' the ex-Guardsmen aimed their autoguns at the hideously mutated holograms. Jaq and party ducked behind a larger-than-lifesize nude female figure of solid white marble. The high-velocity shells passed straight through the holograms, impacting in walls, and into the bodies of the clientele. Chips flew off of the marble giantess as a couple of shells caroomed off the statue.

The live acrobats had ceased their act. Were they not part of the floorshow, which had so terrified the clientele? Shells killed several of the acrobats – even as the fearful holograms were winking out of existence one by one.

* * *

ON THE WAY back to their mansion in the limousine Lex spat out the finger from his mouth. They were separated from the driver by a privacy screen, and insulated fragilely from Shandabar by smoked glass.

Rakel had recovered her voice.

'That could be a Finger of Glory,' she declared, 'if Tod's a true magician–'

'*I am not that,*' snarled Jaq. He had rejected the opportunity which came so terribly close and so unexpectedly.

'Hey, what's a Finger of Glory?' asked Grimm.

'It's a finger from someone who died abominably,' she said. 'You pickle it during suitable invocations. You dry it. If later you light it, it'll show your way and at the same time hide your presence – until it burns out.'

'Just the ticket,' said Grimm, 'for breaking into a courthouse.'

'Superstition,' snarled Lex. He half-closed his left fist, and whispered into it, 'Biff and Yeremi, you aided me back there. I bless your names; and Rogal Dorn's...'

'Not a superstition,' murmured Jaq. 'A morsel of effective daemonry. So I believe.'

'There is only one glory,' Lex affirmed, 'and that is the Column of Glory in His palace on Earth.' There, where the skulls of long-dead Imperial Fists grinned from their shattered armour embedded nobly in a tower half a kilometre high.

'I'll need new boots specially made for me, damn it,' said Grimm. For he and Jaq and Rakel were still as barefoot as Lex.

ALL FOUR WERE shaken by what had happened in the House of Ecstasy. Morale required a feast from Grimm. Fine foods such as imported grox tongues should be accompanied by the best local *djinn* and strong ale.

Initially, it was Grimm who mainly indulged in the *djinn*. Rakel followed his lead. Would the real Meh'lindi ever have allowed herself to become intoxicated, as Rakel was becoming? Jaq sipped, since he had sanctioned this indulgence. Lex also drank the fiery spirit ceremonially, to be detoxed by his special organs.

Presently Grimm, well in his cups, began to hiccup.

'Oh, ancestors – *hic* – I think it's my name-day today. Oh well – *haec* – if it ain't today it must be sometime–'

'Remember your body,' Lex reproved him.

The little man bridled. 'Is your body a temple of glory? Well – *hoc* – in that case mine's a hog-pen. Who cares? When there's havoc, a hog-pen can often outlast a temple.' Grimm raised his glass. 'Here's to you,

Lex, in your temple! Here's to the Sons of the Emperor, wherever they may be, assuming – *hic* – they're anywhere. Here's to them conniving Illuminati. Here's to you, boss!'

Abruptly Jaq seized a flagon of ale – and drank, and drank, to disorder his senses. He swigged from the bottle of *djinn*.

Seated there in the black-curtained dining room, Jaq swayed. Was arcane energy still hovering nearby? Did his vision swim as he gazed at the false Meh'lindi? To Rakel he said bluntly: 'Come to my room, now.' With him he took the amputated finger.

WHAT RITE DID he perform with Rakel – known only to inquisitors who had plumbed depths of perversion by proxy during their investigations of evil?

When both returned later, Rakel was white-faced and trembling. Jaq was sweaty and feverish. Grimm snored by now, his head resting on the table. Lex sat with the waxed thigh bone before him, as if that were indeed the remains of a mastiff's meal. He was polishing the bone meticulously.

'Lust – or Change?' Jaq asked aloud, of the very air. He brandished the finger, now bereft of ring and data-disc. The finger had become stiff and leathery.

'Behold a Finger of Glory! A lumen for my mock-Meh'lindi, my thief, whose body is willing though her soul evades me! Perhaps I'm becoming a magus without recourse to Slaanesh or to Tzeentch.'

Grimly Lex polished.

After a while the Space Marine said to Jaq, 'If you become insane, my lord inquisitor, despite my vow I may need to kill you.'

Jaq swept an empty bottle of *djinn* from the table. The bottle shattered upon the black slate floor. Even this crash did not wake Grimm.

'Killing me,' said Jaq. 'might be righteous, yet it would ruin all hope.'

'Perhaps it would. Use that corpse's finger as you please. My own fingers revere this bone.'

Rakel listened numbly.

EIGHT
COURTHOUSE

JAQ FELT TAINTED and psychotic as he waited with Lex and Grimm in that same warehouse of saddles and bridles near the courthouse. The rear door had been reinforced with a wooden bar. Lex had easily broken the bar. Tumbled racks had been restored to an upright position. Purity tassels had been fastened to them, which the trio ignored. Now that all of the pilgrims had departed from Sabulorb, the rear alley was forsaken but for charred dog bones which rats had gnawed. Here in the warehouse was the rendezvous point for Rakel – who trod alone, right now, inside the courthouse.

As lookout, Grimm had watched Rakel commence her entry by way of a locked manhole cover giving access to a dry sewer which had been wrongly positioned during the long process of construction. Now she was alone amidst hundreds of servants and clerks and detectives and Arbitrators and marshals and judges.

Filth clung to Jaq's soul. The taint of betrayal – of himself, of the devout Space Marine captain, of the memory of Meh'lindi, most of all, of Him-on-Earth. Nevertheless, under the film of gathering psychic scum was his soul not still pure and intent on the light? Was it not through transmutation of foulness that he must aspire to a potent alchemy? Such sensations – and worse – he must endure, without provoking Lex to execute him.

A line from an old song in the creole dialect of a world Jaq had once helped cleanse came back to him: *Two madonna taboo, eh, Johnny Fedelor!*

'Eh, faithful Johnny, Johnny Fidelis, to admire two ladies is forbidden!' was the translation he had been told. There could not be a pretend Meh'lindi and a real Meh'lindi. Might embracing the pretend Meh'lindi ritually invoke the real Meh'lindi – or exclude her?

Surely such musings were the stuff of psychosis. Psychosis might be the instrument of enlightenment.

'What you humming, boss?' asked Grimm.

'Nothing, abhuman!'

'Huh, my ears deceive me. Say, while we're waiting shall I recite one of the shorter squat ballads?'

'If Rakel takes as long as that,' Jaq said dourly, 'she has either been caught or else she's dead.'

'Regard my ballad as a thief-timer. Like an egg-timer. When it runs out, we'd better bugger off. And don't tell me that we'll go into a court-house after Rakel! I shan't do it, boss. The temple was another matter.'

'Actually, you know, there is a *Ballad of the Boot*, about a roguish squat freebooter who tramped all over the galaxy in his pirate merchant ship.' Grimm hoisted a bare dirty foot, and tore at it vigorously with a horny fingernail. He peeled off grime and hard skin. A new pair of custom-made boots had been ordered. They would take a week. Once sewn, they needed to be battered and distressed for comfort, otherwise they would give him corns.

'Two madonna taboo, eh, Johnny Fedelor?' whispered Jaq.

'Eh? Is that some kind of invocation... magus?'

Jaq's skin crawled. '*Esto quietus, Loquax!*' he ordered. 'I must meditate.'

'Likewise,' Lex told the abhuman sternly.

IT WAS TWO hours before Rakel joined them. When she did so, Jaq's heart skipped a beat. His Meh'lindi was suddenly amidst them as if from out of nowhere – as though she had materialized at that moment from out of the sea of lost souls.

'I succeeded,' she said simply.

Between two fingertips of her left hand Rakel was holding up what seemed to be a data-disc. No: it was a greasy wafer from which a last wisp of smoke arose. It was the final residue of Chor Shuturban's Finger of Glory, now consumed entirely. It was this which had hidden her coming into the warehouse – even from Jaq's psychic sense, even from Lex's special ears.

In Rakel's other hand dangled a heavy satchel.

Black-clad and black-faced, with two lethal rings on her fingers, Rakel had entered the courthouse dungeons. Infrequent electrolumens glowed redly like hot pokers in the prevailing darkness. Softly she had padded, hearing distant groans – then laughter from a guardroom. Its plasteel door was ajar, outlined by light from within. She bypassed this place and mounted stone stairs to a higher subterranean level, a maze of storerooms; then she mounted again...

She had spent hours at the mansion studying on screen the layout of the courthouse – multi-level, labyrinthine, a dense and complex fortress-municipality. Otherwise she would surely have become hopelessly lost – as lost as a legal case in a great archive.

Rakel avoided internal courtyards. She favoured dark corridors. She was darkness embodied, slinking from darkness to darkness. As she climbed higher, baroque glowglobes were alight, and there was more nocturnal activity. In vaulted scriptoria, clerks were scrutinizing scrolling screens and scribing. Although this courthouse was only decades old, great mounds of documents had already been generated – as if the place was a vast rich nutrient tank wherein data-bacteria multiplied exponentially without any necessary reference to what lay beyond its confines; where, perhaps, different strains of bacteria contended for supremacy, corresponding to the varying opinions of judges in their high chambers.

Night-ushers prowled with sheaves of printout. Cyborged servitors trundled. These sucked up dust and fallen documents. Slow ceiling-fans, resembling rotating brass pterosaurs, stirred papers into motion, to escape from desks. Were it not for the fans, stale air might accumulate in suffocating pockets. Grilles protected weaponry and ceremonial whips and maces.

Just as truth emerges from perplexing obscurity, increasingly there was illumination. Now Rakel's black garb would betray her. She resorted to the Finger of Glory. She lit its tip with an igniter. Soft shimmery flame fluttered. She allowed herself to be seen – but she was not seen.

As she traversed arcades and galleries, so the finger consumed itself, burning down to the middle phalanx.

A dark-clad Arbitrator emerged from a side corridor. Armed with a lasrifle, he blocked her way. In his mirrored visor she saw the flame of the finger flickering. The Arbitrator was puzzled. He couldn't make out Rakel as she stood silently, holding her breath. Some polarization of light must be letting him see the finger-flame which she held, as if a luminous moth were hovering in mid-air.

'What's there?' came his voice. He spoke in standard Imperial Gothic, being within an Imperial courthouse, and being very likely of off-world origin. The Arbitrator shook his head as if to dislodge the intrusive image. 'Where are you, Corvo?' he called out. 'There's a flaw in this visor. You usually use this helmet, don't you?'

The colleague named Corvo did not seem to be nearby.

The Arbitrator removed a hand from the lasrifle, so that its barrel dipped. He raised his hand to his visor and lifted upward. A thin intense face appeared. Twin pendants dangled from the man's nostrils, like hardened plugs of mucus. Probably those were gas filters. Frowning, he stared directly at Rakel.

Rakel's lungs were bursting. She simply had to breathe out. At the sigh of her breath the gun jerked upward, awkward in a single hand.

Rakel crooked a finger. She had remembered aright this time. The toxic needle hit the Arbitrator in the cheek.

He was convulsing. Darting forward, she caught the lasrifle as it fell. The Arbitrator toppled against her. Her sudden rush had extinguished the finger. In his few last seconds of horrified lucidity, the Arbitrator may have glimpsed Rakel's eyes, in her blackened face, emerging out of nothingness like some predator from the sea of souls, to snatch him.

His body spasmed against her as if experiencing some perverse counterpart of ecstasy. His helmet was slipping. She must drop the finger to catch the helmet. Lasrifle in one hand, helmet in the other, Rakel let herself sink to the floor to break the Arbitrator's dying fall. How he writhed upon her, until suddenly he became limp.

She extricated herself. Found the candle-finger. Dragged the corpse into an alcove. Stripped him of his black uniform. She dressed herself in that, and donned the mirror-helmet. The remaining portion of finger and the igniter, she slipped into a pocket.

THE DATA-STORE she sought was near to a judge's chambers.

Carved doors to the chambers stood open. Fruitily scented oil-lamps burned in a vestibule panelled in intricate mosaics of dark marble spelling out ancient legal judgements.

The thick plasteel door of the data-store was open too. Light spilled forth. She tiptoed.

The store wasn't large. No towering iron shelves of tomes, such as Rakel had already glimpsed elsewhere, nor ladders nor gantries. Instead, there was just one enormous central book, taller than herself and mounted on a turntable. Its sail-size pages of stiff plastic fanned open through three-quarters of a circle. Like so many words upon those pages, hundreds of discs were mounted in lines and columns above reference codes.

A silk-clad clerk was turning a page, searching for a disc. The clerk was singularly tall and thin, as though he'd been stretched on a rack to assist his clerical duties, or bred for height and reach. His long thin arms were those of some spider-crab.

The clerk searched on behalf of a burly figure in gorgeously trimmed ermine robes and a towering black turban. This dignitary's eyes bulged behind incongruously small silver spectacles, betokening minute attention. A collar of goitres, lapped by fine fur, swelled the judge's neck. His head seemed but the summit of a veritable mountain, snow-clad below, capped with volcanic soot. He was fiddling with a metal rod around the end of which a blue energy field flickered. That was his power maul, with which he could clout a malefactor insensible, or on a higher setting smash through a wall.

As the supposed Arbitrator entered, the judge smiled at the image of himself and his power mirrored in the visor.

'Ah, Kastor, you find me still here–' This judge must have been expecting an Arbitrator of that name to visit him in his chambers.

Respectfully Rakel inclined her head and helmet.

'You're early, Kastor. So hurry up, Drork,' the judge said to the clerk. He flourished the maul. 'Surely the disc cannot have been misfiled!'

'Surely not by me, my lord,' replied the skeletal Drork, 'since to the best of my recollection it has never been called for during the whole of my indenture. Misfiled by my predecessor, perhaps.' Apparently there was a certain informality and mutual understanding between this clerk and the judge.

'Alien lingo disc for a hypno-casque,' the judge explained to the false Arbitrator. 'I've finally been able to appoint you a marshal of the court, my trusty Kastor.'

Rakel inclined her head even more lavishly. If only the judge did not demand a verbal response. If only she were able to ask about this 'lingo disc'!

The energy field of the maul faded into virtual invisibility. Thoughtfully the judge rubbed a great goitre with the tip of the maul, massaging his deformity.

'I appreciate your reticence, Kastor! I want you to form a small discreet team. Three other Arbitrators and yourself should suffice. Yesterday our astropath received a bulletin – which I alone am privy to as yet. Several bizarrely-clad aliens landed on planet Lekkerbek, purporting to be itinerant entertainers. Members of the eldar race. Such clowns also appeared on Nero IX. Likewise on Planet Karesh – without any obvious means of transport there. Doubtless they hid their ship somewhere in the wilds. On Karesh a fracas occurred, resulting in the death of two of the trio of aliens. The third alien vanished. In case a similar visitation

occurs here on Sabulorb, I wish you and your team to be ready to arrest
and interrogate these aliens in their own tongue–'

'Ah,' said Drork, 'here is the disc in question.' The clerk plucked the
coin-like data-disc from a towering plastic page.

'Take it and use it, Kastor.'

Rakel inclined her head obediently. She accepted the disc from Drork
and secreted it within her stolen uniform.

How soon would the real Kastor be arriving? Had not the inquisitor
said that she should conduct herself as an assassin, as well as a thief,
here in the heart of the courthouse?

The judge continued to rub at his great goitres with his inactive maul.
'If fortune blesses us, I shall be in the ascendancy amongst my learned
colleagues. Tell me, Marshal Kastor–'

Tell him? That was an impossible demand! Instantly Rakel raised the
lasrifle and fired at that fur-clad mountain of a man. Even as the blast
erupted against the judge, his hand was activating the maul. Blue energy
raged – and promptly died away again. Sidelong he collapsed upon the
floor.

Her second shot threw Drork backward against the book of discs. The
turntable spun. Two tall plastic pages clapped together, trapping the
dying clerk between them.

'Your honour!' A call came from along the corridor. That must be Kastor now.

Try to shoot him too? Noises may have forewarned him. She laid
down the lasrifle. Pulled out the stump of finger. The igniter flared.

Kastor was still lingering near that fruity-scented vestibule, lasrifle at
the ready. When Rakel rushed past him unseen he must have felt the dis-
placement of air. What could account for this sudden breeze?

'Your honour!' she heard him call again.

She was running away as quietly as she could.

Soon Kastor would enter the data-room and discover his judge dead
– *inexplicably* dead – and the clerk too. Now no one remained to explain
anything about eldar aliens, unless the courthouse astropath was questioned. Fearing for his or her own skin, the astropath might deny all
knowledge. He or she had divulged that bulletin only to the judge who
had now been assassinated. The perpetrator of the murder might be
some rival judge...

Rakel paused to extinguish the Finger of Glory. Chor's finger had
burned down as far as the proximal phalanx. She proceeded onward as
a mirror-masked Arbitrator with an urgent errand to attend to – and a
perfect right to be in any part of the courthouse. She would need to light

the finger again, closer to the dungeons where she would discard her stolen costume. She was determined to retain a little stub of the metacarpal part of the finger with which to surprise the inquisitor and his giant and his dwarf.

Let them respect her. Thus might she continue living. Thus Jaq Draco might accept her as an adequate substitute for the dead woman who inflamed his soul as a venomous thorn inflames flesh.

'WHAT'S IN THE satchel?' asked Grimm. 'The head of a judge?'

'No,' said Rakel. 'But I did assassinate one, as instructed.' She opened the satchel. 'I came across *these* in an armoury while I was making my escape.'

Clips of explosive bolts! Well over a dozen clips! Enough for *Emperor's Peace* and *Emperor's Mercy* and Lex's boltgun to utter their opinions many times over.

Reverently Lex reached into the satchel, took out a clip, and kissed it – almost as if bestowing a kiss upon Rakel.

'I did right, didn't I? This theft should confuse the courthouse doubly – these being relics here, and a relic being stolen from Occidens too.' Her speech was fluctuating between standard Gothic and Sabulorb dialect. After her exploit she was tired.

Had the real Meh'lindi ever betrayed fatigue?

'Tell me everything quickly now,' Jaq said, 'in case some accident happens to you. Give me a fast summary.'

Rakel hastily related about the judge and the clerk and the disc and the astropathic bulletin.

'You performed well,' Jaq praised her. 'After we return home I must reinforce your image with that special Tarot card, and with psychic pressure. You shall not suffer flux.'

'Pity,' said Grimm, 'about those eldar closing in, eh boss? If Harlequins do come here, it might have been better if a judge was planning to dungeon 'em.'

'Not at all!' said Jaq. 'If some eldar arrive here mysteriously we'll know for sure there is a webway portal hidden on Sabulorb. If they arrive by passenger merchantman, we'll know that there isn't one. If they arrive in a ship of their own, then the portal's on the outermost rocky planet or else on a moon of one of the local gas giants.'

Indeed. The eldar race had never given rise to the Navigator mutation, whereby human beings were able to pilot warp-ships swiftly from star to star. The eldar only had their webway to rely on, and short-distance interplanetary vessels.

Perhaps eldar seers could have engineered a Navigator gene into some of the children of their race – but the eldar scarcely dared enter the warp. Their fall had given rise to Slaanesh. Slaanesh forever resonated with eldar minds, a perpetual curse upon them, hungry to engulf the survivors. For the eldar to journey into the warp would be to offer themselves as sacrifices. The web was their only safe channel for interstellar travel.

'Besides,' added Jaq, 'once I've learned the language I shall need a tutor to master the reading of the runes.'

'A Harlequin chained in our cellar, persuaded to tutor you by torture?' The little man still remembered his treatment at the hands of Jaq and Meh'lindi in the engine room of *Tormentum Malorum*, before he confessed his dealings with Zephro Carnelian, who had duped him. Meh'lindi and Jaq had duped him too. Grimm's torment had been almost a hundred per cent suggestion, working upon an inflamed imagination.

Jaq said to Grimm: 'I've told you that physical torture is inefficient. There's a much better way to persuade an eldar.'

'What is it?'

'First we need to catch our eldar – rather than them catching us. We must go now – get away from this neighbourhood!'

'Soon be red dawn,' said Lex. 'Soon be red day.'

DURING THE NEXT week, Jaq's nights were spent wearing the hypnocasque. By day he practised phrases which none of the others could understand.

'*Nil ann ach cleasai, agus tá an iomad measa aige air féin,*' he would recite.

Only the real Meh'lindi would have been able to respond. Jaq's verbal exercises constituted a kind of one-sided dialogue with her departed spirit.

Only occasionally did he gloss a cryptic utterance. Rakel happened to be listening when he intoned, '*Nil ann ache cleasai…*' Jaq stared at her achingly familiar yet uncomprehending face, and translated into Imperial Gothic: 'The trickster thinks too much of himself. That,' he commented, 'will be our motto as regards Harlequins.'

While Jaq studied the Eldar language, Lex began to carve the thigh bone with his silicon carbide engraving tool. In lieu of a report to his Chapter – which he must not attempt to make as yet – Lex began to engrave an image of that Chaos world where a daemon had sat fishing from a low sickle moon, and where brave Imperial Fists had died resisting the onslaught by Chaos Marines.

When Rakel happened to peruse his progress a few days later, she said accusingly, 'But you're picturing nightmares!'

Was she herself suffering nightmares?

'Nay, lady,' he said. 'I am picturing reality. Or rather, I picture a hideous *unreality* which nonetheless exists. You should not look upon such things. Those who behold such sights merit mind-wiping.'

'Mind-wiping?' she echoed. 'In that case I shall never look at your art again.' She had fled from the room.

No, she should not look at his etchings. Next, he intended to picture Meh'lindi speared to death by the terrible Phoenix Lady in the webway.

After much minute attention to the details of the Chaos world, Lex strolled into the garden to rest his eyes.

Grimm was staring at the huge red sun.

'It's warmer today,' said the squat. 'Warmer than it's been since we arrived here. Can't you feel it on your bare skin?'

Lex wasn't one to pay much heed to heat or cold. Besides, he'd been focusing his attention upon the fine lines wrought by the graving tool and how well those lines corresponded with appalling memories. Surprised, he agreed.

'But at the same time,' said Grimm, 'that ruddy sun looks, I dunno, smaller?'

Lex mused a while: 'As I recall,' he said, 'that vast red orb is actually the outer atmosphere of the sun expanded across hundreds of millions of kilometres. Deep within, hidden from our eyes, will be a white-hot core, a dwarf core. By the time the radiance of that core reaches the extremities, the temperature is only that of an iron poker in a fire.' His brow furrowed. 'I've heard that the radiation output of white dwarfs can fluctuate. This is to do with the alchemy of elements.' He regarded Grimm sardonically. 'A dwarf can be unstable.'

The short abhuman scratched his head under his forage cap. 'Maybe we're in for a heatwave, eh?'

'We must hope not! Who knows what the upper limit of a heatwave might be?'

'Don't you try to scare me, you big lunk. This world has harboured life for aeons.'

'Aeons are merely seconds on the clock of time.'

'I'm aware of that!'

'Maybe a relatively minor shock might be enough to destabilize the white dwarf core. A warp-storm occurring locally. Even a warp-ship materializing accidentally within the star and disrupting the fabric of space before evaporating.'

'Thanks for the reassurance.'

'The cosmos does not exist for our benefit, little man, any more than a dog exists so as to harbour fleas. The fleas may think so, but they are wrong. Heroism is to accept this fact yet continue to strive in the Emperor's name.'

'Do you know His name, by the way?'

Lex flexed a fist warningly.

'No one knows His name by now,' came Jaq's voice in reply. Jaq too had stepped out into the garden. 'Nor can He possibly know His own name after so many millennia of transcendent anguish and cosmic over-watch.

'*Bionn an fear ciallmar ina thost nuair ná bíonn pioc le rá aige,*' he recited enigmatically in Eldar, and strode forth through the shrubbery.

NINE
JESTER

A FEW WEEKS later, Rakel brought word about a trio of amazing new performers who were drawing audiences to a theatre in the Mahabbat district.

Two of these acrobatic artistes were clad in kaleidoscopic motley, the hues of which changed from moment to moment. These artistes also wore holo-masks which could display a whole gamut of personae. In repose, the faces which these masks displayed were affably human. No one ever saw their actual faces of flesh and blood behind the masks.

The third member of their tiny troupe wore a skull-mask. White bones decorated his black costume. What a grin that skull exhibited! How frolicsome its wearer could be. He was the one who spoke Imperial Gothic, though not the dialect of Sabulorb itself. Much could be accomplished by mime. What fine mimes his companions were.

'Everyone seems to assume they're human,' recounted Rakel. 'Bit tall, maybe. But with arms and legs and heads in the right places.'

These exotic artistes had arrived in Shandabar by camelopard caravan from the city of Bara Bandobast across the Grey Desert. They must belong to some nomad tribe.

RAKEL'S INFORMANT ABOUT these performers was Mardal Shuturban. The man was still ravaged by the fratricide of his brother. His thumbs bore scars where he had finally torn them free from the bones of Chor's skull. Mardal believed that by some unknowable sorcery 'Tod Zapasnik' had saved himself and Mardal too from death during the delirium in the

Sensuality Suite. Sly brother Chor had hoped that the snake-woman would snoop upon Zapasnik's mind. The plan had gone unimaginably wrong. What did it matter if Chor's finger had been bitten off impatiently? Compared with what Mardal had done to his brother's eyes and frontal lobes, a finger was a trivial matter.

Mardal had babbled impetuously to Rakel. He was deeply disturbed by his experience. At the same time, a criminal could not afford to convalesce. Mardal had seemed on the verge of proposing some kind of alliance with Rakel's powerful and scary patron.

'Oh my brother, oh my brother!' he had wailed. 'Oh my wise, thoughtful brother!'

Why was Rakel asking about exotic artistes on behalf of Sir Tod? Chor might have had an inkling of why. Chor was dead. Zapasnik was an enigma.

Had Rakel really entered the courthouse? Members of the caste of garbage collectors who were allowed limited access to bring away toxic ashes from an incinerator had heard cooks talking about a murdered judge. No need for Rakel to say a word about it unless she wished to! Ah, how hot it was right now. How one sweated. Never before in living memory had anyone perspired so much in Shandabar – outside of a chamber of sin in the Mahabbat district! In the Grey Desert dust was dancing thermally.

'Oh brother mine, brother mine!'

Ah yes, those strange artistes… Mardal would keep watch on them for Sir Tod; but he would do nothing impetuous.

'OBVIOUSLY,' JAQ SAID to his companions, 'the eldar Harlequins are searching for the stolen book.'

Rakel's eyes had widened at this new revelation.

'The book contains many dire secrets,' he told her. 'We removed it from the Black Library of the eldar located in the webway which leads through the warp. Only an inquisitor could penetrate such a place. This is all forbidden knowledge – which you now need to know.'

'Knowledge is a curse,' she said darkly, 'not a blessing.'

THE HARLEQUINS MUST be spreading their scouting forces thin, so as to touch as many likely worlds as possible.

Groups of Harlequins very occasionally visited innocuous worlds of the Imperium to present their pageants of dance and mime. A feast for the eyes! An enigma to almost all human spectators! A troupe would generally consist of at least a hundred of the aliens – including costume-makers and operators of holo-projectors, and even the elderly and children, in addition to the core of costumed players who were also warriors. For as few as three players to visit Sabulorb implied that many similar visits were being made by other Harlequins to as many worlds as possible. Often at great risk, no doubt!

Here on Sabulorb, the Harlequins were passing themselves off as exotic masked tribesmen. The local judges now knew nothing about the astropathic bulletin. On other worlds, too, the eldar might pass as human beings of ethereal grace; as visitors from some luxurious Imperial plant where the population knew nothing of rickets or goitres or skin diseases. The eldar would sometimes even boldly reveal their identity as aliens, endowed with lavish funds – as they had reportedly done on Lekkerbek. On many other planets such as Karesh they must be risking their lives, and even losing them, victims of strict judges or zealous preachers or xenophobic mobs.

All to recover the book!

The alien trio had arrived from the direction of Bara Bandobast, not by way of Shandabar's landing field.

Jaq gave blessings that there was indeed a webway entry and exit somewhere at hand. He and Lex and Grimm began to form plans, which should involve Mardal Shuturban and his men.

Jaq's party now had three fully-loaded boltguns, as well as laspistols. Yet how rash to go unaided against three alien warrior-troubadours, particularly when one was a Death Jester. Those Death Jesters were heavy weapons specialists. Ah, but this Jester could hardly have brought a shuriken shrieker cannon fitted with anti-grav suspensors into Shandabar in his gear! If the Harlequins had ridden armed jetbikes through the webway to Sabulorb, they must have hidden those far out in the desert before joining the camelopard caravan.

A problem was that the eldar were far more sensitively psychic than human beings. The population of Shandabar generated a mental babble, a seething slurry of emotions and half-formed images. Doubtless the Harlequins were attempting to sieve this foetid torrent for any relevant nugget – though without the least guarantee of finding any. What might stand out from the babble, as unusual?

Turmoil at a temple, as priests and deacons of Occidens tried to discover whether the Austral temple had been responsible for the theft of the thigh bone…

The mysterious assassination of a judge…

A gruesome Slaaneshi manifestation at the House of Ecstasy, branded in survivors' minds: that should rivet the attention of any Harlequin.

Assuming that the sensitive eldar were able to extract such needles from the haystack of circumstances!

Mardal Shuturban might be radiating intense horror at what had happened in the House of Ecstasy. His horror might be associated with visual images of a certain wizard – a wizard who had access to priceless jewels.

Shuturban needed an aura of protection cast around him as soon as could be. Either that, or kill him. His help was needed.

The walled mansion was far enough from the Mahabbat quarter for mind-noise to drown out any direct trace of Jaq's presence. Jaq could shield his thoughts psychically. Lex had no helmet shielded with psycurium – but Lex could always intone a mantra of *Rogal Dorn, Rogal Dorn...* Could Jaq maintain protective auras for Grimm and Rakel, and for Shuturban too?

'Lex,' said Jaq, 'I want you to start up a prayer-mantra in your mind as a screen against psychic intrusion. Grimm: I want you to start reciting your longest ballad to yourself – silently – and don't stop. Rakel: I need to conjure protection around you. I need to embrace you with protection.'

Did a moan escape her lips?

'Next,' he told her, 'I need you to hurry to Shuturban and tell him that his life is in danger from those performers unless I protect him psychically.'

'He'll believe you're a sorcerer for sure, boss,' said Grimm.

'Maybe,' Jaq said to the abhuman, 'I am becoming one.' Briefly a rictus twisted his face. 'With your faithful help, my squat factotum, and with yours especially, Captain d'Arquebus.'

It was the first time that Rakel knew for sure that the giant was a Space Marine. She gasped – and Lex clenched his fist. In salute, or in reprimand? He loomed over the false Meh'lindi. His heels came together. Had he not been barefoot, those heels would have clicked.

'Lady,' he said formally, 'I present myself properly at last. Space Marine Captain Lexandro d'Arquebus of the Imperial Fists Chapter, travelling incognito as escort for my Lord Inquisitor Jaq Draco. This fist will snap the neck of anyone who betrays my identity, or my lord inquisitor's.'

'Yes,' murmured Rakel. 'I hear you.' She mumbled some prayer to herself. How many terrible secrets could she tolerate?

Jaq told her: 'We'll need to rendezvous with Shuturban somewhere private well away from the Mahabbat district.'

'Somewhere in Bellagunge?' suggested Grimm. 'Now that our boltguns are full of ammo!'

'And empty them for no good reason?' Lex said acidly. 'We can do without a commotion.'

Where, then, could they rendezvous? The ruins of Oriens harboured too many beggars. That saddle warehouse might be booby-trapped by now, by its owners – and it was too close to the courthouse.

The little man piped up: 'How about the cobblers where I got my new boots?' Grimm stamped appreciatively. The successors to his old boots indeed had a long-lived-in look to the leather. 'Meeting there has no obvious rhyme or reason. So it's ideal. It's nowhere near Mahabbat. Mind you, we must turf the cobbler out first to save his skin – I'm grateful to him.'

Jaq nodded. 'Shuturban can bring as many bodyguards as he pleases.' He turned to Rakel, and took the Assassin card from inside his robe. 'Come with me, my mock Meh'lindi, *in nomine Imperatoris*, to be clasped with protection.'

AMIDST IRON LASTS and pincers and buffing wheels, amidst stitchers and scourers and sole-cutting shears – so many boltguns and laspistols and autoguns! The cobbler's workshop could never have seen such a gathering of hardware as was in the hands or belts or holsters of Jaq's party and of Mardal Shuturban's half-dozen men.

The workshop was a long broad room, lit by electrolumens in sconces. Perhaps a hundred pairs of boots and shoes hung on hooks from joists.

The fat bald proprietor, Mr Dukandar, had been evicted into the night along with his stout wife and two apprentice sons. This happened as soon as Jaq's party arrived, in advance of Shuturban and company. The Dukandars couldn't remain in their upstairs quarters in case they eavesdropped. Take a walk for a couple of hours if you know what's wise! Cool though the night air might be, for Sabulorb the temperature was almost balmy. The Dukandars wouldn't catch cold.

'WE ARE MEETING again,' Mardal greeted Jaq, with sombre respect. 'My life being in danger once again?'

'In dire danger from those exotic performers. Being alien psyker-warriors–'

Mardal smashed a fist into his palm.

'Yes, crushing them,' agreed Jaq. 'But I am absolutely requiring one of those aliens as my prisoner, to be questioning about how they were arriving here. Mardal Shuturban, you are reeking of recent sorcerous assault. Your intention soon becoming known to the aliens. The flavour of what was happening to you in the House of Ecstasy attracting those psykers as carrion-flies to gangrene. Needing me to be protecting you with a conjuration of concealment. And then we are striking, _swiftly_.'

'A conjuration?' Sweat pimpled Shuturban's cheeks.

'So that you being immune from psychic surveillance. I shall be extending a mental shield, Mardal Shuturban. Requiring me to be reciting certain anathemas, and blessing you with this.' Jaq exhibited his sleek black force rod, accumulator and booster of mind-energy.

As Jaq led a compliant Shuturban aside, amidst the pliers and rasps and sole-stitching machinery, Grimm smirked momentarily. Oh, the boss could extend an aura of protection around a whole ship. He wouldn't use a force rod to do so. That rare ancient weapon was for blasting at daemonic manifestations. The boss was vamping for Shuturban's benefit. Shuturban was duly impressed.

By now it was well over half an hour since Jaq's party had arrived at the cobbler's premises. They were about to leave together with Mardal Shuturban and company, bound for a certain theatre in Mahabbat.

From outside in the night an amplified voice reverberated: 'BEING HIS IMPERIAL MAJESTY'S ARBITES! PREMISES BEING SURROUNDED. FOUR PERSONS WITHIN ABANDONING WEAPONS, THEN EXITING ON KNEES ONE BY ONE WITH HANDS BEHIND HEAD! SHORT WEARER OF NEW BOOTS BEING FIRST OF ALL!'

'Oh my ancestors!'

Jaq rounded on Shuturban. The man mimed protestations of innocence which seemed perfectly sincere.

'BE SURRENDERING PEACEFULLY FOR LAWFUL QUESTIONING BY ARBITRATOR STEINMULLER!'

The boots, the boots... That was the fatal flaw. A unique pair of boots had been abandoned in the ravaged Sensuality Suite of the House of Ecstasy. Someone had reported this fact to the courthouse. Could have been one of the ex-Guardsmen, acting secretly as an informer for the courthouse. Could have been the lord governor's lascivious nephew, or one of the other patrons, infuriated at how the orgy had endangered or injured them. Someone of status, who could appeal to the courthouse to investigate.

Item: the stunted abhuman who lost his boots had been with a giant slave and with a robed bearded man.

Item: the bearded man had played a part in the trouble rather than being just a victim.

Thus: find the abhuman, and discover the true facts of the case. Proceed astutely, without letting it seem that any investigation was underway. Therefore, amongst other procedures: visit all cobblers throughout the city in the hope that the abhuman needed new boots.

It must have taken Arbitrator Steinmuller a while to arrive at the plan of action. By the time a bailiff of the courthouse had actually visited Dukandar, Grimm had already collected his new boots. When Grimm returned to evict Dukandar, the cobbler had raced to the nearest unvandalized public vox-caster.

Or did he even need to do so? Dukandar would already have revealed the fact of Grimm's earlier visit. On the off-chance that the distressed boots might prove faulty and a grumpy customer might return, the bailiff might have been keeping watch on the cobbler's from another building.

Now a squad was outside, and around.

'ABHUMAN EMERGING WITHIN TEN SECONDS,' came the voice. 'NINE… EIGHT…'

Grimm readied *Emperor's Peace*. Jaq levelled *Emperor's Mercy*. Lex aimed his bolter at the door. Shuturban's men pointed autoguns and laspistols at the shuttered windows. Mardal had produced a laspistol.

When Shuturban and company arrived, the bailiff must have been occupied contacting the courthouse. Those extra unexpected visitors had not been spotted. The Arbites believed there were only four miscreants inside Dukandar's place; not a dozen.

Nor could the Arbitrators know that three were armed with fully-loaded boltguns.

On the count of zero, deafening explosions blasted the front facade of the cobbler's. Rubble vomited; clouds of dust billowed. The whole of the wall and its door and shutters disintegrated. Beams and rafters sagged. Plaster from the ceiling cascaded upon tools and benches. Still sustained by side walls, the upper storey did not pancake down upon the ground floor, yet the building groaned almightily.

The Arbitrators had fired a volley of krak grenades to open up Dukandar's premises. The explosive effect of these were entirely concentrated at the target, without collateral blast. Would the Arbites now be switching to choke grenades to disable those who lurked within? Or tanglefoot grenades?

'Out, out – or gettin' caught!' bellowed Lex at Shuturban's men, remembering to use scum patois. 'Out, and killin'!'

With a roar he launched himself into the wall of dust and scrambled over rubble. As did Jaq, hauling Rakel with him. As did Grimm. As, with only the briefest of hesitation, did Mardal and his men.

* * *

FIVE MIRROR-VISORED Arbitrators were immediately evident, out in the dusty dark street. Two were indeed porting their weapons, busy attaching different grenade tubes to the long barrels.

RAAARKpopSWOOSHthudCRUMP
RAAARKpopSWOOSHthudCRUMP
RAAARKpopSWOOSHthudCRUMP

The first *RAARK* of explosive bolts – like the rowdy growl of some carnivorous terror-lizards or of hell-dogs erupting from the dust – caused the Arbitrators fatal instants of hesitation. Bolts penetrated chest or belly. Bolts exploded, *CRUMP*. Blood sprayed. Autoguns were racketing too. Ducking, two surviving Arbitrators loosed laser pulses which hit one of Mardal's men simultaneously. Each had chosen the very same target. And a lesser target, too! Perhaps Lex seemed more like a force of nature than a mortal adversary. The abhuman must not be shot. As for the bearded man, was he using that woman as a shield? The woman might be important to the investigation. Wrong decisions, wrong.

Emperor's Peace and *Emperor's Mercy* roared adieu to those two Arbitrators.

Which one of the five corpses was Arbitrator Steinmuller?

From an alleyway around the side of the cobbler's three more Arbites were coming to assist. From a passageway on the far side, two more emerged. Crossfire flew. An energy blast caught Grimm on the very edge of his flak-jacket, bowling him over, but the squat was able to scramble to his knees. Another of Mardal's men screamed and fell.

RAARKpopSWOOSHthudCRUMP
RAARKpopSWOOSHthudCRUMP

The raving of the autoguns! The gaudy flowering of energy shells on impact!

Did the fight last for fifteen strobing seconds? Perhaps not as long. Yet it seemed to last for several minutes in slow motion.

The Arbites were all dead, or at least severely injured. Lex roved quickly from one body to another. He checked by starlight for signs of life. Where he found life lingering he ended it, so that the courthouse would be unenlightened.

Where was the cobbler?

'Mr Dukandar!' Grimm called into the night. 'Your shop is damaged!' How sadly the building sagged. 'It's time to salvage your tools, Mr Dukandar!'

Once the victors departed, shadowy beggars might flock to loot the premises of its boots and shoes – and of its pincers and shears and nails and leather. No cobbler showed himself. If Dukandar was wise he was already hastening with his wife and sons to lose himself somewhere in the smoky entrails of Bellagunge.

Did a bailiff still keep watch through a cracked shutter in some neighbouring building? Was he whispering urgently into a vox-caster?

Lex raked the street with his gaze.

'Us gettin' outa here!' he shouted at Shuturban.

'To the theatre!' cried Jaq.

Grimm paused briefly to scoop up one of the dropped lasguns to which an Arbitrator had been attaching a new tube of grenades. The little man jammed the barrel diagonally inside his belt.

TO THE THEATRE, indeed: to the Theatrum Miraculorum on Khelma Street in Mahabbat, like some intoxicated nocturnal revellers eager for even more exotic entertainment.

En route, Mardal Shuturban collected five more men armed variously with shotgun or chainsword.

Mardal's group now totalled nine men, plus himself. Would fourteen persons be sufficient to deal with three warrior-troubadours, sufficient to slaughter two and subdue a third? Mardal's men believed so – especially those survivors of the encounter at the cobbler's. They were flushed with having exterminated a whole patrol of Arbites.

ELEGANTLY CLAD IN silks and furs, patrons of this night's performance were spilling out from the domed foyer of the theatre into Khelma Street to meet bodyguards and chauffeurs. Balloon-wheeled automobiles and gilded carriages pulled by snuffling snake-necked camelopards crowded the thoroughfare. Feet and hooves and wheels stirred dust. Rich perfumes competed with the weed-smoke of cigars and with exhaust fumes and with the odours of camelopard dung and urine.

The irruption of the fourteen through this secure normality seemed almost like a continuation of dramatic spectacle – especially since no armed robbery or abduction or murder seemed intended as regards any theatre-goers. A swift frontal approach through an excited crowd which was venting psychic noise might take the Harlequins unawares. Was this not a time and a place for an inquisitor to act flamboyantly? Let the courthouse suspect the secret presence of an inquisitor – aye, and of an Imperial assassin too! This would perplex and perturb.

Weapons weren't being brazenly flourished, though eye-witnesses could hardly fail to notice the toothed blade of a chainsword or the long barrels of shotguns or of lasguns filched from the dead. Well and good. Had not Shandabar seen a genestealer uprising and a cleansing by Space

Marines, and the pious and bloody riots of pilgrims? At times death was a currency as common as the shekel. Jaq and associates lagged a little, letting Mardal and his men take the lead.

THE DOMED AUDITORIUM was almost deserted. Chandeliers of electrolumens glowed brightly. A spangled curtain hid the stage. As the intruders advanced down aisles, some ushers ducked behind plush seats.

'Master Jadu!' cried one of those attendants piercingly.

Glittering, the curtain swept up and sideways, bunching tableau-style – to reveal the impresario peering from the wings. What a peculiar fellow Jadu was. Exaggeratedly high heels and short skinny legs elevated a little barrel of a body clad in purple velvet appliquéd with crescent moons and comets. With a red coxcomb hat upon his head he resembled a plump, fussy poultry-bird. One could imagine Master Jadu flapping his arms and clucking and crowing resoundingly.

Behind him – much taller than him – multicoloured spangles shimmered where no part of the curtain should be. A ghost of Jadu's own moon-face swayed in mid-air. It was a Harlequin in chameleon mode. Its holo-suit was copying the surroundings. Its psychoactive mask imitating the impresario's own face! A device seemed to float unsupported: a sleek gadget with a sheen to it. Something wrought of psycho plastic or wraithbone – a shuriken pistol!

A stream of what seemed like tiny spangles sprayed along one aisle. One of Mardal's men screamed. Blood laced his clothing. His chainsword fell from a crimson hand, from which two fingers also fell. No spangles, those – but tiny spinning razor-discs propelled at high speed by a compact gravitic accelerator. Those tiny discs would scalpel through flesh, severing arteries, piercing internal organs, cutting bone. The man behind spasmed in a delirium of pain and injury, and collapsed.

Autoguns opened up. The impresario-bird seemed to fluff out his feathers as shells tore into him.

RAARKpopSWOOSH, spake Lex's boltgun, as he fired over seats.

RAARK-RAARK, declared *Emperor's Peace* and *Emperor's Mercy* in chorus.

Explosive bolts ripped through the spangled drape as if through tissue, and one surely detonated in alien flesh. Ethereally tall, kaleidoscopically fluxing, a figure seemed to drift forward. Its false face was now a private nightmare to whoever beheld it. Mardal shrieked, 'Chor, no don't–!'

Rakel squealed, seeing some nightmare of her own. Was that figure on stage the assassin whom she imitated, coming for her?

Shuriken spangles sprayed, scattershot. Blood flew from a nick on Grimm's rubicund cheek. Blood welled from the upper slope of Lex's brow as a new companion to old duelling marks appeared. The blood immediately hardened to a knob of cinnabar.

RAARK!

RAARK!

The Harlequin danced his last dance.

The raiders hurried backstage past a lanky alien corpse masked in horror and past the dumpy, slaughtered-turkey corpse of unfortunate impresario Jadu.

THEY FOUND THE Death Jester lurking in a blue room walled with lapis lazuli.

Oh such a lanky mischievous figure of death he was. His costume was decorated with real bones. His skull mask, framed by a great clownish yellow collar like the fully-open petals of some huge jungle flower. A wild spray of inky hair fountained from his crown.

The first man through the doorway was greeted by a Harlequin's Kiss.

Strapped to the back of the Jester's forearm was a tube bonded to an egg-shaped reservoir. The Jester clenched his fist and punched the air in front of him. Briefly the interloper wobbled as if he had become a jelly; and collapsed. What had been a man had become a bag of minced organs braced with bones.

Such was the consequence of the monofilament wire which had leapt from that tube to pierce its victim's body and uncoil within his entrails. Thrashing about like a whip, the wire had reduced guts and liver and lungs and heart to a slurry.

The wire had leapt back into its container, curling tight.

Already it was jumping out again, kissing the next man with the same consequences.

How swiftly a third! The third was Mardal Shuturban himself. The man jerked. He was a bony jelly containing warm soup. He spilled upon the floor.

The Death Jester might kiss everyone who came for him before they had a chance to fire their weapons.

Dropping *Emperor's Peace*, Grimm hauled out the lasrifle, cranked the grenade tube, and fired several times into the room of lapis lazuli.

Gas billowed within.

Until that moment Grimm hadn't known precisely what type of grenades would pop out of the launcher. It was a fair guess that those

Arbites had intended to capture rather than kill or maim. Now Grimm caught a whiff, and his eyes watered – and he caught his breath.

Jaq had dragged Rakel backward. Mardal's other men were beginning to gasp and cough at the seepage from inside the blue room.

'Ceasing fire!' bellowed Lex. 'Killing anyone who is firing again!'

Unlike the helmets worn by eldar aspect warriors, that Death Jester's mask wasn't sealed against the atmosphere. Inside the cloudy room the tall figure was staggering, bending over, wracked.

Lex was gathering himself. He would rush into the room with his eyes shut tight and seize the Jester and haul him out. Just then, the eldar lurched for the doorway, fending wildly at whoever might be in his way. No longer was he able to use his weapon. He himself might blunder into the wire when it retracted.

Lex seized the emerging alien. He snapped the Jester's wrist. The Harlequin wouldn't be able to clench his fist and punch again. Lex threw the eldar, skidding, along the passageway, away from the gas. Launching himself upon the choking alien, he dragged the long arms behind the bone-cloaked back. Discarding the lasgun, Grimm was beside Lex a moment later. He pulled from a pouch a plastight manacle-loop to cuff sound wrist to broken wrist. Struggles would only tighten the tether. A second loop fettered the Jester's ankles. Quickly Grimm retrieved *Emperor's Peace* before the precious weapon might be stolen.

'This one being ours,' Lex roared at the coughing bystanders. 'Yourselves finding the third Harlequin and killing him!'

Jaq knelt by the disabled choking Jester, and stated in Eldar: 'I have your Book of Fate. We will take you to it, Jester.'

This should ensure that the Harlequin of Death wouldn't try to kill himself by swallowing his tongue or by some other guile.

MARDAL WAS DEAD. Only Mardal had imposed any discipline upon his gunmen. Whatever discipline there had been now quite disintegrated. Orders to search the rest of the theatre for the other Harlequin were heeded only insofar as the gunmen would keep an eye open while they were escaping to safety.

The third Harlequin must also have escaped rather than blending with his surroundings in ambush.

They had left by a door at the rear of the Theatrum Miraculorum. Lex carried the Jester slung over his shoulder at a fast trot by way of inky back alleys. Sirens wailed distantly, and there was an occasional crackle of gunfire.

No Harlequin, dappled in darkness, shadowed their route. Lex would surely have heard whenever he paused alertly. Jaq would have sensed. The third Harlequin must have judged it wiser to flee from Shandabar. To steal a camelopard. To ride it into the Grey Desert until the beast's heart gave out – on his way to wherever the hidden webway entry was.

Would that Harlequin return a few days later accompanied by aspect warriors riding jetbikes? Or might the spy declare that the mission to Sabulorb had proved lethal yet inconclusive?

THE JESTER WAS chained in the cellar near to the lectern, unable to touch it physically. After removing the Harlequin's Kiss, which the Jester bore stoically, his wrist had been splinted and bound up.

Less stoical was his reaction to the removal of his skull-mask. He had bucked and writhed – but off had come the skull to reveal a lean, sinisterly handsome alien face with the highest of cheek bones and slanting turquoise eyes.

Next morning Jaq began learning the runes.

At first the Jester was uncooperative – until Jaq ripped out half a page from the *Book of Rhana Dandra* and lit the vellum with the same igniter as Rakel had used to light the Finger of Glory.

Flame climbed. Runes writhed as if alive. Runes crisped and crumbled to ash. Smoke laced the air as if the consumed words were attempting to maintain a ghostly existence. Jaq swept the smoke aside as brutally as a power gauntlet breaking cobwebs.

This sight wrung such a groan of grief from the Jester, more agonized than any physical torture might have caused. The destiny of his race had been diminished.

'Page by page,' vowed Jaq in Eldar, 'I shall destroy the book before your eyes, Jester. I shall cram the final page into your own throat to choke you!'

'To destroy what you cannot understand – that is the human way!'

'Precisely. So therefore I wish to read these runes.'

The Jester laughed wretchedly.

'Hieratic high eldar runes! Have you a spare month, and the mind of a cogitator?'

'I have all the time in the cosmos, and a mind honed by my ordo, and I shall conjure concentration.'

Jaq made to wrench out the remaining half of the page. Runes squirmed beneath his fingers.

'No!' cried the Jester. 'Enough. I shall teach!'

* * *

THE HARLEQUIN'S NAME was Marb'ailtor, which signified something akin to *Corpse-Joker*.

Jaq waited until the next day to demand, 'Marb'ailtor, where exactly is the webway entrance which you used?'

The Jester demurred. Jaq tore out a whole page from the book and set it alight. Might that be the very page upon which his own involvement with eldar affairs was inscribed?

'Truly you are insane!' shrieked the Jester.

Jaq smothered the half-consumed page against his robe. He displayed the remains tauntingly. Thus he had been taught how to torment a person.

'A day's march east of the city called Bara Bandobast,' confessed the Harlequin, 'there is a labyrinth of rock. Humans regard the place as haunted because holes in the rocks give the wind a voice. Near the centre are six giant mushrooms of stone. There is the gateway.'

'I think you're lying,' said Jaq. He relit the page.

The Jester howled impotently. Evidently he had told the truth.

'How,' asked Jaq, 'can there be stone mushrooms?'

'The wind whirls around stone pillars. Grit in the wind abrades the stone. Big grains of grit cannot rise as high as little grains. The lower part of a pillar wears away faster than the top.'

LATER, JAQ DEMANDED, 'Where do the Emperor's Sons have their stronghold?'

'I do not know, I do not know!' insisted Marb'ailtor.

IN THE MATTER of the runes the chained Jester was certainly cooperative – scrupulously so, sometimes *repetitiously* so. Did Marb'ailtor aim to prolong the period of instruction in the hope that he might be rescued before Jaq could read the prophecies fluently enough?

Yet at other times the Jester seemed almost impatient to accelerate the process. It was as if Marb'ailtor were torn between two conflicting outcomes – both of them undesirable.

One outcome must be that Jaq would soon achieve mastery of the Book of Fate – and therefore he would take the stolen book elsewhere with him, to act upon what he had learned. The other outcome was that he and the book would remain on Sabulorb for a while – with what consequences? The worst consequence must be the destruction of the book so that it was lost to the eldar forever. How was the book likely to be destroyed, other than by the sort of vandalism with which Jaq had earlier threatened the Jester?

Even in that cellar beneath the mansion the air was perceptibly less chilly. Upstairs, despite the permanent black drapes which cloaked the windows, rooms were warm. Outside, the temperature was almost sultry. For what must have been the first time in millennia Shandabar sweated. Discernibly the great red sun had shrunk somewhat.

LEX WAS TROUBLED. Rakel was bewildered.

'How can a sun shrink,' she asked, 'and yet be hotter?'

'Gas shrinks inwards and compresses,' Lex said. 'Thus more gas will burn in the interior. Thus more heat radiates.'

'We've already been through this,' said Grimm. The little man pulled off his forage cap. Derisively he mopped his brow. 'Phew, we'll roast – and the *Book of Dandruff* will burst into flames. Look, Lex, you're talking about oscillations. This planet would already have been cooked to a crisp if oscillations were extreme.'

'That is true,' admitted Lex.

'MARB'AILTOR,' JAQ SAID severely, 'do you believe this planet is about to burn?'

The Jester stared at Jaq with those eerie unmasked turquoise eyes.

'You,' said the eldar softly, 'would play games with forces of Chaos. I have sensed the lure of corruption. According to the doctrine of *Tranglam* – which some call the Theory of Chaos – our farseers declared that a small perturbation sometimes has huge consequences when circumstances are vulnerable to change. A night-moth flutters its wings and causes a subsequent storm half a world away. If this is true of a mere moth, how much more so of energies spilling from the psychopotent warp! The weather gives cause for concern.'

'Continue decoding the runes,' Jaq ordered.

DUE TO THERMAL *gradients whipping up winds in the interior, in the desert which lay beyond the Grey Desert a sandstorm was arising. Ribbons of sand were snaking along, rising higher and weaving together into a speeding, undulating flying carpet.*

In the Grey Desert itself, dust was storming aloft and becoming a dark wall rushing onward. Behind that wall, no sunlight could filter down into a suffocating realm black as night...

TEN

RENEGADES

FLAME-HAIRED MAGNUS *had looked out through the warp from his watchtower, as if seeking a trace of the eldar's lost Book of Fate.*

Oh to gain possession of that mysterious and mutable text! To be able to rove through its alien runes, looting its secret prophecies! By mindforce he might alter the words and twist the very future. How mighty Lord Tzeentch would rejoice. How unholy Tzeentch would bless Magnus and his followers.

Above the jagged crags from which the watchtower soared, the energy of the warp crackled in a stygian sky. Atop the tower there bulged a naked eyeball of elephantine size. At once crystalline and protoplasmic, this cupola pulsed inwardly, scrying through the warp into the realm of ordinary reality far from the Eye of Terror, detecting ripples of psychic activity.

Magnus only had one eye. It was set centrally above his nose. He had been thus when he was the headstrong commander of one of the boldest Space Marine Chapters crusading to conquer the galaxy for his Emperor. Even then, unbeknownst to his battle brothers, he was marked by Chaos, and had hungered for arcane wisdom. He had hungered so eagerly that when the possessed Warmaster Horus rebelled, Magnus must needs be a rebel too, forced to ally with daemonry. And be blessed by daemonic energies and potency!

With his own single eye Magnus spied through the telescope of that other baleful cyclops-eye surmounting the watchtower. In a rapture of rapport he had detected the divinations of alien farseers desperate to recover the Book of Fate thieved from their secret library. His spying was part psychic perception, part symbolic vision, part interpretative intuition.

Through the warp his followers had flown to attack the site of those alien divinations, to disrupt and disorient. Maybe even to deal a mortal blow to that vast half-crippled craftworld, so stubborn in its refusal to submit to its final fate.

The shape-shifting ships from the Planet of the Sorcerers each carried a crystalline seer-scope similar to the eye on the watchtower. By seer-scope they could track the glow of psychic activity.

From his watchtower Magnus had glimpsed, far away from cursed Ulthwé, a halo of sorcerous summons, a prelude to wizardry, allied to that lost book. By now the book so obsessed him that he was as a male musk-moth scenting a single molecule of pheromone released from a league away.

Far away, a Tarot card of Tzeentch was twitching, animated by the ever-scheming Architect of Fate, and by some powerful psyker's tormented passion to unstitch time. A psyker in whose possession was that stolen book of destiny! In whom conflicting urges were at war. Foolish fidelity, and tragic craving. A harsh idealism: to bring a new light into the universe. A lust that change might occur; and yet that the tyrannous cripple on Earth might be sustained or purified.

Change-lust was the signature of that psyker's soul in turmoil. He might succumb to either the Great Conspirator or to the Lord of Lust. The balance might tilt either way. That it had not already tilted was due to a precarious conjunction of forces, and perhaps because of spiritual agony. The Lord of Lust knew how to transmute agony into delight; delight into agony. The Lord of Lust was Tzeentch's rival in the fourfold corruption of the cosmos.

Magnus had sent other shape-shifting ships speeding through the warp. Oh Mutator, oh Master of Fortune, may the Chaos Renegades of Lord Magnus come swiftly to their destination.

NORMALLY IT WAS gloomy inside the curtained mansion at noon. But on this particular noon the world outside was cloaked in deepest darkness. Dense dust stormed suffocatingly across the city. Visibility outside was virtually zero. In the streets, a hand held directly in front of one's face would be hard to see – assuming that one had not already choked to death even despite wet rags tied over nose and mouth.

Thousands of street-dwellers and beggars must have suffocated during the past half hour since the storm arrived. Once the storm passed over, sanitation squads would be busy for days carting bodies to mass graves. In the unaccustomed warmth, uncollected bodies would soon begin to stink.

Such a dust-storm might reach as high as three thousand metres into the sky. Within the lowest reaches of the storm, nearer the ground, airborne sand also swirled. It was the friction of grains and grit which accounted for the sickening headaches which had suddenly afflicted Jaq and Rakel and Grimm and Lex, like an onset of unwelcome possession. The electrical potential in the air must have soared to eighty or ninety volts per cubic metre, grievously disturbing the electrical field of a person's body and brain.

Jaq exerted his psychic power to combat this. Yet it was not a psychic assault.

So hard to think straight any longer. Maybe he ought to relax and welcome nausea as the harbinger of a frame of mind in which he might indeed be vulnerable to derangement and possession.

With this in mind, Jaq had donned the hooded monocle which had been Azul's warp-eye.

Outside, black wind howled, laden with grit and dust. Curtains quivered. All four had gathered in the same room on the ground floor as if the mansion were under attack from more than merely the elements. Was there not a dark sense of something impending?

Something which Jaq might invite, and absorb – while it strove to absorb him – and might then repulse by gazing into a mirror at his own reflection seen through Azul's eye! Was there a minimum time during which he must remain possessed by whichever power came – so as to become illuminated when he freed himself? And while possessed, what rite ought he to enact with the false Meh'lindi?

Did the Assassin card twitch inside his clothing? Was the Daemon card vibrating in anticipation of trumping the Assassin card?

How Jaq's head ached, and his soul as well.

Rakel moaned. 'My head, my head, I could claw it open...' Would Meh'lindi have moaned thus?

'Don't waste your energy telling me you have a headache!' Jaq growled. He must not sympathize. Meh'lindi had always regarded herself as expendable in a higher cause. In that rejection of self had resided the real assassin's perfection. If Rakel were to lose her own self, yielding way to Meh'lindi's soul, then in that moment Rakel would at least participate for a moment in perfection; and that would be Rakel's reward.

But of course they had not yet reached the place in the webway where time might twist. Jaq did not yet know how to reach it. Nor was becoming possessed a necessary precondition for resurrecting Meh'lindi. Or was it, or was it? How Jaq's soul ached with confusion, and his head too. This electrical interference induced such disorder in the mind.

From Grimm: 'Oh it's bloody misery, this. Wonder how our Jester's coping? Hypersensitive snobs, those eldar. So intense! Nervous systems strung like catgut on a harp. Every sensation heightened. Beggar it – but he might be having a brainstorm downstairs! Seizures and paroxysms! I'm gonna check him out, boss. Maybe there's less voltage down in the cellars. You come with me, Rakel. Might clear your head.'

'Go, go,' said Jaq dismissively.

GRIMM CLUMPED DOWN the stone stairs. Rakel padded softly behind him. Along to the cell they went. As soon as the abhuman set stumpy hand on the iron key in the lock he squawked and shook his fingers and spat on them.

'Damn it, it stung me!'

To avoid any further electric shock, Grimm used a grubby kerchief to turn the key.

The Jester sat in his garb of bones upon the pallet mattress which Jaq had allowed him. A chain rattled as he raised a long-fingered hand in sinister greeting.

Grimm slapped his own brow. 'Oh, of course! His chains are earthing the electricity…'

'What is happening?' Marb'ailtor asked; for it was he who spoke Imperial Gothic.

'Just a storm. Particles rub together. Voltage potential soars.'

'The storm is caused by rising temperature,' announced the Jester. 'The sun will burn this world and everyone on it. There will be white skeletons everywhere. Yours and mine and hers.'

'No, there won't be! The sun won't do that – 'cos it never did before.'

'This time it will happen, abhuman. For Death is here. Death will play a prank on Sabulorb.'

'Huh!'

'Free me, abhuman. Help me to reach the webway. The eldar will give you sanctuary.'

'From whom? I'm sure I'd enjoy being looked down on by your sort for the rest of me life.'

The Jester nodded at the locked chest which was out of reach of him. 'The eldar will reward you with bright jewels. A fortune! Your master is insane. He will become possessed. This world will burn. I smell daemonry coming closer. Your master will sacrifice you as pawns.'

Grimm puffed himself up. 'I'm the major-domo hereabouts.'

Rakel shuddered. 'What is really to be my fate?' she asked Grimm.

Grimm eyed her. 'Not to worry. That body of yours will see many years of service yet. Keep up with your exercises, hmm?'

Did a hint of a tear appear in Rakel's eye?

'Shut up, you!' Grimm barked at Marb'ailtor. 'You're scaring the lady.'

Distantly from upstairs came a muted crash as though the wind had racked itself up to a hurricane force and had now exploded through a window. No, that noise was due to something else. Some other violent intrusion.

'Crazy aspect warriors!' A squat's detestation of eldar affectations went hand in hand with a sensible degree of respect. 'Suppose the storm isn't deep. They've come up behind the storm on jetbikes, using it as cover. Now that they've smelled Old Bones here psychically, they've plunged right on in.' Grimm clutched *Emperor's Peace*. Crouching in the doorway, he trained the boltgun along the passageway.

'Get your pistol out, girl!'

As Rakel readied the laspistol, with those eerie turquoise eyes of his and by mime Marb'ailtor implored her to shoot the abhuman. She shook her head.

Risk her body succumbing to flux?

'I 'spose,' mumbled Grimm, 'dust would clog engine intakes, though...'

'A visit by masked Arbitrators?' she murmured. 'Masks all coated in dust. Nothing visible...'

'We don't move from here,' said Grimm, 'until we know for sure what's going on. You,' he called to the Jester, 'no singing out, or else you'll be biting on a bolt!'

The Jester didn't sing. He shivered.

'Daemons,' he hissed. 'Daemons!'

Had Jaq – his brain circuits disrupted by the high voltage – gone critical upstairs?

'Oughta tell the boss to cling on to a chain or summat,' muttered Grimm.

Neither he nor Rakel were intending to move.

THE FIRST TWO raiders to burst through a sheet-glass window and rip black drapes aside with their metal fists would have glimpsed in the room two men: one robed and bearded – the other huge and stark. A barbarian slave in his groin-cloth and webbing, bare-chested, restless. Such thighs, such biceps, such pectorals, such a solid slab of chest – and such vulnerability, to persons similar to himself, especially when those persons were enhanced by power armour! Surely the stark giant was a Space Marine, one of the paralytical Emperor's despicably devout knights such as these raiders themselves had once been long ago! Witness the bygone medical scars on his anatomy!

Such was the glimpse enjoyed by the raiders, before choking dust surged into the room along with them, abolishing ordinary visibility.

But of course these raiders had image enhancers in their helmets.

FOR LEX AND Jaq the brief glimpse was of vanes like axe-blades jutting above angular helmets. It was of monstrous armour utterly harsh in its lines and edges, except for the rotund shoulder pauldrons.

Around the terrible figures electrical discharge flickered. Haloes crackled. Auras sparkled. The armour was damascened with arcane hexes. It was enamelled with badges of jeering bestial faces. One cruel brute toted a heavy bolter cloisonnéd with screaming, fang-bearing lips. That back-breaking bruiser of a gun could knock out a lightly-armoured vehicle, let alone a man. Power armour easily sustained such a weight. The bolter clutched in the other intruder's metalled fist seemed like a toy by comparison.

'*For Tzeentch!*' shrieked an amplifier, over the howl of the wind, as incoming dust blinded and choked Jaq and Lex.

HAD THESE HIDEOUS emissaries come in response to Jaq's tormented soul-searching?

He may have been on the verge of inviting a daemon to possess him. But not of inviting corrupted human minions! Even though those might be sorcerers in their own right! Pride raked Jaq's soul even as he clutched a palm over his nose and mouth – not to prevent vomit from spewing forth, though nausea twisted his guts, but to filter the dust.

Dust stung his eyes. He must shut them. He must rely on tumultuous psychic cues. Oh, to have the near-sense of a blind astropath who could inwardly and exactly detect persons in her vicinity. Jaq himself was blind, and holding his breath.

What use was a warp-eye lens when its intended victims could not see it? Blindly Jaq snatched out his force rod. How sick and confused he felt. He summoned repulsion and disruption and anathema. He discharged these into the swirling gritty darkness, sweeping his rod from side to side rather than aiming it.

The impact of armour hurled him against a wall, concussing him. Dizzily he slid on to the hard slate floor.

LEX HAD LOOSED a bolt from his gun – with what consequence he did not know. Armour embraced him, crushing him in an immense cudbear hug. The gun was plucked from his grasp. To keep hold of the gun would simply have been to lose his fingers as easily as a spider loses its legs to a vicious child. Stray electricity stung him. His nostrils were silting up. He must close down his breathing. Both of his hearts were thumping – in horror at the memory of being captured once before.

Aye, captured in a tunnel inside the world of Antro, deep down away from the ruddy light of a star known as Karka Secundus. On that fearful occasion implacable spiked hoops powered by pistons had immobilized him in his armour. He had been stripped of his armour in preparation for sacrifice to Tzeentch.

Now the armoured strength of Tzeentch's Chaos renegades was dragging Lex out into the inky dust storm. He could not exert himself even in futile resistance. He could not even give vent to a howl. To do so, he must breathe. If he breathed, he would choke.

JAQ ROUSED. DIMLY he could see the room. Ruddy light was filtering through the dust as though he was perceiving the scene in infra-red. The drapes were fluttering like great predatory wings. A great angular suit of armour lay motionless upon the slate floor.

The storm was on the verge of passing over. And the force rod had killed one of the Traitor Marines.

A convulsion of coughing racked Jaq. He hawked up gritty froth. He dragged a handful of robe across his mouth and nose. He coughed again and again as though his lungs might turn inside-out. At last the bronchial spasm subsided. He gulped air through the thick sieve of his garment. Then he forced himself to breathe more shallowly.

Lex was nowhere to be seen. The wind wailed past the shattered windows. Elsewhere in the mansion there seemed to be no sound of turmoil. Chaos renegades from the Eye of Terror were so close at hand! A boltgun lay on the floor. Lex's gun. Jaq pulled out *Emperor's Mercy*, aiming towards the dust-veiled garden.

Those Chaos Marines had come into this room. He had seen two of them before dust blinded him. Probably there had been one or two more. They had proceeded no further. They hadn't attempted – yet – to ransack the mansion. They had left. They had even left Jaq alive.

They had taken Lex as their prize!

'Grimm!' roared Jaq. More coughing convulsed him.

THE ABHUMAN CAME soon enough, *Emperor's Peace* in one hand. On entering the ruptured room, Grimm clapped his forage cap over the lower part of his face. Rakel, who was with him, began to splutter.

Outside the wind was dropping fast. The view was clearing somewhat. The lightest dust would still take hours to settle. Beyond shrubberies and gravel the far boundary wall was flattened – under the bulk of a ship as large as the mansion itself. A rectangular vessel with giant pincers at the bow, and razor fins. Jutting from the ship's snout was what appeared to be a plasma cannon. Other armaments were mounted atop, and to the rear.

'Huh,' spluttered Grimm, 'I see we got new neighbours. Guess there weren't ever too many planning laws in Shandabar.' He eyed the fallen armour with fearful curiosity. His teeth chattered. 'Su-somebody du-deliver a new su-suit of armour for our bu-big hunk?' He squashed his cap against his mouth to control himself.

'Chaos Marines.' Jaq spoke tersely so as not to cough again. He glared at Rakel as if to erase the words from her consciousness.

The shock of proximity to these impious tools of corruption was intense – visceral and soul-searing. That these agents of abomination should be here, in this heartland of the Imperium, was a horrendous development. Chaos seemed to be all-knowing, all-powerful. The Imperium seemed like a vast, star-spanning cobweb seeking to thwart the hornets – and locusts, and viler plagues – of Chaos. The web sought to be of adamantium. How frail and rusty much of it was! Space Marines and Imperial Guard were so many spiders scuttling to sting the toxic hornets which ripped the cobweb. No wonder their stings must be fierce and sometimes indiscriminate. And perhaps the effort was doomed.

A forlorn fierce pride coursed through Jaq; and he grinned crazily. 'Chaos has come calling on us – yet hardly the way I dreamed!'

WHY HAD THE Traitor Marines withdrawn? The logic of Chaos was not necessarily the logic of mortals. Those knights must have come here in response to the Daemon card, and perhaps to seize the Book of Fate, which might well resonate its presence to such as they.

Had Jaq's force rod disrupted their reasoning? Jaq had been enfeebled by the high voltage in the air – and yet one raider had actually died. The force rod had scrambled their thinking. Maybe the strong electric charge had contributed. Would the metal of their suits have insulated them, or caused an accumulation of voltage?

Sickeningly, Jaq recalled Lex's confession. Lex had once been touched by Chaos – by the near presence of Tzeentch. To the Chaos raiders, Lex must have smelled of that past encounter. To control and corrupt a pious Space Marine would give them such perverse joy! Then to use that wretch as a tool against his former associates! How much more perverse than simply to kill Lex.

Had not Jaq assured Lex that the force rod could save him or kill him, if need be?

Grimm interrupted Jaq's reverie. 'Uh, boss, do we just wait here for their next performance? Or do we get the hell out of here with the *Book of Dandruff* and leave the Jester to 'em?'

Does one wait for the approach of a lumbering perverted homicidal giant attired in borrowed Chaos armour? Does one discharge a force rod at Lex – mercifully? Or in vain? Lex had spoken of maybe needing to execute Jaq... How tables were turned, how fate was foxing all hope!

After killing Lex, await the onrush of many more armoured renegades? Try to decamp with the book? Surely they would be detected by some radar or motion sensor aboard the dire vessel. The plasma cannon would gush, consuming the mansion and anything in the vicinity.

'Uh, boss, are you hoping the local vigilantes will take umbrage at the ship in someone's back garden – and fire off their pop guns? We gotta get outa here!'

'*No.*'

'Uh, you hoping Arbites will cotton on that there are hostile Space Marines roosting in this suburb, and send an execution team? Natch, they'll be delighted to save our bacon, if they ain't all fried by plasma, which is much more likely!'

'That's exactly why we can't leave,' snapped Jaq. 'The Chaos ship has this mansion covered.'

If only Arbites, or soldiers of the local garrison, might render assistance. If only those who should rightly be allies might indeed combine! Jaq's lonely renegade status denied him so much.

He gazed at the fallen armour. 'I shall need to board that ship with my force rod. Somehow I shall wear that armour so that they imagine their vile comrade is returning–'

'That's figging ridiculous. It's power armour. You don't have spinal sockets to control it. You ain't enhanced all over, and inside. Lex could hardly move in armour when his power went off, remember?'

'Maybe that Chaos armour is lighter–'

'Made of titanium? Looks like tough steel and ceramite to me.'

'Maybe I can force it to move a step at a time, as if I'm badly injured. Rage may lend me strength. I will pray hard.'

'Oh fig. If only you weren't right about the plasma cannon.' Grimm scurried to the suit and knelt. He wrenched the vaned helmet aside, unsealing it. The dead face he exposed was shark-like, harsh and lean. That face sported dozens of tiny tattoos of vermilion mouths, as though it had been kissed repeatedly by rouged or bloodstained miniature lips. Pink drool had dribbled down the chin.

'Give me a hand, Rakel!'

Painstakingly, off came those rounded pauldrons. Then the sharp angular vambraces. Then cuisses. Then greaves. Then poleyns and groin-guard and cleated boots. Time was passing. Dust was settling slowly.

'There ain't no spinal sockets, boss! Just things like puckered ulcers or suckers down the backbone. Or like lips–'

Lips of Tzeentch, which would open all over that daemon's body, uttering contradictory statements…

'Daemonry!' cried Jaq with a terrible joy. His prayer was answered. 'The suit's sorcerously synched to its wearer. It's psychically synched.' How the words slithered from his lips.

The dead renegade's body was mostly coated in iridescent scales as filmy as those of a fish. This renegade seemed to have been in a state of metamorphosis. One might imagine him, in whatever foul citadel he inhabited, lolling in a marble pool before arising to don his armour. Now the eerily lovely glitter was fast fading from the scales.

With assistance Jaq began to don the unfamiliar armour.

BY THE TIME Jaq stood armoured, with visor still open, visibility outside allowed an even clearer sight of the Chaos ship. Jaq still wore the hooded lens of Azul's eye.

As though to compensate for its progressive exposure to view, that ship wavered. It began to shift its shape, at least in the eye of the beholder. Miniature holo-projectors studding the hull must be generating a false semblance, a faceted camouflage; unless the daemonic power of change could manipulate the very material of that ship into new contours and configurations.

The ship no longer seemed to be a ship, of angular and box-like aspect – but instead a building. It imitated the mansion from which the trio witnessed it. A casual spectator might have been fooled – especially with all the haze of dust still adrift – except that the hoax mansion straddled a crushed wall.

Were the occupants of the genuine adjoining property gaping from their own windows across their own shrubby gardens at this phenomenon, this mirage looming amid the dust-mist? Might it seem to them that Tod Zapasnik was a sorcerer who had shifted his own abode closer to them under the cover of the storm, intruding right over the boundary line? Might it seem that the storm had been so fierce that it had uprooted and shifted Zapasnik's home? Those owners would be well advised to cower, and not approach that trespassing structure.

Due to the freak warmth, and to apprehension and expectation, Jaq was perspiring. He prayed for unity with this unnatural power armour; that it might heed his psyche and obey his will.

'OH ANCESTORS!'

The sight which wrung this yell from Grimm was of Jaq's harsh armour transformed. Like the ship, its appearance had shifted. It wreathed itself in holographic or daemonic illusion. Briefly its colours were fluctuating: brightly green, luridly yellow, achingly blue. Then, as if blessed by some kind of glory, the armour was red, embellished in gold; and remained so. The axe-like vanes rising behind the helmet seemed to have expanded into a blood-red bat-wing of metal. Gilded fylfot crosses adorned the shoulder pauldrons. The knee-protectors were embossed with skulls. On the groin-hauberk was a golden scarab. Surely this was pious Imperial armour, bearing witness to a long-lost purity of purpose.

Within the open helmet Jaq's grizzle-bearded face was distorted by some vision – associated with Rakel? Grimly he squinted at her. He took a step.

'Turn back!' he commanded. 'Do not go onward! You must not!'

AHEAD OF HIM, Jaq saw Meh'lindi lying asleep in that cul-de-sac in the webway. Grimm lay nearby, and Marines, and his own sleeping self – and also the doomed deceitful Navigator.

If Meh'lindi went onward, it would be to her death, speared by a Phoenix Lady. Was this the moment when he could snatch her back from her fate? Was this when her soul could be plucked to safety and enshrined in... in... in... He could not think clearly. His thoughts were in turmoil, as though Chaos were about to submerge him.

From the turmoil arose an image of a wench's oval face, vague as a wraith. Her name came to him: Olvia. Jaq had been intimate with Olvia aboard the terrible Black Ship carrying him and her and hundreds of other young psykers to Earth to be consumed so as to feed Him-on-Earth; and some few of them to be sanctified as astropaths or inquisitors. Not Olvia, though. Not her. She was already lost to her life. Just as Meh'lindi was lost!

Oh loss, oh loss! Oh agony of loss. Oh *damnum, detrimentum!*

Words tore from Jaq: 'Turn back! Do not go onward! You must not! I swear this by Olvia! Go back!'

His other self, there in the webway, roared in repugnance:

'*Ego te exorcizo!*' A fierce repulsive force rebuffed Jaq overpoweringly. That nook in the webway was shrinking to a vanishing point.

Yet he was still staring at Meh'lindi's face! Ach no, at Rakel's face. With his steel gauntlets he could have assaulted that tantalizing face in frustration – except that it was sacred, in a private profane corner of his soul.

'Boss? You BACK with us yet?'

'What do you mean?' demanded Jaq.

'You've just been standing there like some statue, all stupefied and bewitched.'

Aye, caught up in that vision of the webway where time passed differently.

'How long was I thus?' Grimm told him, and Jaq groaned. 'So long!'

The abhuman added: 'If I weren't a loyal sort of tyke I'd have taken off on me own in the meantime!'

'And if it weren't for the plasma cannon,' Rakel reminded Grimm. 'What happened to you, lord?'

'That doesn't matter!'

Jaq could hardly have plucked Meh'lindi's soul from her doomed body while she was still alive and brought it here. His vision, induced by the Chaos armour, was futile.

'He looked so noble in his armour,' Rakel murmured.

'Glorious and red and gold,' agreed Grimm. 'Skulls on the knees, scarab on the groin.'

Now Jaq was harsh and angular once more; and the armour had become a dull blue.

They had seen him exactly as he had seen himself on that earlier occasion in the webway.

'Couldn't help but admire you, boss. 'Cept for your paralysis. Course, how you looked just now wouldn't have impressed any Chaos Marines into imagining you was one of them! Just as well you didn't budge from here.'

Had this been the meaning of the illusion projected by the armour: that true honour and purity still resided within him despite a dalliance with daemonry, despite a pathological addiction to Meh'lindi? That these obsessions were indeed the route to virtue?

When he donned the Chaos armour just now, had the shining path touched him – after so long? Had the Numen transfigured him? Might the Numen now guide him into that Chaos ship, as once it had guided him through the Emperor's palace and into the throne room itself? Guide him unseen and safely?

Was he already illuminated, unbeknownst, without needing recourse to daemons? Without first needing to surrender his soul? Had he not already surrendered himself to this steel suit of Chaos – and exorcised himself?

'I'm going to the Chaos vessel,' he growled. 'Give me my force rod, Grimm.' He was on the point of closing the visor, to hide his face.

'Oh my ancestors,' cried Grimm. 'You're too late.' From the direction of the Chaos ship, Lex came lurching. His face was contorted by a psychopathic snarl.

Eleven
Tzeentch

It was Lex's worst nightmare come true.

Oh, the threat of sacrifice to Tzeentch had been actual enough in that cave within Antro – but Terminator Librarians had saved Lex, Biff and Yeri. Nothing could save Lex now.

Worse still: his present tormentors were corrupted Marines who had rebelled against Him-on-Earth ten thousand years ago. If Lex had been elevated to a superhuman condition by surgery and by the gene-seed of Rogal Dorn, these former Marines had become radically inhuman. Daemonry had sustained their twisted lives, endowing them with hideous powers. Their existence was the vilest blasphemy in the cosmos.

Worst of all: it was not their intention simply to sacrifice him or to torture him to death. They intended to make him into one of them: into a daemon-ridden cadet of Chaos.

Contours inside the Chaos ship were wilfully deviant: askew and slanted and crooked. Ornamentations were tortuous and devilish. To gape at those was nauseous. They seemed to pluck at the mind. Sulphurous incense burned, perhaps to mask a lurking foetor.

With their power gauntlets two of Lex's captors easily held him, by wrists and ankles, upon a grooved iron table. They disdained the shackles which were welded to either end of the table. Thus they could turn him over, like a huge child, to examine his spinal sockets, and to let a comrade in corruption insert a chilly probe into those sockets. The mere touch of this probe made Lex writhe.

How many captives – how many vulnerable psykers – had been examined upon this table until they became insane or became serviceable slaves for these renegade sorcerers?

Now a captive Fist had fallen into their hands. He must strive to hide the actual identity of his Chapter lest it be dishonoured. Would they recognize his cheek-tattoo, his personal heraldry as a Fist?

What a dry chuckling he heard from those who had raised their visors. Facial electro-tattoos, thus exposed, shifted slyly in shape and hue.

WHAT WAS MISSING from a Space Marine's body was a suicide gland. What was missing was the ability to will oneself to die.

How could such a facility ever be contemplated? Even if hideously and fatally injured a Marine must strive to endure, at least until his progenoid glands could be harvested. Else how could a new super-warrior be kindled to replace him?

Sheer pain, Lex would welcome. Pain, he could convert into adoration of Dorn.

Not this impious prying, this intimate invasion.

A black-nailed finger traced the puckers on Lex's forehead from which he had torn out his service studs.

'You would seem to be a deserter,' said his tormentor, his daemonic tattoos pulsing. 'A runaway traitor. You have found your new family, deserter! Yet your hormones reek of loathing for us. They stink of loyalty to your wretched primarch and to that thing on Earth. How can this be, how can this be? Let us see, let us see.'

The voice became hypnotically sing-song. 'All is change, all is mutation and alteration. We shall mutate you and initiate you, so that your soul shall conform to the semblance of a renegade. You shall become one of us – a lesser one throughout the next few centuries, yet one nonetheless. Capable of serving our master, Tzeentch, and of being rewarded with attributes, and of aspiring to potent sorcery. Oh yessss–'

DURING STAGES IN Lex's novitiate as a future Space Marine he had been initiated dauntingly enough – by a feast of foul excremental unfood and by other formidable ceremonies.

The forced rite of initiation which took place like a ravishment within that Chaos vessel was execrable and almost unspeakable. How could Lex obliterate from memory the Kiss of Corruption, the Communion with Chaos, the Prayer of Perfidy, the spells and the invocations? And all the while he was experiencing the slither of tendrils within his spinal sockets. These invaded his nervous system, generating nauseating visions of the fragility of the cosmos, of the feebleness of reality which daemonic fingers sought to unpluck and reknit, with such vile success.

Lex in torment saw the whole cosmos burst forth from a mere bubble in the energy-warp. A sparrow's fart the universe was! That fart inflated suddenly. It caught fire and exploded outward. Gas became matter. Space ballooned to accommodate the gush. Matter became the stars and worlds of a billion galaxies. All was mere froth upon the surging unseen ocean of the warp. Finally the pull of the warp would drag all galaxies and all space back together again, abolishing this temporary interruption which was the whole of space and time, and all of struggling suffering life.

The lusts and rages of life caused terrible entities to coalesce in the warp, and to give rise to sub-entities, to daemons and sub-daemons. Daemons clawed at reality to try to drag it and its denizens back into the warp prematurely. Tzeentch and his daemonic lieutenants especially sought to twist the future of the cosmos askew. Tzeentch would triumph.

The Emperor on Terra was no more than a guttering candle in malevolent darkness. The radiance of Rogal Dorn and other primarchs were pathetic glimmers.

What of the shining path which Jaq sought? What of the good light which might be awakened by benevolence and compassion and self-sacrifice arising universally? A sparrow might as well fart into a hurricane. The spirit of the Numen slumbered, unaware of itself except in dreamlike spasms.

Oh, do tell your tormenting initiators that the name of your Chapter is the Imperial Fists! Oh, do hand over the Book of Fate to the worshippers of Tzeentch! Oh, do join them joyfully in the disruption of this futile cosmos, and be rewarded.

All along Lex's nerves, and in his mind, potent daemonry squirmed like an invasion by tiny ants which were really all one collective manifold beast.

'Which Chapter did you desert?' Lex heard.

He gibbered. His mouth frothed. His very soul was being drowned in vileness, and revived, and drowned again. Soon it would no longer be his soul, but Tzeentch's property; and he would be a willing puppet.

'Which Chapter?'

As he opened his lips to reply, his left hand tore free from the gauntlet which held it. His left hand rose as if to stifle him, to throttle him. That was the hand on the bones of which were inscribed the names of Biff Tundrish and Yeremi Valence of Necromunda, and of the Imperial Fists...

Lex seemed to hear from afar in the sea of souls the voices of Biff and Yeri crying out to him to resist – no, to let them resist on his behalf, to let them be his strength and his salvation. Yeri particularly had always yearned to protect Lex, hadn't he?

Let Biff and Yeri be his own protective daemons who would lurk within; who would snatch his soul back to safety even though it seemed to be lost to Tzeentch. The inscriptions hidden upon the bones of that left hand were the most potent sorcerous runes. By virtue of those runes, his left hand clasped Rogal Dorn's own hand through the intermediary of his dead comrades. Though he fell, they would raise him in the final moment.

Sweating and shuddering, Lex submitted to the Chaos Marines.

The name of his Chapter? He could tell them that without blame, because it was the proudest of names.

The Book of Fate? He could betray that. They already knew it was nearby.

Who should they wickedly send to fetch it, and to kill or be killed, but this traitor, this new cadet kinsman in Chaos?

'*That's* his initiation test!'

'In that house they'll think he has escaped from us–'

'Instead he will kill or concuss–'

How Lex relished the prospect of incapacitating the inquisitor with his bare hands. How he hoped to hand Jaq over to his new brothers in sorcery. How he relished the thought of swatting the impudent squat to death or tearing him limb from limb. As for Rakel, that sham – what fate would be best for her, to torment Jaq the most? To inject her again with polymorphine so that she would go into fatal agonizing flux – providing the visible dissolution of Jaq Draco's stupid ambitions!

There was also the Death Jester, to serve up to these new elder brothers. Lex could relish these deeds and allow his hormones to riot, because his left hand enshrined his salvation. That hand was calm now. It feigned.

Chaos Marines were laughing. What if their new initiate were killed as soon as he returned to the mansion? Why, he would die utterly subverted – traitor to his Chapter of naive musclemen and to the ramshackle Imperium. Then the Princes of Chaos would overwhelm the mansion and seize prizes.

Lex himself was a prime prize – but a prize best enjoyed perhaps in the squandering of it.

* * *

'He's coming for us!' bawled Grimm. He levelled *Emperor's Peace*.

Jaq waved the force rod. 'Don't shoot till I've used this! I may purge him and cleanse him.'

'That's all very well for you to say. You're wearing armour.'

At least Lex wasn't wearing any Chaos armour.

'I order you not to use the bolter. Otherwise I'll kill you.'

'Oh ancestors, maybe I'd rather be killed by you than by what'll follow-'

By what would inevitably follow.

Whatever Jaq achieved with Lex would surely be futile. Suppose Jaq could restore the Space Marine to sanity, what price another pair of hands, however muscular, to fire another boltgun – against armoured Chaos Marines? Ultimately, against a plasma cannon?

'Shall I free the Death Jester?' cried Rakel.

What, and arm the Harlequin? Gamble that the Jester might temporarily ally himself with his captors so as to save the Book of Fate from being seized by the forces of Chaos?

What a trusting – or desperate – assumption that would be.

Lex loomed in the vacant window frame. Promptly his left hand clutched that frame to slow him and hold him back.

His face was a mask of homicidal hatred. How he snarled at the hand. Relaxing its grip, the hand made a defiant fist – which then struck him brutally and dazzlingly on the chin.

'He's at war with himself!'

Urgently the hand gestured at Jaq not to use the force rod. Jaq refrained, temporarily at least.

'He's possessed, and he ain't!'

The hand mimed opening a book. The hand pointed down in the direction of the basement. The hand urged going there. A nimbus of light glowed around the hand, leaving quasi-phosphorescent traces in the dusty air like blazons of a luminous route which should be followed.

How urgently Lex gestured.

This matter was urgent indeed if the renegades aboard the ship were observing – with mounting bewilderment – through oculi.

'Basement's the best place to be when a plasma cannon lets rip! That way we can be buried alive and roasted more slowly-'

The lambently glowing left hand – a whole hand rather than a mere Finger of Glory – reached out toward Jaq, not so as to interfere with his force rod, but to invite Jaq to clasp the hand with his free gauntlet. That hand was becoming translucent, as though it were an alabaster X-ray. Bones showed within, scrimshaw bones with words inscribed upon them, over and over elegantly and minutely in cursive script, words almost too small to read. There was no time for closer scrutiny.

As Jaq accepted the hand, light flickered around his borrowed armour, and once again it wore the guise of glorious red and gold. Would the renegades right now be watching something so inexplicable and occult that the mystery of it might deter them for a few more precious minutes? Might they imagine that Tzeentch was somehow manifesting himself within the mansion? That Tzeentch was causing such strange changes! Such a seemingly noble metamorphosis!

The hand assisted Jaq in his manoeuvring of the suit. The Hand of Glory led him.

'Stay, Grimm, stay!' ordered Jaq. 'Rakel too. The renegades must see someone still up here or they might come to investigate.'

'Oh ancestors...'

Rakel was gaping numbly at a pair of sorcerers about to leave that violated room.

HOW THOSE TURQUOISE eyes widened. How crazily the Jester grimaced at the sight of Lex and Jaq. Jaq, in that spuriously splendid armour. Jaq, led by Lex whose illuminated hand leaked phosphor streaks which lingered briefly in the air. How Marb'ailtor wrenched at his chains.

'*Deamhan diabhal!*' he uttered in dismay. The giant stank of daemonry – although his glowing hand seemed like a living torch which was keeping dark evil at bay. That resplendent armour was a phantasm. It was lustrous silk draped over razor blades. Something momentous had happened, and was still happening. What, what? Surely Death was about to jape the Jester – who would die in ignorance.

Lex and Jaq entirely ignored the captive eldar.

On the lectern the *Book of Rhana Dandra* lay open. With his glowing hand, Lex assaulted the tome. His shining fingers seemed to sink into the vellum as if it were dough. As he lifted his hand clear, did runes drip phosphorescently from his fingers? The runes on the page were writhing.

Marb'ailtor howled at the desecration.

With his Hand of Glory Lex gestured urgently at Jaq's force rod, and then at himself. Lex's other hand, his possessed hand, clamped itself upon Jaq's shoulder pauldron. This contact caused the splendid semblance of red and gold to arc and flash and fade, stripping away that heroic illusion, revealing the renegade armour in its harsh angularity.

* * *

JAQ UNDERSTOOD. LEX was trying to expel the daemonry into Jaq himself, as lightning might arc through a conductor. Thus, to empower Jaq!

Jaq pressed the force rod against Lex's chest.

'Yield up the evil in you! Let it pass into me! *Ego te exorcizo!*' Jaq discharged his rod.

The flash threw Lex backwards ponderously, to crash into the doorjamb. Lex pivoted slowly. His fading fingers of Glory dragged four phosphorescent claw marks down the stone as slowly he slumped to the floor. He rolled over. His eyes were alert with a light of salvation as he gazed, still alive, towards Jaq.

Jaq reeled and might have fallen but for the corset of his armour. The rod fell from his gauntlet. He gripped the lectern to steady himself. He was gazing down upon shifting shimmering runes, flowing like spilled mercury.

What did he wish the book to tell him? What did he want it to yield? His fate, his future...

The location of the place where time could twist...

Or of a place where a soul could be redeemed from death...

A place of redemption, of deliverance.

A place in the warp from which the shining path originated. To arrive there might supercharge the dormant Numen. The Chaos Child might begin to awaken to divinity and to transfiguring power – and might even incarnate a fraction of itself in the illuminated mortal who visited its Chaos cradle.

Surely this was impossible, a megalomaniac fantasy! And yet... at that pivotal place to resurrect someone worthy from death might surely send a shining ripple through the whole fabric of the warp and the cosmos too...

Someone as worthy as Meh'lindi.

Yes, oh yes.

Personal passion and cosmic salvation might both be served. The Imperium might be saved and transfigured, along with Him-on-Earth. Oh to bring healing balm to that wounded God, to reconcile Him restoringly with the Child of Light.

How Jaq ached for Meh'lindi to be resurrected, reincarnated. She was like an amputated limb. Her ghostly presence persisted and persisted.

A haunting cackle lurked in his mind. Yet how his perception was enlarging. How shiningly he saw: a sentence descending circuitously down into the page. The sentence curled around and within itself like some burrowing silver worm. The initial word of that sentence served as a compressed code which now gave rise to a whole stretch of instructions. Instructions which were simple directions. *Clé, ceart, lár:* left, right, middle. Directions through the webway! Directions to Jaq's destiny.

When the rune had appeared to Azul Petrov in his agony-vision, the rune which had revealed the hidden route to the Black Library, the starting point had been precisely where Petrov had happened to be at that particular time.

So it must be with this snaking sentence.

With the tip of a steel-clad finger, Jaq flipped up the hood from his lethal monocle.

Of a sudden the sentence was jagged and forked. No longer was it a sentence at all but an intricate network. What Jaq saw through the lens exemplified rather than described. A particular route through the network was luminously traced. Sometimes it returned upon itself. It crossed itself. Twice it cut over a major axis – those must be wraithship passages.

Of course! That place of power in the webway, that node which Great Harlequins were said to seek, was in no one particular place. It could become present anywhere at all – if and only if you followed a precise combination of routes from any starting point whatever.

No wonder Great Harlequins had never found the place. Potentially it could be anywhere. Yet it never was found, because no seeker had ever yet followed the exact combination. Who in their right mind would cross through the vast tunnel of a major wraithship axis?

Jaq peered. A small gap existed in the route. Another gap, elsewhere.

What could those gaps signify but that the quester must quit the webway somewhere and then re-enter it nearby? Within the craftworld there were too many webway portals to make the right choice except by sheer chance. These gaps must relate to planets upon which there were not one, but two openings. You must travel across the surface of a world from one portal to the other.

The rune of the Black Library had been pared from the warp-eye. Jaq sensed now that the rune of the route to the place of power was inscribing itself psychically in thin black lines upon the warp-eye lens.

As it did so, the page ceased to have hidden depths.

Jaq hooded the lens, as a beetle collector might enclose a fine specimen. Whenever he chose to look through the lens, overlaid upon whatever scene he saw would be the route.

Was the route still implicit in the page? Might others discover it? Roughly he ripped the page out and rolled it up.

Lex was squatting now. His chest was blackened as if by soot, yet the injury seemed superficial and irrelevant to him, a negligible flash burn.

Jaq tossed the scroll at Lex.

'Tuck that into your webbing. Don't lose it. Help me get out of this cumbersome armour! Hurry, we haven't long…'

How yearningly the Death Jester stared at the scroll. He must believe that his captor-wizard had found some prophecy of immeasurable value, outweighing the rest of the Book of Fate!

WHILE LEX HELPED Jaq strip off vambraces and greaves and pauldrons, Jaq probed himself inwardly.

He seemed clean, yet he persevered…

And he encountered a presence.

A sensation had taken up temporary residence in the tip of his right foot. How insignificant it seemed, like a wart. It was hiding as far away from his brain as it could find.

No sooner detected, than the presence reached out like some sea anemone opening up its fronds. Those fronds extended numbingly out and out. Jaq's right foot became numb; wouldn't obey his will. The foot jerked sideways. The presence controlled it.

Jaq's leg was numb to the knee – to the thigh. The invasion was coursing up through him, rising like floodwater up a drain. Hasty incantations had little effect. This energy-thing from the warp was wild to seize a material body for its own use.

Jaq's hands were still his own. But to use the force rod upon himself might injure him severely. Lex had been protected by that luminous hand of his, and the daemon had anticipated transferring into another body. Jaq must rip the daemon from his own marrow and banish it all the way into the warp.

While Jaq still controlled his own voice, he cried out to Lex, 'Don't look at the lens! Hold the armour in front of my face as a shield and a mirror!'

Lex understood. The giant snatched up the rounded pauldron. Even as Jaq beheld the reflection of his own rutted and bearded features with his ordinary vision he flipped up both lens-hoods again. He gazed through the eye of the warp at himself. The rune of the route interposed a filigree lattice. Energy seemed to leap through the lattice into his brain – raw warp-energy, akin to the daemon within him yet without any consciousness of its own nature.

Like a wave which had crashed ashore, this energy began to withdraw powerfully, sucking at his soul. This was when mortal men might lose their lives or go mad. The energy was also sucking at the daemon which was rising up so swiftly within Jaq.

The daemon's momentum became part of that powerfully ebbing force. It was being dragged with the wave, losing identity, shrieking.

Out of Jaq the daemon was sucked.

JAQ HAD SHUTTERED the lens and was breathing deeply.

Lex had discarded the pauldron and had slammed the *Book of Rhana Dandra* shut. With his ceramically toughened fingernail he ripped precious gems loose from the binding, and jammed these into a pouch upon his webbing. He was planning ahead. If they could conceivably escape from the mansion there was little that they could carry with them other than weapons and the condensed wealth of jewels.

'Are you... illuminated?' Jaq asked Lex – in wonderment at what had happened.

Lex ignored the question. How could he possibly have become illuminated when he had never been a psyker to begin with? A miracle had happened. That miracle had been due to the names upon his finger bones, to intervention by the souls of dead comrades, to the intercession of Rogal Dorn the shining light.

'Are you?' Lex barked at Jaq.

Jaq did not know. Analyse himself as he might, an awareness of illumination eluded him. Oh, he had seen luminously into the Book of Fate, assisted by that hand of glory which glowed no more. Oh, he had been semi-possessed, but not profoundly in his soul. When he reached the place of power and reincarnated Meh'lindi, that would be the supremely illuminating moment.

Upstairs, a boltgun began to racket. There came the muffled sound of heavier fire in reply. The renegades must be returning to the mansion in force. Only Grimm and Rakel were in their way.

As Jaq and Lex ascended from the cellars in haste, leaving book and Jester abandoned, a pandemonium of explosions began which could have no imaginable explanation...

THE REASON WAS both wonderful and terrible.

Chaos Marines had spilled from their ship to advance on the mansion once again. Grimm had waited until they came half-way before opening fire. He was determined to die dearly and cause a little delay.

His shots provoked a thunderous response. And then, moments later, flying machines hove into view in the dusty air above the ship. Armed machines. Two-person machines. Half a dozen of them.

These had been classified by the Imperium as Vypers, eldar craft, somewhat larger than jetbikes. Some sported twin shuriken catapults;

others, single shuriken cannons. Three of the Vypers carried heavy plasma guns in addition. The other three carried lascannons. The pilots and gunners were a squad of craftworld guardians wearing pale green wraith-armour and dark green helmets. Green banners rippled.

A seventh Vyper was keeping its distance. In the gunner's, the passenger's seat, was a shimmer of hues. The third Harlequin had indeed reached the webway portal. He had brought vengeance back with him. Vengeance – or reinforcement? In spite of Jaq's psychic shielding had the Harlequin sensed something of the true motive of the attack at the theatre? Had he sensed – or guessed – the link with the lost Book of Fate?

That Harlequin could not have realized that the Death Jester had been captured instead of killed, otherwise there should have been another Vyper with an empty seat for rescue.

Those Vypers had flown to Sabulorb on the very coat-tails of the storm – such an ideal cloak. Had the eldar spied the Chaos vessel descending upon the shrouded city? If not, its daemonic aura must have caught their attention and demanded investigation. Oh, let not the book fall into the clutch of the arch-enemy.

A Vyper opened fire with plasma cannon and lascannon upon that ship which disguised itself as a mansion. Pilots and gunners had seen renegade Marines leaving that place. No mere mansion, that!

Incandescent shells of plasma burst against their target. Waves of heat radiated, accompanied by thunderous shock. Parts of the target were converted into superheated ionized gas. If confined, this would have been thermonuclear in intensity.

Energy shells from the lascannons delivered their massive punch. Camouflage vanished, revealing the boxlike vessel. The giant pincer at the front was crippled. The plasma cannon at the snout had burst open. Part of the hull had stoved in. A razor fin had sheared off. That fin was flying through the air like some flat predatory creature. It impacted in the roof of the adjoining mansion, showering a scurf of tiles. Its blade must have shorted out some power unit, because a moment later the whole roof of that large house erupted, a small fireball rising, followed by gushing black smoke.

The ship's upper plasma cannon discharged itself dazzlingly. One of the Vypers became an expanding ball of scorching lurid gas.

Plasma cannons took quite a while to recharge after the expenditure of such energies. The pilots of the remaining Vypers were turning their attention to the armoured renegades out in the open – just as those renegades turned their attention upon the Vypers. Shuriken discs streamed and cannoned from above. Heavy bolts and energy packets flew upward. Blasted, a blue-clad gunner fell. Punctured a score of times, a Traitor Marine staggered.

Grimm fired almost affably, out into the garden.

It was at this moment that the plasma cannon near the stern of the Chaos vessel opened fire past the blazing mansion, at its vine-clad perimeter railings.

Traffic was coming into view. Half-track armoured vehicles, mounted with heavy stub guns or autocannons. Trotting alongside were ebony automatons, almost, with mirrored faces. Arbites, armed with lasguns.

Plasma disintegrated the railings and caused some casualties. The half-tracks revved and headed directly through the dispersing heat and gas. Before the rear plasma cannon could recharge, the half-tracks were speeding past, on either side of the grounded ship.

What did the Arbitrators make of those alien flying machines swooping and banking, pitted against ferocious angular Marines? The armoured vehicles and the Arbites on foot opened fire impartially on all disturbers of the Emperor's peace. *TUB-TUB-TUB-TUB*. Heavy bullets belched from the big stubbers. Laser-packets rocketed pyrotechnically. They were like fireworks hurled against steel. Those renegades were armoured strongly enough to cause heavy bullets merely to ricochet.

The fight was threefold and insensate. By now Jaq's mansion was suffering enough collateral damage to bring masonry crashing down, interspersed by showers of glass from upper windows. Noises of detonations were deafening.

'Let's get outa here!' shouted Grimm.

Jaq seized his discarded robe to don over his mesh-armour. 'My bone!' exclaimed Lex. What about the thigh bone on which he had carved for the sake of his Chapter, should he ever rejoin them? And for the sake of his soul!

Stray las-fire ignited curtains. Flames climbed to lick the ceiling.

'Gotta leave your bone, you great mastiff,' yelled Grimm.

Lex groaned with grief.

'What about the Jester?' shrieked Rakel.

'Leave him to roast, of course!' shouted Grimm. 'And the *Book of Dandruff* too. Give his snooty pals something to occupy their minds. If those guys can deal with the Chaos boys as well as with the mirror-faces then they'd better take up fire-fighting pretty damn fast–'

Distracted by the nuisance of the Arbites, Chaos Marines were succumbing to the aerial onslaught. The damaged Chaos vessel began to throb and to vent wisps of plasma. Despite its damage it was preparing for take-off. The pilot was preparing to abandon all the surviving Traitor Marines.

AMIDST SUCH BEDLAM it *was* indeed possible to escape to the sidelines and away, blessing the dust which still hung in the air and the smoke drifting from explosions and fires.

As Jaq and his companions were fleeing, a small sun seemed to rise against the hazed ruby immensity of Sabulorb's own sun, which was now reasserting itself in the sky. A small and wobbling minor sun: that was the plasma torch of the Chaos ship.

With a vane missing, and with the other weakening it had suffered, that ship might well be unsteerable. If it achieved escape velocity the renegade ship might only plunge onward through space... until in a few days time – or much earlier, depending on velocity – it fell into the embrace of the vast red sun. How deeply would it penetrate the furnace-hot outer gases before exploding?

Or would the pilot suicidally activate the warp-drive to escape this fate, annihilating his vessel and disrupting space in its vicinity, sending a shock-wave inward through the contracting red giant?

On the vast scale of a sun, this would be a puny enough shock-wave, but perhaps significant. A dying butterfly begetting a tempest.

Twelve
FIRESTORM

It HAPPENED THAT an airborne troop carrier arrived at Shandabar's spaceport from the northerly continent just prior to the storm. On board were two hundred hardened soldiers. They were due to be sent offworld to join the Sabulorb regiments. A transport ship of the Imperial Guard had landed at the spaceport to receive the new intake. Two squads of veteran Guards were escorts.

Half of the Shandabar garrison was routinely stationed near the perimeter of the spaceport, the remainder being near the governor's palace. In the wake of the storm these received a static-crackly vox message from the senior judge at the Arbites courthouse in the city.

Aliens coming from the direction of the Grey Desert on armed, two-person flying vehicles had raided a suburb. That same suburb had already been invaded under cover of the storm by other formidable armoured warriors. Extraterrestrial raiders had chosen Shandabar as the venue for a private war. Many Arbitrators had died. Urgent assistance was requested.

Due to the assassination of a judge and the massacre of a patrol in the city, the courthouse had adopted a policy of rapid response to sightings and reports.

Veterans and hardened recruits disembarked from the spacecraft to be met by all available surface troop carriers of the spaceport garrison, bulging armoured skirt-plates protecting their huge desert-tyres. Shortly after these vehicles had left the spaceport, an unidentified vessel descended from orbit without warning or permission. During the final stages of its descent, it fired a plasma cannon at that almost empty Imperial Guard ship upon the ground. The Guard ship exploded. Scattered wreckage crippled the nearby troop carrier.

No sooner was the intruder down than a burst of plasma demolished the control tower. Next, the terminal was torched. Huge warriors in terrifying power armour emerged from the angular vessel.

Elsewhere in Shandabar many jetbikes were sighted, steered by tall figures in green armour and helmets resembling great smooth hoods...

CITIZENS WHO HAD sheltered from the storm emerged to find dust-choked victims lying dead in drifts of grit in every street. A syncopation of distant explosions and gunfire from various quarters suggested that gangs must be taking advantage of the confusion.

Indeed deacons in camouflage clothing had set out from the Oriens Temple to launch an attack of retaliation upon the Austral Temple – though this was not the cause of most of the crackle and thump.

Viewscreens, set up throughout the city for the ceremony of the unveiling, had still not been dismantled. A judge messaged the Oriens Temple, ordering its high priest to use the camera link to proclaim a state of emergency and immediate curfew via those public screens. City being under alien attack. Arbitrators restoring order mercilessly, being assisted by Imperial Guards.

In the meantime devotees of the Imperial cult had begun flocking through grime-clogged streets to the courtyard of Oriens to pray. As prayers arose, like a portent there appeared above the vast courtyard a small armed flying vehicle – with Death as a passenger. Riding pillion was a bizarre lanky figure with a smoke-blackened skull of a face and a body of sooty bones stitched to a smouldering cloak. Death seemed to be in agony, and insane, and perhaps himself soon to die.

Through a loudhailer Death proclaimed to whoever could hear: *'YOUR SUN IS ABOUT TO MELT YOUR WORLD! YOUR SUN IS ABOUT TO BOIL YOUR SEAS! YOUR SUN IS ABOUT TO BAKE YOUR DESERTS! ALL FLESH WILL CHAR, ALL BLOOD WILL BOIL, ALL LIFE WILL END!'*

The shocked high priest transmitted this scene to dust-coated screens throughout entire districts of Shandabar. Most viewers did not fully savvy the standard ImpGoth of this apparition. Yet the scorched Jester's gist was clear. The sun pulsed heat through the lingering dust. The whole sky seemed aflame.

And then Death the Jester fell from his perch – as if he had been shot in order to silence him. Down he tumbled to sprawl burned and broken.

Rescued from the blazing mansion by the wild bravery of two green-clad guardians who had heeded his psychic cries, rescued together with the smouldering *Book of Rhana Dandra*, Marb'ailtor had suffered serious burns. Even so, Marb'ailtor insisted to his rescuers that this city must be plunged into absolute anarchy so as to allow the eldar to cope with the Chaos renegades and to safeguard the Book of Fate without interference by organized human authority – and so as to be able to track that mad magus-inquisitor who had carried off a crucial page.

Let there be utter anarchy!

Marb'ailtor would endure long enough to bring this anarchy about.

Once the Death Jester had fallen from the Vyper, and once the Vyper had sped off, the high priest finally uttered the curfew order. This command from the courthouse was completely at odds with Death's warning about imminent calamity. Or was it at odds at all? Let the people passively await extinction – while, unimpeded by crowds, the authorities used some escape route!

Panic rippled through Shandabar. Panic, and outcry. The curfew was ignored. If two million people – minus a few thousand suffocated corpses – all disobeyed, what could mere hundreds of Arbites do?

Fires were soon burning here and there in the city. The Austral Temple was in flames.

Fire. Heat. The furnace of the sun, slowly sinking. Dust-haze, heat-haze, plumes of smoke, including one from the direction of the spaceport…

Rumour of an escape route spread like a flash-fire. Not of escape by way of the spaceport! The spaceport was crippled. A hostile warship sat there. Whenever a freighter attempted to power up, a blast of plasma would strike it; a new explosion would rock the city.

Escape by way of the broad Bihishti River? Flight upon its cool waters? Thousands of people mobbed boats. Boats capsized under the burden of bodies. Thousands of people drowned. That could not be the route. Boats were too slow. None of the authorities were fleeing by way of water.

A zealot preached about penitence in the desert, salvation in the wilderness: 'Be confronting your souls in the desert as a test of faith! Be seeking the crucible of tomorrow's dawn!'

The vast majority of people had no clear idea of what was happening except that there was desperate urgency to distance themselves from Shandabar. Shandabar would burn. Soon a massive exodus was beginning. In its hysterical surge this resembled the ceremony of the unveiling, though on a greater scale.

By land-train and by trucks and by limousines, all bouncing along upon balloon-wheels, and by rickshaws and sand-sleighs and carts

pulled by camelopards, and on the backs of camelopards, and on foot
the evacuation commenced in entire disorder. As the sun at last withdrew its ruddy light and intemperate heat, sinking below the camber of
the world, a whole population was fanning out southward across the
Grey Desert in the general direction of Bara Bandobast.

Minor battles accompanied the mass migration. Islands of violence
eddied within the flood of folk. Highly mobile homicidal Chaos
Marines fought running skirmishes with lightning-swift aliens. Imperial
Guardsmen were involved, Arbitrators too. These rolling skirmishes cut
minor swathes through the exodus, serving as further goads to the mass
of refugees. How much dust so many people were raising too. What
with the dust and the setting of the sun, there was soon a blind lem-
ming-surge, illuminated only by the discharge of weaponry.

About the time when Shandabar would have receded to a bumpy line
along the horizon – had there been any visibility – a chain of distant
explosions rocked the desert. Seconds later a scorching gust from the
north carried much airborne dust away, revealing a wall of flame along
that same horizon, a bright and rippling banner, and bringing uncanny
illumination to the desert.

'WHAT IN THE name of all my ancestors...'

Grimm and Lex and Jaq and Rakel were jammed inside the cabin of a
single-carriage land-train. Until now the driver, obedient to the boltgun
held at the back of his neck, had been steering by the hazy beams from
the transport vehicle's lamps. Suddenly: that great brightness from behind
was reflected in the ornate mirrors jutting from either side of the cab.

If nomad bandits ever loomed in those mirrors, sprinting on foot or
riding camelopards, hoping to board such a train from the rear, automated autoguns were mounted at the rear and half way along the
carriage roof to deter them. On the route to Bara Bandobast bandits
were rarely a problem. Yet right now the roof of the land-train was
packed with refugees who had climbed and clung, dense as the fleas on
the head of a swimming cudbear. Jaq hadn't wanted boarders shot off.
Those people were a cloak, comparable to the human cloaks worn by
many other vehicles. They were camouflage.

The goods carriage was full of thoroughbred camelopards from breeding stables on the southern outskirts of Shandabar. According to the
driver, the beasts were being sent to take part in annual desert races at
Bara Bandobast; hence this journey of his, which Jaq and company had
hijacked. The storm had died; he had been setting out when other
events supervened.

Those animals were hobbled to prevent them from kicking each other. They were muzzled to stop them from biting their neighbours. Their weight and that of all the refugees up top caused the land-train's engine to labour somewhat. Jaq did not wish for high speed. If they outdistanced the mass stampede, they might become conspicuous. As things were, how might pursuers of whatever affiliation be able to single them out amid untold vehicles and a fleeing mass of a million people or more?

That light which pierced the dust; that blast which blew dust away temporarily, that wall of flame...

'Has Shandabar been nuked?' exclaimed Grimm.

Lex shook his head. 'I don't think so,' he said. 'Even ordinary dust at a certain number of grains per cubic centimetre in an oxygenated atmosphere can explode if there's a trigger. I think that the force of the storm may have exposed huge deposits of carbon, sulphur and nitre of potassium in the Grey Desert. It bore these aloft and mixed them. It spread them as an aerosol across the city. This thinned to a critical density. Plasma explosions ignited the mix. The city exploded in a fire-storm.'

'Do you mean to say we're travelling across a desert of gunpowder? This can explode too?'

'I doubt it, abhuman, otherwise flame would be reaching us by now. Other factors in the city could be lingering electrostatic charge due to friction, and the effect of Chaos. We ought to offer up a prayer of thanks that Shandabar exploded.'

'In the morning when the sun rises, the temperature will soar. The mob would be wise to return home. But now home has been annihilated. We will continue to be a needle in a very vast haystack. Eldar and Chaos renegades and local peace enforcers might kill each other. They will certainly become fatigued. Not revving too fast, driver!'

They must try to catch some sleep, or half-sleep, in the crowded vibrating cab while Lex or Jaq or Grimm in turn supervised the driver. Rakel could sleep as long as she pleased, or was able to.

How COULD JAQ's party know that a second Chaos vessel had landed at the spaceport?

Why should they need to know, when the fire-storm had already scorched that vessel?

COME THE DAWN, the smoke from Shandabar was a distant smudge upon the northern horizon. In all directions the desert was dotted with vehicles and with the fittest foot-sloggers who had kept up their best pace throughout the menacingly warm night. Amazing, really, that there were still pedestrians in the vicinity. Fear of death was such a fierce spur. But also, bargains must have been made.

Vehicles would have broken down fairly recently, or run out of fuel, shedding occupants and hangers-on. Nearly all functioning vehicles were slowed by the burden of hangers-on.

Vehicles lumbered along surrounded by a gang of would-be boarders like sweat-flies accompanying a tormented and exhausted grox. Social organization had emerged amongst this vast rolling flood of fugitives so that people would take turns to ride and to jog.

The rumour endured that a route to safety existed. Who actually knew the route? Who would wish, in ignorance of that route, to outdistance whoever might possess this knowledge?

Did the route simply lead to Bara Bandobast? If the sun were about to destroy all life on Sabulorb, Bara Bandobast would burn too!

Might the secret of the route involve the fierce aliens? Or those terrible armoured marauders? Dispersed amidst the immense exodus, survivors of both factions continued to skirmish wearily with one another and with local forces. Come dawn, only one armed flying bike seemed to be still aloft. None of the two-person fliers could be seen. Intakes choked by dust, had their pilots abandoned them? Had they been crippled by shots? Who could say? Skirmishes were akin to the dartings of frenzy-fish amidst a shoal of sprats. Where the sprats were so numerous, and the skirmishes comparatively few, the chance of being killed in crossfire was actually quite small – except for the persons actually killed. Sprats and vehicles and camelopards were being used as moving cover by the combatants.

Did one really wish to distance oneself from those fighters who might know the way to safety? Fighters came from off-world. If the world was to burn, safety must be off-world. Rumour spread, pantingly, of a huge fleet of starships waiting in the deep desert to evacuate people whose faith was strong, whose faith was now being tested.

QUIVERING, THE SUN shouldered up over the eastern horizon. Soon heat began to beat a gong upon the desert floor. The sky glared. Mirages burgeoned: of phantom vehicles floating along amidst the actual vehicles. Of floods of spectral people. Of distant shimmering towers. Surely those must be the starships of the rumour. Mirages appeared of a wide shallow river through which far-off refugees seemed to be wading.

How could one be certain which sights were real and which were imaginary? How excellent these many mirages. How confusing for anyone trying to find a needle in all the hay, now that the desert was bright.

OF A SUDDEN the driver slumped over the controls. He was asleep. The land-train swerved and stopped abruptly. A couple of clingers were pitched from their perch. One scrambled to claw his way back up over the front of the cab. He stared in at the congestion within the cab, and at the driver seemingly dead – of a heart attack, of a stroke? The refugee gestured, offering himself as a substitute driver.

Pushing the driver aside, Grimm switched on the powerful dust-wiper to sweep the petitioner away. The man lost his hold. As he fell his hand closed on the wiper arm, dragging it down, bending it away from the windshield.

The driver woke groggily.

'Whaz happening–?' His hand flailed. He was in no state to drive any more. The throbbing engine had cut out. They could hear feet on the roof. They could hear drumming too. The hobbled camelopards were thumping their hooves in complaint.

That other man who fell off must have broken his leg. Grimacing, he stretched up an arm in appeal. And now two inverted heads peered down from above to snoop into the cab through the windshield.

With a grip upon the neck, Lex stilled the worn-out driver. He undogged the cab door briefly, threw the man out, and dragged the door shut. Grimm scrambled into the driving seat. He shouted at the peering faces, 'One of you climbing down and straightening that wiper or else I'll be switching on the guns up top!'

As a man descended hastily, Grimm restarted the engine. While the fellow wrestled with the wiper arm, the land-train moved slowly forward. Maybe the balloon wheels missed the man with the broken leg. To run over him might be kinder than to leave him behind.

THEY WERE TRAVELLING south amidst the migration in the general direction of Bara Bandobast. That labyrinth of rocks and the stone mushrooms, of which the Jester had spoken, was supposedly to the east of Bara Bandobast. A day's march, Marb'ailtor had said. Some fifty kilometres. Soon they would need to change direction towards the south-east.

If a single land-train were to deviate from the general direction of the trek, it would become conspicuous.

The air in the cab was so hot and vapid, so lifeless. It would only become hotter. Sweat trickled; lungs laboured. The cab possessed a ventilation system. A concealed fan whirred. But no vehicles on Sabu-lorb had hitherto needed a refrigeration unit, only a heater. Though the cab heater was switched off, it seemed to be operating at maximum output. Under Jaq's robe his mesh armour was becoming oppressive. Flexible, porous and lightweight it might be – how could he think of forsaking its protection? – yet it taxed him.

Grimm rubbed salty sweat from his eyes. 'We gotta open the windows.'

Jaq agreed. 'And it's about time we changed course.' A manual winding mechanism operated the window against which he was crushed. In miniature the mechanism reminded him of a torment machine he had once studied as an apprentice inquisitor. He wound down the armoured glass and shouted, 'All you up there! Hearing me!'

Heads appeared.

'We are knowing the true way to safety! I am swearing this by Him-on-Earth! We must not be heading to safety in isolation.' He needed to stop and summon up saliva to lubricate his words. It was a while since they had drained the cab's water canteen dry. 'Otherwise aliens and renegades will be stopping us. This whole trek must be veering south eastwards. You must be running to other vehicles to be spreading the word. They must be spreading the word in turn. When enough vehicles are changing direction, only then are we doing likewise. Destination being stone labyrinth in the desert fifty kilometres east of Bara Bandobast.' He swallowed dryly. 'Be going and saying this now! Only we here are knowing whereabouts in the labyrinth. I am guiding you to safety. Be going and returning. Otherwise I am shooting you off the roof on a count of *ten*... And *nine*...'

Grimm halted the land-train. To any suspicious observer it would seem that the vehicle had simply broken down. Men and women were descending. Several gestured at their throats or croaked for water. How could they say anything without a few sips?

Oh but they could. Jaq mimed the absence of water in the cab. A man bit his wrist, and sucked on trickles of blood.

How could they run? Nevertheless, they managed to stagger, casting fearful glances backwards at the stationary carriage. It remained where it was – nor by now were there any other potential boarders in the vicinity.

'Nervous fools,' growled Lex. 'We need them back, as a crab needs its shell.'

* * *

NOT QUITE AS many refugees returned. A few must have collapsed while away from the land-train. Nor could all manage the climb up to their former scorching perch. Nevertheless, once more the train had a coat of people.

Presently the tide of migration began to veer sufficiently, and over a wide enough expanse, for Grimm to begin heading east by south. A mass momentum accumulated. Word of mouth was no longer necessary. Vehicles far away were altering direction merely because so many others were doing so.

FOR SOME WHILE they had been hearing a punctuation of modest explosions. The brisk bangs seemed unrelated to any skirmish. Abruptly an explosion rocked their land-train. The cab lurched to one side.

Another detonation. The train lurched again.

'Someone's shooting at our tyres–'

A third explosion. The vehicle was dragging. The floor was at an angle. How the engine toiled.

'No one's shooting,' Rakel said huskily. She gestured as a nearby limousine subsided suddenly upon ruptured flattened rubber. 'Heat's expanding the air in the tyres. The tyres are bursting.'

THE LAND-TRAIN was disabled, and they had abandoned the control cab.

Far and near, balloons were banging. With boltguns and laspistols Jaq and Grimm and Rakel covered a small crowd of dizzy refugees who had quit the roof. Lex let down a ramp at the rear. He led out the camelopards one by one. Still hobbled, the animals shuffled with mincing steps. Long necks snaked from side to side, attempting head-butts. Out in the open, each instinctively shifted to present the minimum profile to the great hot sun. How stupidly malevolent the beasts' whiskery faces looked. How scrawny their bodies. Ribs and other bones stood out prominently as if hairy rubber were wrapped around skeletons. The humps were like giant erupting boils.

These beasts weren't even sweating. Nor had the air inside the carriage reeked unduly. Camelopards must be able to tolerate higher temperatures than people. Probably the lack of fat on their bodies – apart from in the parasol humps – would allow heat to radiate away more rapidly.

Before the start of human colonization camelopards must have been introduced to Sabulorb with an eye to a possible future rise in temperature. Untold generations of beasts must have shivered for aeons, unable to evolve fat on their bodies because their gene-runes had been locked. At last the beasts were coming into their own. But perhaps not for long. If radiation from the sun continued to intensify, the camelopards' summer of happiness might only last for a few days – until they all died of heatstroke, though rather later than their erstwhile owners.

A dozen animals stood shuffling, too hampered to attempt an escape or too stupid to think of it. Dazed passengers eyed the beasts covetously. Refugees might have surged feebly had it not been for the guns.

'There'll be water in those humps,' Grimm enthused hoarsely. 'A figging cistern of water. I'll stick a knife in as a spigot–'

'Sir, sir,' croaked a dusty woman, whose obesity must be causing her great discomfort. 'Sir, not being so! Humps storing fat, not liquid.'

The abhuman motioned her to advance. 'Be explaining.'

'Fat needing burning for releasing water.'

'Damn it, there ain't no time for cooking humps.'

'The blood, sir, the blood–'

'Damn fool idea drinking salty blood!'

'Blood not being salty, sir. Red bloodcells being filled with water when camelopards drinking. Bloodcells stretching, engorging. Bloodcells expanding to a quarter-thousand times their original volume–'

'Bloodcells swelling two hundred and fifty-fold? Tosh!'

'Being true! Beasts being watered before journey. Be observing how swollen the humps–'

This was indeed the truth.

The land-train's engine was sited mainly beneath the cab. Part jutted forward, protected by a hump-shaped hood. Lex soon unlatched this hood. Wrenching it loose, he hurried back to the camelopards.

A Fist thought. A Fist planned.

With a sand-shovel from the carriage Lex dug a shallow pit to accommodate the hood. The hood was now a big basin.

Litres of blood from two butchered camelopards filled the basin. In turn Rakel and Jaq and Grimm and Lex lapped their fill, under the hammer of the sun. Those not drinking pointed their guns at the increasingly desperate refugees. Lex filled the canteen from the cab with blood. Then they let the refugees loose upon the ample remaining blood.

The other camelopards had watched the fate of their stablemates with what seemed a smug disinterest. From the carriage came reins and rope and four leather saddles.

Lex hauled the fat informant to her feet. Her face was blotched with blood. So was his own face. So were those of his companions. Dried blood and dust would provide protection against sunburn, which no one on Sabulorb could ever have experienced before.

Lex had seen camelopards ridden in the streets of Shandabar. Ordinarily a saddle was strapped behind the hump. These were racing saddles, though, and racing beasts. Maybe different circumstances applied.

'Saddle going behind the hump, eh, woman?' he demanded. The pretence of only speaking scum slang was so irrelevant now.

'Otherwise their heads snaking back, sir, to be biting.'

'Not keeping mounts muzzled?'

'Needing to race with mouths open, for air!' She hesitated, gazing at his bare fused chest abulge with muscle. 'Your weight, sir. Your mount not racing, only cantering.'

Thirst slaked, refugees turned their attention to the two corpses. Knives emerged. The immediate object wasn't meat but hairy hide with which to contrive oozing shawls to cover heads and shoulders.

'How ordering a beast to run?' Lex demanded. 'What words being best?'

'Taking me with you?' wheedled the woman. 'Clinging behind the dwarf?'

'Maybe,' conceded Lex.

'Myself knowing much about 'pards, sir.'

'What about your weight, ma?' interrupted Grimm.

The woman's gaze strayed to those ropes which Lex had brought from the carriage.

'You will be leading spare mounts behind you,' she said in accusation. They would not be abandoning spare mounts for refugees.

'Hurry up!' called Jaq.

They were in no danger of being left behind by the migration. This was still scattered all over the hostile and increasingly hotter terrain, never mind how many hundreds of thousands had fallen behind, or fallen, never to rise. Yet sooner or later someone who hunted Jaq's party must surely find them.

Rakel aimed her laspistol at the woman. 'Be telling the words. If wrong, we are not going far.' True indeed. If the beasts failed to gallop – or at least to canter – then the woman could expect swift punishment.

Anxiously the woman said, 'To be starting, be crying out *hut-hut, shutur!* To be cantering, be crying *tez-rau.* For galloping, *yald!* For stopping, *rokna!*'

Though perceptibly smaller than even on the previous day, the sun was still gigantic. How its heat beat down.

Lex told his companions, 'Listen, we can make it. The heat isn't quite as bad as it seems. Not yet! It's bad by contrast with beforehand.'

'Huh!' All very well for Lex to say so, when he was modified and trained to endure extreme temperatures. Still, squats could tolerate enough heat in the deep galleries of mines. No doubt it was madness to continue this journey by day. Brain-boiling madness. What other choices did they have? Some of the refugees, having flayed shawls for themselves, cut hunks of raw dripping sinewy meat and retired inside the empty carriage for shade.

Jaq shed his robe, revealing the scaly mesh armour beneath. He unpeeled this from his body, resumed his robe, then he rolled the flexible armour up and tied the roll to a saddle like some shrivelled armadillo.

Rakel was swaying. Abruptly she vomited blood, as if some tiny missile had entered her unseen and unheard and ravaged her internally. Ach, that was only camelopard blood she was chucking up.

A shallow depth of liquid blood still remained in the basin, though around the edges a brownish purple rim was coagulating.

'DAMN IT, YOU'LL drink again!' Grimm told Rakel. He grabbed her by the arm. She submitted. She knelt. She lapped.

Lex began roping camelopards behind one another. One spare mount to run behind, for Jaq. One spare for Grimm. One spare for Rakel. And two spares for his own hefty self.

What, canter? When he could try to gallop? At least until his first mount burst its heart.

Lex secured the saddles. He arranged the reins. He unmuzzled the beasts, avoiding a biting. Finally he unhobbled the creatures, avoiding being kicked. The four companions mounted.

One beast remained.

'Last one being for you, ma,' Lex told the fat woman, 'in gratitude for your advice. *Hut-hut, shutur!*' he bellowed. His camelopard lurched into motion. The camelopards' eyes rolled. Strings of spittle flew from floppy lips, peeled back to expose large yellow teeth.

'*Hut-hut, shutur!*' from Jaq.

'*Hut-hut, shutur!*' from Grimm.

'*Hut-hut, shutur!*' from Rakel.

'*TEZ-RAU!*' bellowed Lex. 'And… *YALD!*'

Behind, for a short while through dust one could see the fat woman wrestling strenuously with the final beast. Her fellow refugees were hurrying from the carriage to contest ownership.

How sad that so many striving people must be treated as expendable! But Lex and Grimm and Rakel were all too likely to be expended before the day was out.

Thirteen
Heatwave

The air seemed to be molten glass. The glass was imperfect, full of flaws and distortions. These flaws served as channels for mirages, as lenses for images of far-off vehicles and camelopard riders, and of shuffling refugees on foot – and of corpses, increasing numbers of corpses.

Was this lumbering figure in angular power armour, who shouldered a storm bolter, near at hand? Should Jaq or Lex or Grimm loose off explosive bullets at that renegade? The image wavered and vanished before they could decide.

A natural phenomenon, this! It seemed that the heat might be boiling the blood in one's brain, breeding lunatic fancies.

The hood of Jaq's gown shaded, yet did not cool his head. Grimm had his forage cap to protect his cranium somewhat. Lex had been trained to tolerate the intolerable – but might his brain boil, even so? His exposed spinal sockets looked like holes drilled neatly in him by a marksman's bullets. Rakel wore an improvised hat of vellum folded in a yacht shape, and secured under her chin by the red assassin's sash. The sash lent her the appearance of someone whose throat had been cut bloodily from ear to ear. That vellum hat was the great page which Jaq had torn from the *Book of Rhana Dandra*.

Was the rest of the Book of Fate being carried to safety by a Harlequin somewhere amidst the dwindling migration? Had the book already been rushed to the webway portal by Vyper or by jetbike? Such questions seemed remote and meaningless.

Glare reflected from the ground. They rode upon a glowing anvil, with a hot hammer poised overhead. What an inversion of blacksmithery this was. Those on the anvil would not soften like metal in a forge. They would dry up and harden utterly. No one would pluck them up with tongs to plunge them into cool water to quench them.

They passed bodies which were already almost mummies, their fluid content evaporated.

Yet something might well pluck them up. Great whirling cylinders of grit were wandering randomly amidst the mirages and the real refugees. Localized thermal hurricanes, these, the desert equivalent of water-spouts. One such cylinder picked up a refugee from beside an overturned bicycle-rickshaw – and dropped him a short while later as a skeleton, scoured to the bone by the swirling abrasion of sharp particles. At all costs avoid such roaming cylinders.

Constantly stones were bursting and rocks were cracking, uttering loud reports; such was the exceptional heat.

A vision came to Jaq – of the sky as a womb of light. Therein floated a great bloated pulsing blood-red child, the sun. Or was that red mass itself the womb, and did a white dwarf foetus lurk deeper inside it?

Jaq found himself praying croakingly to the Chaos Child:

'Come into being! Become conscious! Show me the shining path again, the quicksilver way.'

How could a shining path appear when all the world and all the sky seemed ablaze? Was his prayer not heresy?

Lex snarled, 'Let me see the light of Dorn!'

The light was a hot red, edging into white.

Rakel began to babble huskily. 'I am an assassin, aren't I? An invincible assassin who can endure any torment!'

This was fitting. Rakel was conforming to her destiny. Maybe the heat would erase some of the higher functions of her brain, making the transition from herself to Meh'lindi easier...

'Look!' gasped Grimm.

Water was fountaining from the ground ahead, falling back in a rainbow.

'Another mirage–'

'No, no. *Yald! Yald!*'

Nostrils flaring, the camelopards were already galloping faster.

THUS FAR ONLY one of the beasts had collapsed under Lex. Resilient creatures, these. During the time it had taken for Lex to transfer the saddle to his second mount, his three companions had simply sat upon theirs inertly. They could have changed mounts but none could summon the energy to do so.

The camelopards needed no cry of *Rokna!* to halt at the pool which was forming in a depression, fed by that liquid plume. Before Jaq and party could dismount a dozen other dusty burned refugees had arrived from out of the mirages. Three rode on camelopards. Half a dozen more were packed inside a white limousine. Steam billowed from the hood.

The fountain was a shining path, was it not? A vertical path, ascending for half a dozen metres before cascading back, bringing salvation to thirst, at least. Animals and humans crowded together, slaking their thirst and soaking themselves.

Jaq arose, dripping. 'We should give thanks,' he said, 'to Him-on-Earth for this blessing.'

'Might as well give thanks to the bloody heat,' said Grimm. 'Cracking fissures in the rocks. Opening up a water-bearing stratum under pressure.'

Probably this was true. It did not seem to be true. Surely they were the recipients of a miracle.

Lex eyed the steaming vehicle. The turbanned driver, who wore soiled white silks, was carrying water in cupped hands to cool the hood before he would contemplate opening it. A thinker, that one.

'Hey,' Lex called to him, 'you deflated your tyres, eh?'

The driver recoiled at the sound of standard Imperial Gothic, a stranger's speech.

'You were deflating your tyres in anticipation?'

'Yes.' The reply was terse and defensive. Might this armed giant covet the vehicle?

'Doing well, fellow!' How many other drivers would have thought of this? Ten per cent? Five? That would still amount to thousands.

'Place of safety being here,' declared one of the driver's passengers. He sounded simple-minded. 'We will be hiding all but our noses under the water.'

Perhaps he was ingenious, but insane.

'Place of safety being further on,' said another passenger. He spoke patiently, as if it was necessary to reason with the canny madman or else they would break some social bond which had brought them this far. 'Being the haunted stone labyrinth, remembering? First we must be passing the hermitage I was describing.'

'Haunted?' cried a rawly sunburnt young woman who had been riding upon a camelopard. 'How being haunted?'

'What hermitage?' asked her companion, a stouter older woman whose long black hair was stringy with oily sweat.

'Ghosts howling in that labyrinth,' declared the informant. 'Being a former resident of Bara Bandobast, I am knowing this. Labyrinth being taboo, yet we must be braving it. On the way we must be passing the Hermitage of the Pillar Ascetics.'

'Who?' asked the simple-minded soul.

The reply came: 'The Secluded Solitary Stylites are praying for His face to appear in the sun so that our Sabulorb will become the prime pilgrimage planet in the whole cosmos.'

'Excusing me,' interrupted Grimm, 'but how many hermits praying?'

'Hundreds.'

'Excusing me again, but how being hermits if such a crowd?'

'Each hermit sitting alone atop a different pillar of rock!' Was this dwarf stupid?

'Huh, so they'll be praying twice as hard today! Or falling off their pillars like flies.'

From behind a low rise there lurched a tall figure in pale green armour, without any helmet. Although pinkly burned, his features were still graceful and achingly handsome. A plume of black hair spread out like a pathetic tattered toy parasol. One of the eldar guardians. He cradled a lasgun.

Inflamed skin pouched around his slanted eyes. He was squinting. He seemed half-blind. He tripped. Using the long-barrelled gun as a crutch he rose again. Then he pointed the gun in the direction of the fountain, the little crowd, the steaming white limousine.

'Being alien–!'

Out came a stub gun. A bullet flew towards the guardian, missing him entirely. To most ears what difference was there between the crack of that gun and the noise of another stone bursting? The keen-sensed eldar must have perceived a distinction. Shouldering his lasgun, the guardian fired towards the source of the sound.

He missed the gunman, but the energy packet erupted against the rear of the limousine. Bodywork tore open. Fumes gushed from a ruptured tank, igniting. Briefly a flame-thrower was spouting into the air. And then flame flashed back. The whole rear the vehicle exploded. Quickly the limousine was engulfed in an inferno.

How the driver howled. How he shredded his silks in despair at the sight.

RAAARKpopSWOOSHthudCRUMP spake Lex's boltgun; and the half-blind guardian died. Already Lex was remounting. Already he was gesturing urgently to Jaq and Grimm and Rakel to get into their saddles before the stranded passengers could recover from shock. The two women resumed their saddles even quicker than Grimm. They had arrived at the same conclusion. The passengers were stranded. Mounts were available.

Lex brandished the bolter and roared hoarsely, *'Hut-hut-shutur! Tez-rau! Yald!'* A chorus of *Hut-hut* and *Yald,* and the burning limousine and its former occupants were being left behind. At least they were left at an oasis – until such time as the sun might boil the water away. When that time approached would the ingenious madman lie underwater, scalding and boiling?

THE TWO WOMEN were still tagging along with Jaq's party. Well and good. Thus the group might appear more normal – if anything was normal any more.

'Gaskets would have blown in any case sooner or later,' remarked Grimm airily. 'Cylinder block would have cracked. Best efforts don't always produce the best butter.'

'Spare us your squattish cookery mottoes,' said Jaq. 'I wish to meditate.'

'You could have been leaving them your spare mounts,' called out the younger woman.

'You two were hopping in your saddles fast enough!' retorted Grimm.

Rakel glared at the young woman. 'Don't be messing with us,' she warned. Perhaps this was indeed a helpful warning. 'I,' she continued, 'being an Imperial assassin.' Was she oscillating between sanity and insanity?

PILLARS OF DARK stone. Thousands of flat-topped rocky columns, ranging from three or four metres in height to upwards of fifty metres. These rose from the gritty desert over an area of many square kilometres,

This region seemed like the ruins of some prodigious temple. In the interior loomed a vaster hump of rock, honeycombed with cave-mouths. That might have been the inner shrine of the temple.

Atop a column knelt a white-robed hermit. What could be seen of his face beneath his cowl was brown leather. How the heat had baked him, exposed there up on that solitary height. Surely he had mummified.

Carved in the base of that natural column was the inscription: *HIS GREAT RED EYE WATCHING US.*

Further on, another hermit knelt high upon another pillar. This time the inscription read: *PATRIARCH OF ALL.*

Numerous other refugees were moving through the area. Some were on camelopards or balloon-wheeled trikes. Others were exhaustedly pedalling rickshaws. Many were reduced to pedestrianism. Every now and then, someone sprawled and did not rise. Tired tormented eyes barely glanced at the spectacle of the hermits on their pillars.

Many were the places in the Imperium where piety and insanity were indistinguishable. Insanity could often be contagious and persuasive. Pilgrims who had visited the holy city of Shandabar over the years, and been inspired with fervour, may well have been attracted subsequently to this desert hermitage. How many hermits there were, up on their pillars! The extent of the hermitage only became apparent as Jaq's group rode deeper.

All of the hermits were leathery corpses, desiccated by the heat or by the recent dust-storm – mummified into gargoyles in their positions of prayer.

Ordinarily these hermits would have sat high enough to escape storms of grit and sand. Yet during a dust-storm would they not be obliged to retreat inside that honeycombed central shrine to escape asphyxiation? From that place, indeed, their daily food and drink must emerge, transported by servants. Over the centuries or millennia that great rock had probably been extensively excavated, resulting in chambers and storerooms and maybe widespread catacombs beneath.

Obviously the hermits had sheltered from the dust-storm! When the storm passed, they had resumed their places. Then the rising heat had begun to kill them. The rules for these anchorites must include an exemption for dust-storms – yet not for a pernicious rise in temperature. Sabulorb was a cool world, was it not? Consequently the hermits had remained kneeling atop their pillars in ever more fevered prayer.

Within that central shrine-rock were servants grieving impotently? Maybe they were rejoicing to be free of duty. Maybe some mourned while others celebrated. Deprived of a rationale, the servants might even be at each other's throats – as the heat began to invade what may formerly have been a very cool abode.

Camelopards had slowed to a trot, partly because of the many pillars. Hereabouts a gallop might literally be breakneck. Yet this place also seemed to exert a certain charm over the snooty animals. How silent the area was. All pebbles with flaws must have cracked a while since. The 'pards padded circumspectly and refrained from snuffling, as if loath to disturb the serenity.

Again, the inscription: *PATRIARCH OF ALL.*

Why not 'Father of All'? That was the more common usage.

Cold terror tiptoed down Jaq's spine. Upon a stubby spire a hermit opened his eyes, to glare down. Such mesmeric violet eyes those were. Cracked lips parted, revealing pointed teeth.

On other columns other hermits were stirring. Jaq kicked his camelopard in its ribs to urge it past that particular pillar. He hissed to the others, 'These are genestealer hybrids!'

Growling oaths, both Grimm and Lex were readying their boltguns.

The young woman called out, 'What being happening?'

From Rakel: 'What will they do?'

Something inside Jaq seemed to snap. Hoarsely he cried, 'My true assassin knew what genestealers and their hybrids do. She took on their inhuman form. She tore hybrids apart with her claws.'

Genestealers would kiss their seed into a human victim, male or female. Human parents would give birth to baleful offspring, upon which they could not stop themselves from doting, since they had become slaves to their spawn. Some hybrids were monsters. Others almost seemed human, big-boned and bald, though their teeth were usually sharp and their eyes hypnotic.

Such as these hermits upon the pillars.

Purestrain genestealers were so strong and resilient. Their claws could rip through steel. Hybrids shared enough of that vigour and robustness to endure a rise in temperature. The leathery appearance of the hermits must be due to the emergence of some mature stealer characteristics – the horny purplish hide – in response to environmental disaster.

If all the hermits out in the open were hybrids who could pass as human, what monsters might lurk within the central shrine? Hermits and monsters alike would all be brood-bonded in empathy to a hideous armoured hog of a patriarch! Sabulorb had not been successfully cleansed after all. Survivors of a brood had subverted this desert hermitage and multiplied...

If Meh'lindi were only here. If only she were still equipped with genestealer implants, whereby to confuse the hybrids on their pillars. No, that was a vile wish! Her implants had been an abomination.

'She tore hybrids apart with her claws!' repeated Jaq.

Exhausted and almost demented, Rakel shuddered convulsively. 'You have high expectations of your mistresses, my lord inquisitor!'

Shame whelmed Jaq. His voice shook. 'Your imitation of her is sacred,' he declared.

Yet no: it was profane.

Yet no again: Rakel's imitation of Meh'lindi would become sacred when Meh'lindi was reincarnated within Rakel – and when the Chaos

Child stirred in the womb of the warp, sanctifying Rakel's sacrifice of herself and Jaq's baptism of the new soul within her!

'I apologize on behalf of the Ultramarines,' declared Lex as he surveyed pillar beyond pillar, upon which white-clad shapes stirred slowly. 'That the genestealers should have regained such strength so soon! Truly it is better that this world be scorched.'

A hermit had risen slowly to his full height the better to survey the sluggish advent of the residue of the migration. His cowl fell back, revealing a bald head glossy in the glare of light, and the bony ridges of his brows. He stretched out muscle-corded arms. He was inviting that advent onward, blessing it.

The scattered mass of refugees must have seemed like manna – or cause for imminent mania. Other hermits were rising. In time of crisis the absolute imperative was to pass on the genetic heritage of stealers. Here came so many human cattle, to be inseminated.

Maybe this trek of human cattle was also welcome for the nourishment it could provide, if the heat died down rather than increasing. This desert was so barren. Did the hermits' servants grow food in the catacombs? Did hens cackle and lay underground? Were there tanks of algae? A feast of human flesh might be welcome; carcasses for pickling or smoke-curing.

Grimm sniggered hysterically. 'Pad along softly, beast,' he told his mount. 'Keep up the pace, there's a good 'pard.'

They passed another pillar, from the top of which a hybrid regarded them with magnetic eyes.

Thousands of flies were entering a web. The hybrids were like toads whose tongues are awakened by an appropriate flicker across the retina as prey moves within reach.

How soon would hybrids begin to descend? Maybe just as soon as mature stealers erupted from the mouths of those tunnels in the shrine-rock.

This had been a hallucinatory, sun-struck journey – yet now the worst hallucination of all was real.

'TROTTING A BIT faster, there's a good 'pard...'

To break into a gallop or even a canter might precipitate the onslaught. Alas, their informant had not supplied the command for trotting. Grimm urged his mount with his knees.

'Hey,' he called softly to the women who accompanied them, 'what being the name for trotting?'

'Be saying *asan*,' was the reply from the younger woman. '*Easy riding* being the meaning.'

'*Asan, shutur. Asan!*' This word was like a prayer. Grimm's mount picked up some speed. Others followed suit.

How Grimm yearned to be riding a power-trike rather than this lolloping quadruped. His rump was so stiff and sore.

In all directions hermits had arisen. All seemed to be straining to hear some sound. Were they awaiting an audible signal from the shrine-rock – or a psychic cue to attack? Yet their attention was focused northward from where the migration came.

'AIRCRAFT!' ANNOUNCED LEX.

Soon anyone could hear the drone of engines.

Into sight in the glowing sky came a large troop transporter, flying slowly. Lex shaded his eyes and stared as the plane began to bank. It was intending to circle the hermitage.

'Imperial emblems, I think.'

How alert the hybrid hermits were now.

One of the aircraft's four engines spluttered and coughed and died.

'It's almost out of fuel!'

That aircraft couldn't have come from Shandabar. Shandabar was ashes and smouldering wreckage.

'Must be from the northern continent, from the planetary army base or the Departmento–'

After the dust-storm and before the city exploded, some astropath must have sent a message regarding intrusion by aliens and renegade Space Marines. Then Shandabar had fallen totally silent. A troop carrier had flown to investigate. To become so low on fuel, it must have met storms en route. The pilot would have counted on putting down at Shandabar. He would have beheld the utter and inexplicable destruction of the capital city. The plane had carried on. The pilot would have seen the signs of the migration: dozens of kilometres of corpses and abandoned vehicles; then refugees still struggling along, and camelopards – and that veering in the direction of the trek, away from the obvious route to Bara Bandobast. The migration would have seemed to be heading for this place of pillars deep in the desert.

Airspeed would have ventilated the interior of the plane. Conditions on board might not have been too stifling. A hatch opened in one side of the plane. Bodies began to fall out. White chutes opened up. Bodies were drifting down – troops in mottled yellow and grey desert-camouflage, long-barrelled lasguns slung around their necks. Only one soldier's chute failed. He plummeted directly to the ground. Body after body plunged from the door. White blossoms opened. A hundred and fifty of the troops, at least!

One after another the plane's other engines coughed and cut out. Now it could only glide ponderously, its pilot hoping to reach open desert. An especially tall spire of rock clipped a wing. The plane promptly spun over and disappeared. The thump of impact threw up a cloud of dust but no fireball. No fuel was left for an explosion.

Troops were landing. Hermits were descending swiftly from their pillars, familiar with every finger grip. And the tunnel mouths of the shrine-rock vomited monsters!

Creatures with four arms, the upper set equipped with claws! Oh that characteristic loping gait. The speed, the sheer speed. Horns projecting from the spines. Bony sinuous tails. Long craniums jutting forward.

Behind those purestrain monsters boiled forth a mob of hybrids who were far from human in appearance. They were such vile satires upon humanity with their swollen jutting heads and jagged teeth. Even from a distance their distortion was conspicuous. Some brandished a claw instead of a hand. Spurs of bone jutted from the backs of others.

Those hideous hybrids were armed with a motley of autoguns and shotguns and regular swords and chainswords. Of course the purestrain stealers used no weapons nor tools other than their own fierce armoured bodies.

Having reached the ground, hermits were pulling stub guns and laspistols from under their white robes. A hermit cried out, 'Silver-tongued Father, your saliva salving our souls!'

In the largest of the tunnel mouths, to survey the massacre which his brood intended, had appeared the patriarch. Oh what a leering fang-toothed hog of a four-arms! Armour-bones protruding from its curved spine were the size of loaves. Three-clawed hooves raked the rock on which it stood. Too far to make out its rheumy violet vein-webbed eyes.

Yet far too close as well!

Grimm shot the nearest of the hermits, wrecking his chest.

'Tez-rau, yald!' shouted Jaq.

They cantered, they galloped. Already one stealer was racing to intercept them. The bouncing of Lex's camelopard spoiled his aim. A bolt was wasted on destroying the inscription upon a pillar. With a prayer and a bolt from *Emperor's Mercy*, Jaq halted the monster. It remained alive, writhing and ravaging the gravel.

Hermits were waylaying weary, sun-struck refugees, often killing bare-handed. Some stooped to suck blood to slake a thirst. The toughest refugees defended themselves with stub guns. Scattered all over a great area, troops in yellow and grey were firing energy packets wildly as stealers or hybrids rushed towards them. Most stealers reached their chosen victims and tore them apart. Attracted by the sight of the descending chutes – and now by the detonations of this lethal affray – a half-track vehicle came speeding. Upon it was a black-uniformed Arbitrator. He had lost or discarded his mirrored helmet. Skin was peeling from his inflamed face. A genestealer raced from behind a pillar towards the half-track. The Arbites swung the serpent-mouthed auto-cannon mounted upon the vehicle. Shells blazed towards that monster which should not have been present upon Sabulorb. A high-velocity shell took off one of the lower arms of the stealer.

On account of the extra revving perhaps the driver inside the half-track succumbed to heat prostration. Or perhaps he tried to swerve the vehicle away from the oncoming monster. One of the vehicle's tracks locked, hit a rock. The vehicle skidded and began to overturn. The auto-gunner was thrown clear. The genestealer bounded faster. The Arbitrator rolled and tried to pull a side-arm from a holster. Claws closed upon his burned bare head.

The genestealer turned its attention to the capsized half-track. Claws impacted in metal, seeking a hold by which to wrench a panel loose.

A jetbike was coming.

A streamlined aerial shark with a rune on its sloping nose, and short stabiliser-wings each shaped like a double axehead, it dodged its way between pillars, flying at only twice the height of a man. It had made a close approach before being spotted. Such low-level flying risked a stealer leaping and clutching at a wing.

In the seat of that jetbike was a confusing blur of hues – a Harlequin whose holo-suit was in kaleidoscopic flux. From either side of the shark's snout jutted, like tusks, shuriken catapults. The twin guns dipped momentarily, and spat discs of razor-metal ahead almost too swiftly to be seen. A stealer was crippled. Discs had sliced through its rugged carapace into its softer core.

The jetbike was angling towards the shrine-rock from which the patriarch surveyed the carnage. Blatantly. Genestealers were here – and here was comparatively close to an entry to the webway. Guardians of a vile secret, the hybrid-hermits would not have ranged far from their pillars in the past. Not as far as the stone labyrinth. Survival of their brood demanded isolation, not exploration. But now Sabulorb was about to burn. If the patriarch of the brood realized that there was a way to escape, hybrids and purestrains would do their utmost to find that place. Purestrains certainly could survive the mounting heat for long enough. Stealers could be loose in the webway, able, if fate played a black enough trick, to find a craftworld.

This must not happen. The Harlequin angled the jetbike upward toward the shrine-rock, toward the terrible shape in that tunnel mouth.

A hail of shuriken discs bracketed the four-armed monstrosity. A good many discs hit it. The armoured hog staggered but did not collapse. One of its two humanoid hands hung by a single remaining ligament. An eye had burst, but the shuriken disc responsible must have lodged in especially tough orbital bone, not piercing through to the brain. Injuries wept gluey ichor. An armoured knee was shattered. Yet the creature's will was indomitable. Perhaps fatally injured but alive, the patriarch still stood defiantly.

All this the Harlequin would only have a couple of seconds to perceive. Maybe it had been the Harlequin's original intention to destroy the genestealer patriarch – then at the last moment to swoop up vertically, avoiding collision with the shrine-rock. Now he dared not do so.

Still hurling discs, that shark of a flying bike crashed into the patriarch's chest. The impact hurled the beast backwards into the tunnel, along with jetbike and suicidal rider. Then the jetbike exploded, and cleansing flame gushed from the tunnel mouth.

'YALD! YALD!'

Jaq's group was almost clear of the last of the pillars when a hybrid hurled himself at the younger of the two Shandabari women.

The hybrid pulled her from her mount. He sprawled upon her as she writhed and shrieked. The hybrid was screaming incoherently. He made no effort to spring up and seize her 'pard, to leap into the saddle and ride.

'Don't slow!' bellowed Lex, staring back; for Rakel had shown signs of reining in – something that the refugee woman's older friend was already doing. 'Keep up the pace! *Yald, yald!*'

The stout woman was swinging her mount around, to return. 'Helping us!' came her cry.

No help was possible except at the cost of delay. Delay in putting the hermitage behind them might easily outweigh the use of the two women as a show of normality. One must pray that enough combatants amid the far-flung pillars killed or incapacitated each other, so that no effective pursuit would occur.

The hybrid was still shrieking incomprehensibly as if it was he who was pinioned upon the ground. Because of the death of the patriarch, a psychotic tempest must be raging in the minds of the brood, disrupting any lucid behaviour. Maybe the stout woman would be able to knife the hybrid and rescue her friend.

Fourteen
GRIEF

THOUGH THE GREAT sun was well past its zenith, heat and radiance were ramping up by a further increment – like yet another crank of a rack which would finally spring bones from their sockets and craze a body with insensate agony.

The dusty stone mosaic of this part of the desert was becoming a vast griddle, painful even to the splayed hairy pads of the exhausted camelopards. The beasts had no choice but to proceed onward. To relieve the pain briefly required the shifting of a foot forward, and then another foot, perpetually. A permanent smell of singeing hair accompanied the camelopards.

Their riders might well have been dead in the saddles, mummified in position.

Few indeed were the scattered fellow travellers, all likewise now borne by camelopards. Mirage-travellers might well outnumber real ones. If one squinted sidelong into the glare, no vehicles were in sight – not even as mirages. In the quivering lens of hot air you could even spy mirages of yourself. Reality itself might have melted.

How many refugees had succumbed by now? A million and a half? Jaq's party must be in the very vanguard. No one in the thinly travelled vicinity paid them any heed as possessors of special knowledge.

Those untold hundreds of thousands of dead Shandabaris would soon be only a fraction of the global death count – although no one would ever number them.

* * *

OCCUPYING THE TERRAIN from east to west was what appeared to be a desolate city. Nooks of shade were visible, in dark contrast to the glare of the roofs. The camelopards trotted eagerly.

The city proved to be a shallow plateau which had cracked into great blocks, divided by broad canyons and by long narrow clefts. For millions of years gritty wind had been at work, carving out chambers and corridors and lanes, and sculpting bridges of stone. Here was the labyrinth at last. It extended over dozens of square kilometres.

Bone-dry it was. Stone-dry. Dry as death.

They took temporary refuge from the sun's direct heat in a natural chamber as big as the whole of their former mansion. Within the chamber the temperature must have been ten degrees cooler. Or at least: ten degrees less roasting. In other circumstances the place would have seemed like an oven.

They must drink. They must eat. They had long since drained the canteen which Lex had filled at the oasis.

The stone floor was smooth, presenting no natural bowl to fill with blood.

By croaks and gestures Grimm indicated a means. The little man had remembered a method he once saw on a primitive agricultural world.

Off came Rakel's vellum hat. Grimm removed the hat's long ribbon, that assassin's sash which had secured the hat under Rakel's chin – that sash with a garotte concealed inside the fabric.

Summoning a reserve of strength, Lex restrained the chosen beast. He dragged its snaky neck low. Grimm looped the sash around the beast's neck. He tied that red ribbon as a tourniquet. The camelopard tried to buck. It snarled and spat, but Lex held firm.

With the point of his knife Grimm dug into the beast's carotid artery. Blood spurted into the squat's face as the living heart pumped lifeblood strongly through the little hole. Promptly Grimm suckered his lips to the wound. He swigged and swallowed for all he was worth like some sturdy vampire baby.

Briefly he stoppered the wound with his thumb. On that agric world the peasants had used a plug.

'Your turn, Jaq.'

Hardly able to speak, Jaq motioned Rakel to drink next. She was on the verge of expiring. She was precious to him. She was essential to what must transpire at that place in the webway.

Staggering, Rakel latched on to the mount's neck, and Grimm pulled out his thumb.

Already the beast was struggling less, seeming somewhat drowsy. Hopefully the tourniquet wasn't tight enough to kill it. Its brain was simply receiving less blood, and its lungs less air.

Jaq suckled next.

What of Lex, who must hold the beast? Grimm tried to position the empty canteen accurately. Spurts were so erratic. No time to delay. Urgently he gestured at Rakel's hat which lay upon the floor. Couldn't fetch it himself. Thumb in the dyke, holding back the blood flood.

Jaq scooped up that cleverly folded page from the Book of Fate. As if bearing a receptacle in a sacred rite, he tilted the hat. Grimm removed his thumb; camelopard blood pumped into the chalice of vellum.

Jaq held the blood-filled hat for Lex to plunge his face into.

THE BEAST WAS dead now, fully garrotted. Its fellow camelopards rolled their eyes, but perhaps they were only cleaning away dust.

Flesh on the body would be stringy, sinewy. Therefore Grimm butchered the hump. He exposed thick raw fat which he cut into chunks.

The taste was foetid.

'It'll burn like high-octane fuel in our bodies,' Lex assured the others.

All very well for him to say so. Equipped with an extra stomach, Lex could cope with unfood and even toxins.

Yet they forced themselves to feast.

In the heat, the hump fat seemed already to be turning rancid. Nevertheless, Grimm packed fat into pouches; and the canteen had been refilled with blood from the hat, after Lex had done drinking.

THE HEAT, THE heat. Dearly though they may have wished to lie down and sleep, they might wake to incineration. Though the sun had all but set, furnace light remained and the sky was still bright. Press on, press on, before darkness suffocated this labyrinthine place.

Jaq had retrieved the sash. He eyed the makeshift hat, coated within by congealed blood, its eldar runes besmirched.

'May as well abandon the page,' he told Rakel wearily. 'If we haven't found the mushrooms by morning we'll all soon die.' He secured the sash around his own waist for safekeeping.

Lex led Jaq aside.

'Surely we should keep that page,' he murmured. 'I know we couldn't possibly have brought the whole book with us. To toss the last scrap of the text away seems wrong. To use it as a hat... that was the only way to save Rakel from sunstroke. To use it as a vessel for beast's blood, even if I was eager to drink...' Lex shook his head.

'Are you revering *alien* texts, captain?' Jaq asked harshly.

'Doesn't the text undergo changes? Mightn't some reference to the Emperor's Sons appear even in that scrap? Forced by circumstances, we seem to be straying from duty, from sacred vows.'

'Not so! Oh no, Lex, not so at all.' How Jaq strove to convince. 'At the place in the webway where history can change, I shall deny death by resurrecting Meh'lindi. This deed will send a shockwave through the Sea of Souls such as may compress and coagulate the Chaos Child – by at least an iota. Maybe by a crucial iota! The Eldar Theory of Chaos states that the flutter of a moth's wing may trigger a hurricane half a world away. Marb'ailtor said so. How much more potently must this be true at that crucial node in the webway, within the very warp itself!'

Lex looked sceptical.

'I swear this, captain! Did not the Hand of Glory guide you? Did I not take your daemon upon myself and cast it out?'

Lex nodded. This was awesomely true.

'Am I not illuminated? If I am wrong,' added Jaq, 'I pray that you kill me. I would beg you to take me prisoner and deliver me to the Inquisition – except that the Inquisition is infiltrated by conspirators, and at war with itself.'

To what reliable authority could Lex deliver Jaq? To the Terminator Librarians of the Imperial Fists, should Lex ever be able to rejoin his Chapter? The alien Book of Fate, the Emperor's Sons: these matters were altogether too large for a Chapter of Marines to handle. And as Jaq said, the Inquisition was at odds.

'Hear me, Lex: we are participating in a process of perfection of spirit, to be undertaken by a hallowing sacrifice...'

Of Rakel's soul.

Lex shuddered, since sacrifice as such seemed to stink of daemonry. 'Self-sacrifice is sublime,' he murmured.

The fire in Jaq's eyes! 'Do you not think I would willingly sacrifice myself if such sacrifice was possible? Let us pray silently that the luminous path blesses our lady thief with understanding. I shall certainly honour her. She is a sacred vessel. An inquisitor must make hard, devout choices. Painless choices are mere heresy.'

'Aye, pain is pure,' agreed Lex.

'Meh'lindi's reincarnation will be an act of love,' insisted Jaq. 'That will be a seed-crystal of love inserted into the psychic sea. It will be a triumph over death and chaos, which the psychic sea must heed.'

The psychic sea – or the *psychotic* sea?

* * *

IF THERE HAD been any flies in the depths of the desert, those pests would have clustered around the four travellers as they made their onward trek. Flies would have been clinging to skin and clothing crusted with dried camelopard blood.

For a while their gait, especially Grimm's, was more like a duck-waddle, after all those terrible hours in the saddle.

They had abandoned their mounts by now. They had followed a winding, narrowing canyon until it became a cul-de-sac – except for a corridor boring through the canyon wall. That corridor had commenced spaciously but then tapered until they were compelled to proceed on hands and knees through into the adjoining canyon.

Towering stone walls ran parallel to one another. Those walls were only a metre thick, yet fully fifty metres high. Wind had bored holes here and there which were barely big enough to squeeze through.

Thermal winds blew through the labyrinth. Holes in stone gave voice to those winds. *Thees-way, thees-way*, the voices seemed to say – voices of the ghosts of the labyrinth, voices of dead travellers who had become lost here long ago, and who now wished for company in their empty misery.

Despite high-octane hump fat, Rakel had collapsed from fatigue. Lex carried her slung over his shoulder. Sometimes he needed to drag her through low passages behind him.

HIDDEN BY LOFTY walls the setting sun had vanished, though the heat remained as extreme as ever. Unaccustomed auroras danced in the sky, perpetuating light.

They met half a dozen stumbling refugees who were also searching the labyrinth for the place of safety – without any idea of what the place might be. No harm in telling the secret to a few desperate wretches, survivors of the lottery of exodus. Indeed, on the contrary!

'Have you seen a circle of tall stone mushrooms?' Jaq demanded.

These refugees had not come across any such phenomenon. Now they staggered away to search for it. Some went one way, some another. If they did find the place, they vowed to shout out in the hope that their hoarse voices might echo far enough through canyons and passages.

Jaq consulted the eye-lens. The rune of the route was clear to see, yet where in the real world was the starting point?

Lex clenched his left fist. 'Oh Dorn, oh light of my being,' he prayed. 'Help me now. Biff,' he murmured. 'Yeri...'

What could summon the light of Rogal Dorn? The heat was not yet great enough to match the torment of a pain-glove, the unconsuming inferno of punishment which had brought him visionary insight in the past. What agony could summon enlightenment?

'Your knife, Grimm,' Lex said. 'You must stick it slowly in my eye – until I see our way!'

With Rakel still slumped over his shoulder, Lex knelt.

'Come off it, big boy!'

Grimm glanced at Jaq – yet Jaq was nodding anguished agreement. Self-sacrifice was a tool. A tool of transcendence. Furthermore, there was a pattern here, a cryptic equation which the captain must have perceived, an equation between Azul's eye – which Lex himself had once cut out – and his own eye.

'Do you not see the harmony of circumstances?' Jaq asked Grimm.

The little man shook his head.

'An eye for a warp-eye,' Jaq said softly. 'Illumination through torment. The alternative might be our deaths, and total failure. Yours is an inspired soul, captain. Would you rather that I held the knife?'

'I believe that the abhuman will carry out this technical task as efficiently as any servitor.' No, Lex did not wish Jaq to wield the knife. Was Lex some heretic, that he should submit to excruciation by a member of the Inquisition?

'You won't lash out?' Grimm asked the kneeling Space Marine.

'I shall keep my eyelids fully open, abhuman. I swear not to flinch. When eventually I rejoin my Chapter, our chirurgeons and apothecaries can fit me with an artificial oculus.'

Well they might. Yet for a fighting man to yield up the sight of one eye when the future was still so fraught with uncertainty was brave indeed. Or was it folly?

'You must press very slowly to stoke the pain,' instructed Lex.

Grimm commenced his task. Lex held his breath.

AT THE MOMENT when the eyeball burst, and humour flowed, Lex's clenched fist became phosphorescent with such a leprous eerie glow.

His forefinger opened out, pointing. Pointing the way.

As LEX WALKED, still shouldering Rakel, he swung his head from side to side. Thus he compensated for diminished vision. The assassin's sash was tied over his ruined eye now, like a bloody bandage.

Without this blindfold his vision would be hopelessly fogged by light falling upon that naked lens which resembled a pool of pus in a burst abscess. His glowing index finger pointed ahead.

* * *

By AURORA-LIGHT they entered a natural plaza.

Six stone mushrooms rose to Lex's height and half again. These stood in a circle almost cap to cap. Within was an upright disc of light, of misty blue. It was the doorway to the webway. There began a tunnel which led into the depths of elsewhere, far from this labyrinth, far from Sabulorb.

Lex set Rakel down, and shook her. 'We're safe,' he grunted.

Arousing feebly, she gaped at his bandaged face. Her voice wavered. 'What happened to you?'

'A sacrifice,' Jaq said to Rakel. 'There comes a day when we must all make sacrifices, even of ourselves. What are we in the perspective of the godly Child of Chaos? Or of Him-on-Earth? Or of the Sea of Souls wherein all the anguish and rage and lust and also all the virtues of a trillion trillion bygone souls are dissolved, awaiting apotheosis!'

'What does "apotheosis" mean?' she asked in a daze.

'It means to become divine, whether balefully or gloriously! Although we are only flotsam compared with that sea, yet our self-sacrificial actions stir a current which becomes a powerful wave.'

'Fine preaching,' Grimm said. 'How far is it to the first gap in the route where we set foot on some world? We gotta rest. I need a figging lotus world with lotsa food and drink and ease. So does she.'

Jaq uncapped his monocle. He squinted at the misty blue tunnel. 'I count only ten forks until we arrive at a gap. We're blessed.'

Maybe because they were so close to safety, the heat seemed suddenly to become abominable despite the setting of the sun. The night air was searing.

Surely soon, on the far side of Sabulorb, the shallow seas must begin to steam and simmer. Ultimately those seas would boil away. All combustible material upon the continents would ignite spontaneously. Vegetation and buildings and corpses would become smoke. The very rocks and deserts would incandesce.

From the roll call of a million worlds, one name would be erased: that of Sabulorb. Who would pay much heed to this minute subtraction, except for interested citizens of star systems in the neighbourhood, and Navigators, and of course distant clerks of the Adeptus Ministorum (since they would be losing a planetary parish), and clerks of the Departmento Munitorium (since they would be losing a recruiting base), and members of the Adeptus Arbites (since they would be losing a courthouse – though Sabulorb would no longer need policing).

Five thousand light years away across the Imperium, who would even have heard of Sabulorb? The mass of people would continue not to have heard of the planet roasted by its sun. The vast mass of people would continue to be ignorant of almost everything. Might it be that the Emperor, embalmed in his throne, would shed a precious tear from one of his leathery eye-sockets?

ENTERING THE ELDAR webway was like walking into a tunnel of ice. So great was the contrast that three of the four baked and blistered fugitives were soon sneezing and shivering convulsively.

Even Lex was affected to a lesser extent. The transition from excessive heat to a normal temperature – which seemed glacial by comparison – stirred deep memories in Lex of the Tunnel of Terror in the fortress-monastery of the Fists. In that dire tunnel, zones of torrid heat had alternated with zones of absolute chill, and of airless vacuum, and of induced agony – and with teasing pockets of safety.

This whole tunnel through the warp was a place of comparative safety – provided that they met no Phoenix Warrior, such as had harpooned the real Meh'lindi. Apart from such a ghastly possibility, they would certainly not meet any ordinary travellers. At most they might sense a fleeting ghost passing by, out of phase with themselves. Such was the nature of the webway. Each traveller or group of travellers occupied a unique quantum of time. Two groups who set out at separate times from separate places could not coincide at the same time and the same place within this galaxy-spanning network.

Whilst in the webway, one's sense of duration evaporated. Had one set out through the network just a few minutes previously? Or an hour earlier? Or a day earlier? Impossible to say! In the webway even chronometers were completely unreliable, while one watched recording a lapse of several hours, and then only of a few minutes.

It was this timelessness which would sustain the four of them until they could reach a gap in the rune-route, and emerge upon a world. Tramping the webway was akin to travelling in a dream.

Led by Jaq, with monocle uncapped, they reached one fork in the network, and then another, and another. Lex lent support to Rakel. She must not expire. Would the real Meh'lindi have needed assistance? Would Meh'lindi have needed a helping hand until they could reach a world and water and food and some shelter to sleep in undisturbed?

A comforting world? A lotus world, in Grimm's phrase? Why should that be where they emerged? Rather than some bleak and terrible place. Or even some world which had been engulfed by Chaos!

* * *

THEY STEPPED OUT of the misty blue tunnel into a damp and airy cave, green with ferns. Ferns growing around a pool into which a spring prattled over boulders.

A shaggy brindled beast reared and snarled, baring hooked yellow fangs. A tufted tail thrashed from side to side. The cave was a den.

With his laspistol Grimm shot the animal twice. Its charred body toppled into the pool.

Because its snout remained underwater, no doubt it was dead. After a prudent pause, all four joined the dead beast in the water, gulping and dunking.

A STREAM RAN out of the mouth of the cave, into golden woodland under a blue sky. On this world it seemed to be late afternoon, and autumn.

'Just look at us,' grumped Grimm.

Blistered, peeling skin. Grime. Crusts of camelopard blood. Lex with only one eye. Rakel vomiting water.

Some hump fat remained. Grimm moulded this between his hands then smeared it on to his smarting face. Huffing to himself, he anointed Rakel and Jaq and Lex likewise.

What species of beast had they killed? An unknown carnivore. Red meat. Unlikely that the meat would contain natural toxins. The beast had been well protected by its fangs and claws, until they came along. Soon they were chewing raw steaks.

A bland yellow sun was sinking. Lazy cumulus clouds gathered, painted orange and crimson by the evening light.

Hardly wise to succumb to sleep close by a webway portal. Reeling with fatigue, they quit the cave. Lex carried the butchered remains of the beast some distance, to hide behind a fallen tree. Mustn't leave such a marker to betray that armed persons had recently used the portal. While the others waited, Lex returned quickly to bathe once more in the pool and cleanse himself of yet more blood.

They found a dell. It seemed safe to bivouac under a screen of torn-down branches. Half of Lex's brain would remain on guard. Jaq gave thanks for this world, but Grimm was already snoring.

LEX SHOOK GRIMM awake.

Misty morning of pearly light. Dew illuminated thousands of gossamer webs in the gilded crisping foliage. Trivial webs woven by tiny things, which but for the dew would have gone unnoticed. At the exit from the bivouac, strands floated loose and torn.

'Rakel woke and snuck out a few minutes ago,' Lex murmured.

'Huh, you can guess why! Me own bladder's bursting with all the water.'

Yet one must assume that her departure wasn't innocent. Jaq still slept. His head rested upon Lex's arm. Lex didn't wish to disturb the slumbering inquisitor.

AFTER ATTENDING HASTILY to the call of nature, Grimm padded after Rakel, trying to snap twigs only softly. Realizing the folly of stealth, he began to bound through the woods towards the cave. She might have gone in any direction. Yet in all directions except one she would be trackable. If she re-entered the webway...

As Grimm approached the cave there was no sight of her. When he reached the cave, it seemed deserted.

He almost turned back, to look elsewhere.

No. Readying *Emperor's Peace*, he charged into the misty blue tunnel. How his big boots pumped along.

MEH'LINDI, IN THE mist...

No, Rakel. She was hesitating at the first fork.

'Stop right there, lady, or it'll be a bolt in the back!'

Rakel froze.

'Turn round slowly, and let's not be seeing any laspistols.'

Rakel turned. 'Grimm...' How appealing, her voice.

'You shouldn't have stopped to choose,' the little man said almost apologetically. 'Left nor right wouldn't matter, unless you're superstitious. You should have run and run. Come on back now.'

'To choose,' echoed Rakel. 'What choice do I have in my fate? I'm scared...'

Something about her hand, her fingers.

'Hey, don't you crook your fingers at me!'

The hooded rings on her fingers: those digital weapons. One still remained unused.

'I wasn't intending...' Defeat was in her stance. Yet there was also a residue of angry defiance. 'Grimm, tell me truly – by all that we've gone through together! Will I really go into flux if Jaq doesn't reinforce me?'

Oh, so that's why she had paused. She had seized her chance to run – to run into an exotic maze which spanned the galaxy. Thus, to save herself from *she knew not what*. What if she escaped only to succumb to polymorphine spasm?

'That's absolutely true,' Grimm lied brazenly. 'Now don't be a fool, and come on back with me – willingly, not for fear of a bolt. You're going to live. You aren't going to die.'

Her body wasn't going to die. That much was true. However, her mind and soul would vacate that body – if Jaq's sorcery succeeded. Maybe the sorcery might fail. If so, Jaq must somehow wean himself away from an obsessive dream.

'Jaq intends to use me somehow. Using me will destroy me, won't it?'

'I swear that it won't, Rakel binth-Kazintzkis.'

Credit the thief with her full name. Honour and compliment her. Had Lex been reluctant to chase after Rakel because he might be obliged to dishonour himself by lying to someone who was virtually a comrade?

Rakel asked: 'Will you swear by your ancestors, Grimm?'

Grimm's heart thumped. A binding oath, indeed, for a squat. This same squat still winced at how he had been duped by the lies of Zephro Carnelian regarding the supposed Emperor's Sons and the benign eldar custodianship of the long watch of the sensei knights. Lied to, and fooled! Lies were a poison. One poison could sometimes counteract another poison.

'You won't swear, will you?' said Rakel. 'Honest abhuman that you are, more human than most humans.'

'Huh, of course I will.' Grimm strove to improvise. 'That's just the point. I was thinking to meself that an oath on the Sacred Ancestors is binding between us squats – but you regular humans don't have any ancestors.' He contrived a chuckle. 'I don't mean that regular humans are all bastards! Lots of high and mighty lords would take exception! You just don't worship your ancestors like we do.'

'On my home world,' Rakel reminded him, 'our shamans would drink the lichen-juice containing unrefined polymorphine so as to adopt the appearance of dead ancestors and enshrine their spirits temporarily. Communion with our ancestors is sacred.'

She had said so during their first interrogation of her. She had indeed.

Futile to prevaricate any longer. Think of the higher cause, Jaq would have advised.

'Rakel binth-Kazintzkis,' said Grimm solemnly. 'I do swear by my noble and virtuous ancestors. May they disinherit me spiritually and genetically if I lie. May I sire only limbless freaks. May me gonads wither. May I never live to become a living ancestor myself.'

Ashes were in Grimm's heart as he accompanied Rakel back towards the cave. He believed this curse indeed. Now he would never reach a truly mature age and attain powers and wisdom. A spiritual worm would consume him inwardly. Not this year, not next, but after a while.

If he were to tell Jaq about this oath and how much it cost him, would the inquisitor even be able to understand? Would Jaq comprehend how vastly and disproportionately this lie compensated for Grimm's former well-meant duplicity in the matter of Carnelian? Maybe Lex, self-excommunicated from the sacred companionship of his battle brothers, might be able to sympathise?

As Grimm and Rakel emerged from the cave together, the morning sun was already beginning to burn benignly through the early mist. Rakel looked around. She inhaled deeply, as though this was the first moment of a new and sublime phase in life – or as if she was storing such a moment as she might never experience again, the memory of which must be her precious consolation.

For Grimm, no such consolation existed. Ashes, and grief.

Huh, Grimm thought to himself as they walked back, Probably get meself killed soon anyway. Probably better that way. Get my head blown off. No more thinking. No more feelings.

He ached, inwardly. How he ached.

FIFTEEN
HARVESTERS

By the time Grimm and Rakel returned to the bivouac, Jaq had roused himself.

Jaq paid scant heed to the little man other than a quick glance. He and Lex were discussing the other portal which must exist somewhere upon this planet. The map upon Jaq's lens simply showed that there must be another point of entry to the webway – but not in which direction, nor how far away.

Slowly Lex unwound the red sash, to expose the remains of his eye. What he revealed made Rakel squirm. Grimm seemed curiously reluctant to witness the injury his knife had inflicted.

The abhuman gazed anywhere else.

'Seems like a pleasant enough world, this,' the squat muttered disconsolately. 'Give or take the odd carnivore. Huh: trees and streams and a tame sun. Bet it ain't nice at all here! Nothing ever is. Wish I'd died along with me Grizzle in that earthquake.' He rallied himself. 'It's the knife again, eh?'

'I see no other way,' said Lex.

'No other way: that ought to be our motto. Good job I left some of that eye of yours for further surgery. You wouldn't be much use to us totally blind, having to be led around and relying on your amplified ears.'

Rakel said hopefully, 'Maybe we ought to get to know this world a bit better before we do anything drastic? It seems so hospitable. There are bound to be people. People might know where that other portal is. They

721

might think it something else than what it is. They might shun it, or worship it.'

Grimm glared. 'Oh you'd love to dilly-dally, wouldn't you? Have a holiday.'

'We have the jewels,' she said eagerly. 'We can buy information. We can buy people.'

'There aren't bound to be people,' Jaq contradicted her. 'There may be no one at all.'

Grimm licked his lips. 'Or else there may be crazed green-skinned orks who would love to enslave us. Fancy being a painboy's slave?'

'I'm waiting,' said Lex impatiently.

Sighing, Grimm took out his knife. He spat on the blade derisively as though to confer antisepsis. 'This is just the sort of skilful surgery that painboyz love to indulge in!'

'I don't know anything about such creatures,' protested Rakel.

'Well, we'd better get off this planet sharpish before you have a chance to find out!'

'You're saying these things to pressure me. There's no evidence.'

'Huh. Trees are green. Why shouldn't the inhabitants be green too?' Grimm sniffed. 'Doesn't smell polluted,' he granted. 'Proper ork world ought to be heavily polluted.'

'You seem in a foul mood,' Jaq said to the abhuman. 'I think I ought to hold the knife.'

'Foul mood?' Grimm echoed. 'You wouldn't know. Course I'm not!' He grinned, ruddy-cheeked. 'I'm just psyching myself up to torture Lex, that's all.' Having sworn a false oath, he mustn't undermine its effect on Rakel by indulging his inner misery, or else that deceitful oath would have served no purpose.

While Lex knelt as if before an altar, Grimm applied pressure to that giant man – knife-point against lens.

WONDROUSLY, THE FINGER-LIGHT reappeared. The light of Dorn, swore Lex. Or of the luminous path. Maybe both were aspects of the same guiding radiance.

When Lex pointed eastward, his finger brightened. To north or south or west, it dimmed.

They gathered ripe nuts from low branches, and big sweet blue berries from bushes, and meaty fungoids. Lex ate first, to test the fare.

Non-toxic. Nutritious. Hospitable.

* * *

ALL DAY THEY tramped through forest without incident other than the scuttling of occasional half-glimpsed little animals. Towards evening, the trees thinned out. Stumps bore axe marks, some quite recent. Wood had been felled for fuel or for building materials.

Orks would have demolished whole swathes of forest indiscriminately, leaving vast scars. Had human beings wielded the axes?

Maybe wild eldar lived here, those puritanical fanatics who had fled to the fringes of the galaxy before the Slaaneshi spasm devastated their civilization; and who had survived because of their self-denial. Yet such a world should not be linked to the webway. Of course it might have become linked long after settlement.

Yesterday, sheer exhaustion had put the travellers to sleep before daylight departed. So they had not seen the night sky. If this world was out on the fringes, stars might seem thin. Black intergalactic void would be close at hand. Alternatively, depending on hemisphere, the vast bulk of the home galaxy might be radiantly visible all at once. If so, this might indeed be a wild eldar world, of exodites, so called. Except for the webway entrances.

Most likely this was a primitive human planet which had long lost touch with the Imperium, and even with the memory of colonization.

Eventually they came to a great clearing. Grey ash covered hectares of land. Charred stumps of beams poked up here and there. A whole close-packed town must have occupied this space, quite recently. The town had been incinerated. Tramping through the ash, they came upon a few burned broken skeletons. But not many, not many at all.

Had enemies sacked and burned the town? The degree of destruction seemed beyond the technology level of axe-wielders. Why were there so few bones?

A stony rutted road led away through more trees. Warily they followed that route. After some twenty kilometres they came to what must recently have been an even more substantial town. It had also been reduced to ashes. The road continued, utterly deserted apart from themselves. At dusk they bivouacked in a small clearing at a sensible distance from the road.

The sky had been cloudy during much of their march. Now it cleared, as light was quitting it.

Soon they were staring up at a chain of tiny moons strung pearl-like across the zenith. A hundred little moons, perhaps. Each like a bleached snail shell, or like some curled-up fossilized foetus, chalky white. A snail, or a foetus, with a beak perhaps. Stars were scanty – but those moons, those many moons in an unnatural ring!

Even as they watched, one of these mini-moons detached itself from the procession and began to dip down towards the atmosphere.

Lex blasphemed softly.

'What are those?' Rakel asked softly, as if in fear that those eerie moons in orbit might hear her voice.

Lex's reply was as cold and hard as marble.

'You saw genestealers in the hermitage on Sabulorb, Rakel. Now discover a terrible secret. The creatures in those ships up there are what created the stealers. They are more dreadful than genestealers. They are known as *tyranids*. Tyranids harvest whole worlds of their biological material to mould and mutate into abominations. They strip worlds bare. The process had begun here, with the harvesting of the highest lifeform: Man.'

TYRANID HIVE-FLEETS came from way across the intergalactic gulf, two million light years or more. Presumably they had stripped a previous galaxy bare of all life. Life was their raw material. Out of this raw material they made such abominations as screamer killers and fleshborer guns and scavengers.

Of course, 'screamer killer' was merely a name which human survivors of early encounters with tyranids had bestowed – upon heavy rotund battle-creatures which shrieked horrifyingly as they scuttled forward, virtually invincible, flailing their razor-edged arms and spitting toxic bio-plasma. Merely a human label – for something vilely inhuman.

Fleshborers, likewise! Merely a name, screamed by psychotic survivors, in an attempt to describe a hand-weapon which was a brood-nest of vicious beetles, beetles which the weapon would goad to leap convulsively towards a target, to gnaw through flesh and bone like paper…

Their very ships were organic creations, compounded of thousands of modified creatures slavishly linked by an empathic central gland. Throughout the vast fleet of millions of vessels and sub-vessels a collective mind presided. Destroy ten thousand vessels (if only one could!) and still the mind presided. Destroy a hundred thousand (vain hope!) and still the mind would be relatively unimpaired. Its units would continue stripping worlds of life to assemble more parts of itself.

Neither the ravaging warriors – whom the Space Marines knew as tyranids – nor the carnifex screamer killers, were individual entities. Each was only a specialized cell in the colossal multifarious organism of the hive-fleet. The infiltration of the home galaxy had been underway for a couple of centuries or so – a menace as deadly as the powers of Chaos which for aeons had been spreading their cancer within the galaxy.

The tyranid swarm was yet another incontestable reason why the Imperium must conduct itself remorselessly and even mercilessly, lest humanity be devoured...

Might it be that deliverance from Chaos could only come about in the end by the absorption of all life into the tyranid swarm? What a vile and terminal remedy this would be.

Lex pounded his fist into his palm, without extinguishing his finger of glory.

'I have fought them! I have been inside a tyranid vessel on a raid. We were backed by a battle fleet. I was wearing full combat armour–'

Now he was one Space Marine alone, and almost naked. Dressed in mere clothes, his companions might as well be naked. As for their pathetic armoury... If a tyranid even glimpsed them, they were doomed to become raw material.

How could they sleep that night, with those snail-like ivory vessels in the sky? With vessels descending periodically, and others rising into orbit, conveyers of captured flesh!

The first wave of the onslaught had already passed through this region, removing the highest life-forms for use. Lucky old carnivore in its cave, to have escaped harvest, and then to be blessed with swift oblivion!

The four travellers must move on as soon as could be, following the finger, praying that the other portal was not five thousand kilometres away, nor even a thousand, nor a hundred. How could they hope to cover even a hundred kilometres before a new wave of harvesting passed across the surface of this doomed world?

Yet first they must get some sleep. If, during sleep, a harvester might detect and seize them, how could they possibly doze off? Terror would keep them awake, and exhaust them. Unless...

'I'm no assassin,' Jaq said. Did his gaze reproach Rakel that she was no real assassin either? 'I've witnessed a certain assassin kill with the touch of a finger upon the neck. A lesser pressure renders a person unconscious. I understand the principle. I know the vital nerve. The Inquisition teaches us the frailties of the human body. I propose...'

To render unconscious. Unconsciousness might segue into natural restorative sleep.

Lex was trained to be able to nap during any lull in combat. It must be Lex who would numb the others.

Jaq demonstrated. Then he, Rakel and Grimm lay down. 'Don't push too hard,' said Grimm. 'In fact I think I'd rather be bashed on the head with the butt of a boltgun.

A moment later he lay still. Was he unconscious, or dead? Attentively Lex bent low over the abhuman.

'Still alive. Squats are tough.'

From Jaq: 'I commend my spirit...'

Lex rendered Jaq unconscious, checked his vital signs, then turned to Rakel.

'Wait–'

'Yes, lady?'

'These tyranids... I never knew how hideous the universe can be. The genestealers, and those corrupt renegades... And Sabulorb, a whole world incinerated...'

'That was due to variability in its sun. Unless the arch-enemy somehow acted as a catalyst.'

'It's all so terrible...'

'I've seen worse, lady. I've seen a Chaos world itself. Compared with that madness, a tyranid vessel is relatively comprehensible, however execrable.'

'It's too much, too much. We are true companions, aren't we, after a fashion? Four companions in a hell.'

'After a fashion,' he conceded. He would never have dreamed that an Imperial Fist might be asked to regard a thief as a companion. Yet a Space Marine was ever a protector of the vulnerable. Ach, Rakel was an instrument for Jaq to play upon. She had been this ever since she made the terrible mistake of trying to rob the mansion. Could it be that he felt pity at this moment? How futile, in a pitiless cosmos.

'Put me to sleep now,' she begged. Was she really asking for him to kill her, in such a way that she would never know?

'No more talk,' he said, 'or we might wake the others up.'

With his fingers he touched her neck, powerfully yet gently – more gently than he had touched Grimm or Jaq, though with the same result.

JAQ HAD CAST an aura of protection. Would this suffice against a sweeping mass of scavenger creatures endowed with an instinct to harvest life? Or against alert tyranid warriors if any remained in the vicinity?

The stripping and processing of the life of this world was only commencing. The full task might take ten years or twenty. Time was no object to an immortal hive-mind which had coasted through the gulf between galaxies for hundreds of millennia.

Meanwhile the forest remained with its freight of lesser life. Empty, now, of man's presence. Man's burned places were empty alike of dogs or horses or goats. All taken, selectively, as the initial prizes of the harvest.

Eventually even worms and beetles would be gathered, sifted out. Even microbes and bacteria would be gleaned by microscopic nano-collectors, until there was utter sterility, and that sterility was further sterilized by fire.

Lex's finger was glowing more brightly.

Let it be, let it be, that the two portals were close together. Twins, in resonance with one another. Energy-tubes which had divided only at the very last moment of formation.

THE ROUGH ROAD had veered away from the direction which Lex's finger indicated. They were hiking through golden and scarlet woodland untouched anywhere by axe. These trees were both strange yet familiar. A tree was not a species. It was a biological structure, obeying similar constraints of gravity and photosynthesis.

Undergrowth was sparse, probably stunted by chemicals secreted by the roots of the trees in the eternal battle for space and resources.

Steep crags were rising amidst the woodland. Here and there, deep rocky shafts plunged vertically down amidst the loam and humus: deep natural wells. Sometimes snapped branches had fallen across these wells and accumulated a mat of debris. These might have been the lids of traps. To tread this woodland unwarily by night could be fatal.

Deep down in the water at the bottom of one sheer wall, there floated a segmented, horny hunchbacked body – a six-limbed gargoyle. Twice the size of a man, wrought of amber and russet coral, the hue of the autumnal trees.

'That's one of them,' whispered Lex.

Rakel did try to stifle her cry of panic and dismay.

Wasp-waist. Armoured haunches. That long lurid head. Its claws had grooved the sides of the well in vain. Eventually it must have drowned.

Then, deep down, golden eyes opened. Those eyes glared upward. The body convulsed in the water. Claws raked at stone. If only the golden gargoyle could scale the slippery vertical sides. Yet it could not, despite the lure of the flesh peering from overhead.

'Kill it?' asked Grimm.

'No,' said Lex. 'Our guns are too noisy. Even the lasers. The echo in the well shaft would boost the din.'

'Pity we don't have a needle gun.' Grimm glanced at Rakel's expended digital weapon, and shrugged. 'Would have done you good, girl, shooting your fears.'

Rakel swallowed several times, suppressing an impulse to vomit.

Down in the well that great tough coral body doubled up, as if to impale itself with its own barbed tail, thus to boost itself upward like some rococo missile from a silo.

Jaq twitched at the empathy call. The psychic howl impinged on him only slightly, rather as the ultrasonic cry of a bat might register upon a sensitive ear as the faintest twitter. Yet it was perceptible.

'It's signalling its kin. We must run!'

HOW THEY RAN.

Wary of further hidden well shafts. Alert for distant sounds. Lex's stabbing finger was radiant. *Ahead, ahead.*

Soon, from a good way behind – yet ever closer – came a whinnying inhuman shriek of pursuit. That warbling whistle might have been meant to panic or manipulate prey which had ears to hear. Maybe air was squeezing through certain ducts in the external skeletons of the loping pursuers, causing this moaning wail.

Glancing behind: a distant flash of amber and russet – which was certainly not foliage in motion.

Another glimpse. Tyranids were hunting.

ONE OF THE monsters had sighted them. Impossibly, its pace seemed to increase. In its upper set of arms it was clutching what seemed to be a great golden drumstick which might have been torn from some ostrich-like bird.

Lex knew that instrument all too well.

A deathspitter.

One of the vilest bio-weapons used by the tyranids. The organic gun consisted of three types of creature bonded together. In a hot, wet womb, hard-shelled toxic maggots were bred as ammunition. When firing occurred, a slimy spider-jawed creature would seize a maggot and strip it of its shell, laying bare the corrosive flesh. To rid itself of contact with the caustic body-fluids, the jutting bowel of the gun would spasm, ejecting the poisonous maggot-flesh through the air at high speed. The slimy flesh, itself burning in agony at contact with oxygen, was like phosphorus to any victim which it spattered against.

Such nauseating devices did the tyranids turn other creatures into, in their biological conquests.

During the time which the raiding party of Fists had spent aboard a tyranid vessel, Lex had seen armless humanoids whose heads were clamped by organic lamps... To imagine oneself – or Rakel – similarly transformed! Shorn of arms, and of willpower. Converted into a mobile lantern. Perhaps only the prisoners' protoplasm and their gene-runes would be exploited to manufacture such servitor creatures.

Either way, the prospect was unbearable. This ghastly fate was befalling the former inhabitants of this planet right now; and might in a few more minutes befall Lex and companions. That, or caustic high-velocity maggots from the deathspitter...

'What,' panted Grimm, 'what's that thing it's carrying?'

'You don't want to know!'

At that moment Rakel tripped and sprawled.

LEX SKIDDED. HE doubled back. He hauled her, hand under armpit, even as she was trying to scramble up. How he lugged her along. He might have plunged into another of the well-shafts but for Grimm's shout of warning: 'Watch out!'

Pain lanced urgently through his finger of glory. Pain, the signal; pain, the revealer. His finger glowed so brightly that in another moment it might well ignite.

'It's here, right here!' he bellowed.

Grimm paused. Jaq swung around. Lex craned to stare down the shaft, half-blindly, holding Rakel over the edge so that she gasped and writhed.

Lex prayed to see – and prayed not to see – an opening to the webway somewhere down below in the precipitous wall of the well. To see, because then they would have found it. Not to see, because without ropes the entrance would be unreachable. Ropes, and many spare minutes! The tall tyranid was loping nearer by the second, thrusting its deathspitter forward like some anti-grav device which was towing it headlong, aimed at the humans. More tyranids came into view. That wailing warble might have been a war-cry if these creatures had been human or abhuman or eldar or ork, anything individual and of this galaxy.

Lex only saw sheer sides of stone and blank blue water shining at the bottom of the shaft.

Water, so blue.

The entrance was horizontal, not vertical. It was underwater.

'Leap, leap!'

Lex tossed Rakel, shrieking, down the shaft. He seized Grimm and hurled him likewise.

To the robed inquisitor on the far side of the well: 'Jump. Jaq, jump!'

Two disappearances of prey-samples. Capture, no longer a concept. The deathspitter farted its first shrieking maggot-slug from that bowel of a barrel – as Lex dived.

What if he was wrong? When he hit the water, what if Rakel simply surfaced nearby, and Grimm alongside her – and there they would all float impotently, staring up for a few last moments until fierce inhuman heads loomed above?

Lex clove the water.

Blueness blinded him. Down he travelled, down. The water twisted him around. The water was thrusting him upward.

And, oh Dorn, he did break surface, to find Rakel bobbing close by, spluttering, and Grimm bereft of his forage cap, wallowing, and only moments later Jaq's grizzled water-slicked head was breaking surface too; and all four were treading blue water confined by stone.

Above, bending down, were long, drooling, jagged heads.

SIXTEEN
WARWORLD

DISORIENTATION DEPARTED. Above was the roof of a cave. Dripping stalactites grew downward. Those were the heads Lex had thought he saw. To one side the rim of the pool was high. Then it slanted down steeply to water-level. The high side was a smooth weir down which a film of water flowed. The low side was a natural sluice, draining excess water away along a subterranean channel. The spillage of blue light from below the surface of the pool illuminated the smooth mouth of a dry passage. Underground flood torrents must have smoothed the mouth whenever it rained heavily on whatever world was above.

SOAKED, THEY WERE recovering breath upon a slanting mass of rock beside that tunnel mouth. Lex's finger no longer glowed. The only light came from the webway portal underwater, until Grimm produced an electrolumen from a pouch.

Items: boltguns and a couple of laspistols and a force rod, wet yet seemingly sound. Jaq's monocle. His rolled mesh armour which had been secured under his robe. Jewels, and the paraphernalia of Grimm's pouches. Some spare nuts, soon eaten.

'Why ain't we back in the webway?' Grimm was the first to demand of Jaq. 'Flushed down a sewer pipe we were, from one pan of piss into another.' Grimm directed the light beam into the stone passageway. The passageway angled slowly upward before rounding a bend of its own, where it seemed to narrow considerably. 'Let's get going! Those things can follow us.'

731

'I think not,' said Lex. 'They have other business… harvesting.'

Jaq prayed softly, but to what power?

Soon he said, 'If a luminous finger no longer points elsewhere, that is because the proper place is right here. Do we understand all the intricacies of the webway? Do even Great Harlequins understand? The entry to the webway must be right here, in the pool.'

'Boss, this entry leads to a well with monsters up top!'

'This was unlike any other webway link. Hardly a link at all!'

'You mean more like a topological twist? A geometrical anomaly? Sort of like causes the zero-energy containment field controlling the warpcore in a neoplasma reactor?'

Jaq glared at Grimm, who added hastily, 'You'd need to ask one of our engineer guildmasters about that. Me, I'm just an ordinary engineer.'

'An engineer who probably thinks himself superior to the tech-priests of Mars!'

'Those magi,' Grimm muttered under his breath, 'whose devout experiments with squattish warp-core tech resulted in the buggering up of Ganymede.'

'What did you say? Never mind! Here is some such twist, I do believe. Diving back into the portal from this side ought to take us into the true webway.'

Rakel's voice quavered. 'Dive… back in again?' She turned to Lex in appeal.

He rose, still wet. He gripped her by the arm, to lead her. 'Rakel, we'd better dive from the highest bit of rock before we lose our taste for water.'

She fought in vain. 'Those monsters… I never knew the horror!'

'I told you there are worse than those.'

'Our lives are spent in a torture chamber–'

'Nevertheless,' said Lex, 'it happens to be a vastly large torture chamber. Billions of naive people do actually survive relatively unscathed until a natural death.'

'Not I. Not I.'

Rakel screamed as he leapt with her.

THEY HAD EMERGED, sprawling, into misty blue webway. The end of the tunnel was liquid, held back by some membrane which permitted the passage of living beings but not of inanimate matter. Was this membrane a creation of the eldar during an earlier era? Or was it a phenomenon of the webway itself? In this universe, as Jaq knew all too well, the unknown and unknowable vastly overshadowed the entire vault of knowledge.

Quickly they travelled away from this place, with the rune-lens as their guide.

JAQ WAS FIRST to step from the webway – into what seemed at first glance to be an authentic, although deserted, torture chamber.

Lit only by the soft blue radiance from the webway, a sombre crypt housed a succession of fearsome toothed iron machines. Blades jutted from these. Such was the muffled rumbling and thumping percussion which assaulted the ears that one might imagine that these machines were in operation. Yet the equipment was eerily motionless. The muted din came from elsewhere. It came from above. It reverberated through the walls. Such was the vibration that dust descended slowly through otherwise stale and motionless air.

Was a vast factory of the Cult Mechanicus in operation above and beyond this crypt?

A series of sharp *crumps* suggested that, on the contrary, a major battle was in full swing.

Grimm swept the crypt with the beam from the electrolumen. Due to the rays of light shining through dust the air was full of geometrical patterns. It seemed as if subtle force-fields radiated from around those cruel machines. The purpose of all the apparatus must surely be to–

'Don't move!' yelped Grimm – too late.

Jaq had taken a pace forward on to a floor of black tiles, each marked with a dark red arcane symbol. A tile creaked underfoot. With a grinding whirr one of the machines came into operation – to hurl its dozen blades at Jaq.

With a raucous shriek, the device succumbed to age and rust. Its spars and springs and ratchets fell apart. Rust cascaded. The whole machine crumbled and collapsed. Blades clanged down upon the tiles, fracturing apart, so fragile had the metal become over the course of untold centuries.

'They're all booby traps,' cried Grimm.

Aye, they were all devices for flinging blades at whatever might emerge from the webway. And all of them were utterly antiquated. Nothing could have emerged from this webway exit for thousands of years. Pressure of a foot upon a tile would still cause a machine to come into operation – and then it would merely disintegrate.

With a howl of glee the squat engineer capered across the crypt. He danced upon those hex-patterned tiles. A dozen machines wheezed and grated and gave way into piles of rusty scrap.

The dull external clangour and vibration continued.

A sweep of the electrolumen beam revealed no obvious exit from the crypt. No flight of stairs. No iron door. No visible hatch.

Walls were great blank slabs. Supporting the huge slabs of the ceiling, semicircular diaphragm arches sprang from low engaged columns along the walls, unreinforced by any buttress. The effect was of an artificial cave, secure and massive, fortress-like. It might have been a fine shelter against crude missiles hurled by catapults or gunpowder, built by primitive though clever masons – had there been any way in or out. The absence of any exit indicated that the massive masonry existed to confine the webway opening, to incarcerate it forever along with those primitive killing machines. Presumably no one knew any longer that this sealed crypt existed. A building would have been piled on top to cap the seal. That building might have collapsed millennia ago, providing foundations for a subsequent building, which in its eventual collapse would have formed a further layer of footings for some other edifice. Such was often the way. Cities rose high upon the rubble of their own former selves.

Judging by the audible tumult they could not be too far underground. Might as well be under hundreds of metres of stone, even so!

Thump-thump-thump-thump. Sounded as if a massive thudd gun was firing off a quadruple salvo from overhead.

'My stomach's grumbling,' complained Grimm. 'Lex might be able to eat rocks and rust. Damned if I can.'

'I might very well be able to chew such things,' snapped the giant. 'But they would not nourish me. Switch your light off. Save power.'

If they went back through the webway to a different world in search of supplies, they would break the pattern which led to that special place. Here was the second gap in the pattern. They must cross that gap. Not to do so would compel them to commence the sequence all over again. How would they fare, if so? Lex had already lost the humour and the lens from his eye. Only the retina and the optic nerve remained to torment, if need be.

'A thudd gun's a significant target,' said Lex. 'We must hope that a battle cannon or a big beam projector is used to assail it; soon, and devastatingly!' He scanned the unreinforced arches ingeniously holding up the roof of slabs. 'We should shelter just inside the webway portal, and pray for a direct hit.'

Before intoning such a prayer, Jaq thoughtfully unrolled his mesh armour. He cast off his robe, drew on the flexible armour, and resumed the robe again. All four sat within the webway and bowed their heads, in the posture of people awaiting a missile attack. Rakel's teeth chattered. Grimm's utter silence went unremarked, since Imperial prayers were never of any account to a squat.

THE THUNDEROUS DETONATION of a prayer being answered rocked the whole crypt as if it were a crib in the claws of a carnosaur.

The deafening roar continued, increasing in volume. Some edifice was collapsing overhead, ramming tonnes of rubble downwards. The arches of the crypt groaned mightily – then snapped inwards. Choking dust billowed into the webway.

WHEN THE DUST had cleared enough to see through, a slab was half-blocking the portal. Enough gap remained for even a Space Marine to squeeze through.

From somewhere up above, hazy natural light filtered down. Fortunate, indeed, that the masons of this world built massively. Great slabs and blocks were canted upon one another in vast vertical confusion – up which, through fissures and chimneys, it would be possible to clamber... towards the pandemonium of conflict.

SUCH A SIGHT greeted their eyes.

The demolished stronghold, which had been a firing platform for the now-disintegrated thudd gun, was atop a precipitous hill overlooking a sweeping valley. The hill might be the core of an ancient extinct volcano, with the remnant of a crater. The crypt had been built in the crater. Above had been piled the stronghold, now reduced to a jumble of jagged stone teeth like some orkish idea of battlements. Ideal location for a thudd gun, which lobbed shells high in the air. From here they would travel further than usual and descend with a more devastating armour-splitting impact.

Some corpses had been hurled against tilted slabs. Others must have hurtled down the precipice. No signs of life in the immediate vicinity.

Yet the immediate vicinity was of no account whatever compared with the vista!

A rolling sea of men and machines were at war! A multitude of mites were in muddled combat. Such vehicles were in their midst. Battle tanks and superheavy tanks, mobile battle cannons, specialist artillery carriages, four-barrelled lascannon on motorized track-units. Dwarfing all these were numerous Titans, gargantuan war machines with autocannon and plasma cannon and chainsword arms, their energy shields flushing as they soaked up a surfeit of incoming fire.

A thin drizzle drifted down from a uniformly grey sky. Together with the drifting smoke and fumes this mizzle bestowed a pastel impressionism upon the prodigious spectacle.

Those Titans were like stalking, upright tortoises, striding ponderously, their cleated feet crushing whatever infantry were in the way, whether friend or foe. The auto-cannon arm of one hung crippled. Another's leg was rigid, so that it must swing its way slowly forward. A great glowing crater in the distance marked where the reactor of another Titan must have overloaded.

Mites fought mites. Tanks fought tanks. Titans fought Titans. Rapier lasers targeted Titans, trying to bring their four thrusts of energy to converge exactly upon the void shield of a lurching target. Titans blasted at the track-units carrying the massive rapiers. All was in convulsive conflict. Wreckage and corpses littered the battlefield like so many crushed ants. A thousand minor fires burned. If there had ever been villages or fields or orchards in this valley, no trace of those remained.

The ruined stronghold vibrated with shock waves. The air thrummed. How the hordes of humanity struggled. How potent and ingenious the weaponry. Some of the Titans were Carnivore class, armed with multiple rocket launchers and turbo-laser destructors. Some were Warhounds with plasma blastguns and mega-bolters. Oh the cannons and battle claws, oh the gatling blasters and power fists. After an encounter with tyranids, this sight of regular human conflict filled the soul, almost, with the boon of blessed familiarity – rather than with horror. The sight almost restored faith in human endurance.

Rakel whimpered.

Considerably overtopping any other Titan was a red castle mounted upon two flaring rounded bastions. Smoke had veiled it. Now it became more clearly visible. From its topmost spires, plasma cannons and lascannons jutted. Two of the four spires were ablaze. Human mites had taken refuge on the ornate battlements below. Those battlements were borne upon vast metal shoulders. A glaring skull could swivel upon a neck-dome. On either side were two massive pivoting weapons arms – a multi-melta and a plasma cannon, from which flapped the smouldering remnants of battle banners. That dome was set directly upon a horizontal and cylindrical pelvis. Great pistons, surely of adamantium, plunged into the great boot-like bastions. One of the bastions was wreathed in flames.

An entire castle, humanoid in general appearance, and wondrously ornamented all over with golden skulls and double-headed Imperial eagles, with fleurs-de-lys and fylfots!

One vast red boot of the castle moved. It grooved a wide pathway. The whole edifice lurched forward a step. No mere castle that, but a Titan amongst Titans! At the base of the moving boot were wide stairs resembling claws. From an arched doorway troops streamed down the claws.

'Bloody hell,' swore Grimm, 'the Adeptus Mechanicus have been busy!'

Even so, that Titan of Titans was in trouble. Its spires and one huge foot were ablaze. Its plasma cannon was seemingly disabled. The multimelta arm still beamed infernal heat, reducing tanks to puddles of glowing slag. Even as they watched, one of the lesser yet redoubtable Titans scored a plasma hit in the castle's groin. Although the scene almost eluded analysis, it seemed that Imperial forces were suffering a set-back.

A groan drew attention to what they had assumed was a corpse nearby. The golden epaulettes of the man's high-collared greatcoat were like fronds of a sea anemone. Sleeves and breast were adorned with pious icons and honour braids. Miniature steel skulls studded wide gauntlets. The man's face was flash-burned. His legs had been shattered. Very likely his pelvis too. Blood seeped.

His groan, of recovered consciousness and of revival to pain, became a defiant growl of fury at his inability to move. Was his spine broken too? He shifted his head and inhaled.

'In the Emperor's name, assist your commissar!' he ordered. Was the man hallucinating that the giant and the abhuman and the robed man and the quivering woman could possibly be members of the Imperial Guard? Regiments of the Guard were a motley recruited from many worlds, preferably from the cream of planetary defence forces, though often from violent gangs and barbarians. A commissar's duty was to impose obedience and unity and purity of purpose.

How could these four well-armed persons be here upon the obliterated stronghold unless somehow they were participants? If they were rebels – as must seem probable – the injured commissar appeared determined to browbeat them into obedience through awe at his sheer strength of purpose. A plea, or surrender, was inconceivable.

Then Jaq realized: the explosion which destroyed the gun emplacement had blinded the commissar as well as crippling him. The man was guessing that if he had survived then there might be other survivors too. Any such must help him at whatever cost.

Jaq made his way to the ruin of a man and knelt.

'I am an Imperial inquisitor, commissar,' he declared.

'At last,' snarled the man. 'At last!'

'I would show you my palm tattoo, except that you are blind–'

'At last!'

Wondrously it seemed the commissar had been praying for an inquisitor to arrive. Thus what was happening here was no simple rebellion – but some pernicious heresy! That heresy appeared to be triumphing on the field of battle.

This commissar must be disoriented by pain and blindness. Yet one could not take such a dedicated man for granted.

'We were captured soon after we landed,' lied Jaq. 'We succeeded in escaping only recently. We have been searching for you. Those officers of the Guards whom we have encountered hitherto are not exactly subtle men. In your own words, commissar, how would you define the nature of the heresy?'

'Why, the rebel Lucifer Princip claims to be the Emperor's son, and heir to the Imperium. His rank followers believe that this world of Genost will become the new Terra. This is simple enough, and foul enough–' Pain wracked the commissar, and he bit into his lip deliberately.

The news staggered Jaq.

An Emperor's Son! One, moreover, who seemed fully aware of his origin – unless this Lucifer Princip was merely an opportunistic and persuasive liar who had concocted a bogus story.

If Princip was not a liar, had roving Harlequins identified him at some time in the past? Had Harlequins enlightened him? If so, the man had evidently avoided further involvement with the eldar. Had sensei knights found him and informed him of his true nature? Princip was hardly engaged in any secret long watch… What might this Princip know about those knights or about Emperor's Sons? If those did truly exist, and were not a fabrication!

'Is this not simple enough?' repeated the commissar. Was there a growing suspicion in his tone? Commissars were trained to detect deviancy and to root it out.

Simple? How very far from simple!

Said Jaq: 'It is the experience of the Inquisition, commissar, that simplicity may often mask deep deceit and corruption. Tell me, does Lucifer Princip claim to be immortal?'

'Of course he does! Yet no one is immortal, except for our beloved God-Emperor.' A cough wracked the commissar, tormenting his broken bones. He bit his lip again.

Jaq's next question was: 'Is Princip originally from this world of–' For a moment the name eluded him. 'This world of Genost?'

'That's unknown. How did you escape, inquisitor? Who else is with you? My name is Boglar Zylov. What is yours?'

Jaq simply asked, 'Do you know of a mysterious misty blue tunnel, Zylov, within say thirty kilometres of here?'

That other portal, which Jaq must find, may have been used by the eldar to visit Genost, and to discover Princip – if Princip was a native of this world, and if the eldar were at all involved.

Supposing that Princip was indeed immortal, and genuine, how very unlikely it was that he would still be on the planet of his birth over ten millennia after the Emperor had scattered his seed! These enigmas vexed Jaq almost as much as Zylov's broken bones and blindness must vex him.

'No blue tunnel,' growled the commissar, confused. 'What is it? Why?'

The portal beneath this stronghold had been painstakingly sealed in the distant past. The other portal must likewise have been hidden and fastened away in a similar fashion.

'Do you know of any ancient structure resembling this one within say thirty kilometres?'

Zylov's head inclined towards the valley where the war continued to thunder. 'Your questions mystify me, inquisitor!'

Jaq replied, 'I sincerely hope that the intention of our Imperial forces is to capture the rebel alive.'

'The intention right now is simply to survive.'

'Tell me: how many other commissars apart from yourself are with our forces?'

'Three. No, Gryphius was killed. Two – plus myself.'

Gently Jaq said, 'I fear you are no longer fit for duty, Commissar Zylov. Would that you could see my palm tattoo. I need to adopt the mantle of commissar to aid my inquisitorial inquiry. I shall try not to hurt you unduly while removing your greatcoat.'

That ornamented coat, although soiled, would immediately identify Jaq to the Imperial forces as someone requiring absolute obedience.

'Certain inquisitors prefer to work in secret,' Jaq confided to Zylov. 'Thus we learn more, and Princip's heresy requires–'

'*Eradication!*'

'That is a commissar's commendable view. I must take a wider view, *in nomine Imperatoris.*'

Zylov was confused, and agonized. He submitted.

'GRUB!' CRIED GRIMM.

While Jaq had been interrogating the commissar, and while Lex had been watching the progress of the battle from behind a slab, the little man had discovered some scattered ration packs and canteens of water amongst the ruins.

Hands full, Grimm eyed Jaq attired in decorated greatcoat with epaulettes.

'How posh. How ruthless looking. What's the idea, boss?'

To mention Emperor's Sons right now might confuse Grimm, as well as wasting time. It was a supreme priority to discover the true nature of Lucifer Princip. Princip would be utterly protected. It would take a true assassin – not a bogus one – to reach Princip. It would take an assassin of the Callidus temple, whose hallmark was cunning! How utterly Jaq needed Meh'lindi for this mission. She was not really too far away by now. Merely dead, temporarily. Her resurrection – which would cause such a psychic quake, devoutly to be desired as another supreme priority – was merely a dozen or so more avenues distant through the webway.

Jaq said, 'We must find some place resembling this one here. The place may already have been wrecked by battle, and the portal exposed. If not, we shall need to wreck the place ourselves. We require transport and protection and perspective and heavy weaponry. Therefore we are going to commandeer an Imperial Titan.'

Lex cleared his throat. 'Along with my comrades,' he said darkly, 'I once hijacked a heretical Titan.'

Dropping the ration packs, Grimm clapped in morose applause. 'How fortunate for us. Now we can really jump into the frying pan.'

'To know how to operate the Titan,' continued Lex, 'it was necessary for my comrades and me to eat the fresh brains of the crewmen we killed.'

Rakel swayed, aghast.

'It is pointless,' said Lex, 'for any of you to eat brains in the hope of acquiring new skills. You lack an Astartes' omophagea organ. That is essential for digesting the facts of a person's life from their flesh.'

'Huh,' said Grimm. 'I was once advisory engineer with a consignment of Titans shipped out of Mars. So, big boy, I'm already well aware how complicated they are.'

'I said,' Jaq said loudly, 'that we shall commandeer a Titan, not try to climb up one and force entry and kill the crew. The crew will obey us. In my righteous office as inquisitor I am assuming the duties of Imperial commissar, and appropriating that rank. How can the Emperor's forces be losing here unless there is lack of faith?'

Unarguable logic.

'So you see,' said Grimm to Rakel, 'there's nothing to worry about. By my ancestors there ain't! We simply sneak into the valley of death. He flashes his epaulettes. If we haven't already been evaporated or boiled or wasted or blown to pieces we can all take a ride in a colossal target.'

SEVENTEEN
ME, LINDI!

HOW LONG HAD the battle already been raging in the valley? Since dawn? By now sheer exhaustion must have been taking a toll as well as casualties – exhaustion of men and of weaponry too.

Cacophony resounded. Titans still strode and stamped. Outpourings of energies cut swathes through men and machines. Tanks rolled. In many respects the mingled armies were more like a pair of punch-drunk pugilists locked in a clinch, each equipped with several hundred thousand arms. As Lex analysed the situation, some form of disengagement must occur. The Imperial forces had lost the day, yet the rebels could not hope to annihilate such a multitude – unless all discipline and all faith collapsed.

Disentanglement would hardly be easy or quick; any more than if those pugilists, or wrestlers, were smeared in strong glue.

A combination of battle fatigue and luck – and Jaq's aura of protection – finally allowed the four to approach an Imperial Titan. On the way they had been obliged to kill rebels. Jaq's borrowed greatcoat was a provocation. He himself took several hits, which his mesh armour withstood. Lex caught a flesh wound in the upper arm. His welling blood hardened immediately to cinnabar, as if Lex had received a humble chevron of rank.

Ahead towered a largely intact Titan. Skulls and double-headed eagles adorned the splayed fairings of its legs. Its remaining tattered banner displayed a militant white angel slicing off the head of a green serpent. This Titan was partly equipped for close support. One weapons arm

consisted of a power fist – and the other was a laser blaster. On the carapace above its turtle-like head a defence laser pivoted proudly, though a
companion weapon was unidentifiable slag.

Jaq clambered upon the burned-out wreck of a superheavy tank. He
spread his arms wide in the commissar's greatcoat. He semaphored.

The turtle-head took note. The Titan's lurid green eye-shields seemed
to glare directly at Jaq, though of course these eyes were of almost
impenetrable adamantium. Behind those eyes, in the armoured control
bubble, the princeps of the Titan would be staring at two slanted oval
screens which faithfully reproduced the outside view.

Crushing corpses with its huge cleated feet, the Titan paced towards
the tank, then halted. Its defence laser covered the forward terrain, and
the frontal right energy shield ceased to glimmer. Large as a land raider,
the unprotected fist began swiftly to descend.

Usually a crew would board from a gantry. Jaq had expected a flexible
metal ladder to snake down from the rear. Clearly the princeps of this
Titan was an officer who could improvise. Urgently Jaq motioned the
others to join him. Lex carried Rakel bodily up on to the tank.

The metal fist opened its fingers invitingly. The four climbed upon the
palm. Already the hand was rising, carrying them up into the smoky air.
The weapons arm locked horizontally. Along that titanic arm they
scrambled. Ducking under the shield of the carapace, they negotiated a
narrow maintenance catwalk round to the entrance hatch.

INSIDE THE HEAD of the Titan, the temperature was almost worthy of Sabulorb en route to incineration. Hot fumes mingled with the reek of
pious incense. Sweat broke out at once all over one's body. This despite
the laborious inhaling and exhaling of ventilation gargoyles.

Grimm stayed with Rakel in the red-lit escape chamber at the rear,
while Jaq and Lex made their way into the forward cabin to confront the
princeps. For four people to cram up front right away would be confusing.

Graffiti decorated any spare surface of the escape chamber: *Death's the
Destination! Evisceration to our Enemies!* To right and to left, short fat passages led to those pods in the shoulders where four moderati controlled
the power fist, the lascannon, the defence laser up on the carapace,
and… the fourth weapon was slag. Synched to it by servo-motorized
fibre-bundles, its moderatus might have been fatally injured by feedback.

If the Titan's reactor overloaded, the pods of the moderati would cannon pneumatically into this escape chamber just prior to the whole

head blasting free. Should this happen, Grimm and Rakel would be pulverized – unless, at the moment that a klaxon shrieked its warning, they instantly scrambled forward.

Servos whirred. Stabilizing jets hissed. Gargoyles gulped and whistled.

STRAPPED IN THE gimballed control seat, protected by padding and armour, the princeps faced those great slanting eye-screens. Bronze bones framed the screens. Across an array of lesser data screens diagnostic icons scuffled like phosphorescent beetles. A spaghetti of cables led from his reinforced mind-impulse suit into ducts. Cables coiled from his shoulder pauldrons, and wires from his impulse-helmet – which now swung round to scrutinize the newcomers.

Behind a goggle-visor: weary blue eyes. Below the visor: a hooked nose with sapphire rings through each nostril, thin lips, and a depilated chin tattooed with tiny silver pentacles.

Jaq brandished his palm tattoo. 'I am Imperial Inquisitor Tod Zapasnik,' he declared. 'Do you know what an inquisitor is?'

Blessedly the princeps nodded.

'Commissar Zylov is dead,' lied Jaq. Perhaps, by now, he spoke the truth. 'I have assumed his authority, and his uniform. My companion is a captain of Space Marines, undertaking covert reconnaissance–'

'Ah,' breathed the princeps, looking at Lex. He admired that bare giant with the red sash over one eye, and with the boltgun.

'I must not distract you long from controlling this Titan, princeps. I hereby commandeer your splendid machine, *in nomine Imperatoris*, as is an inquisitor's right and privilege. It is vital that we locate a building resembling that former thudd gun emplacement up on the crag to the west. Have you detected any such place within thirty kilometres?'

THE OUTLOOK FROM the Titan was high. Although drifting smoke veiled much from ordinary observation, the eye-screens could operate in infrared. There was also radar.

The princeps summoned a holo-map upon a gridded screen. He willed a cursor to flash.

'Maybe you mean the so-called Tower of Atrocity eighteen leagues east of here. There is little else.'

Lex released a breath. His eye might not need to be ravaged again. Destroying the optic chord would require the implanting of nerve-wires into his brain as well as the fitting of an artificial oculus. He did not wish to burden the chirurgeons of his fortress-monastery unnecessarily.

'Take us there as swiftly as possible,' ordered Jaq.

'With respect,' said the princeps, 'it is well away from the battle zone. Well away from our main force. We may seem to be deserting. A reversal may become a rout. I ought to vox–'

'*No*. The heretics may intercept your message – and then intercept us.'

'Two hundred thousand men may die, lord. We may even lose our base on this world.'

'Nevertheless!' It anguished Jaq to deliver such a pronouncement. More gently he added, 'There are higher considerations, princeps. The apparent defection of one combat unit cannot possibly be a pivot upon which so much hinges.'

Did he himself not behave as though major aspects of the future pivoted upon his own actions?

'*In nomine Imperatoris!*' he repeated. He swirled his filched greatcoat. He rested his tattoo lightly upon the butt of *Emperor's Mercy*. Surely only a person of sublime authority might carry such a precious ancient gun, plated with iridescent titanium inlaid with silver runes. Or an associate of that sublime person.

'Princip's heresy must be crushed!' said Jaq. 'The key may well be in that Tower of Atrocity!'

'I will brief my moderati,' agreed the commander of the Titan.

DISENGAGING FROM THE struggle required some use of the defence laser and lascannon, as well as the hurling aside of battle tanks by the power fist. At one time the Titan's rear void-shields seemed likely to overload and fail. The temperature soared higher as energies radiated. Eventually the Titan was striding at its briskest pace towards the east. It stomped through a carbonized forlorn waste of former vineyards, deserted but for furtive grimy plunderers of corpses.

A sinking sun had at last pierced through the mizzly overcast to paint orange blood across the sky. The cabin was cooling somewhat – as was the escape chamber, where Grimm snored obliviously and where Rakel sat hunched, white-knuckled hands clasping her knees.

LONG EVENING SHADOWS made the tower of slabs, set upon an isolated knoll, seem even more sinister. Embedded in that windowless tower were hundreds of rusted up-curving iron spikes. From some of these, bleached skeletons dangled. A scree of white bones lay around the base of the tower. Its sides were streaked with brown trails. This tower was a place of execution for those who had committed atrocious crimes. It could not have been used as such recently, otherwise some body would surely still be decaying. Some dying malefactor might still be impaled high up, squinting afar in slow agony.

Was this disuse a symptom of Lucifer Princip's heresy?

The tower had survived the ravages of war. No one must have wanted to climb the rungs of those spikes to mount a gun on top. The tower would not survive the attentions of a Titan – which now mounted the knoll.

The moderatus of the lascannon fired energy packets which blasted and shook the structure. He performed a kind of dentistry upon the tower, as if the erection were a vast barbed tooth which required drilling prior to capping with a ceramite crown. Masonry tumbled, blocks with long wicked hooks jutting from them.

The tower appeared to be solid throughout.

On instructions from Jaq, relayed by the princeps, the moderatus blasted repeatedly at the base. A cloud of bone-dust filled the air, swirling snow-like.

The Titan advanced closer. Its power fist punched the weakened remains of the tower repeatedly in the style of a wrecking ball. During this pummeling the princeps edged the carapace against the fabric as a massive lever. With a great groan, the ancient edifice finally uprooted itself and collapsed.

Stooping, the Titan clawed into the foundations. The power fist dragged out chunks of masonry and threw these aside. It excavated soil and stones. Bending almost double, hydraulics shrieking, lamps blazing, it smashed through the roof of a subterranean chamber.

As rubble tumbled into the chamber, murky antique iron machines jerked forth blades – and fell apart in rust.

'You have served the Imperium nobly,' Jaq congratulated the weary princeps.

THE TITAN'S LAMPS no longer glared. Upon the open palm of the power fist the four companions rode down into the breached containment chamber, and into a soft blue glow.

Above, dusk was gathering. Nobody staring down from above would be able to see the portal itself. During daylight hours the glow might not even be visible. By night a spectator would certainly notice. That spill of light would seem to be some baleful form of radiation.

A few thousand years ago, this portal might have been hidden deep in dense wild woodland – which was subsequently cleared. Jaq was sure that the knoll was artificial. Tonnes of stones and soil had been heaped up around the containment chamber to form a base for the Tower of Atrocity.

He would need to come back to this world once he had resurrected his sublime assassin. When he returned, the war of righteousness against the heretic Lucifer Princip would still be continuing. Unless the Imperial forces now present on Genost had been annihilated! Yet if so, others would come. Space Marines might arrive through the void, to cleanse such blasphemy. Eldar forces might sneak through the webway, hoping to seize a self-proclaimed Emperor's Son – or to bargain with him.

Jaq needed the route to remain open, yet protected. Therefore he had told the princeps that with a finger of the power fist the Titan should gouge radiation hexes on the sides of the knoll, amidst the rubble; and never reveal what he had done. Knowledgeable people would believe that a burrowing missile or mole torpedo had destroyed the tower, leaving a stew of lethal long-life radioactivity buried in the site. The ignorant would be too superstitious to investigate.

Thus, once more, they entered the webway, Jaq leading with his monocle.

THE MISTY BLUE tunnel branched several times. And then it opened out, upon immensity.

To right, to left, and above was boundless blue mist. No, not exactly *boundless*. To left and to right the walls of the webway could be seen, now vastly enlarged.

The capillary-tunnel had pierced one of the major arteries of the webway. Here was a channel spacious enough for sizeable ships to fly through from one craftworld to another, or from star to star.

This was as the rune-lens had indicated. The reality was daunting. To hike across the bottom of that gulf without losing one's bearings! To find the blue of the corresponding capillary against the greater blue!

'We shall set out one by one,' stated Lex. 'We shall keep at a right angle to this wall. When the first of us is about to disappear, the second will set out. We shall shout out our names regularly in turn to identify where we are. We'll stay in a straight line, linked by a rope of voices.'

With his enhanced hearing, Lex should be able to detect deviations, and to call out corrections to left or right.

Jaq would go first into the mist. Grimm, second. Rakel would follow. Lex, as anchor-voice, would bring up the rear.

PRESENTLY A CALL came: 'Jaq here! I've found it.'

By heading for the beacon of Jaq's voice presently they were reunited.

More branches ensued. Presently the capillary-passage entered another major artery. How close they were now to the place they sought! Cross this second gulf – and only three more forks remained.

JAQ WAS ACROSS. Grimm was across. Rakel was approaching. Soon Lex would loom.

An eerie throb was discernible at the very edge of audibility. Maybe it was not a sound so much as a vibration of the mist. The throb intensified quickly.

'It's some eldar ship in transit,' yelped Grimm. 'Wraithship rushing this way. Run, Rakel, run,' he yelled. 'Run, Lex! Wraithship coming!'

The mist began to billow and stream. The approaching ship would be out of phase. The sheer size and momentum of even the ghost of a wraithship was bound to have some impact.

What if two out-of-phase wraithships were to fly towards one another through the same artery? They might pass one another by. The artery was ample enough. Or might they pass right through one another? Detection equipment, or some exclusion principle, must surely prevent disaster. The crews of such sizeable vessels must experience drag and disorientation. How much more must travellers on foot experience, so tiny in proportion?

Rakel was arriving apace, her eyes wide with fright at the motion of the mist and the throb and the urgency of Grimm's cry.

Lex came pounding after her.

'Run, run!'

Ever so briefly, a vast white butterfly, wings erect, seemed to rush past. This filled the view momentarily – almost too fast for its faint huge image to be glimpsed. Parting, the blue mists surged in a tsunami of vapours. Suction tugged at the three where they sheltered inside the tunnel.

Lex was bowled away, mist-borne. He was pulled in the wake of a ghost-ship. Turning over and over, he had vanished from view in a trice.

Grimm yelled Lex's name periodically for many minutes.

No answer came.

YET THEY WAITED. Undoubtedly more than one pair of capillaries joined this artery. How to tell one from another except by the presence of comrades who were in phase? What if another wraithship came rushing by? Lex might be carried away across half the galaxy. Yet they waited. Every now and then, Grimm gave a call.

* * *

TIME WAS ELUSIVE within the webway. Was it an hour or half a standard day before they heard a reply? Before Lex came loping out of the mist!

'Huh,' said Grimm, 'the big brute's back.' He wiped a cuff across his eye.

Rejoining his comrades joyfully, Lex breathed deeply to replenish his lungs.

'You took your time,' piped the little man. 'Pass many side entrances, eh?'

'Six,' said Lex. 'Widely spaced. I reasoned that either you had waited, or you had not. The greater gamble was whether I was heading in the right direction. I had spun around so much that even I could not be sure which way I was facing finally. I prayed to Rogal Dorn to guide my choice.'

'You could have tried sticking your finger in your eye.'

'I should stick mine in yours, fool.' Lex clasped Grimm. He squeezed the squat's shoulders, roared a brief laugh, shook the abhuman rag-like, and released him.

THEY HAD COME to a place where four tunnels converged. This crossroad could be no other than the place.

'We're here,' said Jaq, harsh triumph and tragic hope in his voice.

Jaq had shut the monocle and stowed it in a pocket. Two sets of eyes – and one lone eye – regarded Rakel binth-Kazintzkis. She fiddled with the only one of the three miniature weapons on her finger which was still loaded, twisting it this way and that. She trembled.

'I feel wobbly,' she said, as if it was high time for Jaq to reinforce the integrity of her altered body by scrutiny of the Assassin card. 'It is a fearful thing to fall into the hands of an inquisitor.'

'Rakel,' said Jaq, 'in the warp, just beyond the walls of this webway, there is a force of goodness and nobility and truth divine. There is a dynamic towards transfiguration. There is an embryo of a new god who may renew our blessed God-Emperor or who may even supersede Him – may He forgive my heresy! – and, in superseding, release Him from His eternal agony into blissful triumph.' Jaq spoke awkwardly. Could he fully believe in the possibility of such a victory?

Oh, he had experienced the luminous path. He had witnessed Lex's Finger of Glory glowing. Doubt must always remain.

Lex appeared to be racked by mixed emotions. Might Rogal Dorn lend scaffolding to his soul! Let not that scaffold be a gibbet of dishonour, a gallows for an unwitting traitor.

Grimm seemed deeply dour, as if somewhere along the route his soul had deserted him.

Had they not arrived where no one else had ever arrived? Let not doubt subvert this sacred moment.

Jaq and Lex and Rakel knelt in the centre of this four-fold junction bathed in the blue light of the alien webway. Only Grimm stayed standing, defiant of piety, lacking grace.

Jaq prayed aloud to Him-on-Earth, and to the Numen, to the Luminous Path.

He turned to Rakel. Appropriate words would not come. 'You are asking me to accept my own death,' Rakel murmured. Fleetingly she glanced at Grimm.

Frustration coursed through Jaq. 'What have you told her?' he cried at the dwarf.

'Nothing!' howled Grimm. 'I swear by my absent ancestors, nothing!'

'I did strive,' said Rakel in a shaking voice. 'I strove so hard. Please give me oblivion before such nightmares as tyranids seize me. Or Chaos, or other horrors.'

'Indeed,' Jaq said softly. All was well, after all. 'The real Meh'lindi wished for oblivion too,' he told her. 'She denied oblivion to herself.'

Rakel was weeping. 'Now you wish to drag her back into horror and suffering! You see, I understand your desire,' she said quietly.

'You great soul,' exclaimed Jaq, in wonder. He experienced a surge of exalted rapture. This must augur well for what was surely so soon to happen.

'You great soul…'

Yet not a soul as great as that of Meh'lindi, who must soon supplant this woman from her altered body.

'I need Meh'lindi, do you see, Rakel? I need her! I need her by my side – to cope with Lucifer Princip.'

'Oh you needed her,' was Rakel's reply, 'before we ever heard of Lucifer Princip. I do accept my destiny. I accept! Send me into darkness to save my eyes from seeing any more abominations such as I already saw. I cannot face any future. All futures are fearful and foul.'

'All, apart from the Shining Path, which your sacrifice will help kindle. Oh, Emperor of All,' cried Jaq, 'forgive me! Perceive that this is… the way.'

Rakel wept. Yet she also nodded in affirmation. And her affirmation was at the same time the negation of her self – in favour of another, whom she so exactly resembled, even to the very tattoos, courtesy of polymorphine.

Lex was deeply moved. 'Companion,' he said to her. He scratched at his itching left hand as if to scour away the line of life from his palm.

Jaq began to remove the Assassin card.

As before, unbidden, that other card sprang free. The card of Tzeentch shed its wrapping. It fell face up upon the webway floor.

The daemonic countenance leered up at Jaq. He almost panicked. Hastily he slapped the Assassin card down upon the Daemon. The card depicting Meh'lindi but also mirroring Rakel trumped the Daemon card.

Had he not triumphed over Tzeentch in the mansion? Had he not ousted a minion of the Great Conspirator? Had he not overcome Slaaneshi temptations? Jaq felt not lust but pure adoration for this idol of flesh close by him, soon to be reanimated.

'Let us rejoice,' he declared.

Rakel sobbed. 'I rejoice in oblivion.'

Those could have been Meh'lindi's very own words. Already Rakel was not merely Meh'lindi in body but partly so, it seemed, in speech.

Jaq gestured to Lex for the assassin's sash. Lex unwound the red fabric, exposing his ravaged eye-socket. Dangling stole-like, Jaq draped the sash around Rakel's neck as if preparatory to a garotting.

'Stare at the Assassin card,' Jaq instructed Rakel. 'Stare deep into the eyes. Lose yourself in the eyes. Sink into those. You are going into the Sea of Souls to help stir a mighty spirit to consciousness by becoming part of that spirit through your willing self-sacrifice.

'*Spiritum tuum*,' he continued solemnly in the hieratic tongue, '*Ipacem dimitto. Meh'lindi meum, a morte ad vitam novam revocatio.*'

Grimm was shivering. Lex covered the ruin of his eye with his left palm, the better to keep vigil throughout a rite as macabre as any he had endured in the fortress-monastery of the Imperial Fists.

The semblance of Meh'lindi in the Assassin card was squirming.

'At this place,' Jaq intoned, 'where time twists, by the power and the grace–'

SHUDDERING, RAKEL SLUMPED forward. She squirmed. She twisted and flexed. She writhed as if in agony.

And from the writhing woman's lips a cry of defiance and assertion tore: '*Me, Lindi!*'

That was the shriek of identity of a savage feral girl taken from her jungle world to be trained by the Officio Assassinorum. That was the cry which had given rise to her Imperial name, of Meh'lindi.

Jaq gloried immeasurably.

Meh'lindi uncurled. Briefly her hands explored her midriff, where the harpoon of the Phoenix Lady had transfixed her, twisting her guts as on a winch.

'*Me, Lindeeee!*' she screeched.

She rolled. She sprang to her feet. Her eyes were glazed with frenzy. One hand was a fist. The other was slanted, a chopper.

Those eyes! She didn't seem to recognize Jaq at all. Was she even *seeing* him?

Nor, as she flicked her glance, was she truly seeing Lex, or Grimm.

'Die, Phoenix Lords!' Meh'lindi screamed – and launched herself ferociously at Jaq.

EIGHTEEN
ILLUMINATION

COULD SHE BE mistaking Jaq because he wore a commissar's scorched and bloodstained greatcoat with high collar and golden epaulettes, and icons and honour braids upon the sleeves and breast? No! The name she had called him was *Phoenix Lord*. Jaq and Lex and Grimm as well. *Phoenix Lords.*

Those were the eldar hero-warriors who had no craftworld to call their own. They roamed the webway from world to world. Sometimes they disappeared for hundreds of years. They would heed a call of ultimate danger, and suddenly, devastatingly, they would reappear.

Lords? Immortal divinities, almost! Not persons in any ordinary sense!

In the distant past, each Phoenix Lord had been a warrior who had followed the path of war so utterly and absolutely that there was no turning back, ever, to the persons they had been before. If one of them died, his or her soul passed into the spirit stone within their armour. The armour itself would call another candidate to rekindle the same identity, phoenix-like – just as the ancient legendary bird arose anew from the flames of its nest.

It had been a Phoenix Lady, a Storm of Silence, who had speared Meh'lindi to death at the very entrance to the hidden Black Library of eldar secrets.

The resurrected Meh'lindi was mentally locked in those last lethal moments of ultimate combat. She was reliving her last battle. This had occurred elsewhere in the webway, close to the Black Library. Here at this crossroads of time-twist, that previous climactic event dominated her consciousness. The manner of her death monopolized her reincarnated psyche. And she fought.

Meh'lindi fought her final fight all over again, like a soul condemned to a hell of agonizing repetition. Of intensifying repetition.

All three figures were Phoenix Lords. The terrible triple-vision possessed her as surely as a daemon might possess a victim. Such were the energies of the webway, concentrated here, weaving tyrannical illusion.

She would not be a victim! She would not!

HER FIST SMASHED into Jaq's chest under his heart.

The impact should have killed any unprotected enemy. But the mesh armour under Jaq's greatcoat absorbed the bullet-like force of her blow. Aghast, he staggered back, shock scouring his soul.

She seemed to realize instantly about the armour. She was upon him, her hands seeking grips. She paused briefly so that the mesh armour might relax its stiffness. He stared appalled into her spellbound unseeing eyes.

'Meh'lindi…' he gasped. Still she did not know him.

With implacable force, applied smoothly, she hoisted and levered.

JAQ'S ELBOW SNAPPED. Pain lanced through him as if the very marrow of his bones was lava, boiling, spurting. Momentarily he shrieked.

In his agony, she pivoted him across her hips. Jaq crashed to the floor of the webway. The collision stiffened his armour for several tormenting seconds.

He had fallen heavily. A pang in his own hip must be from the monocle lens, crushed by his fall.

Meh'lindi swung; she leapt. The heel of her foot connected with Lex's wrist – just as he was bringing the boltgun to bear from behind his back. The gun sprang loose from his hand.

This Jaq saw through a mist of pain. The mist blurred Meh'lindi's motions. Lex was fending her off with a mighty arm. Her clawing fingers tore at his ruined eye. She feinted. She was going to try to blind Lex entirely. Instead, she somersaulted – and she stumbled, although she recovered swiftly. Grimm sprawled upon his back. He was swearing, so he was still alive.

It could only be Meh'lindi's unfamiliarity with her new body – its lack of perfect training – which had saved the little man. She wasn't quite as co-ordinated as she expected to be. This perplexed and incensed her.

Lex flexed potent muscles. He half-turned his head as if to avert his good eye. He hesitated. Meh'lindi's hostility was inexplicable – unless she was mad. Unless she had returned from the Sea of Souls deranged and demented! Unless a daemon was in her body.

Yet she cried out again: '*Me, Lindi!*'

She adopted a feral crouch, her hands splaying out.

And now the three hooded rings on her fingers caught her attention. The miniature weapons. The toxic needle gun. The flamer. The laser. In exasperation, she howled. Not to have noticed straight away! Not to have realized! To have been so bound up in sheer body. In limbs and spine and nerves!

Meh'lindi stabbed a finger towards Lex. Whirling, she stabbed another in Grimm's direction. Swinging, she jerked a final finger at Jaq.

INSTINCTIVELY JAQ INTERPOSED his uninjured arm. Energy exploded upon his hand, which no armour nor even a gauntlet sheathed.

The shockwave stiffened the mesh upon his arm, all the way to his shoulder. Briefly his arm remained raised, like some crooked staff which might display regalia. The regalia consisted of scorched stubs of carpal bone to which blackened ribbons of flesh and gristle clung. The energy packet hadn't amputated his palm and his fingers. It had vaporized his hand.

Pain hesitated... before surging into tyrannical existence. Even though Jaq's hand no longer existed it seemed that it was being roasted. Tears started from his eyes. A greater grief moaned within him, all-gnawing. Despair consumed him. All hope was crushed. Not only his own proud tragic hopes! Hope for humanity too. Hope that the Imperium might endure. Hope that salvation might emerge.

MEH'LINDI GLANCED AT the giant Phoenix Lord who still stood upright and alive. At the dwarf Phoenix Lord who was recovering himself. She spared not a flicker of attention for the enemy whom her digital laser had disabled. Meh'lindi glared at her own betraying hand.

The miniature needle-gun had failed. The tiny flamer had failed. Neither had been loaded.

How could this be, how could this be? Why was her body imperfect, inaccurate? Around her neck – not around her waist! – was her assassin's sash. She plucked it into her fist.

These Phoenix Lords were playing a terrible game with her. It was as if she must fight with a hand fled behind her back. Oh, this she could have done! Or else died, attempting to! Something more fundamental was at fault.

What could it be? How could she have no knowledge that two of the digital weapons were useless? How could it be that her body did not perfectly obey her will? Oh, she was trapped in a nightmare! She must fight or flee. She was Callidus. She was cunning.

How short a time had passed. Before the giant or the dwarf could react, Meh'lindi fled at random along a blue misty tunnel of the webway.

She raced, her long legs pumping. An intimation of fatigue registered. She forced herself to maintain her pace. Were Phoenix Lords rushing after her, armed with weapons of wizardry? Her gulping breaths were not as rich as they ought to be. Fireflies seemed to flicker in her vision. The blue tunnel forked: At random she ran to the right.

JAQ WAS RUINED, in body and in soul. An arm, shattered. A hand, seared away. Agony flayed him. Tragedy scarified him. He might almost be partaking of the Emperor's own illuminated anguish.

The Emperor would fail. The Imperium would fail. Its death throes would be so appalling that honour and nobility and faith and proud perseverance would be mere drops of water in a cauldron of boiling blood. No new god-child could possibly awaken then. Humanity would succumb. Out of its screaming downfall there would vomit forth a great new power of evil unimaginable. Chaos would surge to engulf reality.

Despair gnawed Jaq like some ichneumon parasite devouring his innards. He had committed heresy and betrayal. Meh'lindi's resurrection had been an abomination. If only she had destroyed him completely!

Lex had vowed to do so, if necessity demanded. The captain had recovered his boltgun. With the stump of his wrist, Jaq thrust himself up, snarling as he did so. He must not cause any more ghastly heretical harm.

He sagged upon his knees. He forced himself to withstand. He knelt, self-condemned. He riveted Lex with a glare of homicidal, psychotic hatred.

And he blasphemed. How he blasphemed.

'May the puny human Emperor shrivel! May the light of your primarch wink out like a candle! Glory to Tzeentch! *Chi'khami'tzann Tsunoi!*'

Jaq was evoking the greater daemons of Tzeentch, in their own language. He must have become possessed anew.

Jaq bared his teeth in a bestial snarl. This time daemonry owned him utterly – so it seemed.

Lex steadied the boltgun. With Rogal Dorn's name upon his lips, he fired at Jaq's head.

RAAARK–

A VIOLENT BLOW upon the vault of a skull might leave it intact. If the bolt had only struck a glancing blow a compression-wave would have been transmitted around the skull to the rigid base, which might fracture.

An explosion within the skull was another matter. It tore the great jig-saw pieces of the skull apart. And even though Jaq's head had not entirely disintegrated, what had been knitted together since childhood was separated now. The frontal plate was divorced from the sundered parietal plates of the cranium, and those in turn from the occipital plate at the rear. Liquified pulp of brain had gushed out of its broken container.

GRIMM DID TRY to wrench enough of the commissar's greatcoat loose so as to hide the sight. He quit.

Lex had arisen from prayer.

Bitterly Grimm exclaimed, 'I didn't think that a daemon could thrust its way through the walls of the webway!'

With his one intact eye, Lex scrutinized the corpse. Slowly he asked the little man, 'What are you implying?'

Grimm babbled, 'As I savvy it, the eldar don't dare travel through the warp in ships the way we do – because they would attract daemons all too easily. That's why they use the webway for travel. The webway acts as a barrier to daemons. How did a daemon get into Jaq?'

'Because of the unique nature of this crossroads!'

Grimm shook his head disbelievingly.

'Because the daemon was still hiding inside him!' declared Lex. 'Ever since he exorcised me!'

'Where would the daemon go to from here?'

'I'm not responsible for the problems of daemons, abhuman!'

'If there ever *was* a daemon–'

Lex clutched his boltgun as if it were the hand of a battle brother offering support. 'Explain yourself!'

'I think that Jaq despaired!' cried Grimm. 'He despaired utterly. Because of *her*.' He jerked his head in the direction which Meh'lindi had taken. 'It was insane to resurrect her. And she was insane.'

'He despaired? Despite all vows?'

'I know what despair is! I can recognize despair.'

Menacingly, Lex demanded: 'How is that?'

Grimm sighed in grief. 'I don't want to say.'

'You will say – or I will squeeze it out of you!'

Wretchedly Grimm confessed: 'I swore to Rakel that she would live. That she wouldn't be destroyed. 'I swore *by my ancestors*. I knew I was lying!'

'What does that false oath signify to you?'

Dully, Grimm told him, 'It's as if you betray your primarch. A squat who perjures himself in this way will never sire any offspring. He'll never become a living ancestor.'

Dread seemed to harrow the giant. 'I have not... betrayed... my primarch,' he insisted softly. 'I have not... betrayed... my Chapter. Yet I have been led far astray. I must make amends. I must... redeem myself.'

The little man wrung his sturdy hairy hands. 'Don't do it by blinding your other eye! Don't disable yourself!'

'That would be blasphemy, you fool! We must return to Genost where those rebels rampage. We must find out all we can about their leader, Lucifer Princip. Surely my battle brothers will come to Genost on a crusade to purge the rebellion. In another year. Two years. Three. Space Wolves or Blood Angels or Ultramarines. It does not matter which.'

'When I was trying to adjust Jaq's coat... I felt in his pocket. The rune-lens is ruined.'

'I can remember the route, abhuman! By Dorn, but it's time to take that route, away from this place of failure!'

Grimm blew his nose in his hands. He wiped himself. He grimaced. Bleakly he said: 'Back to Genost, eh? A pretty rainbow beckons fools onward constantly in hope of hidden gold. Just so does a black rainbow beckon us onward – towards death or madness!'

'Nay,' said Lex, 'that is sacrilege. To succumb to despair is blasphemy.'

Firmly Lex clenched his free hand into a fist – and Grimm may have thought that the Marine was going to strike him. But instead Lex smiled, contortedly. However far away Lex was from his fortress-monastery and from his battle brothers – and although he was half blind and near-naked – he remained an Imperial Fist.

'Come, little comrade,' he barked. 'And redeem yourself by serving Him-on-Earth.'

RAAARK –

For the merest moment–

–*pop*–

Jaq knew.

–SWOOSH–

Then the universe exploded.

BODILESS, HE WAS *afloat within blue light. He was no longer a man, but only a point of view. From that point of view he looked down upon his corpse, lying ruined and defunct.*

He looked down upon Lex, who was kneeling in prayer. He looked down upon Grimm who was trying in vain to cover the corpse's shattered face.

An astonishing serenity filled Jaq's soul, almost to overflowing. Tunnels of blue light led in four directions. He knew that by a mere act of will he might rush afar along any of these tunnels. Or he might simply accelerate his vision along one tunnel or another, as though he were going through an expanding telescope.

He did exactly this – and his vision overtook Meh'lindi. She was loping headlong like a hunted animal.

Stop, stop! He wished her to hear his voice. But she could not hear.

As his vision accompanied her, he perceived a scintillating aura about her – in a way that he had never perceived before. He realized that she had behaved as she behaved because she was in a trance of combat, mesmerized by her dying moment. She had been akin to a Phoenix Lord, possessed by the path of combat to the exclusion of personality. Her lethal rapture would surely abate as her intelligence asserted itself.

That aura of hers was so complex. Could it be that Rakel was not entirely evicted from her former body? Could it be that deep down Rakel still lingered? That, in a sense, Rakel possessed Meh'lindi? Not directly, as a daemon might possess a person. But present, nonetheless. Or that Meh'lindi's spirit possessed Rakel's body, daemon-like?

Yes, yes… Rakel was not entirely dead.

Meh'lindi would be volatile. She would be unstable. Pray that her fierce will would prevail!

He could not communicate with her. He could not contact her, however much he might wish to do so.

Therefore Jaq let his vision range far beyond Meh'lindi – until a blue tunnel reached its terminus, inside a cave a-sparkle with crystals. His vision could travel no further. It could not leave the webway.

ONCE MORE, HE *was gazing calmly down upon his own corpse.*

Grimm was grieving. He was mourning for himself as well as for Jaq. Such despairing hues polluted the little man's aura, unseen by Jaq until now. Oh Grimm, Grimm! Grimm believed himself damned, because he had sworn a false sacred oath to Rakel. Yet he was wrong. For Rakel was not extinguished utterly.

If only Grimm knew. But there was no way that Jaq could inform the squat.

Four blue tunnels led away, branching and dividing into routes leading to anywhere in the webway – to everywhere in this vast network spanning the galaxy. The immensity of this vision exalted Jaq. And in his exaltation, he sensed presences. It seemed that the four tunnels corresponded, in some manner, to the eldar Phoenix Lords. Their transcendent identities intruded upon him. He understood their titles.

Maugan Ra, the Harvester of Souls.

Baharroth, the Cry of the Wind.

Jam Zar, the Storm of Silence.

Karandras, the Shadow Hunter.

They were such potent foes of Chaos.

And he realized that because he had died at this special crossroads, his spirit had not entered the Sea of Souls but had become attached to the webway instead. His vision could ride the webway – although his spirit could not leave it. By riding the webway, knowledge would suffuse him. He sensed, afar, the spirits of dead eldar seers. He might commune with those seers in a way impossible to any other member of the human race.

He would be more illuminated than any living human Illuminatus could ever be!

LEX AND GRIMM *were trudging away from the place where Jaq's corpse lay. Why hadn't they taken the force rod with them? The precious force rod! Neither Lex nor Grimm were psykers. Neither could use the rod. In vain Jaq strove to call out to them, to reassure them that his spirit had survived. To explain about Meh'lindi. To encourage them.*

In vain.

Rapture filled him, at the promise of impending revelations. It was as if he was uniting with the Numen. He was becoming a tiny part of something wondrously noble, yet as diffuse as hydrogen atoms in the void, which would one day condense into a resplendent star.

If only he could commune with tormented humanity! The eldar could commune with the souls of the dead through spirit stones, through wraithbone, through the infinity circuit. Jaq's personal Tarot card might have been a means of contact with the living. His Tarot card was long since destroyed, consigned to ashes scattered in space.

FOR A LONG WHILE, *riding the webway, Jaq's vision followed Lex and Grimm as they retraced the route back to Genost, back to the heretic, Princip. In his sublime transcendence Jaq was impotent to intervene.*

ABOUT THE AUTHOR

Ian Watson received screen credit for the Screen Story of Steven Spielberg's movie *A.I. Artificial Intelligence*, on which Ian worked previously with Stanley Kubrick. *Playboy* published his reminiscences. Ian started writing science fiction as a way of staying sane while teaching in Tokyo years ago, after living in East Africa, and his first SF novel, *The Embedding*, won the French Prix Apollo in translation. His books have appeared in 16 languages so far. In 2001 Ian mutated into a poet when DNA Publications issued his first book of poetry, *The Lexicographer's Love Song*; and Golden Gryphon Press also published his ninth story collection, *The Great Escape*. His newest novel, *Mockymen*, also from Golden Gryphon Press, is about Nazi occultism and mysterious aliens. Recently released by Immanion Press is his Arthur C. Clarke Award finalist, *Whores of Babylon*, completely rewritten thus almost a new book.

His website is: www.ianwatson.info